By Juliet E. McKenna

The Tales of Einarinn
THE THIEF'S GAMBLE
THE SWORDSMAN'S OATH
THE GAMBLER'S FORTUNE
THE WARRIOR'S BOND
THE ASSASSIN'S EDGE

THE ASSASSIN'S EDGE

The Fifth Tale of Einarinn

JULIET E. McKENNA

www.orbitbooks.co.uk

An *Orbit* Book

First published in Great Britain by Orbit 2002

Copyright © Juliet E. McKenna 2002

The moral right of the author has been asserted.

A CIP catalogue record for this book
is available from the British Library.

ISBN 1 84149 124 1

Typeset in Ehrhardt by
Palimpsest Book Production Limited,
Polmont, Stirlingshire
Printed and bound in Great Britain by
Mackays of Chatham plc, Chatham, Kent

Orbit
An imprint of
Time Warner Books UK
Brettenham House
Lancaster Place
London WC2E 7EN

For Marion and Michael, Corinne and Helen, Rae and with fond memories, George.
So much support, in so many ways, for so many years.

Acknowledgements

The truth always bears repeating, so once again, I am grateful to Steve, Mike, Sue, Helen, Robin, Lisa, Penny and Rachel, for ideas, criticism, encouragement and forbearance over ever-extending book loans. In addition to her wider contribution, Liz deserves special mention for serving as on-call plants-woman as does Louise for the medical notes. Thank you, Tanaqui, for the photos, most useful and much appreciated. Angus, thanks indeed for reminding me about Otrick's ring.

The support network continues to evolve and Gill and Mike have proved true friends time and again. As always, I remain indebted to Ernie and Betty for their help beating the tyranny of the working diary over the domestic one.

I couldn't wish for better than the teams at Orbit, in sales, publicity and most of all, editorially. Sincerest thanks go to Tim, Simon, Ben and Julie, Kirsteen, Adrian, Richard, Bob and Nigel. There isn't space for me to list all the booksellers who've impressed me with their professionalism, nor yet all the readers who've brightened up my day with a few lines of appreciation, either personally or in a review. That doesn't mean I'm not grateful, because I most certainly am.

Finally, I would like to thank all those curators and custodians of museums, stately homes and assorted castles who've answered my questions, offered up fascinating extra snippets and been intrigued rather than baffled when I explain just what it is that I do.

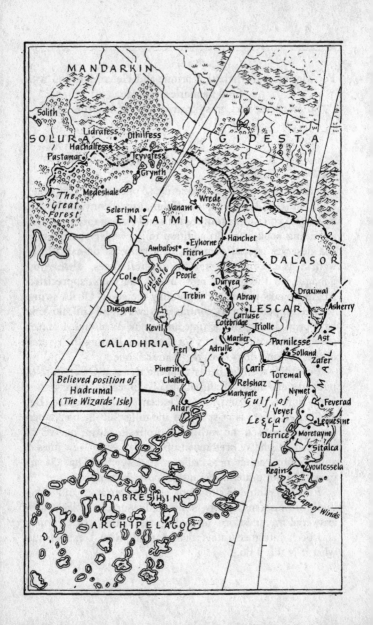

MANDARKIN

Solith

SOLURA
Lidrafess
Othilfess
Hachalfess
Pastamar
Teyvafess
Grynth
Medeshale

GIDESTA

The
Great
Forest

Selerima
Vanam
ENSAIMIN

Wrede

Eyhorne
Hanchet
Ambafost
Friern

DALASOR

Col
Peorle
Gulf of Peorle
Duryea
Draximal
Trebin
Abray
Asherry
Dusgate
Carluse
LESCAR
Kevil
Cotebridge
Triolle
Ast

Marlier
Parnilesse
CALADHRIA
Ferl
Adrulle
Solland
Carif
Zafer
Pinerin
Toremal
Claithe
Relshaz
Nymet

Believed position of
Hadrumal
(The Wizards' Isle)
Markyate
Feverad
Atlar
Gulf of
Veyet
Lequesine
Lescar
Derrice
Moretayne
Sitalca
Regin
Zyoutessela

ALDABRESHIN

ARCHIPELAGO
Cape of Winds

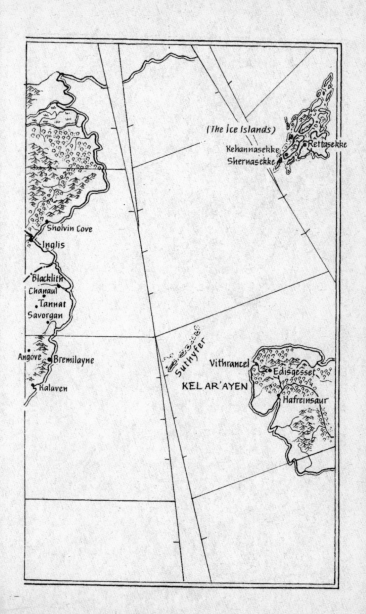

(The Ice Islands)

Kehannasekke
Shernasekke
Rettasekke

Sholvin Cove
Inglis

Blacklith
Chanaul
Tannat
Savorgan

Angove • Bremilayne

Kalaven

Suthyfer

Vithrancel
KEL AR'AYEN

Edisgesset

Hafreinsaur

CHAPTER ONE

Notice from the Prefecture
of the University of Col
To all Resident Mentors and Scholars

By long tradition festivals at the turn of every season are a time for this university to welcome visitors from other seats of learning. We are accustomed to do so with every courtesy and luxury afforded by this city's extensive trade, our contribution to the commerce that is Col's lifeblood. Students and scholars alike mingle with visitors and townsfolk, broadening their experience of life. Accordingly, the Prefects of this university will not tolerate any repetition of the incidents disgracing this most recent spring Equinox.

In choosing a life of study, we all suffer accusations of idleness, and rebuke for perceived failure to produce anything of tangible worth to the unscholarly mind. We rise above such taunts, secure in the knowledge that learning outlasts any achievements of merchants and architects, artisans and their guilds. All of which tolerance is rendered worthless when students, scholars and even several mentors are clapped in irons by the Watch for brawling with visitors from Vanam's university in taverns frequented by common dockers.

Worse, word now circulates that these arguments were not over money, some business disagreement or a lady's favours, but over points of scholarship. This university has become an object of ridicule among the populace. The Prefecture considers this an offence graver than all of the damage done around the city. Broken windows, doors and wine bottles may be redeemed with gold. A reputation once tarnished may never recover its lustre.

To obviate any recurrence of such offences, the Prefecture offers the following for the immediate consideration of mentors and scholars and the judicious guidance of students.

Denying Temar D'Alsennin is who he claims to be is as irrational as refusing to accept the accounts of that restoration of him and his people through the offices of Archmage Planir of Hadrumal. It is equally nonsensical to claim this is all falsehood in service of some all encompassing yet curiously ill-defined conspiracy involving the Archmage, the Mentors of Vanam and even Emperor Tadriol himself. Such foolishness does this university's standing immeasurable harm.

However, and notwithstanding the overweening arrogance of certain scholars of Vanam, the return of Temar D'Alsennin to Tormalin will not answer one hundredth of the questions as to why the Old Empire collapsed. He cannot tell us why the dethronement of Nemith the Reckless and Last precipitated the Chaos rather than orderly transition to a new Emperor and dynasty. D'Alsennin's attempt to found his colony has no bearing on any of these events. It was a minor undertaking compared to other ventures the Old Empire was then engaged upon, most notably the ultimately fruitless conquest of Gidesta. That this colony was of little or no consequence to the Convocation of Princes is plain. Rather than divert resources to helping D'Alsennin, the Annals record every House turning its efforts to quelling secessionist revolts in Caladhria and opportunist uprisings in Ensaimin.

D'Alsennin can offer only a limited account from a very partial perspective as a young and untried esquire of a minor House long distanced from the councils of the powerful. He had already crossed the ocean to Kel Ar'Ayen before the final, crucial years of Nemith's reign and had long been rendered insensible by enchantment before the most violent period of warfare between the Houses of Aleonne and Modrical. While his reminiscences may offer some interesting sidelights on those momentous events, they are insignificant in the wider context of the established historical record.

Granted, it seems likely that the as yet only partially explained deterioration in the usages of aetheric magic contributed to the collapse of the Empire. Judging the impact of such a blow, set alongside the attested assaults of famine, civil strife and the recurrent devastation of the Crusted Pox will certainly be a fruitful area for study. Similarly, a full assessment of the role of this aetheric magic in the governance of the Old Empire must now be made. We of Col should not be laggard in undertaking such enquiries. We need not concern ourselves with boasts from Vanam that their mentors' links with Planir's expeditions to Kel Ar'Ayen give their scholars unassailable superiority in such studies.

Col is the main port through which travellers to and from Hadrumal pass. We should set aside our habitual reserve in dealing with wizardry and invite mages to refresh themselves in our halls and join in our debates. We may usefully encourage our alchemists to correspond with those wizards studying the properties of the natural elements. This university was founded by those scholars who salvaged all they could from the burning of this city's ancient temple library during the Chaos. It is now evident that such temples were centres of aetheric learning in the Old Empire. Resident scholars and mentors must seek out such valuable lore hidden in our own archives. We can claim more peripatetic scholars than Vanam and many now tutor the sons and daughters of Tormalin Houses as well as the scions of Lescari dukes and Caladhria's barons. All such archives may yield invaluable material for further study and this prefecture is writing to enlist the aid of all entitled to wear this university's silver ring.

Rather than wasting time and effort in vain attempts to prove this university's supremacy over Vanam through fisticuffs, it is the duty of every mentor, scholar and student to establish our preeminence through the ineluctable authority of our scholarship.

Vithrancel, Kellarin,
15th of Aft–Spring, in the Fourth Year of Tadriol
the Provident

In that instant of waking, I had no idea where I was. A crash of something breaking had stirred me and the muttered curses that followed took my sleep-mazed mind back to the house of my childhood but as I opened my eyes, nothing seemed familiar. Insistent daylight was entering unopposed through a door in an entirely unexpected wall. Come to that, when had I last slept with a heedlessly open bedroom door?

Wakefulness burned through the mist of sleep. I wasn't back in Ensaimin, for all that someone outside was muttering in the accents of my childhood. This was half a world away, clear across an ocean most folk would swear was impassable. This was Vithrancel, newly named first settlement of Kellarin, a colony still finding its feet after a year of digging in its heels and setting its shoulder to hacking a livelihood out of the wilderness.

Well, whatever was going on outside, it could happen without me. I wasn't getting out of bed for anything short of a full-blown riot. Turning over, I pulled the linen sheet up around my shoulders, pushing my cheek into the welcoming down of the pillow, plump with my spoils from the festival slaughter of geese and hens. How many more days up to my elbows in chicken guts would it take before I had a feather bed, I wondered idly.

No, it was no good; I was awake. Sighing, I sat up and brushed the hair out of my eyes to survey the little room. I'd slept in better, in stone-built inns with drugget laid to mute the scuff of boots on polished floorboards, tapestries on walls to foil stray draughts and prices just as elaborate, never mind the extra copper spent to keep the potmen and chambermaids sweet. Then again, I'd slept in worse, down-at-heel taverns where you were lucky to share a bed with strangers and picking up whatever vermin they carried was all part of the price to pay. The most wretched inn was better than a freezing night beneath a market hall's arches, giving up my last copper to persuade a watchman to look the other way.

I went to open the shutters to the bright midmorning sun. No, I wasn't about to complain about a warm, clean room, floor newly strewn with the first herbs of spring. The breeze was cool on my bare skin and I looked for a clean shirt among clothes and trifles piled on my fine new clothes press. Ryshad had bought it for me with three days trading his skills with plumb line, mallet and chisel to a nearby carpenter. My beloved might have decided against his father's trade in the end but he'd not forgotten his lessons. I really should tidy up, I thought, as I sat on his old travel chest pulling on my breeches.

The bright leather of a newly bound book caught my eye among the clutter on my press. It was a collection of ancient songs that I'd found the year before, full of hints of ancient magic. In an optimistic ballad for children, there'd have been some charm within it to summon sprites to do the housework for me. I smiled, not for the first time, at the notion. On the other hand, any number of darker lyrics warned of the folly of meddling with unseen powers, lest the unwise rouse the wrath of the Eldritch Kin. I'm too old to believe in blameless strangers turning into blue-grey denizens of the shadow realms and turning on those who dishonoured them but there were other reasons for me to shun some of the more tempting promises of Artifice. If I used aetheric tricks and charms to read an opponent's thoughts or see their throw of the runes ahead of time, I'd blunt skills that had seen me through more perils than Ryshad knew of.

Chinking noises outside drew me to the window instead. A stout woman in practical brown skirts bent to retrieve shards of earthenware scattered on the track between our house's ramshackle vegetable garden and the neater preserve over the way. A spill of liquid darkened the earth at her feet.

'Dropped something, Zigrida?' I leant my elbows on the sill. She straightened up, looking around for who had hailed her as she brushed a hand clean on her dress. I waved.

'Livak, good morning.' A smile creased her weathered face agreeably. 'It's Deglain standing the loss.' She sniffed cautiously at the base of the pitcher she'd been stacking the other pieces in. 'It smells like the rotgut that Peyt and his cronies brew.'

I frowned. 'It's not like Deg to come home drunk, not at this time of the morning.'

'Swearing fouler than a cesspit and throwing away good crocks.' Zigrida's voice darkened with disapproval. 'But he's a mercenary when all's said and done.'

'Not like Peyt,' I objected. Granted Deglain had come to Kellarin paid to stick his sword into whoever might wish this colony venture ill, but a year and more on he'd returned to skills learned in some forgotten youth and half the colonists simply knew him as a tinsmith.

Zigrida grunted as she tucked a wisp of grey hair beneath the linen kerchief tied around her head. 'I can't see any more pieces.'

'There aren't many passing hooves to pick them up,' I pointed out.

'That's not the point, my girl.' Zigrida looked up at me, shading warm brown eyes with an age-spotted and work-hardened hand that brushed the lace trimming her kerchief with a hint of frivolity. 'It's time you were out of bed, my lady sluggard. You can get a bucket of water to wash this away.' She scraped a stoutly booted foot across the damp ground before glancing towards the steadily retreating trees that fringed the settlement. 'I don't care to know what the scent of strong liquor might tempt out of that wildwood.'

I grinned. 'At once, mistress.' I'll take Zigrida's rebukes as long as a twinkle in her eye belies her scolding and besides, doing her a favour always wins me some goodwill.

Tidying up could wait. I dragged the sheets across the mattress brushing a few stray hairs to the floor, bright auburn from my head, curled black from Ryshad's. Our bed was a solid construction of tight-fitted wood finished with golden beeswax and strung with good hemp rope. Ryshad wasn't about to sleep on some lumpy palliasse or a box bed folded out of a settle. Lower servants slept on such things, not men chosen for preferment out of all those swearing service to the Sieur D'Olbriot, nigh on the richest and most influential of all Tormalin's princes.

Then I looked rather doubtfully at the sheets. The mattress was still fragrant with bedstraw gathered in the golden days of autumn but the linen wanted washing, if not today then soon. I had a nice wash house out behind the house but spending the day stoking the fire to boil the water in the copper and poking seething sheets with a stick was scant entertainment. Before I'd come here, laundry was always someone else's concern as I'd moved from inn to inn, earning my way gambling and with the occasional less reputable venture.

I pulled the top sheet free of the blanket and dumped it on the battered chest at the foot of the bed. Ryshad stowed his possessions inside it with neatness drilled into him from ten or more years of barracks life. He deserved a clothes press like mine, I decided. Ryshad's help had set Kerse up with a better workshop than any of the other woodsmen of the colony. They were all turning to joinery now they could spare time from shaping joists and beams. Now spring Equinox had opened the sailing seasons, Kerse needed to consider the markets for work this fine right across the countries that had once made up the Tormalin Empire. I knew quality when I saw it; in a girlhood seeming even more distant than the lands we'd left behind, I'd been a housemaid polishing up prized pieces not worked with a fifth the skill of our new bed.

But Zigrida had asked me to fetch some water. I'd better do that before thinking about laundry. I abandoned the sheet and went down the cramped stair boxed into a corner of the kitchen that took up the back half of our little cruck-framed house. Using the belt knife laid on a stool with the jerkin I'd discarded the night before, I carved a slice from the ham hanging by the chimneybreast, savouring the hint of juniper and sweet briar that had gone into the curing. Chewing, I went in search of a bucket in the tiny scullery that Ryshad had screened off from the kitchen. I ignored the flagon of small beer keeping cool in the stone sink my beloved had painstakingly crafted. If I was going to the well, I'd make do with water. Ale was never my first choice for breakfast, nor Ryshad's, but the winter had seen supplies of wine from Tormalin exhausted.

As I opened the kitchen door and crossed the rudimentary cobbles Ryshad had laid to get us dryshod to the gate, a girl came running up to Deglain's house, across the track. It was twin to our own, sunlight white on lime wash still fresh over the lath and plaster solidly walling the timber frame. It had been interesting watching them being built; Ryshad had explained exactly how the weight of one part leant on another that pulled something else, the tension keeping the whole house solid.

The buttercup yellow shawl over the girl's head gave me a moment's pause but then I recognised the lass. 'Catrice! Is everything all right?'

She ignored me, hammering on Deglain's door. Deg opened the door, only a crack at first. Seeing Catrice, he flung it wide and tried to fold the girl into his arms.

She resisted his embrace with a forceful shove. 'You stink!'

Deg's reply didn't have the piercing clarity of Catrice's outrage so I couldn't make out his words but his blinking eyes and unshaven disorder were eloquent enough.

'I'll not sleep in the bed of any man who falls in it half dressed and full drunk,' she shrilled, hysteria sharpening her tone.

'Do you suppose her mother knows she's here?' Zigrida came to the fence on her side of the precisely delineated alley separating our two properties. With a whole continent to spread ourselves over, there would be none of the squabbles over boundaries that plague the higgledy-piggledy burgages of Ensaimin's close-packed towns.

'She'll be none too pleased when she finds out,' I commented. Catrice was the only and much cherished daughter of one of the southern Tormalin families come to make a new life in this untamed land the year before. They were still apt to take their consequence rather too seriously for my taste. Zigrida was from the north, close to the Lescari border and, as such, considerably more down to earth.

Whatever Deg had to say for himself was enough to set Catrice to noisy weeping. She didn't resist as he pulled her into an awkward hug, clumsily wiping at her tears with the edge of her shawl.

Zigrida watched the pair disappear inside. 'You reckon something's boiling up?'

'Could be something, could be nothing,' I shrugged. 'But we'd best be ready to stick in a spoon to quell any froth.' In general, colonists and the mercenaries hired to defend them rubbed along easily enough together but there had been a few awkwardnesses. The sons and daughters of sober yeomen occasionally found the free and easy attitudes of the soldiery rather too enticing for their parents' peace of mind.

'Are you going to send for the corps commander?' Zigrida asked.

'Perhaps.' Halice, currently in charge of the mercenaries, had been a friend of mine for years and I served as her unofficial deputy when I had nothing better to do. 'Did you see Ryshad this morning?' I'd got used to staying asleep when Ryshad rose with the dawn to pursue one of his myriad projects around Vithrancel.

'That Werdel came calling first thing. They'll be out at the clay fields.' Zigrida's tone was warm with approval. She liked Ryshad.

I smiled too. I was more than content with a cruck-framed house, it's how four-fifths of Ensaimin's towns are built but Ryshad considered wooden buildings as nothing more than temporary. Before the previous autumn's Equinox had barred the ocean to ships, he'd recruited the son of a brick-maker known to his stone-mason brothers in Zyoutessela and had half the men of the colony digging clay on the promise of a share in the bricks and tiles. As soon as the scarce frosts of Kellarin's mild winter had passed, Ryshad reminded everyone they'd promised to help build a drying shed while Werdel puddled and shaped the weathered clay for a successful trial of his new kiln. Fired with enthusiasm, my beloved had bored me to sleep these past few nights with explanations of how to turn quicklime into mortar.

I swung my bucket idly by its rope handle. 'You've been baking bread this morning?' Zigrida had a smudge of flour by the spray of colourful flowers embroidered around the laces of her sober green bodice.

'What's it to you?' She cocked her head on one side.

I hefted the bucket. 'Water for you today in return for a loaf or so?'

Zigrida laughed. 'Fresh bread will cost you more than a few pails.' A frown deepened her wrinkles as she pursed thin lips. 'You can give me an afternoon in my garden, helping with the fruit canes.'

I shook my head in mock consternation. 'You drive a hard bargain.'

'Then do your own baking, my girl.' Her smile lifted a generation from her laughing eyes.

I waved a hand in capitulation. 'I'll get some water and then I'll call round for the bread.'

Zigrida nodded and disappeared within her own doors. I headed for the nearby outcrop of rock offering plentiful clean water from one of Kellarin's many springs. It was a pleasant walk. Halcarion's blessing loaded the knot of trees around the wellspring with richly scented blossom as soon as the Winter Hag had quit her watch. Maewelin hadn't disputed the Moon Maiden's authority with late frosts or sudden storms and even people who barely paid lip service to either goddess had celebrated all the traditional rites of thanks at the recent Equinox.

With winter keeping everyone close to home and making improvements, a broad stone basin had been built around the spring so I didn't have to wait long before I could dip my pail beside busy goodwives and less eager maidens about their mothers' bidding. I sympathised with the sullen faces; I'd walked out on hearth and home at much the same age, fleeing the drudgery of service to someone else's whims and malice, buoyed up with all the ignorant confidence of youth. But I hadn't sulked about my errands when I had been my mother's least reliable housemaid. I'd taken any chance to get out of the house, to learn more about life and pocket any coin I could win with a smile or a jest.

'Livak, good morning to you.' One of the bustling women nodded approval at my brimming bucket. 'Wash day at last, is it?'

That immediately raised my hackles. 'Not that I know of, Midda. Tell me, you haven't heard who it is setting up as a laundress, have you?'

Midda looked puzzled. 'No.'

'Oh well,' I shrugged. 'Still, if you come across her, pass the word that I'll be on her doorstep with a hefty bundle every market day.'

I smiled but Midda was frowning at the thought that something might be going on that hadn't reached her ears. With luck, once she set about interrogating her gossips, the spreading word would prompt some woman or other to set up her own wash tubs to steal a march on my mythical would-be laundress.

Mind, I'd still have to find some way to pay for someone to do my washing. I felt a little mildewed as I walked back, swinging the bucket to see how far I could tilt it before I risked slopping the water. There was a sizeable share of what little coin the colony boasted secure in a coffer beneath our bedroom floorboards but that was precious little use to me. Work was the currency of Kellarin and it was Ryshad's skills that were putting credit in our ledger to buy me the prettiest plates from the potters or the softest blankets bright from the looms.

It wasn't as if I didn't have talents of my own but there was just precious little scope for them. I could usually find a friendly game of runes or someone happy to play the White Raven against my Forest Birds to while away an evening but these placid craftsmen and farmers weren't in the habit of laying bets against their luck with the fate sticks and, after the first half season or so, were hardly inclined to wager against my chances of driving their raven clear off the game board.

I lifted the bucket and cupped myself a drink of water. Halcarion save me but I'd hand over that whole coffer of coin for a decent cask of wine. Mind you, I thought wryly, I wasn't the only one fed up with water and ale. Whatever fruit Zigrida's canes might produce after my untutored ministrations wasn't destined for pies; she'd told me as much. But fruit cordials would never match the velvety seduction of Angovese red or the aromatic coolness of Ferl River whites.

That idle thought prompted another that stopped me in my tracks. Aft-Spring's winds would soon bring ships and it was a safe bet they'd carry trifles and trinkets to tempt the colonists as well as the necessities of life we couldn't yet make for ourselves. Traders from Tormalin would be wanting coin on the barrelhead, not unquantifiable promises of bartered labour. If I found some opportunity to set people like Midda fretting about that, I might get more takers for my money staked against their sweat. Come to that, traders in an anchorage without any of the usual amusements would probably be only too eager for a casual game of runes. It would take more than a winter's idleness to leave my fingers too stiff to lighten some Zyoutessela merchant's purse.

My spirits rose as a new notion occurred to me. Those ships would surely be carrying wine. If I bought up as much as I could, I'd have something better to trade for goods and services than the donkey work I'd been taking on, just so I wasn't sitting on my hands and living off Ryshad's efforts. I wasn't about to do that here in Kellarin, any more than I'd have taken his coin to be called his whore back home.

Those same ships could take letters back to Tormalin for me. I considered how I might have them carried to the more distant trading centres of Relshaz and Peorle. As sworn man to D'Olbriot, Ryshad had had the right to use the Imperial Despatch and I wondered if they ever carried any unofficial correspondence from men who'd left their Prince's service. In the right places, I had friends who could ship an entire cargo of wines and liquors across the ocean with my name branded on every barrel. If I became the woman the colony turned to for its wine, where might that lead me?

Feet marching in ragged step behind me interrupted such speculations. Midda and her friends scattered like hens in a farmyard, white aprons fluttering, sweeping skirts aside lest some heedless soldier tread on their hems. Not that Ryshad would have called this rabble soldiers and even Halice would have admitted they were barely worth a mercenary's hire. I picked up my pace a little as the unshaven mob passed me to halt milling around outside Deglain's door with the usual unfocused malice of a gang of drunks.

'Deg! Hey, Deg, we didn't finish our game!'

That was a voice I recognised and one I didn't like. Peyt hadn't taken the hint when Halice had offered to pay him off the previous autumn, suggesting he head back for more profitable wars, as so many other mercenaries had done once the colony had thrived unmolested for a full year.

Most of those warriors who'd stayed had taken up old trades like Deglain or turned unskilled hands to hunting and foraging in the woods, stripping bark from felled trees for the tanners, hauling cut lumber to wherever the next house was being built. There was more than enough work to go around, after all. But I couldn't recall Peyt and his cronies lifting a finger, not beyond grudgingly using cudgels on fleeing rats when the sheaves stooked in the new fields won from the forest had been taken for threshing. For all their supposed skill with blades, they'd shirked Aft-Autumn's gory cull of the pigs, sheep and cattle we had no fodder to see through the winter. Ryshad had been scathing in his contempt for Peyt more than once, likening him to one of the fat black leeches lurking in the swampy stretch of land to the east. The only work I'd seen the idle bastard do since the turn of the year was drowning the few hound pups too sickly to find takers, once Ryshad had pointed out to Temar that Vithrancel could do without any pack of masterless dogs.

I reached my own gate and, once inside, latched it carefully, alert to the swelling murmurs, picking out accents from gutters all the way from Toremal clear across to the Great Forest. The door across the way burst open.

'You shut your mouth before I shut it for you!' Deglain's bellow rang out before his voice was lost beneath a flurry of voices, some calming, some goading.

'No one's looking for trouble here,' said one unlikely optimist.

'Peyt only says it like he sees it.' That interruption was larded with malicious expectation. 'She looks a well-thumbed lass to me.'

The ragged ring of men spread out to corral two figures now circling each other.

'I'd carve a slice off her ham,' someone agreed with the misplaced earnestness of the truly drunk.

I moved to lean against the fence as a growing number of people from nearby houses emerged to do the same.

'Her thighs open like a gate on a windy day.' The speaker squared up to Deglain, smiling nastily as he made an ostentatious adjustment to his groin. He was a rangy man with a few days' growth of beard shadowing a hatchet face beneath slicked back, oily black locks. His red, embroidered clothes had once been expensive but rough living and worse table manners had left them bagged and stained. 'I'm not the only one who's combed her quiff.'

A cackling laugh at the back raised the old mercenaries' toast. 'Here's to loose women and well-fitting boots!'

'You're a lying bastard, Peyt.' Deglain took a step closer and Peyt backed away. Deglain was a few fingers shorter but broader across the shoulder and with plenty of muscle beneath the fat that a winter of leisure had left padding him. He was wearing no more than a shirt and tan breeches and the slight breeze flattened the fine linen to outline his solid bulk. His blunt face was twisted in a scowl, thick brows all but lost in his unruly brown hair.

'She's the one carrying the bastard and you're the fool letting her father it on you,' taunted Peyt. 'But you're welcome to my leavings, if you can stomach them.'

'I'll make you eat horseshit for spreading such lies!' One of Catrice's brothers forced his way through the crowd, face scarlet with rage, all youthful long limbs like a heron on stilts. One of Peyt's cronies tripped him and the youth went sprawling to unsympathetic laughter. But Glane hadn't come alone and an angry lad punched the man with a deft fist brutal in his kidneys. Some colonists were picking up mercenary tricks.

'Saedrin's stones!' The man buckled at the knees and was surprisingly slow to get up. Seeing Peyt distracted, Deglain stepped in with an uppercut solid enough to rattle the mercenary's teeth. But it wasn't enough to fell him. Clean living among the colonists had made Deglain forget how hard and fast a mercenary fights and he was a breath too slow in stepping back. Peyt drove a swift, instinctive punch into his belly and with a noise half groan, half curse, Deglain doubled over.

'Go back to your little hammers,' Peyt sneered. 'You fight like a cat with gloves on.'

He looked for the adulation of his hangers-on but he was celebrating too soon. Deglain rammed a shoulder like a bullock's rump into Peyt's skinny ribs, dumping him on his arse.

'If I had a dog as worthless as you, I'd hang him.' He pinned his tormentor long enough for a few good blows then two others dragged him off, their boots and fists going in brutally.

'I'll kick your arse so hard your gums'll bleed!' Peyt was back on his feet, resilience being one mercenary quality he did possess. Blood pouring from a gashed eyebrow, he swore foully as he headed for Deglain.

The big man was holding his own against Peyt's hangers-on with a man at either shoulder to help him, each dressed in the sombre breeches and old-fashioned jerkins of colonists. As more mercenaries stepped up to back Peyt, so men who'd just come to watch found themselves taking a stand to stop Deglain and the others being outflanked. Mild blows to ward off attack were taken as outright assault by the mercenaries for whom fighting came as naturally as breathing. Finding their attempts to defend themselves provoking vicious retaliation, the colonists rapidly abandoned restraint.

'Are you fetching Halice?' Zigrida was by her door, scowling disapproval at the spreading mêlée.

'Let's see how this plays out.' I leaned against the fence that would protect the burgeoning nettles in our plot from these trampling boots well enough. My neighbours' smug turnips were similarly defended with hurdles and hedges set to foil browsers sneaking down from the woods.

'Mercenaries.' Zigrida's contempt was withering. 'Fighting for no more reason than cats in a gutter.'

I held my tongue. Brawls were hardly uncommon in the mercenary camps I'd traversed over the years, especially at the end of a long and boring winter as the men geared themselves up for the perils and profits of a new season's battles. Halice wouldn't be that concerned, as long as no one suffered any real hurt. There was plenty of blood staining shirts and jerkins but no one was on the ground where boots might splinter ribs to gut a man from the inside out. Some had paired off in wrestling holds, feet digging into the dirt before sweeping forward to try and cut the foe's legs out from under him. I saw two men falling all of a piece as neither would let go the grip they had under each other's armpits. Scrambling apart in the dust, one offered his hand to the other, pulling him clear of Glane who was fighting his own little battle. From what I could see, he wasn't the only colonist glad of a chance to let rip, paying back slights imagined and intentional stored up over the last few seasons.

As the swirling fight swept the pair in my direction, I recognised the mercenary Glane was punishing with lightning fast blows, heedless of the damage to his own fists. The lad would learn that lesson the hard way. His victim was a burly bruiser called Tavie, blood staining his grimy shirt as it dripped from a split lower lip. A winter's laziness had left a belly on him like a woman scant days from childbed and he was paying a heavy price for such sloth. Then I saw Tavie decide to level the odds and reach for a dagger at his belt.

'No you don't!' I snapped my fingers in Zigrida's direction but didn't take my eyes off the fat mercenary. Knife poised, he was advancing on the hapless Glane who at least had the sense to retreat as fast as the scuffles all around him allowed, chance sending him scuttling towards me. I scooped up a stone from a pile I'd dug from our supposed vegetable patch in an uncharacteristic fit of enthusiasm the previous autumn. I weighed the stone in my hand, hard and heavy with one jagged edge raw against my palm. Halice is the one with the height and heft to take up a sword alongside the men and make them eat their mockery. I've neither the skills nor the inclination so I've cultivated an accurate throwing arm. What I needed now was the chance to hit Tavie without braining some other fool who got in the way, and preferably before he caught up with Glane.

I saw my moment and took it. The rock hit Tavie hard in the meat of his knife arm. The distraction gave Glane an instant to gather his flagging strength and fraying nerve. The smack of his fist into the side of the mercenary's head was clearly audible over the uproar all around and I winced.

It was Glane's bad luck he knocked Tavie into Peyt. The fortunes of the fight had temporarily driven the tall mercenary away from Deglain. Furious, he turned to find out who had just dropped his man at his feet.

'Fighting for your sister's honour?' A predatory smile curved Peyt's lip as he leered at Glane. 'What a waste of effort!'

'You lay one filthy hand on my sister and I'll cut it off.'
A treacherous break in Glane's voice betrayed his youth.
Young enough to be stupid enough to get himself killed, he
pulled out his own workaday belt knife and levelled the inadequate blade. Peyt stepped back but only far enough to scoop
up the longer, sharper dagger that Tavie had dropped.

'Tell you what, I'll give you a turn on the spit, when I've
beaten a bit of humility into you, see how you compare with
your sister? How about I ram that oyster-sticker up your
hairless arse when I'm done with it?' I knew Peyt's taste
didn't run to boys but the threat disconcerted the lad, just
as Peyt intended. He dropped into the crouch of the practised knife fighter. I could see Glane's hand trembling, his
back to me and our fence blocking any further retreat. The
boy tried to edge away. Peyt darted forward and I made my
move.

My bucket of water caught the mercenary full in the face.
The chill and the shock left him gasping in momentary confusion, his startled yell harsh enough to startle everyone into
stillness now the first rush of enthusiasm for bloodshed was
passing.

'Glane!' I snapped with biting emphasis. 'Put that knife
away and get yourself home.'

A nicely brought up boy, the habit of obedience to an older
female voice had him turning tail before recollection of his
manly duty prompted him to go and hide behind Deglain
instead.

Deprived of his target as he scraped sodden hair out of
his eyes, Peyt turned an ugly scowl on me. 'Livak! You pox-
ridden bitch!'

'Good morning to you too.' I smiled at him. 'I saw you
hadn't bathed yet, so I thought I'd save you the trouble of
fetching your own water.'

He jabbed a menacing finger at me. 'I'll give you trouble,
rag-mop.'

'You don't want to do that,' I assured him, still smiling.
The fence was high enough that Peyt would have to vault it

to get at me and I'd be inside the house and bolting the door before he got a foot on the palings.

'Who's going to stop me?' Peyt took a menacing step towards me. Everyone else abandoned their scuffles to watch this new entertainment. 'Where's your man? How about a torn smock from me to teach you your place is on your back and lifting your heels?'

'You lay a finger on her and I'll make you eat your own stones,' snarled Deglain but Peyt's cronies were a solid barrier between him and me.

I looked past Peyt and smiled. 'Thanks all the same, Deg, but Peyt's got to learn that size really doesn't matter.'

Peyt's glower turned into an unpleasant smirk, as aware as anyone else that he topped me by a head and more. 'I think you'll find it does, you draggle-arsed whore.'

I shook my head, taunting him with mock disappointment. 'When are you going to learn, Peyt?'

He was within a stride of the fence now, face intent like a fox with a mouse in its sights. 'Learn what?'

I took a pace back to keep him coming. 'Which women are good for more than easing the ache in your breeches. We can take care of ourselves.'

'You're backing yourself against me?' He barked a curt laugh. 'That's worth a prince's ransom!'

Then Halice punched him hard in the back of the head. Before he could recover enough to think of raising his knife, she had one hand twisted in his lank black hair, jerking his head back to apply an expert stranglehold all the more effectively with her other arm. Much the same height and with broader shoulders, she had no trouble holding him.

'No, but I'll back Halice against you any day from Solstice to Equinox,' I told Peyt. The fury in his eyes faded to an instant of panic and then to bitter blankness as Halice choked him senseless. Zigrida's grandson was wide eyed and out of breath behind her and I winked at the child who scurried back to his grandam.

Halice dropped the limp, unconscious Peyt to the ground.

'Dump him in his bed and when he wakes up – if he wakes up – he can come to me and take his punishment for this little nonsense.' She turned to scowl at the shifty crowd, none of whom dared challenge her authority. 'When you've dumped him, get yourselves down to the riverside and tell Minare I sent you. If you're idle enough to be this stupid, he'll make use of you. Move!' Her words goaded the mercenaries into a hasty retreat. Peyt half carried, half dragged away, by two of his cronies.

Halice turned her scorching glare on the colonists, dark eyes hard and unreadable. 'You don't have better things to do than this?' She bent to pick up Peyt's fallen dagger and threw it to me.

I picked the knife out of the air and idly tossed it a few times. That should remind people I wasn't just some insipid little twirl Ryshad kept to warm his sheets. Everyone instantly remembered ten tasks requiring immediate attention and took themselves off.

'Halice—' Deglain stepped forward, twisting grazed knuckles in the palm of his other hand, teeth marks plain on his forearm. Glane hovered behind him, bruises darkening on cheek and forehead.

'I'll see to you later.' Halice shaded her promise with threat, holding Deglain's gaze until he turned away. Squaring his shoulders, he ushered Glane towards his house where Catrice waited on the threshold, buttercup yellow shawl pressed to her tear-stained face.

Halice rubbed a broad hand over the dun-coloured hair she kept cropped as short as any other soldier. Now there was only me to see, her coarse-featured face turned amiable. 'I may as well take an early lunch since I'm here. You can tell me what that was all about while we eat.'

The Island City of Hadrumal,
15th of Aft-Spring

'Do you suppose there are many of those dust-ups between mercenaries and colonists?'

The speaker was a wiry man with thoughtful brown eyes and a reddish beard worn close trimmed, whose sparse sandy hair was cut so brutally short it was nigh on invisible. He was young to have gone all but bald, much of an age with his companion still boasting a full head of black hair, long enough to reach his shoulders if he were to untie the scrap of leather holding it back. The two men shared a sinewy build but that was as far as any similarity went. The dark-haired man had a sallow complexion and was noticeably taller than his companion whose fair skin showed freckles as they emerged from the shadow of a doorway into the early morning sun.

'Livak and Halice looked to have everything well in hand.' Breezily confident, he stuck his hands into the pockets of his grass-green jerkin, a garment significantly more relaxed in cloth and cut to the sober buff of his companion's clothes.

'Livak's got more than her fair share of wits,' the sandy-haired man said thoughtfully. 'What did you make of Halice when you travelled with her?'

'She's as shrewd as she's plain faced.' The taller man smiled. 'I don't imagine there'll be trouble with those hired swords but we can mention it if you like, if our esteemed Archmage needs some excuse for having Hadrumal send representatives to Kellarin.' From his tone, he plainly didn't think this would be necessary.

The two men turned off the long curve of Hadrumal's high road and through an ancient gateway of weathered stone that pierced a tower rising dark against a still sky all but colourless with the first light of the day. Footsteps loud on the flagstones, they crossed a courtyard where most windows were still firmly shuttered, their fellow wizards not yet stirring to a new day about the age-old study of magic.

The black-haired man opened an iron-studded door on to a dark staircase. A single window at the top shed scant light on the oak treads and both men paused to accustom their eyes to the gloom. Ascending in step, obvious expectation lightening their feet, the pair exchanged a grin as the sandy-haired man rapped a brisk knuckle on the door at the top.

'Enter.' The summons was curt enough to startle the pair into identical looks of surprise.

The dark-haired man opened the door. 'Archmage.'

'Shiv.' The man within had his back to them, standing by a table piled high with books and documents. He looked round to greet them with a brusque nod. 'Usara. What can I do for you?'

'We thought we'd invite you to share some breakfast with us.' Shiv's words tailed off into uncertainty.

'You're expecting someone?' Usara didn't hide his surprise at the Archmage's formal robe, an expensive gown of silk as dark and glossy as a raven's wing, arcane symbols picked out on the fronts in matt black embroidery. Planir's hair was as black as his robes but for a touch of frost at his temples.

'As you can see,' the Archmage replied tersely.

Hesitation checked Shiv's smile. 'We wanted to discuss Kellarin.'

'What about it?' Planir made a neat stack of the small volumes he'd extracted from his pile of books.

'There'll be a lot happening there this year,' Shiv began rather lamely. 'The colony was set fair to expand by the end of last autumn and now we're past Equinox, there'll be nothing to hold them back.'

'There's a whole new continent to discover,' Usara

chipped in. 'Hadrumal can offer all manner of assistance. Wizardry will make exploration far quicker and safer.'

'That's wizardry in general or you pair in particular?' Planir turned shadowed grey eyes on Usara. The early light through the lancet windows made harsh angles of his clean-shaven face.

'You know we have an interest in Kellarin, Archmage,' the younger man said slowly.

'Any ship wanting to make the ocean crossing needs a wizard aboard,' Shiv shrugged. 'It may as well be us as anyone else.'

'I beg leave to disagree,' said Planir with a weary hint of humour. 'That's a task ideally suited to mages fresh out of their apprenticeship who need a lesson in the differences between the theories they have learned and the practical application of magic.'

'We could keep a weather eye on them from Kellarin,' Usara suggested. 'Use our own experience of the oceans and the coastal currents to help them.'

'You don't see your duty here as more important?' The faint smile faded from Planir's face. 'It is customary to pay for the learning you've gained by passing it on, turn and turn about with your contemporaries. What about your own apprentices?'

Usara looked uncertainly at the Archmage. 'I think we've taught them all we can. Equinox always means apprentices moving on to new masters, so we thought we'd be free—'

'Did you consider who might be planning to pass their apprentices on to you? Herion's already mentioned two lasses he thinks would benefit from your assistance, 'Sar.' Planir gestured towards the long roofs of Hadrumal's buildings visible through the windows, tall towers and lesser buildings subservient to them. 'You're both of some standing in the Council now, respected among the halls. More than one mage is interested in your notions of working magic cooperatively.'

Usara opened his mouth but Planir cut him off with a curt sweep of one hand. 'Do you imagine you've learned everything Hadrumal has to teach you? I don't recall Shannet releasing you from your pupillage with her, Shiv.' He fixed the dark-haired mage with a hard look. 'What does she think of your plans? I take it you've told her?'

'No,' Shiv replied slowly. 'She hates any mention of Kellarin, as you know full well.'

'Because Viltred, love of her youth, died there and Otrick, friend of her old age, returned moribund.' Planir's eyes were flinty beneath fine black brows.

'You don't need to remind me of that,' retorted Shiv, stung.

'No?' Planir's voice was cold. 'Have the dangers that proved so fatal for them vanished?'

'Elietimm have made no move against the colony in more than a year,' said Shiv with determined composure.

'But the possibility remains, of course. Which is all the more reason to send mages with more up their sleeves than a talent for keeping a fire in overnight or picking the best place for a well,' Usara pointed out.

'They worked enough malice in the north last year, as you know better than any.' The Archmage folded his arms carefully over his robe. 'Despite your success in foiling their plans, 'Sar, I don't suppose they've given up their hopes of alliance with the Mountain Men. If you're in Kellarin you could be seriously wrong-footed if we suddenly find we need the benefit of the contacts you made among the Forest Folk and the upland strongholds.'

'Whenever we've countered an Elietimm threat, they've tried something else, not the same thing again. There's been no sniff of them in the Archipelago since Ryshad exposed their conspiracies.' Shiv took a step forward. 'And the Mountain Men will be full on their guard, any fool can see that. Elietimm eyes will start looking south again. Apprentices will be hardly able to defend the colony if they attack. If we're there, we'll know what we're dealing with and how best to fight it.'

'So do you consider them a threat or not?' Planir looked puzzled. 'You just said there'd been no sign for over a year. Perhaps you should think through whatever your argument is before we discuss this further?'

Shiv coloured but didn't say anything.

'Kellarin has mercenaries and magic of its own, don't forget that.' Planir smiled thinly. 'In any case, the Tormalin Emperor and I have come to, shall we say, an agreement over Kellarin. He'll allow the colony its independence as long as Hadrumal does the same.'

Usara looked perplexed. 'I don't see the two of us threatening that.'

'Your modesty does you credit, 'Sar.' Planir's tone warmed a trifle. 'Consider the reputation you have in Toremal as the mage who drove the Elietimm out of the mountains all but single-handed last year. Of course, such power and valour was only to be expected from one of the wizards who rediscovered the lost land of Kellarin the summer before that, fighting with mighty mages like the admirable Shiv to defend its people, even to the death of such worthies as Viltred.'

'I hardly think sarcasm is called for,' said Shiv curtly.

'Forgive me, I didn't mean to mock.' Planir looked tired despite the early hour. 'I appreciate you have an interest in Kellarin and close ties to people there but you can keep your weather eye on them from here.'

He glanced at Shiv who tried and failed to look innocent. 'Don't tell me you've not been scrying for them because I won't believe you. No, don't worry about it. Scry all you want as far as I'm concerned and if trouble does come floating down from the Ice Islands, then you can give Kellarin all the assistance you want. The Emperor will be too glad of it to quibble and the first to cheer Elietimm ships burnt to the waterline with magical fire or drowned like rats in a barrel with a conjured storm.'

'I appreciate your confidence but we've no great record

of success against the Elietimm enchanters,' said Shiv bitterly.

'Then wouldn't you be safer here?' queried Planir. 'You're contradicting yourself again, Shiv.'

'We're scarcely any further forward in understanding aetheric magic.' Usara's frustration was evident. 'I need to work with those adept in Kellarin if I'm to make any sense of the little we've learned over the winter, if I'm ever to see how Artifice relates to wizardry. We might even see how the two magics might work together rather than stifling each other.'

'A hope I hold before the Council each and every time some sceptic calls the value of your studies into question.' Planir raised a quizzical brow. 'Surely you'll make better progress surrounded by twenty generations of learning documented in Hadrumal's libraries than struggling to fit in your studies around keeping ships away from dangerous currents and tracking lodes of ore for the colony?'

'I need to discuss my theories with the Demoiselle Guinalle,' Usara insisted. 'She's the leading adept, after all.'

'Ah yes, Guinalle.' Planir slowly inclined his head. 'But what about Aritane, 'Sar? She can't go back to her people in the mountains. These Sheltya who hold their lore, they'll assume – and rightly – that's she's told you all she knows about their ancient aetheric magic. You told me that would mean death for her if the Sheltya ever caught her.'

'She's safe enough in Hadrumal,' said Shiv with a dismissive shrug.

Planir kept his stern gaze fixed on Usara. 'You've complained to me often enough about the scant respect she's shown, 'Sar. You hear all the arguments that Artifice is no more than some second-rate magic unworthy of Hadrumal's notice. You're going to leave Aritane to face all that alone?'

'Then she can come to Kellarin with us.' Usara was looking exasperated now.

'You've managed to persuade her?' Planir was astonished.

'I understood she sees herself as exiled to Hadrumal for life. It's the only place where she can stay hidden from Sheltya working Artifice to hunt her down, isn't it?'

'I'm sure Guinalle could protect her in Kellarin,' said Usara stiffly but his face belied his words.

'You don't think her race's ancient kinship with the Elietimm will make her even less welcome than she is here, among colonists who suffered so dreadfully at their hands?' Planir hazarded. He frowned. 'And of course, if Elietimm enchanters do seek a new target for their hatred as you suggest, Shiv, and were to attack Hadrumal for instance, then we'll find ourselves with both Guinalle and Aritane, the only two with any real knowledge of such magic and more crucially how to counter it on the far side of the ocean.'

'Why are you making so many difficulties, Archmage?' Shiv demanded bluntly.

'Why haven't you two thought through all the consequences of your actions?' snapped Planir. 'Haven't I taught you better than this? Is this notion entirely your own? Did someone else suggest it? Troanna for instance?'

'I don't answer to Troanna,' Shiv replied in the same breath as Usara's protest.

'I'm your pupil, Planir, no one else's.'

'Then why is this plan leaving you so blinkered to wider considerations?' Planir said abruptly. 'Tell me 'Sar, is your desire to see Guinalle entirely academic? You've set aside your romantic inclination for the lady?'

'No, but that doesn't interfere with my duty to Hadrumal.' Usara coloured furiously beneath his beard. 'No more than you're hampered by your attachment to Larissa.'

'I think we'd better talk about this some other time,' Shiv said hastily. He caught Usara by the sleeve. 'As you say, Archmage, there are other aspects to this that we'd better consider more fully.'

He forced Usara through the door and closed it quickly

as the sandy-haired wizard shook himself free with visible annoyance. They descended the stairs in mute irritation.

'What was that all about?' Usara burst out as they reached the courtyard. 'I know he's been short-tempered lately but that was just impossible!'

'Maybe we just picked the wrong moment,' Shiv said dubiously. 'He looked dog-tired. What do you suppose is keeping him burning the midnight candles? Larissa?'

Usara shook his head. 'She's spending a lot less time with him. I hear the gossip is upsetting her.'

'What did she expect, letting Planir charm her into his bed?' There was little sympathy in Shiv's response. 'She's his apprentice.'

'He's genuinely fond of her,' Usara insisted.

'But she's a diversion from his cares, not someone he'd share them with. He must miss Otrick.' Shiv's voice was sad as he trod on the patterned shadow cast by a leaded casement now opened to the morning air.

'We all do,' Usara sighed. 'And who's Planir got to talk to, now the old pirate's dead?'

'Pered doesn't think Planir's taken time to grieve for Otrick properly,' Shiv observed. He grimaced. 'I win the washing up till next market day. Pered bet me Planir wouldn't just give us leave to go.'

Usara looked back at the Archmage's lofty window. 'Perhaps we should have told him the whole plan.' His words tailed off into uncertainty.

'We agreed we'd take it one step at a time,' Shiv said firmly. 'Anyway, who do you suppose is coming to see him first thing before breakfast? Maybe that's why he was in such a contrary mood.'

They passed through the gateway and fell silent as a couple of yawning apprentices crossed their path. Usara led the way out to the less exalted buildings of the high road where Hadrumal's tradespeople were setting about the more mundane occupations of their day.

'What do you say to some bread and cheese?' Shiv nodded towards a small shop whose solid shutters were now let down to form a counter stacked with flagons of water and wine and baskets piled high with rolls fresh from some nearby bakery.

'It wouldn't hurt to see who came and went for a chime or so,' agreed Usara.

Vithrancel, Kellarin,
15th of Aft-Spring

'If you want anything else to drink, we'll have to raid your cellar.' I dumped the flagon of ale on the table in front of Halice.

She fetched earthenware goblets from the dresser and poured. 'What makes you think I've got any wine left?'

'Knowing you better than your own mother did.' A knock sounded at the front door and I wondered who was being so formal. We were in the main room, too small to be called a hall for all the house boasted the dignity of the separate kitchen. 'Come in.'

The door opened to reveal Zigrida's grandson Tedin. 'Grandam's compliments and it's a loaf for the corps commander's lunch.'

'My thanks to her.' Halice smiled at the lad standing barely eye-level with her belt buckle. 'And you did well this morning. You kept your head and ran fast.'

Tedin ducked his head on a gap-toothed grin of pleasure as he set the bread on the table and scurried away.

'What's that man of yours got in the pantry?' Halice asked as the boy pulled the door closed behind him.

I went to look. Well aware I should barely be trusted to pod peas, Ryshad was responsible for all our cooking and food stocks. 'There's a fresh cheese.' I sniffed the moist muslin bag hanging on its hook cautiously. 'Mutton and onion pie and some pickled mushrooms.' Ryshad must have done some notable service to get such precious remnants of a good-wife's winter stores. I peered dubiously at the label of a small stone jar sealed with waxed cloth and twine. 'Pickled broom buds?'

'I haven't seen those since I was a child.' Halice came through to carry food to the table. 'The old women made them to offer at Drianon's shrine.'

'Ryshad wouldn't have put them in the pantry if we couldn't eat them.' I shrugged and cut bread. Halice opened the jar and tasted one before nodding approval and taking more.

'What will Minare have Peyt's mob doing to earn their crusts?' I asked through a mouthful of tasty mutton pie.

'Setting fish traps in the river.' Halice grinned. 'An afternoon up to their stones in cold water should damp down their embers.'

I tried one of the broom buds, finding it mildly aromatic with a faint bitterness, not unpleasant. 'What are you going to do with Peyt?'

Halice spread soft white cheese on a heel of bread. 'He'll be upriver to Edisgesset.' Mouth full, she stumbled over the name the colonists had bestowed on the mining settlement in the hills. 'He can fetch and carry for the charcoal burners for a season or so.'

'Will they have enough ore for smelting this summer?' I queried.

'They opened up the diggings well before Equinox,' Halice pointed out. 'And the sooner we've got metal, the better for trade. Shipping back fur and wood's all very well but cargo like that takes up a cursed lot of room for its value.'

'The right furs can be worth their weight in gold. So can pretty feathers for Tormalin ladies' fans.' After a visit home last summer Ryshad had been full of notions for trapping any bird with a gaudy tail.

'Hmm.' Halice gestured with her knife as she swallowed. 'What I want is to find some of those grubs that make silk. If Kellarin could break the Aldabreshin monopoly, we'd be set for life.'

'If hums were hams, beggars would go well fed.' I took a slow drink of ale. 'I'm thinking about trying my luck in the wine trade. Do you think Charoleia would be interested? Will she still be in Relshaz?'

'She was overwintering there.' Halice applied herself to her meal. 'I don't know which spring fair she was planning to visit, Col or Peorle, and there's no telling where she'll head after that.'

'Let's hope we hear from her by an early ship.' Charoleia would doubtless be charming travellers riding home across the length and breadth of the countries that had once made up the Tormalin Empire, relieving them of their spoils from the Equinox fairs of the great cities. I thought a trifle wistfully of the gaming that had gone on without me.

Halice's thoughts were still in Kellarin. 'Are you thinking of setting up as a proper wine factor with your own warehouse or just taking orders and a commission for settling them?'

'I hadn't really thought.' I took an apple from the bowl on the table.

'Then think and get your pieces on the board before someone else has the same notion,' Halice told me firmly. 'It's too cursed good an idea to let slip. My cellar's as dry as a drunk in the morning. And talking of drunks, has Peyt really been sniffing round Catrice?'

'I've no idea where she was flirting her petticoats before Solstice.' I peeled the apple, wrinkled from the store and soft beneath leathery skin but sweet with the memory of last summer's sun. 'She's kept company with Deglain since the turn of For-Spring. I can vouch for that.' There'd been precious little entertainment to brighten up the winter beyond keeping track of the neighbours.

Halice looked thoughtful. 'So it's his babe.'

'Unless Peyt caught her in a dark corner and wouldn't take no for an answer.' I offered half the apple to Halice.

Halice shook her head. 'He's all mouth and hair oil but he wouldn't risk that. Not with nowhere to run but the wildwood. He knows I'll flog any man till his ribs show for rape.' She cut another slice of pie with her belt knife. 'Who threw the first punch?'

'Deglain,' I said reluctantly. 'But Peyt came looking for a fight. Deg just wanted to sleep off his drink.'

'Raeponin's scales don't tell gold from lead.' Halice grimaced. 'Mercenary rules mean the one who started it gets the heavier punishment, even if only by pennyweight.'

'You're going to send Deg to Edisgesset?' I reckoned we should try weighting the god of justice's scales. 'Is he still a mercenary? He's been working at a trade since before the turn of the year.'

Halice scratched her head. 'I'll tan Peyt's arse for him if I've picked up his lice,' she muttered. 'That's a good question. If Deg's thrown in his lot with the colony for good, he'll be D'Alsennin's problem.'

'He'll be tied to a colony family soon enough, if Catrice's mother has anything to say about it,' I pointed out.

Halice chuckled. 'I never thought I'd see Deglain chivvied with a copper-stick.'

'He won't be the only one, not by Solstice,' I opined.

Halice nodded at the auburn hair brushing my collar. 'You're growing a wedding plait to lay on Drianon's altar, are you?'

I made a derisory noise. 'What do you think?'

'What does Ryshad think?' she countered with the direct gaze of a friend close enough to take such liberties.

'Save your breath to cool your broth,' I told her firmly. 'Think about this instead. The line between who's a fighting man and who's a colonist will only get more scuffed with every match and every passing season. We should draw up some rules before that game really gets into play.' Which would make a more interesting day than doing laundry.

Halice nodded. 'Let's see if we can pin D'Alsennin down long enough to talk it through. It's time that lad faced up to his responsibilities,' she added with relish.

We finished our meal and I avoided Halice's amused eye as I dutifully cleared the table and washed up. You'd need a knife at my throat to make me admit it, especially to my housekeeper mother, but truth be told, I didn't particularly begrudge such necessary tasks. And Ryshad had more sense than to expect the constant clean linen and immaculate house his mother devoted her every waking moment to. I still considered that a waste of time, even now the novelty of so much leisure hanging on my hands was wearing off.

Outside, the generous sun of Kellarin encouraged neat lines of seedlings in gardens vivid green from a sprinkling of rain the night before. I took an appreciative breath of clean air, far better than the stench of foetid gutters that plagues even the best of towns. Cruck-framed houses dotted the rolling landscape in all directions, a few already showing wings added to accommodate growing families. There was plenty of room for such expansion and every plot had been liberally measured to allow for a pigsty and a hencoop as well as a sizeable kitchen garden. Not that such bounty was much use to me who'd grown up in a city where fruit and vegetables arrived on costermongers' carts.

'You want to be getting your plants in,' Halice observed. For all her years with a sword at her side, she'd grown up a smallholder's daughter in that border district where the hilly land's too poor for Lescar, Caladhria or Dalasor to be bothered who claims it.

'Getting dirt under my fingernails?' I scoffed. 'I'll see who's willing to wager some sweat. A day digging my vegetable patch should make a decent stake for someone.' Someone who'd want coin to spend when the first ships arrived.

Goats were tethered on the common grazing cut by tracks already taking on the breadth and permanence of roads. We passed a lad struggling to get a peg in the ground while his beast prodded him with malevolent horns. 'Peyt's less use than that billy,' I observed, 'and he smells worse. Can't you just ship him back to Tormalin?'

Halice laughed. 'Peyt could have his uses. Getting between me and some Ice Islander for one.'

The chill that made me shiver had nothing to do with the fluffy white clouds fleeting across the sun. 'We've none too many decent fighters left, not since Arest took his troop to Lescar.' I wondered which of the continuously warring dukes had the gold and good fortune to secure his services.

'We'll see familiar faces back before the sailing season's half done.' Halice was unconcerned. 'Allin tells me there's been camp fever all over Lescar through the latter half of winter.'

'Lessay should be smart enough to get clear of that.' But Arest's lieutenant had still opted to leave last summer. Land may be valuable, he'd said over a farewell flagon, and granted, it can't be stolen or tarnished, but it's cursed difficult to spend a field on drink or a willing whore. I couldn't argue with that.

Genial, Halice swapped pleasantries with toiling colonists busy in burgeoning gardens and met sundry acquaintances bustling about their errands. Village life was what she'd grown up with, everyone living in each other's pockets. I picked pockets when pressed into a tight corner and moved on swiftly. I'd been raised as a Vanam servant's daughter in the midst of that busiest of cities where my mother kept herself to herself and not just to avoid the pitying glances of those inclined to patronise an unwed woman with a minstrel's by-blow at her skirts.

I smiled and chatted but still found it unsettling to be so readily recognised by folk I barely considered neighbours. After half a lifetime making sure I went unremarked, I found this an unwelcome consequence of living with Ryshad. He'd helped half these people with something to do with their building and had dealings with the rest in his unofficial capacity as Temar D'Alsennin's second in command. I'd yet to find a subtle way of letting these people know that gave them no claim on me.

Eventually we reached the wide river curling through the broad fertile plain between the hills and the sea. Indistinct in the mouth of the spreading estuary, I saw the solid bulk of the *Eryngo*, Kellarin's biggest ship, riding secure at anchor as the crew made ready for their first ocean voyage, just as soon as the holds were full with goods to raise Kellarin's credit back home. Closer to, the bare ribs of half-built ships poked above tidal docks hacked out of the mud the year before.

Halice's gaze followed mine. 'Our own caravels should be exploring the coasts before the last half of summer.'

'Do you think the Elietimm will try their luck this year?' I didn't mind letting her hear my apprehension. 'They're not dogs, to take a lesson from the whipping we gave them.'

'We'll be a match for anyone looking for trouble.' Halice sounded equal to the prospect. 'Peyt and his mob will step up smart enough if it's a choice between fighting back or having your skull split and I've told D'Alsennin I'll be drilling any colony lads bright enough to swing a sword without braining themselves.'

I knew for a fact Ryshad wasn't keen on that idea, concerned that the lads would find their loyalties split between D'Alsennin and the mercenary life. Well, that wasn't my problem, and anyway, I had more serious concerns. 'What about Elietimm magic? Swords don't do so well against that.'

'Arrows and crossbow bolts kill an enchanter just as dead as anyone else.' Halice looked out towards the distant ocean. 'I can't see Guinalle and young Allin letting their black ships sneak up unnoticed. Let's hope for the best while we plan for the worst. With Saedrin's grace, all those ships will have to do is surveying.'

Halice turned to follow the track leading upstream towards Temar's newly finished residence. A woman passed us, full skirts sweeping the grass, decorous kerchief around her head.

I looked after her. 'That's Catrice's mother.' The woman hailed one of the boats busy about the placid waters of the river.

'Off to see Guinalle, I'd say. Let's see what the demoiselle reckons to all this before we corner D'Alsennin.' Halice used her fingers to blow a piercing whistle and a mercenary called Larn promptly turned his boat towards us. A native of

Ensaimin's lakeland, he was currently earning his bread ferrying up and down the river.

'Want me to wait?' He showed Halice the deference of all sensible mercenaries.

She shook her head. 'We'll see ourselves back.'

I got carefully into the boat, bigger than the cockleshell skittering across the estuary with Catrice's mother but still none too secure to my mind.

'You really should learn to swim,' commented Halice.

I stuck my tongue out at her. 'It's hardly a necessary skill for a travelling gambler.' Vanam is as far away from any ocean as it's possible to get in the erstwhile provinces of the Tormalin Empire.

Sitting, I took an unobtrusive grip on the thwart. As Larn leaned into his oars I studied the far bank of the river. The all-entangling vegetation had died back from the stone ruins over the winter and had yet to reclaim them. That laid all the more starkly bare the decay of Kellarin's first colony, founded generations before Vithrancel was even thought of.

More than attitudes and priorities separated the colonists and the mercenaries. Temar D'Alsennin and his hopeful followers had crossed the ocean an astonishing thirty generations ago, turning their backs on the dying days of Tormalin's Old Empire. From their wistful recollections, all had seemed paradise for the first couple of years but then they'd suffered the first fatal onslaught of the Elietimm, ancestors of those same Ice Islanders who'd plagued both sides of the ocean for the past few years. Those early settlers who hadn't been slaughtered fled upriver, hiding themselves in caves discovered while prospecting for metals. Ancient magic had hidden them all in a deathless sleep until the curiosity and connivance of the Archmage had unearthed the incredible truth, lost for so many years thanks to the Chaos that followed the death of Nemith the Last.

I'd enjoyed witnessing the discomfiture of Hadrumal's conceited wizards when the ancient magic of Tormalin had proved to be nothing to do with their own mastery of air, earth, fire and water. I'd been intrigued to discover the same aetheric enchantments could be worked through those ancient songs of the Forest Folk, whose blood ran in my veins thanks to my wandering father's fancy alighting on my maidservant mother. On the other side of the coin, that Artifice had been able to lock those colonists helpless and deathless in the shades between this world and the next still gave me the shudders and then there was Ryshad's distrust of Artifice. I wasn't so interested in it to risk losing him. I realised I was absently twisting the ring he had given me round and round on my finger.

As always Halice's thoughts were more immediately practical. 'Why's Ryshad so set on making bricks? Isn't there enough stone here to keep him happy?' She nodded at bright scars marking the age-stained grey masonry. Beyond using the place as a quarry, most colonists had no use for these uncomfortable reminders of years lost while they lay insensible under enchantment.

'Not with him and Temar insisting that everyone's cesspit is stone lined,' I told her. 'Have you seen all the warehouses, market halls and workshops they're planning?' I'd been shown the drawings, in exhaustive detail; every footing to be set firm with stone and topped with all the bricks Werdel could turn out. Vithrancel's past would underpin its future as D'Alsennin took the lead in turning his face to the here and now rather than the long lost past.

I got carefully out of Larn's boat on the far side. Breeched and booted, we easily gained on Catrice's mother, her strides hampered by the petticoats rustling beneath her hurrying skirts.

A lofty hall appeared round a turn in the gravel path, surrounding wall newly repaired in sharp contrast to the tumbledown ruins on either hand. This time-worn dwelling had been built by the long-dead Messire Den Rannion who'd invited the colonists on their ill-fated venture. It had been their first sanctuary in that confused season when Planir had reawakened them. We had all fought with our backs against these walls, mercenaries, mages and ancient Tormalin alike when the Elietimm had attacked, determined to kill any rival claimants to this land. Guinalle, more formally Demoiselle Tor Priminale, had tended the wounded in the ancient steading using her life-giving Artifice in despite of Elietimm enchantments. By the time the sufferers had either died or recovered, Guinalle had quietly had the place re-roofed and the perimeter wall made secure. No one had had any luck since suggesting the highest-born surviving noblewoman of the original colony move herself across the river, which at least kept the stink of boiling medicaments away from the rest of us. As an apothecary's customer whenever I had the chance rather than a devotee of the still room, I'd never realised quite how much pungent preparation woad needed.

'You can do the talking,' I said to Halice.

Halice shook her head. 'You can't blame her on Ryshad's account for ever.'

'I don't,' I said indignantly.

Halice shot me a sceptical look. 'A blind man in a fog can see how he mistrusts Artifice.'

'I've done more than half the scholars in Vanam to unearth lost aetheric magic,' I protested. 'I brought back no end of lore from the Forest and the Mountains last year.'

'You still walk stiff-legged around Guinalle because of what happened to Ryshad,' said Halice mildly.

My dismissive noise came out rather more non-committal than I intended. Drianon be my witness, I occasionally caught myself watching Ryshad as he slept, wondering if any trace of the enchantment that had enthralled him remained. The bodies of the colonists had been sealed away in the Edisgesset cavern when Guinalle worked the enchantment that locked their true selves, the very essence of their lives, into rings, jewellery and, in Temar D'Alsennin's case, into his sword. Those vital tokens had been sent back to Toremal to summon aid but the few who escaped the destruction of Kel Ar'Ayen found their Empire in the toils of anarchy. No rescue had ever come.

I didn't know how body and consciousness had been separated. The thought of what Guinalle called Higher Artifice
gave me gooseflesh. Eventually – and the scholars of Vanam
continued to argue with Hadrumal's wizards as to why –
these sleeping minds had stirred the dreams of whosoever
chance or some god's fancy had left holding the artefact. The
first hints of the lost colony's true fate had emerged from
the contradiction and exaggeration of legend.

But Planir the Black, fabled Archmage of Hadrumal wasn't
ever one to leave things to chance or even to Saedrin himself.
He'd made sure Ryshad was given Temar D'Alsennin's sword,
hoping similarities between the two men would form a bond
to reach across the shades and bring back the answers Planir
wanted. It had worked, after a fashion, but I still considered
the way Ryshad's body had been possessed by Temar's
questing mind too high a price.

But only fools argue over a hand that's been played out.
All those runes had been gathered for drawing anew and I
planned to make the best of my luck and Ryshad's.

We followed Catrice's mother through the darkly stained
gate now reinforced with pale new timber. The courtyard of
the ancient steading was busy; Guinalle wasn't alone on this
side of the river. Masons cleaned stone reclaimed from the
ruins and men studied a plan, pegs and cord for marking
something in their hands. I recalled Ryshad mentioning a
kiln wanted hereabouts to burn rubble into lime for his
precious mortar.

The outraged matron ignored everyone as she hurried into
the wide hall. 'Demoiselle, Demoiselle, a moment of your
time, if you please.'

We followed and I wrinkled my nose at a faint smell of
paint. Looking up I saw the roof had been repanelled since
my last visit, its decoration begun. The first pious scene
completed showed Saedrin sorting his keys by the door to
the Otherworld while Poldrion poled his ferry of newly dead
across the river that flows through the shades.

I looked for Guinalle and found her by a long table

covered with a pungent array of greenery dotted with early flowers in blue and yellow. A woman a touch below my own height, she was neatly made with a trim waist to balance rounded hips and a bosom to catch a man's eye. Dressed in the same work-stained broadcloth as the other women, the golden chain that girdled her nevertheless marked her rank, carrying a chatelaine's keys, knife and small mesh purse. The women sorting herbs for immediate decoction or bundling sprigs for drying looked up with ready curiosity at Catrice's mother. The busy hum of conversation took on a speculative note.

'Mistress Cheven.' Guinalle ushered the red-faced matron into a side aisle where withy screens separated bays into an illusion of privacy. I favoured the inquisitive women with a sunny smile while Halice leaned on the doorpost, dour faced, prompting most to tend their steeping jars and tincture bottles.

'One of those filth—' Catrice's mother struggled for words to express her contempt, accents of Toremal strengthened by emotion and echoing round the stone walls. 'He calls my girl a slut, says she lays with any who asks, claiming her babe as his.' Fury choked her to silence before abruptly deserting her, leaving her plump face slack with the threat of tears.

'Calm yourself.' Guinalle looked past Mistress Cheven as she pressed the woman to take a stool. 'Corps Commander Halice is here and I imagine about the same business.' She beckoned to us with unconscious authority.

Halice walked over unhurried, me a pace behind. 'Mistress Cheven, Demoiselle Tor Priminale.' She bowed and Guinalle sketched a perfunctory curtsey out of archaic habit. 'I came to warn you about Peyt right enough. He's out to make trouble for Deglain and slandering Catrice was the best thing he could think of. There was a fight—' Halice raised a hand to soothe Mistress Cheven's inarticulate distress. 'Peyt came off second best and he'll feel the sharp edge of my tongue as well as due punishment. It was Deg I wanted to talk to you about, Demoiselle.' She looked at Guinalle. 'Back in Lescar, hired as a corps, I'd have him flogged for messing with a girl, if she was unwilling. If she was willing but found with child, I'd pay him off and promise him all the torments of Poldrion's demons if I ever found he'd abandoned them. But I'd still be calling him to account for throwing the first punch in a brawl.'

'But this is not Lescar,' Guinalle concluded Halice's unspoken thought.

'Deglain's a good man, not one to fight unless sore provoked.' Mistress Cheven looked concerned. 'Me and her father, we're glad to see Catrice keep company with him. They've been talking about wedding this Solstice coming. Back when, that is, if we still held to old customs, they'd be handfasted long since.'

'Deglain's been working as a tinsmith since before the turn of the year,' Halice pointed out. 'Does he come under my jurisdiction these days? I wouldn't argue for it.'

Guinalle sat on a stool herself. 'No, I don't suppose he does.'

'I don't want Peyt to sniff an excuse to go stirring up any bad feeling between mercenaries and colonists. This seems as good a time as any to agree a few rules about exactly where D'Alsennin's writ runs and where my authority holds.' Halice studied Guinalle's heart-shaped face before turning to Mistress Cheven with firm assertion. 'But Peyt definitely comes under my lash and I'll see it bites him. He won't sully Catrice's name again.'

'That answers your complaint, doesn't it?' Guinalle brushed absently at the chestnut braids coiled high on her head and I noticed green stains on the ladylike softness of her small hands, grime beneath her precisely pared nails.

The habit of obedience to anyone noble born prompted the older woman to stand. 'I suppose so.'

'Send Catrice to see me,' Guinalle smiled reassurance. 'I can see how far along the babe is.'

'That would be a kindness, Demoiselle.' Mistress Cheven looked relieved. 'It being her first – well, there are things a girl won't ask her mother.' She glanced at Halice and me, colouring as she curtseyed a farewell to Guinalle.

'Didn't women ever wear breeches in the Old Empire?' I watched her go with amusement.

'Not that I'm aware,' replied Guinalle with a smile too brief to reach her hazel eyes.

'Can Artifice tell you if Deg truly is the father?' Halice asked bluntly.

'I might get some sense of it.' Guinalle hesitated. 'Does it matter, if he loves Catrice and acknowledges the child?'

'I'd like to be forewarned, if it'll come out wearing Peyt's nose.' Halice looked stern. 'I'll ship him back across the ocean before Catrice's due season for a start.'

'Which will almost certainly be For-Autumn.' Guinalle's unguarded face showed an instant of weariness. 'Another one. Drianon only knows where we're going to find enough Bluemantle.' She looked at the long table where her women were still diligently sorting herbs between whispered comments and snatched glances in our direction. 'I wonder how anything got done over the winter, there are so many babes expected between hay and harvest.'

I couldn't decide if Guinalle sounded disapproving or envious. No matter, midwifery was none of my business and I'd make doubly sure of that with a little herb gathering of my own, as soon as Halcarion's Vine came into bloom on this side of the ocean.

Halice had other concerns as well. 'We need D'Alsennin—' She broke off as two men with belligerent expressions hurried into the hall and hailed Guinalle.

'Demoiselle—'

'My lady—'

One was a colonist I vaguely recognised; the other a craftsman come over the previous year after D'Alsennin had taken ship to Toremal to settle a few matters with Emperor Tadriol and start recruiting new blood and necessary skills.

'It's the piglets,' one began.

'I'll pay with a share when it's killed,' protested the other.

His Tormalin lilt was already coloured with the ancient intonations and mongrel mercenary accents that were blending into Kellarin's speech.

'There's ten in the litter,' the first man appealed to Guinalle. 'Me and the wife can't eat that much sausage! We need firewood. He's got it stacked up to the eaves—'

'And I sweated for every axe stroke,' protested the craftsman. 'And Estle's boar did the work on your sow, not you!'

'I was talking with the demoiselle.' There was an ominous edge to Halice's voice and both men took a pace back.

The colonist twisted his cap awkwardly in square hands. 'Beg pardon, Mis—' He swallowed the word 'Mistress' as Halice glared at him.

'If you want D'Alsennin to extend his authority over Deglain, Corps Commander, take it up with him.' Guinalle stood, smoothing the front of her plain gown. 'I have more than enough to do here.'

'So I see.' Halice frowned and the men with the squabble took another step back but I didn't think her anger was directed at them. 'Have you any adepts trained to share your duties yet?'

Guinalle stiffened. 'We've managed some study over the winter but time is limited with so much to do.'

'And it's always quicker and easier to do things yourself rather than show someone else. Why risk them fouling it up?' Halice's voice was firm but not unsympathetic. She looked down at Guinalle with a rare smile. 'Which is all well and good but you need to let folk learn by their own mistakes.'

'It's for me to judge how best to train practitioners of Artifice.' Guinalle's chin came up, her expression one of frosty hauteur. 'Haste is often at odds with wisdom, especially when we can ill afford even the most trivial errors. Good day to you.' Guinalle nodded a brusque farewell and swept back to her waiting women, leaving the men with the squabble looking blank.

Halice strode out of the hall and I followed, noting she

was rubbing absently at the thigh she'd broken a couple of years back. Guinalle's skills with the healing power of Artifice had saved Halice from life as a cripple and Halice was ever one to honour her debts, whether the noblewoman wanted her help or not.

'That girl needs to take a bit more time for herself and ask a lot more of other people. I can't recall when we last talked without someone interrupting to ask her to judge a barter, solve a quarrel, or advise on some triviality.' Halice shot me a glare. 'There wasn't one of the adepts she's supposedly training around that table.'

'Don't look at me,' I warned her. 'My tricks with the Forest charms are only Low Artifice and that's as much as I'm interested in.' That Guinalle barely concealed her disdain for such minor magic didn't exactly endear her to me.

'You could learn the Higher Artifice,' Halice challenged. 'You've shown an aptitude for enchantment.'

'I don't want to,' I told her bluntly.

'You mean Ryshad doesn't want you to,' countered Halice.

'When did I last hide behind a man's say-so?' I scoffed. Ryshad hadn't told me he didn't want me studying Artifice with Guinalle. He probably wouldn't, even if I did. But he wouldn't like it all the same and that was enough to tip the balance in favour of my own reservations, even if I was curious to learn how Guinalle worked her enchantments without the songs that were the only way I knew of using aetheric power. I wasn't that curious. Tricks to light fires or smooth over footsteps are all very well but I knew better than most how Artifice could get inside people's heads, even leave them dead without a mark on them. I could count the people I'd trust with that kind of power, even with the best of intentions, on the fingers of one hand.

Halice was scowling. 'D'Alsennin's some skill with aetheric magic, hasn't he? He should lean a bit more weight on the traces.'

It was a safe bet who'd be telling him that. Which would certainly be more interesting than going home to do the laundry. A new thought occurred to me. 'Sutal will probably come back if Lessay does. She'd take some of the load off Guinalle.'

Halice nodded grudgingly. 'We could do with a proper surgeon, regardless.'

We got a ride back across the river on a flat-bottomed boat laden with salvaged masonry and I scrambled gratefully ashore at the jetty that marked Vithrancel's first proper landing. I spotted Werdel among the men piling stone up beyond any risk of flooding.

I waved to him. 'Where's Rysh?'

He rested dusty hands on his thighs. 'Taken D'Alsennin up to the drying sheds.'

I looked at Halice. 'Do you want to go after them?'

Halice looked around the buildings that were finally giving Vithrancel some appearance of a real town. Colonists and mercenaries alike had tacked haphazard shelters on to ancient remnants of walls and roofs, scant defence against that first uncertain winter. A full eight seasons later, the last of these makeshifts were being cleared as new buildings staked firm claim to the land and we even had an irregular space people were calling the market square. A brewer had claimed the first plot to universal approval and his solid establishment now offered Kellarin's only taproom where I occasionally found a friendly game among those keen to quench their thirsts. The long low building beside it sheltered looms shared informally by men and women with the skills to use them and I saw the usual throng of people with wool to swap for yarn or finished cloth around the door. The loft above served as a store for the dyers and fullers who'd set up pungent work further downstream.

Halice was glaring at an impressive building at the head of the market square. It had a definite air of authority, roofs neatly slated with stone rather than wooden shingles and walls scoured clean of the mottled stains of age. A splash of bright green on a ground of azure blue hung bashful from a lanyard, waiting for Temar's return to hoist it to the foremost gable. Held out by a helpful wind, it would show a device of three overlapping holm oak leaves.

'It's all very well Temar hanging out his flag but as soon as anyone fussing sees he's never there, they head straight for Guinalle. What we want is some magic to stick the lad's arse to a chair every morning,' said Halice with a glint in her eye. 'Artifice or wizardry, I don't care which.'

I chuckled. 'Shiv might oblige. Let's see what's trading while we're waiting.' I gestured towards the large hall to the offhand of Temar's residence. That had rapidly become the centre for barter and bargaining among colonists and mercenaries alike. I might find something worth the promise of a few of Ryshad's bricks.

The Island City of Hadrumal,
15th of Afi-Spring

'Hearth Master, Flood Mistress.' A startled maidservant bobbed a curtsey to the stout man sweeping into the quadrangle. He spared her a lordly wave of the full-cut sleeve of his velvet robe. The woman with him ignored the girl, cutting directly across the flagstones towards Planir's door, unyielding determination on her weathered face. She held the door for her companion with visible impatience but remained silent, setting a punishing pace up the stairs. The man rapped a fat hand on Planir's door, ruby rings dark on three fingers.

'Come in.' Planir sat in a high-backed, comfortably upholstered chair by the empty fireplace, a book in one hand, a goblet of fruit juice in the other, a crumb-strewn plate on a small table at his side. 'Troanna, Kalion, please, help yourselves. There's caraway loaf or sunrise breads. Something to drink?' He got to his feet.

Kalion, flushed from the exertion of the stairs, smiled at the generously laid table. He tucked a cushion behind him as he sat and unbuttoned the high collar of his scarlet gown, its nap still fresh from the tailor's brush. 'Thank you, Archmage, a little plum cordial, with plenty of water,' he added hastily.

'Just a glass of water, if you please.' Troanna sat unsmiling in an upright chair and ignored golden glazed buns still warm from the oven, split ready for fluffy sweetened cream and the preserves to hand in crystal dishes. As Kalion filled an eager plate, she settled the skirts of an emerald gown in the Caladhrian style favoured by most of Hadrumal's women. Troanna's dress was as severe as her expression, without even the usual embroidery to lighten it. Her hazel eyes studied

Planir with an intelligence that made it plain she was no mere gap-toothed matron subsiding into dumpy middle age and greying hair. 'We came to discuss appointing a new Cloud Master.'

'Or Cloud Mistress.' Kalion looked up from the breakfast table with instant alertness. 'Archmage, have you seen the conclusions Velindre drew from her voyage around the Cape of Winds last summer? She's proving extremely talented.'

'I've not had the pleasure of reading her journal as yet.' Planir smiled as he poured drinks at an expensively inlaid sideboard. He waved a hand at the books stacked higher than Troanna's head on the reading desk. 'I have so many calls on my time.'

'You should make time to consider all candidates,' Troanna said, unimpressed, hands laced in her lap.

'Such excessive delay is causing talk around the halls,' Kalion warned as he spread damson jam with precise knife strokes.

'I'm assessing every candidate most thoroughly.' Planir gestured towards the book he'd set aside. 'That's Rafrid's treatise on the interaction of the southern sea winds and the winter winds from the northern mountains.' He handed a crystal glass to Troanna and set a carafe of water together with a goblet of ruby liquor by Kalion's elbow.

'If Rafrid had ambitions to be Cloud Master, he shouldn't have accepted mastery of Hiwan's Hall.' Kalion emphasised his words with a jab of an empty cream spoon.

'Master or Mistress, we need someone coordinating the proper study of the element,' insisted Troanna.

'Quite so.' Kalion added a little water to the cordial in the goblet. 'Archmage, what am I to do when some apprentice appears with a query that should properly be referred to a Cloud Master?'

'Your talents with the air are well known.' Planir resumed his seat, resting his elbows on the arms of the chair as he steepled his fingers. His face was amiable. 'I imagine you're both equal to such questions.'

'That's no answer and you know it.' Troanna's response was curt. 'Those coming here to explore their affinity deserve guidance from the leading proficients in each and every element.'

'I agree.' Planir's expression was more serious. 'Which is why I won't rush such a crucial decision.'

'All delay gets you is dirt and long nails,' Troanna retorted.

Kalion took another bun with a casual air. 'It would be quite proper for you to nominate two or three candidates to the Council and ask for a vote. There's plenty of precedent for such appointments.'

'The Council won't select Rafrid,' Troanna warned. 'He can't be Cloud Master and run a hall.'

Kalion's laugh was forced. 'He can't run with the hare and hunt with the hounds.'

Planir looked at him, unsmiling. 'You have a point to make?'

Troanna was unmoved by the chill in the Archmage's voice. 'You say you're so busy? Perhaps you should set aside some duties. Let the Council choose a new Stone Master at the same time as the Cloud Master we need.'

'Or Mistress,' interjected Kalion.

Planir shrugged dismissively. 'I'm hardly the first Archmage to be an Element Master at the same time.'

'Sooner or later, they all relinquished the lesser duty,' said Troanna bluntly. 'I thought you'd have the wit to see the necessity sooner, Planir.'

'Archmage, you've naturally been preoccupied with guiding Hadrumal through the last few years' upheavals in the wider world.' Kalion's sincerity was unaffected by the cream smudging his plump chin. 'It's no reflection on your abilities but can you honestly claim to have time for assessing some apprentice's notions on the cohesion of rock?'

'What if these Elietimm with their peculiar enchantments reappear?' Troanna spoke mercilessly over him. 'Can Hadrumal stay uninvolved if they threaten Tormalin or Kellarin again? As Archmage, you'll have Emperor Tadriol, the dukes of Lescar, the Caladhrian Parliament and whoever else come running in a panic and asking for our aid.'

'What if they attack Hadrumal itself?' Kalion's ruddy cheeks paled and recollection haunted his eyes. 'We've seen their abhorrence of wizardry. You'll need a full nexus of Element Masters backing you to work quintessential magic to stop them.'

'I hardly think it'll come to that.' Planir took up his fruit juice and sipped it with unconcern.

'No?' Troanna's scepticism was biting. 'Otrick was my friend and this Artifice left his mind dead within him. I can't forget that. Nor do I want to sit vigil over any more living corpses because you were tied up in disputes over pupillage agreements when you were needed to defend someone else.'

'Set the Elietimm aside, Archmage.' Food abandoned, Kalion leaned earnest elbows on the table. 'Even without them, your duties as Archmage increase with every season from what I can see. Hadrumal is committed to helping these people in Kellarin. They need our magecraft to sail the very oceans, never mind anything else. You've extended invitations to any wizards in Solura who might care to study here. You've been talking about pursuing Usara's discovery of magebirth among the Mountain and the Forest races. We have Mentor Tonin trying to search out Artifice's secrets and Vanam's scholars visiting here while our mages travel to their university. The pace is hardly going to slacken. All we ask is you consider setting aside some of your other burdens.'

'Perhaps.' A line appeared between Planir's fine black brows. 'I'd be a fool to let my scones burn because I wouldn't let anyone else at the griddle, wouldn't I? If Hadrumal needs a new Stone Master, Usara's the obvious candidate.'

Troanna narrowed suspicious eyes. 'What dedication has he shown to the proper study of magecraft lately?'

'He and Shiv have been seeing how mages might work together in lesser combinations than a full nexus,' Planir offered.

'I fail to see how he'll have made much progress when he

spent all last summer traipsing round with the scaff and raff of the mainland backwoods.' Kalion leaned back to fold thick forearms over his substantial girth. 'Not even representing Hadrumal to anyone of influence.'

'Then he wasted the winter breaking his nails trying to pick aetheric lore out of that collection of old Forest songs and whatever myths that Mountain lass he dragged back here could think up.' Troanna was contemptuous. 'Mentor Tonin is welcome to indulge such intellectual curiosity but it's hardly the province of wizards.'

'You wouldn't welcome some Artifice of our own to counter the Elietimm?' Planir asked blandly.

'I would if there was any sign of it, Archmage.' Kalion sounded genuinely regretful. 'But there's none beyond the simplest tricks, is there?'

Troanna looked at him unsmiling. 'We would do better to meet any aetheric assault with tried and tested magic worked by a full nexus of Element Masters.'

'There are more candidates for Stone Master than Usara.' Kalion barely let the Flood Mistress finish speaking. 'Galen has been examining the fundamental assumptions under-pinning our understanding of the element of earth.'

'I had no idea.' The Archmage shook his head thoughtfully. 'But he hasn't initiated any discussion that I'm aware of and I do keep current with such things, the earth being my own affinity. Kalion, you should drop Galen a hint to share his conclusions, otherwise people will only think him good for the latest gossip.' There was a barb in Planir's casual geniality.

'Usara is far too young to have any credibility with the older mages,' Troanna said with finality. 'He hasn't the experi-ence to claim pre-eminence in his element, no matter what his recent reputation as an adventurer might be.'

'While Galen has spent so long in Kalion's shadow, he has no reputation of his own at all.' Planir met Troanna's stern gaze calmly. 'Who could be confident he'd be sympathetic to some apprentice's adolescent confusions or could summon the necessary diplomacy when two mages dispute a pupillage?

There's more to mastery than pure study, as you know better than anyone.'

He sprang to his feet, crossing the room to stand by the window. 'There's no obvious candidate for Cloud Master – or Mistress – any more than there is for Stone Master. True, I could offer a handful of each to the Council but do you think any would command a consensus? I don't – and I certainly don't want Hadrumal splitting into factions and backbiting when, as you so rightly say, Troanna, we must be wary of threats from outside. The Elietimm have been quiescent since their attempt to stir revolt in the Mountains was foiled but we cannot relax our vigilance just yet. Kalion, your hopes of greater influence on the mainland may finally be realised with this new understanding we've come to with Tadriol over Kellarin. Even the appearance of dissension among ourselves could undermine all the work you've done to convince people of Hadrumal's potential to help them. It never takes much to revive the suspicions and misinformation that plague wizardry's reputation in the mainland.'

'Ifs and buts are no excuse for inaction, Planir.' Troanna was unimpressed. 'This situation is intolerable and, as Archmage, your duty is to resolve it.'

Kalion's jowled face creased with dissatisfaction. 'And quickly.'

'Hasty with the whip and the horse may stumble,' warned Planir. 'I'm sure the best candidate will become apparent in time.'

Troanna snorted. 'Or you'll spend so long looking, you'll pass over an adequate one. Better ride a donkey that carries you than a horse that's always bucking.'

'I'll find a proverb to trade you for that one tomorrow,' Planir smiled.

Troanna stood. 'This is no matter for levity.'

She looked at Kalion and the stout mage reluctantly rose to his feet. She ushered him out of the room, neither mage saying anything further before she closed the door with an emphatic clunk.

Planir looked at the plain oak panels for a long moment before slinging his robe haphazard over the back of his chair. Weariness at odds with the early hour carved deep lines in his face now as the animation left it. He moved to the window, looking down as Kalion and Troanna disappeared beneath the arched gateway. Holding out his hand, he studied the great diamond ring of his office, sunlight catching the faceted gem set around with emerald, amber, ruby and sapphire, all the ancient tokens of the elements of wizardry. On the finger beside it, he wore a battered circle of silver. Whatever device had decorated it was long since worn to obscurity.

The Archmage clenched his fist and closed his grey eyes on a grimace of regret and frustration. The glasses Kalion and Troanna had used began to tremble slightly, a faint rattle from the table beneath. The dregs of plum cordial suddenly ignited in a startled flame while the untouched water in the larger goblet began to seethe before breaking into a rolling boil. The fluted bowl of the cordial glass folded in on itself, the long stem wilting. The water glass sank beside it, empty of all but a fugitive trace of steam, the broad foot spreading into a formless puddle. The gloss of the polished wood beneath was unmarred.

'Childish.' Planir said reprovingly to himself before opening his eyes with a wicked grin. 'But satisfying.' Tossing the now cold and solid glass into an ash bucket by the hearth, he pulled a well-worn jerkin from the back of the door, shrugging it on as his light tread echoed rapidly down the stairwell.

Vithrancel, Kellarin,
15th of Aft-Spring

'Why are people always so eager to give you gifts?' I followed Halice out of the trading hall.

'It won't be my beauty, so it must be my charm.' Halice offered me the little mint-lined basket of withy strips.

I took a sticky sweetmeat and nodded at Temar's residence. 'His lordship's back.' The bold flag fluttered jauntily.

'Let's see what he's got to say for himself.' Halice curled her lip.

'Mind your manners,' I warned, mock serious.

'Me? Who served the Duchess of Marlier?' Halice pretended outrage.

'Who got dismissed for giving her mouthy daughter a slap,' I pointed out.

'She deserved it.' Halice laughed.

We turned down what looked to be a lane at first glance, running between the trading hall and Temar's residence. Inside the latter, hammers still echoed and saws rasped over the much interrupted and delayed business of making it fit for a Sieur's dignity. Two lads barely older that Tedin sat in a doorway dutifully straightening scavenged nails. One scooped a few from rain-dulled tiles at his feet. Their broken patterns beneath the gravel and the stumps of pillars buried in the new stone of the walls on either side were the last remnants of a great hall that had once stood here. But the roof was long since fallen and the mighty walls only offered a few broken courses so the colonists had merely taken them as a guide for new buildings raised around the shell of the old hall. We passed carved embellishments worn featureless by generations of rain.

The one elegant doorway that had survived above head height was now the entrance to Temar's private quarters at the back of the tall building. Halice pushed open the door without ceremony. Once the carpenters had fitted out the reception rooms, archive and private salons necessary for the rank the Emperor had confirmed him in, Temar might be able to turn this into suitable accommodation for the Sieur D'Alsennin's servants but for the present, the lower floor was undecorated with crude screens at one end inadequately masking a kitchen and a private chamber for Temar above reached by a plain wooden stair.

Temar and Ryshad stood behind a long table up at the far end, poring over a slew of charts with a couple of other people bending their heads close.

'Master Grethist got an ocean boat up to this cataract.' Temar tapped the map with a long finger. 'With sail barges, we can explore further.'

So they were planning another expedition. If Ryshad was going, perhaps I should tag along. Summer in Vithrancel didn't promise to be overly interesting without him.

'Portage over that ground will be a trial and a half.' A black-haired woman, sedate in a homespun tunic over undyed skirts traced a line with a chipped nail. 'It's far more broken than the slope on this side.' She looked up at our approach.

'Rosarn.' Halice greeted her with a familiar nod. The woman's homely appearance was deceptive; Rosarn had been a mercenary longer than any bar Halice and as soon as Temar gave the word, she'd be in boots and leathers, daggers sheathed at hip and wrist, ready to cut her way through thickets a squirrel would rather go round. Half the corps commanders in Lescar went looking for her if they needed an enemy position scouted out or a potential advance reconnoitred. She specialised in tasks demanding light feet and the wit to think fast on them.

'How far did you get, Vas?' Ryshad, the love if not of my life then certainly of these past three years, brushed at his black curls in absent thought.

'Here at autumn Equinox.' Vaspret set a stubby finger on the parchment. Stocky, weather-beaten and with manners as ill made as his much-broken nose, he had come to Kel Ar'Ayen as one the original venturers and sailed on the first explorations of the continent's coasts with the long-dead Master Grethist.

'To retrace Vahil Den Rannion's route, we should really be using the caves.' Whatever they were planning, Rosarn was clearly looking forward to it. I'd heard her say more than once a whole continent to explore without risk of a Lescari arrow in the guts was a gift from Talagrin.

Temar was fair-skinned by nature and the spring sun had yet to tint his winter pallor but I saw him blench from where I stood. Ryshad looked sharply at Rosarn and a shadow darkened his amber-flecked brown eyes. Then he saw me and smiled, affection softening the stern lines of his long jaw and broad brow. I smiled back and the minor discontents of the day vanished like morning mist on the river.

'We want an overland route to join the two rivers,' D'Alsennin said with a touch too much firmness. He searched for some other map. 'We can hardly take wagons or mules through caves, even if the route Vahil used is still passable, by some miracle of Misaen's grace.'

And you'd rather face invading Elietimm single-handed than spend any time out of reach of daylight, my lad. I'd no idea if it was Temar who'd originally been afraid of the dark or Ryshad in some childhood fastness of his mind. Perhaps it was some echo of the imprisonment in Edisgesset's sunless caverns that they'd both tasted, caught in the toils of Artifice. Whatever the case, both men now shared an abiding fear of enclosed spaces and I kept waking to an open bedroom door because Ryshad couldn't sleep with it shut.

But Ryshad was older than Temar by a double handful of years and more. He set his jaw, visibly ignoring his own qualms. 'Is there any chance the missing artefacts could have been lost in the caves, before Vahil got to the ships?'

Vahil Den Rannion, Temar's boyhood friend and now twenty-some generations ashes in his urn, had borne the

task of taking the sleeping minds of Kellarin's people beyond
the greedy Elietimm grasp. He'd found a way through the
caves that riddled the high ground between Vithrancel's river
and another that ran down to a second settlement in the
south barely founded before the Elietimm scourge arrived.
I wouldn't have wagered a lead penny on his chances but,
against all the odds, Vahil had won back across the ocean,
only to find the Empire collapsing around Nemith the
Worthless's ears. Every noble House had been too busy
saving its own skin to spare any thought for a colony all but
written off a year or more since.

So the treasures had been scattered, their true value
unrecognised down the long years. Then mages consulting
with alchemists at Vanam's university had piqued Planir's
curiosity with tales of bizarre dreams tantalising scholars of
the days before the Chaos. Since waking to find himself
required to lead the colony, Temar had striven to recover all
that he could, even challenging the Emperor of Tormalin to
help him but there were still a few poignant sleepers insen-
sate in the vast emptiness of the cavern that had protected
the colonists for so long. Guinalle visited them every Equinox
and Solstice, searching her learning for any clue as to how
she might rouse them without the artefacts that bound them
to the enchantment.

'I suppose that's possible,' Temar acknowledged reluctantly, ice-pale eyes hooded like a hawk's under narrow brows.
His hair was as black as Ryshad's but fine and straight,
cropped like a trooper's.

'We should send someone to search,' Ryshad said firmly.
His commitment to finding the lost artefacts was equal to
Temar's. That had been one factor in the Sieur D'Olbriot's
decision to release him from sworn service, the prince seeing
how Ryshad's sense of obligation had him increasingly torn
between D'Alsennin's interests and D'Olbriot's.

Temar's angular face lifted with relieved inspiration.
'Guinalle could devise an incantation to find anything holding
enchantment in the caves.'

'Why not improve your own skills with Artifice rather than always relying on her?' asked Halice sharply.

Temar looked at her with surprise. 'I've scarcely time to study Artifice.'

'A Sieur decides where to spend his time.' Halice flicked the corner of a map hanging over the edge of the table. 'What is it now? Charting coasts? Prospecting for metals?'

'Scouting a route to Hafreinsaur,' said Temar defensively. Fired with enthusiasm when the Emperor had decreed independence for Kellarin, as present day speech rendered the ancient name, one of Temar's first and thus far few acts as Sieur had been naming the settlements to honour the original founders: Vithrancel for Ancel Den Rannion, Hafreinsaur for Hafrein Den Fellaemion. He'd wanted some such name for the mining settlement but that had failed in the face of mercenary tongues mangling colonists' colloquial references to their cave sanctuary in Old High Tormalin. The compromise that was Edisgesset was now firmly established.

Halice gave him a look that would have shrivelled any mercenary. 'I can name ten men who'll do as good a job as you.'

Temar rubbed a cautious hand over his mouth. 'You think I should be doing something else?'

'Spend more time in and around Vithrancel,' Halice told him frankly. 'Do some of the pettifogging work that weighs down Guinalle from sunrise to dusk. Someone's asking her advice every second moment because you're never around. She'd have more than enough to do if she were only working Artifice, what with fools falling sick or injuring themselves and her insisting on warding all the crops and animals every chance she gets. She's exhausting herself and it's the willing horse that gets worked to death, my lad.'

'We'll discuss this later.' Rosarn rolled up her maps with a rattling sound. 'I'll see what progress the boat-builders have made.'

'I think—'

Rosarn deflected Temar's indignation with an apologetic

smile, gathering up Vaspret as she headed for the door. Never mind Tadriol the Prudent, 5th of that House to rule as Emperor of Toremal decreeing Temar was now Sieur D'Alsennin, prince of that House and overlord of Kellarin. Rosarn answered first and foremost to her corps commander.

Temar took a seat at the head of the table, squaring his shoulders. For lack of any ready response, he raised a lordly hand. Bridele, a young woman widowed before the first fall of Kellarin, scurried up with a tray of glass goblets and a jug. Temar had servants if no one else did.

Ryshad and I cleared space among the parchments and she poured suspiciously pale wine for us all. Halice didn't wait for an invitation to sit but Ryshad waited for D'Alsennin's nod.

'Of course I'll help Guinalle,' Temar said stiffly. 'She only has to ask.'

'Can you see her doing that?' Halice's disarming grin lightened her coarse features. 'Forfeiting her noble obligations, never mind her pride? Tackle the easier problem. With you away so much, folk all got into the habit of running to Guinalle. You need to let people know to come to you.'

'Guinalle doesn't have any truly competent adept to share her burdens, does she?' Ryshad commented with careful neutrality.

'I do not have the time to study Artifice,' Temar repeated, colouring slightly.

Ryshad and I exchanged a glance. It wasn't only pride that had Guinalle keeping her own counsel so much and Temar taking every opportunity offered to go off and explore Kellarin, leaving her to rule Vithrancel. They had shared a brief passion before the ruin of the colony's hopes and as inexperienced lovers so often will, they'd wounded each other deeply in tearing themselves apart.

'I don't think many folk hereabouts do,' I remarked in the same light vein as Ryshad. 'Not with the dedication Guinalle demands of them.' I didn't imagine I was the only one whose general curiosity about Artifice had retreated from the rigorous study the demoiselle demanded of would-be adepts.

'Perhaps we should see if Demoiselle Tor Arrial is ready to return from Toremal,' Ryshad suggested.

'You're welcome to ask but don't expect me to,' said Temar bluntly. 'It will take more than Tadriol designating me her Sieur before I try claiming lordship over Avila.' The Demoiselle Tor Arrial was a formidable older noblewoman who'd known Temar since his extremely callow youth and seldom let him forget it.

I looked at Ryshad. 'Avila's doing valuable service where she is, sending us news of Tormalin and making sure we get decent goods, not the dross of dockside warehouses.' And making a new life in Tormalin meant she could put the bereavements of Kellarin's destruction behind her somewhat.

'Without her there to use her Artifice, we have no means of sending word to the Emperor.' Temar set his jaw. 'I will not recall her.'

No one was going to argue with that. If the Elietimm ever reappeared, we all wanted some way of calling up reinforcements and quickly.

Halice nodded. 'But where can we find more people with aetheric skills?'

I had an idea. 'What about those scholars from Vanam who visited Guinalle last summer, all curious about lost aetheric teachings? They've had all winter to study the lore we found in the Mountains and the Forest last year. Surely they'll have some competent practitioners by now?' Even before these recent additions to their knowledge, Mentor Tonin and his scholars had had enough Artifice to break the enchantments in Edisgesset's cavern. That was how we'd roused Temar and Guinalle in the first place.

'What about recruiting a few more wizards?' Ryshad mused. 'Whoever Hadrumal sends with the first ships might agree to stay for a season or so.'

'When are we expecting those?' I looked for an answer.

'I did ask Guinalle to find out from Avila.' Temar couldn't quite keep his composure as he caught Halice's exasperated glare.

'You're as bad as the rest of them.'

'Allin could bespeak any number of mages in Toremal to find out,' Ryshad pointed out.

'So where is she?' demanded Halice.

'She's helping Werdel with modifications to his kiln,' Ryshad admitted a little sheepishly.

Halice snapped her fingers at Bridele's sandy-haired son who served as Temar's ever-eager page. 'Go and find Lady Allin.'

The lad grinned at her and took to his heels. I sipped at wine watered almost to tastelessness and grimaced.

'Bridele can make you a tisane,' offered Temar.

'From the last dust of her spice jars?' I asked 'Or some unknown herb? My thanks but I don't need poisoning.' At least one recent death had been some obsessive steeping himself a quick route to Poldrion's ferry in a vain attempt to eke out his tisanes.

I saw Temar was looking pinched around the mouth. Maewelin had exacted precious little due from Kellarin over the winter but Temar took each and every loss hard. 'Is there news from Edisgesset? Are the miners ready to start smelting?'

He was successfully diverted. 'As soon as possible.'

'What are you going to do with the copper?' I asked.

'Trade it with Toremal.' Temar looked puzzled then smiled. 'For tisane herbs and decent wine, perhaps.'

'We need iron.' Ryshad was serious. 'We've found no trace of ironstone and our smiths are reusing every rusty scrap of chain as it is.'

'Coin would simplify trading with Toremal.' Ryshad raised an eyebrow at me but I looked at him with bland innocence. 'Ready copper around here wouldn't come amiss either. It would save you and Guinalle adjudicating barters and such.'

'Coining is a skilled trade.' Temar frowned.

'I know a man who could do it,' I offered. 'Make it worth his while and he'll cross the ocean.'

'That Gidestan with the cropped ears?' Halice recalled his name. 'Kewin?'

Temar chose his words carefully. 'I hardly think the Emperor would take kindly to us making free with his currency.'

I looked at him, exasperated. 'I'm not suggesting forgery. What about your own head on a few pennies?'

'It would make a fine statement of independence.' Seriousness underlay Ryshad's amusement. 'Kellarin needs to stand on its own two feet.'

Temar looked doubtful. One of his more appealing qualities was a lack of the usual arrogance that goes with noble blood. Halice and I were agreed he wouldn't get the chance to develop it.

Ryshad on the other hand wanted to see Temar stamp his authority on Kellarin a good deal more firmly. 'It's certainly worth considering.'

I saw Temar sneaking a glance at his maps. 'If you want to trace those caves why don't you see if Hadrumal could help? Shiv could follow the rivers and Usara should find any hollow from a rabbit scrape down.' I'd travelled the wild fastnesses of forest and mountain with Usara and watched experience broaden the mage's horizons far beyond the narrow vistas of Hadrumal.

'That's a good notion.' Ryshad reached for the parchment he'd been covertly studying. 'Two mules make a better plough team than one.'

'Perhaps.' Temar's aristocratic politeness didn't fool any of us. He wasn't past the youthful folly of jealousy because Usara showed an interest in Guinalle.

'If we want more mages, they're the obvious ones to invite.' I knew Halice was thinking the same as me. In her self-possessed fashion, Guinalle had shown signs of welcoming Usara's attentions. A friendly wizard knowing all too well the demands and frustrations of magical arts might prompt the stubborn girl into admitting her own limitations.

'Where's Jemet?' snapped Temar, sipping his pathetically weak wine.

I caught Ryshad looking compassionately at the younger man. I wasn't so indulgent. Granted Temar had a hard row to hoe to make a success out of Kellarin but I wondered if my beloved was a little too inclined to give the young nobleman the benefit of the doubt.

The swish of the door broke the awkward silence and Allin hurried in behind Jemet the page. Of all the wizards I'd met since a chance venture introduced me to Shiv and repaid me with more trouble than I could have imagined, Allin was the least like an Ensaimin balladeer's fantasy. She was no willowy mage-woman sweeping all before her captivating beauty, earth-shaking, lightning-swift powers snaring all men with lust in the same breath as scaring the manhood out of them. Allin was short, round, plain enough to make Halice look passable and frequently unflatteringly red in the face. At the moment, out of breath, she was quite scarlet.

'Sit down.' I offered her my stool and the watery wine. I liked Allin and her ready habit of sharing any skill, magical or practical, had won her many friends in Kellarin. Not that she realised this. The last child of a long family, her humility bordered on the ridiculous and Temar wasn't the only one determined this mage-girl learn to value herself as highly as other people did.

'How can I help?' Her hectic colour faded as she drank the wine.

'Could you please bespeak Casuel?' Temar asked politely. 'See if he knows when we might expect the first ships?'

Allin turned to the expectant Jemet. 'A candle, if you please, and a mirror.'

The lad scurried to fetch the paraphernalia for Allin's spell and then stood at Temar's shoulder, blue eyes avid.

Allin snapped her fingers at the candle to kindle enchanted flame and carefully captured the unnaturally ruddy light in the mirror. She went about her wizardry with far less ceremony than most of the mages I'd had the dubious fortune to encounter but even this understated display had Jemet in silent thrall, Bridele sneaking a look from the kitchen door. The lately come craftsmen still retreated awkwardly when magic was worked but the original colonists had lived in an age when Artifice was a readily acknowledged skill. They made no distinction between Guinalle's aetheric enchantments worked for their benefit and the different abilities of the mageborn. As far as they were concerned, magic of any stripe meant Kellarin would never again suffer Elietimm attack undefended and unable to call for aid.

The reddish glow on the metal shrank to an eye-watering pinpoint of brightness and then spread once more in sweeps across the mirror like wine in a jolted glass catching the light. Concentration lent dignity to Allin's plump face as the radiance faded to a burning circle around the rim and the mirror reflected a miniature scene. We saw an elegantly appointed bedchamber where a familiar figure was stepping hastily into his breeches.

'Casuel, good morning,' Allin said politely.

'What's so urgent it couldn't wait until after breakfast?' Casuel fumbled with his buttons before running a hand over tousled brown hair, not yet pomaded into fashionable waves.

'Esquire D'Evoir.' Temar came to stand beside Allin and inclined his head in a well-bred bow. 'I beg your pardon. It's rather later in our day.' He spoke with the aristocratic precision that Casuel always took as due respect but I generally felt it was D'Alsennin's way of hiding his irritation with the wizard's pretensions.

'Sieur D'Alsennin.' Casuel's tone turned abruptly from brusque to ingratiating. Temar's House might have vanished in the Chaos but if the Emperor decreed it be raised again, that was good enough to win a grovel from Cas.

'Everyone else in Toremal will have eaten their breakfast long since by now.' Ryshad's murmur was for my ear alone as he moved behind me, folding strong arms around me.

I craned my head back to whisper. 'Since when's our Cas been Esquire D'Evoir?' In those same ballads where Allin's appearance would have been as appealing as her personality, Casuel's all-encompassing knowledge of the fragmentary history of the Old Empire would have been arcane learning essential for saving a princess or restoring a king to his throne. As it was, his self-serving scholarship had been entirely focused on proving his merchant family's claim to ancient rank. Then Planir had seconded his scholarship for his own mysterious purposes and Cas had inadvertently helped save Kellarin's people.

'Temar helped fill in the missing twigs on his family tree.' Ryshad nodded at the distant image. 'Imperial grant of insignia at Solstice, he's now Planir's liaison with Tadriol and official conduit for any prince wishing to communicate with Kellarin.'

So Cas had been rewarded with all the access to the great and the good of Toremal that his snobbish heart could wish for.

'We need to know when we might expect the first ships from Bremilayne or Zyoutessela,' Temar was explaining as Allin somehow brought Casuel's face closer to the mirror.

'But the first one will have arrived by now.' Casuel fiddled with a tasteless gilt fish brooch pinning the frilled collar of his silk shirt.

'I would hardly be asking if it had,' Temar said with more courtesy than I'd have managed.

'It set sail on the twelfth of For-Spring,' insisted Casuel.

There was a pause as we all mentally tallied up the days and the phases of the greater and lesser moons.

'That's very early to be setting out.' Ryshad knotted doubtful brows. Raised in the southern port of Zyoutessela, he knew more about the seasons' vagaries than the rest of us.

'Especially when you have neither mage nor aetheric adept aboard to cope with ocean winds and currents.' Unpleasant satisfaction turned Casuel's well-made face ugly.

'I don't understand,' Temar said sharply.

'The ship was backed by Den Harkeil gold,' began Casuel pedantically.

'Avila told me that was arranged,' Temar interrupted.

'The Sieur Den Harkeil has set his clerks loose in every archive he can secure access to.' Casuel looked momentarily envious. 'They've dug up every scrap of parchment detailing Den Fellaemion's voyages and the Sieur's convinced it should be possible to cross the ocean without magical aid. There's no mention of it in any of the tales of Nemith the Sea-farer.'

'Because no one with a grain of sense would think of venturing into the open ocean without an adept aboard in those days,' said Temar tightly.

'Why does Messire Den Harkeil feel entitled to ignore both Planir and the Demoiselle Tor Priminale saying a ship needs a mage or an adept or ideally both?' Halice was scornful.

'He believes the islands in the mid-ocean are the hidden secret that enabled Den Fellaemion to reach Kellarin,' Casuel said reluctantly.

Temar bit his lip. 'Suthyfer?' It was a measure of his concern that he used the mercenaries' everyday name for the islands, not the fanciful Garascisel he'd decreed.

'Is that possible?' Ryshad looked from Temar to Allin who was looking distressed.

'Has the vessel come to grief?'

'I don't know.' Temar chewed a thoughtful knuckle.

'Just because something hasn't been done, doesn't mean it can't be.' Halice had other concerns.

'Ships nowadays are sturdier than the ones Den Fellaemion used.' Ryshad looked apprehensive. 'Mariners are more used to sailing the ocean, with the growth of trade up to Inglis.'

'Half the noble Houses in Tormalin want a taste of the Kellarin trade,' I pointed out. 'They'll be sticking down their own colonists without so much as kissing your hand if they can get away with it.'

Allin shook her head emphatically. 'Cloud Master Otrick himself always said it would be impossible to cross the ocean unaided.'

'Did he say the same after he learned about Suthyfer?'

Halice studied a map. 'If a ship could reach the islands, take on fresh water, take bearings on the right stars and check the sun from solid land, that would set them fair for the second leg of the journey.' She looked at Allin. 'Did Otrick factor that into his calculations?'

'I don't know.' Allin faltered with sudden self-doubt.

'The Emperor has decreed that any land grant must have my seal,' Temar insisted but he looked worried.

'We're going to throw people back into the sea, when their prince has sent them here on the promise of a new life?' Ryshad said dourly.

'Tadriol's going to sail up and down the coast to enforce his writ in person, is he?' I chipped in.

Halice jabbed an emphatic finger at Temar. 'What about people who don't recognise Tormalin writ? Land hunger's been a goad in the Lescari wars for I don't know how long.'

'Let's not go begging for trouble.' Temar was scowling. 'If the ship is lost—'

'—we'd best look for wreckage or survivors.' Ryshad completed the thought.

'Could you tell us where currents might have carried them?' Temar looked to Allin.

'The *Tang* will discover its fate.' Casuel spoke over her with irritating condescension. 'Naldeth's on board. I warned him Den Harkeil's arrogance would doubtless lead to disaster.'

'The *Tang*? Den Castevin's ship set sail?' Temar waved everyone else to silence. 'When can we expect that?'

Casuel looked affronted. 'They left on the 37th of For-Spring.'

'Just before the full of the greater moon.' Ryshad narrowed his eyes. 'They should make landfall any time in the next ten days.'

'The lesser at dark won't have been a problem, not with a mage aboard.' Halice was doing her own calculations.

Allin didn't look so sure. 'Naldeth's affinity is with fire, not air or water.'

'Parrail's on board as well.' Casuel's dismissiveness made my palm itch to slap him. 'One of Mentor Tonin's pupils. He has sufficient Artifice to assist.'

'Thank you for this news, Esquire D'Evoir, and for your time. We need keep you no longer.' Temar nodded to Allin who snuffed the candle with a prosaic puff. Casuel's obsequious farewells dissolved like the thread of blue smoke unravelling from the wick.

Temar rubbed a hand through his close-cropped hair, leaving it in unruly black spikes, his blue eyes haunted. 'Dastennin forgive me but I could almost hope Den Harkeil's ship has foundered.' He wasn't invoking the god of the sea out of habit or hypocrisy.

'They knew the risk they were running.' Halice was no more inclined to sympathy than me. 'Folly's generally a capital crime sooner or later.'

Ryshad moved away from me towards a half-completed map of the coast between Vithrancel and Hafreinsaur. 'Where do we suppose they might land, if they're looking to set up their own standard?'

Halice twitched the map out of his reach. 'We're only guessing till one or other ship turns up. We'd be better off organising ourselves so we're ready to meet any challenge. Temar, you're calling yourself Sieur; it's time you started enforcing your writ. If you're going to do that, we need to know where it runs.' She grinned. 'Which is what I came to discuss in the first place. Are you going to claim fealty from any of my lads who throw in their lot with colony families. Are they going to get the restraint they need if you do?'

'What's brought this up?' Ryshad sat on the edge of the table, dark eyes alert. He knew the value of discipline among fighting men and had suggested more than once it was time Temar swore men to his own service in the manner of Messire D'Olbriot's militia. Temar kept avoiding the issue, claiming he didn't understand the customs that had been devised in the uncertain days of the Chaos.

I sat on Ryshad's abandoned stool and took out my belt

knife, idly cleaning my nails as Halice explained about Deg and Catrice. Temar rallied his wits and proposed reviving some of the ancient customs his grandsire had relied on. Ryshad advised a few modifications in the light of the greater independence Tormalin princes allowed their tenants these days. Halice grudgingly approved a few changes he suggested to the rough and ready sanctions she used to keep the mercenaries in line. Even Allin ventured a few hesitant observations on Hadrumal's parallel systems of influence and power.

The only interest I've ever had in justice is keeping well clear of it. In some towns that means playing an honest game, watching my manners and trusting to Halcarion to keep my luck polished up. In other places it means taking every chance that offers and making my own besides. Sometimes, you just have to trust to a fast horse waiting to take you out of reach when some fool with an empty purse goes crying to whoever thinks they're in charge.

I pared my nails and wondered if it mightn't be more interesting to go home and wash the bed linen.

CHAPTER TWO

To Cadan Lench, Prefect and Mentor of the University of Col,
From Aust Gildoman, Registrar to the Magistrates of Relshaz.

Dear Cad,

You asked me to keep a weather eye out for any news of interest in aetheric magic hereabouts. Don't think this counts as interest, exactly, but I thought you'd like to know how high some people's feelings can run.

Your friend,
Aust

A Warning to All Rational Men in the Face of New Superstition From the Sciolist Fellowship of Relshaz

Every clear-thinking man has rejoiced in this generation's rise above the falsehoods and myths that so encumbered our forefathers. The pernicious influence of wizardry over the fearful is finally quelled just as the malign grip of religion upon the credulous has been broken. Now we must take a stand against insidious new fables as we are assailed by a mendacity combining the worst elements of magic and dogma.

Aetheric magic, also called Artifice, is noised abroad as the answer to every woe that afflicts the feckless. It will bring bread to the idle, succour those suffering through their own debauchery, and provide undeserved wealth for the inadequate. If half the powers ascribed to this ancient lore are to be believed, Artifice could bring the very moons down from the heavens. It takes but a little rational thought to see all such hopes have no more value than the silver of moonshine reflected in the gutter. Those few with any knowledge of these supposed enchantments are far from our shores and Tormalin nobility besides. Whatever slight benefits might accrue from their lore will inevitably be reserved for those born to rank and precedence. The commonalty is offered mere garbled cantrips barely understood by priests eager to snare the gullible once more with the comforting deceptions of piety.

Counter such folly with insistence on the study of the tangible. Remind any friend tempted by lies and half-promises of the proven benefits accruing from advances in every field of natural philosophy. We must not return to those naive days when the study of proportion was the realm of the mystic rather than the objective man, when anatomists were shunned for encroaching on Poldrion's privilege and alchemists and apothecaries won only derision for their pains. Let us look forward to the advantages we will secure through rigorous application of the intellect explaining the richness of the living world, unlocking the secrets of death and disease, charting the cycle of the heavens and seasons and answering a myriad other questions besides.

Magic of whatever nature promises unearned boons but let us never forget the heavy price paid in the past by those succumbing to such temptations. No rational student of history can deny the Chaos enveloping the Old Empire must have been less comprehensive in its destruction, had not ignorant rulers summoned the unprincipled powers of mages in undisciplined pursuit of selfish aggrandizement. Malevolent magecraft wrought misery through every land from the ocean shore of Tormalin to the Great Forest beyond Ensaimin. No renewal could begin until amoral wizardry was driven from our shores, exiled to that isle where the mageborn skulk to this day.

Artifice may not offer such dramatic distortions of air and earth but its insidious threat is no less ominous. Consider the testimony of this Temar D'Alsennin, lately feted in Toremal. He tells of enchantments woven into every aspect of governance. Their false promise encouraged the Old Empire to spread ever further, ever thinner, relying on frail cords of Artifice to link all together. There was no understanding underlying this magic. In using enchantments to attack an enemy rather than honest strength of arms, D'Alsennin's ignorant sorcerers cut the bridge from beneath themselves as well as their foe. With one thread cut, the web of Artifice unravelled throughout the Empire. The seeds of the Chaos were sown, ready for the fire and water of heedless mages to bring them to full bloom. D'Alsennin credits aetheric magic with his salvation and that of his people without ever acknowledging that same sorcery held them all senseless beneath the earth for more than twenty-four generations. This was not salvation but mere cowardly postponement of an evil day. What rational man would ever consider such a fate preferable to an honest death?

Ignore those who assure you latter generations of wizards have both wisdom and discretion. Remain vigilant lest misguided sentiment over this archaic Artifice seduces anyone into thinking magic of whatever nature has any claim on these enlightened times.

Suthyfer, the Western Approaches, 18th of Aft-Spring

The islands rose from the vast ocean with shocking abruptness; sharp ridges strung out across the waters. Closer to, tree-clad hills hunched defiant shoulders beneath the infinite blue skies, steep bulwarks drawn up close beneath serried spines grudging the barest suggestion of a beach to the all-encompassing seas. The sea matched that niggardliness with a paltry band of surf, meagre waves lifting listless sweeps of white before retreating to the coruscating deeps. No hint of reefs threatened the ship shunning the lesser islets, intent on a narrow strait just visible between two emerald promontories.

Clouds drifting unfettered cast light and shade on restless waters already brilliant with fleeting shimmers like fish darting away from inquisitive eyes. The isle ahead offered an impassive mosaic of greens unruffled by the steady wind carrying the fast-approaching ship inshore. Stalwart trees carried sober hues beneath the verdant highlights of new growth and underbrush, motionless patterns framed by the dark mossy bulk of the rising peaks. The wind shifted and moist earthy scents momentarily won over the scouring salt of the sea breeze and seabirds' cries pierced the creak and thrum of rigging and sail.

'I'll be so glad when we land!'

'That sounded heartfelt, Parrail.'

The man clinging to the rail of the ship greeted this new arrival with a weak smile. 'Naldeth, good day to you.'

'Duty to you, gentlemen, but clear out of the way.' A sailor hurried past, bare feet deft on the swaying deck, oblivious to the chill wind despite his sleeveless shirt and ragged knee breeches. 'Can't you go below with the rest of the passengers?' He didn't wait for a reply before hurrying up the ladder-like ratlines running from the rail to the crow's-nest where the top half of the mast was securely stepped to the lower.

Parrail looked apprehensively at Naldeth. 'I don't think I dare.'

'Over here.' Naldeth led the way to a stack of securely netted cargo. He cast a wary eye up at sailors deftly reconfiguring the creamy sailcloth billowing on the *Tang*'s tall square-rigged fore and main masts. 'Still no sea legs?'

'It's not so much my legs as my stomach.' Parrail took a reluctant seat, lifting his head to see past the intricacies of ropes and pulleys. 'It's better if I can see the horizon. One of the sailors told me that.'

'I do what I can to keep the ship on an even keel,' said Naldeth lightly.

Parrail managed a faint smile. 'My thanks to you, Master Mage.'

'My pleasure, Master Scholar.' Naldeth made a comic attempt at a seated bow. Leaning back against the shrouded lump of canvas that was the ship's boat, he yawned widely before looking around. Animation and intelligence lent distinction to an otherwise unremarkable face. 'This trip's taught me just how much I don't know about the workings of water, but the winds have been favourable so I don't think we've lost too much time.'

'Dastennin be thanked.' Parrail's intensity had little to do with devotion to the god of the sea. Much of an age with the wizard, the scholar nevertheless looked appreciably younger thanks to a snub nose, boyish features and wiry brown hair teased by the wind.

Naldeth idly tapped a foot on the tightly fitted oaken deck. 'Master Gede was saying we should be anchored and ashore in time for lunch.' He laughed. 'I take it you didn't want breakfast?'

Parrail took a deep breath. 'No, thanks, and I'd rather not

talk about food.' He tugged absently at the laces of the plain linen shirt he wore beneath an unadorned broadcloth jerkin.

'Sorry.' Naldeth looked up towards the sterncastle of the ship where captain and senior crewmen stood in purposeful conclave before the lateen-rigged aftmast. They broke apart, each one sliding deftly down the ladder-like stair, intent on his allotted task. The captain remained behind, scanning the vista ahead as he talked to the helmsman whose broad hands cradled the whipstaff that governed the ship's massive rudder. The captain was a tall man, hair pale grey in contrast to brows still black and knitted in the scowl fixed on his weathered face by years of peering into sun and wind. He wore soft half boots and long breeches of plain blue broadcloth beneath a comfortably loose-cut shirt much the same as wizard and scholar wore. Where Naldeth had opted for the same leather jerkin worn by half the crew, the captain maintained the dignity of his rank with a sleeveless mantle of warm grey wool belted with a tooled leather strap and a fine brass buckle.

'So is Suthyfer just the name of this island or the whole group?' Parrail asked more for the sake of distraction than wanting an answer.

Naldeth obliged regardless. 'I think it's the whole group. I don't think anyone's actually named the individual islands. I'm not sure anyone's ever stopped here to do a proper survey.' With the fast growing bulk of the largest isle now dead ahead, his hazel eyes were bright with curiosity. 'Whoever does should name at least one rock for himself, don't you say? That would be something.'

'You're interested in doing it?' queried Parrail.

Naldeth was visibly taken aback. 'No, I'm bound for Kellarin.'

Parrail hesitated. 'You didn't seem overly taken with the colony when we were last there.'

'I was glad to see the back of the place.' A scowl threatened Naldeth's cheery countenance. 'I'd never seen people killed before. I mean, people die, don't they? Poldrion rolls

the runes but when it's people you know . . .' He fell silent
for a moment, face vulnerable. 'I'm sorry. You lost friends, I
know.'

'I want to help Kellarin for their sake.' Parrail's
unguarded reply wasn't a rebuke but Naldeth's swift
response was defensive.

'I'd done as much as I could, hadn't I? I thought I'd best
take what I'd learned back to Hadrumal. The Archmage and
the other wizards left long before me.'

But Parrail's soft brown eyes were looking inward on
remembered sorrow. Awkwardness hung between the two
young men as sailors' shouts of encouragement and warning
sounded the length of the ship. The hills loomed closer.
Manoeuvres with ropes and rigging were punctuated by
bellows of command from the rear deck and the snap of
obedient canvas. The strait between the central island and
its slighter neighbour threaded a silver ribbon between the
green shores. White birds darted towards the *Tang* and
wheeled above its wake, cries of alarm and curiosity loud.

'When did you go back to Vanam?' Naldeth's question
held the faintest hint of accusation.

Parrail dragged his wits back to the present. 'For-Autumn
last year, not long after you sailed. We reached Zyoutessela
for Equinox and I was back in Vanam by the middle of For-
Winter. I swore I'd never set foot on a ship again.' He shuddered before his expression brightened. 'But Mentor Tonin
persuaded me. I take it you're on your way to consult with
Demoiselle Guinalle as well? I heard Usara went looking for
aetheric lore with that woman with the Forest blood, Livak?
Did he truly bring one of the Mountain Artificers to
Hadrumal?'

'Yes, a woman called Aritane but I've nothing to do with
that.' Naldeth looked surprised. 'I'm just lending a hand to
keep this ship on course. I'll want to see what's to do in
Kellarin. My affinity's with fire and I hear the Edisgesset
miners are planning on refining ore this year.' He grinned.
'But you're welcome to woo the demoiselle if you want.'

'I've no notion of wooing anyone.' Parrail tried to cover his chagrin with firm dignity. 'I thought you worked at the Archmage's orders.'

'When I'm one of three mages standing and Elietimm enchanters are knocking everyone else out of the game. Back in Hadrumal, I'm just a middling fish in a busy pond.' Disappointment lent a strained note to Naldeth's offhand answer.

Parrail nodded. 'I know what you mean.'

'I thought I could make more of a splash in Kellarin.' Naldeth's talkative nature won out over any impulse to discretion. 'It's all very well endlessly debating theory and specu-lation but it's nice to have ordinary folk glad of your help, not looking as if you've got two heads, if you offer to light wet firewood.'

He would have said more but the sailors' calls rose to a new urgency. Master Gede bellowed a sudden command and the *Tang* heeled round on sweeping canvas wings to dart into the sound. The rolling swell of the open ocean gave way to calmer waters between the two islands, glassy smooth where they reflected the bright sun, crystal clear in the shallows of a frowning cliff, dark skerries visible just beneath the surface.

Naldeth spared a wary glance for passing sailors before urging Parrail to the side rail. 'Let's get a look at this place.'

The ship followed the curve of the shore past a precipi-tous cliff. Below a hollow in the hills some way ahead, a shingle spit offered a gently shelving anchorage. The shore of the lesser island broke into shallow promontories hiding little bays, with folds of land beyond rising in green swells.

Parrail sniffed. 'Is that meat smoking?'

'They did it!' Amazed, Naldeth pointed to a vessel beached on the strand, masts lopsided as the retreating tide left it unsupported. It had the same long hull as the *Tang*, suited for open or inshore waters, square rigged on fore and main masts, shallow fore- and aftcastles in the most recent style and rails guarding the waist of the ship, low to ease the loading and unloading of cargo carried in the capacious hold.

'Den Harkeil's ship?' Parrail squinted but no flags flew.

'I can't tell.' Naldeth shook his head, visibly annoyed. 'Just because this lot got lucky, that doesn't mean anyone else will.'

Parrail sought a better view. 'Perhaps it's a Kellarin ship?'

'Sail ho!' Looking up at the shout, both saw the lookout in the crow's-nest was pointing astern.

'Another ship?' Naldeth wondered aloud.

'Master Mage, Master Scholar!' The captain's harsh summons set them hurrying for the sterncastle.

'Have either of you had word of other ships?' demanded Master Gede as Naldeth reached the top of the stairs.

'No one's bespoken me.' Naldeth shook his head.

'Nothing from Bremilayne?' Gede peered aft, trying to identify the newcomer. About a quarter as long again as the *Tang* with the same long lines, it carried a formidable weight of sail rigged for speed and attack. Fore- and aftmasts carried three courses of canvas compared to the *Tang*'s two and that wasn't counting the square-rigged bowsprit and two lateen-rigged mizzens on the aftdeck. Fancy carving adorned rails and the wales and the beakhead at the bow was carved into a threatening shark. As it closed, the boldly painted name below was plain: *Spurdog*. 'Master Parrail?'

'I've heard nothing but Artifice isn't always effective worked over the ocean,' Parrail hastily qualified his reply.

'Ware sail forrard!'

Gede gauged the speed of the rapidly approaching vessel behind before looking to the front where a second ship emerged from concealment behind a curve of the shore. The newcomer could have been built from the same plans as the *Spurdog* but a sterner shipwright had fashioned the plain rails ringing the crow's-nests and deck castles. The bow was unadorned but for a brass spike and the name *Thornray* carved and painted black beneath.

'Dast's teeth, it's a god-cursed trap!' spat Gede.

'We've barely steerage, this slow,' the helmsman hissed, testing his whipstaff with a leathery hand.

'All sail!' Gede bellowed. 'Wizard, raise us a wind!'

'Flag astern!' The lookout clung to the rope stays at a perilous angle.

As the *Spurdog* ran a vivid scarlet pennant up its mainmast, the *Thornray* answered with its own.

'That's no Tormalin insignia,' said Parrail dubiously. 'Who raises snake flags?'

'Pirates,' said the captain with loathing. He narrowed his eyes to judge the course of the *Thornray* now intent on blocking their path. Naldeth didn't look up from a spark of blue light he was cherishing between his hands. He drew his palms a little wider and the light grew into an iridescent sphere, azure threaded through with brightness painful to the eye.

'Quick as you like, wizard.' The helmsman glanced over his shoulder as the *Spurdog*'s sails stole what little breeze the *Tang* could hope for between the confining islands.

The lookout yelled with fear and fury as a shower of arrows rattled among the *Tang*'s sails. Several sailors cried out, arms or legs bloodied. One unfortunate thudded heavily to the deck; screaming and clawing at a vicious shaft piercing his belly.

Parrail knocked Naldeth clean off his feet. The mage's curse went unspoken as he saw bright arrowheads biting deep into the planking where he'd stood. Master Gede was dragging the helmsman beneath the inadequate shelter of the stern rail, the man choking on his own blood, an arrow deep in his chest. Shocked, Naldeth's magic scattered in a haphazard flurry of feeble gusts.

Master Gede knelt on one knee by the whipstaff, the other booted foot braced and his hand steady. 'We need wind, Master Mage.'

'Can you use the water to slow them?' Parrail's voice shook.

'It's too antithetical.' Naldeth fought to steady his hands as a faint sapphire glow suffused the empty air between them. He'd done this before, he reminded himself. If he was ever going to be the equal of Kalion or Otrick, he had to meet challenges like this. If he lived that long.

A second deadly wave of arrows came from the rigging of the pursuing ship. 'They're looking for magelight.' Parrail cowered by the stern rail trying to help the helmsman.

'Curse it!' Raw power burst from Naldeth's hands. At the last moment, he managed to fling it up at the main mast and the *Tang* lurched as the sails suddenly filled, dragging the vessel bodily through the water.

'Ware rocks!' A sailor high on the foremast pointed urgently off to one side.

'Ware boats!' The cry came up from the waist of the ship, frantic sailors gesturing ahead and astern. A flotilla of long boats was darting out from the lesser island's hidden bays where they'd been lurking for the *Thornray*'s signal. Parrail risked a glance over the stern rail and saw a second hungry pack come fanning out on either side of the *Spurdog*. Sweating rowers leaned into their oars, each boat full of raiders, swords in hand. In every prow, a man swung a menacing grappling iron.

Naldeth's face contorted as he struggled to master the gusting currents of air buffeting him. Livid glints of magic swirled around him but at last a steady wind billowed the *Tang*'s sails. The pirates astern hurled abuse as the ship pulled away, the enchanted wind stronger than the toiling men at their oars. Shouts of alarm ahead sounded beneath the questing prow, splintering sounds of wood drowning them an instant later.

Gede shook his head at Naldeth. 'Stop or we'll ram her!'

The *Thornray* was dead ahead, her rails lined with pirates. Her captain was steering directly into the *Tang*'s path, confident his heavier hull would withstand the impact.

'What can I do?' Naldeth stood stricken with indecision.

'Lend a hand to turn her!' Gede was struggling to steer his ship past the predatory pirate's stern.

Parrail cowered beneath the rail, trying to staunch the

helmsman's wound. '*Zistra feydra en al dret.*' His voice cracked as he tried to work the enchantment. The helmsman coughed a gout of scarlet blood and drew a deep shuddering breath before falling limp beneath Parrail's hands.

Thuds sounded all along the ship's sides. The long boats had reached the *Tang*. Pirates flung their grapnels with practised precision and for every rope a desperate sailor cut, two more gripped with irons claws biting deep with the weight of men climbing the lines below. The pirates swarmed over the rail, sailcloth jackets soaked in pitch to foil the few blades that the sailors could muster. Once on the deck, every raider drew short swords or daggers in either hand, hilts wrapping round into brazen knuckles for a brutal punch if close quarters foiled a stroke with a blade.

'*Zistra feydra en—*' Parrail choked on his enchantment as a grappling iron soaring high over the rail hit a sailor at the bottom of the aftcastle stair. The man shrieked, razor sharp points ripping open his face and chest.

Instinct brought blazing fire to Naldeth's outstretched palm. He threw it full in the face of the first pirate to set foot on the deck by the screaming man. Crimson with magic, flames wrapped around the pirate with a furnace roar. Hair blazed in a passing flash then the man's naked scalp blackened and split, face beneath contorted in tortured shock. Raw flesh oozed for a scant breath before the all-consuming fire scoured the man's silent scream to the rictus grin of a skull. He fell, head charred and naked bone, arms scorched and blistered, booted legs untouched. Sparks took hold of the pitch in his smouldering jerkin and the magical fire ran greedily across the deck leaving barely a scorch mark. It leapt to the grappling iron, melting it into a shapeless lump before consuming the rope as it went in search of fresh victims in the boat below. Unseen screams lifted above the ear-splitting din of the vicious struggle aboard.

'Wizard, yonder!' Master Gede waved at a new sail. A gaff-rigged ship, deft and manoeuvrable was swooping down the anchorage. Barely two thirds the length of the *Tang*, the single mast carried triangular headsails rigged to the bowsprit and cut back all the better to spill wind and turn the ship in its own length. The square topsail and fore-and-aft mainsail drove her on and a bold red pennon streamed from the masthead, a black snake writhing down the length of it.

Frenzied, Naldeth snatched at the roiling air around him but a hail of slingshot thudded all around, bruising him cruelly. He wove a frantic, fragile shield but it was too late. Master Gede was down, bleeding from a gash to the head, the *Tang* drifting forlorn without his guiding hand.

Parrail had been vomiting but struggled towards the captain on his hands and knees. Tears poured down the scholar's face but he gritted his teeth and mouthed the measured syllables of a charm.

Naldeth looked wildly into the waist of the ship where the crew fought with pirates swarming aboard from all directions. Gede's boatswain went down to a slashing blade, the shipwright beside him struggling to defend himself with a belaying pin at the same time as stretching a hand to his fallen comrade. The pirate hacked it from his arm and raised his weapon for a killing blow but the sailor who'd fallen first kicked out with his last breath. The one-handed sailor smashed the pirate's face to a bloody pulp with his length of solid oak but another raider cut him down, stamping for footing on the bodies of ally and prey alike.

'*Nis tal eld ar fen.*' Parrail wiped bile from his chin. He knelt beside Master Gede but his eyes were fixed on the murderous pirate below. The man yelled and clapped his hands to his face, swords forgotten as he swung this way and that rubbing at his eyes.

'I have him!' Naldeth exulted. He pulled a shaft of lightning from the confusion of grey and white clouds overhead and seared the man dead but a blue echo of his magic flashed all around him drawing several arrows. Worse, pirates below made a concerted move towards the rear deck.

Parrail grabbed at the mage's tunic. He drew a deep breath, enunciating an incantation with meticulous care. Naldeth was simply frozen with fear until he saw the pirates intent on his death had halted, confused like a pack of questing hounds who'd lost their scent. Faces turned to the aftdeck seemed to be looking straight through him.

Parrail's eyes were hollow with consternation. 'What do we do now?'

'Take hold.' Naldeth held out a shaking hand, hoping he was equal to his sudden inspiration.

Parrail snatched at it like a drowning man. 'But Master Gede—'

Too late. An azure spiral of power bound his arms to his sides, his feet leaving the deck for an instant before he was plunged into darkness. Parrail groaned with misery as his abused stomach sought to empty itself once more. Then he realised they were in the dimness below decks. Panicked voices rose in the broad hold where those hoping for a life in Kellarin had been waiting out the long days at sea among their hammocks and chests of treasured possessions.

'What's happening?' demanded a man's voice.

'It's pirates!' Naldeth replied, anguished. 'They're killing everyone!'

The consternation that provoked threatened to turn to outright hysteria but everyone fell silent a few moments later when a hatch at the far end of the deck opened to the white and terrified faces below.

'Out!' A swarthy Gidestan beckoned with a bloodstained glove.

The hapless youth at the bottom of the ladder looked around wildly for guidance but everyone else dropped their gaze.

'Out, all of you.' The Gidestan sounded menacing.

The lad climbed slowly up the ladder, yelping as his head reached deck level and unexpected hands hauled him bodily through the hatch.

'And the rest!' What little patience the Gidestan had was plainly exhausted.

Someone else was half pushed, half urged up the ladder

and others followed. A surge of bodies carried Naldeth and Parrail closer to the shaft of pitiless daylight, whimpers of fear and ragged breaths of distress all around them.

'We work no magic or enchantment.' Parrail dug painful fingers into Naldeth's arm as the wizard opened his mouth. 'We have to live long enough to get word out to Hadrumal or somewhere, anywhere.'

The press brought the two of them to the ladder and they had no choice but to climb, Parrail first then Naldeth close behind him. Scrambling on to the deck, rough hands shoved them towards the motionless crowd clustered around the main mast. Homespun folk with the honest faces of craftsmen and farmers huddled together, watching the pirates casually tossing the bodies of the slain overboard. Parrail recognised the ship's sailmaker, the helmsman, a farmer from Dalasor whose name he couldn't recall.

A few were looking wide-eyed at the forecastle where a bare-chested pirate was tying up the remaining sailors. A few struggled with the pirates restraining them, more went with sullen obedience but one man managed to break free. He hit out wildly, felling one and then kicking out to catch another in the groin, shouting some incomprehensible abuse. The defiance died on his lips as the bare-chested man smashed the back of his head with an iron bar. He twisted his fingers in the blood-soaked wavy hair and held the corpse up to warn sailors and passengers alike. 'That's what making trouble gets you!'

Naldeth's gorge rose at the sight of the dead man's misshapen pate, bone gleaming white around grey pulp and gore. He swallowed hard and his terror unexpectedly receded in the face of desperate calm as he forced himself to assess his plight. At least he and Parrail were dressed much the same as the rest of the passengers. For the first time since his childhood he breathed a thanks to Saedrin. The showy robes and elemental colours fashionable in Hadrumal would have condemned him as a mage at once.

With the unresisting sailors now bound, pirates were

moving among the prisoners, cutting knives and purses from belts, ripping the few pieces of jewellery visible from necks and wrists, dumping all the spoils in a prosaic wicker basket once destined for a goodwife's trips to market.

'Your rings.' One gestured at a yeoman's gold-circled fingers with a bloodstained knife and an evil grin on his under-nourished face. 'Take 'em off or I cut 'em off.'

Naldeth offered no resistance as rough hands searched his jerkin and breeches pockets, his coin purse torn from the cord he wore beneath his shirt. Then the rat-faced man reached for Parrail's hand.

'The ring,' the pirate ordered.

Parrail's stricken expression was little different to those all around but Naldeth saw the added pain in the scholar's eyes as he surrendered the silver emblem of Vanam, hard-earned symbol of long years of study and self-denial.

That distraction left the mage slow to realise why everyone had fallen silent. All the pirates standing upright and ready, faces turned to the far rail. Naldeth saw the single mast of the ship that he'd failed to hit with any useful magic, snake pennon whipping to and fro in lazy mockery.

A taller man than any Naldeth could recall climbed over the rail with a deftness belying his bulk. The pirates raised a loud cheer, boots stamping, swords smacked together in raucous celebration. The tall man swept a courtly wave to acknowledge those on the forecastle and Naldeth noticed he was lacking the little finger on his sword hand. He had black hair with a curl to it, long enough to fall below his shoulders if it hadn't been pulled back into a merciless queue. Those shoulders looked broad enough to bear any burden but the man was dressed like a noble who'd never had to soil his hands.

As he turned to share his approval with his pirates, Naldeth saw a delighted smile deepening creases beginning to claim a permanent place around the pirate's eyes. He was a man in the prime of life, teeth white against the trimmed and disciplined beard that showed just a touch of grey. 'Well done, my lads. Now, let's have a little hush.' His voice was a carrying boom well suited to his barrel chest. The pirate approached the terrified colonists, heedless of his polished boots as he kicked some bloodied body aside.

'Good day to you.' He bowed low with ostentatious politeness. 'I am Muredarch and I am the leader of these—' His smile turned feral. 'We're pirates. You're prisoners, though you'll get a choice about that. We're taking everything we find on this ship. You don't get a choice about that.' He grinned at a stifled squeak of protest. 'But we'll be handing out fair shares because that's the way we do things in my fleet. If you want a share, all you have to do is swear fealty to me and do as I say until I say different. Show a talent for our life and you'll find it's recognised. Birth means nothing here but ability counts for a lot.'

He brushed a casual hand over his sea-blue tunic, embroidered velvet and belted with silver, the breeze ruffling the lawn sleeves of his shirt. 'I don't promise a long life but by all that's holy, it's a merry one while it lasts. We take our pleasures as readily as we take our plunder,' he continued airily. 'Wine, women, good food and if you're hurt, we'll see you doctored and kept in comfort. If you're left unable to fight, we don't cast you off; there's always jobs to be done that don't need a sword. When you've earned me enough loot to pay me for sparing your lives, you are free to go, with whatever you've saved for yourselves. But most stay on and make themselves richer still.'

The lesser pirates hanging on his every word laughed but Naldeth heard genuine merriment, not the sycophancy he'd expected and found that worried him more.

'You ladies can work for us as you choose.' Muredarch turned a serious face to a mother clutching a daughter just blooming into girlhood. 'No man will take you against your will, not without being gelded for it. Share your favours and be paid for the courtesy or earn your keep with cooking, washing, nursing.' He shrugged. 'Or you give your oath with the men, sign on the roster and earn an equal share. Where's

Otalin?' A chorus of approval rose from the pirates as one stepped forward from a blood-soaked foursome on the forecastle. 'We don't keep women to firesides and distaffs if they don't care for such things.'

Otalin shouted something derisory at the bound sailors, proving her womanhood by pulling jerkin and shirt apart to bare her breasts. It was, Naldeth decided, quite the least erotic display he'd ever seen.

Muredarch clapped his hands, which brought instant silence. 'Anyone endangering the fleet in any way dies for it. Anyone starting a quarrel on board ship hangs for it,' he said with quiet menace. 'You can settle a score in blood ashore as long as you don't involve anyone else. If you can live by our rules, you'll earn more gold than you ever dreamed of. If you can't, we'll take our price for your life out of you in work but I warn you, that's the long way to earn your freedom. The quickest way out is not to work, then you won't eat and you'll die soon enough. If that's your choice, so be it. You've till dawn tomorrow to think it through and then I'll want a decision from each and every one of you.'

He turned to nod to the pirates on the sterncastle. 'Bring him here.'

Naldeth heard a sharp intake of breath from Parrail as Master Gede was pushed down the ladder to the deck. He fell heavily, blood dark and matted in his grey hair. The woman Otalin jumped down lightly beside him and hauled him to his feet. The master sailor was pale, eyes bruised, arms bound behind him and looking unsteady but his jaw was set.

'Good day to you, Captain.' Muredarch inclined his head, one equal to another. 'I take it you understand you're in my fleet now?' He didn't wait for an answer. 'A captain should always stay with his ship, shouldn't he? I always do my best to see to that. So you have a choice to make.'

'Turn pirate and prey on honest men?' growled Gede with contempt. 'Never.'

'I said you had till tomorrow to make that decision.'

Muredarch smiled that feral smile again. 'No, I've something else to ask you. Who's the wizard?'

Gede's eyes fixed on Muredarch, face expressionless.

'Who's the wizard?' Muredarch repeated, soft and venomous. 'Give him up. He didn't do you much good, did he?'

Naldeth's heartbeat sounded so loud inside his head it deafened him. The breath caught in his throat and his groin shrivelled with fear.

Gede stayed silent, eyes focused only on the pirate chieftain. He didn't dare look anywhere else in case he gave some hint away, Naldeth realised. Numb with shock, he wished he could look away from the appalling sight but he dared not turn lest he meet someone else's accusing eyes, see some pointing finger handing him over to this brute. His thoughts disintegrated into wretchedness and terror.

Muredarch was studying Gede intently. 'No, you won't give him up, will you? Not without a little persuasion. But I'm a man of my word. I'll let you stay with your ship.'

The pirates laughed and Naldeth saw savage expectation on their faces all around. Otalin shoved Gede towards the main mast and the passengers scattered in alarm. Muredarch casually drew one of several daggers sheathed on his silver ornamented belt and the bare-chested man jumped down from the foredeck. He carried a hammer and sharp iron spikes as long as a man's forearm. Muredarch cut Gede's bonds but two pirates were waiting to grab his hands. Their chieftain stepped aside as the pair pulled Gede's arms behind him, one either side of the mast, forcing his hands flat to the wood.

At Muredarch's nod, the bare-chested man drove a spike through Gede's hand, nailing him to the mast. The captain couldn't restrain a yell of anguish. 'Dast curse your seed!'

Muredarch was unmoved. 'Show me the wizard.'

Gede shook his head, biting his lip so hard blood ran down his chin.

Muredarch nodded and the second spike hammered home. Gede's cry was joined by sobs and distress all around.

'Show me the wizard.' But Gede stayed silent.

Despite the murmurs of distress all around him, Naldeth made no sound. He couldn't have done so to save his life.

The pirate chieftain shook his head with regret as Gede's chin sank to his chest. He wound strong fingers in the sailor's hair to yank his head up. 'Till tomorrow.' Turning his back on Gede he walked unhurried to the rail. 'Get them ashore.' He swung himself down to his gaff-rigged ship.

As soon as Muredarch was off the deck, the pirates moved, belaying pins and the flats of blades herding the comprehensively cowed passengers. Parrail caught Naldeth by the elbow, urging the shocked mage forward. An older man with a dyer's stained hands shot them both a fearful look from beneath lowered brows. The scholar swallowed hard on his own fear, foul bitterness in his mouth, gullet and belly sour and scalded. Surely these people wouldn't give them up to these torturers, not when magic might be their only salvation? He dropped his own gaze, concentrating on moving with the crowd, on keeping Naldeth moving, terrified lest either of them do something to attract unwelcome attention.

The pirates simply counted off their captives into the waiting longboats like so many head of sheep; the pockmarked ruffian in charge didn't tolerate delay. The woman with the daughter baulked at the rope ladders strung over the side of the ship and at his nod, two burly raiders swung her bodily over the side where she dangled, whimpering.

The man waiting below laughed until her flailing shoe caught him in the face. 'Watch what you're at, you clumsy bitch!' Snatching at her petticoats he pulled her down with an audible rip of cloth. If another pirate in the boat hadn't caught her arm, the woman would have fallen into the dark waters but she was too frightened to realise he was saving her and pulled free with a cry of alarm.

The man laughed with scant humour. 'Lady, I don't want your notch on my tally stick.'

'Not given the choice.' The pirate rubbing his bruised face was looking up at her daughter's legs hanging helpless above him. He grabbed her calf and the raiders above dropped the girl. The man slid his rough-skinned hand up her stockings and beneath her skirts as he caught her around the waist with his other arm.

The lass jerked rigid in his embrace and in panic, she spat full in the pirate's face. 'How dare you!'

'Beg pardon, my lady.' He removed his hands with elaborate care and a lascivious smile. 'You come find me, if you change your mind.'

Parrail and Naldeth were pushed towards the rail. The scholar kicked the mage hard on the ankle and saw bemused realisation of pain burn through the shock fogging the wizard's eyes. Parrail nodded at the rope ladders and to his relief, Naldeth managed to fumble his way down to the longboat. Parrail gripped the rungs with trembling hands, nails digging into the tarred rope, trying to go as fast as he could, fearful lest he fall but more scared of the consequences if he did.

'That's your lot!' The pirate with spittle still glistening on his unshaven cheek waved to the ship and urged his rowers to their oars. 'Get on!'

The passengers huddled on the central thwarts of the boat, the mother sobbing into her daughter's breast. Naldeth was still staring ahead with unseeing eyes but Parrail twisted to try and gain some idea of where they were being taken.

He saw a crude stockade of green timber some little distance inshore, bark still on the trees, fresh axe marks still pale on the sharpened ends. A scatter of rough shelters, lean-tos and tents sprawled over the close-cropped turf between the stony beach and the thick underbrush that cloaked the rising land. Returning pirates were stirring fires to life, cauldrons and kettles swung over the flames. The few who'd stayed hidden ashore came out of the undergrowth and from the stockade, shouts of congratulation audible over the smooth waters of the anchorage. The sun was warm, the breeze gentle and the islands looked verdant and hospitable. Parrail felt utterly desolate.

The boat crunched to a halt on the shingle spit. 'All out and sharp about it!'

As they scrambled over the side, stumbling in the knee-deep water, Parrail risked a quick look round for any hope of escape. He wasn't the only one.

'Nowhere to run, sorry.' The scornful pirate wasn't looking at him but Parrail still coloured, humiliated by the mocking laugh of several brutes waiting at the water's edge.

'You're in the stockade for tonight.' A thickset man with a shaven head in sharp contrast to his plaited brown beard stepped forward. He wasn't dressed for raiding but wore buff breeches and jerkin of a cut and quality Parrail would have expected on any Vanam street. 'Give us your oath that you'll join us in the morning and you can set up your own patch.' He indicated the ramshackle camp with an expansive gesture.

Parrail shoved Naldeth into the centre of their group as they headed meekly for the stockade. The scholar hoped the grey despair on the wizard's face would be taken for the defeat that hung heavy on the rest. Their captors seemed keen to dispel such gloom.

'Muredarch's a great leader,' volunteered a muscular youth, tanned beneath a sleeveless shirt unlaced to the waist. 'You should think about his offer. It's the best chance for serious wealth for the likes of us this side of Saedrin's door.'

'It's good living,' his companion agreed, slapping at the gilt and enamel decorations on the expensive baldric that carried his sword. He swung a flagon of wine in the other hand, cheery in the bright sun that mocked the prisoners' misery.

Parrail wondered where the wine had come from and who had died for it. They reached the stockade and were roughly shoved inside the crude gates. Parrail was hard put to stifle abject tears when he heard the rough-hewn bar outside secure it. He dashed them angrily from his eyes and grabbed Naldeth. The wizard looked at him numbly and Parrail shook him bodily before urging him into the narrow shadow cast by the crude walkway that offered their few token guards a vantage point.

'We have to send word.' He quailed lest anyone overhear his urgent whisper.

Uncomprehending, Naldeth struggled to find some response but none came.

Parrail found the first stirrings of anger fighting to rise above his fear and nausea. 'We're the only ones who can send for help.'

Naldeth shuddered and rubbed a shaking hand over his mouth. 'Who?' he managed to croak.

Parrail licked dry lips. 'Hadrumal?' The great mages had defended Mentor Tonin and his scholars before; Planir, Otrick and Kalion wielding mighty magic to send Kellarin's foes screaming before them. That seemed so very far away and long ago compared to his present predicament.

Some animation was returning to Naldeth's face. 'I need to conjure a flame if I'm going to bespeak anyone.' He looked around. 'And something shiny, something metal.'

Parrail looked around as well. 'They haven't left anyone so much as a hair pin.'

'Nor any fire.' Naldeth shivered. 'It's going to be a cold night.'

'Any flame will give you away as the mage.' Parrail wished he hadn't spoken when he saw stifling dread threaten Naldeth's fragile composure again. 'Think, man! What are we going to do?'

The wizard drew a deep, shuddering breath. 'Can't you use Artifice?'

Parrail hugged his aching belly. 'I can try but what if someone hears me?' He looked round at the other prisoners but all were sunk in their own misery, some clinging to each other, others lost and alone in their shock.

'Do you think they'll give us up?' Naldeth asked in a hollow voice.

'Master Gede didn't.' Parrail's voice cracked.

'He's not dead yet – and neither are we.' Naldeth grasped

the scholar's shoulder in a clumsy attempt at comfort. 'I've just thought of something; I can weave air to cover your incantations, can't I?'

Parrail managed a wan smile. 'Let's see who I can reach.'

He moved to the negligible protection of a rough-hewn upright supporting the walkway and sat facing the blank wall of the stockade. Naldeth dropped down beside him, sitting with bent knees and feet flat to the trampled grass, elbows resting on his knees, head and hands seemingly hanging limp. Only Parrail could see the utter concentration holding the mage rigid. This was no time to let any hint of magelight escape his working.

'When—' The silence that swallowed his tentative query told the scholar he could attempt his own enchantment. Parrail forced himself to breathe long and slow, concentrating on the memory of Vanam's university quarter and banishing the reality of this nest of pirates. He pictured the scholarly halls where learned men shared their theories in lecture and demonstration, the dusty libraries where long-dead rivalries stood shoulder to shoulder in the chained ranks of books. With a longing that twisted his heart, he focused his thoughts on the cramped house where Mentor Tonin shared his enthusiasm for the lost lore of the ancients with his students, conscientious in tutoring even those he only took on for the sake of their fathers' fat purses, their gold keeping the roof over the heads of those poorer but diligent like Parrail.

He mouthed the words of the enchantment that should carry his words to Tonin but felt nothing. The image in his mind's eye was as stiff and unresponsive as a painted panel. He tried again but there was none of the thrill he recalled from his past use of Artifice. Where was the vivid connection, the wondrous sense of touching the aether that linked all living things, thought speaking to thought, free from the fetters of distance or difference? Vanam was as unreachable as the sun sailing high and untroubled above them.

Was he doing something wrong? Parrail wondered. But he'd worked this Artifice with Mentor Tonin even before he

had helped the scholar rouse the sleepers of Kellarin. He had
worked it so much more effectively after Demoiselle Guinalle
had explained the apparent contradictions in their lore,
untangling the contrary incantations that had been hampering their attempts at enchantments. Hopeless longing seized
Parrail. He'd been so eager to share the winter's discoveries
with Guinalle, not least those woven into love songs that he'd
be able to sing to her.

Perhaps he should try that older, simpler form of Artifice.
Parrail closed his eyes, the better to hear the silent melody
playing in his head. What was the song Trimon had used to
call to Halcarion, lost as he wandered in the depths of the
Forest, calling on the Moon Maiden to light the stars to guide
him home? Would it work, sung unheard in the elemental
silence all around him? Could he keep the pitch and beat?
He'd never been a good singer. Determination gripped Parrail
as he concentrated every fibre of his being on the mythic
ballad.

> The malice of elder dark wove shadows to snare and
>   bind him.
> Trimon took up his harp and sang that his love might
>   find him.
> Driath al' ar toral, fria men del ard endal
> Cariol vas ar jerd, ni mel as mistar fal

It was the jalquezan that held the enchantment, wasn't it?
The incomprehensible refrains of Forest Folk songs worked
their long-forgotten Artifice. Parrail sang in mute resolve,
weaving his cherished memories of Guinalle through every
nuance of the travelling god's desperation and desire for the
remote goddess of maidenhood and mystery. The rhythm of
the song pulsed in his blood, warming him from head to toes
in an exultation that bordered on ecstasy. He gasped and the
rapture was gone.

'Well?' Naldeth released his spell, looking at Parrail with
the intensity of a desperate man.

A shiver seized Parrail and it was a moment before he could speak. 'I don't know,' he admitted lamely.

A shadow fell across the pair of them and they looked up guiltily. Relieved, they recognised the yeoman absently twisting his ringless fingers.

'So what are you two going to say when they come for us in the morning?'

'Messire D'Olbriot doesn't favour these open meetings, does he?' I looked around the rapidly filling hall. The door barely got a chance to close before some curious face opened it again. I had to admit Temar's new reception room looked impressive. Ryshad had spent the last few days cajoling people into lending a hand and they'd set to with a will. The wooden panelling I was leaning against still wanted paint or varnish but it was a considerable improvement on cramming everyone between the trestles and boards of the trading hall.

'No Sieur does these days.' Ryshad was counting heads. 'This is the old style; the way Temar remembers his grand-sire doing things. It has its points; the Caladhrian Parliament's open to all and half the Lescari dukes hold their assemblies in the open air.' Sworn to D'Olbriot, Ryshad had ridden the length and breadth of Tormalin and half the countries beyond. 'Deals behind closed doors send rumours of bad faith hopping around like frogs in springtime.' He scratched a scar on his arm, token of such rumours that had nearly been the death of him and Temar the summer before in Toremal.

'Can he stop it turning into a shouting match? What if everyone tries to have his say at once?' I looked up to the dais where Temar sat on a high-backed chair; arms orna-mented with saw-edged holm oak leaves. He was wearing a sleeved jerkin in the Kellarin style rather than the gaudy fashions of Toremal that I knew he had crushed in a trunk somewhere. It was still a superior garment; Bridele must have been squinting by a candle half the night to finish the green leaves embroidered on the grey silk.

Guinalle sat beside him on a plainer chair upholstered with rich russet leather. The colour complemented her smoky blue gown, cut neither ancient nor modern but calculated to flatter her figure at the same time as using the minimum of precious damask. A modest swathe of lace obscured the low sweep of the neckline and discreet diamonds glinted beneath the glossy fall of her unbound hair. The two were deep in the first conversation I could recall them sharing since Equinox. 'What if Guinalle takes a contrary view to him?' I asked Ryshad.

'They'll save any arguments for later. They both grew up in courtly Houses; they know the importance of appearances.' We claimed two of the stools arrayed around the edge of the room and Ryshad stretched long legs out in front of him. 'They know Kellarin runs on goodwill. Neither will risk undermining that with a public squabble.'

I wondered if Temar appreciated how much that goodwill depended on Ryshad's talents. As D'Olbriot's man, he'd often had to unite some disparate band of men, getting a task done with a joke and a laugh, asserting his authority with steel in his voice and, if need be, in his hand. He'd been doing the same for D'Alsennin since we got here.

My beloved was watching Guinalle with a slight smile. 'Did she tell you Artifice was used to curb anyone letting their mouth run away with them in the Old Empire courts?'

She had and I wasn't entirely happy with the notion. I surveyed the crowd, some intent faces among the merely inquisitive. 'Who steps up first?'

'For the moment, first come, first heard.' Ryshad looked at D'Alsennin with faint impatience. 'I told Temar he'd do better to have people bring their business to his proxy before an assembly meets and to let them know he'll hear them in order of importance.'

'You're not taking that on?' I hoped it was plain I expected a denial.

'I'm no clerk.' Ryshad said emphatically. 'It's time young Albarn took on a few responsibilities of the rank he's so eager to claim.'

As Ryshad spoke, Albarn Den Domesin appeared on the dais from a door in the back wall. This sprig of ancient Tormalin nobility had certainly welcomed the Emperor's edict that the few remaining noble lineages of Kellarin should henceforth be considered cadet branches grafted on to the D'Alsennin tree. Perhaps someone should tell him that Tadriol had simply been circumventing the snarl of legalities threatening to entangle Temar as aggrieved and opportunistic Sieurs had laid ancient claims and spurious grievances before Toremal's law courts.

Albarn settled himself at a table to one side of the dais where an unsullied ledger lay open beside an assortment of pens and ink. He didn't look too enthusiastic for someone eager to be acknowledged as Temar's designated successor.

'Poor lad, taking notes himself rather than lording it over copyists,' I said with light mockery. 'Still, if you want to reap, you've got to sow.'

'I haven't seen you doing much sowing.' Ryshad shot me a quizzical look. 'But I tripped over Fras making a mess in our garden this morning. Why is that?'

'He's as handy with a spread of runes as he is with that hoe.' I spread my hands, unconcerned. 'He'll get the job done.' And I'd washed the bed linen, so felt entitled to some entertainment today.

Halice strode through the crowd and pulled up a stool. 'How long are we going to be sitting on our hands?'

'We're waiting for their nod.' Up on the dais Guinalle was emphasising her point to Temar with sharp gestures. 'What does she reckon to this notion?'

'A sensible custom long overdue some use.' Halice grinned. 'If we can convince her to turn away anyone plaguing her outside of these sessions, she might learn to relax a little.'

Ryshad laid a hand on my thigh to silence me. 'Here's the old wether to break the snow.'

The crowd stilled as a white-haired man stepped forward, nodding a polite bow to Albarn before standing below Temar and Guinalle. 'My duty, Messire, Demoiselle.'

'Master Drage.' Temar inclined his head and Guinalle favoured the man with a courteous smile.

He coughed. 'It's about these land grants. I'm wondering if we can't break them up a bit. Back home, we held land in different parts of a demesne, some meadow, some plough land, all different tracts, so no one got all stones or bog.'

Temar nodded. 'But there's sufficient land here to give everyone good soil.'

'But what about hail or storm?' Drage spoke with the confidence of age and experience. 'Larasion be blessed, we've mild enough weather here but if all a man's crops are in the one field, any misfortune could ruin his harvest.' A murmur of agreement supported him but I could see a few belligerent faces determined to dispute this. Yeomen newly come from Tormalin liked knowing exactly where their boundaries ran and their precise rights to enforce them.

Temar bent to confer with Guinalle before answering Master Drage. 'You raise a valid concern and I imagine others share it. But equally, many folk prefer their grant within a single enclosure. We suggest anyone wishing to swap a portion of their holdings with another gather in the trading hall tomorrow. We can have exchanges recorded by formal charter—'

Guinalle's scream came like lightning from a clear sky. She stumbled to her feet, head shaking like a horse tormented by hornets, hair lashing wildly as she clutched at her temples. Temar barely caught her as she fainted, falling to his knees on the hollow dais with a thud that echoed around the stricken silence.

Ryshad's long legs ignored the stairs, me taking them in two strides. Halice was barely a pace behind us.

'Is she breathing?' I demanded. Her colour was ghastly, lips bloodless, face slack.

Temar ripped at the lace secured around her shoulders with a silver and sapphire brooch. 'Her heart's racing.' We could all see the beat in the pale hollow of her neck.

Ryshad scooped her up in his arms.

'Through to the back.' Halice lent a steadying hand as he got to his feet.

'Keep them here.' I held Temar back before pushing him towards his seat of authority and the open-mouthed consternation below. 'Carry on or gossip will have her dead and on her pyre before sunset.'

Halice was holding the rear door for Ryshad. She beckoned me with a jerk of her head. 'We'll send word as soon as we know what's wrong.'

Temar visibly composed himself and turned to the astonished gathering. 'It seems the demoiselle is taken ill.' His voice strengthened. 'But she would be the last one to wish for any fuss and the first to urge us to continue.'

That much was true but the thought did little to relieve my anxiety as I closed the door on his words.

Ryshad was standing in the middle of Temar's hall, frowning. The walls were still bare stone but Bridele was doing her best to make the place more comfortable. High-backed settles flanked the wide hearth, mismatched but well made and softened with linen-covered cushions bright with more of the housekeeper's embroidery.

Halice was tossing them to the floor and delving in the hollow bottom of the settle to find a blanket. 'Livak, have that woman find us some decent wine.'

I ran to hammer on the kitchen door. Bridele opened it, startled.

'Demoiselle Guinalle's taken ill,' I told her rapidly. 'Fetch wine or white brandy if Temar's got a bottle hidden away.'

As she scurried away, I went to look for kindling in the cluttered inglenook. Ryshad laid Guinalle gently down. 'Is she stirring?'

'Barely,' said Halice, chafing the noblewoman's fragile wrists between her own muscular hands. 'Have either of you heard of any contagion?'

We all looked at each other, relieved to see mutual head shakes. Drianon save us from another outbreak of the fever that had left Tedin orphaned and in his grandam's care, I thought. Especially if we didn't have Guinalle to curb its virulence this time.

Ryshad snapped open the clasp of her chain girdle. 'Where are the laces on this cursed gown?'

'Under the arm.' I pointed before turning back to the hearth. '*Talmia megrala eldrin fres.*' A flame sprang up among the twigs and I fed it with bigger sticks. Guinalle might scorn such Lower Artifice but she couldn't deny it was useful. I saw a feather poking through the linen of a cushion and, recalling my mother dealing with a light-headed housemaid, plucked it out.

'On there.' Ryshad directed Bridele to set her tray on the low table between the settles. Guinalle moaned, a low sound of acute pain. He knelt beside her. 'Can you tell us what's wrong?'

He didn't tell her she was going to be all right, dark eyes scanning her pale skin for any sign of a rash or some other ill omen. Ryshad's sister had died of a spotted sickness and Halice and I have seen people healthy at dawn and dead before dusk.

Halice brushed Guinalle's disordered hair aside, testing her forehead for fever. The girl caught her breath and opened frantic brown eyes like someone roused from nightmares. She tried to raise herself but Halice restrained her. I poured a goblet of dark ruby wine and stood at Ryshad's shoulder.

Guinalle's eyes were disconcertingly distant. 'Parrail?'

'What about him?' Halice demanded.

'Is he in trouble?' asked Ryshad.

She seemed deaf to their questions. I lit the feather and waved the smouldering fragment beneath her nose. Guinalle coughed on the acrid smoke and her indignant eyes focused on me.

'Parrail's in the most dreadful distress!' She sat up, a rush of colour to her lips and cheeks reducing her corpse-like pallor.

I handed her the wine. 'Is it the ship?'

'He's terrified.' The demoiselle took a shuddering breath.

'It's a wonder he could work any Artifice!'

'Could you tell where he is?' Ryshad got to his feet, trying not to press her too hard.

'On land or at sea?' I amplified the question.

Guinalle drained the cup of wine before speaking. 'On land, I think, but not on Kellarin. Or perhaps not. I felt the ocean hindering his enchantment.' She set down the goblet and knotted her fingers in her lap, knuckles white.

'Trouble at sea comes fast and furious.' Ryshad's concern was plain. 'Especially if they're making landfall. Can you reach him with your own Artifice?'

Guinalle's dogged self-possession was returning. 'Give me a moment.'

I perched with Halice on the low table, trying not to look too impatient.

Guinalle sat on the edge of the settle, smoothing her skirts as she took a deep breath. She spared a vexed look for her torn lace before folding her hands slowly beneath her breastbone. Closing her eyes she spoke with measured calm.

'*Lar toral en mar fordas, ay enamir ras tel. Parrail endalaia ver atal sedas ar mornal.*'

Her squeal made us all jump and Halice's grab for a non-existent sword hilt sent the tray and goblets crashing to the floor.

'What?' Ryshad was braced for action.

'He's in fear of his life.' Guinalle was shivering like someone cloakless in the depths of midwinter.

'From the sea?' I recalled the lad was as bad a sailor as me.

'He's not alone. He fears for the people with him.' Guinalle's brow furrowed, eyes dark and inward-looking. The demoiselle raised a hand and I saw marks on her palm where her fingernails had dug in. 'He's surrounded by dangerous men, thieves and killers.'

'Elietimm?' Ryshad looked murderous.

'No,' Guinalle said slowly. 'I've no sense of them.'

'Can you talk to Parrail?' Ryshad was all but pacing the floor with frustration.

'He's scared out of his wits.' Guinalle shook her head, distraught. 'He won't hear me and for me to see through his eyes with Artifice—'

I wasn't waiting for explanations. 'We need scrying. I'll find Allin and set Temar's mind at rest.' I added with a smile at Guinalle. Embarrassment at the realisation of her public collapse wiped away the last of her pallor and, mortified, she looked surprisingly young.

I left her to Ryshad and Halice, slipping discreetly on to the dais in the reception hall through the rear door. Albarn had his head down, scribbling rapidly and Temar looked to have kept the business of answering appeals to his authority as Sieur going fairly smoothly so far.

'Make an offering to a shrine, that's where it stays.' A woman with a figure like a peg-dolly was standing before Temar, hands on hips.

'Mistress Beldan, you have said your piece. Please let Mistress Treda have her say!' I was impressed by Temar's firmness.

His chair hid the second woman from me but from her accent, she was one of the original colonists. 'I know nothing of practice over the ocean nowadays but we hold to an older custom.' Her effort to sound placatory was obvious. 'If I give a cooking pot to Drianon by way of thanks, I expect the goddess to bring someone with the need for it by her shrine and have them find it there. I don't look for it to gather dust for all eternity.'

'A cook pot's no fit devotion—'

'Thank you.' Temar cut across Mistress Beldan's scorn. 'Does anyone claim responsibility for the shrine? Is anyone willing to take on a priesthood?'

I saw people looking at each other with confusion and reluctance. Priesthoods and confraternities for the upkeep of shrines have been hereditary for generations out of mind on the other side of the ocean but there was no such tradition here.

As uncertain muttering occupied everyone, I stepped up

to Temar's side. 'Guinalle's all right, just fainted.' That reassured him even if I wasn't entirely sure it were true. 'Parrail's in some sort of trouble and used Artifice to call for help. It took her completely by surprise and he's none too adept, so that made things worse.' I noted people stepping eagerly forward to listen and considered how much bad news to chew on would stop their vivid imaginations supplying worse.

'What kind of trouble?' Temar's pale blue eyes fixed on me.

I wasn't going to speculate with all these ears around. 'We need Allin to scry for us. Do you know where she is?'

'With Master Shenred.'

I patted Temar on the shoulder. 'You're doing well. Keep it up.'

Temar allowed himself a grimace of frustration before I took myself out by the back door. I heard him return to the matter in hand with tense deliberation. 'We should establish a confraternity to agree such practices for the shrine. Anyone willing to serve should give their name to Albarn and lots can be drawn. Those who prefer a different rite can set up their own shrine.'

Back in Temar's residence, Bridele was cleaning the floor and Halice was tending the fire while Guinalle sat frozen on the settle. Ryshad looked up from searching among Temar's charts and spared me a brief smile.

'Any idea where Shenred is?' I asked him.

He thought for a moment. 'Try the slaughter ground.'

Hurrying down the tiled lane, I ran down river past the hillock that shielded the sights and sounds of the bloodier end of a master butcher's business. Allin was by the hanging store, apron over her gown, sleeves rolled up and one hand carefully testing a vat of brine. 'It's all a question of evaporation,' she said earnestly. 'With water antithetical to my fire affinity, it's a delicate balance.'

'Sorry to interrupt, but D'Alsennin needs a little magic working.' I smiled briefly.

Shenred sighed. 'Go on then, lass.'

'I'll be back as soon as I can,' Allin apologised earnestly.

'It'll keep, lass.' He smiled at her. 'That's what brine does.'

I forced a rapid pace to take us out of earshot as soon as possible. 'How well do you know Parrail? Well enough to scry for him?'

'I don't think so.' Curiosity followed Allin's honest regret. 'Why?'

'He's in trouble and we need to know how bad,' I told her bluntly.

'Naldeth's on the same ship, isn't he?' She dried her hands on her apron. 'I know him, and his brother.'

'Then that's who you scry for.' We returned to Temar's residence as fast as I judged we could go without attracting undue attention.

Allin stripped off her apron as we entered. 'Do we have – good, thank you.'

Ryshad was already filling a broad silver bowl from a prettily glazed ewer while Halice added to a motley collection of bottles on the table. 'We've got you all the inks and oils Bridele could find.'

Allin rapidly selected a glass vial of green oil with sprigs of herb in it. She uncorked it with care, letting a few drops fall on to the surface of the water. 'I may not be able to hold the image for long,' she warned.

The vivid green of the oil vanished as it spread across the water, a hint of thyme scenting the air. Allin cupped her hands around the rim of the bowl and set her round jaw resolutely. I joined Ryshad on one side of her, Halice and Guinalle on the other, all of us trying not to crowd the mage but increasingly anxious to see what her magic might reveal.

The invisible film of oil shone as if sunlight were playing on it. The green-gold sheen thickened, trails of radiance falling through the water, spreading and diffusing until the colour filled the bowl. It deepened to a grassy hue, then to a mossy darkness and, faint at first, a reflection formed on the glassy surface. 'Don't jog the table.' Allin concentrated on the bowl, her tongue caught between her teeth.

'Is that the ship?' I saw an ocean vessel drawn up on the shingle strand of Suthyfer's best anchorage.

'That's Den Harkeil's.' Ryshad pointed to a ram's head carved on the stern rail.

Halice scowled. 'Hardly fit to sail.' The wheeling magic showed us where planking had been stripped from the ribs of the ship, leaving it broken like the carcass of a dead animal.

'What do they want the wood for?' As I wondered, Allin sent the spell searching across from the shore. We saw crude shelters sprawling over the grass, some canvas, others built from hatch covers and doors. Chests and casks were stacked beneath crude nets weighted with pulley blocks.

'Who are they?' Halice put careful hands behind her back as she bent closer to study small figures, some barefoot in shirtsleeves with an air of purpose, others more leisurely in boots and cloaks.

'Pirates,' said Ryshad coldly. 'Scum of the seas.'

'Where's Parrail?' Guinalle's eyes went from the image to Allin and back, frustration chasing anxiety across her face.

'I'm looking for Naldeth.' Allin's voice was tight with concentration.

It was like flying over the camp on the back of some seabird. The spell carried us to the edge of the scrub that fringed the forests and we saw a rough-hewn stockade below.

'They're not just stopping to take on water,' murmured Halice.

Ryshad glowered. 'Who's inside there?'

Splintered spikes and the heavy gate were no barrier to Allin's magic. We surveyed the crushed captives within.

'That's him.' I hadn't seen Naldeth since the year before last but a gambler cultivates a memory for faces.

'Parrail.' Guinalle cupped her cheeks with her hands, eyes dark with distress.

'Allin, can you show us the anchorage again? Looking north.' The mage-girl nodded at Ryshad's request and the shifting image made my stomach lurch.

'That's their ship.' He nodded. 'The *Tang*.'

We saw a second ship anchored in the sound. 'They're not stripping that one for timber,' I commented.

'They're looting the cargo.' Halice pointed to laden longboats heading for shore.

'But Kellarin wants those things,' said Guinalle with anguish.

'And the pirates want the ship.' Halice pointed at a scarlet pennon snapping at the top of the mainmast.

'With all those wharf rats to crew it, they're not worried about killing the original company.' Ryshad scowled as a longboat's oar shoved a floating corpse aside.

Halice hissed as a sleek-hulled, single-decked pinnace appeared in the sound, followed by two substantial ocean ships built and rigged for speed. All three flew the scarlet flag with the black line of the snake device. 'That's a god-cursed fleet.'

'I'm sorry,' Allin gasped as the image abruptly blinked into nothingness.

'We've seen enough,' Ryshad assured her. 'I'm getting D'Alsennin.'

As he turned on his heel, the rest of us stood in pensive silence.

Halice looked at Allin. 'Could you bespeak Naldeth?'

'And let everyone know he's a wizard?' I looked sceptically at her. There were some advantages to the more discreet workings of Artifice.

Halice grimaced. 'Which could get him killed out of hand.'

'Can't you lift him out of there?' I asked Allin. Shiv's wizardry had once got me out of a prison cell.

'Not without a nexus,' the mage-girl said sadly. 'Not so far away.'

'The Elietimm used Artifice to move people over great distances.' Halice looked at Guinalle. 'Could you—'

'I cannot rely on the strength of the aether over such a distance, not over water.'

The two magic wielders looked at each other with mutual regret.

'We'll just have to do it the old-fashioned way then,' I said bracingly.

'Pirates?' Temar hurried in, open face betraying his shock.

'Holding Suthyfer, if we don't do something to shake them loose.' Halice moved to pick up the map Ryshad had been studying.

'How soon can we set sail?' Temar planted his hands on the table.

Halice looked up. 'You're not thinking of going in alone?'

Temar jutted a single-minded jaw. 'We've the *Eryngo* and the coast ships besides and men enough to fill them with blades.'

'Ploughmen and artisans.' Halice stuck her thumbs through her belt, clasping her buckle. 'We need trained swords against pirates, my lad.'

'I led my cohort—'

Ryshad spoke over Temar's hot indignation. 'Granted the *Eryngo*'s bigger than the pirate ships we've seen so far but it's also heavier, higher and slower. They'll run rings round us if we're not careful.'

'The coasters are more nimble.' But Temar was looking less sure of himself.

Ryshad gestured at the blank bowl. 'No more than the *Tang* and they captured that.'

'We need a full corps of mercenaries,' stated Halice firmly.

'How long will that take to arrange?' Ryshad demanded. 'Give that lot half a season to dig themselves in and we'll never get them out. Speed's as important as weight of response.'

'Can you whistle up ships loaded with fighting men?' demanded Halice.

'Yes,' replied Ryshad. 'As soon as Allin has Casuel tell D'Olbriot the peril we're facing.'

'Casuel can send letters to all the corps commanders who owe me favours,' countered Halice. 'He can use the Imperial Despatch.'

'No.' Temar was almost as pale as Guinalle had been. 'I

won't run to D'Olbriot like some child failing his lessons. Nor will I put Kellarin any deeper in anyone's debt, not Tormalin princes or mercenaries, not unless my back's to Saedrin's threshold.'

Halice and Ryshad turned on him like twin halves of a double door.

'We call the miners down from Edisgesset.' Temar lifted his chin defiantly.

'Where do we find swords for them all?' Halice challenged.

I raised a reluctant hand. 'If you bring all the miners down here, who guards the prisoners in the diggings?'

That silenced everyone.

'They have all given their parole. None is a threat.' Guinalle's voice shook.

Ryshad, Halice and Temar studiously avoided each other's eyes. I was glad they all realised this was no time to reopen that particular argument.

Allin had no such qualms. 'They came here to kill everyone. They're Ice Islanders!'

'They surrendered as soon as their leaders were killed,' Guinalle insisted.

Which was true and, Saedrin forgive me, had been cursed inconvenient. Seeing no prospect of ransoming them back to the Elietimm, Halice had been for killing them out of hand and Ryshad would have called that deserved execution under the fortunes of war but Temar had baulked at yet more bloodshed. So the silent, sullen captives had been sent upriver to dig for ore under the watchful gaze of miners used to a life of hard knocks. Accident and disease was culling them fairly effectively from what I heard, if not fast enough to suit Halice. Guinalle on the other hand protested such treatment every time she visited Edisgesset to torment herself over the sleeping figures still in the cavern. Temar did his best to ignore both issues by seldom going up river at all.

'D'Olbriot can send all the help you need,' Ryshad told Temar firmly. 'Or if you're worried about being obligated, call on Tadriol. He's your overlord, you're entitled to his aid.'

'Which makes his suzerainty plain in fact as well as in theory,' Temar retorted. 'If Tormalin blood's shed for Kellarin, half the Sieurs who wanted to throw us off here last year will insist Tadriol claim a share in our land and offer their own people to defend it for him.'

'We can call up a couple of mercenary corps as quick as any Imperial cohorts,' interjected Halice. 'Once they're paid off, that's an end to it.'

'Paid off with what?' Temar threw up his hands with irritation. 'If they don't demand gold up front, it'll still cost us land granted to men with no idea how to till it and less interest.'

'Why risk death or injury to anyone?' said Guinalle, agitated. 'Artifice and elemental magic both can bring a ship safely over the ocean without having to stop at Suthyfer.'

'Don't be so foolish.' Temar made no attempt to hide his scorn. 'They'd have a stranglehold on our very lifeblood.'

'No one would risk the crossing with pirates camped on the route,' Halice said more courteously. 'Even without any need to stop.'

'The threat would kill all our trade.' Ryshad looked at Temar. 'And from that base, they'll plunder the whole ocean coast. With the Inglis trade at their mercy, the Emperor will act with or without your agreement. If Tormalin cohorts set foot on Suthyfer, you want it on your terms, not Tadriol's.'

'Which is why you want mercenaries.' Halice slapped a roll of parchment against one booted leg. 'Pay them with the pirates' loot.'

'No!' Guinalle objected. 'We'd be no better than those thieves!'

I'd had enough of this. 'What about Hadrumal? Numbers don't count for so much with wizards chucking handfuls of fire or skewering people with lightning. Any size ship will sink if magic lets in the sea below its waterline.' I'd done my best to steer clear of magic for most of my life but since I'd found myself reluctantly involved in such matters, I'd come to appreciate its uses in the right place at the right time.

'What will the Archmage demand by way of recompense?' challenged Temar.

'If you want to make a break with Tadriol, bringing Planir in will do it,' Halice pointed out. 'Tormalin suspicions of magecraft's ambitions will have a field day.'

'That could do as much harm to Kellarin's trade as pirates,' said Ryshad reluctantly.

'I don't think Planir could help.'

Allin's soft words nearly went unheard but Temar stopped and looked at her. 'Go on.'

She went pink. 'Obviously he could use his magic, but I don't think he'll want to, not involving Hadrumal on his authority as Archmage. The Council's badly split over whether or not wizardry should be involved in mundane affairs—'

Ryshad hushed Temar's indignant exclamation. 'How so?'

'Fighting the Elietimm was one thing,' Allin said with an apologetic glance at Guinalle. 'They're a magical threat, but pirates are just pirates. Planir's being pressured to nominate a new Cloud Master—'

'Such concerns are so very much more important than life or death for Kellarin,' Temar interrupted scathingly.

Even though his anger wasn't directed at her, Allin blushed scarlet and ducked her head so that all we could see was her coiled braids. I promised myself that sometime soon I'd wake Temar up to the lass's silent devotion for the insensitive clod.

'But what about Parrail?' Guinalle's distress was giving way to anger.

'Let's see the lay of the land.' Halice unrolled her parchment on the table.

'At least we can see what forces we'll need,' Ryshad said to Temar.

I looked at their three heads bent close together. If Halice was as stubborn as an offside ox, Ryshad and Temar made a matched pair just as bull-headed. Their deliberations were going to take quite some time.

Guinalle shot Temar's oblivious back a fulminating glare

and stalked off to sit on the settle by the fire again.

I tapped Allin on the shoulder and she looked up. 'Planir can't actually keep an eye on every wizard's doings, can he?'

Allin looked puzzled. 'How do you mean?'

'If we had mages helping us without Planir necessarily knowing, so no one could blame him for it, maybe we could find a quicker route through all this than sending in any swords.' I spared a glance for Ryshad who was plainly trying to stop Halice and Temar falling into outright disagreement. I was never going to share his or Halice's relish for a fight and if magic could keep my friends from risking a pirate sword in their guts, I'd try any way I could to make the runes fall my way.

'I'll do my best,' quavered Allin.

'I'm not asking you to take them on alone!' I let slip louder exasperation than I intended and caught a curious look from Ryshad. 'Let's get some air.'

We left for the tiled lane. I didn't dare look back and wondered how long we had before Ryshad came to find out what I was up to.

'Can you bespeak Shiv?' I asked Allin. 'You're not too tired?'

'Not for something using fire.' She ventured a modest smile. 'He's right, you know, Shiv. The more magic I work, the stronger I become.'

I realised some of the people who'd come to Temar's assembly were watching us from the end of the lane with lively curiosity. I smiled blandly at them and turned to lead Allin into the creditable start of a kitchen garden that Bridele had planted behind the hall. 'Where can we find a little peace and quiet for you to work?' I wondered.

'The shrine?' Allin suggested. 'No one will disturb us at our devotions.'

'Good idea.' It would take some while before Ryshad would think of looking for me there. I led the way to the sanctuary the older women of the colony had dedicated to Drianon out beyond the marketplace. The small stone building stood in its own little garden, not a weed to be seen among the burgeoning flowers. The door was already dotted with ribbons and scraps of cloth pinned as token of some boon sought from the goddess. I'd been thinking of hanging one there myself, just to hint that the coming summer's ships could usefully bring hopeful girls willing to earn their place in this new life as maids of all work. Well, that wasn't going to happen, not till we'd got rid of these pirates.

Inside, the walls were empty of the serried ranks of funerary urns that we'd have seen back in Ensaimin and I for one was glad of that. In the centre was a statue of Drianon, elegance at odds with the rustic shrine. That had been Temar's doing last summer. He'd searched among half the sculptors in Tormalin before fixing on one he felt both skilled and pious enough to craft the Harvest Queen's ripely beautiful figure, her serene and mature face crowned with wheat, autumn fruits spilling from her cupped hands.

A few offerings were laid at her sandalled feet, mostly the everyday trinkets that had so offended Mistress Beldan's sensibilities. There was one garnet necklace more akin to the ostentatious displays of devotion customary these days and I wondered what might constitute me having sufficient need for it to placate Drianon. I dismissed the notion as Allin picked up a polished pewter plate.

'A spill, please.'

I handed her a slim scrap of wood from a box by the incense burner and watched the mage work her magic with flame and metal. 'Shiv?'

I edged round to stand at the mage-woman's shoulder. 'Shiv, it's me, Livak.' I looked into the brilliant circle burning a hole in the pewter to see the wizard sitting peacefully at his own kitchen table.

'To what do we owe this pleasure?' Shiv looked amused and his lover Pered raised a friendly hand in greeting. Allin dimpled and gave a little wave that nearly set her fringe alight with the flame.

'No pleasure,' I said grimly. 'We need your help. Pirates

have set up camp on Suthyfer and they've seized two of this year's ships. Scry for yourself.'

Shiv looked dubious. 'Planir—'

I cut him off abruptly. 'I don't want to go to Planir. Allin says there's a miser's hoard of reasons why he won't help. I want you and Usara, if he's willing.'

Allin spoke up. 'Everyone else who might help will want their piece of Kellarin in payment or they'll just argue till Poldrion claims everyone over whether or not they should get involved.'

Shiv leaned back, trying to find words for something troubling him.

'You owe me, Shiv,' I warned him. 'You and Usara. You blackmailed me into working for Planir in the first place and you've been racking up the debts ever since.' I smiled just enough to let Shiv know I held all the winning runes in this hand. 'I'm calling in your marker.'

Allin stifled a giggle and the spill's flame flickered.

'It was Darni put the thumbscrews on you, not me,' Shiv objected. 'Anyway, I've saved your skin enough times to balance the ledger.'

'Who got you off the Ice Islands in one piece?' I challenged him. 'Who got Lord Finvar to hand over that rancid old book you needed so badly?'

'Just what is it you want me to do?' Shiv asked. 'Besides risking Planir's wrath.'

'Naldeth and Parrail are prisoners,' I told Shiv bluntly. That got his attention and Pered's too. 'Along with crew and passengers and whoever else was on those ships. Those ships are full of things Kellarin needs too.'

'You're not going to get all that back with just me and 'Sar,' said Shiv with undeniable truth. 'There'll have to be a fight for it. We'll translocate ourselves to you and bring our magic to bear,' he offered.

'And me,' Allin added at once.

'Ryshad, Halice and Temar are all arguing about how best to go in at the moment,' I admitted. 'But Kellarin barely has the men for it.' I considered the problem. If Shiv said magic wouldn't do it, I'd have to believe him, no matter how many ballads might claim otherwise. Well, we needed another shipload at very least. 'You could help there couldn't you? Bring in a ship from the other side of the ocean, play the anvil when Temar's men go hammering in?'

'Raise mercenaries?' I could see Shiv was dubious even through the spell. 'From where?'

'Bremilayne, Zyoutessela, wherever you know well enough on the ocean coast to magic yourselves to. There are always sailors hanging round docks who'll sign on for a fight if you offer them enough coin,' I urged. 'Then with you along, the whole job will be done and dusted a good deal quicker. The faster we can act, the fewer people will find themselves queuing for Poldrion's ferry.'

'I'll scry for myself and see what I think,' Shiv temporised.

I judged I'd pushed him far enough for the moment. 'Tell Usara it'll be a splendid way for him to impress Guinalle. Most suitors just turn up with a bunch of flowers or some ribbons.'

Pered laughed and I blew him a kiss. I liked Pered.

'I'll bespeak Allin at sunset, our sunset.' Shiv still looked severe and broke the spell with a snap of his fingers.

I looked at Allin. 'Let's keep this to ourselves for the moment, shall we?'

The Island City of Hadrumal,
18th of Aft-Spring

'Skewered like a rat to a fencepost,' Shiv said with distaste but his light touch on the wide earthenware dish that framed his scrying didn't waver.

'I don't think he's dead.' Usara looked sick and gripped the fronts of his sombre brown gown.

The wizards were in Shiv's neatly appointed kitchen, every pan on its hook above the wide hearth, plates and bowls racked by the window.

'It could take days.' Pered scrubbed a blunt-fingered hand through his dark blond curls. 'You wanted a copper-bottomed excuse to go to Kellarin, didn't you?' He swung a kettle above the glowing heart of the slow-burning fire and chose a spice jar from the colourful array on a shelf.

'Be careful what you wish for, you may just get it,' Shiv said without humour.

'He can't forbid us now, surely?' Usara absently ran a finger over the grain in the table raised by years of scrubbing.

'Let's ask.' Shiv abandoned his spell. He rolled down the sleeves of his leaf-green linen shirt and threaded silver links through the cuffs with deliberate precision.

'Don't let Planir turn you into a toad,' Pered warned lightly as he emptied the ink-tainted water from the bowl into the stone sink.

Shiv paused, catching up a light cloak discarded on a chair. ''Sar will find a bucket to bring me home in if he does.'

Usara grinned and sketched a wave of farewell. He followed Shiv through the front room of the narrow house where an iron-studded door opened on to an unremarkable street. Outside, an identical terrace of grey stone houses faced Shiv's, the cobbles between dotted with detritus brushed from the flagway by proud housewives.

A diligent youth hovered where the side street met the high road, offering his services as crossing sweeper. Shiv tossed the lad a copper but didn't wait for him to wield his broom. He walked rapidly through booths and stalls set out along the centre of the wider road, oblivious to the blandishments of the traders.

Usara waved aside an urchin offering him a basket of fish. 'How are we going to play this?' he demanded.

'By ear.' Shiv stepped around a barrow piled high with waxed ochre rounds of cheese. He didn't slow his pace as they left the market behind and started up the shallow sweep of the hill where the halls that were the heart of Hadrumal loomed. Lesser dwellings lined their route, each storey jettied out an arm's length further than the one below, homes and workshops for victuallers, cobblers, drapers and tailors and all the rest who supplied this sanctuary of wizardry with the mundane necessities of life.

''Sar!'

The mage looked to see who had hailed him. 'Planir, we were just on our way to see you.'

'I thought I'd run a few errands to get the archive dust out of my throat.' The Archmage tucked a couple of small paper-wrapped and well-sealed packages into a pocket of his jerkin, whose original rich purple was faded to a midnight indigo, bare patches rubbed in the velvet.

Shiv cocked his head to study Planir. 'There's news from Hadrumal.'

'Bad news,' Usara amplified.

Planir raised an eyebrow. 'Let's hear this somewhere a little less busy.'

He led the way to a narrow gate all but invisible in the dark shadows cast by the tall houses on either side. Planir touched the lock and it opened with a grating whisper. He ushered Shiv and Usara through before securing it with another brush of magic and a smile. 'We don't want children or animals poisoning themselves.'

Trees lined the walls that enclosed the garden divided into quarters and eighths by low walls and hedges. Every bed was patterned with herbs and flowers, some tall, some creeping, dull green and bright shoots mingled. On the far side of the physic garden a second gate gave access to a small orchard where bees bumbled among blossoms in the sunshine. Heady fragrances came and went on the fitful breeze, refreshing after the dry stone breath of the highroad.

'Let's sit,' Planir suggested genially.

'Pirates have landed on Suthyfer, those islands in the mid-ocean,' Shiv told him bluntly.

Usara glanced around but there was no one else among the orderly ranks of methodically labelled plants. 'It's more than one ship and a formidable count of men.'

Shiv gestured to the limpid pond at the heart of the garden. 'Scry for yourself.'

Planir shook his head, walking slowly towards a stone bench set in an arbour of aromatic vines. 'No, no, I trust you, both of you.'

'So what are you going to do about it?' Shiv demanded.

'They've already captured two ships bound for Kellarin.' Usara's face was grim. 'Made slaves of crew and passengers.'

'Those they haven't already killed,' added Shiv. 'The captain's been nailed to his own mast.'

Planir winced, then frowned. 'Why do that?' He took a seat.

'Naldeth and Parrail were on board the ship that was taken.' Usara perched on the edge of the bench.

'They're alive for the moment.' Shiv stood shifting his weight from foot to foot. 'But who knows for how long.'

'What are we going to do?' asked Usara urgently, looking from Shiv to Planir.

Planir plucked a sprig of camomile from a wooden trough. 'Has Naldeth bespoken you?'

'No, but I don't suppose he's able to.' There was faint rebuke in Usara's voice.

'So D'Alsennin's sent word? By Allin's good graces?' Planir savoured the faint apple scent of the bruised herb.

Shiv's boots crunched on the gravel and he folded his arms. 'Livak got Allin to send word.'

Planir pursed thoughtful lips. 'So this is no formal request for Hadrumal's aid. Do we know what D'Alsennin's planning?'

'They're talking about raising men and ships,' Usara said slowly.

'But you can see the complications there,' urged Shiv. 'Mercenaries—'

'It's a sensitive situation.' Planir nodded. 'As is everything concerning Kellarin.' He tossed aside the camomile. 'I appreciate the warning. As soon as D'Alsennin asks for my help, I'll bespeak Cas. I'm not sure how much leeway the Emperor will allow us but we'll do what we can, always assuming the Council doesn't raise too many objections.'

Shiv and Usara stared at him, aghast.

'But Naldeth's one of our own!' Usara sprang to his feet. 'And Hadrumal's name will be cursed in Vanam if Parrail dies.'

'The mentors know as well as anyone else that taking passage to Kellarin entails risk,' said Planir curtly.

'Storm and shipwreck, maybe.' Shiv looked belligerent at Usara's shoulder. 'Not being abandoned to pirates.'

'We can help resolve this with the least bloodshed,' urged Usara.

'Perhaps.' Planir looked up at the two infuriated wizards. 'We can do so much, can't we? Involve ourselves, brandishing the threat of raw wizardry and no mainland prince or powers could curb us, if we chose to ignore them.' He smiled. 'But we've had this conversation before, more than once.'

Shiv wasn't amused. 'Yes, Archmage, and I for one am tired of it.'

'What is the use of power if it's never brought to bear?' Usara was barely less confrontational than Shiv.

'Dear me, you're allying yourself with Kalion and his

ideas.' Planir's voice grew a little cold. 'I had no notion.'

'Forgive me, but that's not true and you know it.' Usara swallowed his indignation with difficulty.

'Kalion wants to be fed and feted by the rich and powerful and have them hanging on his every word, doing only as he tells them,' said Shiv with contempt. 'We just want to save lives in imminent danger of being lost!'

'It's pirates, Shiv,' Planir said patiently. 'They're a running sore on Tormalin's ocean flank and, yes, they could prove a serious problem for D'Alsennin. But they're nothing new. The oceanward Sieurs have scourged the coast clean of wreckers and raiders for generations. This is no sudden catastrophe that needs the Archmage to save Tadriol's neck. Hadrumal's action without justification will just stir up every old prejudice against magic and doom-laden ballads of wizardly arrogance will do the rounds of every tavern from Inglis to the Cape of Winds.'

'What do we do to counter that ignorance?' challenged Shiv. 'It's all very well saying we don't get involved with the mainland, not unless it's a matter of life and death and some ruler comes begging on his knees but what does that get us in the long term?'

Usara spoke with rather more moderation. 'If the commonalty only ever see magic as a scarce resource for the powerful, they're bound to resent it.'

'Mages work everyday sorcery clear across the Old Empire.' Planir sounded indifferent. 'Apprentices go back to their homes with the turn of every season.'

'But they don't go back to spread any knowledge of magic,' countered Usara. 'Most just tire of our isolation here or find a life of study holds little appeal once they've learned sufficient control of their affinity not to be a danger to themselves and others.'

'It's fear that brings them here in the first place,' Shiv nodded. 'Or has them sent, thanks to age-old bias. How many who leave here ever work anything more than cantrips to ease their way through life or impress the gullible?'

'Wouldn't you rather mageborn sons and daughters were sent to Hadrumal eager to learn useful skills?' pleaded Usara. 'Knowing they'd be welcomed back home and valued for what they can do?'

'I don't recall hearing of mages starving by the wayside.' Planir plucked another sprig of camomile. 'Even the least of wizards can earn their bread with their magic.'

'If their hide's thick enough to put up with snide remarks like all I heard in Ensaimin last year,' Usara said with exasperation.

'And jibes from the Rationalists,' snapped Shiv. 'I don't know what's worse. Ensaimin, Caladhria and the rest with their credulous dread of tales from the Chaos where every wizard's a threat, or the so-called forward-thinking Rationalists who say magic's as much an irrelevance as outmoded piety in their search for quantifiable explanations of the world's workings.'

Planir smiled at Shiv's indignation. 'The most blinkered natural philosopher or wooden-headed Rationalist cannot deny the reality of elemental fire singeing his toes.' He turned to Usara. 'And the rediscovery of Artifice should put paid to their scorn for religion. How much old lore have you unearthed in the temples of Col and Relshaz?'

'More than I expected, but the greater part has been lost since the Chaos, thanks to ignorance and prejudice.' Usara looked steadily at Planir. 'Are we going to see Hadrumal's learning lost to worm and decay as well? Wizardry withering, disregarded?'

'Look at Aritane's people in the Mountains,' Shiv invited with an outstretched hand. 'Their Artificers, the Sheltya, they won't act to stop the Mountain Men being driven from their land, their forests, their mines – and they lose respect with every step and with every generation.'

'As I understand Aritane's explanations, the Sheltya hold back because aetheric powers were gravely abused in the past, by those clans who were driven into the ocean and became the Elietimm. You've seen the tyranny of Artifice in the Ice

Islands at first hand.' Planir's grey eyes were bright with challenge. 'When the Elietimm offered help and the Mountain Men seized their chance, brutal Elietimm Artifice brought them to the brink of warfare with the lowland cities and further discredited the innocent Sheltya.'

'There has to be a middle path between disuse and abuse,' insisted Shiv. 'Look at Kellarin. Before the Chaos, aetheric magic was an everyday part of life. The colonists don't fear magic of whatever hue or nature.'

'Aren't we rather getting off the point?' Planir stood up. 'What has this to do with pirates?'

The two mages hesitated.

'Our help in Vithrancel would show Tormalin merchants wizards helping everyone, not just the rich and powerful,' said Shiv slowly. 'And Dalasorian traders, whoever takes word home.'

'I believe Guinalle and Allin work together as much as they are able.' Usara looked hopeful. 'Seeing how their skills complement each other could be valuable to Hadrumal.'

'That's something to lay before the Council.' The Archmage's face was inscrutable. 'What if you fail?'

Shiv and Usara looked uncertainly at him.

'When you're worn to exhaustion by trivial demands after a season or so in Kellarin?' Planir waved an airy hand. 'I can't see even the most bored apprentices joining you to spend all their time mending broken pots. What will there be to interest our more skilled mages? Will we see the rarified magic of Hadrumal's masters cosseting sick beasts or digging out a mine collapse thanks to some fool thinking magic should save him the cost of shoring timber? What if some catastrophe does befall Kellarin and you prove unequal to the task? On the other side of the coin, what if you do drive off some disaster and everyone assumes you'll be saving them from every peril from a cut finger up for ever more? Perhaps it's not fear of failure that checks the Sheltya, but fear of the consequences of success.'

Planir pointed a questioning finger at Usara before turning

it on Shiv. 'How exactly do you plan to rid the islands of these pirates? How do you plan to reach Suthyfer? You've neither of you been there, so you'll need a ship. Where will you find that? The power to guide wind and wave is all very well but you'll still need hands to reef sails and pull on ropes or whatever it is that sailors do. They won't be doing it for the love of Naldeth or in hopes of a better future for wizardry. Have you got enough gold to hire them?'

'We'll find some from somewhere,' said Shiv crossly. 'We want to help rescue Naldeth, Parrail and any other poor bastard who manages to stay alive. Do we have your permission to go?'

Planir studied one well-manicured fingernail. 'No.'

Usara looked at him closely. 'You're forbidding us?'

'Oh, no.' Planir glanced up. 'As Archmage I'm duty bound to curb dangerous ambition but I trust you, both of you.'

'So we can go?' Shiv asked with a touch of confusion.

'That's entirely up to you.' Planir smiled. 'As I said, anyone can take passage to Kellarin, at their own risk, naturally.'

Planir rose and the two mages moved apart as the Archmage walked away. 'Lock the gate behind you.' He disappeared between the tall houses.

'So we're going?' Shiv looked at Usara.

'He didn't say we couldn't.' The sandy-haired wizard scratched at his beard.

Shiv took a deep breath. 'Right then. Where do we find a ship?'

'Zyoutessela?' suggested Usara. He looked doubtful. 'Have you spent much time hanging round docks?'

'Let's deal with one problem at a time.' Shiv looked rueful as they left the garden. 'I've got to tell Pered before we do anything else.'

They walked in silence through the busy morning bustle of Hadrumal.

'What's going on?' Usara's surprise as they turned the final corner startled Shiv out of his musing. He watched, mouth half open, as two less than competent lads manoeuvred a bed through the narrow entrance of his home.

Pered appeared just as the two mages reached the doorway. He stepped aside for a grey-haired man who counted solid gold coin into his palm. 'And here's the luck back.' Pered delved into one pocket and handed the man a silver penny.

'Morning, Shiv.' The grey-haired man nodded before following his purchase to the third doors up the row.

'Master Wryen.' Shiv followed Pered into the house, Usara avidly curious behind him.

The front room was still dominated by the broad slope of Pered's copying desk but new ribbon tied all the parchments into neat bundles now, every stage of work from the first faint lines ruled for pen and ink to bright illuminations needing only the final burnish of gold. Pered picked a slim wooden case out of a small casket full of coloured bottles and began putting pens into it. 'I told you; the next time you went off on some quest for Planir or whoever, I wasn't being left behind again.' His voice was affectionate.

Usara ducked his head on a smile.

'We're not exactly leaving on Planir's instructions,' Shiv admitted.

'So much the better.' Pered put a careful lid on his pens. 'You've been talking over your tisanes about striking out on your own for long enough.' He grinned at their guilty faces. 'I've heard all your plans for setting wizardry to rights in the kitchen while I've been working in here.'

A knock at the door saved Shiv from having to find a reply.

Pered opened it to a thin woman who peered inside with lively interest, adjusting her tawny headscarf with nervous fingers. 'So you're off then?'

'That's right, Abiah.' Pered led the goodwife through to the kitchen. 'So you're welcome to whatever linens or pots you want, for coin on the table.'

'Off to Col, are you?' The woman looked at Pered. 'You've your sister there, haven't you?' Her eyes brightened as she looked at the exotic array of spice jars. 'You won't be wanting all them weighing down your bags. Make a nice spot of colour in my parlour, they would.'

'We'll manage a few pennyweight of spice.' Pered's voice was friendly but he stood protectively in front of his collection.

'Rent's paid up till the quarter year.' Abiah shook her head, at the same time continuing to make interested inventory of the kitchen. 'Must be urgent business to call you away and leave that for old Barl's profit. He'll have someone in here before the hearth's cold, you do know that.'

Pered was proof against the invitation to confide in her. 'If he does, you tell him to send the rent he owes us to my sister.'

Abiah laughed. 'I will, at that. You'd best write down her direction for me.'

'Tell Barl I can keep an eye on him no matter where I am,' Shiv added.

Abiah looked unsure that this was a joke. 'I'll do my best to see he does right by you lads.' She gave Pered a quick hug. 'I only hope we get neighbours as good as you've been. You know, my daughter's getting wed at Solstice. She's no great store in her bottom drawer so I'll go and get her, if that's all right.' She hugged Pered again but Shiv stepped deftly out of her reach so she had to content herself with a wave of farewell.

Pered took her through the house and closed the front door behind her. He turned. 'You needn't laugh, 'Sar. You'll have half the hall wanting to know why you're packing up.'

Usara set down a small portrait he'd picked up from Pered's desk. 'We're leaving for good then.'

Pered looked at him and then at Shiv. 'You don't seriously imagine you'll be coming back? Not after all that's been said?'

Suthyfer, Fellaemion's Landing, 19th of Aft-Spring

'Are you awake?'

'I barely slept.' Naldeth roused himself, heavy-eyed and dishevelled. 'What is it?'

'Food, I imagine.' Parrail sat creased and grimy beneath the shelter of the stockade's wall walk. He hugged his knees as the heavy gates swung open just wide enough to admit three men and a woman lugging a basket.

Naldeth looked nauseous. 'I'm not hungry.'

Parrail's look of grim determination sat oddly on his boyish face. 'We have to keep our strength up, if we're to get out of here.'

'How are we to do that?' Naldeth looked around hastily in case anyone had noticed his incautious despair but everyone else was already forming a sullen line. Parrail returned with a soft loaf of bread tucked under his arm, hands occupied with a slab of yellow cheese and a succulently meaty haunch. 'This is what they were smoking. It's some beast from the woods.'

'Ugly as an unwed maid but good eating,' a voice above them remarked. Startled, they looked up to see a pirate on the parapet. He nodded a cordial greeting. 'We don't do so badly.'

Naldeth and Parrail exchanged a wary glance and applied themselves to their food.

'You two with your soft hands and new-bought clothes, I don't reckon you've gone hungry too often.' The pirate raised his voice and caught the eye of three lads huddled some way beyond the magic wielders. 'Join Muredarch and the ache of an empty belly'll be but a memory, my oath on it.'

'Where do you hail from?' Parrail asked cautiously.

'Me?' The pirate leaned against the splintered bark of the stockade. 'A village called Gostrand, three days up the Dalas from Inglis and just where the hills reach high enough to keep your feet out of the floods.'

'You're a long way from home.' This wasn't the Gidestan who'd dragged them out of the hold the day before, Naldeth realised.

'Fifty times richer than I'd be on my deathbed if I'd stayed. A man in Muredarch's crew sees full value for his work.' The pirate gave the three youths another significant look. 'I'd had enough of breaking my back for whatever pittance some silk-gowned bastard in Inglis would pay for a year's digging, and of watching him sell it off down the coast for ten coin in gold for every silver he paid for it.'

Sudden activity drowned out the man's words; bellowed commands, obliging shouts answering and the thud and crash of casks and bales outside the stockade. Parrail nudged Naldeth and nodded towards a ladder that another pirate was setting firm in the trampled ground so the prisoners could get on to the wall walk. Naldeth looked doubtfully at the scholar but followed him up.

The looted contents of the *Tang* had been piled beneath rough shelters of sailcloth and raw lumber in the open space in front of the stockade. Muredarch surveyed the booty, strolling along in a scarlet linen shirt over black breeches, gold chains braided around his waist and catching the sun. A dark-haired woman in dull green walked at his heels, a ledger cradled in one arm, pen poised.

Muredarch's whistle carried clearly across the encampment and summoned women and pirates who'd been busy about the scattered tents and huts.

'Can you hear what he's saying?' Parrail asked Naldeth in a low tone.

Naldeth shook his head.

'It's all written up, so there can't be no quarrelling,' said the pirate with approval. 'Them as drew the tail end lots last time around step up first.'

A man and woman waited for Muredarch's nod before taking a bolt of cloth and a barrel. The woman in green made a note in her ledger as the man wheeled the heavy barrel carefully away, his companion balancing the cloth on her shoulder. Both were smiling broadly. The next man stopped to speak to Muredarch before departing with a heavy casket whose rope handles strained at the weight within it.

'That'll be my uncle's tools,' said the lad glumly. 'And my apprenticeship gone with them.'

'Swear your oath to Muredarch and earn something to trade for them.' Another pirate came up, a saturnine man with scars on his forearms both long healed and freshly red. 'Indentured to your uncle? No masters here, my lad, to take all the coin and begrudge you half the pay they promised you. Anyway, I wouldn't go back to a journeyman's full day rate.' He laughed and flourished a lavishly beringed hand marred by filthy nails. 'I earn thrice the coin in half the time!'

'You'd be Tormalin, by your accent,' Naldeth commented cautiously.

The pirate looked at him. 'Savorgan bred. What's it to you?'

Naldeth shrugged. 'Nothing, just making conversation.'

The pirate turned back to the apprentice lad. 'You've got an answer for Muredarch yet?'

The lad looked scared. 'I'm not sure.'

'You'll be asked once the shares are made.' The pirate nodded at the patient knot of people waiting with pails and pannikins as barrels of salt fish and dried peas were broached. The woman in green had joined a sandy-haired pirate who was opening a succession of small bottles and flagons. He took a cautious taste of one before holding it up. 'Green oil.'

A woman raised her hand and hurried forward to take it. Spiced vinegar and mustard oil were claimed with similar alacrity but the woman in green waved away a man wanting a jar of physic oil. The sandy-haired pirate rinsed his mouth from a waterskin at his belt and spat before continuing his sampling.

'Who's she?' Naldeth watched as a growing selection of condiments and luxuries were stacked at the woman's feet.

'Ingella.' The scarred pirate sounded wary. 'Muredarch's woman.'

The woman looked around and shouted to a grey-headed man in the rags of a sailor's breeches. His feet were bare, lash marks criss-crossing his naked back. He flinched as if he expected to be hit when the woman pointed to her new possessions.

'That's your lot if you don't take the oath,' the pirate commented with friendly concern. 'Every man's slave and no man's friend.'

Parrail tugged at Naldeth's sleeve and they edged away along the wall walk. 'What are you going to do?'

'Swear, I suppose,' the mage whispered uneasily.

Parrail paled beneath the dirt on his face. 'It doesn't bother you, being forsworn?'

'I don't suppose Raeponin will hold it against me.' Naldeth's feeble attempt at a smile failed.

A new flurry of activity caught everyone's attention. A burly pirate was dragging a youth up from the shoreline. The lad tried to hold on to his unlaced breeches but lost his grip and stumbled as they fell down around his ankles. He was pulled along regardless, naked buttocks pale in the sun, humiliation burning his face scarlet.

His captor dumped him prone before Muredarch, expression eloquent of outrage even if the gusting wind snatched his words away. Muredarch listened with close attention and then turned the lad over with a booted toe, bending over to talk to the cowering youth.

'Which hand will it be?' chuckled the Tormalin pirate.

'What's he done?' asked Parrail.

'Shat in the wrong place.' The pirate sucked condemnatory teeth. 'Muredarch says no one's to foul the sound. You drop your breeches where the tide'll clean the rocks or that's what you'll get.'

A heavyset man came up, shirtless beneath a buff jerkin and swinging a five-stranded whip. Parrail recognised him as the one who'd nailed Gede to his own mast and winced as the lad was stripped of his shirt and tied to an upright spar planted down by the water. Muredarch held up a hand for everyone to see. It was the four-fingered hand, prompting a general murmur of approval.

The Tormalin pirate nodded. 'That'll learn the lad without crippling him.'

But the man with the whip still set to with a will, barbed lashes ripping into the boy's skin, blood spattering in all directions. Naldeth and Parrail both turned away, sickened, but saw more pirates had come into the stockade to chat apparently idly with their captives.

'Do you suppose many turn pirate just for the chance to dress like whoremasters on market day?' The mage watched a bald-headed pirate in an incongruously lace-trimmed shirt advancing on a meek-looking girl.

Parrail watched the raider's expansive gestures, doubtless offering all manner of inducements. All smiles, he wasn't about to let the girl escape him, rough fingers stroking her hair and her cheek.

'Muredarch did say rape was forbidden.' Parrail looked sick as the girl's feeble protests waned. She stood mute with misery as the pirate put a proprietorial arm around her shoulder.

'Holding a lass down and ripping up her petticoats, maybe.' Naldeth rubbed his hands together as if his fingers pained him. 'Scaring some poor poult into laying herself down seems allowed.'

A ship's bell rang and the pirates amiably socialising inside the stockade abruptly changed tack.

'Down the ladder,' ordered the Tormalin on the wall walk, sharp face brooking no argument. Naldeth and Parrail hastily obeyed, hurrying to the back of the huddle of captives as the gates opened wide.

Muredarch stood in the centre, his smile welcoming, his height forbidding, eagled-eyed henchmen stern on either side. 'You first.'

He summoned a middle-aged man nervously twisting a kerchief between his hands. 'I'm just a miller, your honour,' he blurted out.

Muredarch nodded. 'And now we've got wheat, thanks to your ship. Will you grind it for us? I've a fancy for fresh bread after a season and a half of twice-baked biscuit.'

The miller's face creased with confusion. 'I can't think what's best—'

'Take all the time you need.' Muredarch laid a reassuring hand on the cowering man's shoulder before nodding to a flat-faced brute with tattoos all down one arm. 'In the meantime, you can start paying your debts.'

The tattooed pirate held the miller fast while the man who'd flogged the boy stripped him of gown, shirt, socks and boots. The tattooed pirate knotted a thick leather strap securely around the miller's neck and, using it as a handhold, hauled him away. 'If you won't grind the wheat, you can carry the sacks, old fool.'

'Let me know when you've made your mind up,' Muredarch called genially before pointing at the next man who met his eye.

The erstwhile sailor ducked his head in a hasty bow. 'I'll swear but I won't go raiding.'

'Fairly spoken,' said Muredarch in an oddly formal tone. He drew himself up to his full height. 'Do you swear to obey me in all things, to treat all so sworn as your brothers and sisters in oath? Do you put your fate in my hands according to the vow we all trust in?'

'Yes.' The sailor managed a strangled whisper.

'I so swear,' the whip man prompted with a ferocious scowl.

'I so swear.'

Muredarch looked at his new recruit for a long contemplative moment. 'Go see Ingella. Set your mark or your thumb to your name in the muster book and she'll sort you out a pitch.'

The next few all swore the oath, some with visible reluctance, two women stammering through their fear to insist they wouldn't take part in any piracy. Muredarch treated them both with exquisite courtesy. The defiant few were stripped and either dragged off to some toil or thrown to the back of the stockade. Naldeth and Parrail watched glumly as pirates came to pick over the heap of clothes and boots on offer. Some of the apprentices who'd sworn Muredarch's oath with suspicious enthusiasm joined them.

'Do you swear to obey me in all things, to treat all so sworn as your brothers and sisters in oath? Do you put your fate in my hands according to the vow we all trust in?' Muredarch was smiling at the woman who'd nearly been dropped in the water the day before.

'I so—' She broke off and swallowed hard. 'I so—' She tugged at the neck of the chemise below her bodice but the collar was neither high nor tight. 'I so—' The woman coughed, face scarlet as she choked. She fell to her hands and knees, struggling for breath as Muredarch looked down impassively.

'Mama!' Her daughter screamed and would have run to her but the tattooed pirate caught her, one broad hand slapping over her mouth.

The woman collapsed, panting like a stricken animal, lips fading to a deathly blue.

The remaining prisoners stood frozen with shock but few of the raiders, men and women alike, spared more than a passing, regretful shake of their heads.

Parrail's eyes were wide with horror as he nudged Naldeth. 'Artifice,' he mouthed silently.

Naldeth was trembling, fists clenched, sweat beading his forehead.

'It's her own fault.' Muredarch explained in conversational tones. 'She tried to take the oath without meaning it. Oh, didn't I say? We'll have no falsehoods here. Try it and you'll die like this poor fool. Think on that before you decide.' He smiled at the dead woman's daughter whom the tattooed pirate released to sob out her heart over the corpse.

After that, the prisoners gave their oath or refusal with terrified speed and, finally, there was no escape for Parrail or Naldeth.

'I cannot swear to you.' The scholar shakily pre-empted Muredarch's question.

The pirate chief assessed the scholar with merciless eyes, examining him from head to toe. 'You might like to reconsider. Ingella tells me she wants a clerk.' He nodded and Parrail was handed over to the tattooed pirate and the lash man. They stripped him with ungentle hands and flung him into the dank shadow of the parapet where the other prisoners cowered.

He'd barely got his breath back when Naldeth landed on the trampled grass beside him. The mage winced, easing the leather collar away from the weal it had scored on his neck. 'Bastard didn't give me a chance to stand up.'

'On your feet.' The tattooed pirate surveyed the cowering prisoners. 'You're nameless and friendless and that's how you'll be unless you swear to Muredarch. You take any order you're given and you'll eat. No work, no food. Right, you can start by gathering firewood.'

Parrail reached out to help Naldeth up but a vicious stick smacked his hand away.

'If he can't stand, he can sit there till he starves.' It was the Gidestan pirate, no hint of friendship in his eyes now. 'It's every slave for himself, soft hands and all.'

Parrail retreated, hugging his arm to himself.

Naldeth watched in wary silence until the Gidestan

advanced on the dead woman's daughter who was vainly trying to preserve her modesty in her torn shift, the mark of the tattooed pirate's hand still scarlet on her ashen face.

'If they're using Artifice, we have to let Guinalle know,' the wizard whispered urgently to Parrail.

The scholar's face was tight with pain. 'I'll try tonight.' He winced. 'But I think that bastard broke my wrist.'

CHAPTER THREE

To Keran Tonin, Mentor at the University of Vanam,
From Rumex Dort, Archivist to Den Castevin, Toremal.

This is all I can find of recent record about pirates but we're
seldom involved in such things. I'll ask around and see what
else I can have copied for you. Next time you're passing
through this way, you can buy me a drink and explain what
all this is about.

R

*Roll of the Autumn Equinox Assize held in Chanaul
in the second year of Tadriol the Provident
Esquire Burdel Den Gennael presiding as Justiciar beneath
the Imperial Seal
Attestors to the Assize drawn by lot from the tenantry
of Den Hefeken, Den Fisce and Tor Inshol
Summary of cases relating to maritime concerns
brought to judgement and attested as fairly dealt by
those called to that service*

The captain of the ship Periwinkle *was brought before the
court after being taken by vessels of Den Fisce on the 35th of
Aft-Summer on suspicion of piracy. The captain refuses to
give his name and it cannot be ascertained from the crew, even
after such prolonged close confinement. Three names have been
given for the man but none can be found to be reliable. The
ship contained goods proven as stolen from the docks at
Blacklith and as looted from the wreck of the* Shearwater, *a
ship owned by Tor Inshol and cast away on the rocks below*

Oyster Head. Captain and crew are sentenced to branding on the right hand as thieves and flogging on the dockside at Blacklith, that all ships' masters may learn their faces and spurn them in future. Those who can prove title to their goods may reclaim them from Den Gennael's Receiver of Wrecks. Any property remaining will be turned over to the Shrine of Dastennin, to be used by the fraternity for the relief of seamen's widows and orphans.

Malbis Cultram was brought before the court by Den Hefeken's Sergeant at Arms, arrested after three separate accusations of his involvement in piracy were laid. Silks, wines and fine spices were found in his cellars but Cultram can provide neither accounts nor yet trading partners to prove his title to such goods. He claims they were purchased for his own use but can show no trade or profession to justify either the quantities of coin found in his strongboxes or such excessive stocks of luxuries. Witnesses from Blacklith examined separately have identified Cultram as associating with known pirates. A series of coastal charts drawn up by the Pilot Academy of Zyoutessela were found among his private papers. Cultram has never been entered on the muster of the academy and his possession of such charts is therefore unlawful. Further, the Master of Pilots has sent his affidavit that these particular charts were issued to the helmsman of the Brittlestar. This ship of Den Rannion was lost to pirates in the tenth year of Tadriol the Prudent with all aboard put to the sword but for a few surviving by chance and Saedrin's grace. One such sailor, Evadin Tarl, was brought to the court and identified Cultram as one of those same pirates. Cultram is sentenced to be hanged in chains on the dockside at Kalaven at Solstice, his body to be tarred for its better preservation and the continued warning thereby to any tempted to follow his example.

Kemish Dosin stood before the court of his own volition to meet the repeated accusations made by his neighbour Rumek Starn that he, Dosin, is in the habit of sailing with pirates. Dosin is resident in Savorgan, a man of no formal skills, having given up his apprenticeship as a joiner some years since. His former master will supply him with no character. Witnesses presented agreed that Dosin occasionally works as a labourer on river barges but deny that he has ever sailed on an ocean vessel. Harbour Masters at Kalaven, Blacklith and Zyoutessela find no record of him on any ship's muster. Starn could bring no evidence beyond his unsupported accusation. Dosin called on the owner of the Black Rat tavern to confirm Starn's considerable gaming debts to Dosin. The accusation is accordingly dismissed and an exaction of twenty-five Crowns is to be paid by Starn to the shrine of Raeponin in Savorgan no later than Solstice. Should he forfeit, he will be committed to the pillory for the duration of the festival.

Fulme Astar, lately apothecary of Tannat stood before the court at the insistence of the Sieur Den Sacoriz, that these rolls may record his abjuration of the Empire in its present bounds. Den Sacoriz would otherwise require explanation of Astar's presence on the pirate vessel Dogcockle, *taken on the 7th For-Autumn by ships of Den Hefeken after witnessing an unprovoked assault on the Inglis merchant vessel* Petrel. *The court accepts that while the crew were taken in blood and duly hanged from their yardarm, there is no evidence that Astar participated in the raid. Den Hefeken's shipmaster was therefore correct to return him to Den Sacoriz's justice as an erstwhile tenant of that House. Extensive enquiry has found no evidence to support Astar's contention that he was kidnapped off the street in Tannat by pirates to provide them with medical assistance. He was not restrained aboard ship; there is no evidence that he was ill-treated or coerced. Den Sacoriz's Sergeant at Arms also bore witness that Astar's wife has made numerous complaints to the Watch that he was using both her and her children violently. Enquiries into the death of one child from a surfeit of laudanum have not yet been satisfactorily concluded. Astar undertakes to leave Tormalin lands before the turn of this present season with no more possessions than he can carry in his two hands and with only the clothes on his back. The court accepts this plea and will not pursue him further. Should he return, his life is forfeit and any who takes it may apply to Den Sacoriz for the appropriate bounty.*

'Get every piece exactly where you want it before making your crucial move.' I moved my apple thrush across Temar's expensive game board to force Allin's white raven away from the safety of the little marble trees. An agate screech owl blocked the sanctuary of a thicket figurine and hooded crows lay in wait beyond. We were playing at the table in D'Alsennin's residence. Everyone else was busy about preparations for the expedition Temar was insisting on. Ryshad and Halice had grudgingly agreed, since neither could get their own way.

Allin sighed. 'Naldeth was so nice to me when I first went to Hadrumal, him and his brother. Do you think I should bespeak Gedart?'

I leaned back in my chair. 'I'm sure 'Sar will give him the news.' He might have done but that wasn't my concern. I didn't want Allin exhausting herself, not when she was our only wizardly resource. I'd seen Shiv and Usara leave themselves virtually senseless by too much elemental exertion and the lass had spent most of yesterday scrying to help Vaspret draw up a detailed map of Suthyfer. Halice had been almost unbearably smug when Allin had found a fourth pirate ship, even if it was only a gaff-rigged single master.

Allin studied the game board without any sign she saw the opening I'd left her. 'Seeing that man beaten . . .' She shuddered.

'Half naked and someone's prisoner is no fun,' I agreed. I knew that for cold, hard fact. 'But they're fed and the weather can only get warmer. And Saedrin grant it won't be for too much longer.'

Allin nodded but was still looking wretched when Guinalle opened the door from the tiled lane. 'Where's Halice?'

'Talking to the copper miners.' I nodded in the direction of the reception hall. 'With Temar and Rysh. They shouldn't be too much longer.' They were debating how many men to bring down from Edisgesset without leaving the mines at risk of some revolt by the Elietimm captives there.

'Has Halice got all her mercenaries together?' Guinalle demanded.

I nodded. 'Me and Halice have been convincing Deglain and all his pals that whatever crafts they've been polishing up, they're still under her command.' Over the course of a few long evenings in the taproom. Ryshad had been in bed by the time I got back last night and gone before I'd woken this morning.

'I had Peyt come tell me his men reckon their hire ends at the shores of Kellarin.' Guinalle's mouth pinched with disapproval. 'He says he's not going to Suthyfer.'

'Halice will convince him he's mistaken,' I assured her. Halice would relish a chance to beat the error of his ways into the oily rabble-rouser.

'Wait with us.' Allin offered Guinalle the platter of sweet-cakes Bridele had given us.

Guinalle took one grudgingly. 'I hope Temar's not insisting on taking all but the halt and the lame. Driving out these pirates will do no good if Kellarin withers on the vine while he fights.'

'Did you contact the *Diadem*?' asked Allin with sudden urgency.

Guinalle nodded. 'Master Heled was none too pleased but Emelan is confident he can guide the ship well out of reach of danger. What about the *Rushily*?'

Allin took a cake and nibbled it. 'Braull will let the current take them south and then cut back towards Hafreinsaur.'

'A long voyage,' I commented.

'Long but safer.' Allin shrugged. 'And with Braull on board, they'll not lack fresh water.'

'An advantage ships carrying mages have over those with Artificers,' acknowledged Guinalle ruefully. Still, discussing magic seemed to improve her mood.

'Have you had any success contacting Parrail as yet?' I asked casually.

'No.' Guinalle smoothed already immaculate braids. 'I thought I might be able to reach his dreams last night but the link slipped away.' She adjusted the chatelaine at her waist. 'He was barely sleeping deeply enough to dream.'

'That's hardly surprising,' I remarked.

'And no reflection on your skills,' offered Allin earnestly.

'Perhaps.' Guinalle smiled tightly. 'The distance over the water is the biggest problem, that and all the anguish disrupting the aether.'

'How so?' frowned Allin. She was always interested in learning more of the workings of Artifice, intrigued by the notion that Guinalle somehow drew on the collective, unknowing will and belief of other people.

'It may be easier once Master Gede dies.' I was surprised to see the normally imperturbable Guinalle shamefaced. 'His pain is truly dreadful and disordering the aether. The distress of all his people at his suffering overlays their thoughts.'

'It must be like trying to work cloud magic in the middle of a rainstorm.' Allin nodded with an understanding quite beyond me.

Guinalle glanced in my direction. 'Imagine trying to hold a tune when someone is screaming in your ear.'

Tears welled in Allin's dark eyes. 'Gede was still alive this morning when I scried.'

'The central thought in his mind is protecting Naldeth,' said Guinalle sadly.

I thought about what Halice had told me over a private glass of white brandy the night before. Inside information was essential for an assault with comparatively few men attacking such a defensible position. Any mage bespeaking Naldeth would betray him with their magic, which left speaking to Parrail across the aether our only hope. I looked at the little white raven figurine, choosing my next words carefully. 'Could either of you release Master Gede to Poldrion's care?' I wasn't seeing those I loved going into any danger I could lessen, not if there was anything I could do about it.

'There's nothing I can do.' Allin was shocked, as a nicely reared daughter of a rural Lescari household that still observed traditional pieties.

Guinalle looked at me and I met her gaze steadily. She held to ancient faiths long since consigned to myth and ballad but her training in the Artifice of healing meant she'd worked with the sick and dying often enough. 'He'll be dead in a day or so.'

'Does Ostrin demand that death be pointless anguish?' I'd seen mercenary surgeons routinely invoke the god of healing and hospitality as they gave some hopeless case a final drink of something to ensure Saedrin wasn't kept jangling impatient keys.

Something in Guinalle's eyes that told me she'd done the same. 'If I were actually there, perhaps I could offer him some ease.'

I looked at the game board and imagined I was playing the raven instead of Allin. Challenging an opponent to swap sides is always a good trick in a taproom, as long as he'll wager against you winning from the hopeless position you've forced him into. It's lined my pockets a good few times and, more importantly, it teaches you there are always more options than are first apparent. 'Guinalle, have you ever tried working Artifice on someone you can see through a scrying?'

The demoiselle shook her head. 'Usara has suggested it but I've never tried.'

Allin looked uncertain. 'Artifice and elemental magic so often preclude each other—'

'You might save Master Gede some pain,' I suggested.

'Which might clear the aether sufficiently for me to reach Parrail.' Guinalle looked narrowly at me and I wondered if she was using Artifice to read my thoughts. 'Very well. Allin, would you scry for me?'

Allin looked uncertain but was too used to being told what to do to demur. I still intended stiffening her backbone but for the moment was glad the mage-lass remained so pliable. 'Of course, Demoiselle.' She moved to the far end of the table where water, bowl, inks and oils were now a permanent fixture. It didn't take her long to summon an image of Master Gede, ashen faced, head lolling and mouth gasping, either for air or from thirst. His eyes were open but vague and drowsy. Black blood spread from his pinioned hands down the wood of the mast. Fresher flows welled when fatigue or cramp forced involuntary movement to add to his agonies.

'Mercy is a duty from highest to lowest,' Guinalle muttered to herself with sudden resolve. '*Ferat asa ny, elar memren feldar. Ostrin agral fre, talat memren tor.*'

The rhythm of the enchantment recalled a lament my minstrel father had played over the dead child of one of my aunts. A sudden ripple ran over the surface of the scrying though no one had touched the bowl. All at once the vision of the stricken mariner vanished.

'I'm sorry.' Allin was intent on the bowl. 'There was something running so counter to the magic.'

Guinalle looked distraught for an instant before her customary composure walled off such vulnerability. 'It didn't work. I felt that much.'

I felt belatedly guilty for asking such a thing of her. 'You did your best.' At the same time, I was sorely frustrated.

The door to the reception hall opened to admit Temar, Ryshad and Halice intent on a new dispute.

'So we've a fighting force, just barely.' Halice cut off Temar's protest with a brusque sweep of her hand. 'How do we outflank Suthyfer without more big ships?'

I held up a hand. 'I know where we'll get one more.' I'd achieved at least one thing today.

Halice looked at with ready interest, Temar with sudden hope and Ryshad with affectionate suspicion.

'Shiv and Usara are in Zyoutessela,' I explained. 'They bespoke Allin this morning.'

'I told them about Naldeth. They insisted on helping.' She barely blushed at this embroidery on the truth.

Temar smiled at her with delight. 'How many men can they raise? What's Planir's advice?'

'Would you bespeak them for us?' Ryshad asked urgently.

Halice nodded. 'If you're recovered from yesterday.'

Allin coloured a little but hopefully the others thought that was bashfulness rather than guilt. She had been ordered to work not magic until at least noon today but it had been her insisting to me that she was sufficiently rested to find out what Shiv and 'Sar were up to. Halice and I stepped back to let the mage-girl reach for the broad silver mirror and candlestick scavenged from Temar's bed chamber.

'Oh, for a handful of mages to link a few good corps together,' Halice commented in a low voice as Allin worked her spell. 'I could hand the Lescari throne to whichever duke made me the highest offer.'

'How do you think Tormalin's ancient cohorts managed to defeat Caladhria's armies so comprehensively?' Temar said unexpectedly. 'Coordinating your forces by magic's as good as having half your number again.'

'Which is what we're going to need if we're going to come out ahead of this fight,' Ryshad pointed out.

'Which is why the morality of Artifice is drilled into any would-be adept.' Guinalle levelled pointed criticism at Temar.

'Shiv? It's Allin.' She smiled into the mirror. 'How are you getting on?'

The spell showed us Shiv and Usara in a wood-panelled room furnished with simple elegance. The light had that translucent quality that comes from overlooking water.

'Where are you?' asked Ryshad.

'On the ocean side,' Usara answered. 'An inn called the Griffon Garden.'

Ryshad whistled with amusement. 'Still nothing but the best for Planir's men.'

The ochre-toned image in the mirror shook for a moment, the bright band around it contracting. 'Allin?' Temar laid a hand on her shoulder.

She nodded. 'It's just Shiv and Usara bracing the spell.'

The image clarified and Shiv's voice lost its tinny quality. 'Rysh, what's the best way of hiring a ship hereabouts?'

'Try the Harbour Master,' Ryshad advised.

Shiv grimaced. 'He says everything is either already at sea or about to sail for someone else.'

'Then do the rounds of the dockside taverns and find a captain who's looking peevish. Make him a better offer than the one he's got.' Ryshad hesitated for a moment. 'You'll need coin on the table though, not the promise of a share in the final payout.'

Shiv and Usara exchanged a glance that needed no words to speak clearly across the spell.

Ryshad cracked his knuckles. 'There's a moneylender called Renthuan works out of a goldsmith's on Angle Street, back on the Gulf side of the city. Tell him I sent you for Kitria's dowry.'

With Ryshad's only sister long since ashes in her urn, that was a useful password.

'I'll make good every penny,' Temar assured Ryshad stiffly.

So he'd better, I thought privately. That would be the gold that was token of Messire D'Olbriot's esteem for Ryshad, notwithstanding the pragmatism that had prompted the Sieur to hand him back his oath.

'You need a captain who won't get all prissy about filling his holds with fighting men rather than cargo,' advised Halice. 'And who can rustle you up those wharf rats.'

'Don't get arrested for planning piracy yourselves,' Ryshad said hastily.

'We don't want word of this getting back to the Emperor.' Temar bent closer to the mirror, voice low and conspiratorial.

'Or to any chosen or proven man,' added Ryshad. 'Remember Zyoutessela's a D'Olbriot town.'

'Have you spent much time around docks, Shiv?' I asked.

'No.' He looked indignant. 'I don't know why people keep asking me that.'

Temar looked at Ryshad. 'Do you know anyone who might assist them?'

Ryshad shook his head. 'Not and be sure D'Olbriot won't hear of it.'

'I'm not at all sure they can do this,' Halice muttered to me. 'Not without getting their throats cut. This needs you or me over there.'

'But we're needed here.' I considered who else might have both the skills necessary and the willingness to help us out. 'Did Charoleia mention where Sorgrad and 'Gren fetched up for the winter?'

Halice shook her head. 'Last I heard they were in Solura. Even the Imperial Despatch couldn't get a letter to them in time to do any good.'

Either Allin's bespeaking skills were improving or Usara had uncommonly sharp ears. 'I could bespeak Sorgrad.' He looked like a drowning man who'd spotted a rope.

'Could you fetch them to you by magic?' I asked.

'Probably.' Shiv looked thoughtful. 'If we work together.'

'Who are these people?' Temar asked Ryshad.

'Mercenaries, among other things.' Ryshad spared me a speculative glance. 'We've not met but Halice and Livak speak highly of them.'

He came to slip an arm around my shoulder. I slid my hand around his waist and hid my face in his chest for a moment. The comfort of his embrace helped soothe the qualms I was feeling about what I'd asked Guinalle to do and also meant Halice couldn't catch my eye. I'd seen a burning question on her face that I didn't want to answer just yet.

Halice turned her attention to Shiv. 'See if you can find out anything about snake-flagged pirates without getting your throat cut.'

Temar squeezed Allin's shoulder. 'You're tiring. That's enough for now.'

Shiv nodded. 'I'll bespeak you once we've made contact

with Sorgrad.' He gestured and the link over the endless leagues snapped, leaving the mirror an empty circle.

Halice turned on me. 'How's he going to bespeak Sorgrad? I thought wizards can only talk to other mages.'

I shrugged. 'It turned out last summer that Sorgrad's mageborn.'

Halice's jaw dropped and then anger darkened her face. 'You didn't tell me!'

'Not my business to tell,' I retorted. 'Take it up with Sorgrad if you're looking for a fight.'

Halice shook his head. 'When I think of all the times I could have used a wizard—' Like me, she'd always considered mages something to steer well clear of but since we'd been caught up in Kellarin's affairs, she'd come to appreciate their uses.

'Bring magic into the Lescari wars and all you'd do is unite every other duke against the one you were fighting for,' Ryshad pointed out. 'Which might at least help end their cursed wars.' He grinned but Halice was still looking dour.

'Sorgrad would have been no use to you,' I told her bluntly. 'He's had no real training. It was magebirth got him exiled from the Mountains so all it's ever been to him is a bane.' If we in the lowlands were chary of wizards, that was nothing compared to the abhorrence the Mountain Men under the guidance of their Sheltya felt for them. Once I'd seen that for myself, I'd found it no wonder Sorgrad had spent his life suppressing his unwanted affinities.

'We have more urgent concerns than arguing among ourselves.' Temar spoke up with surprising authority. 'We were taught in the cohorts to learn all we could about our foes. Who could tell us more about these pirates?'

'If only we still had Otrick to call on,' I sighed. The raffish and much missed Cloud Master had studied the workings of the winds through a lifetime of sailing with who'd ever give him passage. That had been pirates more than once.

'Velindre spent a lot of last year sailing the ocean coast,' Allin said hesitantly.

'She trawls round the rougher ends of the docks, does she?' I was amused. In our scant acquaintance, Velindre was one of those mages who presented a front of serene aloofness. Perhaps she had hidden depths.

Temar looked at Allin, concerned. 'You mustn't tire yourself.'

Allin laid her own small, soft fingers over his long and work-hardened ones. 'I'm all right, truly. It's fire magic after all, and Shiv's right, you know. The more magic I work, the more I find I can do. '

I caught Guinalle looking at Temar and Allin, her expression fixed.

'She's in Hadrumal.' Allin set up a fresh candle and lit it with a snap of her fingers. 'I really think she has hopes of being chosen for Cloud Mistress.'

If she was deceiving herself, the mage-woman was doing a lot of work for nothing. Allin's spell caught Velindre in a library, sat at a broad table covered in open tomes stacked two or three high.

'Allin?' Velindre didn't sound best pleased, drawing an anonymous sheet of parchment over the crabbed and faded writing she was studying.

'Hello, Velindre.' I heard the nervousness in Allin's voice. 'The Sieur D'Alsennin needs your help.'

'What manner of help?' The blonde wizard's face was pale against the oak shelves loaded with age-darkened books.

'You're more familiar with the ocean coast than anyone else we can think of,' Temar said courteously. 'We find pirates have landed in Suthyfer and wondered if you might have some knowledge of them.'

Velindre looked cautious. 'Possibly.'

'The leader flies a scarlet pennon with a snake on it,' Temar told her. 'He's dark, uncommonly tall and bearded.'

Velindre raised pale eyebrows. 'That sounds like a villain called Muredarch.'

Ryshad's arm tightened round me and we both took an involuntary step closer.

'He was a privateer working out of Inglis,' Velindre began.

Temar looked at Ryshad for explanation. 'Traders play by Inglis rules or they don't trade,' he said with contempt. 'The Guild Masters post bounties on ships that ignore their tariffs or sail out of embargoed ports. Privateers go after them.'

'Most take any honest ship that falls foul of them as well,' added Velindre.

Ryshad nodded, severe. 'They sell on the cargoes to traders who don't ask questions or to Sieurs who pass off the goods as coming from their own estates. So where's this Muredarch been lately?'

'Regin, I believe.' Velindre shrugged.

Temar wasn't the only one looking to Ryshad for answers.

'The most southerly port on the Gulf coast and a real nest of snakes,' he explained. 'Pirates know any law-abiding House's ships won't pursue them round the Cape of Winds. They'll risk it when the alternative's hanging in chains on the dockside. If they make safe landfall in Regin, they can sell all the evidence to the Archipelagans.'

'Before sailing happily up the Gulf coast with an innocent shipload of Aldabreshin spices, silks and gemstones,' concluded Velindre.

'Why's this Muredarch in Suthyfer?' I wondered.

'He's holding a mighty grudge against Inglis,' offered Velindre. 'He took a guild letter condemning a Den Lajan ship but after Muredarch had set sail, the Sieur bought off the bounty.'

'So Muredarch didn't get paid?' hazarded Ryshad.

'Worse,' Velindre told him. 'He'd caught the ship and sold off the goods in Blacklith then came to Inglis looking to ransom the crew back to Den Lajan. The Guild Masters repudiated the bounty and told him to make Den Lajan's losses good out of his own pocket. He refused and they posted a bounty on his own head and ship.'

'So every other pirate's looking to nail his hide to their mast,' speculated Ryshad.

Velindre shook her head. 'Not at all. No one will touch

him. He's a clever man and knows how to inspire loyalty as well as respect. Even if Inglis raised the bounty high enough to tempt some desperate captain, fear of the consequences would have his crew mutinying. For every tale of Muredarch's bravery or boldness, there are two of his ruthlessness.'

'Where does he hail from?' I'd found clues to a man's weaknesses in his origins more than once.

'There are a double handful of stories doing the rounds.' Velindre counted off fingers with incongruously bitten nails. 'Bastard son of some noble House. One of two sons of an Inglis Guild Master who runs legal trade and piracy in tandem. Dispossessed chieftain of some Dalasorian nomads who took to the seas to escape his enemies. Those are the less fanciful speculations.'

'Where he came from is less important than where he is now,' Temar said firmly. 'Madam mage, we would welcome—'

'My regrets, Esquire, I'm sorry, Messire, but I'm staying in Hadrumal.' Velindre addressed herself to Allin. 'There are all manner of possibilities opening up here. You studied under Master Kalion and his influence seems to be on the rise. Troanna's swaying the Council to her way of thinking as well. We could see ourselves with a new Stone Master as well as Cloud Master.' Was it my imagination or did a speculative look enter Velindre's eyes? 'Allin, you don't happen to know where Usara's got to, do you?'

The radiance of the magic circle dimmed. 'I'm sorry,' Allin gasped. 'I'm too tired.' The brilliance flared for an instant then dulled to shut out Velindre's inquisitive face.

'I'm not really tired.' Allin looked guiltily up at Temar. 'But I don't want to get Shiv and 'Sar into trouble. Do you think she believed me?'

'So Hadrumal doesn't know what they're up to?' Ryshad was looking at me in a way that promised interrogation rather than pillow talk at bedtime.

I smiled blithely at him. 'I imagine the Archmage knows

what's going on behind his back as well as under his nose. He always has before.'

Ryshad raised a quizzical brow at me.

'If we don't involve him on Temar's authority, that fat bastard Kalion can't use his interest in Kellarin for a stick to beat him with.' I managed to sound entirely reasonable. I smiled at Ryshad again and won a grudging grin that eased my heart.

Zyoutessela, Toremalin,
20th of Aft-Spring

Shiv looked uneasily across the snowy linen tablecloth. 'You really want that pair in on this?'

'Show me some alternatives,' invited Usara. 'We've had no luck hiring a ship dealing with honest men.'

'So we deal with two we know to be dishonest?' Shiv grimaced. 'Who could vanish with Ryshad's coin quicker than butter in a dog's mouth.'

'I'd rather risk that than being knifed in some dockside alley,' said Usara bluntly. 'Anyway, they wouldn't betray Livak, nor yet Halice.'

'You're the one who's travelled with them.' Shiv still looked unconvinced.

'I liked them.' Pered spoke up from the corner where he was stocking a leather satchel with bottles and brushes from a brass-bound chest.

'I'll allow they were charming house guests but I've heard stories from Livak that threatened to curl my hair.' Shiv ran a hand over his dead straight locks. 'And they're like Livak; never do anything without looking for something to show for it. What have we to offer?'

'Sorgrad may claim he wants no schooling in his magic but Livak hinted that's what he went looking for in Solura.' Usara's eyes grew distant. 'You know he's got a double affinity?'

Shiv nodded. 'Which makes his going untrained even more of a waste.'

'Think it through,' said Usara impatiently. 'Sorgrad's attuned to fire and air. That gives us the four elements between the three of us.'

'You're thinking we could create a nexus with an untrained Mountain Man?' Shiv was incredulous.

'Maybe not a nexus,' allowed Usara. 'But it's a chance to see how we could use our elements in common that we'll never get in Hadrumal, not without someone running tell-tale to Kalion or Troanna.'

'Perhaps.' Shiv drummed his fingers on the table before stopping with a decisive thump. 'Planning a fire won't boil the pot. You'd better bespeak Sorgrad and see what he thinks.'

Pered slung the strap of his satchel over his shoulder. 'I'll go earn you the cost of a few more candles.' He caught the hand Shiv raised to him. 'Let me know as soon as you can fix a sailing date. A few portraits in oils would fetch a sight more coin than ink and watercolour sketches.' He squeezed Shiv's fingers and went through the door with a spring in his step.

Usara looked after him with embarrassment. 'We do have enough money for such things.'

'He doesn't paint or draw for the coin.' Shiv laughed. 'That's just a handy excuse. He'd spend his last cut piece on parchment scraps or charcoal before he'd even think of bread.'

Usara rubbed his hands briskly together. 'Let's see if we can find Sorgrad.' He reached for a small travelling mirror. 'Fetch me a taper, would you?'

But the door opened again before Shiv had reached for the pot on the mantelshelf.

'Look who I met on the stairs,' announced Pered.

'Larissa.' Shiv's greeting was barely civil.

Usara gaped. 'What are you doing here?'

'Good day to you.' Larissa took the chair Shiv had just vacated and tucked demure lavender skirts around booted ankles. She unlaced her short grey travelling cloak and let it fall back to reveal a close-buttoned, high-necked bodice to her long-sleeved gown. For all her sober garb, the mage-woman carried herself with an unconscious sensuality. Pered absently dug sketching materials out of his bag.

'To what do we owe this pleasure?' asked Shiv curtly.

A faint wash of colour highlighted Larissa's strong cheek-bones. 'I want to come to Kellarin.'

Left without a seat, Shiv sat on the bed's richly embroidered counterpane. 'Did Planir send you?'

'No.' Larissa avoided his eye as she brushed her thick, chestnut plait back over one shoulder.

'Then how did you know we were here?' asked Usara mildly.

'Planir told me you were sailing for Vithrancel.' There was a hint of defiance in Larissa's reply. 'You had to be here or in Bremilayne. I can scry.'

'You expect us to believe Planir's not watching your every move?' said Shiv caustically.

'Shivvalan!' Pered objected.

'Why should he?' Larissa rounded on the lanky wizard. 'I've no real talent to merit his interest, isn't that what they say? Dual affinity, but it doesn't amount to half a true aptitude. How else would I have advanced to the Council without playing the Archmage's warming pan? What use could I possibly serve there beyond passing on anything I learn inside Planir's bed curtains.' Bitterness spilled over her sarcasm. 'Or perhaps you're in the camp who think I do have some talent, not for magic obviously but for sleeping with the right man and learning his secrets when I've slaked his lusts? Are you one of those imagining I'm playing a deeper game, just waiting for me to betray him to Kalion or Troanna?' She flapped a mocking hand.

Usara rubbed a hand over his beard. 'I see you're well up on current gossip.'

'There are always plenty of folk who think I really ought to know what's being said about me.' Hurt tempered Larissa's resentment.

'Not that they agree, naturally.' Pered glanced up from his sketch with a meaningful look for Shiv. 'And they defended you, they really did.'

'You're the Archmage's pupil and you sleep in his bed,'

Shiv said reluctantly. 'Blow in the dust and it's bound to sting your eyes.'

'Have you never been a fool for love, Shiv?' The faintest quaver threatened Larissa's composure.

'Of course he has.' Pered's tone left no room for argument.

Usara cleared his throat in the brittle silence. 'Why exactly do you want to join us?'

Larissa sniffed inelegantly. 'If I'm a fool for love, Hadrumal gossip says the same of Planir. Or according to Kalion, he's a fool for lust, which keeps things simpler, the way the Hearth Master likes them. Troanna just seems to disapprove on principle which is a bit rich coming from a woman twice married and with Drianon knows how many children.' Larissa looked unhappily at Usara. 'Whoever you listen to, I'm undermining Planir. That bitch Ely was hinting he won't appoint a new Cloud Master until he can concoct some charade to support my nomination. According to her, he'd use his own abilities to mask my inadequacies before the Council.'

'That's ludicrous.' Shiv was shocked.

'If I'm weighing the balance against the Archmage, I'm taking myself off it.' Larissa's tone strengthened. 'I'll prove my aptitudes with something not even Kalion and his toadies can gainsay. You're exploring how mages might work magic together in less formal ways than a nexus. I have a double affinity; I have insights to offer.'

'That's not actually why we're here.' Usara scratched his beard. 'Pirates have seized Suthyfer, those islands in the sea route to Hadrumal. We're going to help D'Alsennin drive them off.'

'Then I can help too,' said Larissa promptly.

'The Archmage doesn't want it to look as if Hadrumal is playing a part,' Shiv said firmly. 'The Emperor won't stand for it, for a start. If you come with us, that involves Planir.'

'Nobody in Toremal knows I share Planir's bed,' scoffed Larissa.

'Everyone in Hadrumal does,' Shiv pointed out. 'Kalion

will be the first to pass on that tasty gossip, if he thinks it'll discredit Planir among the influential Houses.'

'Surely it's for the Sieur D'Alsennin to decide if he wants my help,' said Larissa defiantly. 'Ask him.'

'I'm not sure—' Usara began hesitantly.

'If you've only just arrived you'll need a room.' Pered stepped forward to forestall a forceful interruption from Shiv. 'Shall we see if we can find you one here?'

'That's a good notion.' Larissa accepted this adroit offer of a dignified exit gratefully. 'We can continue this later.'

Shiv closed the door with an emphatic shove, green eyes indignant. 'This is a complication we could do without!'

'You don't feel sorry for her?' Usara obviously did.

'She's only herself to blame.' But Shiv's condemnation was half-hearted.

'You think Planir should live like some Soluran anchorite because wizards prefer gossiping about the Archmage's lovers to pursuing their proper studies?' countered Usara.

'We can't take her, 'Sar!' Shiv threw up his hands.

'You're going to tell her she can't come?' challenged Usara.

Shiv pursed his lips. 'We could just leave without her? She's never been to Kellarin or Suthyfer, so she couldn't translocate herself there.'

Usara picked up the silver mirror in his hand. 'Let's just get on our way as soon as possible. That means we need Sorgrad's help, even if we don't want Larissa's.'

'This is choosing between rotten apples,' growled Shiv.

'Stop complaining and pass me a candle.' Shiv obliged and Usara set it aflame with a cursory wave of his hand. 'Let's remember we're looking to help Kellarin, not bicker among ourselves.'

Shiv swallowed some retort. 'Can you reach all the way to Solura?

'If I can't, you'll have to go scrying for them.' The bearded mage was intent on his spell. In the next moment, the mirror lit with an amber radiance that startled Usara backwards. 'Sorgrad, it's me.'

Shiv stood at Usara's shoulder to see two familiar figures scrambling away from the spell that had opened up so unexpectedly next to them. Huddled in a ditch beyond the bank of a hollow road, both had the fine blond hair and brilliant blue eyes of the truly mountain born. The first to peer cautiously into the magical void was stockier than his brother but at first glance they looked similar enough to wear the same collars.

"Sar?' Sorgrad's initial distrust softened into a broad smile. 'What are you up to these days?' He brushed a few sere leaves off his blanket and sat cross-legged upon it.

'This is what bespeaking looks like from the other side, is it?' 'Gren dropped down beside his brother with sudden amusement. 'Have you ever caught someone ploughing his lady's furrow? Or someone else's?'

'We've had word from Livak.' Usara spoke without preamble. 'Pirates have landed on those islands in the mid-ocean that ships bound for Kellarin use as a staging post.'

'I recall the maps.' Sorgrad's azure eyes were astute. They hardened. 'I'm sure Planir has some cunning plan to sink them.'

'Pirates?' 'Gren raised a curious finger to poke at the spell before Sorgrad slapped it away.

'Planir says it's none of his concern, nor yet Hadrumal's,' Shiv said tartly.

'Ryshad and Halice are raising a force from Kellarin and we're in Zyoutessela looking to do the same.' Usara matched the Mountain Man's directness. 'Livak said you could help us.'

'Zyoutessela?' Sorgrad elbowed his grinning brother in the ribs to forestall some comment. 'Don't know it but docks are much of a muchness, Col, Peorle, wherever.' He frowned. 'We're the wrong side of Lagontar.'

'We'll hitch a ride to Nestar Haven and pick up a ship for Col.' 'Gren was already securing his blanket with a leather strap and foraging among the leaves for a battered leather backpack.

'Col to Attar, then across the Gulf of Lescar. We can't get to you soon enough to be any use.' Sorgrad shook his head. 'But I can give you a few hints to save you getting robbed yourselves.'

'We can't leave Livak and Halice twisting in the wind.' 'Gren looked mulish. 'And why should they get all the loot?'

'That's an interesting point.' Sorgrad smiled. 'Even advice should be worth some silver.'

'You won't just help us for Livak's sake?' Shiv looked disappointed.

'You should take to acting in masquerades, wizard,' Sorgrad laughed. 'Livak would be the first one to take a rise out of me for not asking a fair price.'

Usara shrugged. 'D'Alsennin can pay you a share in whatever loot the pirates may have.'

'We get to pick it over,' demanded 'Gren.

The wizards looked at each other. 'If Halice agrees,' Usara said cautiously.

'But we want more from you that just advice. We want to bring you here to do this yourself.' Shiv bent closer to the mirror. 'Sorgrad, how much elemental magic have you learned in Solura?'

Sorgrad's face hardened. 'Not enough to make this trip worth my while.'

'Have you any notion of translocating yourself?' asked Usara.

'The spell's closely tied to air affinity,' Shiv assured him. 'You should at least be able to try.'

'Pigs can try whistling but they're still ill suited to it.' Sorgrad shook his head obstinately.

'Then we'll bring you here ourselves.' Shiv absently rubbed his palms on his thighs.

'You drop me in the ocean, wizard, and I won't drown until I've made you sorry for it.' 'Gren was looking wary and accordingly threatening.

'Sorgrad, I know you can summon a candle flame. You can hold this bespeaking steady to help us.' Usara set the mirror down on the table and Shiv hurried to sit opposite him.

'How?' Sorgrad asked with reluctant interest.

'Feel for the fire,' said Shiv. 'Use it to maintain the circle of light.'

With the mirror now flat, Usara allowed himself a sceptical look at the other mage.

Shiv didn't respond, concentrating instead on the mirror. 'All you have to do is sustain the reflection.'

The spell dimmed and Sorgren's cautious voice took on a metallic echo. 'Like this?'

'That'll do,' Usara assured him. 'If we work cursed fast,' he added to Shiv in a low voice.

He planted his hands on the table and took a deep breath, staring unseeing at the white cloth. As he drew his hands round in opposing swirls, an azure trace lingered on the linen like a memory of blue sky behind fine cloud. Usara lifted his hands to cup them before him, cradling a swelling ball of slate-blue magelight. The sphere grew, paling as it did so from slate through indigo to the faint gold-tinged colour of a summer evening sky. The eggshell blue washed over the wizards and disappeared beyond the confines of the room.

Shiv's eyes were tight shut as he pressed his palms together, arms outstretched. He spread his fingers wide and turquoise brilliance netted his hands. Fleeting, like lightning from a clear sky, it was gone almost before it was seen. The mage frowned and new strands of light appeared but still no more substantial than a spider's web reflecting moonlight. Shiv took a deep breath and the tracery of power strengthened to ultramarine. He drew his hands apart with infinite care and the strands of magelight thickened and twisted, threads snapping and rejoining, coiling and spiralling upwards. As the weave extended, it grew thinner, paler. It reached the window and fled.

'Is something supposed to be happening?' 'Gren's interested voice rang out from the silver mirror.

'You tell me,' responded Sorgrad curtly.

Usara's head dipped towards the table and Shiv scrubbed sweat from his forehead with the heel of his hand. 'Shit!'

'So we flag down a cart after all?' Sorgrad's mockery betrayed a trace of disappointment.

'It's too far,' Usara gasped. 'When we're reaching outside our own affinities.'

'We nearly had them.' Shiv flexed his hands and scowled. 'We should be able to manage one.'

'We go together or not at all, wizard.' Sorgrad's muted voice was uncompromising.

Usara looked at Shiv. 'We could do it with Larissa's help.'

Shiv groaned. 'You're not serious?'

'Show me another way?' Usara brushed faint traces of power from his hands. 'Besides asking the Imperial Despatch to pack Casuel in a crate and send him along?'

Shiv rubbed at his temples. 'I don't know who'd be more trouble.'

'We have to do something,' snapped Usara. 'Or we may as well go back to Planir with our tails between our legs.'

'Larissa can help us bring them here.' Shiv sounded distinctly unenthusiastic. 'That'll give her some insight into combining affinities that she can wave in front of Kalion's cronies. But we're not taking her to Suthyfer, agreed?'

'I don't know if you're interested but I can barely see you.' Sorgrad's chagrined voice was fading fast.

Usara gestured and the wavering spell rallied. 'We need help from another mage to bring you here. Don't go far and we'll find you when we need you.'

'You don't think we've got our own plans for the day?' 'Gren's distant voice challenged mischievously. Sorgrad's response was too muffled to be audible and then the bespeaking shattered into glittering fragments that sank away into the mirror's reflection.

'Curse it!' Usara snuffed the candle with an angry hand.

'Come on.' Shiv was heading for the door. 'They can't have gone far.'

Pered and Larissa proved to be the only people in the

wide room occupying most of the inn's ground floor. Too big to be called a parlour, too salubrious to be merely a taproom, its well-scrubbed tables and ladder-backed chairs could offer comfortable intimacy for two as well as convivial circles for larger gatherings. Curtains fluttered at open windows as a fresh sea breeze scoured the scent of the previous night's wine and revelry out of the corners. Larissa and Pered were sitting by the wide arch of the hearth, a tray on the table between them. Pered expertly measured herbs into a hinged sphere of silver mesh, snapped it shut and dropped it into a fine ceramic cup. 'Tisane?' he offered as Shiv approached. 'It's a local blend, decent enough, if a bit heavy on the linden leaves.'

'Please.' Shiv took a seat. 'Larissa.' He hesitated as an aproned maid brought a jug of hot water from the kettle hanging over the fire.

'We find we need your help in working a spell.' Usara pulled a chair over from a nearby table and sat astride it.

Shiv waited until the maid had delivered more cups. 'But please reconsider sailing with us after that. This whole voyage promises to be extremely dangerous.'

Larissa studied her cup, prodding the metal ball of steeping herbs with a spoon. Her hazel eyes were reddened and she clutched a handkerchief that Shiv recognised as Pered's. 'What do you need me to do?'

'Join us in a translocation.' Usara looked to see the maid was out of earshot. 'We need to bring two people from Solura.'

'Solura?' Larissa looked up, startled.

'Western Solura,' Shiv offered, adding cold water to the tisane Pered handed him.

'It's still a cursed long way.' Larissa wrinkled her nose in thought. 'We need as much air around us as possible, some-where outside, high up for preference.'

Pered passed a crystal pot of honey to Usara as the bearded mage grimaced at the taste of his drink. 'You can take a carriage up to the top of the portage way. Everyone goes to see the views.'

'As long as we can find a reasonably discreet corner.' Usara looked at him.

Pered nodded. 'There's a park full of monuments off to the side of the square on the actual crest. Sieurs Den This and Tor That have spent coffers of coin to get themselves noticed, without realising no one gives them a second thought once they're a generation dead.'

Shiv grinned. 'Have you drawn everything in Hadrumal by now?'

'At least three times,' Pered assured him.

'Let's get on, shall we?' Usara stood up.

Larissa drained her cup and raised an expectant brow at Shiv who sighed and set down his half-finished drink.

The bright sun outside was warm enough for Larissa to fan herself and unbutton her high collar. Swathed in silks and layers of muslins rather than wool, the ladies of southern Tormalin swept past, elegant in more unstructured styles than the formal tailoring of Hadrumal.

'Here!' Pered raised a hand as a hireling carriage deposited a flurry of giggling girls at a milliner's opposite. 'Up to the vantage point, if you please,' he told the driver.

Usara handed Larissa in beside Shiv who looked silently out of the window. The sound of iron-bound wheels on cobbles filled the coach.

'I wonder if Ryshad's family built any of these?' Pered mused as the shops and inns of the commerce quarter yielded to sprawling houses; hollow squares of ruddy-tiled roofs above whitewashed walls shaded by trees fragrant with blossom. Stout walls encircled such dwellings, occasional open gates offering glimpses of busy households within. On the flagway either side of the road efficient servants delivered sacks and barrels, workmen carried tools and materials. Nursemaids gathered little ones skipping with delight safely away from rumbling carts and carriages while footmen escorted youths sullen at the prospect of lessons and maidens impatient at such chaperoning.

Usara studied the passing city. 'Ryshad's brothers live on

the other side of the isthmus, don't they?' he said at length. 'Anyway, these houses would be five, six generations old, before the Inglis trade really started bringing in the coin. When would you say these were built, Shiv? Aleonne the Gallant's reign or Inshol the Curt?'

Shiv didn't reply. Larissa was studying her hands again so Pered and Usara exchanged a shrug and sat in silence.

The horses leaned into their collars to pull the carriage up the road that snaked ever higher towards the pass cutting a deep cleft in the saw-edged mountains north and south of the isthmus. Houses became smaller and more closely packed and the cobbles gave way to hard-packed earth. Each frontage showed three or four rows of windows and garret rooms besides beneath the brown and ochre tiles. Hurrying out from behind a loaded dray, a girl with a scarlet fan startled a saddle horse, which whinnied its indignation as it shied away and startled their coach's team. The driver's rebukes and the girl's defiance added sharp notes to the murmur and bustle all around. Within the carriage, the silence persisted.

'Here we are,' Pered announced with determined cheerfulness when the coach drew to a halt. He paid off the driver as Usara got out and offered Larissa a courteous hand. She waved it away with a tight smile.

'So where are we?' Shiv surveyed the broad square that had been hacked out of the rock to flatten the crest of the pass. On either side jagged cliffs fell back towards the ocean, broken by uncertain slabs and screes, doughty herbs and flowers scrabbling to maintain a foothold on the sparse, sun-scorched soil.

'The princes who built the road joining the two harbours made sure that the Emperor granted them the dues in perpetuity. This is where they collect them.' Pered nodded towards several heavy wagons plodding across the flagstoned expanse, just arrived up the wide road that led to the unseen port of the city's larger, older half that faced the calmer waters of Caladhrian Gulf rather than the uncertain currents of the ocean. Galleys looking little larger than a child's playthings dotted brilliant blue waters that reached to the horizon.

Usara watched a liveried man wearing the badge of some Tormalin princes stroll up to a laden cart's driver. He produced an amulet that won him a nod but those that followed were waved towards a long row of water troughs beneath wind-tossed shade trees. 'It must be worth the cost, to avoid the time and risks of a voyage around the cape.'

'Mind your backs!' Pered pulled Larissa aside as toiling horses snorted behind her, sides heaving as their driver slackened their reins. 'Ferd, get that manifest to Den Rannion's clerk! Jump to it, lad!' A child leapt from the back of the cart and ran off as the driver urged his reluctant team towards a space beside a gang of men dividing the cargo they had just carried up here between two wagons waiting impatiently for goods from Caladhria, Lescar and countries beyond.

Shiv surveyed the constant activity all around. 'They must have paid for the road ten times over by now.'

'More like a hundred times,' Pered opined. 'But a Sieur can always find a use for more coin.' He nodded at the detachment of armed men relaxing around the base of a massive statue of Dastennin. Crowned with seaweed, the god of the sea's robe broke into roiling foam around his feet, his weathered bronze hands green with age, outstretched in benediction towards both seas.

Larissa closed her eyes and turned her face to the steady breeze, face rapt. 'I feel I could touch the sky up here.'

'It's a splendid place to work with the air,' agreed Usara with hopeful anticipation. 'Even I can feel that.'

Shiv turned to Pered. 'Working magic in the open isn't exactly against the Emperor's writ but I don't relish debating the point with Den Rannion's sworn men. You said there were more private places up here?'

'This way.' Pered led them towards a mighty tower on the southerly side of the square. With its flared base of tightly fitted stones seamlessly married to the rock beneath, it looked like some marvellous tree grown of living stone.

'Wasn't the Sieur Den Rannion one of the original patrons of the Kellarin colony?' Larissa queried, nodding towards the men with silver eagle's head badges bright on their copper-coloured jerkins who shielded the tower's door with crossed pikes.

'That was his brother, Messire Ancel.' Shiv glanced up at the broad balcony circling the slender waist of the tower. 'The present Sieur is no friend to Temar.'

Excited voices floated out across the great square, exclaiming over the views. Above, where the tower was capped with a sturdily built watch-room, sworn men kept vigil to east and west. A great eagle spread vast bronze wings over them, poised eternally on the moment of flight.

Larissa tilted her head to one side. 'If you can get mages with the right affinities working together, we could well bring ships safely around the Cape of Winds. Then D'Alsennin wouldn't have to pay for the privilege of this rigmarole of portage across the isthmus.'

'I'm not sure Temar would want to put the Emperor's nose out of joint like that.' Shiv waved away a hopeful lad offering a tray of sweetmeats.

'Where are we going?' Larissa looked uncertain as Pered led Usara towards the queue of well-dressed merchant folk and comfortably humble townspeople waiting to gain access to the fabled tower and its balcony with letters of introduction or the simpler expedient of a few well-chosen coins. Smiling lackeys offered them wine and tisanes beneath an awning fluttering in the constant wind.

'I'm not sure.' Shiv picked up his pace and Larissa hurried with him.

'I can't imagine anyone building a greater monument than Den Rannion's,' Pered was saying to Usara. 'But that doesn't stop them trying.' He waved a hand at the miscellany of commemorative stone and metalwork planted haphazard in an irregular space between the mighty tower and the ragged, fissured mountainside beyond.

Shiv raised an eyebrow at the blatant panegyric to some

long-dead Tor Leoril engraved on a massive marble urn. 'You said we could find a discreet corner?'

'This way.' Pered led the mages through monuments ranging from the blandly functional to the frankly bizarre. They passed a granite bull, big as life and pawing ferociously at its plinth, and reached a mighty bronze dragon leprous with verdigris and fighting against chains that ran from a collar to metal posts embedded in the ground. Its bating wings cast a deep shadow over a creature half fish, half hound that lounged unconcerned on a high drift of scallop shells carved from a single slab of marble. Behind, an empty space was effectively blocked from passing view and any curious eyes on the tower's balcony.

Shiv nodded approvingly. 'We'd still better work fast.'

'I'll stand guard.' Pered took himself off to sit apparently idly some way beyond the dragon, digging charcoal and parchment out of one pocket. Usara stifled a smile.

Shiv raised questioning brows at Larissa who braced herself and held out hands that betrayed her tension with a faint tremor. Usara completed the triangle and all three mages concentrated on the empty air between them. The only sound was the stealthy scrape of Pered's sketching.

'Dear heart,' Shiv said conversationally. 'This would be easier without distractions.'

'Sorry.' There was an apologetic rustle and then silence from Pered.

Larissa's gaze hadn't wavered. She focused on a shimmer of blue at the very mid-point between them. The strand of magelight was barely a hair's thickness but startling in its sapphire intensity. A faint smile curved Larissa's full lips as the magic split, doubling and redoubling, threads blurring and fluttering in the curious wind coiling around the mages. 'Usara?' she invited.

Usara was painstakingly summoning a grey-blue haze from the rock beneath them. It hovered on the very edge of sight like a memory of mist. Ever more dense as it drew closer to Larissa's cerulean sorcery, the cold colour was drawn into her spell like smoke up a chimney, brightening to a vivid blue. 'We can do this, Shiv,' he breathed, exultant.

Turquoise light pooled below the dancing tendrils of light, ripples edged with radiance. Aquamarine waves leapt to join Larissa's magic, colliding with the sun-burnished blue. Flourishes of white light bleached the green hue of Shiv's working to that same sapphire clarity. The breezes playing around the monuments danced around the wizards' linked hands, any that ventured too close swept into the sorcery.

With a suddenness that startled an oath from Pered, two figures tore through the impossibly narrow line of the spell. The magic blew away on the wind like fragments of a dream.

'It's me!' Pered backed hastily away from the naked dagger in Sorgrad's hand.

Sorgren had somehow tripped as he came through the spell. He rolled like a fairground tumbler, back on his feet in an instant. 'Ouch.' He grinned as he sheathed his own blade. 'You really have to learn that spell, 'Grad.'

Pered looked past him to Shiv, wide-eyed. 'That was incredible.' He shook his head. 'How could I ever paint those colours?'

Sorgrad tossed his knife up high, catching it as it tumbled. He halted to survey Larissa. 'My lady.' His voice was warm with admiration.

'This is Larissa.' Usara wondered how best to introduce her. 'Planir's—'

'—pupil.' Larissa offered her hand. Sorgrad bowed deep and brushed it with his lips.

'Gren contented himself with grinning at her in blatant appreciation. He tugged at his collar to settle his crumpled shirt and something chinked in a pocket of his tattered jerkin.

'What were you running from?' Shiv frowned at the younger Mountain Man.

'Watchmen.' Sorgrad held two backpacks in his off hand and tossed one to his younger brother. By contrast with 'Gren's dishevelled appearance, his shirt was clean, the silver buttons on his jerkin polished and his boots well oiled.

'Gren's hair was long and tied back all anyhow with a scrap of leather. Sorgrad's was neatly trimmed and brushed back with a touch of expensive oil.

'What did the Watch want?' Usara asked before he could stop himself.

'There was this goldsmith,' began 'Gren with a happy smile.

'We don't all have Planir's bottomless bags of gold.' Sorgrad took a handful of silver chains out of one pocket and stowed them in his pack. He looked blandly at Shiv.

'Does Planir earn his coin or does he make it?' 'Gren was next to Larissa, pale against her darker colouring, azure eyes engaging. 'Alchemists go to Hadrumal, don't they? Everyone says they're looking for magical help to turn base metals precious.'

'Shall we get on our way?' Pered suggested, offering Larissa his arm. 'Gren sauntered along on her other side. The others followed some paces behind.

'So let's go look for a ship,' said Sorgrad. 'No sense in delaying, not if there's a fight in the offing.'

'We've tried the harbour master and all the various princes' factors,' Usara said gloomily.

'I'll find someone who sees the sense of taking your coin.' Sorgrad's confidence was laced with a hint of menace.

Pered looked back, shading his eyes with a hand. 'Are we all going down to the docks?'

Sorgrad shook his head. 'I only need these two to sit still, look rich and keep their mouths shut.'

'You're lodged at a decent inn?' 'Gren smiled obligingly at Larissa. 'Let's wait for them there.'

'Larissa's rather more than just Planir's pupil,' Shiv murmured to Sorgrad.

'I don't see him hereabouts.' The Mountain Man shrugged. 'Your choice: risk 'Gren cutting a slice off Planir's loaf or taking him down to a dockside after your magic just spoiled his hopes of a good fight.'

'Pered will keep things decorous,' Usara offered.

'As long as he doesn't go off trying to work out how to paint a spell,' frowned Shiv. 'All right, let's find two coaches.'

Pered was already whistling them up and 'Gren ushered Larissa inside the first with exquisite courtesy at odds with his grimy clothes.

'Somewhere near the pilot academy, if you please.' Stifling his qualms, Usara followed Sorgrad and Shiv into the second vehicle and the coachman whipped up his horse. Once down from the heights, they rattled through streets thronged with people intent on the buying and selling that kept both halves of Zyoutessela rich.

After some distance, Usara cleared his throat. 'Sorgrad, how did you get on in Solura?'

The carriage swayed round a corner before Sorgrad shook his head with disgust. 'Everything Gilmarten told me was true. Every mageborn must be apprenticed to some other wizard and every master mage is under vow to some baron or other. The best I found were earnest do-gooders desperate to sign me up with someone in their circle. The worst were pig-headed bastards who locked me up and called for the local headsman to brand me as an untrained mage.'

'You escaped, obviously.' Shiv looked at him speculatively. 'Using magic?'

'Picklocks and 'Gren's talent for breaking heads,' Sorgrad said without humour.

'We could share a few things with you,' Usara said with studied casualness.

'Just so you can help out Livak and Halice,' added Shiv.

'Good of you to offer.' Sorgrad smiled, this time with satisfaction. 'That was going to be a condition of my cooperation.'

'I thought we'd already agreed your price,' said Shiv with mild indignation.

'That was 'Gren's price,' Sorgrad assured him earnestly.

Usara laughed. 'It's not far now. What do we do when we get to the docks?'

'We find a likely tavern where you two sit still, look rich

and don't so much as clear your nose like a wizard. In the kind of tavern we want, that'll mean knives coming your way.' Sorgrad's tone was simply matter-of-fact.

'So we're looking for our own crew of pirates?' guessed Shiv.

Sorgrad smiled. 'No, we're looking for a ship. I'll go looking for crew after dark and I'll take 'Gren because I probably will be dealing with freetraders. If it takes a fight, I'd rather have him at my back, if it's all the same to you.'

'We can get ourselves out of trouble,' protested Shiv.

'You won't see how to keep yourselves out of it in the first place,' countered Sorgrad.

'If we're caught using magic in some brawl, the word will get back to D'Olbriot quicker than bees to honey,' Usara pointed out to Shiv.

'What's D'Olbriot's stake in this game?' Sorgrad looked from Usara to Shiv and back again. 'I think it's time you told me what's going on. Let's start with why you two are playing truant from Hadrumal?'

With Shiv's frequent interjections, Usara's explanations lasted all the way through the grimy, gimcrack terraces cramped between the generous holdings of the merchant classes and the unyielding sprawl of the dockside districts. Warehouses loomed high on either side with blank walls and doors barred from within. They passed the much extended building where ship owners and captains paid for their helmsmen and pilots to learn the mysteries of the ocean coast, its winds and currents. The coachman drew up in a small square dank with the scent of the retreating tide and hammered on the roof. 'This is as far as I go.'

Shiv stood with Sorgrad as Usara paid the man off. 'Where do we start?' he wondered aloud.

Sorgrad nodded at a man selling freshly cooked shrimps from a bubbling pot on a small brazier. 'Got a cup on you?'

Neither wizard did so each had to pay for a misshapen reject from someone's kiln to hold a steaming spoonful. Sorgrad produced a short-stemmed silver goblet from some pocket and exchanged a few words as the shrimp seller filled it.

Nodding to the mages, Sorgrad led them away, holding a shrimp between his teeth to pull off its head before crunching the rest. 'Our friend tells me there's a captain about to be left high and dry by a merchant whose creditors will be breaking down his doors any day.'

'He told you that for the price of three pots of shrimps?' The difficulties of peeling one with one hand and his teeth didn't mask the fact that Shiv was impressed.

Sorgrad shrugged. 'I told him it'd be worth ten times that if the word turned out to be sound.'

Usara was licking a burnt finger. He passed a hand over his shrimps, which abruptly stopped steaming. 'Where do we find this captain?'

'A dive called the Moon and Rake, so watch your step,' Sorgrad warned. 'And if you use magic again, 'Sar, I'll break your fingers.' He led them down a noisome lane running between a barred storehouse and a yard with high walls topped with broken glass. A few more turns brought them out on to a raucous dock. Sorgrad hailed a man hauling a laden sled on iron runners over the slick cobbles. The docker directed them with an unsmiling jerk of his head.

'Yonder.' Sorgrad led the way towards the tavern whose battered sign showed a man dragging a pole through shallow water beneath the lesser moon casting the secretive light of her full round. Her bolder sister was no more than a blind crescent. The building looked more respectable than Shiv had expected and he raised his hand to the door already ajar.

A dagger thudded into the jamb barely a finger's width away from his startled hand. 'No, this way.' Sorgrad retrieved his blade and gestured to an alley beside the tavern.

The wizards did as they were told. Sorgrad watched from the shadows for a moment before pointing to a big man. 'Now what do you suppose he's doing here?'

Much of a height with Shiv he was half as broad again across the shoulders, muscles emphasised by a close-cut shirt in faded red linen beneath a buckled jerkin. He was deep in conversation with a man handing bundles of clothes, baskets of bottles and a few crates of battered fruit down to a lad standing in a broad, flat-bottomed rowing boat tied to the stubby posts on the dock. The trader paused to consider several of the ocean ships anchored safe in the embrace of the curving arms of the harbour and surrounded with boats like his own tempting their crews to spend their coin on a few trifles.

'Darni!' Shiv was furious. 'So Planir trusts us, does he?'

'He's shaved off his beard,' Sorgrad noted with approval. 'Passes better for Tormalin that way, I reckon.' With his black hair and dark colouring the big man certainly bore more than a passing resemblance to the incurious passers-by.

'He might have some business nothing to do with us,' Usara suggested doubtfully.

'Even when he's hiring out as a mercenary Darni's about some scheme of Planir's,' said Shiv grimly.

'Can we get rid of him somehow?' wondered Usara.

'You really want to break with Hadrumal?' Sorgrad looked surprised, then considered the task. 'I can take him with a knife in the back down some back entry but I'm not going up against someone that size in broad daylight. We'll get some gang of sworn men running in to spoil the fun for one thing.'

'I didn't mean kill him,' protested Usara, horrified.

'What do you suppose he's doing?' Shiv watched as a woman came to see whom the trader was talking to. She was tall and stout with improbably dyed hair and rouged like a child's doll. Several other women hovered close by, gowns cut low and legs bare beneath their soiled skirts. They flanked a couple of malnourished girls, one with her wrists held tight by her hard-faced elder. Darni turned to talk to her, gestures curt, face intimidating. The whoremistress had plainly faced his type before and shook her head, unimpressed. Darni turned on his heel, heading further down the dock. The trader and whoremistress looked after him with resentment.

'Wait here.' Sorgrad darted across the cobbles to be welcomed by the woman with an avaricious smile. They exchanged a few words and then Sorgrad headed back towards the wizards with the youngest whore released from her captor.

'What do you suppose he wants her for?' asked Usara with alarm, seeing Sorgrad's protective arm around the girl's thin waist.

'I'll get Pered to draw you a picture.' Shiv was quite nonplussed.

Sorgrad ushered the girl into the alley. 'How much coin are you carrying?' he demanded of the mages.

'Pardon?' Usara looked blank but Shiv was already reaching for the purse he'd tucked prudently inside his breeches.

Sorgrad unbuttoned his shirt and pulled several gold and silver chains over his head. 'Right, I told the old bitch there were three of us, so you should have time to run before they come looking for you.' He scooped up the marks and crowns that Shiv offered and pressed them into the girl's trembling hands, bruises banding her wrists. 'Buy a ride on some carrier's cart to the far side of the pass before nightfall.' He stowed the jewellery in the girl's meagre cleavage with impersonal efficiency. 'Sell that before you sell yourself, chick.'

She looked at him with huge, hopeless eyes. 'My da drowned last year and the scour took the babe and my mam with it. My auntie took the little ones but—'

'There's a goldsmith on Angle Street,' said Usara with sudden inspiration. 'Find a man called Renthuan there. Tell him Ryshad Tathel wants him to help you.'

A spark of life lit the girl's fearful face. 'Yes, masters.' She turned and ran down the alley away from the docks, fists clutching the coin to her bony breast.

Sorgrad watched her go with a shake of his head. 'Whoring for sailors is no task for children.'

Shiv was looking at Usara. 'Sending her to his money lender isn't going to flatter Ryshad's reputation.'

'Shall we go before that fat madam comes asking what we've done with her?' Usara looked apprehensively at the whoremistress who was fortunately busy with a handful of newly arrived sailors. 'Did she say anything about Darni's business?'

'He's looking for a girl who he reckons is looking for a passage over the ocean. From the description, he's after your Larissa.' Sorgrad was watching the woman now deep in negotiations. 'Now, quickly.'

Neither Shiv nor Usara delayed as Sorgrad led them out of the alley and, unseen, away down the dock. He passed the first tavern beyond the Moon and the Rake but ushered the mages into the next; a sour-smelling, ramshackle place. 'Over there.' He led them past a gang of men waiting for a boatswain to pay them off according to the figures chalked on their broad-brimmed, oiled-leather hats or the offside shoulder of their dark leather jerkins. A thickset man with a cudgel stood ready to discourage anyone keen to take more than their share from the coffer of coin.

'I think we should offer Darni a seat at the game,' announced Sorgrad.

Shiv leaned against a pillar. 'Livak doesn't like him.'

'Livak's not rounding up a crew willing to fight pirates with just you two dancing masters to back her up.' Sorgrad grinned at Shiv. 'Besides, Livak takes the runes as they roll, just the same as me. Darni's big and scary and he's useful with a sword. We worked together well enough in the Mountains and that counts for a lot.'

'If Planir's concerned enough about Larissa to send Darni after her, we should surely let him know she's safe.' Usara realised he was standing in a sticky pool of ale and looked down with distaste.

Shiv pursed his lips. 'Do you think he's here to haul her back to Hadrumal?'

'Possibly,' said Usara cautiously.

'If we're taking a pretty piece like her on this voyage, she'll need her own guard dog,' Sorgrad pointed out. 'Otherwise you'll find 'Gren playing her champion and slitting the throat of anyone stepping too close.'

'Darni's no fool.' Shiv looked at Usara. 'He'll find us or her sooner rather than later. Don't we want to have that conversation on our terms rather than his?'

Usara nodded. 'He might let slip what Planir thinks of our little expedition.'

'Let's go find him.' Sorgrad was already heading for the door.

Shiv grimaced. 'It's more cursed complications every way we turn.' He pointed a firm finger at Usara. 'You can tell Livak.'

For someone who so dislikes the sea, I was spending entirely too much time aboard ships.

'Still feeling queasy?' The ship's carpenter passed me leaning on the rail of the *Eryngo*.

'No, thanks all the same.' I glanced up to the crow's-nest where several sailors were keeping as eager a vigil as me. 'Any sign of the *Dulse* or the *Fire Minnow*?'

Lemmell shrugged. 'You'll hear it the same as everyone else.' He came to stand beside me, one hand smoothing the rail like a man caressing a favourite hound. He loved this ship, always keen to point out some virtue to me, explaining to anyone who'd listen that the *Eryngo* was a quarter as long again as the biggest of the pirate ships, never mind half as broad again. That's right, Haut the sailmaker would agree, and we carried more canvas and better rigged. I couldn't decide if they truly knew the ship better than anyone else or were just hopelessly biased. Captains came and went at the whim of an owner and crews were hired from voyage to voyage but I'd learned boatswain, helmsman, shipwright and sailmaker stayed with a vessel from the first laying of the keel until it was either broken or rotted as a hulk. Some even kept wives and families in their canvas-walled cabins on the lower decks but Temar had forbidden that on this voyage.

'Don't you worry about pirates, my girl,' Lemmell continued. 'We've high sides and a steep forecastle ready to repel boarders and the rear deck stepped to give D'Alsennin the best view of any fight.'

As the carpenter went on his way, I glanced towards the stern but D'Alsennin wasn't up there. He was down on the main deck and seeing me, came over. 'How much longer, do you think?'

I looked back across seawaters calm with the stillness of early morning. Somewhere, just out of sight, were the islands we'd come to reclaim. Somewhere, beneath the featureless cloak of trees, Kellarin's mercenaries were prowling with murderous intent. Quiet as a squirrel too mean to share his nuts, Ryshad on one headland, Halice on another, they would be creeping up on the watchposts Allin's scrying had betrayed to us. Somewhere, two of Kellarin's coasters lurked in the inlets they'd crept into under the scant cover of the moonlit night and every mask of magecraft and Artifice that Allin and Guinalle could summon. Dastennin, Halcarion and every other deity grant the ships would bring our people back to us.

'Not long.' I spoke with more hope than certainty.

'We'll make those bastards sorry they ever thought of staking a claim to Suthyfer,' Temar muttered. Kellarin men still asleep in the *Eryngo*'s capacious lower decks would help make sure of that.

I glanced up at the sun, still broad and soft gold this early in the day. 'It'll take as long as it takes.' That would be Ryshad's answer and Halice's too but they'd better hurry, if we were to launch our attack to catch the pirates still fuddled with sleep.

The deck swayed beneath my feet as the *Eryngo* made a slow turn. The *Nenuphar* and the *Asterias* did the same, square-rigged mainsails furled like the *Eryngo*'s, just relying on the triangular sails on their stubby aftmasts for steering in circles. I sincerely hoped all the sailors were pulling the right ropes to stop us colliding as we marked time in the same patch of sea.

'I should have gone too,' muttered Temar, frustrated.

'This is a very different fight to sweeping across the Dalasorian plains with half an Imperial army at your back,' I pointed out.

'As Ryshad and Halice keep saying with all their talk of skulk and strike and cut and run.'

I made a non-committal sound by way of reply. It was plain his exclusion from the fun still rankled with Temar but Ryshad and Halice had been adamant. The Tormalin wars of lordly conquest back in the days before history had been a very different affair from the base civil war that was Lescar's running sore. It was dirty fighting that was wanted here.

Still, I didn't like sitting on my hands aboard ship any more than D'Alsennin. This inaction came all the harder after the ceaseless hectic days since Parrail had raised his alarm. All of us had roused yeomen, miners and artisans to hone their tools and fury to a murderous edge. Halice and I had set every mercenary to scouring rust from swords and summoning old ingenuity for scavenging supplies.

Temar turned to look at the sterncastle and the doors to the rearward cabins under the raised afterdeck. 'Allin may have news. Guinalle might be able to reach Parrail without so much water between them.'

'We let them sleep,' I told him firmly. If I couldn't help my friends with a weapon in my hand, I could ensure this expedition's magical resources were carefully husbanded. Guinalle was an even worse sailor than me and the stresses of working Artifice while actually afloat left the noblewoman with a headache like a poleaxed cow. Allin wasn't so tired but seeing the pirates' captives daily beaten, degraded and filthy distressed the mage-girl dreadfully. After breaking our backs to get Vithrancel's ships sailing, we'd had to stand off the islands for three frustrating days waiting for Shiv and Usara's ship to make the longer crossing from Toremal, even with wizardry clearing a path through the waves and swelling their sails with mageborn winds.

Temar glared at the closed door. 'I want to know how Shiv's men are getting on.'

'Sorgrad and 'Gren have been fighting for more years than you've been living.' Saedrin curse it, I sounded more patronising than reassuring thanks to my own apprehension. The runes can always roll wrong, no matter how much skill my friends might have to weight them. 'Oh, come on then.'

Temar took time to smile and wave reassurance to curious sailors, as nobles always seem to, no matter how fast the ground's crumbling beneath their feet. I knocked a brisk double tap on the door.

'Come in.' Allin sounded contemplative and sad but that was better than outright anguish. She sat scrying at a table hanging from the beams of the deck above. Its raised wooden rim and a dampened cloth offered her bowl some stability but pools of fading radiance showed where ensorcelled water had slopped over the edges.

'So much for me trying to make sure you got some rest,' I chided her. Next time I'd empty the cabin of anything she might use for magic. Then she'd probably go back to scrying in the butt of water kept on deck for the sailors' refreshment. She'd only stopped when she realised none of them wanted to drink from it, even if all she were using was citrus oil.

'How goes it to the north?' Temar twisted his hands absently together.

'It's all over bar the grieving.' Eerie reflections turned Allin's sombre face into a mask of light and shadow.

I looked into the scrying bowl to see a triangular cove between two spurs of brittle grey rock where even the hardiest plants were defeated by the combined assaults of wind and wave. Temar's pennant was waving on the roof of a sizeable if crudely built hut tucked beneath a crag. Bodies lay among the stumps of a recently felled grove of trees.

'Kellarin's writ is in force on this islet at least,' said Temar with satisfaction.

'It's a start,' I agreed. An important one; Shiv's scrying had detected a sizeable outpost of pirates on this jagged diamond north of Suthyfer's westernmost isle.

Allin looked up. 'If you want me to bespeak Usara, I'll have to give up the scrying.' A gleam betrayed the sorrow brimming in her eyes.

'Don't waste your tears on these vermin,' Temar said severely but he gave her half a hug for comfort.

I tried to pick out familiar outlines among the anonymous

figures looting the bodies, a yellow head bent over a dead man's hand. 'Gren, surely? I bent closer but stepped back with an oath as a sudden conflagration erupted on one side of the cove.

A smile teased Allin despite herself. 'Is that your friend Sorgrad?'

Sure enough, I saw a blond man warming ostentatiously casual hands at the blaze. 'It is, and burning longboats by the look of it.' He looked small within the miniature world of the scrying, more so beside a hulking figure that could only be Darni. I still felt a sour resentment as I looked at the big warrior. I wouldn't be here if he hadn't blackmailed me into working for Planir. All I'd wanted was to sell the bastard a valuable piece of silver before its unpleasant owner realised it was missing, but Darni had recognised it and my cooperation had been the price of staying out of irons. Still, I reminded myself, reverse those runes and I'd never have met Ryshad. That put me ahead of the game, didn't it?

'None escaped?' Temar's voice was tight with concern.

If they had, our venture wasn't exactly sunk but it would be taking on water fast. To beard this pirate captain in his lair, we needed to attack from both ends of that crucial inlet dividing the two main islands of Suthyfer. We had to know nothing lurked behind us ready to stab us in the back.

'No one got away.' Allin gestured and her spell swooped backwards over the water to show the pirate fleet's pinnace prostrate in the surf, barnacles and green fouling on her shallow hull exposed to derision from the deck of a tall three-masted ocean ship drawing close to the wide beach.

'That must be the *Maelstrom*,' breathed Temar.

'Something to show for Ryshad's coin,' I commented. Shiv and Usara had found a ship easily the length of the pirate predators, more heavily built with higher sides and deck castles but rigged for sailing just as close to the wind. As we watched, it anchored well clear of the pinnace's three mast-heads now digging deep into the pale sand and the tangle of sodden ropes and sails on useless spars. Corpses bobbed among nameless flotsam and the beach sand was stained muddy red with the blood of those few who'd made it to shore.

'Whose work was that?' asked Temar with admiration. For myself, I was none too keen to see how easily a ship could be knocked on its beam-ends.

'Larissa and Shiv between them.' Allin gazed into the bowl. 'I wish I had such power.'

'When you're working your own element, you do.' Guinalle was lying on one of the cabin's bunks with a damp cloth on her forehead. I'd thought she was asleep.

'Feeling better?' Temar's eyes stayed fixed on the scrying bowl.

'No,' replied Guinalle curtly.

'Can I get you anything?' I was glad of the distraction. The way the scrying was swaying at odds with the motion of the *Eryngo* made me distinctly nauseous.

Guinalle managed an infinitesimal shake of her head, mouth tight.

'I wish you'd try some of Halice's tincture.' They say let a lame dog that snarls well alone but my beloved might need this stubborn girl up and ready to hunt. I looked at Temar. 'Shiv used some sorcery to cure me of seasickness once. When we meet up, he can treat Guinalle to it.'

The demoiselle flapped an impatient hand, which at least proved she wasn't entirely incapacitated. 'All I need are some of the right herbs fresh picked.'

'Have you managed to sense anything of Parrail?' I wondered if Temar's neutral tone masked a mutual irritation with Guinalle. Sympathetic as I was to her seasickness, I found her manner increasingly irritating.

Guinalle swung her feet down from the bunk and sat up, putting her cloth carefully in a lidded jug. 'He's hurt his arm. I can't tell how badly.'

'So the chances of working Artifice between you are on a par with me winning a game of Raven against Livak.' Temar's rueful attempt at a joke fell flatter than my baking.

Guinalle coloured furiously. 'I have done the very best—'

'Have you any idea if Naldeth's hurt?' Allin interrupted with what was either supreme lack of tact or the precise opposite.

Guinalle visibly reined in her emotions. 'I've no sense of that.'

'It shouldn't matter.' Temar patted Allin on the shoulder. 'We'll have them out soon enough to heal any hurts.'

Allin looked up at Temar with irritation. 'Wizards in pain or delirium often have trouble controlling their influence on their element. They work magic without meaning to. That's what set Planir looking into Soluran healing traditions in the first place.'

Which were based on fragments of aetheric lore. Which had set the Archmage on the trail first of Artifice and ultimately the lost Kellarin colony. I wondered if Planir felt like a man at a Solstice fair who's seen his winnings doubled and redoubled in a series of lucky bets at the racetrack. Or did the Archmage know the hollow disbelief of walking away from a gaming table with cumulative losses to indebt his unborn grandchildren?

'While we who use Artifice find ourselves entirely unable to work enchantment if pain distracts us,' Guinalle commented sourly.

'Things bursting into flames all around him will betray Naldeth as a mage at once.' I'd bet enough loot to gladden 'Gren's heart that things would go badly for the wizard after that.

'The sooner Shiv and Usara can lift them out of there, the better,' Allin breathed fervently.

'We just have to get close enough,' agreed Temar.

Running feet sounded on the deck outside. 'Messire!'

Temar only got to the door before me because I was the wrong side of the table.

'They're on the way back.' The sailor was grinning from ear to ear.

Temar and I ran to the rail to see for ourselves. The *Dulse* and the *Fire Minnow* were indeed labouring towards us, favourable winds needing no wizardly assistance but the run of the tide already turning against them. D'Alsennin pennants streamed from their mastheads and cheering men lined each vessel's rails.

'How far does noise carry over water?' I asked Temar in sudden alarm.

'The wind's in our favour,' he assured me with a boyish grin.

I masked my impatience better than him but it still felt like half a season before the *Dulse* drew alongside with exquisite care. The *Eryngo*'s crew dangled woven straw fenders over her rails and sailors on the *Dulse*'s deck below held boathooks ready to save us from too hard a clash. They need not have worried. The ships came together as gently as a lover's kiss and climbing nets and ladders were flung down from the *Eryngo*. I looked down from the height of our ship's three additional decks.

'Ryshad!' Temar saw him and hailed urgently. He tucked the oily red cloth he'd been cleaning his sword with into his belt, sheathed his blade and came to climb up to us. He leaned on the rail for a moment and kissed me before swinging himself aboard.

'We were on top of them before they knew it.' Ryshad grinned through smears of leaf mould and green grime. A dark stain on his buff breeches was probably blood and the rusty smears on his shirtsleeves certainly were.

'They were barely keeping a watch,' Vaspret amplified behind him. 'All tucked up nice in a nest in the woods.' He dug in a pocket and began untangling a waxed cord garrotte.

'Not a rat escaped,' Ryshad said before Temar could ask.

'You took no prisoners.' Guinalle was in the cabin door, face accusing.

Temar stifled a snort of irritation but Ryshad met the noblewoman's gaze calmly. 'No, but we did take casualties who'd appreciate your care.'

A few mercenary men and women, with bloodied dressings

around slashes to arms and legs, were being helped across the *Eryngo*'s rails.

'Here's the *Fire Minnow*.' Allin had come out on deck as well and pointed to Halice's ship. The *Eryngo* lurched as it came alongside with less precision and Halice was already climbing a rope with a fine disregard for the crushing gap between the smaller ship and the *Eryngo*.

'How many got away?' Ryshad demanded.

'A handful, maybe more,' spat Halice, bitter as aloes. 'Some cursed hunting party dallying their way back but sharp enough to take to their heels when they realised what was afoot.'

'We chased them,' protested Rosarn, her face taut with chagrin.

'It was a difficult assault,' Temar offered but Halice's expression was perilously close to a sneer.

'Even if they know the ground, they'll be slower through forest than we'll be over water.' Ryshad was thinking through the implications. 'We've seen no sign of beacons so they shouldn't raise an alarm before we can attack.'

'We're committed, whatever they do. The tide's already on the turn.' Halice was determined to take full advantage of the phases of the moon. With the greater at full and the lesser at half, the tides wouldn't be running this strong again until the double full towards the end of For-Summer. 'Sieur D'Alsennin, who can I have to make up my numbers?' The *Fire Minnow*'s wounded were coming aboard.

As Temar hastily produced the list of those who'd thought themselves unlucky to draw a rune to miss out on the initial assault, Guinalle unbuttoned the cuffs of her grey gown and shoved the sleeves above her elbows. 'Come on, Allin.' The women headed for a man writhing in silent agony as he clutched gory belly wounds, head pressed back against the board he'd been tied to.

Ryshad looked after them. 'I do wish Shiv had been able to raise a surgeon,' he muttered. I caught him in a fierce embrace. His shirt smelt of age-old trees and wood smoke.

He kissed the top of my head. 'Have they taken the sentry island yet?'

I nodded, catching his chin and hearing his teeth click. 'Sorry. Yes, Allin was just scrying.' I tugged at the red cloth in his belt. 'What's this?'

'A present for you.' He pulled it free with a wicked smile. 'The watchpost's snake.'

'You're sure none of your family ever turned pirate?' I teased. 'You're taking to this like a cat to cream.'

'Just doing what I've been trained for.' He drew me to him for a lengthy kiss that promised a sleepless night as soon as we got the chance.

'Just be careful.' I looked deep into his velvet brown eyes.

'I will.' He gazed down at me for a moment of heart-warming stillness. 'You too.'

'I can't come to much harm nursemaiding Allin and her ladyship,' I said caustically.

'You're the best woman for the job.' Ryshad's smile acknowledged my frustrations.

A piercing whistle from Halice called him away. They exchanged a few words before returning to their respective ships. Temar intercepted Ryshad who nodded his head reluctantly after a moment. D'Alsennin ran across the deck and disappeared over the side, intent on getting himself to one of the other coastal boats. He didn't see the resigned shake of Ryshad's head that I did.

'Livak!' Allin was beckoning, on her knees beside a wounded man, a coarse apron from somewhere protecting her gown. She swabbed blood from an encrusted gash across his chest, pausing only to throw his torn and stained shirt to me. 'See what you can salvage from that.'

I got out a knife to strip the cleaner cloth into bandages. The *Eryngo* heaved beneath me as our reunited flotilla headed directly into the sound between the islands. The run of the tide carried us ever faster while I cleaned, salved and band-aged blessedly trivial wounds, binding wrenched ankles and bloodied knuckles, fetching and carrying at Guinalle's command and Allin's polite requests. The Lescari mage-lass applied those skills learned at her mother's side in the battle-worn dukedom of Carluse. She kept up a murmur of reas-surance while Guinalle worked with a steady litany of soft incantation. I'd wager the Old Empire owed a good measure of conquests to its adepts' ability to limit casualties with Arti-fice. Most aetheric learning had centred on the Bremilayne shrine to Ostrin in an age when the god had been more concerned with healing than hospitality. I had no quarrel with that, not if Guinalle's skills meant more of our people came home unscathed.

The waters narrowed as the land advanced on either side, hills leaning ever closer to the strait's edge. The trees were taller than our mast and here and there an outcrop of dark rock hung ominous overhead. Sailors in the *Eryngo*'s crow's-nests looked in all directions for any sign of the enemy. Lookouts in the prow fixed their eyes on the shadowed waters, searching for reefs and skerries. The *Dulse* and *Fire Minnow* slid stealthily in our wake, their sister ships *Asterias* and *Nenuphar* not far behind.

'Allin, we're nearly there.' I was counting off the land-marks we'd scried for along the inlet.

'I'm ready.' She made to untie her gore-smeared apron.

'No, keep that on,' I told her. It wasn't much of a disguise but it might keep the enemy from picking out the mage among the ordinary folk on deck. 'How well can you see from here?'

Allin frowned. 'Not very.'

'Try standing on the steps to the rear deck.' I didn't want her up in plain view on the sterncastle but, Drianon curse it, the girl was unhelpfully short. Guinalle began ordering the lightly injured to carry the worst wounded below decks, her face grim but her hands steady as she folded them on the plaited cord girdle at her waist.

'Sail ho!'

After a frozen instant, the cry set everyone about their allotted tasks. Temar, Ryshad and Halice had gone over this plan time and again and if anyone fouled their duty, I'd personally see that they got to explain themselves to Saedrin.

The first of the signal flags, red saltire on a white ground, ran up the mast, rope humming like an angry hornet. The four coastal ships fanned out from behind the *Eryngo*, blocking the seaway. As we swung around rocks long since tumbled down from a shattered cliff, I saw the first of the pirate ships flying a scarlet pennant with a black snake twisting down its length. The shark at the beakhead below the bowsprit identified it as the *Spurdog* and it looked unholy imposing in these confined waters.

The deck was cleared but for Kellarin's fighting men ready and eager for action. Guinalle joined me by the doors to the stern cabins while Allin perched on the broad treads of the ladder-like stair to the afterdeck. The wizard-woman's eyes fixed on the slowly approaching vessel with burning determination. Longboats surged out from behind the *Spurdog*, each packed with pirates, blades cutting bright swathes in the sunlight. The oars dug deep into the water as the rowers fought the strengthening run of the tide.

'Gently,' murmured Guinalle.

'I know.' Allin's attention was fixed on the raiders' ship.

I held myself ready, for just what I couldn't say. I had nothing to say and nothing to do.

The *Spurdog*'s longboats spread out like a pack of wolves intent on harrying some hapless deer but our flotilla was carefully placed to deny the pirates passage past us in one of the narrowest parts of the strait. Then the foremost longboat lurched abruptly as if it had hit a rock hidden beneath the dark water. The man with the rudder yelled rebuke at the man in the prow whose protestations were lost beneath cries of alarm as the boat shuddered again but there was no sound of wood grating on stone. The one behind it stopped dead in unyielding water while a longboat on its other side rocked violently from side to side, wale dipping beneath the water. Some struck out for shore as the boat sank, a few disappearing as the weight of blades and boots dragged them under the glassy waters. Others had no luck seeking help from their fellows. Hands reaching up were met with kicks and pommels smashing grasping fingers. Three or four men reached one longboat together but trying to haul themselves aboard all at once they overturned it, casting the entire complement into the water in a confusion of shouts and curses.

'They're doing Shiv's job for him.' I tried to see beyond the pirate vessel but it was impossible to get a clear view. No matter, not as long as we held all their attention to the front.

Allin was still intent on the *Spurdog*. Some sailors were casting ropes and nets over the sides, shouting at men struggling in the water. More crew were aloft, trying to rig sail but the canvas was fighting back, tugged this way and that by hostile winds, ropes snatched out of questing hands, billows snapping in all directions. We were sailing on a gentle breeze just strong enough to give us headway but the pirates found themselves attacked by their very own private storm. With a crack like a thunderbolt, the great stay cables that controlled the flex of the masts snapped. One lashed a man who fell screaming to the deck. Another pirate was snared in the rigging and strangled as he lost his footing. As more ropes snapped, the solid wooden pulleys and blocks swung like morning stars to smash flesh and bone. The raiders abandoned all thought of setting sail, hanging on like Poldrion's demons to masts now swaying wildly and creaking ominously.

'There!' Guinalle pointed in the same instant as another shout from on high and the second signal flag shot up its lanyard, gold cross on a red ground. The pirates were sending in their second ship.

'Ready, Allin?' I stood beside her. The *Thornray* came forward cautiously, trying to evade the unnatural squalls plaguing its dock mate.

Allin was scanning the masts and forecastles of both hostile vessels. As I heard the first evil chirrup of an arrow, her hand shot forward. Gouts of flame flared in the air as arrows ignited, the acrid stink of burnt feathers drifting in the still air as the metal heads pocked the sea with a rash of stifled hisses.

'Crossbows,' I warned her as a bolt thudded into the *Eryngo*'s main mast. I spared a thought to hope Temar had the sense to keep his head down.

Allin laced her fingers tight together. Men on our ship ducked as crossbow bolts knocked astray from their aim still came clattering in hard enough to do damage. One went skittering down the deck beside us, glowing red hot to score a charred line on the planking.

Wizardry or just chance swept a sheaf of blazing arrows back into the *Spurdog*'s sails. 'Come on, Allin,' I encouraged her. 'You know what you have to do.'

Her plump face twisted in distress but the heavy, salt-laden canvas still went up like gossamer swept into a candle flame. Rags of searing fire fell away to set other sails alight. Flames ran the length of the rigging like fire devouring a spill of lamp oil. Spars cracked and flared and the iron bindings holding the upper lengths of the main mast together melted in the inferno that was the crow's-nest. Gouts of molten metal fell to kill men on deck instantly and then the whole section toppled, felled like the mighty tree it had once been in some distant forest. Crashing backwards, it wrecked the aftmast, the deck of the sterncastle disappearing beneath a murderous crush of wood and sail.

A precisely tailored tempest now wrapped around the *Thornray* and shouts from the ship took on a new urgency as the *Dulse* and *Fire Minnow* swung round for the gravel strand where the plundered *Tang* and Den Harkeil's barque were drawn up. The *Nenuphar* and the *Asterias* backed the *Eryngo* in a solid blockade, Vithrancel's archers ready to pinion any remaining longboats struggling back to the landing.

The *Spurdog* was burning with a furnace roar and, with the *Thornray* helpless, the pirate vessels drifted apart. I thought I glimpsed something akin to heat haze wrinkling the air beyond. No matter. I had more immediate concerns as the *Fire Minnow* and *Dulse* prepared to send Ryshad and Halice's forces ashore to do battle with the pirates. An

ominous force was gathering among huts and palisades built
with the blood and tears of their hapless captives.

Allin took a resolute breath and magefire leapt from the
Spurdog to the *Thornray*. The masts caught light like trees
in a wildfire and her crew began jumping, despairing into
the water, some burning as they fell.

'No!' Guinalle was ashen with horror.

'This is battle.' Thinking she was going to faint, I caught
her arm.

'They have Artifice, my lady, they have Artifice! I don't
know who but they use it to kill.' To my astonishment,
Parrail's frantic voice echoed inside my head. 'Anyone
forsworn chokes on their oath. They're trying to find your
mages, I can hear them searching. They'll kill any wizard
they can reach.' He was gabbling and his anguish seared my
mind like an unexpected scald.

'Stop your magic,' I yelled at Allin. 'Now!' We couldn't
have her reduced to a barely breathing corpse by hostile
enchantments.

She stared at me, bemused.

'They've aetheric magic seeking you,' gasped Guinalle.

Even Allin's high colour fled at that. 'We have to warn
the others.'

I looked beyond the now blazing *Thornray* again but still
could barely see more than shimmering haze. 'How?' We'd
agreed signal flags for every other contingency but who'd
expected this?

'I'll bespeak Usara.' Allin found a ragged tuft of bandage
in her apron pocket and caught up a scored metal cup that
had held some wound salve.

'You're too easy to attack,' I objected.

'We can armour her with Artifice.' Guinalle's face was set
as stone and she grabbed my hand. 'Just follow my lead. Remember when we worked Artifice together against Kramisak.'

Usara has this theory that belief is the key to aetheric
magic. I resolutely thrust all doubts away, summoning instead
vivid recollection of Guinalle breaking down that enchanter's

wards when the Elietimm had attacked before. She had sung and I had echoed and we'd confined the bastard's malevolence with her own, so Ryshad and Temar could cut him in pieces.

'*Tur amal es ryal andal zer, fes amal tur ryal suramer.*'

The archaic words were all but meaningless but the lilts and rhythms were as familiar as breathing. Was it bred into my bones by Forest blood or simply a memory from distant childhood when my wandering minstrel father had sung me to sleep in a garret room?

I heard Allin, muffled as if she were surrounded by fog and a good way off at that. 'Parrail says the pirates have Artifice. We have to stop our spells.'

As she spoke, I felt something brush past me but there nothing to be seen. Guinalle strengthened her grip until my fingers started numbing. She was staring straight through me as she repeated her incantation with biting emphasis. I found myself shuddering with that irresistible shiver old folk call the draught from Poldrion's cloak. I held Guinalle's hands as tight as she held mine. I had to believe she could do this or we were both lost. If this was all that stood between the wizards and aetheric magic scouring the wits out of their heads, I'd chant until my tongue dried up.

Allin was shouting orders and I could hear urgent activity all around but I couldn't drag my eyes away from Guinalle's face. Then the young noblewoman dissolved before me to hang in the air like a shadow. I blinked and Guinalle was there again but the cabin doors behind her, the sterncastle of the ship, Allin, everything else was as insubstantial as smoke. Everything faded to a mist of featureless grey, the *Eryngo* and everyone aboard a mere trick of my vision like the memory of a candle flame snuffed in a darkened room.

I bit my lip and tasted the metallic tang of blood. I could still hear Allin shouting. I could still smell the rank sweat of my own fear and the charring of the burning *Spurdog*. I could still feel the deck beneath my feet and Guinalle's vice-like grip on my hands. I pictured her face, every detail of her dress. She'd got me into this and, Drianon save me, she'd get me out of it or I'd know the reason why.

Colours gathered around the edges of the grey mist, fleeting if I tried to look at them but soon gathering strength and depth. Shapes emerged, hard to make out at first, as my true surroundings overlaid everything I saw like a shadow from Poldrion's realm.

We were inside the prisoners' stockade. I would have ripped my hands free of Guinalle but she held me fast. 'We're no more than shades here.' Her words echoed unspoken inside my head and I remembered I'd once vowed I'd rather be raped than feel that unholy intrusion of someone else's will into my own again.

A gang of pirates slammed open the gates, swords and clubs swinging. Two prisoners too close to the entrance were dragged to their feet, arms twisted cruelly behind their backs. The rest retreated, too scared to run the gauntlet of the pirates, broken in spirit as well as body, their rags of clothes beyond repair. I tried to pick out Parrail or Naldeth among the bruised and filthy huddle.

Three newcomers ran full tilt into the stockade, two men and a woman, none overtall and all within a year or so Temar's age or Guinalle's. The woman wore a mossy skirt, the men dun breeches and all were fair enough to pass for Sorgrad's kinsmen. All wore shirts laced high to the neck but I still caught the unmistakable glint of silver beneath. The only aetheric enchanters who wore gorgets were—

'Elietimm.' Guinalle's hatred rang inside my head.

The first man clapped rough hands around a prisoner's head and the captive writhed in the unforgiving grasp. I couldn't hear his screams but his pain echoed through Guinalle's enchantment and I felt it like a blow to the back of the head. The enchanter abandoned the man, gripping the next with the same savagery. The man jerked with one convulsive spasm and, again, the agony battered me but the Elietimm tossed him aside in baffled fury.

The woman barked some order and the pirates advanced.

The prisoners scattered in futile terror like penned sheep who've just found a wolf in their fold. One lad ran for the gate but two pirates wrestled him to the ground. Seeing him pinned in the suffocating mud, the second Elietimm man laid a hand on the boy's rancid hair. After an angry shake of his head, the enchanter caught a cudgel from a pirate and smashed the lad's skull in brutal frustration.

I could see Naldeth and Parrail. Both were trying to keep as many people between themselves and the hunting Elietimm as possible but so was everyone else. It was like watching a flock of geese harried by a pack of dogs. As the prisoners struggled with each other, the weaker stumbled away, easy prey for the waiting pirates. His innate gentleness betraying him, Parrail soon fell victim.

A pirate, his nose rotting from some pox, dragged the lad to the waiting Elietimm woman. The scholar was filthy; shirtless, ribs showing and bruises charting the daily round of brutality. Parrail tripped but the bullying raider wouldn't let him find his feet, hauling him bodily over the foul ground. He threw Parrail face down before the woman, kneeling on the back of the lad's legs, pinning his hands behind his back. Parrail twisted his head from side to side, trying in vain to escape the woman's questing touch.

To my inexpressible delight pain racked her face as soon as she laid a hand on him but her cry only brought her fellow enchanters running.

'Who are you? Where do you come from? Who do you speak to?'

I don't speak the Elietimm tongue but I heard their harsh demands echoing all around my thoughts, their voices mingled.

'I will not say.' Parrail wrapped himself in defiance.

'Who has taught you?' Fear and hatred tainted the Elietimm's questions but his skill with Artifice cut Parrail like a knife.

Like the glimpse of a page in a book opened and shut, I saw Mentor Tonin, Parrail's tutor in distant Vanam.

'You cannot defy us.' Vicious gratification coloured the Elietimm's chorused thoughts. That instant of unity passed and all three attacked the scholar with ruthless interrogation.

'Who are you?'

'Where are your friends?'

'Who has betrayed Muredarch?'

Was there nothing we could do? I wanted to shake Guinalle by the shoulders, insist she get the lad out of there, do something, anything, but what if I alerted these bastards to our eavesdropping? Fear for myself as well as fear for Parrail soured my throat like bile.

Colourless fire lit the shadows with reality for an instant, the distant stockade fading as I saw the *Eryngo* more clearly. The sick agony of a broken bone ached in my wrist even thought I knew it wasn't my injury.

'Curse them!' Guinalle's bitter words tied me tight to her will again. Vivid once more, I saw the stockade, saw the brutal pirate twisting Parrail's discoloured forearm this way and that. The lad sobbed, banging his head on the ground, tears streaming from his screwed-up eyes.

All three Elietimm crowded round the boy like buzzards not even waiting for their prey to die. The pirate man scrambled away, plainly terrified of these slightly built strangers. Parrail curled into a helpless ball, cradling his injured arm, knees drawn up, head tucked down, his defiance as futile as a tiggyhog's.

The Elietimm joined hands and, as plainly as they did, Guinalle and I saw Parrail's life laid bare. Cherished memories fluttered past me like so many coloured pages torn from a child's precious chapbook and scattered on the uncaring ground. He'd been a beloved child, all the more when childhood frailties had carried too many of his brothers and sisters to Poldrion's tender care. His father, humble clerk to a merchant house, had scrimped and saved to send his promising son to Vanam, mother wiping away her tears and consoling herself that such sacrifice was for her darling's good. No idle student, nor yet a rich one, Parrail had run errands for wealthier scholars to pay his way but even then, going hungry when some tempting scroll or parchment emptied his purse. Mentor Tonin's pride had warmed the young scholar, bolstering his confidence in his abilities, spurring him on to tease threads of meaning out of the tangle of superstition and garbled litany that was all that the Chaos had left of aetheric lore.

The Elietimm ripped such memories apart, desperate for whatever Parrail might know that they did not. With the burning agony of his broken arm consuming him, he lay helpless, unresisting. They held recollections of his first visit to Kellarin up to cold scrutiny. They saw him nervous and excited in Master Tonin's party, thrilled to see his studies turn from dry theory to flesh and blood reality before being terrified by Elietimm assaults. With friends and mages dead all around, Parrail was left the most likely to succeed in reviving the sleeping colonists. Travelling to the hidden cavern of Edisgesset, he summoned steely determination to defeat his frail self-doubt.

To my surprise, I caught a fleeting notion that Parrail had been scared of me but that vanished like smoke in the burning light of his devotion to Guinalle. His wonder at her beauty held her sleeping face before us all, frozen in the dimness of the cavern when Parrail had first seen her. That first rapture deepened to an abiding admiration where he saw her every word as grace, her every action proof of her nobility and virtue. Even his return to Vanam hadn't shaken that devoted loyalty and when the chance to return had come, Parrail's longing to be of service to his lady coloured his every thought and action.

I was enraged, repelled, outraged as if I'd seen the poor lad stripped naked for some howling mob's amusement. The Elietimm woman's head snapped up and she stared straight at me.

'Darige, Moin!' The bitch could see us both, no question, eyes boring right through whatever veil of enchantment Guinalle had used to cloak us.

They abandoned Parrail and moved towards us.

'Guinalle?' Surely she could see the danger as easily as me?

'You foul the very aether with your touch.' Guinalle's contempt lashed out and the Elietimm trio recoiled. 'I should sear that corrupt knowledge from your very minds. What tainted lore do you think you can use against me?'

She raised her hand, an insubstantial wraith but the Elietimm stumbled backwards as if they faced some mythic warrior all tricked out with a blazing sword and shining armour.

One of the men, the one called Darige tripped over Parrail. Quick as a biting fox, he grabbed the lad's hair. 'If we cannot touch you, he's in our hands.'

He kicked Parrail viciously in the groin. The second man, Moin, stamped on Parrail's broken wrist. The scholar barely reacted and I felt Guinalle's sick worry echo my own concern.

This unholy world of illusion flickered around me. The man Moin smiled with feral satisfaction. 'Are you strong enough to maintain your magic in the face of his pain?'

'Yalda!' Darige didn't take his eyes off Guinalle as he beckoned the woman forward.

She caught up the pirate's club and with a venomous smile brought the solid oak down on Parrail's head. Blood oozed from his nose and ears. She swept it down again and again as Darige kicked him in the gut, Moin taking nailed boots to his unprotected back.

The innocent lad's final torment faded like a dream but I knew this was no nightmare even as the *Eryngo*'s deck grew solid and reassuring around me once more. Guinalle covered her face with shaking hands and fled to the stern cabin, racked by shuddering sobs.

Allin was wide eyed in consternation. 'What happened?'

'They've got Elietimm enchanters,' I told her. 'We have to get out of here.' I realised I was soaked with sweat, my shirt stained dark and my breeches clinging to my legs. The wind chilled me but I was already as cold as ice inside.

'We're already going.' Allin pointed to the black and yellow chequer flags hoisted to signal a retreat. The *Dulse* and *Fire Minnow* were heading towards us, those pirates who'd have cheerfully slaughtered everyone aboard left frustrated on the gravel of the landing. 'We haven't the men to fight without wizardry to help them.'

The *Eryngo*'s sailors brought all their efforts to bear to ease us past the smouldering wrecks of the *Spurdog* and the *Thornray*. The *Maelstrom* was turning in the wider strait beyond the burning hulls, plain for all to see now its cloak of magic had been dropped for fear of aetheric attack on Shiv, 'Sar and Larissa. So much for our plan to get them close enough to gather up the prisoners with their newfound confidence in using the element of air. Vithrancel's flotilla closed up behind us as we fled north up the strait, taking every advantage from wind and tide, our hopes broken behind us.

'What about Parrail and Naldeth?' Allin asked, her voice shaking.

'Parrail's dead,' I told her grimly.

'What about Naldeth?' she quavered.

'I don't know.' Though I could guess his fate if he betrayed himself.

CHAPTER FOUR

To Cadan Lench, Prefect,
From Sul Gavial, Librarian.

It's all very well you asking me and my staff to search through boxes of litter our forebears were too idle to throw away but have you any idea what a thankless task this is? What isn't faded to illegibility is either shredded by mice or noxious with beetles. This pious claptrap is the sole prize from an entire annal compiled by some priest in the first year of Nemith the Last's reign.

A Welcome to the Shrine of Ostrin

I am delighted to learn that you will be joining our family of adepts and bringing a flavour of Col's celebrated harmonies to our liturgies. You will join acolytes from the great temples of Relshaz and Draximal as well as the myriad lesser shrines of Caladhria and beyond. We are born to all degrees of rank, from the lowliest Names with the honour of but a single hall to shelter Sieur and tenants alike, to the lofty privilege enjoyed by the mightiest Princes of Convocation.

Distinctions are meaningless in our isolated retreat. In the hospitality enjoined by Ostrin's favour, we welcome all as equals. Come to this lonely place with humility and a mind relieved of all distractions of precedence and you may learn all we can teach you. Study the lore of Artifice with diligence and piety and you will return with redoubled skill to serve your first allegiance and those loyal to your House by birth or sworn by choice.

We seek to perfect the arts of healing, to honour Ostrin to whom we are sworn above all. Beneath Drianon's guiding hand, we watch over those making the hazardous journey from the Otherworld into this by way of a mother's womb. As the year turns, we learn how to read Larasion's promises of storm and sun and beseeching Drianon, we may increase the fertility that is her blessing on the earth. Attain the discipline to lift your mind from things seen to the unseen and you may seek Arimelin's help in speaking to those far distant. Under Halcarion's tutelage, you may travel the infinite paths marked by the moons.

As the gods grant rewards of power, they exact solemn duties in return. As those set above you uphold justice within their domains, you will swear to answer to Raeponin for the truth you prompt from a silent tongue or lift from an unwilling mind. Your sincerity will be tested never so sorely as when you comfort those passing into Poldrion's care. It will be laid upon you to ease the fears of the dying as their lives are come before Saedrin's scrutiny.

We are entitled to satisfaction and even a measure of pride in the execution of our Artifice but let us always remember that such skills as we master, are granted only by the grace of the gods whom we honour, as is their due. In their service, we of this shrine are sworn to curtail the arrogance of any who might be tempted to abuse the lore we entrust to them.

Suthyfer, the Northern Sentry Island,
1st of For-Summer

I walked to the far corner of the bay and looked out to sea. White ruffs of foam trimmed mysterious waters shining like black silk beneath the clear silver light of the greater moon. She was gliding serene in the cloudless night sky, perfect circle framed in subtle radiance. Her lesser sister hovered near the horizon, face half hidden as if by a veil drawn aslant, modest handmaiden to that pale beauty, waiting her own turn in the dance of the heavens. The sea breeze perfumed the air with a cleansing freshness, every now and then overlaid momentarily with the sweetness of some unknown blossom unseen in the darkness of the untrodden forest cloaking this hitherto untroubled speck of land. The rhythmic rush of the waves on the sand soothed like the rock of a cradle for a fractious babe while low voices behind me went about some unhurried business. I turned a flat stone over and over between my fingers.

'Beautiful, isn't it?' Pered joined me.

'Hmm.' I managed a non-committal noise.

'What's wrong?' He wasn't being nosy, just offering a friendly ear. I'd noticed his talent for that before.

I cleared my throat. 'Did Shiv ever tell you about Geris?' Gentle, trusting Geris. I'd never had the chance to teach him it was just agreeable flirtation and casual lust landing me in his bed, not the high-flown romance of his imagining.

'The scholar from Vanam.' Pered nodded soberly. 'Elietimm killed him.'

'Same as Parrail.' At least I was managing not to cry. 'Well, worse. They tortured him.' Sudden anger surprised me. All Geris had been doing was sniffing out ancient lore for Planir, with Shiv and Darni along to keep him out of trouble. How did that warrant kidnap by the Elietimm, a death broken and mutilated, all his innocent illusions brutally shattered? 'It's time we stopped these scum bringing murder and misery wherever it suits them.' I spun the stone out across the water to vent my fury. It struck silver sparks from the blackness once, twice, six skips in all.

'That's quite a trick.' Pered looked around his feet. 'Do you want another?'

'No, thanks all the same.' I'd hold on to the rest of my rage. Its heat was better than cold emptiness beneath my breastbone when I thought of all those dead at Elietimm hands. 'Did you want something?'

Turning to Pered meant acknowledging the noise behind me was no comfortable everyday bustle. On this side of the beach the dubious crew Sorgrad had gathered for Shiv were still allocating supplies from the caches in the nearby woods and rocks that Rosarn and Vaspret had unearthed. Vithrancel's mercenaries had long since divided their spoils and were bedded down around their own campfires on the far reach of sand. Spread in desultory knots between them were those ordinary men of Kellarin who remained after the *Eryngo*, *Nenuphar* and *Asterias* had been hastily provisioned from looted stores and sent to battle wind and tide all the way to the southern end of the strait. We had to block that before any pirates could get some ship seaworthy and try to escape.

'It's past midnight.' Pered shivered though it wasn't particularly cold.

I glanced at him. 'Never thought you'd rue the day you weren't mageborn?'

'What's it like?' He struggled for the right word. 'To be used for Artifice?'

The skin down my spine crawled with distaste but I fought to quell the feeling. Having an Elietimm enchanter inside my head had been worse than any rape – and I knew enough of violated women not to say that lightly. How to describe being used for Guinalle's convenience? More akin to the sale and purchase of a disinterested body for a purse of silver?

'It's not so bad,' I said, offhand.

'I'd still rather not.' Pered's usually insouciant eyes were shadowed with more than the dark of the night. 'But I don't suppose we have a choice.'

'Walking away from a bad run of luck only guarantees your losses,' I said lightly. 'Staying to play is the only way to come out ahead.'

'Even when someone doubles the stakes?'

An ear-splitting whistle saved me from having to find an answer to that. I saw 'Gren waving at me, oblivious to annoyed glares from those he'd startled from sleep.

'Time to go,' I told Pered bracingly.

We walked around the scored and soiled sand where a pit had hastily been dug for corpses attracting too many crabs and flies for anyone's peace of mind. Picking our way past snoring heaps of blankets and upturned boots, we reached the rough-hewn cabin that the raiders had helpfully built for us. I caught Darni looking at us from an efficient shelter rigged from oilskin but ignored him. The last thing I wanted was his abrasive intrusion into this.

'Gren was by the door, eyes bright with anticipation, fair hair all but colourless in the half-light. 'She says they should all be asleep by now.'

'I wouldn't argue with that.' Usara came up yawning and we all went inside. Guinalle stood by some board salvaged from the wrecked pinnace and set on two hastily lashed trestles. Ryshad and Temar were setting out stools. The cabin smelt damply of green lumber with a musty undertone of stale sweat. Lamps threw shadows over gear discarded by pirates hopefully too dead to intend reclaiming it. The acrid heat of burning oil caught in the back of my throat.

Guinalle looked up. 'Let's begin.'

I sat beside Ryshad, Temar and Pered on the other side of the table. Everyone showed varying degrees of reluctance, apart from 'Gren at the end whose enthusiastic eyes were fixed on the noblewoman still standing at the head of the board.

'We must find out all we can about these Elietimm without alerting them. The best way to do that is to skim their dreams. To do that, I need a strength in the aether that I'm just not finding, not with the ocean all around and lacking the usual resources of the shrines.' Apart from these somewhat unnecessary explanations, Guinalle was as self-possessed as I'd ever seen her, no trace of the hysteria that had seized her earlier. 'With you all to help me, we should manage.'

I sincerely hoped so. Back in Vithrancel, the placid belief of Mistress Cheven, Master Drage and all the rest provided a solid foundation for Guinalle's enchantments. Out here, she had mostly mercenaries and sailors sailing just close enough to the wind not to be hanged for pirates themselves. I'd noted precious little piety in either contingent.

'Livak has some knowledge in the lesser uses of Artifice as well as her Forest instincts. Ryshad should share something of your training, Temar, thanks to the Artifice that linked you.' Guinalle favoured D'Alsennin with a smile that evidently surprised the lad.

I reached for Ryshad's hand beneath the table. Only I knew the full depths of the horror he'd known when Temar's trapped mind had broken through the confining enchantment, fighting blindly to take Ryshad's body for his own.

Guinalle continued, perhaps setting all this out for Usara's benefit, more likely to instil some confidence in the rest of us. 'I'm still not sure how but it's undeniable Sorgren has been proof against assault from both Sheltya and Elietimm in the past.'

'No one comes looking inside my head without a by your leave,' shrugged 'Gren.

'I'm just here to make up the numbers, am I?' Pered's quip was a little forced.

Guinalle looked steadily at him. 'You're an artist; you see beyond the immediate and the physical. That's much the sensitivity demanded of an adept. Just concentrate on following my lead.'

She sat and held out her hands to Temar and Ryshad and

we joined in a circle. Ryshad's strong grip held my off hand
and 'Gren's blunt fingers gave my knife hand a gleeful
squeeze. I narrowed my eyes at him in mute warning but all
I got was a cheery wink. Temar and Pered were fixed on
Guinalle who had closed her eyes. Temar did the same and
after a moment, so did Ryshad. I considered it but couldn't
bring myself to do it.

Guinalle caught her breath and opened her eyes. I shut
mine guiltily.

'I'm sorry, Ryshad.' Guinalle shook her head. 'Your
mistrust of Artifice is too strong.'

Ryshad's face betrayed an instant of chagrin. He dropped
Guinalle's hand before giving mine a courtly kiss. 'I'm sorry,
everyone.'

'You can keep watch with me for anything going awry.'
Usara was by the door, all the while watching Guinalle
intently.

'What do we do if it does?' I heard Ryshad mutter under
his breath as he went to join the mage.

'Let's continue, shall we?' Temar set his jaw and held out
demanding hands.

'Gren and I shuffled our stools to draw the circle tighter.
Guinalle began a low incantation as soon as her hand touched
mine and the crude cabin faded around me much as the
Eryngo had done. The others were clear enough but everything outside our linked hands was as indistinct as smoke.
This time I didn't see a new place but rather a face. It hung
in the air between us, motionless, expression slack in sleep.
It was the woman, Yalda, the silver gorget that marked her
as enchanter among the Elietimm bright around her neck.

Guinalle opened her eyes. 'Concentrate on her.' In some
distant recess of my mind, I could hear the first incantation
still binding us with its rhythms but Guinalle was somehow
separating her thoughts into several, separate threads, each
with its own focus. Was this the secret to Higher Artifice, I
wondered, no more complicated than remembering the roll
of the runes at the same time as anticipating an opponent's

next wager and all the while keeping a weather eye out for
the Watch?

I still wasn't sure I wanted to learn this Higher Artifice
though. Emotions swirled around our circle. Pered had
framed the girl in the imagined oval of a miniature frame,
picking out details to paint like the gathering creases at the
corner of her eyes. 'Gren was comparing her, none too flat-
teringly, to a golden-haired dancing girl of his acquaintance
and I did my best to ignore his speculations about what lay
beneath Yalda's nightgown. Temar saw her only as an enemy,
determined to secure whatever knowledge might aid our
cause.

All that was to be expected. What unsettled me was
Guinalle carefully masking her hatred, lulling the girl's
sleeping mind with an insidious charm that she spread to net
first the man Moin and the younger Darige. There was none
of the brutality the Elietimm had used on Parrail but I knew
beyond doubt that Guinalle's revenge could more than repay
them for his murder, if she so chose. I made a mental note
never to play against the demoiselle for money or favours
and then wondered if everyone else knew I'd thought that in
that instant.

Guinalle began a new incantation quite different in pitch
and pace and new images hung in the empty air. The fluid,
distorted shapes were nothing like the vividness of scrying
or bespeaking and I wondered what Ryshad and Usara might
be seeing.

The images slowly coalesced to a grey stone keep on a rise
above a harbour cutting sharply into a meagre, dune-swept
coast. I couldn't help a sharp intake of breath as I recognised
the place where Ryshad, Shiv and I had been held prisoner,
caught in our fruitless quest to rescue poor Geris. Me,
Ryshad, Shiv and Aiten. Aiten's was another death we owed
these scum.

'Do not rouse them with your anger,' Guinalle chided me
soundlessly. The image drifted to show us the garden within
the keep. It was much as I remembered it; no mere pleasaunce

but closely planted with vital crops while glasshouses on all sides reared plants too tender for the harsh climate. The chill I felt owed nothing to the cold winds of the far north. Fear, pure and simple, was raising the hairs on the back of my neck but, to my surprise, I realised this wasn't my dread.

A white-haired man was tending a climbing plant, clipping undisciplined shoots from the base and training wayward tendrils within the strict confines of a trellis. This was the bastard who'd set all the confusion of these last few years in motion. This was the man who'd sent Elietimm spies to Tormalin and beyond. They had robbed and murdered with the help of his Artifice as they hunted for those artefacts that would enable their master to kill all who might oppose his seizure of Kellarin's rich lands. I sensed Temar throttling his own rage and tried to contain my own hatred but our detestation was a muted note beneath the resounding apprehension of all three sleeping enchanters. They saw themselves as much subject to him as the mindless vine. They must seek nothing but his bidding, so their skills and knowledge of Artifice might flourish under his guidance. Painful awareness lurked just beneath such thoughts. Any deviation from his will would be cruelly punished, their freedom curtailed with every last person they loved sharing their fate for any dire transgression.

'Ilkehan,' breathed Guinalle with satisfaction. 'Now we have his name.'

We'd just called him the Ice Man when we'd been his captives. It had suited his dead white hair, fleshless, merciless face and his calculated brutality, lethal and indifferent as winter's bitterest chill.

Faces flickered across our vision like memory slipping out of reach. A baby, too small to be identified as boy or girl, came and went almost before we realised but we all felt a surge of fatherly love from the sleeping Moin. A couple, elderly by Ice Islander reckoning, prompted filial affection from Darige that touched even me, who'd walked away from such ties without regret. The girl Yalda kept her devotion for a barrel-chested warrior looking not unlike Sorgrad, his leather armour studded with emblems of rank.

'He's that bastard Eresken's father,' remarked 'Gren with interest.

'Who?' Temar frowned.

'The warrior?' I was puzzled as well.

'Yon Ilkehan.' At 'Gren's naming of him, we saw the Ice Man again. He was addressing cowed Elietimm among a scattering of squalid hovels, who waited in rags for grain doled out by Ilkehan's well-fed minions. We couldn't taste their hunger but we felt their trepidation. On every side, black-liveried troops stood alert for any dissent.

'No, who's Eresken?' Temar let slip exasperation.

'The Elietimm enchanter who tried to rouse the Mountain Men to war last year.' Pered summoned sufficient confidence to join our silent conversation. 'The one who seduced Aritane from the Sheltya.' She'd been all too ready to believe Eresken's promises that Artifice would right the many and manifest wrongs the Mountain Men had suffered as recent generations of lowlanders encroached on their territories. Personally I'd have been suspicious, given Eresken openly acknowledged his descent from a clique long exiled from the Mountains for the highest crime of using enchantment to serve their ambitions. But I hadn't suffered the frustrations of Aritane's celibate life and the curbs the Sheltya voluntarily imposed on their own so-called true magic.

The image suddenly shifted. We saw Eresken's face, coldly handsome and then a ghastly mask of blood, neck half hacked through.

'I thought cutting his head off was safest,' 'Gren explained genially.

Eresken vanished to whatever punishment Poldrion's demons had prepared for him. Then we saw another Elietimm enchanter, the one who'd sought Ryshad's death by conniving at his enslavement among the perils of the Aldabreshin Archipelago, for the sake of the D'Alsennin sword he carried.

Temar knew this one's name. 'Kramisak.' Quick as imagination, I saw Ryshad's sword foiling the bastard's mace stroke and ripping out his throat when their rival quests for the lost colonists had brought them face to face.

'Ilkehan's sent three because one alone is too vulnerable.' Guinalle nodded to herself.

'But they're not as strong as either of the other two.' Inadequate as Temar's Artifice might be, it was showing him something hidden from the rest of us. I shared a shrug of incomprehension with Pered and 'Gren.

'He keeps so much learning to himself.' Guinalle looked thoughtful as she read the blank, sleeping faces. 'He has no one stronger to send.'

'Why doesn't this big man come himself?' 'Gren's eyes lit with his unvarying readiness for a fight.

'It's not in his nature.' As Temar spoke, we saw Ilkehan in the study I'd at least managed to loot of maps and sundry other records before we'd escaped the Ice Islands. Pen in hand, he was making notes on some chart. This bastard was a schemer, a conniver of other men's deaths who seldom got blood on his own hands. I didn't need magic to tell me that.

'Other concerns keep him close to home.' Guinalle's words threw the image into confusion so abruptly we were all startled.

This slaughter had none of the riot of battle we'd known today but the shadowy Elietimm lay surely dead. Two armies were meeting on a barren pewter shore, broken rocks behind them strewn over a scant stretch of faded grass, stark heights behind still topped with winter's stubborn snows. Warriors' boots churned up the shallow grey-green sea as they hacked each other to pieces. We couldn't feel the cold spray or the cutting wind, the treacherous sand beneath our feet but turbulent emotions roiled around us. Panic lest his own entrails be ripped out spurred one man on to gut another. Rage burned a youth so fiercely that anyone within sword reach was mere blood for spilling to quench his anger.

Ilkehan's men were clad in the black leather we'd come to know and loathe while their opponents wore a dull brown.

'Is this real or imagined?' Temar studied the aetheric vision.

'Hard to say,' Guinalle murmured. 'That's Moin, though.'

We saw him on an arid turf bank. Liveried like a soldier, gorget bright at his collar, he raised a hand and brown-clad figures began dropping like medlars from a frosted tree, gashes in their faces and chests showing red like the flesh of burst fruit, the only splash of colour in the pallid landscape. Moin's livery sprouted new adornments and his gorget blurred from silver to gold. We saw Eresken again, at Ilkehan's shoulder, then his face blurred and became Moin's.

'Our boy's looking for promotion,' commented 'Gren.

'So he's the one to watch?' I felt Temar promise himself the man's early death.

Guinalle shook her head slowly. 'He's just the one whose thoughts are closest to his skin.'

I noticed the woman Yalda tossing and turning in her distant sleep. 'What happens if they wake up?' As I asked, I felt alarm from Pered and perverse anticipation from 'Gren. In a nauseating instant, I learned how Eresken had come to grief. It seemed getting out of 'Gren's head was nowhere near as easy as getting in. The Mountain Man was eager to try driving another intrusive enchanter into insanity and death using only the untrammelled force of a mind blithely untroubled by conscience.

Guinalle spared 'Gren a faintly repelled look before focusing her attention once more on the sleeping Elietimm. 'I just want to see what they know of this pirate.'

She coaxed memories from their dreams like a musician drawing music from a lyre. We saw a broad haven sheltered by a mighty headland offering sanctuary from the savage rocks and seas of Toremal's ocean coast. A town sprawled behind the tufted dunes and rowboats ferried men and goods between the shore and ships swaying at anchor.

'Kalaven.' Pered was surprised. 'We stopped there before setting course for Suthyfer.'

'Sorgrad found some good crewmen there,' 'Gren observed.

'So did Muredarch.' Guinalle encouraged Yalda's recollection of a startlingly tall man with wiry black hair and a savage cast to an otherwise handsome face, if you made allowance for the ragged beard and the crow's-feet of age and disillusion framing his eyes. He'd been down on his luck back then, breeches dirty, shirt stained and boots inadequately patched. He was talking to Darige.

'So much for Emperor Tadriol smoking every Elietimm spy out of his thatch.' I'd always had my doubts about that, hearing Ryshad tell of frustrating pursuits of rumour and suspicion as his prince set him hunting the thieves who'd cut down a younger son of the House for an heirloom ring. He'd only learned later it was a Kellarin artefact when his path crossed mine and Darni's and Shiv's.

'Guinalle,' Temar warned.

'Very well.' Her lips narrowed with frustration before she soothed the air to emptiness with a lilting incantation. The sleeping faces vanished and I was abruptly aware of crippling stiffness in my neck and shoulders and the promise of a truly spectacular headache.

'I need some fresh air.' Pered got unsteadily to his feet and Ryshad promptly opened the door.

'I'll settle for a drink.' Even 'Gren was looking unsure of himself and that was as rare as a moonless night.

Resting my forehead on my upturned palms, I felt Ryshad's strong fingers rubbing my shoulders. 'So what did you see?'

Ryshad took a moment to answer. 'Colours, shapes, nothing I could make sense of. 'Sar couldn't even see that much.'

'Another instance where Artifice and elemental magic don't mix?' I rubbed my temples with cautious fingertips and squinted up at Ryshad. 'What now?'

''Sar's gone to get the others. Are you all right?' His grimness promised trouble for someone if I wasn't.

I nodded carefully. 'I will be.' Kneeling, he gathered me to him. I laid my head on his shoulder and thought very seriously about going to sleep and leaving everything to the rest of them, at least until the morning.

'Where's Allin?'

I opened my eyes to see Temar scrubbing his face with the heels of his hands.

'With the rest of the mageborn. They were going to discuss just what wizardry they might venture without risking Elietimm attack.' Ryshad stood and lifted me to my feet before sitting on the stool himself. I sat on his lap, arms loose around his shoulders.

'Usara was saying Aritane's helped him devise certain defences over the winter.' Guinalle's voice was weary.

We sat in silence for a short time until Halice kicked open the door to wrestle a cumbersome basket of bottles inside. 'If you're done, let's hear what you know and make a plan.'

We all winced at the crash and clink of glass apart from 'Gren who perked up immediately. 'Always best done with a drink in your hand.' He helped himself to a fat-bellied bottle studded with a blobby wax seal.

Halice handed out a motley selection of wines. 'So what did you learn?'

By the time Temar had explained, to no one's great surprise, that our old enemy was the driving force behind the pirates, the wizards had arrived. Shiv had an arm around Pered, eyes searching for the least hint that Artifice had hurt his beloved. Usara went to press some wine on the largely silent Guinalle with detached courtesy. He had even managed to find a gold-trimmed silver goblet from somewhere.

'Can we get Naldeth out of there?' asked Allin. She'd been preoccupied with the mage's fate ever since we'd had to leave him behind.

'He's one of ours, is he?' Sorgrad had helped 'Gren shift

the table to the side of the room and the brothers sat on it, swinging their feet idly. He downed a hefty swallow of white brandy.

'Guinalle?' Temar passed Allin his pale green bottle of Caladhrian white and she took a hesitant sip.

'I don't think we dare try reach him.' The demoiselle sighed with eloquent frustration before looking round at all the mageborn. 'You had better limit your magic to things within reach, things you can see. The Elietimm shouldn't be able to attack you unless you're seeking something beyond your immediate senses.'

'So we can still blow pirates out of the water with fire and lightning?' Sorgrad winked at Larissa who was standing a little apart from Shiv and Pered, silent and watchful. She smiled shyly back at him.

'Which will be useful,' observed Ryshad drily as he took red wine offered by Halice.

Sorgrad shot him an enigmatic look, which Ryshad met with level imperturbability. With all that had been going on, they'd had no real chance to take each other's measure as yet but that would happen sometime soon. I took the bottle from Ryshad and swallowed a mouthful of Sitalcan, its bracing bite cutting through the weariness fogging my mind. I'd better make sure I was around to stop my oldest friends and my newest love coming to blows over their undoubted differences. I wasn't expecting them to like each other but I hoped they'd at least respect each other's talents.

Halice had other concerns. 'We'll not get rid of those pirates as long as they've aetheric magic backing them.'

'We've aetheric magic to use against them.' Usara smiled at Guinalle but we could all see the worry in his eyes.

'Are you certain you're proof against these three? We're barely adept enough to back you.' Temar sketched a circle to include me, 'Gren and Pered. 'Usara, might that Sheltya woman be induced to help us?'

'Aritane?' Guinalle shook her head regretfully. 'Even if

she were prepared to leave the sanctuary of Hadrumal, I don't believe she's come to terms with Eresken's betrayal of her and her people. That alone would leave her horribly vulnerable.'

'So we've a cursed sight more than pirates to worry about now.' Ryshad swirled the wine around in his bottle thoughtfully. 'What does Ilkehan want with Suthyfer?'

'Elietimm holding these islands will be a dagger at Vithrancel's throat and all the Tormalin ocean ports,' glowered Halice.

For some reason, I thought about the Ice Man pruning his creeper. I remembered how my mother had waged constant warfare on knotgrass that had the temerity to continually reappear among the herbs and flowers she cultivated in the modest patch permitted her by the wealthy merchant who owned the big house. Every time my mother thought she had the thing beaten, another stem of jaunty little leaves capped with red-trimmed white flowers would spring up to mock her. As a fat-legged little girl I had played uncomprehending through one long afternoon while my father, on one of his rare and longed-for visits, had carefully dug up every cherished gillyflower and clump of heartsease, each woody sprig of spikenard swathed with leathery green leaves. He'd laid them all tenderly in moist shade before digging out every last root of that cursed knotgrass, following every stubborn rootlet down to its end. I recalled his conspiratorial grin as he lay flat on the black earth to reach as far as he could, soil dusting his coppery hair and smudging his face. Joining him in the normally forbidden delights of digging and dirt, I'd been just as filthy by the time we'd finished but at least my mother had never seen the knotgrass again.

'We have to get rid of Ilkehan.' It was remarkably easy to put such a momentous notion into words. As easy as casting the handful of runes that could make your fortune or break your neck. 'Everything leads back to him.'

'When you say "we"?' Ryshad inclined his head as he looked at me and I knew he understood.

'Kellarin could never raise an army to fight the Elietimm.' Temar plainly didn't. 'Would the Emperor go to war on our behalf? Could he raise the ships, the men?'

'Stop thinking with your cohorts,' chided Sorgrad.

'I don't think this will be something the Emperor can risk being linked with,' Ryshad said slowly. 'He came out of last summer's confusion well enough placed but the Sieurs of the leading Houses will still be watching him for any excessive independence.' Temar's unexpected arrival had seriously disrupted the complex game of checks and balances that the princes of Toremal played among themselves and the Emperor had had to walk a fine line between keeping them in check or seeing them turn on him instead of D'Alsennin.

'Overlord or not, Tadriol rules with the Sieurs' consent. They won't be overly reassured to see him killing people who irritate him out of hand. ' Halice rubbed a thoughtful finger round the wide neck of the flagon she held. It made a soft squeaking noise. 'Anyway, the back of a knife makes a neater job of cracking an egg than a rock the size of your head.'

'A knife's what you want,' said 'Gren with relish. 'A raiding party to cut the bastard's throat for him will settle this nonsense.'

'Get the drop on them and hit them hard, you can kill pretty much anyone,' Sorgrad stated firmly before grinning suddenly. 'Why do you suppose your noblemen spend so much money on sworn men and mercenaries?'

'Assassination?' Temar looked startled. 'That's hardly honourable.'

Guinalle opened her mouth but shut it again without speaking.

'We're mercenaries,' Halice pointed out mildly. 'Honourable doesn't pay, as a rule.'

'It would be an execution,' Ryshad corrected Temar sternly. 'That man has lives without number to pay for, even if other hands swung the blades at his command.'

'Parrail,' snapped Halice with sudden anger.

'Geris,' I said shortly.

'Aiten.' Ryshad's nostrils flared as he struggled to contain the rage and sorrow that I knew always lurked in some locked corner of his thoughts. Aiten had been his friend for many years, sworn to D'Olbriot, at Ryshad's side as they hunted whoever had left the House's young esquire for dead. We'd all but escaped the islands of the Elietimm when Ilkehan's enchantments had stolen away his mind, setting him to kill us all. I brushed a kiss across Ryshad's forehead and felt his arms tighten around my waist. In those intense conversations lovers keep for the midnight hours of troubled nights, Ryshad had told me he'd vowed revenge, for the sake of the oaths they'd shared.

I wouldn't try talking him out of it, not when I owed Ilkehan a full measure of vengeance for leaving me the only one with the chance to kill poor Aiten before he became the death of the rest of us. Could I wash that blood off my hands with Ilkehan's own? 'What of the missing artefacts? Could Ilkehan hold them?'

Guinalle looked stricken. I recalled what Halice had told me of her Equinox and Solstice visits to the Edisgesset cavern, her anguished prayers as she burned incense to Arimelin at the altar she'd had set there.

'Quite possibly.' Usara looked thoughtful. 'And we surely want to restore those last few, now that the danger you saved them from is past.' He smiled at Guinalle but, as always, she was too racked with remorse over their present predicament to credit herself with saving these people from bloody death hands in the distant past.

If 'Sar's words didn't strike a chord with Guinalle, they certainly did with Ryshad. 'We'll only be visiting his own practices on the man,' he said forcefully. 'He kills by stealth to serve his own ends, heedless of the innocent. Justice will weight our actions against his in Raeponin's balance.'

'The man's crimes would condemn him in any court from Toremal to the capital of Solura,' Shiv said perfunctorily.

'How do you propose administering this summary justice?'

Ryshad and I looked at him and saw the mage already knew what we were thinking.

'We're the only ones who know the layout of his keep,' I pointed out reluctantly.

'You're the only mage who's been there, who can translocate us all,' added Ryshad with an apologetic glance at Pered. The artist set his square jaw, pale beneath his freckles, but didn't speak.

'Then we're coming too.' Sorgrad's tone brooked no argument. He jabbed a finger at Ryshad. 'You're not taking our girl there into some enchanter's snake pit without us to back her up.'

'No Chosen man ever made a good assassin.' 'Gren took a blithe swig from his bottle. 'Too much honour in you, but that's your problem. Me, I don't care who I kill.'

'So I've heard,' replied Ryshad blandly.

Sorgrad gave him another measuring look before addressing himself to Temar. 'We owe this Ilkehan for the Mountain dead that Eresken's plots and deceit piled up.' He grinned, predatory. 'What say we just walk in there, saying we met Eresken last summer, offering some new alliance? We could cut out Ilkehan's heart and be done inside half a day.'

'You've no interest in getting out alive?' Halice set her flagon on the table with a sharp smack. 'If—'

'No,' said Ryshad firmly. 'If we're going to do this, it just takes the handful of us. Any more and we might as well send a fleet blowing horns and flying flags.'

'You'll still have Muredarch to deal with,' I pointed out to Halice. 'He's hardly going to throw up his hands just because his pet enchanters lose their master all of a sudden.'

'I cannot take on these pirates without your help, Halice,' Temar said hastily.

'We can deal with them in short order as long as there's no threat of Artifice.' She looked a little mollified. 'Will killing this Ilkehan knock out those three enchanters?'

'Guinalle?' Usara's gaze hadn't left her.

'I think so.' The noblewoman looked up and continued with studied neutrality. 'If his death is public, certainly public knowledge and widely known as fast as possible. A shameful death, something grotesque or humiliating, that will undercut all the awe he inspires.' Her voice was cold. 'His power is founded on fear rather than any true devotion so his death will leave his adepts on little better than shifting sand.'

Ryshad raised an eyebrow at me and I shrugged. I'd been thinking more of sticking a poisoned dagger in the bastard's back and discreetly running away.

'Shall we cut his head off?' Sorgrad and 'Gren on the other hand were swapping bottles and ideas with conspiratorial glee. 'Stick it on a pike for all his folk to see?'

'From everything we know, Ilkehan holds some preeminent position among the Elietimm clans.' Usara was looking thoughtful again. 'If we can knock him off the top of the tree, that might well leave the rest of them more interested in squabbling over the spoils than attacking us.'

'Especially once we've made it plain taking on Kellarin leaves you so very nastily dead,' Sorgrad agreed with relish.

'Men like Ilkehan keep tight hold on power by cutting down any poppies growing taller than the rest,' said Ryshad slowly.

'Which is a coin with two sides.' I saw the potential weakness in Ilkehan's armour as plainly as Ryshad. 'With Kramisak and Eresken dead, he has no obvious successor.'

'Certainly not if we kill these three here.' Temar looked determined.

'I'll settle for a likely pay-off, not hold out for bonuses. Killing Ilkehan should leave Muredarch's enchanters leaderless and that should buy us enough time to deal with the rest of the scum.' Halice looked at Guinalle who nodded reluctant confirmation.

I handed the wine back to Ryshad. 'We saw his soldiers fighting those people in the brown liveries again.'

'That other mob who snuck about over here, stealing things and ransacking shrines.' Ryshad pursed speculative lips. 'We never did find out what they were about, did we?'

'Let's find out while we're there,' suggested 'Gren obligingly.

'This isn't some trading trip.' Sorgrad gave his brother a withering look. 'But we might find ourselves an ally, somewhere safe to run while we're there.' He raised his brows at Ryshad who nodded slowly. I was relieved to see the two of them showing cautious acknowledgement of the other's battle wisdom.

'What do we tell Planir?' demanded Usara abruptly.

'Why tell him anything?' countered Shiv. 'He made it plain enough we were on our own.'

'But that was before we knew Ilkehan was involved,' protested Usara.

'He said we had a free hand to act for Kellarin as we saw fit.' Shiv shook his head. 'Anyway, the Archmage of Hadrumal can no more afford to be associated with summary executions than the Emperor of Tormalin.' Sarcasm sharpened his tone.

'We won't tell,' said Sorgrad with spurious innocence.

'Not as long as he makes it worth our while.' 'Gren raised a mock serious finger.

'Planir wouldn't object.' Larissa spoke up defiantly from her corner. 'He wouldn't shirk from exacting such a penalty from any wizard whose abuse of magic truly warranted death.'

'He let that madman Azazir go free.' Shiv let slip a sceptical aside to Pered.

'You don't know half what Planir does to keep Hadrumal on an even keel, Shiv.' Larissa glared at him. 'Wizardry would be in a parlous state without him.'

'I don't know about that but then I don't know a lot about wizardry.' Sorgrad jumped down from the table and turned a charming smile on Larissa. 'If I'm to be any use backing

Shiv on this trip, my lady mage, I could do with some more instruction from you before we leave.'

'Livak!' Guinalle left off studying her hands to get my attention. 'I had better drill you in your Artifice, just to make sure it's all clear in your mind.'

'Very well.' That wasn't the most appealing prospect.

'Let's get some sleep and set the pieces in play tomorrow.' Halice started gathering up bottles, nodding to Pered to open the door.

I looked at Ryshad. 'Even lower Artifice could save our necks somehow.'

'Indeed. We certainly want every kind of shot in our quiver.' He kissed me before setting me on my feet and standing himself. 'Are we sleeping on board ship or ashore?'

'Ashore, please,' I said fervently.

'I'll get some blankets.' Ryshad ushered Shiv and Pered out, the tall mage still scowling. Sorgrad followed, escorting Larissa out with flattering courtesy, 'Gren sauntering along behind.

'Would he be so admirably eager to learn if the lady mage were not quite such a beauty?' Temar wandered over, face disapproving.

'What was it interested you in studying Artifice with Guinalle, back in the way back when?' I smiled just enough to take the edge off my words. I was certain Sorgrad's main ambition was getting his hands on Larissa's staylaces but no one criticises my friends but me. Well, me and Halice.

Temar coloured. 'It's late. I'll see you in the morning.' Allin jumped up from the stool where she'd sat all but unnoticed and hurried after him.

'Good night.' I left Usara finding comforts for Guinalle that she'd never have looked for herself and went outside, yawning, to meet Ryshad just where the crushed plants around the hut yielded to gritty sand. He had an armful of blankets and we made ourselves comfortable in a discreet hollow.

He lay back and held out an arm. I curled into his embrace and he held me tight.

'Are we doing the right thing?' I asked him. Bold plans made with trusted allies and a reinforcing drink in your hand have to stand up to scrutiny in the cold light of dawn, if they're not to lead to disaster.

I counted five echoing heartbeats in his chest before he replied. 'I can't see what else to do.'

'Oh, very reassuring,' I grumbled.

'No, I didn't mean that.' Ryshad shifted slightly so he could wrap both arms around me. 'We have to get these pirates out of the islands and we need magic, wizardry to do that. We daren't risk Shiv and 'Sar or anyone else, if these Elietimm can use Artifice to leave them for dead while they're at it. For all Guinalle's skills, she's certainly no inclination to use aetheric magic to attack people and, frankly, I doubt she'd know how to, even if it came down to a fight between them. It's just not her way. So you're right. We need to kill the Ice Man. We've seen him trying to cause trouble every-where he can; pirates this time, in the Mountains last year, in the Archipelago before that. Kellarin will never be safe as long as he's there. It's simple.'

'Simple.' I echoed. 'I hope it will be.'

'We got out alive last time, didn't we?' Ryshad kissed my hair. 'And we didn't know what we were facing, nor yet have magic to back us, not after Shiv got that smack on the head.'

I turned my face to him, dim in the darkness. 'Geris or Aiten didn't get out.'

'Geris didn't have an aggressive bone in his body, from what you've told me, nor yet a suspicious one.' Ryshad cleared his throat. 'So he never stood a chance. Ait, poor bastard, he was just cursed unlucky.' He sighed. 'But he always said if the dawn turns up your death runes, there's nothing to be done about it.'

'I prefer to make my own luck,' I muttered.

Ryshad hugged me close. 'We know what we're dealing with and we've got Shiv, Sorgrad and 'Gren to back us.'

'Yes, we have.' I craned my head back to kiss his bristly cheek. 'You need a shave.'

'In the morning,' he yawned. 'Now go to sleep.'

Since there was nothing else I could do, I did.

Shernasekke, Islands of the Elietimm, 2nd of For-Summer

With everyone agreed that Ilkehan must die, we'd woken to a day of ceaseless activity that somehow managed to be incredibly tedious. By the time we were standing between Larissa and Allin, with Usara and Shiv discussing who should act as focus for their nexus of magic, all I felt was relief that we were finally leaving. That was before I remembered just how revolting it felt to be flung across the leagues by wizardry. I can't begin to describe the solace of gravel crunching beneath my boots. I ground my feet just to hear the noise again. A few deep breaths helped settle my stomach and the painful ringing in my ears faded to be replaced by a soft murmur of surf. I knuckled my eyes to try and clear the yellow flashes obscuring my vision.

'Are you all right?' Ryshad steadied me with concerned hands.

'Just about,' I said with some irritation. 'You seem fine.'

He grinned sympathetically. 'I don't get seasick either.'

I looked round for the others. 'How are you feeling?'

'Fine,' Sorgrad said absently, deep in thought about something.

I managed a slight smile. 'How long before you work out that trick?'

'Give me time,' winked Sorgrad.

'Don't try translocation without me or 'Sar around,' Shiv told him seriously. 'Not until you get the hang of it. With a dual affinity, you'll end up—'

'Why are we waiting for someone to come and cut our throats for us?' demanded 'Gren impatiently.

Ryshad looked around the rocky beach. 'Let's find some cover.'

There was precious little on offer. Dark rubble was strewn over sands the colour of wood ash, the grey sea lapping the shallow shore. Slews of stinking weed tangled between the boulders, hiding hollows and pits to sink the unwary up to their knees. Out to sea, the mists of the late afternoon blurred the line between water and sky. They could have been hiding a double handful of ships for all I could tell. We had to get off this exposed shore.

Ryshad headed for a scar worn by feet, human or animal, where the pebbles rolled up beneath a sharply undercut bank topped with a stretch of dusty green turf. We all looked cautiously over to see a stretch of scrubby grassland running up to a steep ridge of broken rock. Greater heights beyond were blunt and sere and, even in this first half of summer, topped with a rime of white that could only be snow. These dismal islands felt half a world away from the rich lushness of Suthyfer, even if Temar's charts said different.

'Does this look familiar?' Sorgrad shifted the satchel he wore to his other shoulder.

'Yes.' I'd have laughed in the face of anyone who'd told me I'd come back to these islands. But here I was and, worse, it was my own god-cursed idea.

'Close enough, Shiv.' Ryshad grinned at the mage whose answering smile betrayed his relief.

'Come on.' 'Gren was already on the top of the bank, looking in all directions, dagger ready.

'We want to bear that way.' Shiv had a map, thanks to Pered's assiduous work with pen and ink all morning while the three of us scoured every memory of our previous visit here. 'That village is over yonder, so hoods up.'

Ryshad and I obliged while Sorgrad ostentatiously ran a hand over his own golden head. 'Try to look like we belong, 'Gren.'

'For the moment,' Gren chuckled with happy anticipation.

'Let's not get close enough for anyone to wonder.' I didn't imagine there were too many redheads hereabouts and we didn't want anyone seeing we were armed, never mind Ryshad and Shiv's dark colouring.

We moved off and, away from the scour of the wind, I saw summer had swathed the few stunted trees in leaves. 'There's barely enough forage for an unfussy donkey,' I said uneasily to Ryshad. 'We should have brought more food.'

'Carrying too much will just get us noticed.' He continued scanning the flat plain.

'Don't worry,' Sorgrad smiled. 'We'll be honoured guests before nightfall and fed to suit.'

'What was that?' 'Gren halted and we all stood still.

I heard a faint scrabbling and what could have been a warning voice, muffled and incomprehensible. 'Where's that coming from?' A faint shiver ran down my spine.

Sorgrad dropped to his knees and we all did the same.

'What are you doing?' he said, surprised.

'The same as you,' I told him tartly. 'Why?'

He nodded to a hole in the turf. 'Whatever's making your noise is down there.'

'That'd be a tight fit for a hungry rabbit.' Ryshad got up, brushing fine, dusty earth from his breeches. 'I don't think we need worry.' Wary amusement lessened the tension in the air.

'I wonder what it is.' 'Gren knelt, hand reaching for the burrow.

'Something that could bite your fingers off and leave you with festering stumps?' I suggested. 'Just leave well alone.'

'There's someone coming.' Shiv tucked his map in the breast of his hooded jerkin. We saw a solitary figure carefully removing the larger stones that served for a gate in one of the low walls dividing this barren hinterland.

'Move.' Ryshad set a pace just fast enough to suggest purpose but not so hurried to attract attention.

The edge of my hood hid the figure from me, which left my back itching. 'What's he doing?'

'Nothing. Just keep going.' Sorgrad led us towards a low notch in the jagged ridge. 'Gren didn't bother with the narrow path, heedless boots crushing the few flowers crouching in the coarse grass, bruised herbs momentarily sweetening the gusting breeze.

'Keep a weather eye out for goats,' I warned him. 'We could barely move without tripping over the cursed things last time.'

'Let's see that map, Shiv.' Sorgrad ducked into a sheltered hollow between two tall boulders sticking through the grass like broken teeth.

Ryshad and I each held a corner flat against the lichen-spotted stone.

'We need to go north.' I traced a line on the parchment.

'Giving that village a wide berth.' Ryshad jabbed it with an emphatic finger.

Shiv ran a thumbnail along a faint blue line and a darker brown one. 'Once we're over that river, we follow the road inland.'

Sorgrad looked dubious. 'Follow it or shadow it? I don't fancy being asked to explain myself if we run into someone nosy.'

Ryshad shook his head. 'We'd attract more attention off the road than on it.'

'We have to take the road, regardless. It's mostly sheer rock and screes where it cuts through the high ground.' I held Sorgrad's gaze until he decided I was telling him the truth, not just siding with Ryshad.

'Let's get going,' 'Gren complained.

We crested the ridge and headed down the far side. More stone walls scored dry lines across close-cropped grass. Dark splodges of muck were the only sign of goats and I was wondering where they were, when I nearly tripped headlong into a ditch hidden by rushy grasses.

'Watch your step.' Ryshad caught my hand and we stepped carefully over the dark brown water.

'I can smell food.' 'Gren was looking at the distant roofs

of the village we were avoiding. Bluish smoke rose from a few stubby chimneys.

'At this distance?' I scoffed. 'You're imagining it.'

'You'll have walked up a better appetite by the time we get there,' Sorgrad told him sternly.

'What if this man with the brown troopers doesn't want to help us?' 'Gren enquired thoughtfully. 'Do we kill him as well?'

Sorgrad shrugged. 'Depends what he says, I reckon.'

The pair of them moved ahead to scout out our path. Ryshad and Shiv were some little way behind me.

'Just what did Usara reckon to travelling with these two?' I heard Ryshad ask the mage.

'Sorgrad's the one you have to make listen to reason,' Shiv answered in an undertone. ''Gren's just interested in drinking, eating, fighting and tumbling pretty girls, in whatever combination he's offered. As long as he thinks he's in with a chance of one or more, he'll go along with whatever his brother tells him.'

I smiled to myself and picked up my pace, so I could keep Sorgrad and 'Gren in sight. Comparatively sheltered between the ridge and the high ground, the grass grew thicker, softer underfoot and dotted with bell-shaped blue flowers trembling on fragile stems. Bolder white flowers drifted around clumps of frilled and leathery green leaves topped with red flowers clasping some secret in their petal globes. I wondered again where all the goats had gone to let such prettiness bloom uneaten.

'Gren was soon bored with casting around like a badly trained hound and came to walk beside me. 'This isn't so bad.'

'You want to try it here in winter,' I told him. We'd only been here at the very start of the season and that had been bad enough.

'Soft lowlander,' he chided. 'Me and 'Grad, we're used to harder living.'

'Hard living and your life and death at the whim of some Ilkehan's boot heel?' I queried.

'Gren was unconcerned. 'We'll put an end to that.'

I was about to ask him what augury he'd seen when a sharp whistle from Sorgrad prompted Ryshad and Shiv to catch us up. We joined him at the top of a rise, just short of the river. He'd propped his rump on a handy lump of rock, the ever-present breeze ruffling his fine yellow hair, and was rummaging in one pocket.

'Apricot?' Sorgrad held out a little washleather pouch.

I took a sticky lump of dried golden fruit, tucking my other hand through my belt. 'What's to do?'

'Over yonder.' Sorgrad waved casually at the land running down to the river. The flow was narrow enough for crossing stones here, widening out below us into a broad estuary of sandbars and glistening channels. Black and white and pied birds waded and prodded for worms or some such in the shallows, darker shapes wheeling above them in the washed-out blue.

'There.' Ryshad pointed as a wide, triangular net suddenly swept up and around just beyond a shallow knoll crowned with yellow flower spikes.

'What's he after?' wondered Shiv.

'Those.' I pointed at a squat, short-winged bird all black but for a white belly and a comical tuft of scarlet and yellow feathers behind each eye. 'Look, he's got one.'

The hunter had indeed netted one from a small flock coming in to land. The rest hit the ground with less of a bump than I expected from such clumsy-looking fowl and vanished down burrows. I laughed. 'That's what made those noises.'

'Gren studied the hunter's lair. 'What are we going to do about him?'

'We cross there and we leave him alone,' said Ryshad firmly, pointing at the stepping-stones.

'Do we?' 'Gren demanded of me and his brother.

'We've no need to kill him unless he comes after us,' I told Sorgrad.

He shrugged. 'Fair enough.'

That was enough to send 'Gren heading for the stepping-stones. They were slick with slimy green growth and Shiv hurried past me. 'Wait a moment, 'Gren.'

The weed began to steam, drying from shining emerald to a muted green that crisped into a dull brown, the unceasing wind carrying the lightest wisps away. Sorgrad watched, intent, while 'Gren looked downstream, still keeping watch on the hunter.

'He'd kill him in a moment, wouldn't he?' There was concern beneath Ryshad's distaste. 'And never give it a second thought.'

'It gives him an edge over the rest of us.' I shrugged. 'That's kept him and me alive more than once. Believe me, I'd rather be with him than without him on a trip like this.'

'I know he's your friend but I wouldn't have him under my command,' said Ryshad slowly.

'I'm not asking you to like him and, anyway, he wouldn't serve under your command,' I pointed out to my well-drilled beloved. 'He's a mercenary, though, and he understands discipline in a fight. Halice wouldn't stand for anything less.'

'Just as long as he realises I won't,' muttered Ryshad as we made our way down to the river and over without incident. As soon as we were across, all 'Gren's attention turned to the way ahead, the bird hunter forgotten, as I'd known he would be.

Hills rose on either side as we followed the road inland. We all stayed alert for any other travellers but as the day lengthened into a long evening, no one came from either direction. I even began to relax until that realisation made me frown.

'Where is everyone?' I turned to Ryshad and Shiv who were bringing up the rear again.

'How many times did we have to hide last time?' Shiv nodded at the tangled bushes lining the route, their vicious thorns currently hidden by flourishes of leaves and the rosettes of pink-tinted blossom.

'Not even goat shit to tread in, is there?' frowned Ryshad.

I realised something else was wrong. 'Weren't there pillars marking this road?'

'What is it?' Sorgrad and 'Gren came back towards us.

'Gren slapped at something buzzing around his face as I explained. 'Cursed midges.'

Shiv looked at a stretch of flatter land where the pass the road was following widened out a little. 'They're coming from over there.' As if he'd given some signal, a cloud of little black bloodsuckers came roving towards us.

'Must be the time of year for them,' I grimaced.

'Hurry up and we'll leave them behind,' urged Ryshad.

Shiv was still studying the peaty stretch beside the road. 'These people are willing to kill to get off these rocks, because there's so little decent land, isn't that right?' He pointed to deep chevrons cut into the bog. 'So why let those ditches clog up? This is usable land, if it's drained.' It didn't look halfway usable land to me but I'd take Shiv's word for it. He'd grown up in the Kevil fens of Caladhria and there aren't many bigger swamps.

'Livak, I found your pillars,' Sorgrad called out.

'And here.' 'Gren was a little way beyond his brother, looking in the gully that edged the road.

We joined them to see dark stones broken and stained with the muck pooled around them.

'What's this?' Sorgrad jumped down for a closer look and ran a finger down deep chisel marks obscuring overlapping lines set in an incised square.

'It was clan insignia of some sort.' Ryshad was studying 'Gren's pillar. 'This one's defaced as well.'

Shiv hissed with frustration. 'Usara might know how to read something from the stone.'

'We brought the wrong wizard.' 'Gren was ready to make a joke of it but no one else was inclined to laugh.

I looked up and down the road whose emptiness was taking on a sinister aspect. 'Let's get on.' I told myself not to be fanciful but kept a hand on my dagger hilt just in case.

'Here.' Ryshad handed me a few long, oily-looking leaves. 'Rub those on yourself. It'll keep off the midges.'

Sorgrad immediately began searching the side of the road until he came up with some smaller, hairier plant. 'These are better.'

I smiled at them both and rubbed Sorgrad's on my wrists and Ryshad's on my neck. The sooner they both got the message I wasn't about to choose between them and no one could make me, the better we'd all get along. More importantly, the midges didn't bother me after that, be it thanks to one plant, the other or both. That was relief because I wouldn't have put it past 'Gren to count my bites and make a score out of them, just to see who'd be more put out, my lover or his brother.

Ryshad and Shiv forced the pace with their longer legs until we shorter ones were half walking, half jogging. No one complained and we made good speed until we reached the jutting rise of stark grey rock that hid our destination.

Sorgrad recognised it too; he only ever needs one look at a map. 'Who's going first?' 'Gren took a pace forward, eyes bright with expectation.

Ryshad looked at me and Shiv and then nodded to Sorgrad. 'Just a quick look and come straight back here.'

'Sit tight, my girl.' Sorgrad winked at me and the pair disappeared around the outcrop.

'I can't hear anything.' Ryshad cocked his head.

I listened. 'Birds, breeze.' But no voices, no sound of tools or the bustle we'd seen here last time.

Shiv rubbed his hands together. 'Shall I—'

Sorgrad's whistle interrupted him and we hurried round the curve in the road, my dagger ready, Ryshad's sword half drawn.

'What in Saedrin's name happened here?' I exclaimed.

'Dast's teeth!' Ryshad's sword hissed all the way out of its sheath.

'I don't think we're going to find any allies hereabouts.' Shiv surveyed the scene in the hollow of the flower-speckled hills.

The road was lined with small houses, a scatter of others on the grass beyond. Even allowing the Elietimm were generally short folk, I'd thought before these people risked bumping their heads on their rafters. Now I realised the floors of the low-roofed houses were actually dug a good half span below the ground outside. I could see that because every roof had been ripped off, walls left defenceless before the harshness of wind and weather. Every house looked to be built to the same pattern; a windowless, stone-paved room at one end, something that looked like a quern stone set in the wall that separated it from a wider room beyond. That had windows and a flagged floor, open hearth backed by an upright slab of stone to foil the draught of doors to the front and to rooms beyond. Earthen floors and tethering rings in those suggested byres or stables, finally more storage ending in a circular arrangement of tumbled stones above a stoke hole. That could have been a corn kiln, a brew house, a laundry vat or some other domestic necessity but no tools or utensils remained to give any clue.

'Look for some clue as to what happened here,' Ryshad ordered. 'Keep someone else in view all the time.'

'Let's not disturb too much,' I added. 'We don't want it too obvious we've been here.'

Ryshad nodded, sword at the ready as he strode down the road, Shiv at his side. Sorgrad cut off to one side, blade in hand. I reckoned me staying with 'Gren would be safest all round.

'Nothing.' He was poking his dagger in a soggy mess of part-burned thatch. 'Whoever did this stripped the place.'

'Not quite.' I looked down into a house some way down the track. The central room was black with soot and charcoal where timbers had been stacked and burned. 'How many trees have you seen big enough to make roof trusses? This is like melting down a stack of coin hereabouts.'

'So someone was making a point.' 'Gren shied a stone at something scurrying through the mire of the deep ditch separating the houses from the road. 'There's nothing here to say what or who, though.'

I looked at the devastated houses. Birds much the size and hue of hooded crows were building nests on the ragged walls, plundering the scattered straw and turf that had once covered the roofs. Their chucks and caws emphasised the empty silence.

'Let's see what the others have found.' We ran down the track to join Ryshad in front of what had been this settlement's central stronghold. He held out his hand to me. 'Think you can get in there again?'

'If you give me a boost.' That was a joke. When we'd come looking for Geris, the wall around this formidable house of stern grey stone had risen well above my head. Now I could step across the blocks marking the foundation.

'Not one course left upon another,' murmured Shiv in a portentous voice.

'Like something out of a bad ballad,' I agreed. But this was no comfortable tale to while away a winter's evening.

'Let's see if there's anyone still in residence.' I took a cautious step up and over the broken wall, dagger in hand. Ryshad began a slow circuit from what had been the guard-house while Shiv headed for the opposite corner. Sorgrad and 'Gren spread out to reconnoitre the far side of the compound.

'Didn't we think this was a forge?' Shiv stopped to look at tumbled stones blackened with fire. There had been a whole range of buildings along the inner face of the wall when we'd sat and spied on the place before.

'And this would be the mill.' I kicked at the last charred heartwood of a tangle of roof timbers.

'Someone had wanted this house razed beyond hope of repair.' Ryshad was walking cautiously through the rubble where the whole front face of the house had been pulled down, side walls and back reduced to broken outlines barely waist high.

'This is where I got in last time, where the window was.'

I stepped through the empty air above the chipped stones. Broken wooden frames and splinters of horn were strewn across a floor hacked and cracked by malicious axes. The stubby remains of the internal walls sheltered sodden drifts of grey ash bleeding black stains across the pale flagstones. I shoved a piece of timber with a boot to reveal a stark white outline where it had lain. 'I'd say no one's been here since this disaster struck.'

'But what was the disaster?' wondered Shiv.

'Or who,' said Ryshad grimly. I could make a guess.

There had been rugs on these floors, carefully woven hangings, polished stone tables. A family had lived here and many more besides within the compound and in the village beyond, making what passed for a decent life on these rocks. Now there was no one, beyond vermin lurking in the drains and the nesting birds rearing their chicks in a quiet corner. Where had the people flown? Or had they been netted like the fat little fowls on the riverbank?

Ryshad's thoughts were following the same scent. 'I can't find any bodies, nor yet any bones,' he said as he joined me.

'Is that good or bad?' Shiv was unsure and I had no answers.

Ryshad looked up. 'Where's Sorgrad? Or 'Gren, come to that.' He looked annoyed.

'You just said keep someone in view,' I reminded him. 'I'll bet they can see each other.' I used my fingers for the whistle the three of us had used for more years than I cared to recall.

Blond heads appeared above a ridge behind the derelict stronghold and Sorgrad beckoned to us. 'Come see.'

'What were you looking for up here?' To my relief Ryshad kept his tone mild.

'Goat shit,' 'Gren answered brightly. 'Catch a goat, it squeals, brings someone running. We want answers—'

I waved him to silence.

'What do you make of this?' Sorgrad invited as we scrambled to the top of the rise.

We hadn't come this way on our previous circumspect

visit so we hadn't seen the stone circle the brothers had found. That was a shame because it must have been quite a sight before the sarsens had been toppled.

'Wrecking this wasn't a quick or easy job,' said Ryshad.

I didn't need a mason's skills to tell me that. Each stone must have been twice my height, massive blue-grey rocks roughly shaped and raised with some trick I couldn't begin to guess at. The colossal fingers of stone had been the inner-most circle within numinous rings of ditch and banked mound. Once we left the rise behind us, this was the highest point on a wide expanse of tussocky grass running away into mossy hollows and a few scrubby thickets. I couldn't see anything else before the plain blurred into the muted colours of distant hills.

'What was this place for?' 'Gren had a foot up on one of the prone megaliths like a hunter celebrating his kill. Splin-tered scraps of timber and a snapped-off length of braided hide rope were discarded close by. Perhaps that's how the wreckers had brought the giants down.

'We found one before. That was a grave circle.' Ryshad wrinkled his nose with unconscious distaste.

Sorgren squatted and casually pulled a finger bone from spoil dug from the pit where a stone had stood. 'Sheltya lore links the bones of a people to their land and I don't suppose these Alyatimm are any different.' He used the ancient Mountain name for the exiles. 'You lowlanders are all for burning your dead but taking bones, breaking them, that's a desecration in the Mountains, an act of war to the death.'

Ryshad nodded. 'Break a rival's house to rubble and dig up his ancestors, no one's going to gainsay your victory.'

'If this is what passes for a shrine hereabouts, wouldn't it be a pretty effective way of scuppering your enemy's magic?' I couldn't see anyone having a lot of confidence in the leader of the brown-liveried men now, even assuming he wasn't already dead.

Sorgrad was scowling. 'We're not going to find an ally here.'

I'd been thinking the same thing. Still, I reminded myself

firmly, we had Shiv and that meant magic to call on, as long as he could summon it without getting himself attacked. No matter, we'd got out of here without magic last time, thanks to Ryshad's fortitude. Come to that, I'd been in tight corners when I'd worked some risky deceptions with Sorgrad and 'Gren. This was no different. We had our plan, we'd do what we'd come for and then we'd leave. Why did we need anyone else?

'No chance of supper,' grumbled 'Gren.

'Or a bolthole.' Ryshad's face was grim.

'Someone's still coming here.' Shiv was skirting around the edge of the circle, stopping here and there to poke a stick into the ditch that divided the sacred enclosure from the profane land around it. He pointed at a square stone set to one side within the circle.

'Gren, keep an eye out.' I followed Ryshad for a closer look and the brothers came too.

The stone was about the height of a table made to feed a farmhouse and maybe half as long again. The top was scored with interlaced circles and some had narrow hollows at their centre, steep sided and filled with rain. Judging by the grass growing thick all around, it had been left undisturbed by the wreckers.

I poked a long grass stem into one. 'A handspan deep.'

'Gren blew at a crude mimicry of a boat fashioned from a scrap of wood and a dry furled leaf. It bobbed on the dark water. 'What's this?'

Sorgrad used his dagger to probe and fished a bedraggled lump of cloth out of another cup-shaped hollow. 'Solurans are great ones for votive offerings at their holy places.'

'A prayer to keep a ship safe at sea would make sense here-abouts.' Ryshad tapped the little boat with a finger. 'It's not been there long.'

Sorgrad squeezed water from the sodden lump. 'Token for a baby maybe, wanting one or to keep a newborn healthy?' Cords tied the coarse cloth into an unmistakable swaddled shape.

Ryshad stepped away to study the nearest toppled stone. 'When would you say this was done?' He appealed to Shiv who was completing his circuit of the ditch.

The mage paused. 'Well before last winter.'

'Someone still comes here.' Sorgrad dropped the baby poppet back in its hollow.

'Loyalty's harder to kill than people,' I agreed.

Ryshad looked at us all. 'Whoever might be coming could well have some answers.'

'And no reason to love Ilkehan, if he did do this.' I looked around at the devastation.

'Let's set a snare.' Ryshad gestured. 'We hide in the ditch, well spaced out, until whoever comes to make an offering is well inside.'

'What if nobody comes? It could be days,' 'Gren challenged. 'How long do we wait?'

'Give it till dark?' suggested Ryshad equably. 'It'll be safer for us to travel by night in any case.'

'Where to?' 'Gren countered. 'And night's a long time coming, pal, this far north, this far into the year.'

'Shut up, 'Gren.' Sorgrad looked at Shiv. 'If we catch someone, we don't want him yelling for help and bringing trouble. What can you do about that?'

Shiv ran long fingers through his hair, face thoughtful. 'I don't want to work magic within the circle, that's for certain but I can wrap silence around the outside.'

Sorgrad nodded. 'You don't want spells inside the stones. Two people finding they can't hear each other talking will soon start wondering why.'

'It's not that.' Shiv shook his head. 'Last time we were here, there was some aetheric ward that went off like a temple bell when I'd barely summoned magic.'

'I can sing a charm to hide us.' I dug a folded parchment out of my belt pouch. While Pered had been adding every last detail to Shiv's map, I'd been copying out seemingly nonsensical words culled from Forest Folk ballads whose verses sang of enchantment. Guinalle had insisted and, in the circumstances, I hadn't been inclined to argue. Besides, I was the one who'd been proved right when I'd insisted aetheric lore lay hidden in the lays sung in blithe ignorance by minstrels like my father. That surely entitled me to use the Artifice of my ancestors.

Sorgrad flicked the parchment with a mocking finger. 'Think it'll work?'

I stuck my tongue out at him. 'Better than your magic, prentice wizard.'

'Let's get settled.' Ryshad gestured to Shiv. 'You and me opposite each other?'

'I'm thirsty,' 'Gren said abruptly. 'Where's the nearest water fit to drink?'

'Where's your waterskin?' Ryshad let slip exasperation.

'Empty.' 'Gren waved it provocatively.

'Fill it from the ditch,' Shiv said curtly. 'I can make sure it won't poison you.'

'Gren was about to object and I didn't blame him when movement in the distance caught my eye. 'Something's up over yonder.'

That settled that squabble as we all ducked into the ditch. I looked out cautiously, my head barely over the lip. 'That's smoke.'

Grey smudges rose listlessly to lose themselves against the leaden sky. The wind carried incautious shouts to us and I began to make out figures among the lumps and bumps of the uneven ground.

'Someone's setting fires.' Ryshad raised himself cautiously up on his hands for a clearer view. The smoke was marking out a distinct line by now, slewing across the grassland.

'I don't think they're coming this way.' I began to sing the hiding song under my breath nevertheless.

'What are they doing?' Sorgrad wondered, frustrated at not being able to see.

We all watched as the men slowly came closer and I picked out some with nets, spreading out ahead of those carrying slowly smouldering torches. 'They're smoking something out.'

The dense tussocks burned sluggishly with plenty of smoke but precious little flame. With the mossy dampness of our ditch, we were safe from any blaze with ambitions to better itself but being smoked like a Caladhrian ham became a distinct possibility. The shifting wind carried rank fumes to sting our eyes and throats.

'Someone's coming.' Ryshad flattened himself.

I concentrated on the hiding charm as I watched a single figure falling behind the fire setters who were veering off towards a low saddle in the distant hills. Something long-tailed and russet-furred sprang up almost beneath the man's boots but he paid no heed as it jinked and bounced away, all his attention on escaping notice as he headed for the fallen stones.

''Gren, Shiv, round the back. Sorgrad, you take that side.' Ryshad gave his orders and no one disputed them. We spread out around the ditch, me between Sorgrad and Ryshad, which suited me very well. As I crouched and waited, all the while trying to keep the charm running under my breath, I considered swapping my dagger for a handful of throwing darts. There was a small vial of poison in the same belt pouch, thick paste in a sturdy jar sealed with wax and lead and sewn around with leather. I settled for untying the pouch so the darts were ready to hand if I needed them. I left the poison untouched. We wanted this man fit to give us answers and he'd be hard put to talk if he was frothing at the mouth. Besides, I wanted that venom for whatever blade was going to cut Ilkehan's malice short. If the opportunity arose I'd happily see him disgraced if that's what Guinalle advised, but mostly I wanted him dead. Dead, with the least chance possible he'd see his fate coming or have any chance to ward it off. Ryshad could call it justice if he wanted to and perhaps Raeponin would agree. I'd settle for vengeance, quicker and more straightforward.

'Let him get right inside the circle.' Ryshad was braced and ready in the bottom of the ditch. I huddled down as small as I could, all my concentration focused on the incantation.

The Ice Islander didn't even glance in my direction. All his thoughts were on the pitted stone and fulfilling whatever errand had brought him here. He was stocky beneath his crude shirt and a tunic that was little more than a length of folded cloth sewn roughly up both sides. As blond as Sorgrad and 'Gren, his hair was coarser, more dry grass than finished flax. A smouldering torch hung slackly in one hand and I hoped the idiot wouldn't set light to the old yellowed grass all around.

'Now,' Ryshad shouted in the same breath as Sorgrad's whistle and we all sprang up to encircle our prey.

'Run and we'll kill you.' 'Gren took a step forward to level his viciously sharp smallsword at the man's eyes.

'Shout and no one will hear you.' Sorgrad held his own sword point down, voice more soothing than his brother's.

Our captive seemed to understand them well enough, for all the generations separating their bloodlines. Eresken's antics in the uplands had shown us the Mountain and Elietimm tongues had stayed mutually comprehensible.

Shiv and Ryshad were standing silent but needed no language to promise the man a fight if he tried anything. He looked warily at them before giving me a hard look. I held his gaze with all the threat I could muster.

The man's shoulders sagged but it was only a feint. He wheeled round towards me, swirling his firebrand to raise sudden flames from the smouldering pitch and jabbed the thing full at my face.

I ducked to one side, bringing my dagger up to slice down his forearm. Ryshad and Sorgrad were almost on him from behind, so I just sought a wound deep enough to give him pause. It was his bad luck he was still trying to take my head off with the torch. He brought it down as my blade went up and the steel went straight through his wrist. I felt it grate between the small bones and hold fast. Recoiling, he pulled the dagger's hilt out of my hand and the burning brand spun out of his nerveless fingers. I had my arm up to block it but it hit me hard all the same.

'Livak!' Ryshad looked up, horrified as he and Sorgrad pinned the man to the ground.

'It's all right.' I rubbed a painful bruise but I'd settle for that over being scarred for life. The molten pitch was cold and solid before it hit me. 'Thanks, Shiv.'

'My pleasure.' The mage grinned and kicked the torch into the ditch where it landed with a heavy clunk.

'So much for not using magic inside the circle,' observed Sorgrad lightly. 'What were you saying about aetheric wards?'

As Shiv looked first chagrined and then puzzled, 'Gren grabbed the Elietimm's collar. 'Let's get our prize out of sight.'

The three of them dragged him backwards, his heels scoring lines on the turf as he struggled vainly to dig in his feet. Shiv and I followed as they held him against the pitted stone. Ryshad pulled his shoulders back just enough to curve his spine uncomfortably against the unyielding stone. 'Gren had the arm with the dagger still in it; heedless of the blood running down to lace his fingers.

Sorgrad stood in front of the man, Shiv on one side, me on the other.

'I believe your life would be forfeit for coming here, still more so for leaving tokens.' Sorgrad spoke in conversational tones as he searched the man's pockets to find an embroidered ribbon tied in an elaborate bow. 'More lives than your own, I wouldn't wonder.'

The man's eyes darted frantically between us, desperate for some hint of hope. Shiv conveyed a convincing threat, black brows slightly furrowed. Our prisoner wasn't to know he had no clue what Sorgrad was saying. I at least knew enough to follow most simple conversations but Ryshad would be as hampered as Shiv by lack of the Mountain tongue.

'Let's get on with it,' 'Gren said with happy malice. 'Before his pals come looking for him.'

'Do you want me to try a truth charm?' I asked Sorgrad in the fast colloquial Tormalin we all used in Ensaimin.

'Not for the moment.' Sorgrad switched back to the Mountain tongue. 'You're fortunate we're no friends to Ilkehan.'

The prisoner stiffened at that name.

'Tell us what happened, here and over yonder, ' Sorgrad invited. The man winced as he glanced at the dagger still stuck into his arm, blood soaking his sleeve. He kept his mouth firmly shut.

Sorgrad gave me a nod and I rattled off the liquid syllables of an incantation to leave those speaking falsehood voiceless until they opted for truth. Panic flared in the prisoner's eyes as he saw we had Artifice to call on and I smiled warmly at him. Inside, I was chilled by how easily I'd terrified him. Elietimm Artifice was a more potent weapon than steel for ambitious men like Ilkehan. No wonder the Sheltya kept such resolute watch lest any of their number be seduced by the potential for power within their magic.

'What happened?' Sorgrad asked again.

'Ilkehan attacked last year,' gasped the man bitterly. 'Ashernan paid full price for his folly in trying to challenge Ilkehan. When Evadesekke fell, we were encircled. Rettasekke might have come to our aid but Ashernan had dishonoured the truce. Olret held his own borders against Ilkehan but would not cross them.' Despair pained him worse than his wound. 'His house is burned, his line sundered from past and future. We are no longer his people; we have no hargeard.'

We all did our best to look as if we understood what he was saying. Then puzzlement wrinkled his brow along with his suffering. 'Are you of Rettasekke? None other stands against Ilkehan. Or does some eastern sekke still hold out?'

Sorgrad nodded at 'Gren. 'We're Anyatimm. Our companions are of Tren Ar'Dryen.'

The ancient name for the Mountain Men who'd driven out the Elietimm forefathers meant no more to this man than the archaic name for the lands to the west of the ocean. Despair quenched the fleeting glimmer of hope that had chased across his square features. 'Then all you bring is war upon us and death on yourselves.'

Sorgrad considered this. 'We should not challenge this Ilkehan?'

'He is a monster.' Hatred thickened the man's accent. 'He raises armies that none can withstand and backs them with the strongest magic in these islands. When he took Evadesekke, he bridged the very bogs around the citadel with the bodies of his own dead. He will make truce upon a sacred islet and defile it that selfsame day. He has no honour yet he turns a kindly face to those who acquiesce when he declares himself their overlord. Many submit rather than face his wrath.' Now our captive's face twisted with the anguish of uncertainty. 'He claims the Mother's favour, that her blessing dwells in his hargeard. He swears he is the sword of the Maker, forged in the fires of these testing times. Many believe it; how could they not?'

He was genuinely asking a question but Sorgrad stayed silent, face as bland as I'd ever seen him waiting for an opponent to betray the runes held close in his hand. Our prisoner shook his head fervently. 'The mountains speak with tongues of flame and destroy Ilkehan's foes in floods of ice and fire. Those uncertain starve, no choice but to fall to their knees before him, if they would not perish. He will be overlord, whether all will it or none. If you are no friend to Ilkehan, you are his enemy. He will not have it otherwise.'

Our captive fell silent.

'So Ilkehan killed Ashernan and now holds his land?' Sorgrad smiled his understanding. 'If you accept his rule, you go on much as you did before.'

I explained as much to Ryshad and Shiv who were both visibly frustrated by now.

'So you're not about to cross him. You're already thinking you've said too much.' The prisoner stayed motionless, watching Sorgrad warily.

'I'll get him to talk some more,' 'Gren offered obligingly. He made to twist my dagger in the man's wound.

'No.' Ryshad glared at him.

'Gren shrugged and pulled the blade out in one swift movement. Our captive gasped; suddenly weak at the knees and
blood ran free from the oozing wound. 'Gren reversed his
grip and cut the man's throat in a single backhanded stroke.
He was dead before his life's blood choked his final breath.

'Shit!' Ryshad let go and the corpse fell forward on to the
dry grass.

'Gren crouched down, stabbing my dagger into the turf
to clean it. 'That wants sharpening, my girl.' He handed it
back, disapproving.

'What did you do that for?' Shiv was shocked, Ryshad
scowling blackly.

'Gren looked puzzled. 'He'd said all he was going to.'

Sorgrad had taken a prudent step aside to avoid the spray
of blood. 'You heard him; he was Ilkehan's man, willingly or
not. We couldn't risk him trying to garner some favour by
betraying us.'

Shiv couldn't argue with that, though his face suggested
he'd like to.

I looked at Ryshad with silent appeal. 'Even if he kept his
mouth shut for the sake of his own skin, that wound would
set people asking questions in a place like this. Then Ilkehan's
adepts could pull the answers out of his head whether or not
he wanted to give us up.'

'True enough.' Ryshad was still looking thunderous. 'It's
still a coward's trick to cut a man's throat when he's not
expecting it.'

'It's easier than when he does,' said 'Gren irrepressibly.

'Shut up.' I didn't like being in the middle of this argument any better than I liked the fallen stones encircling us.
'It might have been better not to kill him here, if this is some
kind of shrine.'

'It's done, so we move on,' announced Sorgrad. 'We came
looking for an ally but this Ashernan is deader than last year's
mutton. If this Olret's still holding out against Ilkehan, I say
we find him.' He turned to Shiv. 'Where?'

The mage slowly got out his map. 'If we're here, that's the island with Ilkehan's stronghold. He pointed to a long, wide island with a broken chain of mountains running through it. A river cut deep into a central plain.

'Kehannasekke.' Sorgrad nodded impatient understanding. 'So where's this Olret?'

'Rettasekke?' I pointed a tentative finger.

'Gren looked dubiously at the islands scattered across the substantial patch of sea between us and the possibility of an ally. 'How do we get there?'

'You say there are fords and causeways over the sands and shallows?' Sorgrad raised his brows at me. 'Travel by night and take it slow and careful.'

Ryshad laughed with precious little humour. 'I take it you pair are as handy with boats as Livak?'

'There's not much call for them in the uplands, pal.' There was an edge to 'Gren's voice.

Ryshad smiled at him. 'I grew up on the ocean side of Zyoutessela and Shiv's a Kevilman. We steal a boat.'

'It'll be easier to steer clear of other people if we're on the water.' I looked appealingly at Sorgrad. 'And it'll be faster.'

'Fair enough.' The notion plainly appealed as little to Sorgrad as it did to me.

Ryshad was looking at the corpse with barely concealed displeasure. 'We can't leave this to start a hue and cry after us.'

'We've nothing for a pyre and anyway smoke'll bring people looking for the fire.' I wondered what to do. If Saedrin was marking down my share in this unfortunate's death against the day when I had to explain myself to him, disrespecting the corpse wouldn't win me any favours.

'His shade won't thank you for burning his bones, you ignorant lowlander,' Sorgrad rebuked me. 'They should lie where his beliefs held despite all his terror of Ilkehan.' At his nod, 'Gren helped him carry the body to one of the pits beside a fallen sarsen.

'Let me.' Shiv spread his hands and the earth, hard packed by a full year and more of rain and sun, crumbled into fresh-turned tilth, flowing up and over the tumbled corpse. It jerked and twitched with a nauseating parody of life as the soil shifted beneath it and soon disappeared from view.

Sorgrad muttered something sounding vaguely liturgical in Mountain speech too archaic for me to understand.

Untroubled, 'Gren gazed down into the pit. 'The Maker can hold his bones until the Mother takes back his spirit.' He used the same terms as the Elietimm had.

'Misaen and Maewelin?' I guessed. Those two gods had been sufficient for the ancient Mountain Men and even these days, the uplands paid scant respect to the rest of the pantheon.

Shiv drew a deep breath and continued to concentrate on the pit. The soil sank down, smoothing itself to the sides of the hole, soon as compact as if it had never been disturbed.

'Nicely done, Shiv,' Ryshad approved from the far side of this new grave. 'Now let's go and steal a boat.'

Suthyfer, Sentry Island,
3rd of For-Summer

Halice came striding across the beach, the early sun throwing a long shadow behind her. 'You're not scrying, are you?' She looked into the pool left shining among the scoured slabs of rock by the retreating sea.

'No,' Usara assured her. He dusted sand off his hands. 'Though Guinalle thinks working with a natural pool would make it harder for the Elietimm enchanters to find me.'

Halice looked uncertain. 'I thought you needed antique silver bowls and priceless inks.'

'Hedge wizards and charlatans can't work without them,' Usara told her with some amusement. 'And granted, ink or oil makes it easier but I can scry in anything.'

Halice looked at Guinalle who was swathed in a soft grey cloak against the dawn chill. 'Have you any Artifice to show you how they're getting on?'

'I think it best to let well alone,' Guinalle said without emotion. 'Shiv was taking them to a place well outside Ilkehan's domains. If some mischance shows these enchanters my interest there, that could just give him reason to go looking.'

'It's not worth the risk,' said Usara firmly. 'For anyone.'

'You didn't feel any hint of that Ilkehan noticing them arriving?' Halice looked out at the placid ocean barely troubled by so much as a rippling wave, gilded by the sun huge and orange on the horizon. The tide had washed away most of the evidence of the slaughters.

'Not a suspicion.' Guinalle looked north and east to the unseen Ice Islands as well.

'His kind suspect everyone and everything, every waking

moment,' Halice said sourly. 'That's how they avoid knives in the back.'

'They've got Shiv,' Usara pointed out. 'He can bespeak wizards from here to Hadrumal if they fall foul of Ilkehan's malice.'

'Which could leave him no better than a drooling idiot.' Halice put her hands on her hips.

'Not if he's careful, and he will be,' insisted Usara. 'And now we've worked together, it need only be me, Larissa and Allin bringing them back. We don't even need Shiv in the nexus.'

'Ilkehan won't be able to touch mages at this distance, not with Artifice warding them,' Guinalle added.

'As long as he doesn't somehow rope in those adepts of his to help.' Halice scowled at the central islands of Suthyfer secretive across the dark blue waters.

'The best way we can keep Ilkehan from realising he has enemies close at hand is to keep his attention turned to his people's fight here.' Usara nodded at Guinalle. 'We've been discussing how best to do that. Do you fancy working a little magic, Halice?'

'Me?' The mercenary was startled.

'You can hold a tune can't you?' Usara asked innocently. 'Sing a marching pace or a rope song along with a ship's crew?'

Guinalle had a book in one hand, her fingers pale against the age-darkened patina of ancient leather. Whatever gold leaf had once illuminated the spine was worn to an indecipherable shadow. 'The Artifice in these songs is ancient but none the less effective for that.'

'What are you thinking of doing?' Halice was intrigued, despite herself.

'The pirates have one sailing ship left. It's only a single-masted sloop but it could make a break for the open sea,' the noblewoman replied composedly. 'We're discussing how we might discourage it.'

Halice looked out to sea again. 'The *Eryngo*, *Nenuphar*

and *Asterias* have closed off escape to the south. We've the other three ships keeping watch up here.'

Usara raised his eyebrows 'Wouldn't six ships north and south be better? Maybe nine?'

Halice folded her arms, head on one side. 'How?'

Usara's grin widened. 'Aetheric illusion.'

'I'm certain the jalquezan in the ballad of Garidar and his hundred sheep creates mirror images to baffle an enemy.' Even Guinalle, tired as she was, couldn't restrain a smile.

Halice nodded but frowned an instant later. 'There's no chance these enchanters are making fools of us with some Artifice masquerade? Showing you what you want to see while Muredarch's lads come sneaking up the strait?'

'No chance at all.' Guinalle shook her head. 'That's one advantage aetheric far-seeing has over scrying.'

'You're sure?' Halice plainly wasn't. A new thought occurred to her. 'If you could see through any illusion they wrought, why won't they just see straight through this trick?'

Guinalle looked affronted. 'Because I can ensure that they don't.'

Usara stepped in. 'Halice, please allow we're as competent in our duties as you are in yours.'

'Of course.' A rueful smile lightened the mercenary's severe expression and she bowed with mock solemnity. 'I beg your pardon, both you and your lady mages. So, how will this work?'

Guinalle held the book up. 'We convince one man on every ship that this will defend them and then he can lead the rest in singing it as they work.'

'Then you want the boatswains. They love their ships better than their mistresses.' Halice stretched out her well-muscled arms before easing her broad shoulders with a grimace. 'Very well, we'll have mystical ships as well as wooden ones to blockade these wharf rats. The next thing we need to make is a plan for attacking their hole.'

Usara was watching Guinalle who had paled. 'We need to be ready to act as soon as Ilkehan dies,' he said gently.

'I wish I knew how long it'll take them.' Halice was looking out to sea again. 'The sooner we can attack, the less time Muredarch's mob have to dig themselves in. On the other hand, the more we can drill Temar's haymakers and Sorgrad's dock-sweepings, the more chance we'll have something approaching a corps. Well, that's something I can make a start on. Let me know what your far-seeing shows you.'

Mage and noblewoman watched Halice walk away across the beach, kicking sleeping feet, pulling resentful blankets away from blinking faces aghast once they realised how early it was. 'All of you, boots on. Let's see if you're as good with those weapons as you are with your boasts. As soon as we get the word, I'll want you going through those pirates like scald through a cheap whorehouse!'

Usara smiled before turning serious once more. 'Shall we ask the *Maelstrom*'s master when the best time to contact the other ships might be?'

Guinalle didn't reply and when the mage looked to see why, he saw desolation in her eyes. He held out an impulsive hand but she affected not to see it, hugging the ancient songbook close to her breast like a talisman. Usara looked away, tucking his hands through the braided leather strap he wore buckled around his waist. He hesitated before continuing with studied casualness. 'You said something about finding a way to knock the wits out of those enchanters?'

Guinalle closed her eyes before replying with determined composure. 'The question is, which wits should I harass first?'

Bemusement replaced the faint injury in Usara's eyes. 'I'm sorry?'

Guinalle looked at him, puzzled in her turn. 'What do you mean?'

'You say "which wits"?' Usara spread uncomprehending hands. 'I don't understand.'

'I cannot decide which of the five wits I should try undermining first,' said Guinalle slowly.

'Five wits?' asked Usara with lively curiosity.

'Are you going to repeat everything I say?' Amusement animated Guinalle's weary face.

'Please explain,' Usara invited. 'Talk of five wits means nothing to me.'

'It was the first thing I was taught at the Shrine of Ostrin. The least of adepts would have known it before—' Guinalle bit off her words. 'Very well. There are five wits that make up the whole mind, as I was taught anyway. Common wit; the everyday intelligence that we use to live by.' She tucked the songbook under one arm and held up a hand, ringless fingers spread. She tucked her thumb to her palm before continuing. 'Imagination; weaving ideas of the practical kind. Fantasy; giving free rein to unbounded notions. Estimation; the sense to make a judgement. Memory; the faculty for recollection.' Guinalle folded her little finger down and considered the fist she had made before opening her hand as if releasing something. 'Artifice is the working of stronger and more disciplined will upon the wits of another. Surely Aritane told you that? You said you'd been working with her all winter.'

Usara shook his head slowly. 'There's nothing like that in the Sheltya tradition. They liken their true magic to the four winds of the runes; calm, storm, cold dry wind from the north, warm wet wind from the south.' He sighed with frustration. 'We really must find time to sit down and go through your initial instruction. If we're to find any correspondences between aetheric and elemental magic—'

'I fear that will have to wait.' Guinalle gestured towards the pirates' cabin. Temar was heading in their direction, picking his way between men hastily cooking scavenged breakfasts.

'Usara, Allin needs your help.' He waved a hand back towards the rough-hewn hut.

'Is there word from Shiv?' Usara was instantly alert.

'No, no,' Temar reassured him. 'Allin's thinking of ways to make the pirates' lives that bit harder. She was wondering if the pair of you couldn't combine her fire affinity and your power over the earth to dry up the wells and springs around their encampment.'

Usara rubbed a hand across his beard. 'That's an interesting notion.'

'See if you can do it,' Guinalle suggested.

'It can wait until after breakfast.' The mage looked at her. 'You could do with something to eat.'

'In a moment.' She didn't meet his eye, turning instead to the sea. 'Halice wanted me to work a far-seeing to the southern ships. Temar can spare a moment to help. It'll put my mind at ease as well.'

Usara looked as if he'd like to argue the point but settled for giving Temar a warning look. 'Don't take too long about it.'

Temar watched him go. 'What was that all about?'

'Nothing.' Guinalle coloured and held out a hand to Temar. 'Help me?'

Something in her voice made Temar uneasy. He scanned the encampment. 'I see Pered over there. Let's get you some breakfast first and then we can both support you.'

'Halice will have Pered copying maps all day.' Guinalle reached for Temar's hand. 'We can do this between us. We've done it before.'

'When we were surveying upriver for Den Fellaemion?' A laugh of recollection surprised Temar. 'I was going to say that feels like an age ago, but then it was, wasn't it?'

'Not to me.' Guinalle tightened her grasp.

Temar gasped. 'I don't think this is wise.'

'Let me be foolish, just for a little while.' Guinalle closed her eyes. 'I want to remember something better than all this strife.'

Memories wrapped Temar in peace and contentment. High on a hillside above an irregular bay, a perfect circle of dry stone devotedly fitted, offered sanctuary from the sternest weather that might storm in from the ocean. On the inland face, away from the prevailing winds, the gate stood open to welcome any seeking knowledge in this distant place. The path to that gate met the lines of rounded tiles covering conduits bringing water from a springhouse some way further up the slope. Within the wall, a neatly worked garden surrounded each modest dwelling, round beneath a conical roof of slate slabs. In the centre, three bigger square buildings with steeply pitched roofs had larger windows to throw light on the adepts within, unshuttered now that winter's squalls were past.

Guinalle's memory bathed the sanctuary in wistful sunlight. She dwelt on the plain house she had shared with two other girls, all of them happy to escape the intricate formalities of noble etiquette and dress. Her mind's eye turned to the library where nascent aptitude for Artifice won her merit, not blood and heritage. Her piercing sorrow for her gentle, long-dead teachers pricked Temar's eyes.

'I was so happy there,' she said softly.

'You'd never recognise Bremilayne now,' he began bracingly. 'When I was there last year—'

'I don't want to know.' Guinalle's grip was painful. 'Don't you wish it could all be as it was?'

A rush of recollection assailed Temar. A hammer-beamed hall decked with green boughs, a massive fire roaring in the hearth, silks, jewel bright in candle- and firelight, as dancing gowns swished across the rush-strewn floor, matrons as deft as their slender nieces and daughters. Their partners were just as gaudy, gold and silver buttons bright on doublets and gowns woven with shimmering brocade. Double doors opened into a broad room of tables set with every delicacy and temptation that a noble House could command. Laughter echoed silently in Temar's head, floating above a merry mix of celebration and flirtation laced with pious thanks to Poldrion for another year safely past.

'Festival's nothing like how you remember it either.' Temar tried to turn to his own recollections to the summer Solstice he'd passed in Toremal. It was a futile effort. Guinalle held stubbornly to her memory and she was far more adept at this than he. Temar gritted his teeth and summoned the thrill and exhilaration of the vivid, sunlit city of Toremal. He recalled his astonishment at the sprawling districts that dwarfed and surrounded the old walled town they had known, at the elegant Houses Sieurs new and old had built to ring the city with all the artistry gold could buy. 'The world's moved on, Guinalle. You should come and see for yourself.'

'See what?' Behind the mask of Guinalle's relentless self-control, Temar felt grief for her family so long dead, rage at the House that had so long forgotten and then disowned her.

'There's no use pining for what's lost.' Temar did his best to quell his unease, trying instead to let Guinalle see how his own sorrow and rage had run their course. 'We have to look forward, not back. Tormalin rebuilt itself from the ruins of the Chaos; we're doing the same for Kellarin.' If the people of Kellarin no longer had any place in this new Tormalin, by all his hope of Saedrin's mercy, Temar would build them a new home, raise a new power across the ocean.

'Is that what we have to look forward to?' Guinalle's low voice was strained. 'Some mockery of the colony we planned, built on the charity of these Sieurs who rule this changed new world of yours? Oh, I've tried, Temar, I've really tried. I spend my days curing bellyaches and dressing blisters while people bring me petty squabbles over patches of dirt or smelly animals. Is this to be my life? I was a princess. Tor Priminale was a name to claim precedence in any gathering, honoured for husbanding vast lands and tenantry numbering thousands.'

'Which you turned your back on, as I recall.' Temar kept his tone light with some effort. He didn't want to provoke her to outright hysteria but, curse her, Guinalle wasn't going to get away with this nonsense.

'I set my rank aside to study the arts of enchantment. Acolyte of Larasion, Adept of Ostrin: that means nothing now,' Guinalle answered, stricken. 'I cannot even reclaim my own Name, I'm just handed over to a House all but dead before we even sailed.'

'Thanks to the Crusted Pox,' said Temar coldly. 'That

plague and my grandsire taught me a hard lesson very young, Guinalle. I could weep and howl all day and all night but my father wouldn't hear me in the Otherworld. No brothers or sisters could repass Saedrin's threshold to comfort me. All I could do was strive with the life that was granted me, to honour their memory.'

'It's just that I miss them all so; Vahil, Elsire, the Sieur Den Rannion, his maîtresse, all those others cut down in their blood.' Guinalle's brittle belligerence crumbled and a single tear spilled from her brown eyes, dark pools of misery. 'My uncle, Den Fellaemion, a byword for boldness and success. He had such hopes, such plans, but he always told me, if it all fell to pieces, we could just go home. Now where do we go? Where do we belong?' She choked on a bitter laugh. 'You say so much has changed. Not everything. We flee black-hearted invaders and I hide everyone who escapes beneath enchantment, since it can't be more than a season before help arrives. But we wake to find I've condemned us all to a life where everyone we ever knew and loved is dead, but these same foul marauders are still trying to kill us! Then I learn that my enchantment threw the balance of the Aether into such disarray that adepts clear across the Empire were cast into confusion. With that last prop shattered, chaos destroyed our world, Temar, and it was all my doing!'

'It's not your fault.' Temar chose his words with exquisite care. 'I know how difficult this is, Guinalle. I've thought just the same in the silence of the night, and wept for lack of answers and simple misery. Anyway, Nemith did more to bring down the Empire than you ever could. You know what he was like.' He faltered. 'But we are alive and where there's life, there must be hope and however much the world has changed around us, we can still look for warmth and succour to heal our hurts.'

'Can we?' Guinalle took both Temar's hands and held them tight.

Vivid as a dream on waking, he remembered his desire the first time he'd seen her, his nervous awareness that she wasn't some easy conquest like those many who roused his passing lust in his carefree youth. Memory sped through his painstaking courtship to linger on his astonished delight when she'd first accepted his kiss, permitted his decorous embraces and soon encouraged more. 'Oh, don't, Guinalle.' He tried to curb his embarrassment but felt a blush burning his cheeks.

'Couldn't we offer each other a little solace?' she asked defiantly.

'You're a fine one to talk about the ethics of Artifice, if this is how you're going to behave!' Temar said crossly.

'You wanted to share everything with me.' Guinalle rebuked him with a memory of uncovering her nakedness in a secluded glade. 'You wanted to marry me.'

'You declined that honour, Demoiselle,' Temar retorted, stung. But that wound was not as tender as it had been, he realised with some surprise. 'Anyway, you were right; we were never meant to be more than friends.' The sour taint of Guinalle's unguarded jealousy surprised him. 'What's Allin ever done to you?'

'Oh, no more than any other mage. Just dismissed my Artifice as quaint enchantment from a forgotten age, good for healing but no challenge to their crude and gaudy magic.' With the Artifice linking them, Guinalle's sarcasm could not hide her hurt.

Temar found he wasn't inclined to sympathy. 'You're exaggerating and you know it. Usara's all but split his skull trying to work out where aetheric magic and wizardry might meet. He has nothing but respect for your lore. Saedrin's stones, Guinalle, Artifice can leave a wizard mindless! Isn't that enough superiority for you?' Temar fought a desire to take the demoiselle by the shoulders and give her a good shake.

'Once Usara's worked out how to defend himself against such things, how much more interest will he have in me then?'

Temar saw she was mired in confusion over her feelings for the mage.

'Don't you dare pity me!' she gasped, dropping his hands at once.

'We can't go back, not any of us, Guinalle.' Temar rubbed at bruises left by her fingertips. 'I'm not doing this with you, not now, not ever again.' He swallowed hard and glanced involuntarily across the beach. Mercenaries, yeomen and sailors were all going unconcerned about their business while he was knee deep in anguished emotion. 'Let's concentrate on the matter in hand, shall we? Debates over present, past or future will be entirely pointless if we're dead at the hands of these pirates or their Elietimm friends.'

For a tense moment, he wondered if Guinalle was going to weep, storm off, or slap him in the face. Instead she girded her customary self-possession tight once more and held out her hand. 'Halice will want to know what far-seeing has shown us.'

Temar seriously considered not taking it. Then he recalled what fits of pique had cost him in the past. Abandoning his aetheric studies to pay Guinalle back for her rejection of his youthful love, for instance. If he hadn't done that he could work this far-seeing himself. If he were to truly lead these people as their Sieur, he had to know what their enemy was doing. Temar set his jaw, took Guinalle's hand and tried to summon up every defence she'd taught him in case her feelings got the better of her again.

But Guinalle had turned her back on her own inner turmoil. Her seeking mind rose high above the islands of Suthyfer, intent on the echoes of hopes and desires whispering through the unseen aether. Her stern purpose brought them to the *Nenuphar*, captain and crew keeping alert watch. Guinalle wove their myriad thoughts into a vision of the empty sea between the headlands that marked the strait between the islands, bright sunlight dancing on the water. Temar saw the *Eryngo* reassuringly massive in the water, bright red paint weathered to a satin coral hue. Pennants at every masthead declared the ship's determination to bar the way to any pirate. The *Asterias* cut broad circles in the sea a little way off, foam scoring the rippling surface as the lesser ship made sure no pirate lurked in the hidden corners of the coast. Her master stood by the foremast, feet solid, watchful and at one with his ship and men.

'This looks well enough,' Temar said with relief.

'Let's see what else they're up to.' Guinalle sounded as if her adamant discipline had never so much as splintered, let alone cracked to reveal her vulnerability.

Temar silently thanked Ostrin for his long-dead adepts and the way they had trained her and then winced as the poisonous discord around the pirates' camp rang like a tocsin in his head. 'Can you find Naldeth?' Allin was sure to ask him.

'I daren't go so close.' Guinalle held herself aloof, the gravel strand a distant vision. 'There's precious little subtlety to their Artifice but even they'd feel me coming any nearer. I daren't lead them to him.'

'That's their sloop being rigged and readied.' Temar closed his eyes the better to study the picture painting itself inside his mind. 'They're up to something.'

'He's not sure what he's dealing with as yet.' Guinalle watched dispassionate as Muredarch walked to the water's edge. 'He can't make a plan until he does.'

'We're not dealing with a fool.' Temar didn't need Artifice to tell him that.

'They're coming north.' As Guinalle spoke, Muredarch stepped into a battered longboat with pale new wood hastily patching its wounds. The oarsmen pushed off for the deeper water of the channel. 'His enchanters have told him we're here.'

'What are they doing?' frowned Temar.

'Waiting for instruction.' Satisfaction coloured Guinalle's thoughts. 'It seems Ilkehan doesn't encourage initiative.'

Temar watched the pirates coaxing the sloop against the discouraging wind Larissa was carefully spinning from the breeze of the open ocean.

'He's going to offer a parley.' Guinalle dropped Temar's hand.

He opened his eyes. 'We'd better tell Halice.'

The corps commander's reaction was immediate and uncompromising. 'Vaspret! Signal the *Dulse*. We want her underway as soon as maybe. Ros! Get your troop together and ready for anything. This Muredarch wants to talk.'

'I'm coming too.' Temar caught Halice's sleeve.

She looked at him, considering. 'All right. Darni! You're in command here. I can't see how they could try anything but that doesn't mean they won't.'

The mercenaries sprang into action leaving Temar and Guinalle looking apprehensively at each other.

Usara and Allin came out of the cabin.

'What's all the commotion?' the mage-girl asked, concerned.

'Muredarch's sailing to parley with us,' Guinalle replied, voice steady.

Usara was watching her closely. 'Do you suspect some deceit?'

Guinalle's brow creased. 'I don't believe so.'

'I would welcome your presence.' Temar looked from Allin to Usara. 'Both of you. Just in case.'

'You'll need me.' Larissa had come, unnoticed, to stand a few paces off.

Temar was uncertain. 'Darni won't like it.'

'Darni's not my keeper,' snapped Larissa.

'No, I mean that will leave him without a mage, should he need one, should we need to send him some message.'

'Any mage can bespeak Darni,' Larissa said quickly. 'He's an affinity, for all it's too weak to be any use.'

That left Temar on the wrong foot. Before he could think what to say, Allin spoke.

'It's all right. I'll stay.'

Temar found either prospect bothered him; taking Allin into possible danger or leaving her here where some unforeseen trouble might come down on her.

'It's better you take Larissa,' Allin continued. 'Her element's the air, after all.'

'Very well,' he agreed reluctantly.

'Come on!' Halice was waiting by a longboat on the water-line. 'We want to be waiting to meet the bastard. He needs to know we're wise to his every move.'

Temar hurried down the beach, flanked by Usara and Larissa. He managed not to look back for Allin until he was on board the *Dulse*. Then he found her close by Darni's reassuring bulk.

'He'll keep her safe.' Usara stood by him at the ship's rail.

'And she him, no doubt.' Temar turned to look at the afterdeck where Larissa stood by the helmsman, ill-concealed triumph on her face as she raised her arms and summoned skeins of sapphire power to swell the sails. 'Just what is she trying to prove, 'Sar?'

'I'm not really sure.' The mage paused. 'I don't think she is either.'

Whatever drove Larissa, Temar had to acknowledge her skills as her wizardry drove the *Dulse* through the water so fast that foam surged beneath her prow. By the time the labouring pirates had coaxed their sluggish ship all the way up the strait, the *Dulse* had been waiting long enough for Halice to become visibly impatient.

'At last,' she muttered as the lookout hailed the expectant gathering on the aftdeck.

'They look exhausted,' remarked Temar with satisfaction.

Larissa giggled, bright eyed. 'Shall I slacken the breeze a little?'

'Can you encircle them?' Temar asked. 'Make sure they've no chance to make a run for it?'

'Oh yes,' Larissa said confidently.

'Mute your magelight,' Usara said suddenly. 'He knows we have magic but not necessarily who are the mages.' Larissa blushed and did as she was bidden.

'Temar.' Halice nodded to the pirate's snake-crested pennant, which was sliding to halfway down the sloop's single mast. 'Time to play the Sieur for all you're worth.'

Temar took a deep breath as the mercenary ushered him down the steps to the main deck. Usara followed him to the side of the ship as, at Halice's nod, the helmsman skilfully swung the *Dulse* closer to the pirates. Not too close. Not within the reach of a grapnel.

'That's a rich man's plaything,' commented the *Dulse*'s boatswain. He gestured towards the gilded carving all around the sloop's stern, the leaded glass in the cramped single cabin's windows. The aftdeck above it was barely big enough to give the helmsman room to wrestle the whipstaff but it was adorned with two highly polished lamps and a carved dolphin springing along the stern rail. Another one arched beneath the bowsprit.

'I wonder who he killed to get it,' Temar murmured. He took a deep breath to calm his stomach. This was no time to get seasick.

Muredarch stood amidships by the leeboard that could be lowered or raised to adjust the vessel's draught. He gave Temar a lordly wave that set sunlight striking blue fire from the diamonds studding his rings.

'Dressed fit for an audience with Tadriol, isn't he?' Usara leaned on the rail and studied their foe.

'He's certainly prospered since he met those enchanters in Kalaven,' said Temar. 'What is it?' He saw concentration furrowing the wizard's brow, which did nothing to calm his nervousness.

'I'm making the water run counter to Larissa's spell.' Usara kept his attention fixed on the sea. 'Just so they're going nowhere without our permission.'

Guinalle appeared on Temar's other side. 'None of the Elietimm are aboard.'

'That's good to know.' Though Temar hadn't thought they would be.

'Esquire,' Muredarch called. 'I'm offering a parley as you see. May I come aboard?'

'No!' Temar's reply rang out half a breath ahead of a chorus of refusal from the *Dulse*.

'You will address the Sieur D'Alsennin with proper courtesy,' bellowed Halice.

'Messire.' Muredarch bowed from the waist and the sloop's sparse crew did the same. Temar felt sure he was being mocked and anger drove out the qualms in his belly.

'Can you work a truth charm for me?' Temar murmured to Guinalle. 'Just for a little while.' She nodded and stepped a pace back, murmuring an incantation under her breath.

'That's close enough,' warned Halice from the aftcastle as the pirate vessel came almost within reach of the catheads supporting the *Dulse*'s anchor.

'So, Messire D'Alsennin, what can I do for you?' Muredarch stood up, strong legs in black broadcloth and polished boots set wide to balance easily on the swaying boards.

'It's your parley.' Temar rested his hands lightly on the rail. 'It's for you to offer me something, isn't it?'

'I feel I should explain myself first.' Muredarch's words carried easily across the water, a resonant note to his voice. The man could probably make himself heard in a hurricane, Temar thought.

'You doubtless think me merely a pirate.' Muredarch held up a hand though no one on the *Dulse* was disputing this. 'Well, perhaps. In my youth, yes, I strayed among the free traders but that's my point really. Pursuing letters of marque, bounties and the like, that's a young man's game and you can see my grey hairs from there, can't you?' His self-deprecating laugh invited them to join in. Temar stayed stony-faced, Usara unmoved beside him, Guinalle's expression unreadable on his other side. The pirate scanned their countenances, glancing up to Halice high on the aftdeck. His face hardened and Temar looked to see the mercenary commander wasn't bothering to conceal her disdain as she sneered down on the pirate.

'I'm looking for a new role for myself, something more suited to my years and experience,' Muredarch continued conversationally. 'These islands belong to no one and I've a mind to set up here.' He smiled amiably before adding with a first hint of menace, 'You can't show me any writ of yours running here, nor yet Tadriol's.'

Temar ignored that. Halice might not think much of his training with the Imperial cohorts but even he knew better than to pick a fight on hopeless ground. 'What exactly are you hoping to set up?'

Muredarch's smile broadened with growing confidence. 'You'll be hoping to trade across the ocean, when you get this colony of yours on its feet. I could run a nice watering station for you here, offer a place where cargoes could be bought and sold maybe. That would cut everyone's journeys. Surely, that would be worth a share in the coin you'll all be earning? Good anchorage, secure warehousing and the men to make sure everyone keeps honest would look a handsome offer to most merchants I know.'

'I find it a remarkable offer from a pirate who's been preying on our ships,' Temar replied with chilly formality.

'What if I agreed to leave your ships well alone? You don't bother me; I don't bother you. No, wait, I can do more for you than that.' A confiding note warmed Muredarch's voice. 'You'll be a powerful rival to Inglis inside a few years, if you've any sense. They won't like that, now will they? There'll be letters of marque issued against your ships; they'll find some reason to do it. If I were to be sitting here, a few good ships to back me, I could turn hunters into hunted. Curtailing the Inglis trade at your nod, I could improve your markets just when you needed it.'

'I hardly think so,' said Temar coldly.

'You know what they're saying around Inglis, do you? And Kalaven, Blacklith?' Muredarch challenged him, beard jutting. 'That you're an untried boy holding one small corner of a vast land, gold in the rivers for the picking, gems in the sands of the beaches. They're saying land and riches are for the taking, for anyone with the courage to risk the ocean. What are you going to do when ships land up your coast and set up a town for themselves? I could put a stop to all that before it starts and no one will write me off as some weakling.' The threat in his last words was unmistakable.

Temar matched his forcefulness. 'Why should I grant you

anything when you have stolen my colony's goods and made slaves of innocent people?'

'You do have some spirit!' Muredarch laughed. 'You want those people back? They're building my trade town for me just now.' His face turned sly. 'Well, perhaps that's a trade we can discuss. I need rope, sailcloth, pitch for a start.'

'You misunderstand me,' Temar told him coldly. 'You surrender your prisoners and your loot and then I will consider letting you live rather than hanging you for the crows for your crimes.'

'There's spirit and then there's foolhardiness, lad.' Muredarch scowled at Temar. 'Don't think you've got the hand on the whipstaff here. What makes you think you can do anything to stop me?'

'This parley is over.' Temar addressed himself to Halice, striving to equal his long-dead grandsire's autocratic manner.

She nodded and turned to the helmsman.

'You're young and you're foolish, boy,' Muredarch shouted angrily. 'Shame you won't live to learn the error of your ways.' As quick as the snake on his pennant, he whipped a hand back and threw a knife at Temar. The small blade flew hard and accurate before a gust of wind suddenly flung it upward. As it fell to the water, everyone saw the blade bend back on itself, crushed by unseen hands before it disappeared into the depths.

Temar shook his head slowly. 'You forget that I have other advantages to counter your years and experience. You're as much a prisoner here as those unfortunates you've kidnapped. Don't think your little ship can slip past our blockade.' He flicked a contemptuous hand at the sloop, barely two-thirds the beam or length of the *Dulse*.

'You'd do that, would you?' Muredarch sounded interested. 'Run away and leave your men to die unheeded? No, my lad, I'll be leaving here with all my men and all your goods and in my own good time.' The pirate didn't look in the least disconcerted. 'I have magic to call on too, boy.'

'We're leaving.' Temar gestured to Halice. The *Dulse*

surged forward, heeling away from the single-masted ship. Temar hurried to the afterdeck, to keep the pirate in sight. 'None of you let any magelight slip,' he said anxiously as Usara joined Larissa and an implacable swell gathered to drive Muredarch back between the islands.

The mages looked at each other with some amusement. 'No, we'll be careful,' Larissa assured him.

'I wish I knew I could set a magic working and just leave it like that.' Guinalle watched the seas push the sloop down the strait.

'It's not an easy as it looks,' Usara said with feeling. 'And a spell left unchecked can cause chaos, believe me. Azazir—'

'Magical theory can wait.' Halice tapped him on the shoulder. 'Where does this leave us, Messire?'

'He won't leave things like this, will he?' Temar gnawed on a thumbnail. 'We make sure he goes nowhere and see what he comes up with next time?' He looked for agreement.

'He certainly thinks you'll trade something for the prisoners,' Guinalle said slowly.

'Can we ask for Naldeth by name?' asked Larissa, hopeful.

'Not without Muredarch doubling whatever price he puts on his head,' Halice told her tartly.

'I would not make any deal with him, over anyone,' Guinalle said with evident distress. 'He has no intention of keeping his word about anything.'

'I hardly need Artifice to tell me that,' said Temar without thinking. He smiled hastily at her but Guinalle was too pre-occupied to notice.

'He's a pure opportunist,' she continued. 'No fool and not given to ill-considered impulse, so we mustn't make that mistake. He can plan ahead and on a grand scale; he's determined to make himself overlord of some free traders' fiefdom in these islands. He's quite confident he can do it. But that's as much as he intends. He doesn't see himself ruling Kellarin for instance, just plundering it judiciously.'

'Where do the Elietimm fit in to his plans?' demanded Temar.

'He really has no idea what he's dealing with.' Surprise and concern coloured Guinalle's reply. 'He sees them as a tool for his use and believes them entirely loyal to his ambitions.' She smiled without humour. 'They have made sure of that. As far as Muredarch knows, Ilkehan is sole ruler of another group of islands, a predator on trade and the Dalasorian coasts much the same as himself, just more successful at keeping himself hidden. He sees him as an equal and a potential ally in gaining a stranglehold on as much ocean trade as possible.'

'So what do we do now?' Temar looked from Usara to Halice and back again.

Halice didn't seem to see it warranted a question. 'Keep them penned in until Ilkehan's dead. Go in and kill the lot of them.'

'Couldn't we trade a few things?' Guinalle pleaded. 'Not enough to get a ship seaworthy but just to get a few people safely out of there.'

'This isn't a game of Raven,' Halice warned her. 'Don't try being too clever; we're dealing with real lives and deaths.'

'We want him concentrating on us, don't we?' Temar looked at her. 'Even with this other Elietimm leader's help, it going to take time for Livak and Ryshad to reach Ilkehan's keep. Then they've to find some way of killing the man. Keeping him talking might keep that pirate off balance. Then our final attack will be all the more effective, if they're wrong-footed.'

Halice nodded with a twinkle in her eye. 'A fair point, for someone trained in the Imperial cohorts.'

'If Muredarch's concentrating on us and our deeds, those enchanters will be doing the same,' Usara said seriously to Guinalle who was still looking upset. 'That should draw Ilkehan's attention south and lessen any chance of him suspecting attack closer at hand. Do you want to sit down? Shiv was showing me how he helped Livak—'

But the noblewoman shook off his hand and went to stand at the very stern of the *Dulse*, looking out over the waves towards Suthyfer.

'Come on, 'Sar.' Temar ducked as the mizzen sail unfurled above him with a rattle of canvas and ropes. 'Let's get back to our island and work out how best to make Muredarch's life difficult, shall we?'

CHAPTER FIVE

Thoughts on the Ancient Races
Presented to the Antiquarian Society of Selerima
By Gamar Tilot, Scholar of the University of Col

As students of history in our various degrees, we are invited to regard the ancient races of our lands as set apart, an impassable gulf of time dividing their lives from our own and rendering them unknowable. Why must they be so very different from ourselves? I argue these peoples are as easily understandable as the gentleman sitting beside you in this hall. Consider the question thus.

The Forest Folk of old are known through the ballads of wandering minstrels and the legends we tell our children. We entertain ourselves with tales of unicorns and griffons, with myths of women born from living trees and unearthly voices heard in dark and sacred groves. We imagine the people living with such wonders as innocent as children, unfettered by possessions, blithe in romances uncomplicated by marriage or settlements. Such an ideal life is a wonder that has passed beyond our ken.

But who sings us these songs? Why, travelling bards who come out of the Forest, boasting that same red hair celebrated in every chorus. They leave greenwood families living not in indolent ease but in the straitened circumstances of any who must forage for food among root and bough. Minstrels carolling the romances of Viyenne or Lareal do not exalt a lost ideal but merely solicit coin to clothe their children and fill their bellies with bread. Their songs are not mystical history but idle entertainment, to distract their folk from their own cold and hungry existence. Look around your city and you will see plenty of copper-crowned heads. Over the generations, many a Forest man has forsaken the woods for the practical comforts of settled life and trade. The Forest Folk are not distant paragons of a nobler age; they are your tradesmen, your servants. We all share the same concerns for our children, our prosperity, and our posterity. Those so inclined worship the same gods. Why should we imagine it was not ever thus? One can tell a tree by its fruit, after all and the apple never falls far from the tree.

Consider the Mountain Men. Read the sagas copied in the libraries of Vanam and Inglis and you see a race remote and forbidding as the very peaks of Gidesta. Incomprehensible myths speak of men unyielding as stone, dangerous as dragons reputed to haunt their peaks. Scholars nod wisely of the cruel climate that makes such men so harsh. The miners and trappers among the hills and forests north of the Dalas would laugh at such wilful ignorance. Where have the towns of northern Ensaimin learned their noted skills in smelting and smithing if not from the countless sons of Mountain blood who have settled in softer climes and married there, quite content with their lot? There can be no such great differences between us if they do not divide those sharing the honesty of the marriage bed. Tales of ancient warfare among the snowbound crags may send a shiver of steel down the spine when told around a fireside but the truth is that the Mountain Men are as familiar and as slight a threat as the knife you use to cut your meat at table.

What though of the Plains People? That is the greatest mystery of all, or so it is whispered around the chimney corners. We see no trace of them, only gazing in awe at the earthen walls that ring their sacred places, at mighty barrows raised above their honoured dead. Gentlemen such as yourselves dig into these and wonder at copper pots and axes. Why were they buried? Did they truly believe such possessions could be carried aboard Poldrion's ferry? Every discovery turns up more questions than pebbles. The earth-stained bones cannot speak so we invent answers for the silent skulls. Just as children make monsters out of fear and the shadows cast by candles, so we weave the darkness of ignorance into the myth of the Eldritch Kin, masters of a realm beyond the rainbow, rulers of the unchancy lands of water meadow and sea strand, the Plains People gone away into the twilight where we cannot follow.

Nothing could be further from the truth just as no race could be closer to us. The turfed forts of Dalasor may be remote and eerie but the prosaic ploughs of Caladhria and Ensaimin turn up copper rings and brooches with every spring sowing. We live among the ancient dwellings of the Plains People; we cannot see them only because our barns and houses, streets and shrines are raised upon their remnants. We cannot see descendants of this ancient race as we do of Forest and Mountain because those born of the Plains are our very selves. As we have lived for untold generations on these wide and fertile lands, so we have passed from primitive lives and beliefs to wed with the civilisation that the Tormalin Emperors brought from the east. As warp and weft in one cloth, so we wove together the superiority we enjoy today, as the growing child sets aside his toys and takes up the tools of manhood. The Mountain Men have followed our lead and in time the Forest Folk will turn from their amiable idleness and heed their lessons in turn.

Islands of the Elietimm,
5th of For-Summer

'Be careful, there's ice melt coming down there.' Shiv looked back over his shoulder. He was sitting in the prow of the wooden-framed, hide-covered boat we'd stolen. He shook seawater from his white, wrinkled hand. 'Curse it, that's cold!'

Behind me, Ryshad was steering, long tiller tucked under his arm, both hands gripping it firmly. He narrowed his eyes at the milky flow running across the dark grey beach to bleach the greenish water of the sound. 'Put your backs into it.'

Sorgrad and 'Gren exchanged a mutinous look but both renewed their grip on their oars. I smiled encouragement at them and did my best to keep my feet out of the water puddled in the bottom of the boat. My back ached from sitting on the hard thwart and the non-stop wind was cutting through my jerkin. I shivered and began rubbing my arms to try and get a little warmer.

'Sit still,' Sorgrad told me curtly.

'I'm freezing,' I retorted.

'There's nowhere to go and nothing to do. You'll only get more chilled fidgeting,' he said sternly. 'Who's spent more time in the mountains, you or me?'

'Just make sure you keep your hands and feet moving,' Ryshad advised. 'You don't want frost nip in your fingers and toes.'

I could see Sorgrad scowling at that but it seemed he couldn't deny that was fair advice, much as he might want to.

'You could always cursed well row,' 'Gren said as he pulled hard. 'That would soon warm you up.' He certainly boasted a rosy glow.

'I don't want to risk grounding,' said Shiv with some alarm.

'It's all sandbanks round here,' scoffed 'Gren. 'We'd be all right.' There were certainly none of the vicious skerries that had threatened us like vicious claws as we'd negotiated the uncomfortably exposed shore of Shernasekke.

'Let's not take the risk,' suggested Ryshad.

Sorgrad said nothing, just shooting 'Gren a warning look.

'So you stay sitting like a noblewoman on a pleasure jaunt,' 'Gren grumbled. If he wasn't having a good time, no one else was going to.

I refused to feel guilty for having neither the heft nor the weight to match anyone else's stroke. I'd tried spelling both brothers and no one could dispute Ryshad's decision that I stop, after we found ourselves veering so unexpectedly off course.

'Pull, now!' Ryshad leant all his weight into the tiller and the brothers bent over their oars, hauling them back with breath hissing through their teeth. From the concentration on Shiv's face, he was doing his part with magic. All I could do was hold tight as the light boat bucked and swerved. Ashore, a surging stream laden with fine white sand cascaded down a mountainside thick with ash. It drew a stark line across a black sand bar, which itself cut abruptly across the paler grey of the beach where huge boulders, raw edges unweathered, lay scattered like a haphazard throw of knuck-lebones. Pale fingers reached through the dark waters towards us but everyone's efforts took us safely past.

"Sar would dearly love to see a fire mountain burning," Shiv remarked, gazing at the mountain rising high above the shallow swell of the island we were passing. Yellow-tinted grey, the jagged peak had faint wisps of cloud clinging to the topmost pinnacles. No, not cloud but smoke or steam, ever renewed to defy the constant winds. I wondered if Misaen would heed a mongrel lass like me asking him politely to keep his fires banked until we'd quit this unnerving place.

'See, that's all rock spewed up recently.' Shiv pointed to

a formless mass of black stone sprawling across the beach and dusted with white. 'It was so hot, it boiled a barrel full of salt out of the sea before it was quenched.' He smiled, intrigued at the notion.

I decided I preferred land that had the decency to stay as it had been made.

'Livak, put your hood up.' Ryshad spared me a blown kiss when I turned to see him covering his own head. I would have responded but this third day of harsh wind and such sun as burned through the recurrent mists had cracked my lips painfully. We'd taken a laboriously circuitous route in order to keep a long low, grass-covered island between us and the forbidding bulk of Ilkehan's mountain-spined domain.

Our little boat crawled with aching slowness past a rocky islet in the midst of a treacherous sprawl of dunes and grass. A squat watchtower stood on the scant solid footing, the walls around it were stained and broken in several places. Small figures were making repairs with new, paler stone and several paused to look in our direction.

Sorgrad winked at me. 'We leave them alone, they'll leave us alone.'

But the builders on the fort weren't the only people to see us coming in from the shallow seas between the outer Elietimm islands and the deeper ocean. To reach this mysterious Olret's fiefdom, we had to navigate the inner channels winding between dour grey islands fringed with saltings claiming equal kinship with sea and land. We saw men, women and children up to their knees in mud, digging for whatever the grudging sand might yield. Wading birds, black and white and trimmed with flashes of yellow or red hopped around in eager anticipation.

'Why couldn't we steal a boat with a god-cursed sail?' grunted Sorgrad as some unseen current slowed us.

'Why don't you take an oar, if you Tormalin know all about boats?' Puffs punctuated 'Gren's words as he favoured Ryshad with a disgruntled glare. 'I'll bet even I could steer with a wizard smoothing the water under this thing's arse.'

'That's called the hull, 'Gren.' I grinned.

'Your man been making you an expert?' he began.

'We need to make landfall soon,' Shiv interrupted, turning to hide his map from the inquisitive wind.

'That's going to be easier said than done,' grimaced Ryshad.

I studied the coast of Rettasekke curving ahead of us. Black pillars of rock piled in steps and stacks offering no foothold to anything bigger than a seabird. Screaming hordes of them clustered on every ledge and spilled whiteness neither salt nor snow down the cliffs. The sun suddenly appeared to strike rainbow glints from the wet rocks. The colours vanished and I looked up to see dappled cloud spreading across the sky.

'We'll want to be under cover before long,' Ryshad observed.

'Before nightfall, I aim to be an honoured guest at this Olret's fireside, drink in one hand, meat in the other,' said Sorgrad with determination.

'Drink and a willing lass will suit me.' 'Gren chuckled.

'You keep your hands to yourself,' I chided my irrepressible friend. 'Touch the wrong stocking tops and you could find yourself flogged or worse.'

'Foul this up and you'll be explaining yourself to Halice,' added Sorgrad. That was one of the few considerations ever to give 'Gren pause for thought.

'Let's try over there.' Ryshad pointed to a steep stretch of mottled shingle below a stretch of turf breaking the serried black columns.

'Solid ground again,' I murmured fervently.

'Did I mention that coming ashore's the most hazardous bit of a voyage?' said Ryshad conversationally. I turned my head to stick my tongue out at him as Sorgrad and 'Gren chuckled.

'Fast as you can.' Shiv was concentrating ahead. 'We must get above the waterline at once.'

Sorgrad and 'Gren picked up the pace of their rowing. I gripped my seat and trusted to Ryshad's firm hand on the tiller. As we drew closer, I could see the long spill of gravel making a natural ramp down into the deeper water. The instant the hull bit into the stones, Shiv jumped out, splashing through the cold sea with the painter over his shoulder. Sorgrad and 'Gren tossed their oars into the bottom, sprang over the sides and joined in hauling the boat up the slope. Ryshad was over the stern, shoving from the rear. I stayed put until the boat was solidly grounded.

'Would my lady care to come ashore?' Ryshad swept a florid bow and offered me his hand with a grin.

I handed him his satchel and tossed the others their burdens before gingerly getting out of the boat. 'These boots are new. I don't want salt stains on the leather.'

Shiv was passing his hands over his sodden breeches, dry swathes appearing. 'I thought you had more faith in my magic,' he said, mock sorrowful.

'When are you going to learn some useful spells like that?' 'Gren demanded of his brother as he tried to wring water from the bottom of his jerkin.

Sorgrad narrowed his eyes and steam began rising from his own clothes, leaving 'Gren open mouthed.

'Careful,' Shiv warned. 'You wouldn't be the first apprentice to set himself alight.'

'So Larissa said.' A moment later, Sorgrad let out his breath with a triumphant grin. 'What do you think of that?'

I ran a finger over his shirt cuff. 'Just about dry enough for ironing.'

'Find me a nice flat stone and I'll try heating it.' He grinned at me.

'I hate to play sergeant at arms all the time but we don't have time to waste,' Ryshad pointed out.

'I hate being wet,' countered 'Gren.

'Permit me.' Shiv drove the water from 'Gren's clothes with a brisk gesture. 'Let's hide the boat.'

'I don't plan on rowing anywhere else,' 'Gren said firmly.

'I always plan on keeping every option open.' Sorgrad went to help Ryshad and I lent a hand as well. We wedged the vessel between two splintered black pillars and weighed it down with a few substantial stones.

'If we get separated, we'll use this as a rendezvous.' Ryshad stowed the oars neatly beneath the thwarts.

Everyone nodded agreement as Shiv studied his map. 'This way.'

We dutifully followed him up a steep hill shaped like an overturned boat, the blunt stern made by the stark cliffs. It was a punishing climb but the crest offered us a good view across the sound separating this island from Ilkehan's domain. A line of rocks threaded between the sandy channels, the larger ones crowned with uncompromising cairns of ownership and one all but invisible beneath a small but sturdy fort. Ilkehan's island beyond was hidden in secretive mists.

'This must be Rettasekke.' Shiv tucked his folded map away and we looked down on a fertile stretch of land dotted with a few houses, divided with neat stone walls and, in the distance, boasting a more substantial settlement.

'This is a clan leader's holding, is it?' 'Gren looked distinctly unimpressed. 'What do they reckon their wealth in? Rocks?'

If they did, this Olret had a plentiful supply. Beyond the narrow band of scrupulously tended land, jagged grey soon ripped through the thin coverlet of grass. Crags and outcrops ran away inland, ever taller and bolder, joining in daunting ramparts, massing to join the abrupt upthrust of the mountains at the core of this island. Some slopes were freckled black and grey like a rabbit pelt, others striped grey on black like a mousing cat, the patches of coarse scrub here and there doing little to soften the harshness of the landscape.

'There's your goats,' Sorgrad pointed out as our path across the hill showed us more of the grassland below.

It was a scene of considerable activity. A massive wheel-like structure had been built from the ubiquitous grey stones, one gap in the rim admitting a protesting herd of what looked like every goat on the island. Men drove the beasts between walls too high for leaping into the hollow centre, where the axle for this supposed wheel would have fitted. Other islanders were somehow identifying goats and shoving them into wedge-shaped pens formed by the walls that made the spokes.

'What are they doing?' I wondered. Ryshad handed me the spyglass he'd been using and I saw men wrestling the unruly beasts to a standstill for women deftly threading orange, black and green threads through holes clipped in their floppy ears

'Suckling kid for dinner?' 'Gren suggested hopefully.

'Let's get past without anyone asking us our business,' said Ryshad.

I don't think anyone would have asked, had we walked along the shelving shoreline accompanied by a travelling masquerade complete with flutes and drums. For one thing, I doubt they'd have heard us over the ear-splitting din of outraged bleating and curses provoked by a billy goat's horns or some nanny's razor-sharp hooves. It was a relief to leave the commotion behind as we approached the settlement at the far end of the stretch of tillable land.

'That'll be the grave circle, I take it.' Shiv nodded at an enclosure considerably larger than the one we'd seen ravaged. Hereabouts the rock evidently split into handy slabs because this was made from a double ring of rectangular stones fitted precisely edge to edge, a barrier needing no ditch beyond the merest scrape. Two reddish-yellow monoliths framed the single entry to the solid circle and inside more stood in pairs and singletons with no readily apparent pattern.

'I've not seen stone of that colour before,' Ryshad frowned.

'Where are you three going to hide up?' Sorgrad shaded his eyes with a hand.

'You're going in, just the pair of you?' Shiv looked to Ryshad for confirmation.

He nodded. 'That was the plan before. No need to change it as far as I can see.'

That satisfied Sorgrad and we all studied the prospect

before us. Long, low houses were dotted between the grave circle and a formidable keep rising four square and four storeys high within a solid wall. Beyond, a long range of buildings boasted upper floors and chimneys as well as stone slates to their roofs rather than the bundles of coarse vegetation thatching the smaller houses. More of those were scattered on the far side of the keep and its storehouses, the settlement ending in a line of open-sided goat shelters. Beyond, a surprisingly substantial causeway dammed a paltry stream to create a wide pond.

'Barely big enough to spit across.' That was 'Gren's usual Ensaimin idiom for the more wretched villages we'd visited over the years.

'Only if you caught the wind right.' But I had to admit it wasn't very impressive.

'Catching the wind wouldn't be a problem.' The notion prompted a shiver from 'Gren and he was right. The whole settlement was exposed to whatever weather came sweeping up the channel, which was doubtless why nets fringed with substantial stone weights weighed down the thatch of the lesser houses.

Ryshad on the other hand approved of the place. 'Even if this isn't the only landing on this stretch of shore, that pond blocks anyone coming over that headland.'

'No one's going to sneak up on Olret,' Sorgrad agreed. 'Not with such a reach of open land between the houses and any ground that offers cover.'

'If we hang around here, we'll be spotted,' warned Shiv.

There certainly were plenty of people about but, fortunately, most looked too busy to be glancing our way. Between the keep and the sea was a broad open area where men walked barrels to and from large troughs surrounded by women. Lads carried bushel baskets brimming with the unmistakable silver of fish from long sheds on stone jetties that reached out into the water, tethered boats bobbing at their far ends. The sun was back, striking sparkles from the water, and turning greedy seabirds wheeling overhead a brilliant white.

The birds squawked and jinked to dodge small children throwing stones to keep them off racks of drying stockfish. Earlier catches were stacked like cordwood and weighted with the handily flat rocks.

Ryshad was making a stealthy survey. 'Ask to be taken to whoever's in charge,' he told Sorgrad as he snapped his spyglass closed. 'We'll wait over there.' He indicated a spread of dark green patches of some crop being raised between the closest house and the grave circle. The plants looked sparse and thirsty but offered more cover than anything else we could see.

Sorgrad nodded and the pair of them trotted off straight for the keep. The three of us skirted the grave circle, using its solid walls to shield us from view as best we could.

'Will they be all right?' Shiv wondered as we lost sight of the brothers.

Ryshad didn't answer so it was left to me to reassure him. 'Sorgrad's gone into enemy camps before now. Halice often trusts him to negotiate safe conducts or exchanges of wounded, ransom prisoners for food. Believe me, when he sets his mind to it, he can convince anyone of anything.'

'It's not Sorgrad I'm worried about.' Ryshad's tone was concerned rather than caustic. 'What if these people use Artifice to check he's telling the truth?'

'We've come to look for an ally against Ilkehan,' Shiv pointed out. 'That's the truth.'

'What about 'Gren?' persisted Ryshad.

'Whatever Sorgrad tells him is what he'll choose to believe.' I tucked myself behind a clump of unappetising-looking plants which proved to be growing within yet another stone wall, barely knee high this time and filled with something truly foul smelling.

'Dast's teeth, what is that stink?' Ryshad and Shiv joined me, crouching more awkwardly with their greater height.

'Seaweed.' Shiv stifled a cough and peered over the little wall. 'And gravel, half a year's table scraps and what looks like a dead goat.'

I shuffled round until I could lie on my belly and get a decent view of the keep past the plants. Roughly clad Elietimm in dun and brown milled around the buildings, more gold heads together than I'd seen anywhere but in the most distant mountains. 'Gren and Sorgrad were nowhere to be seen.

I was about to heave a sigh before the stench on the other side of the meagre wall stopped me and I settled for sucking at my sore lip. Ryshad sat with his back to the reeking plants, keeping a watch inland and Shiv crouched beyond him to watch the way we'd come.

I made a silent wager with myself and won it when the lanky mage finally complained. 'I'm getting cursed cramped.'

'Stand up!'

But it wasn't Ryshad speaking. Whatever else charms culled from that ancient songbook might offer, Forest myth and Mountain saga remained stubbornly silent on whatever gave the Elietimm their disconcerting ability to step out of thin air. Down on the ground, we were in no position to defy the elderly Ice Islander who glowered at us, not when he had a handful of younger men behind him, armed with vicious maces of wood and iron. All were dressed in a steely grey livery of leather decorated with copper studs. We got to our feet with as much dignity as we could muster.

'We await our friends,' I said in careful Mountain speech.

A thin smile cracked the older man's weathered face. 'You are to join them.'

I translated and Ryshad swept a polite hand to indicate that our new acquaintance should precede us. He did so and his henchmen followed us, maces sloped casually over their shoulders but faces stern.

'What now?' Shiv asked beneath his breath.

'See how it plays out.' I couldn't see what else to do.

'They're not taking our weapons,' Ryshad pointed out, 'nor tying us up.' He was walking on the balls of his feet, hands ready, alert to every man's pace and position.

We were led past people still working in an overpowering

stench of fish guts and through the main gate of the keep's outer wall. Guards in the same leather armour ducked respectful heads to our guide. Elietimm battles must be remarkably simple affairs, I mused, given every enemy was handily identified by his garb. In the chaotic civil wars of Lescar you'd be lucky if all your side carried the same battlefield token or half of them remembered the recognition word. More than one battle had petered out in confusion when both contingents had plucked the same handy flower for their field sign and claimed Saedrin's grace as their battle cry.

Such idly inconsequential thoughts kept my apprehension at bay as we were taken through a busy courtyard where a waiting throng eyed us with curiosity and suspicion. Our guide ignored them all and led us up a flight of forbidding stairs to double doors of weathered and iron-studded oak. At his nod, another grey-leathered warrior opened one to admit us.

The great hall's echoing emptiness took up most of the ground floor by my quick estimation. Pale flagstones were swept bare beneath a skilfully vaulted ceiling rising from thick pillars of polished reddish stone sunk into the grey walls. Clouded glass in tall, thin windows muffled the bright sunlight but we all knew panes an Ensaimin peasant would sneer at betokened wealth and status in these indigent islands. Heavy curtains of soft beige wool, bright with geometric patterns in muted green and soft orange, hung around the far end where a shallow wooden floor offered a suggestion of a dais.

'Drink?' 'Gren proffered his goblet with a broad grin. He and Sorgrad sat on backless cross-framed stools at one end of a long table so aged and polished it was all but black. An Elietimm man wearing a well-cut grey mantle over tunic and breeches of fine quality stood beside them, amusement creasing his plump face. He was as blond as Sorgrad, with a wiry curl to his receding hair but his eyes were dark, something I'd noticed more than once among these islanders.

'Those who hid,' barked the old man who'd brought us

in, gesturing at the same time as bowing deeply to his over-lord.

Sorgrad set his own cup carefully by an array of small platters on the table. 'I have explained that we did not wish to trespass on anyone's hospitality until we had made ourselves known,' he said smoothly. 'Master of Rettasekke, I vouch for Ryshad, sworn to one of those mainland lords whom Ilkehan has raided.' He indicated me next with a courteous hand. 'Livak will speak for the Forest Folk who suffered at the hands of Eresken last summer while our friend Shivvalan comes from Caladhria. The lowland peoples were very nearly brought to war with the uplands by Eresken's treachery and that is his concern.'

All of which had the virtue of being true, if not the whole truth, if someone somewhere was murmuring a charm to test Sorgrad's veracity. He turned to our host.

'This is Olret, who graciously offers us the shelter of his house for the duration of the ancient travel truce.' Sorgrad smiled with a nice balance between humility and self-assertion. 'So we see that our two races are not so sundered, despite the generations between us.'

The Mountain travel truce lasted three days and three nights and I wondered if that meant we'd be spared aetheric curiosity for that period. As I was trying to find a way of hinting as much to Sorgrad, a booming blow on the double doors made me jump. I wasn't the only one and I saw Olret stifle a smile behind a polite hand as this peremptory demand was repeated. He said something to Sorgrad that I didn't catch.

'Olret has business to attend to,' Sorgrad told us. 'He wishes us to stay and observe as his guests.'

Someone somewhere was watching, perhaps behind one of the floor-sweeping curtains, because lackeys instantly appeared from a side door with stools for us all. Maidservants hurried after with more plates of titbits and pottery flasks of pale liquor as well as goblets various goats had sacrificed horns for. One corn-haired lass poured me a generous measure, which I sipped cautiously. The stuff was smooth, light on the back of the throat and innocuously flavoured with caraway. It drawled long, slow lines as I rolled the small goblet casually around in my hand. Too much of this and our host wouldn't need Artifice; we'd all be confiding our innermost thoughts to our new best friend.

On the other hand, refusing to drink would probably be an insult. I took an anonymous finger-length of meat from a plate. It wasn't unpleasant with a rich gamey taste beneath the subtle smoke but I couldn't have said if it were fish, fowl or beast. What it was, it was salty, excellent for provoking thirst.

The great doors were opened and the throng from the courtyard filed in, heads dutifully bowed. Our host moved to a high seat skilfully wrought from dark wood and yellow bone carved with blunt and ancient symbols. Shiv cleared his throat and I looked at him, curious as to whether he might recognise any of these symbols. The mage glanced meaningfully at my goblet as he passed his hand casually over his own. I held my own drink absently to one side as I reached for what I fervently hoped was a morsel of cheese. Shiv's hand brushed my own as he moved to offer Ryshad a dish of small crimson berries. When I took a sip from my goblet to try and quell the unexpectedly acrid taste of the cheese, I found the intense liquor had been diluted to a more manageable potency.

The man who'd led us into this well-baited pen was back again. He stood at the edge of the wooden floor, carrying a long staff carved from one single, mighty length of bone, some tantalising gems set around the ornately carved head. He struck the wooden planks and the crowd shuffled obediently about until a line of men pushed to the front, each carrying a leather bag.

'Proceed.' Olret looked on impassively as each man stepped up to empty his offering on to the long table.

The haul proved to be birds' beaks. The nearest tally proved the death of a goodly number of hooded crows along with several ravens. That chilled my Forest blood; my father had always told me killing a raven prompted dreadful luck. I saw the predatory yellow curve of an eagle's beak as well. Plainly no one worshipped Drianon hereabouts.

The men who'd come forward surveyed the competing piles and those who'd been less assiduous backed away. That left about half looking smug and expectant as the man with the bone staff walked the line and offered a tooled leather pouch to each one. Faces intent, every man pulled out a slip of horn that he held up for the man with the staff to see. He turned to the gathering and I picked enough words out of his declarations to learn three different sorts of rights were being granted.

'Driftwood without tool marks on the Fessands.'

'Worked wood brought ashore on the Arnamlee.'

'Stranded seabeasts from Blackarm to the Mauya Head.'

Olret looked expectantly at Sorgrad as the ritual was concluded.

The Mountain Man bowed politely. 'Those that work to defend your territory from predators share in the chance-brought wealth of the seas.'

Olret smiled with satisfaction. 'Ilkehan keeps all such bounty for himself.' His words carried and a shudder of fear and disapproval rippled through the gathering.

The bone staff thudded on the floor again and the crowd parted like a flock of goats as Olret's grey-liveried hounds brought a handful of men before him. Each one wore only a filthy shirt, wrists securely bound in front. However enlightened this Olret might think himself compared to Ilkehan, his prisoners suffered the usual brutalities. One man's eyes were all but closed with bruises while another's hair was clotted dirty brown with old blood.

Each prisoner was hauled forward in turn and Olret pronounced sentence, expression unchanging. If there was such a thing as arguing a case at trial hereabouts, it must have happened earlier.

'White.' The man's face turned hopeless.

'Green.' Someone unseen at the back hastily stifled a sob of relief.

'White.' For some reason, that came as a relief to that man.

'Red.' That provoked some disturbance on the far side of the hall that had the guards wading in to haul a struggling youth outside so fast his feet barely touched the floor.

'White.' The final judgement disappointed someone but they had the sense to shut their mouth after an involuntary exclamation.

The man with the bone staff waved it in unmistakable dismissal and the crowd melted away as fast as it had gathered.

'He works a deal faster than Temar,' I quipped to Ryshad.

The great doors closed to leave us alone in the vast hall with our host. Alone, apart from whoever was keeping watch behind the curtains. Of course, we were all still carrying our weapons and I reminded myself not to condemn the man out of hand for simple prudence. He left his impressive chair and pulled up a stool, helping himself from the spread of food.

'What had those men done?' My command of the Mountain tongue was sufficient for that but Olret ignored me, addressing himself to Sorgrad.

'Do you still administer the three exiles in the lands of the Anyatimm?'

'I don't know what you mean by that.' Sorgrad looked genuinely puzzled.

Olret seemed faintly disappointed. 'The red exile is from life itself. That man will be flung from the cliffs. The green exile is from hearth and home but that man may find himself some shelter within the sekke and his friends may save him from death with food and water. The white exile is from the sekke and its people. Those men must leave our land before nightfall and none may offer them the least help.' Olret's polite smile turned a little forced. 'That was the exile the Anyatimm of old imposed on our forefathers. We fled north and east over the ice, little thinking that we would find these lands held fast in the cold seas. Then Misaen melted the path and, as many would have it, left us here for some purpose.'

Shiv and Ryshad were both growing visibly frustrated as I struggled to listen and to translate at the same time. Olret waited for me to finish speaking before surprising us all.

'Forgive me. I only know your tongue from the written word and speak it poorly.' His Tormalin was entirely comprehensible, for all his hesitations and harsh accent.

'You have the advantage of me, my lord.' Ryshad spoke slowly with all the practised politeness he'd learned serving his Sieur. 'It is you who must forgive our ignorance.'

'May I ask how you know our language?' Shiv smiled but I could see he was thinking the same as the rest of us. Now we'd have to watch every word we said, even among ourselves.

'I have visited your shores.' Olret could barely conceal his satisfaction at astounding us with this news. 'Not often and never for long but we have long traded with the men of the grasslands.'

A frisson ran through me. 'The Plains People?' I enquired blandly.

'Just so.' Olret had no trouble recognising the Tormalin term for the last of the three ancient races. 'A select few have long made such crossings, defying the sea-roving shades, though ill fates befall the unworthy who risk themselves.'

'I have never heard tell of such visitors.' Ryshad was hiding his scepticism behind a well-trained face.

'We do not linger,' Olret assured him. 'The men of the grasslands lay curses on those who outstay their welcome by overwintering, so we permit no such ship to land. Too many return laden only with stinking corpses, carried here by the sea shades.'

Could there still be remnants of the ancient Plains People in the northern vastness? Tormalin history would tell us they'd all been driven out or married into the Old Empire's high-handed delineation of their provinces of Dalasor and Gidesta. On the other hand, I'd known a fair few cast adrift from the wandering herdsmen of those endless grasslands to skulk like me on the fringes of the law. A lot of them had the sharp features and dark slenderness that legend attributed to the lost race of the Plains. Besides, plenty of those herding clans still passed down ancestral resentment of Tormalin dominance and that could well keep them silent about sporadic visitors bringing something worth trading. I wondered what that something might be.

Olret was talking to Sorgrad again. 'Forgive me, but you will not find a welcome if you bring trouble upon my poor people. We've suffered a full measure of grief in these last three years.'

'The mountains have been burning?' Sorgrad was all solicitous concern.

Olret nodded grimly. 'The Maker first struck sparks from his forge two years since. At first we hoped the Mother's judgement had finally come upon Ilkehan but every isle was shaken or riven. Fish floated dead from the depths of the seas. Goats choked with the ash or died later, poisoned by their fodder. Whole families smothered as they slept when foul air filled the lowest lying hollows.'

'Then we appreciate your generosity all the more,' Shiv said seriously.

I took another piece of the smoked meat and a sliver of flat bread and avoided Shiv's eye. It was Planir, Kalion and a couple of other mages who'd set the mountains erupting hereabouts, to give Ilkehan something to think about besides chasing us as we fled his clutches. It looked as if the Archmage had started something reaching a good deal further than he'd intended.

Olret managed a wry smile. 'We searched out what favour the Mother showed us. There were turnips cooked in the very earth for the hungry. With so many beasts dead, we had fodder to spare for strewing on the hot ash.' He saw we were all looking puzzled at that and hastened to explain. 'It prompts new growth, that we may recover the land as fast as possible.' His face turned sombre again. 'But many have died for lack of food these two years past and Ilkehan preys on the weaker isles like a raven following a famished herd. He piles trouble upon trouble on them before claiming the land by force of arms and saying the people will it thus. Then he grants the starving food to keep them alive enough to work but too hungry to spare strength to resist him.'

'Is that what happened to the westernmost isle?' I asked politely.

Ryshad saw Olret was ignoring me again and asked his own question. 'Have you no overlord or any union of Ilkehan's equals to deny such conquest?'

Olret stiffened as if he'd been insulted before forcing a smile and asking Sorgrad, 'Do the Anyatimm now submit to some king?'

'Never,' Sorgrad replied forcefully, half a breath ahead of 'Gren. 'Every kin manages its own affairs and answers to none but its own blood.'

'And all who share blood ties work together for the common good?' Olret smiled with satisfaction as Sorgrad and 'Gren nodded. 'Thus is ever with our clans.'

Which was all very well and entirely necessary in the mountains north of Gidesta, when the nearest neighbours were ten days' travel over hard ground in good weather and thirty in bad. Everyone pulled together through that self-same bad weather because they risked being the straggler who died if they didn't. I wasn't sure how well the notion would work here with everyone cheek by jowl in these meagre islands. 'How are your leaders chosen?'

Olret ignored me again. 'What is Ilkehan to you?' he demanded abruptly of Sorgrad.

'An enemy,' he replied simply. 'To all of us.'

'Gren spoke up unexpectedly. 'He merits death by our law and by yours too, if that's the price for wintering over the seas.'

Olret looked at him with sharp curiosity. 'How say you?'

'Eresken was Ilkehan's son?' 'Gren answered Olret's nod with a satisfied smile. 'I got it from Eresken himself that his mother was a slave taken from the grasslands and Ilkehan got her with child overwintering there.'

Hope in Olret's dark eyes was soon quenched. 'What is one more misdeed among Ilkehan's manifest crimes? Do you not think we would have stood shoulder to shoulder and marched against him if we could?'

'Why can't you?' asked Ryshad carefully.

'He draws the true magic from every hargeard and wields it like none since the time of the wyrms. The rest of us are left without the strength to ride the oceans in safety and even should we try, Ilkehan uses his dark rites to find and sink our ships. ' Bitterness choked Olret. 'I do not know where he gets such lore. He kills any who see into the realm of enchantment apart from those cravens who crawl at his heels, learning his secrets until he sends them to curse his enemies to death.

'Do you not think we would have thrown him down to break on the rocks below his stronghold if we could? He is proof against any attack. We could pile up our dead to reach his very ramparts and he would still be laughing as he watched us die beneath the lash of his magic.'

'Have you considered sending a single man to kill him?' Sorgrad asked. 'One might escape the notice that a host attracts.'

Olret shook his head. 'Ilkehan kills any exile who reaches his territories, lest they be some spy. As if I would let any man risk the Mother's curse by making such a profane claim just to enter Ilkehan's domains.'

'What's a hargeard?' 'Gren demanded, picking berry seeds out of his teeth.

'You do not know?' Olret looked both wary and confused.

'We do not know the term,' said Sorgrad smoothly. 'It will doubtless be called something else in our tongue.'

'The hargeard is sacred to the Mother and the Maker both,' Olret said guardedly. 'Where we lay our ancestors to rest that the true lore may bind our past to our future.'

Sorgrad nodded reassuringly. 'For us, such rites are centred in the tyakar caves.'

That meant nothing to me but visibly mollified Olret. 'We use the Maker's stones.'

Because anyone laying a body to rest in one of these curse-stoked mountains would probably come back the next day to find their revered forefather nicely cooked for carving. I decided that was better left unsaid and tried one of the berries before 'Gren took a quite unfair share.

'We have hopes of making Ilkehan pay for his crimes.' Sorgrad had decided we'd spent enough time with shuffling positions and measuring up the other players. It was time to cast the runes and see who came up a winner. He looked Olret straight in the eye. 'We have come to kill him.'

That spark of hope flared again in Olret's eyes and this time it burned brighter. 'By your faith in the Mother?'

'By the bones of my soke.' Sorgrad was in deadly earnest.

Olret drew back a little. 'But he has powers none can withstand.' That really galled him.

'I killed Eresken,' 'Gren piped up.

'We have the lore of the Forest Folk to protect us,' added Sorgrad with a nod in my direction.

Olret barely spared me a glance, all his attention on Sorgrad. If we'd had him at a gaming table, he wouldn't have walked away with breeches or boots, his emotions showed so plainly on his face. He desperately wanted to accept we could rid him of his hated foe but every pennyweight of sense tipped his scales to disbelief.

'We have come to risk ourselves, not to bring danger to the innocent.' Ryshad spoke with his usual measured courtesy. He'd judged Olret aright, I noted, as the Elietimm betrayed relief at that. 'But if Ilkehan were to be distracted, if some feint held his attention as we crossed into his lands, then our chances of success would be greatly increased.'

'Is there not some insult, some predation of Ilkehan's that you plan on avenging?' Sorgrad asked casually. 'We need not know where or how but if we knew when you intended to act, we could make our crossing while Ilkehan was looking in another direction.'

Olret was looking tempted but shook his head abruptly. 'Were you captured crossing from my territory to his, Ilkehan would have his excuse to bring death to us all.'

'So we make a dogleg and cross from someone else's lands.' 'Gren patently didn't see a difficulty.

'Perhaps.' Olret's eyes narrowed to give him a rather shifty expression. I guessed there was someone he wouldn't be sorry to drop into Ilkehan's line of sight. 'Let me think on this. In the meantime, I welcome you as my guests, though I'm afraid we're too busy to give you much entertainment. The Mother sends her bounties at this season and bids us gather all we can to see us through the grey days of winter. So, ease your travel weariness with a bath and then we shall offer what we can by way of feasting and music. Maedror!'

Olret was talking a little too fast and with rather too much forced friendliness but for the present I'd settle for getting clean and dry and filling my belly. The man with the staff appeared as soon as Olret shouted for him and we dutifully followed him up to the first floor of the keep. The building proved to have a stair on either side joined by a corridor running through the centre, rooms on either side. I was ushered into a snug cubbyhole barely big enough for the bed blanketed with weaving which made best use of all the shades of the local goats. This was presumably to protect my virtue since the others got a larger bedchamber to share. Maid-servants scurried hither and thither with ewers of hot water as lackeys hauled in baths. They mostly managed the care-fully blank faces of servants interrupted by unexpected guests but one lass betrayed anxious glances at the stairs leading up to the higher levels. I guessed she had duties above that had to be completed, irrespective of other calls on her time. That kind of thing had been one of the many injustices that had set me against a life in service to others.

The bath was bliss. To be warm all the way through again was utter rapture and, as well as scented soaps, someone thoughtful had set a pot of pale salve out on the tiny dresser next to the narrow bed. It soothed the split in my lip and my chapped hands wonderfully. I was rubbing in a second application when a knock sounded on the door.

'Livak?' It was Ryshad.

'Come in.'

He shut the door and leaned against it, smiling with blatant appreciation at my nakedness. Freshly shaven, black hair curling damply around his ears, he wore clean breeches and a shirt which he hadn't bothered lacing.

'What's everyone else doing?' I sat up and hugged my knees.

'I drew the lucky rune so Shiv's only just got his turn in a bath. Sorgrad and 'Gren are arguing over who's going to wear the one smart doublet they've got between them.' Ryshad held out a towel and I stepped into his embrace.

He held me close and kissed me with an urgency that roused my own desire. 'Shall I lock the door?'

'There's no key.' I kissed him back, running my free hand up into his hair. 'But I could take care of that.' I let the towel fall disregarded to the floor.

'That might cause comment, if someone tried the door.' Ryshad bent to kiss the base of my neck and I shivered with delicious anticipation as his breath tickled. He cupped my breast and I could tell someone had given him a salve for softening roughened hands as well.

'Stand the dresser by it?' I suggested when I could concentrate again.

'Good idea.' He slapped my rump with gentle approval.

I had the coverlets turned down on the bed before Ryshad had the door blocked and he swept me off my feet with a flurry of kisses, caresses and laughter. I pulled the shirt over his head as he kicked himself free of his breeches and we lost ourselves among the soft woollen blankets. If I'd thought the bath had been ecstasy, I'd been wrong. I didn't care if Olret had adepts spying on us. All they would have learned was how completely the two of us could become one, when it was just the two of us, open either to other, giving, yielding. No differences of upbringing and experience could come between us, no divergence of attitude or expectation could distance us, no friends or ties of loyalty could pull us apart. Moving in instinctive harmony, every sense alive to touch and kisses, coming together in the ultimate intimacy, I knew beyond question that I loved Ryshad and he loved me. In that simplest of moments, nothing else mattered. We lay entwined, breath slowing, a lazy smile on Ryshad's face as I brushed curls from his forehead now damp with sweat.

A single apologetic knock sounded softly at the door. 'If you're ready, we're invited downstairs for more food.'

I smiled at the barely concealed amusement in Sorgrad's voice. 'We'll be out in a few moments.'

Suthyfer, Sentry Island,
5th of For-Summer

'Temar!' Allin waved from the door of the cabin.

'Finally,' breathed Temar. 'Excuse me, Master Jevon.'

The *Dulse*'s captain looked expectant. 'Them pirates on the move?'

'Let's hope so,' Temar said fervently. He walked briskly up the beach, noting Halice abandoning some animated discussion with the *Maelstrom*'s boatswain and heading for the hut. So he wasn't the only one frustrated by these past few days of tense boredom. Nervousness teased Temar. What would Muredarch's new challenge be? Would he be a match for it?

'What is it?' After the bright sun outside, he blinked in the gloom of the cabin. It was still stuffy and oppressive even after he had drafted some of Kellarin's carpenters to cut windows through the walls and hang shutters.

Larissa and Allin flanked Usara who was looking intently at Guinalle.

'Muredarch just set sail in the sloop. He's coming north.' The demoiselle was pale in the dim light, shadows like bruises beneath her weary eyes. 'They brought a prisoner out of the stockade but muffled in a sack. I can't tell who it is, not with the Elietimm warding the place so closely.'

Temar looked at Usara. 'These enchanters aren't harrying you so much you can't maintain the blockade?'

'As long as we're working within direct sight, we're proof against them,' Usara assured him.

'The winds are still against Muredarch, no matter what direction he might try fleeing in,' said Larissa pertly.

'Those Elietimm only ever work together, which limits

their scope.' Contempt enlivened Guinalle's tone. 'If they stray too close, I warn our mages to cease their working.'

Halice frowned. 'Which is all very well as long as they stay stupid. What if they start working separately?'

'Separately, they will be vulnerable to me.' Guinalle didn't sound as if she relished that prospect.

'Let's go and see what Muredarch has to offer,' Temar suggested.

Everyone moved towards the door, Guinalle the most reluctant. Temar hurried ahead to warn Darni what was afoot. 'And Larissa will stay with you this time,' he concluded, deliberately not reacting as he heard the mage-girl's protest behind him. Darni's reply drowned out whatever it was Usara said to her.

'That's well enough by me.' The big man grinned ferociously before raising an almighty bellow. 'On your feet! First corps, take the watch! Second corps, you can use the time for some sword drill. If those bastards think they're coming here, you can meet them with a blade in your hand.'

Halice's mercenaries were the heart of the first corps, along with those of Sorgrad's recruits whose skills matched up to their often vague claims of experience in battle. Deglain and Minare each took a detachment to the headlands now readied with treetop vantage points and fuelled beacons. The second corps gathered on the beach with eager faces. Kellarin's men were determined to outshine the sailors who were in turn set on improving Halice's opinion of their skills. As the *Dulse*'s crew lofted her sails, Temar watched his men cut and thrust and parry and stab with growing pride.

'What do you think?' he asked Halice as she came to join him.

'I want them a cursed sight more practised before push comes to shove.' Halice looked towards Suthyfer. 'And I want to know what goad Muredarch thinks he's found today.'

Temar looked up at the aftdeck where Usara and Allin were deep in conversation with Guinalle. 'How much more do you think the demoiselle can stand?' he asked Halice in a low voice.

'Hard to tell,' the mercenary admitted frankly. 'She's a will of iron, that much is certain but one hard blow can shatter iron. It all depends if she's cast or wrought.'

That was precious little reassurance to Temar but, as he kept covert watch on Guinalle, he was encouraged to see some of the strain lifting from her face as she discussed whatever it was with Usara.

The *Dulse* sailed on, flags signalling to the circling *Maelstrom* that this was an unplanned voyage rather than the expected relief. With the bigger ship resigned to a longer wait, they headed for the entrance to the sound between the islands. Some little while later, Muredarch's toiling sloop came slowly into view.

'My duty, Messire!' The pirate hailed Temar genially.

Temar bowed his head in curt acknowledgement. 'What do you want?'

'What I wanted before.' Muredarch stood high in the stern of the boat, dressed in his customary finery. 'Rope, sails, nails and bolts.'

'We've already had this conversation.' Temar tried to see who it was a couple of Muredarch's men had subdued on the single-master's deck.

'This time I've got something I know you want.' Muredarch nodded to his subordinates and a heavy-set, thickly bearded man hauled up an unresisting prisoner.

'He should go bareheaded before his Sieur, Greik,' Muredarch said in mock rebuke. The pirate pulled the sacking off the prisoner's head.

Temar fought to keep his face impassive and his voice level as Naldeth was revealed. 'I want all of my people, not one at a time.'

Naldeth was pale with fear beneath bruises and filth, and a scarlet sore festered on one arm. He wore nothing beyond ragged breeches belted with a strip of cloth, bare feet cut and swollen. Temar's stomach turned as he saw the wizard's cringe of fear at an unexpected movement by the pirate Greik.

'You want some more than others.' Muredarch nodded to another man who heaved the contents of a bucket over the rail. Blood and entrails floated across the gently rippling sea. 'My friends from the north want this lad given over to them,' Muredarch continued conversationally. 'Seems he's one of your mageborn.'

'Is he?' Temar's attempt at bluff was futile at best.

'Any man I can't brand is touched with some sorcery,' snapped Muredarch before recovering his poise. 'My friends from the north are all for turning his head inside out with their enchantments but I thought you might like to trade your boy for a few concessions.'

He nodded to the man with the beard who promptly punched Naldeth in the kidneys. As the mage's knees buckled, the pirate knotted a rope securely around his chest.

'Let's see just how much you value your friends.' Muredarch's voice was silky with menace and he stepped aside as Greik hauled Naldeth on to the tiny afterdeck. A second sailor flung a noisome bucketful of blood and butchered bones into the sea. Temar saw sharply angled fins cutting the water beneath the sloop's stern but these were not the dolphins that frolicked on the ship's carvings.

'Sharks,' growled Halice at Temar's side. 'I'd heard tell this was a game with the worst of pirates.'

Dark ominous shapes were gliding below the surface of the sea, vanishing only to reappear in the shadows of the boats, blue-grey fins broaching the ruffled waves, some tipped with white, some with black.

'All I want is to refit a ship and have your seal agreeing my writ runs in these islands.' Muredarch spoke with the reasonable air of a peaceable man. 'I can be of considerable service to you and yours.'

Temar cleared his throat. 'Rule over these islands is not mine to grant.'

Muredarch leaned back on the stern rail as Greik tied off the other end of the rope holding Naldeth. 'You have the

Emperor's ear, you have highly placed friends in Hadrumal. With your word backing me, they won't argue the roll of the runes.'

'You have an exaggerated opinion of my consequence,' Temar said coldly. 'Neither Emperor Tadriol nor Archmage Planir will accept my decree on this.'

Muredarch shook his head. 'But your man here, since he's so desperate to convince us he's worth less than the shit on my shoe, says Emperor and Archmage both have left you to your own devices and won't come running to rescue him or anyone else. Well, they can hardly complain when you make dispositions of land and trade as you see fit. Especially when you're forced into it.'

Temar stared at Muredarch, determined to avoid catching Naldeth's eye. 'We will not be intimidated by scum like you.'

'Then we have a problem. Or rather, your friend here does.' Muredarch considered the quaking wizard, head on one side. 'Not enough blood on him, Greik.'

The bearded man forced Naldeth towards Muredarch who drew his dagger with slow, deliberate malice and scored burning lines across Naldeth's bare chest. The mage writhed in a vain attempt to evade the torment but the bearded pirate held him firm.

'Planir may not involve himself in Kellarin's affairs but harm one of Hadrumal's own and by Saedrin's very keys, he'll involve himself in yours!' shouted Temar furiously.

At Muredarch's nod, Greik turned Naldeth to show everyone aboard the *Dulse* a bold letter M carved into the mage, flourishes at the end of every stroke. 'Can't brand him but can carve him.' Muredarch shook his head. 'If only I'd thought of that earlier. But then, we'd never have uncovered your wizard. Some good comes from every mistake, that's what my father would say.'

'You witless son of a poxed whore,' Halice called out. 'If you knew your father it was only thanks to him being some brothel-keeper's runner.'

Muredarch ignored her. 'Now, do we start high on the

tally and I come down a notch or so for every mouthful you lose of your man? No. Let's see if you've the stones to play for high stakes, boy. Give me what I want and you have him back whole. Hold out and the price goes up.'

'I'm playing no games with you.' Temar turned from the rail to see the horrified faces of Usara and Allin. Guinalle stood between them, face pale as bone and her eyes like hollows in a skull.

A despairing cry and a splash forced Temar back to the sea. Greik had thrown Naldeth overboard and the wizard was struggling to tread water, looking in all directions, hands searching for any hold on the harsh planks of the boat, new scrapes only adding to the blood in the water. Predatory fins swept towards him in long inquisitive arcs.

Greik laughed as Muredarch jerked the rope tied beneath Naldeth's arms and then took hold himself. 'Steady,' warned Muredarch. The rest of the pirates balanced the trim of the sloop, every face showing they'd seen this game played out before.

A notched fin flew straight as an arrow at the struggling mage. It disappeared beneath the water and Naldeth's scream was a rising note of pure agony cut short with a gasping gurgle as something wrenched him beneath the roiling water. More fins jostled in an ever-decreasing circle.

'Pull!' Muredarch was intent as any fisherman casting a lazy line over a peaceful pond. He jerked the rope and the two of them hauled Naldeth bodily from the sea. The mage hung limp, white body dripping with seawater, scarlet blood gushing from the ragged stump where one leg had been bitten clean off just below the knee.

A questing snout broached the surface, black eyes like jet in the blunt grey head, gaping mouth lined with teeth more terrible than the most murderous mantrap. The shark dropped back into the water, pale belly uppermost for a moment before it disappeared into the perilous depths. An arrow, shot without sanction from the *Dulse*, struck the water and floated away, useless.

Naldeth began coughing and retching up salt water. Greik reached down to haul him up and the mage clung on the stern rail, remaining foot flailing in midair. To Temar's astonishment, Muredarch briskly tied a tourniquet around Naldeth's bleeding thigh.

'We can keep this up for some while, boy,' the pirate said confidently. 'Well, depending on how lively Greik manages that rope. We've had a man live through the loss of both arms and legs, haven't we, lads?' He patted the wizard's sodden and matted head as the sloop's crew dutifully chuckled.

Halice gripped Temar's forearm. 'Give the word and I'll fill that bastard so full of arrows, they won't need wood to build a pyre under him!'

'Can we kill them all?' Temar set his jaw. 'And who takes that privy rat's place? Most likely one of Ilkehan's enchanters. Do we raise the stakes that high?'

'We want him looking this way, don't we?' Halice was not deterred.

Temar could hear Usara and Allin whispering urgently to Guinalle. Were they as appalled at what he was doing as he was himself?

'Nothing to offer?' Muredarch sighed with false regret. 'Time for another dipping.'

Greik pushed the hapless mage off the rail, heedless of his cries of anguish.

'Then do it as fast as you can!' Guinalle hung back, face twisted with concentration as Allin and Usara stepped forward to the *Dulse*'s rail.

A crack of thunder from the clear blue sky silenced Muredarch even as a shaft of lightning hissed into the sea by Naldeth's head. Another and another split the water with blinding light and scattered the sharks. Muredarch raised his bloodied dagger at Temar but his words went unheard among shouts of alarm as the seas beneath the pirates' hull bucked and heaved. Muredarch clung to the stern rail, face ugly, only to recoil a moment later as a golden shaft of lightning split the wood, cutting the rope holding Naldeth. The polished lamps exploded, shards of glass cutting Muredarch's hands and face. A pirate tumbled screaming into the water but even with the sharks fled, no one threw him a rope.

'Allin, quick!' gasped Guinalle as Naldeth's unconscious body was lifted on a swathe of dusky light. Usara was still intent on the pirates, a blazing thunderbolt shattering the sloop's single mast and exploding into knives of light to shred the tumbling sails.

'Sink the bastards!' Halice raised one hand as archers on the *Dulse*'s ratlines waited for her signal.

Usara's face twisted with concentration. Magic-tainted mist like bloodstained gossamer rose from the hostile sea to thicken around the pirates who slapped with rising panic at coils tightening around their arms and heads. The magic dissolved at their touch but the threatening tendrils reappeared a moment later. The pirates' shouts cracked with fear.

'Stop, all of you!' screamed Guinalle. The noblewoman pressed her hands to her temples, eyes closed and face white. Naldeth thudded senseless on to the *Dulse*'s deck.

'Help me, somebody.' Allin was on her knees beside him, breaking her nails on the viciously tight tourniquet. His swollen thigh was dark with blood, cruel contrast to his pale, wasted body.

'One shot! Make 'em pay!' Halice swept her hand down. Shafts hissed through the air and pirates cursed and yelled as the arrowheads bit home.

'If we've no sails then we cursed well row! Get the sweeps out!' Muredarch was down among his men, tossing a corpse overboard before dragging at a long oar himself. 'So, Tormalin Sieur, this is how you dishonour truce.' Muredarch stood up, unafraid. 'You've a lot to learn, boy, if you're ever to have men keep faith with you!'

With the long sweeps now deployed, the pirates strained to pull themselves out of bowshot.

'You broke faith first!' Temar's rage got the better of him before he realised he sounded like a petulant child.

Muredarch laughed scornfully. 'I've a whole stockade full

of slaves and the ocean's full of sharks. Let's see who sickens of this game first!' He turned his back on Temar to lend a hand and encouragement as his sweating men fled for the sound between the islands.

'Can't you sink it?' Halice demanded of Usara.

'Not with Muredarch's enchanters ready to pounce.' Usara looked to Guinalle who nodded tight-lipped confirmation.

'We have to get him ashore.' Allin looked up at Temar. She had the stump of Naldeth's leg raised across her lap, swathing the torn and ragged flesh in linen torn from someone's shirt. Crushed splinters of bone were impeding her, blood running between her fingers and staining her cuffs. Guinalle dropped to her knees to cradle Naldeth's head.

'I can raise us a wind,' Usara offered.

Guinalle opened her eyes for a moment. 'No. They're seeking us with every art they can summon.'

'Back,' Temar waved to the *Dulse*'s captain. 'Fast as you can.'

Usara glared after the vanished pirates. 'I could slaughter that whole nest of vermin with every torment of magic I could think of.'

'Help us lift him,' Allin demanded. 'Careful. Keep that leg raised.'

With Guinalle steadying his head, Temar and Usara carried Naldeth into the stern cabin, Allin looking to his wounded leg and remaining foot. For all their care, a lurch of the ship caught them unawares, jolting Naldeth and forcing a moan from beneath his gritted teeth.

'On the bunk.' Usara and Temar laid Naldeth down and Allin began stripping away linen already soaked with blood to study the open wound. She covered it again with a light layer of clean cloth. 'We have to stop this bleeding and that means cautery,' she said bluntly. 'I daren't use magic, not with him being mageborn and in such pain. It'll have to be hot irons.'

The cloying scent of blood was rapidly filling the cramped

cabin. Temar realised he was feeling sick and swallowed hard. That left him feeling both empty and nauseous, his mouth dry. The cabin darkened and Halice filled the doorway. 'I'll see to that,' she said grimly.

'Will you be able to?' Temar took the stained dressings Allin held out to him and then wondered what to do with them. 'I mean, if they couldn't brand him.'

Allin stroked Naldeth's forehead. 'Go and find anything that might dull the pain; tahn, thassin, spirits. Ask all the sailors.'

'Let me do that.' Usara followed Halice out of the cabin. Temar would have gone too but Naldeth suddenly writhed on the bunk. 'Hold him,' Allin cried in alarm and Temar forced the mage's shoulders back on the blankets. Naldeth's eyes stayed closed, lips drawn back from clenched teeth, panting breaths rasping in his throat. A pulse beat fast and ragged in the hollow of his neck. Temar held him, expecting heat to sear his hands at any moment.

'Apple brandy.' Usara appeared at the door, offering a dark bottle sewn into a leather sleeve.

'Use liquor to clean the wound,' said Guinalle from the corner where she was standing, eyes unseeing as she worked some Artifice. 'It won't help the bleeding to have him drink it.' She looked at Usara. 'The enchanters are trying to read Muredarch's intentions. Now we are retreating, they have no interest in harassing us. You could speed us home with some small magic worked just around the ship. But I cannot keep watch for you,' she warned, eyes huge, 'not if I'm helping Naldeth bear the pain of the cautery.'

'Usara knows some elemental defences against Artifice,' Allin was still concentrating on Naldeth's stump, fingers pressing tight to stem the bleeding. Temar moved closer to the door and seized the chance for a breath of fresher air as the mage departed.

Guinalle laid a gentle hand on Naldeth's forehead. 'Concentrate on my touch, on my voice. Let me take you away from the pain.'

The stricken wizard flinched but Guinalle persisted with gentle, inexorable hands bending close to whisper her incantations. Naldeth swallowed a sob, deep in his throat, eyes rolling beneath flickering lids. Gradually his laboured breathing slowed, the rigid tension lessening down his body.

Temar saw tears trickling down Allin's face. She sniffed irritably, trying to scrub her cheek dry on her shoulder. Temar dug in a pocket for his kerchief and went to dry her face. As she mouthed her gratitude, he thought how remarkably sweet her smile could be.

'Mind your backs.' Halice held the cabin door open as the *Dulse*'s shipwright carried in a small brazier held tight between thickly padded leather gloves. His apprentice followed, lugging a hefty slab of slate. 'Set it down there.' The shipwright steadied the brazier as it rested on the tile. 'I don't know what irons you might want, my lady, so I brought a fair selection.' The lad ground pincers, tongs, a small prybar and a plain length of iron into the glowing charcoal.

Allin pulled on a glove the apprentice offered her. As she took the iron bar from the coals, the end glowed with a white heat the brazier could never have imparted. 'Hold his leg for me,' she appealed to Temar.

Catching his lip between his teeth, Temar knelt to grip Naldeth's thigh as steadily as he could. Allin quickly uncovered the butchered flesh, fresh blood flowing from the ruin of torn skin, chewed muscle and sheared bone. Temar had to turn his face away. He'd seen his share of battlefield injuries but this was worse, a man so savaged by a mindless seabeast.

Allin bent closer to wield the thick bar with the delicacy of a fine pen picking through a manuscript. Naldeth whimpered and Temar felt his thigh tense beneath his hands. This close to Guinalle and with all that linked them, he sensed her fighting every impulse that screamed at the mage to rip himself away from this torment. The stink of burning flesh assaulted Temar's nostrils, stinging his eyes but he could not turn away, lest he hinder Allin, lest he meet Naldeth's eyes.

'Nearly done,' Allin murmured. The second application

of the iron only took a moment but the smell was just as bad. Feeling Naldeth falling slackly unconscious, Temar couldn't help clapping a hand to his mouth.

'He's out of his senses.' Guinalle tried to stand but her knees gave way and she would have fallen if Temar hadn't caught her. She began to retch, catching them both by surprise.

'Outside.' Temar gripped her around the waist. 'Come on.'

Allin, moisture beading her forehead, continued determinedly dressing Naldeth's stump with fresh linen. 'Not for the moment.'

Temar realised sweat was sticking his own shirt to his back as he half escorted, half dragged Guinalle out on to the main deck. The noblewoman was ashen but the salt-scented breeze saved her from vomiting.

'It's working Artifice on water,' she said faintly. 'I just need a moment before I go back.'

'Is he going to die?' Temar dragged clean air deep into his lungs and his own nausea faded.

'Not just at present.' Guinalle smoothed her braids with shaking hands.

'Then you work no more healing on him until we are safe on land,' Temar told her bluntly. 'You push yourself too hard.'

'Who else is there?' Guinalle glared at him.

'For combating the Elietimm enchanters, no one,' Temar retorted. 'So I will not permit you to exhaust yourself tending Naldeth. Sailors and mercenaries have lost legs before now and lived through it without aetheric healing. I'm sure Halice and Master Jevon know what to do.'

'You will not permit me?' Rage lent a spurious colour to Guinalle's pale cheeks. 'How do you intend stopping me? What right have you to command me when your callousness cost that poor boy his leg in the first place?'

'Me?' Temar gaped at her.

'You could have had him safe and whole!' Guinalle stabbed an accusing finger in Temar's chest. 'For the sake of some nails and some sailcloth!'

'And that would have been the end of it?' Temar folded his arms to stop himself slapping Guinalle's hand away. 'Don't be so foolish! Yield once to a bully and he comes back asking for twice and thrice.'

'What price a man's life?' cried Guinalle.

'What price would Muredarch settle for, once he had me on the run?' countered Temar angrily. 'He plans to hold these islands for his own and Kellarin can go hang for all he cares. We stand against him now or he'll bleed us dry and spit out the husk.'

'This has been a trying day for all of us.' Usara's hand closed on Temar's arm, catching him unawares. 'Why don't you leave this discussion for some other time, somewhere a little less public?' For all his peaceable words, the wizard's voice was tight with anger.

Guinalle blushed a ferocious scarlet, turning her face out to sea, back stiff with outrage.

Temar took a measured breath. 'What have you there?'

Usara carried a haphazard collection of jars and bottles in a frayed wicker basket. 'Half the sailors seem to have some shrine-sanctioned cure-all in their sea chest, or a salve with the seal of the Imperial Apothecary.'

Guinalle looked over her shoulder. 'Do you know what's in them?'

Usara shrugged. 'Not really.'

'I'll see what Allin and I can make of them.' Guinalle took the basket without ceremony. Usara would have followed her to the cabin but Temar caught him by the arm.

'I didn't start that. It was Guinalle.' Sounding like a whining apprentice again, Temar thought crossly.

'What has that to do with anything?' Usara was unforgiving. 'You're our leader and you should be setting an example.'

'By refusing to give in to extortion?' Did no one appreciate his impossible position? Temar shook his head. 'Never mind. It's Guinalle I'm worried about.'

Usara's annoyance softened to wary concern. 'You and me both, but she insists she's all right.'

Temar waved a hand in frustration. 'She's like a lyre some fool's tuned to too high a pitch. We may get some fine music for a while but she could snap without warning and then we'll have no strings to our bow at all.'

'I believe that expression refers to the weapon rather than the music tool.' Usara tried for levity with a resounding lack of success.

'Adepts are trained to suppress their emotions away from their enchantments. Guinalle's so very effective at using Artifice because she's so very good at divorcing herself from her feelings.' Temar hesitated. 'But she used to allow herself to feel pleasure, to relax, enjoy a dance, a flirtation, just like any other girl.' He gave the wizard a hard look. 'Don't you admire her?'

'I hold her in the highest esteem,' Usara said awkwardly. 'She has a remarkable mind.'

'Take it from me, she's as much woman as intellect,' Temar said fervently. 'But she's forgotten that and that's just making things worse. You're probably the only person who can remind her, soothe her to some proper relaxation.' He gave the wizard a meaningful look.

'Are you suggesting I roll her into a handy bunk and tumble her into a more amenable temper?' Usara was caught between incredulity and outrage.

Temar blushed scarlet but held his ground. 'If that's what it takes. Don't tell me you don't want to.'

'I'll tell you to mind your own business.' Usara rubbed a hand over his beard. 'And I'll write off your crashing lack of tact against the stresses of today. And since we're talking so frankly, Messire, may I suggest you look to your own affairs?' He turned on his heel and disappeared into the stern cabin before Temar had any chance to reply.

That could have gone better, Temar thought gloomily. No, curse it, someone had to get through to Guinalle and Usara was the man to do it. He wondered about joining Halice on the forecastle where she was talking to Master Jevon. Would she congratulate him for defying Muredarch or blame him for Naldeth's mutilation? Would she just be furious with him for not killing all the pirates out of hand, parley or no? How many such outrages would Raeponin have tallied against Halice's name when she came to render her account to Saedrin? Temar wondered sourly. Maybe it was different if you were a mercenary.

The *Dulse* sped on, cleaving through the great swells rolling in from the endless ocean. The vessel swayed as the helmsman turned their course to ride the waves. Temar stared at the rise and fall of the waters, catching every detail of windblown spume, every glint and shade of sunlight on the dense blue. How did those birds so blithely riding the vanishing crests find fish in this vast emptiness? Did they sleep on the waters or fly back to land to roost for the night? Had anyone ever seen those birds but those few who'd discovered these isles lost in the deepest ocean?

No, he decided, he wasn't going to think about Suthyfer. He'd been telling Guinalle she needed to set her problems aside for a while so the very least he could do was take his own advice. But how was he going to find an answer to Muredarch's threat? Never pull a rope against a stronger man, that's what his grandsire had always said.

A soft step beside him roused Temar from his fruitless thoughts. It was Allin, her sombre brown dress stained with blood and water, a smear of unguent greasy on one sleeve. Her round face was sad, brown eyes vulnerable, and a quiver tugged at the corners of her downturned mouth.

'Am I needed?' asked Temar, bracing himself.

Allin shook her head, silent for a moment before answering. 'No, Guinalle and Usara are sitting with Naldeth.' She managed a wry smile. 'They're debating theories of magic so I thought I'd get some fresh air.'

'Theories of magic?' Temar was confused.

The mage-girl nodded. 'Usara recalls some ages-old treatise arguing elemental affinity is an extension of the five physical senses into the unseen realms of nature. They're trying to decide if there are any correspondences between this theory and this doctrine of the five wits that Guinalle says underpins Artifice. He's always had this notion that there must be fundamental balances underpinning everything.' She sounded sceptical.

'Guinalle needs to rest, not boil her brain with puzzles,' said Temar, exasperated.

Allin's short laugh surprised him. 'Actually, I think they both find a little intellectual debate welcome distraction from the bloody reality we've been dealing with.'

Then they were welcome to it, Temar thought. 'How is Naldeth?'

Allin drew an abrupt breath and squared her shoulders. 'Insensible but the bleeding has stopped.'

'He owes you his life.' Temar sought to comfort her.

'For the moment.' Allin's mouth pressed into an unhappy line, tears welling in her eyes. 'It's all rags and gobbets of skin and flesh that will turn to green rot given half a chance and that'll have him dead inside a couple of days. We have to take the rest of his leg off, mid thigh somewhere and find enough skin to cover the stump.' She was struggling not to weep. 'But he's lost so much blood already, I don't know he'll be able to stand it. But, if we delay, we risk the wound festering.'

Not knowing what to say for the best, Temar just gathered her to him, holding her close, silky hair smooth against his cheek.

'If only we could get him to Hadrumal,' Allin sobbed. 'But Guinalle says the enchanters will be watching and we'd all be at risk, Naldeth most of all. What do I tell Planir if he dies?'

'Why should he blame you?' Temar fumbled awkwardly for his kerchief to wipe the tears from Allin's face again. 'I'm the one bears the guilt for defying Muredarch.'

Allin gazed up at him, reddened eyes wide. 'You couldn't give in to him!'

'Thank you for that.' Temar kissed her forehead absently. 'I only hope a few others agree with you.' Allin's arms tightened around his waist in mute support, warming him.

'I'm not playing this game again.' Halice's arrival took them both by surprise. Allin would have moved away but Temar resisted and she stayed in his embrace.

'Muredarch may think he's got all the runes in his hand but I aim to spoil his fun.' Halice was looking as dangerous as Temar had ever seen her. 'He can't torture us by killing prisoners if we take them off him.'

'You can't attack while we're still waiting for Ryshad and Livak to kill Ilkehan.' Temar just about managed to keep his words a statement rather than a question.

'I'm talking a raid, on that cursed stockade of theirs.' Halice's face was hard and cunning. 'We loose the prisoners and take them into the forest. That'll give Muredarch and his cursed enchanters something new to worry about while we wait for 'Gren to have his fun.'

Temar realised he'd never quite appreciated just what qualities had raised Halice to such pre-eminence among the mercenaries of Lescar.

'These people have some bizarre ideas about what's edible,' I murmured to Sorgrad. The time of day suggested this was breakfast but we were served much the same food at every meal. 'Didn't we see a lot of this last night?' Olret might consider himself master of all he surveyed but my mother, mere housekeeper to a prosperous merchant, would have scorned serving up the previous night's leavings.

'Pickled moss?' Sorgrad innocently offered me a bowl of soused green lumps.

'Thank you, no.' I reached for some tiny sweet berries, topping them with something halfway between thick cream and underpressed cheese that, remarkably enough, didn't taste of goat. 'Oh, you're not going to eat that!'

'Gren was contemplating a plate of glaucous grey lumps that I'd thought looked unappetising even before I realised that's where the smell halfway between rancid milk and a plague house privy pit was coming from.

He raised a golden eyebrow at me. 'Why not?'

'Suit yourself.' I picked up my spoon. 'I'm not sitting near you if you do.'

'All right.' He gave up his teasing and pulled a leg from a vaguely goose-shaped bird. I'd tried some of that the previous evening and would have sworn I'd been eating fish, if I hadn't carved it for myself.

'Where's Ryshad?' Shiv cut into a slab of meat too dark and substantial to be a goat so I guessed it must be some seabeast flesh. Perhaps meals would be easier if I just stopped trying to work out what was what.

'Just coming.' I nodded towards the door as I took some

bread. There was plenty of that and if the grain and texture were unfamiliar, it did at least taste recognisable.

Ryshad brushed his hand across my shoulder as he passed behind me and pulled up a stool. 'This is all very informal.'

'Compared to last night,' Sorgrad agreed, looking the length of the long table at people we'd yet to be introduced to, gathering in small groups, chatting as they helped themselves from the array of bowls and platters.

'What were all those stories about?' asked Ryshad. We'd sat through an interminable if well-presented banquet, all of us seated as Olret's guests of honour, and the evening had rounded off with endless recitations resounding with the heavy rhythms of ancient Mountain sagas. With upwards of a hundred of Olret's people packed into the hall and all rapt attention, Sorgrad hadn't liked to translate.

'Wraiths and wyrms, the usual stuff,' 'Gren answered, mouth full.

'One warned of travellers who turned out to come from behind the sunset.' Sorgrad chewed and swallowed. 'It reminded me of a Gidestan tale about the Eldritch Kin, though that's not what they called them.'

'Pass the water, please.' Shiv looked thoughtful. 'Geris reckoned myths of the Eldritch Kin were half-remembered tales of the Plains People.'

I took some of the wonderfully clean-tasting water for myself after pouring a horn cupful for Shiv. 'What do we make of that?'

'Another curiosity for the scholars of Vanam?' Ryshad hazarded.

'There were a good few tales of life among the Elietimm here.' I looked to Sorgrad for confirmation.

'Which bear out what Olret was saying about no over-lords,' he nodded. 'And it seems the lowest born can end up ruling a clan hereabouts if he can convince enough people to back him.'

'If he's got the stones for it.' 'Gren was unimpressed.

'Half those tales were about someone with a bit of gumption coming to a bad end. Where's the fun in that?'

'Bad and bold got exiled or worse while meek and mild got enough to eat and saw his grandchildren thrive,' I said to Ryshad.

He considered this. 'So while anyone could rise to rule in theory, in practice, the strong hand their power to their sons?'

'Sort of.' I frowned. My knowledge of the Mountain tongue had been found wanting a good few times. 'I wasn't quite clear on the daughters, Sorgrad.' According to Mountain custom, the wealth of their mines and forests was always passed down the female line, which did make sense when you wanted to keep such resources within the family. There will always be women to vouch for a child being born to a particular mother but independent witnesses to a conception are never going to be easy to come by.

'From what I could work out, marrying into an established clan bloodline certainly strengthens a claim to power but it's not set in stone like Anyatimm tradition.' Circumspect, Sorgrad surveyed the hall and the people coming to and from the table.

'They don't like their women getting above themselves,' I commented. Several tales had mentioned in passing wives who'd abandoned their husbands for some intrepid lover and either starved in exile or died a bloody death with every hand raised against them.

Sorgrad was still considering Ryshad's question. 'Their songs praise hard work and keeping your head down but if you don't, just as long as you win, no one condemns you for it. That final song started with a woman who shirked her duty to expose a child born to her husband's concubine. The boy lived, ran wild as he grew and finally returned from exile to burn his father's house down around his ears, killing everyone inside. The son ruled and no one gainsaid his right, by conquest as well as by blood.'

'That was the song Olret cut short?' asked Shiv.

I nodded. 'Doubtless because that's the kind of tradition Ilkehan relies on.'

'And there's no overlord or union of the other rulers to keep anyone inclined to abuse his power in check.' Ryshad grimaced. 'It used to be any two leaders with a dispute would agree on a third to act as mediator, lawspeaker,' Sorgren looked grim. 'But that's a tradition Ilkehan seems to have killed off.'

We all fell silent as a maidservant appeared to collect empty plates and make up full dishes from half-emptied ones.

A resounding blow on the double doors interrupted everyone's meal. The leathery-faced retainer Maedror entered, swinging his bone staff as if he'd like to hit someone with it. A liveried guard followed, apprehension naked on his face as he dragged in a cowering hound. Brindled and bred for coursing by its long slender legs and narrow head, it was a pitiful-looking beast, cowering on its creamy under-belly. As it fought against the leash with heart-rending whines, we all saw the bloody socket where some scum had gouged out one of its eyes.

Furious, Maedror shouted at a maid who took to her heels. We all sat tight, along with everyone else caught unawares by this turn of events. Those servants who could, vanished behind the wall hangings. Olret soon came into the hall at a run, tunic unbelted over loose trews and shod in slippers of soft cured hide rather than his lordly boots. He skidded to a halt when he saw the brindled cur.

'What is that?' With Olret spacing his words with delib-erate cold calm, I easily understood.

Maedror's reply was too hasty and stumbling to be clear but I caught the word Ilkehan. A chill ran through the room as if someone had opened a window on to a blizzard.

Olret walked slowly down the hall. He circled the whim-pering dog, bending to look more closely at its rump. The beast crouched low, tail tucked between its legs. Infuriated, Olret snatched Maedror's staff and smashed the wrist-thick bone down on the dog, snapping its spine with an audible crack. The beast howled its uncomprehending anguish, back legs useless, bowels and bladder voiding on the floor. Its front paws scrabbled at the flagstones for a nerve-shredding moment then Olret brought the butt of the staff down to stave in its skull. But that was not enough. He pounded the sorry corpse, blood and brain spattering everywhere. Heedless of his footwear, he kicked the ruined mess of skin and bone time and again, sending gory smears across the floor.

Revolted, I didn't dare look away. No one else had moved so much as a hair, not even the guard with the leash biting into his fingers. Maedror stood as still as a statue, even when Olret, panting with exertion, flung the staff at him. The heavy bone, dull with blood and muck clattered to the floor as Maedror failed to catch it. Olret glared at his retainer with almost the hatred he'd shown for the dog. Maedror bent to recover the staff and even halfway down the hall, we saw the fear in his face.

'Gren nudged me with a whisper. 'If that's the local sport, I don't reckon much to it.' Fighting for 'Gren is only fun if your opponent can appreciate the pain and danger coming his way.

'Shut up,' Sorgrad said quietly.

Olret bent over the ravaged corpse of the dog and lifted one back leg. Whatever he saw warranted a slow nod. The ill-fated guard ducked away, expecting a blow as Olret whipped round but he simply marched up the hall, face like carved stone. His soft, stained footwear betrayed him and, slipping, he nearly fell. No one so much as smiled as he paused to strip his feet bare.

'You, come with me.' He summoned us with a bloodied finger.

A lackey got to the door barely a breath ahead of his master and flung it open. We followed hastily as Olret took the main stairs of the keep two and three at a time. With Maedror hard on our heels, we passed the floor with the rooms we'd been granted and continued without pause for breath up the next flight of stairs. Olret turned down the corridor and halted before a solid door.

'Ilkehan sent me that dog as a gift for my son.' Emotion cracked the cold mask of his face. 'They met on neutral ground at Equinox to agree truce terms. If they had not met, Ilkehan could claim the right to do whatever he pleased. You may see how Ilkehan returned my son to me.'

He opened the door and beckoned us into a hushed and shuttered room, richly furnished by local standards, coffers set along one wall, cushioned chairs along the other, bed hung with embroidered curtains. A still figure lay in the bed beneath a light coverlet. The boy was Temar's age, perhaps a little younger. It was hard to tell with the bandages swathing the youth's corn-coloured head. Yellowish matter stained the linen over what I could only assume was an eye socket as empty as the dog's. A nurse looked at us warily from her cross-stool where the slats in the shutters offered light for her sewing. Olret summoned her with a peremptory hand. Her slow movements betrayed her reluctance as she lifted back the blanket with gentle hands. The lad was naked beneath the soft wool but for the bandages covering his groin which were stained with unmistakable foulness. Now I understood Olret's reaction to the dog.

The pitiful figure on the bed stirred and his nurse re-covered him, Olret hustling us out of the room. 'I do not know whether to wish that he lives or he dies to be spared the knowledge of such mutilations.' He spoke as if every word were torture. 'I cannot stand to see how he looks at me.'

'Which is why Ilkehan didn't take both his eyes.' Sorgrad was coldly furious. In all the years I'd known him, I could count the number of times I'd seen that on the fingers of one hand. I'd also seen the bloody consequences. What people didn't appreciate was Sorgrad was really far more dangerous than his brother. 'Gren only ever acted on impulse. Sorgrad thought out precisely what mayhem he intended.

Ryshad's face was a study in disgust. 'Do such crimes go unpunished?'

Olret looked at Sorgrad and to Shiv. 'Will you truly kill

Ilkehan or spend your lives in the attempt? If I help you, will you tell him at the last that you act for my son?'

'I'll carve the boy's name on his forehead myself,' promised Sorgrad. My heart sank a little since that was no idle boast.

Olret held his gaze for a long moment then nodded with satisfaction. 'Carve Aretrin, down to the very bone.'

'Perhaps Forest lore can ease your son,' I offered slowly. Halcarion help me, if there was some charm to at least save the lad the agonies of death by wound rot, I should try it.

'I will attack one of Ilkehan's outposts, that you may reach his lands unnoticed.' Olret ignored me, addressing Sorgrad, Ryshad and Shiv. 'Come, I will show you.' He turned down the corridor towards the lesser set of stairs.

I stayed put, to see what the reaction would be. There was none. 'Gren stood beside me, watching the others go. 'We're the spare donkeys in this mule train.' He didn't seem concerned. 'Nice to know this Olret's got as much reason to hate Ilkehan as we have.'

'Hmm.' I wasn't so sanguine. 'Olret might have provoked him. Sow thistles and you'll reap prickles after all.'

'You don't trust him,' said 'Gren with eager curiosity.

'I don't know,' I shrugged. 'I don't know who we're dealing with and that always makes me uneasy. Remember that business with Cordainer?'

'Our man's certainly got something to hide,' agreed 'Gren. 'Did you see that gate on the stair?'

'No.' What had I missed?

'This way.' 'Gren led me back to the main stair. A metal gate barred the turn on the next flight, mortared firmly into the stone and secured with the first half-decent lock I'd seen on these islands. 'What do you suppose he's hiding up there?'

A liveried guard appeared on the stairs below and stared up at us with undisguised suspicion. I turned 'Gren with a firm hand and we went down past the guard. I favoured him with a reassuring smile but all I got back was a mistrustful glower.

'What now?' 'Gren demanded sulkily. 'I'm not sitting around getting bored while they fuss over maps and tactics and all the rest of it.'

Not eager for more of Olret's snubs, I'd already thought of a better use for my time. 'Why don't we see what these people reckon to our host? If his own folk like him, maybe we can trust him.'

'Where shall we start?' asked 'Gren obligingly.

'Shall we see what keeps everyone so busy?' I led the way out through the main hall. The yard around the keep was empty apart from a few guards practising with wooden staves bound with leather to save them from splintering. Scarce wood was well looked after around here.

'They move well.' 'Gren's was an expert eye.

'They probably start training them in their leading strings,' I commented. Even without Artifice to back them, we'd have found any Elietimm fighting force formidable opponents.

We passed through the main gate without anyone raising a question.

'Let's see what the boats have brought in,' 'Gren suggested with lively interest.

It was more basketfuls of glittering fish about the length of a man's hand poured in silver torrents into long troughs where mothers and grandmothers ripped them open with practised knives. Lads barely higher than my shoulder dragged baskets of gutted fish to another set of troughs where girls of all ages washed them clean. Several whistled and hummed tunes with a compulsive lilt to put a spring in a step. I wondered idly if there was any Artifice in the music, to drive these people on beyond weariness and tedium. That would suit what I knew of Elietimm cold-heartedness. Beyond them, a square of sombre old men layered the cleaned fish into barrels, adding judicious handfuls of salt and spice. A cooper stood ready to seal them.

'Fish to eat all winter,' said 'Gren without enthusiasm.

'More than enough for the people hereabouts.' None of

whom so much as paused in their work to glance at us.

'You heard them last night. There's farms and holdings all over this island.' 'Gren shrugged. 'They've all sent people to help with the glut.'

Such rural concerns never bothered me in Vanam where I bought fish, pickled or dried from those merchants my mother favoured with her master's coin. Some of them made a tidy profit from the trade. Questions teased me as we watched the islanders work. Did Olret's people truly eat all the fruits of their labours? Where did he get the spice to flavour the brine? I'd eat one of those little fish raw and unboned if pepper grew anywhere in these islands. Come to that, where did he get all the wood for these barrels? I reckoned he was being a little too coy about what trade he had with the world beyond these barren rocks. No wonder Olret was keen to see Ilkehan dead, if the bastard was sinking any ships but his own venturing on to the ocean. That was some reassurance; I'll generally trust a motive that can be weighed in solid coin.

'Gren coughed. 'Let's go somewhere fresher.'

Beyond the gutting and salting, men and women were carving bigger fish into long fillets with wickedly sharp knives. More lads were hanging them on racks set to catch the wind while a gang of smaller children gathered discarded heads and spread them out to dry. An earlier harvest of stockfish was stacked flat beneath heavy stones and the last moisture drained slowly into a fishy slick coating the beaten earth, lapped at by eager cats just waiting for a chance to sneak closer.

A young woman saw me looking at the fish heads and paused in her work, bending a wrist to brush back a blond lock straying from her close-tied headscarf. 'For winter, for the goats.'

'Ah, I see.' Then they'd even have milk that tasted of fish.

'You are visiting?'

'From the west.' 'Gren beamed back blatant appreciation of the shapely figure beneath her coarse and salt-stained bodice.

She would have replied but froze at a sharp rebuke from an older woman further along the stone workbench. 'Gren swept a bow to the sour old hag but she was intent on her filleting.

'Maybe you'd better rein in the charm,' I suggested as we strolled towards the distant edge of the settlement.

'You can't ask that, not with so many fine-looking women,' he protested. 'And precious few men to go around.'

He was right. 'They're all out fishing?' I guessed.

'Not at this time of day.' 'Gren shook his head. 'Let's see if these beauties have any answers.' We'd reached a high-walled enclosure holding more of the elusive goats. I was surprised to see how patiently they stood as girls combed the winter's growth from their thick coats, filling baskets with soft tangles of woolly hair.

A buxom lass stood upright to ease her back and smiled shyly at 'Gren. Two other lasses looked up from their work with ill-concealed interest. 'Good day to you.'

'Gren rested his chin on his hands atop the wall. 'Don't let me disturb you.'

An older woman, possibly the girls' mother, certainly looking out for their interests, assessed him in much the same way she was sorting the hanks of goat hair.

I smiled at her. 'That makes wonderfully soft blankets, doesn't it?'

If I'd been a goat, she wouldn't have treated me to any fish heads. 'Gren on the other hand was winning covert approval from all of them.

'See what you can get out of them without me around.' I slapped 'Gren on the shoulder, speaking in the gutter slang of Selerima. 'I'll meet you back at the keep in a while.'

'Gren nodded, his eyes on one lass bending forward to tease leaves from a goat's shaggy forelock and artlessly offering him a fine view of her cleavage.

'We're here to make friends, not babies,' I reminded him.

'I'll stay chaste as a dowerless maidservant – until I know

what the penalty for flipping a girl's frills might be,' he added with a sly smile.

I poked him in the chest. 'I was a dowerless maidservant, so you'd better stay a cursed more chaste than that.'

'I'm hardly going to tumble the first girl who flutters her lashes at me,' he protested. 'Not when there are so many to choose from.'

'I'll see you later.' Given how much 'Gren enjoyed flirtation, I judged I'd be back before he was ready to risk all our necks for the sake of some lass's white thighs.

As soon as I turned my back, the girls all started talking. As long as he kept his wits out of his breeches, he was well placed to find out a good deal about this place.

The only thing beyond the goat sheds was the pond and the causeway. A narrow-windowed building stood solid in the middle of the rocky dam and closer to, I realised it was a mill. All I'd find there would be busy men who wouldn't welcome interruption. Where might I find something useful like bored guards ready to gamble and gossip?

I walked idly back towards the keep, passing a building both open-fronted laundry and bathing house. Women pounded coarse, unbleached cloth in tubs filled from a spring that steamed as it bubbled up from the ground. On balance, I'd rather heave wood to boil my water than risk the ground melting beneath me for the sake of easier laundry. Unselfconscious as they stripped, girls were washing themselves clean after their fish gutting, pouring water over each other and soaping themselves with what looked like lengths of fatty hide. 'Gren would be none too pleased to have missed this treat but, given how obsessive these people were about cleanliness, I imagined he'd get another opportunity.

Other girls were giggling and chatting as they sat combing out their damp hair in the sun. I wondered about joining them but they were watching youths wrestling on a smoothed expanse of sun-baked clay. The lads were naked but for belts around their waists linked to leather bands around each thigh by plaited leather straps and a brief loincloth to prevent an opponent getting an unexpected handhold. The object seemed to be to drag your opponent off his feet by these straps. I spared a moment to appreciate the game as well as the players but decided the lasses wouldn't welcome me.

Then I heard a hastily stifled giggle somewhere behind the laundry. A seemingly casual stroll took me round to a drying yard where shirts and blankets flapped in the breeze. I ducked beneath a swathe of sodden cloth and found a huddle of children shirking whatever tasks they'd been set. Some were throwing knobbly bones from some sizeable fish's spine into a circle scored on the ground while others tossed a turnip studded with feathers between themselves. They all looked at me with vivid curiosity.

'Good day to you,' I said with a friendly smile.

'What's your name?' asked a pert little girl with an upturned, freckled nose and dark eyes telling of mixed blood somewhere in her line.

'Livak,' I told her. 'What's yours?'

'Gliffa,' she answered promptly. 'You're not from here.'

'No, I'm not.' I swept a vague arm in the direction of the sea. 'My people live in a forest that covers the land with trees taller than your houses.' That should intrigue youngsters from a land where trees rarely reached above knee height.

'What brings you here?' Gliffa was clearly a child always asking questions.

'I wanted to see the sea.' I shrugged.

'What happened to your hair?' demanded a small boy, his own locks close-cropped to little more than gold fuzz.

'Nothing.' I sat down, cross-legged. 'It's always been this colour, same as all my people.'

'Are you gebaedim?' the child asked suspiciously.

That was a word I'd caught last night. I shook my head. 'What's that?'

'Gebaedim live in the western lands.' One of the older girls leaned closer to study my hair and eyes. 'They look like real people until they're out of the sunlight. Then you can see they have shadow-blue skin and black eyes like a beast's.' Smaller ones who'd been looking distinctly nervous relaxed at her authoritative pronouncement.

So Sorgrad had been right. I smiled again. 'We call them the Eldritch Kin.'

'You've seen them?' The crop-headed lad's blue eyes were awestruck.

'No one has, not in a long age.' I shook my head reassuringly. 'We tell tales of them. Would you like to hear one?' That won me eager nods all round.

'There once was a man called Marsile who chased a hare inside an Eldritch man's earthen fort. The Eldritch man made him welcome and offered him guest gifts.' The story of Marsile was one I could tell in my sleep and I gave the children the version my father had told me as a little girl, full of miraculous things like the leaf that prompted fish to throw themselves out of the water when Marsile tossed it into their pond, and the sprig of blossom that made him proof against any fire, even a dragon's breath. My personal favourite was the purse that called coin to keep company with any he put in it.

'When evening came, Marsile told the Eldritch man he must return home to his wife.' I lowered my voice and leaned forward, the children unconsciously doing the same. 'The Eldritch man was angry. He said he had only given the gifts because he thought Marsile intended to marry his daughter and, truth be told, she was a great beauty.' Versions I'd learned later in life detailed the Eldritch maid's charms in terms emphatically not for children, as well as elaborating on just what Marsile did with her to make the Eldritch man so angry. I moved on to Marsile's desperate bargaining for his freedom.

'Finally, the Eldritch man agreed to let Marsile go, but,' I raised a warning finger, 'only if he remained for one night, while the Eldritch man went to Marsile's house and took what he wanted, in return for the gifts he had made him. Because, as we all know, a gift once given cannot be taken back.' The children all nodded solemnly; that rule evidently held even in these poverty-stricken lands.

I told them of Marsile's frantic night worrying about what he might lose, rather than his enthusiastic romping with the Eldritch daughter according to the taproom version. Some stories had the Eldritch man making just as free with Marsile's wife. In those the hapless man returned to find a year had passed for every chime he'd spent within the earthen ring and the Eldritch man's final gift to him was a brood of black-haired brats at his hearth and a wife who ever after burned his food as she pined for her magical lover. But that wasn't a tale for children either. What they wanted was a rousing finish.

'As the sky began to pale, the Eldritch man returned and told Marsile to leave. He warned him he'd release his hounds if Marsile wasn't beyond the river by daybreak. Marsile ran but the sun came up and he hadn't reached the river. He heard howls behind him and running paws,' I drummed my hands on my thighs and the little ones shivered. 'He ran for his life with barking ever closer. He dared not look back, even when something caught at his cloak. He ripped it off and threw it away, hearing the dogs stop to worry at it. But he soon felt their icy breath on his heels again so he threw away his bag, then his jerkin. He emptied his pockets, he lost the leaf, he lost the enchanted blossom and the magic purse but just as the sun came up over the eastern edge of the land, he reached the river. He threw himself in and swam to the other side.' The children all heaved a sigh of relief.

'He scrambled out and finally looked back.' I paused, looking at the intent faces. 'Huge black hounds prowled on the far bank. They had eyes as white as snow and frost dripped from teeth like icicles.' I sat back. 'Then the sun melted them into smoke.'

The children cheered and clapped but as always, there was one less appreciative in my audience. 'They couldn't have reached him anyway.' An older lad at the rear of the group spoke up with confident disdain. 'Gebaedim can't cross water.'

'Then how did they get to Kehannasekke—' The lass broke off and looked guiltily at me. I might tell a good story but I was still an adult and I'd bet her braids this wasn't something they were supposed to discuss.

'We're safe as long at the hargeard holds.' The older boy scowled at her. 'My father said.'

I saw him nervously tumbling three conical shells and a pea-sized reddish stone from one hand to the other. 'What's that game?'

'Just nonsense for the little ones.' He looked slyly at me. 'Could you find the stone?'

I pursed my lips. 'How hard can it be?'

'It's easy,' he assured me, with all the instincts of a born huckster.

'You're not supposed to play that,' piped up some sanctimonious miss.

'I won't tell,' I grinned.

The lad glared at the dutiful one. 'We're only playing for fun. That's allowed.' He sounded a little too defiant for that to be strictly true.

I was happy for him to think we weren't playing for anything of value as I studied the shells beneath his rapidly moving hands. We play this trick with nutshells and a pea back home and call it the squirrel game. I had been a handful of years older than this lad when I'd first learned it, practising till my fingers cramped once I realised a penniless lass on the road had to choose between deception or prostitution and I had scant inclination for whoring. I knew exactly where the lad's piece of gravel was and put my finger unerringly on the shell next to it. 'There.'

'No!' He'd need to learn how to hide his triumph if he wanted to keep people playing long enough to empty their pockets.

'Let me try again.' We went a few more rounds. I let him win often enough to start feeling cocky but got it right a few

times, with suitably feigned deliberation. That kept him keen
to prove he could outwit me. Most of the other children
returned to their own games.

'How does a hargeard keep you safe from gebaedim? No
tale tells how to ward off the Eldritch Kin where I come
from.' I picked up the shell to reveal the stone. That was
twice in a row.

The lad set his jaw, determined to best me somehow or
other. 'Gebaedim live beyond the sunset where there's no
light or water,' he told me with lofty superiority. 'Where the
dead go.'

Which was a fair description of the shades, where the
pious would insist those barred from the Otherworld by
Saedrin ended up. 'What then?'

'The dead have power.' He spoke as if that were self-
evident and it certainly fitted with what I knew of Mountain
Men's reverence for their ancestors' bones. 'The hargeard
ties their power to the living. As long as we have the lore to
use that power, the gebaedim cannot harm us.' He glanced
towards Olret's keep.

'And Olret holds the lore.' I nodded as if he was saying
something I already knew. In one sense he was; I'd suspected
Olret had some Artifice at his disposal. 'But your friend said
there are gebaedim in Kehannasekke?'

'So my father says.' The boy looked all too young as he
said that, fear shadowing his eyes. 'He says Ilkehan uses them
in his army, that's why he's never been beaten.'

'But Olret holds your hargeard and that keeps you all
safe,' I reminded him. I didn't want nightmares of evildoers
arousing parental suspicions about whom the children might
have been talking to. I picked up a shell. 'There it is. I've
got the trick of this now.'

Three times is always the charm and it worked on the
lad. 'I've played enough. I have work to do.' He stomped
off, too cross to fret about Eldritch Kin. As he thrust a sheet
out of his path, I saw a small child trying to hide as she was
revealed.

'Go away!' Gliffa flapped an angry hand at the little girl. 'You're not to come here.'

The intruder fled, bare feet showing dirty soles. All she wore was a ragged shift, which struck me as odd given the others all wore neat skirts or trews, loving embroidery around the collars of their coarsely woven shirts and chemises, feet snug in tight-sewn leather footwear halfway between boots and stockings.

'Will you tell us another story?' Gliffa asked shyly.

'Maybe later.' I smiled at her. 'I'd better go. My friends will be wondering where I am and I wouldn't want to get you into trouble.' I gave her a conspiratorial smile before walking away just fast enough to see the ragged little girl scamper through the crudely cobbled yard running along the back of storehouses. Adults busy about their tasks ignored her, apart from one man who raised his hand to her in unmistakable threat. She cowered away and vanished through a sally port in the wall around the keep.

The jalquezan refrain from the ballad of Viyenne and the Does should keep me unseen if I could only keep it running through my mind. '*Fae dar amenel, sor dar redicorle.*' Sure enough, no one so much as glanced my way as I ran silently to catch up with the child. I reached the sally port just soon enough to see the girl scramble in through a window that quick calculation told me must open on to the lesser stair.

Hitched up, her shift showed a painfully thin rump and legs barely more than skin and bone. That starveling little lass wasn't eating her fill of fishy-tasting birds or meaty seabeasts and sneaking in through a window suggested she was up to no good. Neglected like this, all she'd have to fill her belly was resentment. If I could catch her, I might be able to tempt her to tell me some less pleasant truths about this place.

There was no one in sight but I still kept up the charm as I squeezed myself through the narrow window. I could hear the lass's breathless running up the stair, bare feet whispering on the stone. She didn't halt at the floor above the great hall, nor yet at the next, hurrying on up. I kept pace with her, flattening myself against the wall and peering around the corner to see her meet another of those iron gates. Which were all very well, unless you were thin enough to squeeze through the bars. I watched as the child threaded herself carefully through, the fattest thing about her the woolly animal she clutched by one leg. That was easily squashed and pulled after her. She paused to reshape her treasure, kissing the nameless beast with passionate apology before disappearing up the stairs.

A memory struck me with all the force of a blow to the head. I'd seen that woolly beast before now and I could recall exactly where. That little girl had been barely walking but she'd carried it through the halls of the Shernasekke house that we'd seen reduced to ruins. How had she escaped that destruction? If Olret had saved her, he wasn't taking particularly good care of her now.

What else was he keeping behind lock and key? I crept cautiously down to the corridor where Olret's mutilated son had his room. That was empty so I ran lightly down the next flight and ducked into my own cubbyhole. The bed bore no trace of our passionate exertions the previous night, coverlets straight and smooth. My bag hung on the footboard and I saw that the hair I'd left in the buckle apparently caught by chance, was now snapped. No matter; I didn't keep anything of interest or value in there. I sat on the bed and opened my belt pouch. Slipped into the stitching of the inner seam was a fine steel picklock and I patiently teased it free, tucking it into the sheath of the dagger I had strapped on the inner side of my forearm. I also took out the parchment bearing my scant knowledge of Artifice and smoothed it flat. That in hand, innocent face all eagerness to help, I marched boldly up the stairs to the floor above. There was still no one around, so, tucking the parchment back in my pocket, I disappeared up the curve of the stair.

There was no way I could squeeze through the bars so I knelt by the locked gate. I could have opened most locks in these islands with a piece of wet straw but this was different. As I probed its hidden working, I wondered where Olret had got such a thing. There wasn't enough metal hereabouts to give any Elietimm the chance to hone such craftsmanship. No matter, it wasn't as complex as the Mountaincrafted locks Sorgrad had trained me on. It yielded with a softly rolling click.

I went cautiously up, low to the ground to look over the topmost stairs since any guard would be keeping watch at head height. There was no one there but a rank smell like a stable drain wrinkled my nose. I stood up and walked softly down the corridor. Doors ajar on either side opened on to unfurnished rooms, bare walls, scrubbed floors and no sign of the little girl, not even cowering behind a door. After checking every room, all I was left with was one shut up and, unsurprisingly, the source of the stench. The door wasn't locked but bolted high and low.

What was inside, besides the little girl? Whatever it was, it was something Olret kept safely locked away and that meant it had to have some value. I reached up to the top bolt and then stopped. How had the child got in here and then bolted the door after herself? No, she must be cowering in the other stairwell. I lowered my hand and was about to turn away when both bolts began to move of their own accord. They glided smoothly through the hasps and the latch lifted. A frisson ran through me.

The door stayed shut though. Opening it would have to be my choice. Where had that notion come from? I studied the blank timber. Could I walk away and not know what it concealed? Curiosity got Amit hanged, as my mother used to say. Perhaps, but that had never stopped me before. I pushed at the door and it swung open on well-oiled hinges. I managed not to choke on the stink it released.

The room was the biggest I'd seen on the keep's upper levels and it was full of cages. In a land so poor in metals, I was looking at a fortune to choke the greediest merchant back home. Still, I didn't imagine the women looking through those bars appreciated being surrounded with such wealth. They ranged from a frail-looking grandmother to two maidens barely blooming into womanhood. The other three were much of an age with myself and one held the fugitive child close to her skirts. All were Elietimm by their colouring and features and, by local standards, their gowns were well cut and expertly sewn. But the clothes hung loose on them, gaping at the neck and slack in the waist. All the captive faces were drawn with hunger kept just short of starvation by a prudent jailer.

The little girl looked at me, hugging her woolly animal. Her mother's sage dress was stained and creased with wear, the hems dirtied where she'd been unable to avoid the spreading pile of ordure she'd done her best to keep in one corner of her prison. Could Olret not even grant his prisoners a chamber pot? Or was that the point? How better to humiliate these women than by denying them even the most basic dignities? All had fingernails rimed with black, fair hair lank with dirt, filth engrained in the creases of faces and necks. They had nothing to sit on, not so much as a blanket to soften the iron bars beneath their feet. Only a crude hide spread out below each cage, edges curled and tied into corners to catch the soil before it reached the floorboards and threatened the ceilings below.

I hadn't exactly decided to leave but was considering backing out of the room when I realised I couldn't. Nothing hindered my feet but I knew for a certainty that the only way I could move was forward. All the women watched intently. It was a fair bet one of them was using Artifice on me but, oddly, I didn't feel particularly threatened.

'Good day, ladies.' A step forward was easy enough but I knew instantly I still couldn't take it back.

'Please come beyond the door.' The mother spoke urgently, her Tormalin as good if not better than my Mountain speech. That was a fair point. I moved and the door swung closed behind me, bolts sealing me in with a soft rasp as the grandmother muttered a rapid charm.

'Who are you?' the mother demanded. Locked in a stinking prison, I wouldn't have bothered with niceties either.

'A visitor, from over the ocean.' It may be mere childhood myth that giving the Eldritch Kin your name hands them power over you but I wasn't taking any chances with unknown practitioners of Artifice. 'Who are you?'

'I was wife to Ashernan, master of Shernasekke.' The mother wasn't bandying words with anyone who might help her. 'We are all of that clan; my mother, my sisters and their daughters.'

'I thought Ilkehan destroyed Shernasekke.' I matched her directness, aware someone might interrupt us at any moment. Then I'd be in trouble but we'd deal with that as the runes fell.

'Ilkehan with Olret yapping at his heels.' The grandmother spat copiously in wordless disgust.

Her back against her bars, one of the sisters sat with coppery gold skirts rucked up to pad her rump. 'What Evadesekke sees, he covets. What Evadesekke covets, Kehannasekke steals. What Kehannasekke steals, Rettasekke hides.' The obscure pronouncement had the bitter resonance of old, acknowledged truth in the Elietimm tongue.

'How do you come to be here?' I asked the lady of Shernasekke.

'Olret stole us out from beneath Ilkehan's nose.' She waved a disdainful hand at their foul prison. 'He offers us a choice: marriage with his blood or this squalor.' Her mother barked with weary laughter.

'Marriage will give Olret a claim on Shernasekke land to rival Ilkehan's right of conquest?' I guessed, glancing at the two nubile girls. Marriage by rape is a long and dishonourable tradition in Lescar, where inheritance squabbles fester from generation to generation and more than one duchess took her wedding vows with a dagger at her throat.

'He will only have a claim when the bloodlines are joined by a child.' The other sister scowled from her foetid cage, twitching her mossy green skirts as she stood.

The lady of Shernasekke smiled. 'He may have cut us off from home and hargeard but we can summon power from our common birthright to rule within this room.'

So this neglect might be more precaution than calculated torment.

'It is both,' the woman in green told me.

'Are you reading my thoughts?' I asked warily.

She shrugged. 'A simple enough trick.'

'One that Olret cannot master.' The grandmother came to the front of her cage, eyes webbed with age and sunk deep in her wrinkled face. 'That's the other reason he risks Ilkehan's wrath to keep us in this captivity. We hold all that remains of Shernasekke's lore and Olret would dearly love to add that to his own.'

'Mother!' protested the sister in the green gown.

'Why dissemble?' argued her other sister. 'Olret condemned our clan to be crushed beneath Ilkehan's heel without us to defend Shernasekke.'

'This one is no friend to Olret.' The old woman stared at me. With her clouded eyes I doubted she could see much beyond the length of her arm but something was giving her uncomfortably accurate insight. She grunted with satisfaction. 'Nor her friends.'

'You're here with others?' One of the young girls spoke for the first time, hope naked on her face.

'Can you get a message to Evadesekke?' The woman in gold scrambled to her feet. 'We have ties of kinship there.'

'Dachasekke will help us once they know we are still alive,' her sister in green insisted. 'Froilasekke too.'

'Our quarrel is with Ilkehan,' I said carefully. 'We've little interest in involving ourselves in strife we have no part in.' If you can't see the bottom of the river, you don't start wading.

'Olret will trade us to Ilkehan if some turn of fate makes that worth his while or if our surrender proves the only way to save his own skin.' Shernasekke's lady looked at me and I knew her words for simple truth.

These women had some powerful Artifice among them and, like Guinalle, the skills to work their enchantments without constant incantations. It was also a relief to know Olret wasn't able to look inside my head and learn I'd been up here. This wasn't the brutal, damaging enchantment that Ilkehan had wrought on me and around me but all the same, none of these women were showing any qualms about taking what they wanted from my thoughts or imposing their will on my body. Was that the resonance of undeniable truth I heard in their words or treacherous magic convincing me of their lie? There didn't seem to be any of Guinalle's ethical tradition in Elietimm Artifice; it was either brutal or insidious.

'Are you truly speaking honestly?' I raised my eyebrows at Shernasekke's lady.

She shrugged. 'You can only decide such things for yourself.'

'When I've done so, I'll come back.' I found myself unhampered by enchantment as I turned to leave. The bolts slid back at a whisper from the younger maiden. As I slid through the door, I saw her looking at me with a misery that her elders refused to admit.

I hurried along the corridor. Those women were getting food and water, however inadequate, and I didn't want to meet whoever was bringing it. Slowing on the stairs, I dug a vial of perfume in my belt pouch and dabbed a little in the hollow of my throat. The scent cleansed the prison stink from my nostrils and hopefully masked any clinging to my clothes. Then I heard steps in the corridor where Olret's son slept his fevered dreams and froze. Creeping silently down, I stole a glance around the corner and saw the nurse walking away from me. I hurried on down but heard boots coming up below me. Turning, I fished my parchment out of my pocket and walked back up as if I had every right to be there.

There was no answer when I knocked so I waited by the door for the lad's nurse. Olret's son wouldn't be joining his bloodline with either of those lasses up above. Presumably that was Ilkehan's excuse for cutting his stones like some colt not wanted for stud. Did Shernasekke's lady know that had happened?

Was I going to tell the others what I'd discovered? How would they react? It was easy to see 'Gren could no more leave something like this alone than he could keep his fingers out of a tear in his breeches. He'd be all for storming the upper floor and setting the captives free. Come to that, Sorgrad would need some convincing reason why we shouldn't.

Ryshad might consider losing even a distasteful ally like Olret too high a price to pay for the women's freedom. Our purpose here was killing Ilkehan, not involving ourselves in wider dissensions. Ryshad would certainly find their casual domination of unknown Artifice sufficient argument to mistrust the women and leave them be, at least until we knew them to be friend or foe.

But Shiv would surely argue we needed any and all aetheric lore working for us and against Ilkehan. Would the mage be wrong? Could we have this out among ourselves without Olret getting wind of it?

I'd jotted a few scores from a meaningless game of runes with 'Gren on the back of the parchment. Just what kind of game was this three-cornered strife between Ilkehan, Olret and the lady of Shernasekke who seemed to have taken her dead husband's seat at the table? I didn't owe her any more than I trusted either of the others. Would stepping up and making my own random throw pay off handsomely for us or not?

'What do you want?' It was the nurse come back.

I flourished my parchment. 'My people, we of the Forest, we have songs to soothe the sick and injured.' I wasn't going to claim aetheric skills, not when I couldn't be certain I'd be able to help the lad.

The woman considered this. 'For a little while.' Her face said as plainly as speaking that if I couldn't do any good, I couldn't do any harm and there was little enough hope for her charge in any case.

The room was still dim and the sour sweetness of corruption was stronger than before. The lad lay motionless on his back, an unhealthy flush on his cheeks below his bandaged eyes.

I cleared my throat and began to sing softly. Guinalle reckoned 'The Lay of Mazir's Healing Hands' had Artifice hidden in its jalquezan refrain and I'd seen a wise woman of the Forest Folk sing it over a half-drowned girl who'd certainly recovered faster than she'd any right to. The nurse sat at her window sewing and I caught her smiling at the tale of Kespar who'd lost a wager with Poldrion, that he could swim the river between this world and the Other faster than the Ferryman could row his boat across. He'd paid the price in blood when the god's demons caught up with him. Mazir had healed her love with herbs and wise words, all the while teasing him for his folly. As I sang, I wondered if this poor lad had anyone to love him and comfort him. We'd seen no sign of any wife or mistress to Olret, nor yet any other children. Still, as Sorgrad would say, that was none of our concern. Ever softer, I drew the final refrain to a close. It may have been my imagination but I thought the lad's breath rasped less fast and desperate in his throat.

The nurse set aside her sewing and came to lay the back of her hand gently against his forehead. 'He sleeps more easily.'

'He may yet recover,' I suggested, though Saedrin knows, I couldn't think of a man who would relish such a life.

The woman shook her head regretfully. 'In cutting him off from his future, Ilkehan has cut him off from his past. Without the blessing of those who have gone before, he cannot live much longer.'

I couldn't think of anything to say to that. 'At least he will know a little peace.'

'It's best that you do not come again.' The nurse's face was unreadable.

'Very well.' I turned as I reached the door. 'I shall not speak of this. Will you keep silent as well?'

She nodded.

I did the same and left the room. That would be best for everyone. I didn't relish trying to explain to Ryshad or Sorgrad what I'd done, not when I had no clear idea just why I'd done it myself. Besides, as Sorgrad and Ryshad would both surely tell me, there was no reason for Olret to know what Artifice we might have to call on.

CHAPTER SIX

A riposte to Gamar Tilot and his
Thoughts on the Ancient Races
Presented to the Dialectic Association of Wrede
By Pirip Marne, Scholar of the University of
Vanam

Scholar Tilot makes a worthwhile contribution to the debates among the learned and leisured with his reminder that many with Forest and Mountain blood live among us. I allow we strive too hard on occasion to find arcane explanations for the mysteries of the past, when the fears and desires that drive us all might prove a wiser guide. The ancient races doubtless wished to eat, thrive and procreate just as we do today.

Nevertheless I take issue with Scholar Tilot. True, a proportion of our populace share a heritage with the Forest and the Mountain, but in no sense has either race vanished beneath a tide of common blood. I suspect Tilot's travels have been extensive within the libraries but seldom beyond them. I have journeyed widely, to meet Forest kinships where children stood amazed to see my brown eyes, when all they had ever known were green or blue. Such families live a comfortable life in the trackless depths of the greenwood, supported by knowledge of their world that town dwellers cannot hope to appreciate. I have scaled the passes of the mountains dividing Solura from Mandarkin and similarly found Mountain clans with scant knowledge of lowland tongues and less interest in our lifestyle, content as they are with their own customs and comforts.

As a young student, I even hoped I might travel to some

remote reach of the Dalasor grasslands and find the stocky linea-
ments and swarthy skin of Plains blood in some isolated nomadic
clan. Alas, I now chide myself for such fancies, not because I
believe legends of the Plains People fleeing beyond their rainbows but rather because I learn the brutal cohorts of the Old
Tormalin Empire did their work all too well. Tilot's progress
through his libraries has unaccountably failed to bring him to the
innumerable records of the strife that marked the Old Empire's
conquest of unwilling lands. This is no tale of peaceable union.
Nowhere was this fighting more fierce than in the grasslands of
Dalasor. Time and again, the archives of Tormalin Houses speak
of the unfamiliar race already dwelling beyond the Ast marches.
Those tied to vills and burgages in Caladhria and Lescar may
well have yielded to the invaders rather than see homes and liveli-
hoods burned over their heads but the herders between the Dalas
and the Drax could vanish into the distance whenever the cohorts
advanced, returning under the cover of night to strike at their
tormentors.

We have copious journals and letters written by the young
esquires leading those cohorts. All see the Plains People as entirely
different from themselves. They speak of them wrapping themselves in shadow to pass unseen. We read of plans thwarted when
news known only to a captive is communicated to his fellows
beyond, enabling them to evade pursuit or launch some pre-
emptive attack. In contrast, acts of mercy and kindness are
rewarded with gifts brought by unseen hands, found by men who
had told no one where they intended to hunt or bathe. These real
and doubtless unnerving experiences have been handed down to
us by way of children's tales of the Eldritch Kin. Even the most
inventive fancy could not build such chilling notions without some
foundation.

A few years since, I could not have explained that foundation but let us not join Tilot in ignoring the issue of Artifice. The
comprehensive studies of our estimable Mentor Keran Tonin offer
the best guide to any curious on this subject but, suffice it to say,
I am convinced by his argument that this ancient magic was
known to all three of the earliest races and inextricably woven

*into their religions. It was from them that the emerging powers
of Tormalin learned their lore and turned it to their advantage.
Now we see that power ultimately proved a double-edged sword,
as its loss brought disaster to Toremal's Emperors at the height
of their powers. For the Plains People, it proved no salvation but
it unquestionably provides the origin for the Eldritch Kin's
mystical talents.*

*What has this to do with Tilot's arguments? Consider this:
prompted to look outwards and beyond our easy assumptions by
the events of the past few years, scholars of Vanam have discovered aetheric magic hidden among the Mountain Men and Forest
Folk both, well hidden from prying eyes. If we of Ensaimin and
the other erstwhile western provinces of the Old Empire are indeed
descended from the Plains People, how is it that we have no recollection of such lore? Alas, I fear the secrets of the Plains magic
were scattered on the wind as the nomads fell beneath Tormalin
blades. As the re-emergence of Artifice holds out its intriguing
promise, I am surely not the only one to mourn such a loss.*

Rettasekke, Islands of the Elietimm, 7th of For-Summer

'You're either bored or plotting something.' Sorgrad studied me after looking round my door to find me sitting cross-legged on my bed.

'Bored,' I said with a rueful grin. I was playing an idle game of runes, one hand throwing against the other. 'No one's overly inclined to gossip with me.' I'd done my best to be helpful and friendly after another strangely assorted breakfast but none of the women about the keep would give me more than a couple of words.

I threw a cast of runes on the bed and totted up the score out of old habit. With the Sun dominant, dagger hand had the Reed, the Pine and the Chime beating the off-hand's Horn, Drum and Sea.

'They're just jealous.' 'Gren peered past his brother's shoulder. 'With you so devastatingly beautiful and this shocking shortage of men.' He sighed in mock regret.

'Where did you sleep last night?' I asked as I put away my rune sticks.

'Next to me and snoring fit to shake the bones that guard our homeland,' Sorgrad replied with faint malice.

'I could have tucked up a pretty girl five times over.' 'Gren shook his head. 'But my so-chaste brother here thinks it better we keep ourselves to ourselves.'

'Five would be a record, even for you.' We were walking down the corridor now. 'Why does a runt like you get welcomed like Halcarion's best idea since sex itself?'

'Gren stuck his tongue out at me. 'Because they've lost four ships since Equinox, all hands drowned, all thanks to Ilkehan according to the word at the wellhead.'

I winced. 'That's a lot of widows and orphans.'

'A drain on Olret's resources just when he lacks strong arms and backs to get the hay cut and the harvest in.' Sorgrad shrugged. 'Ilkehan's not stupid.'

'He will be when he's dead. Do we have a plan yet? ' 'Gren looked eager.

'There's a chunk of rock towards the northern end of the strait between here and Ilkehan's territory.' Sorgrad smiled. 'It used to be part of Rettasekke and Olret's been wanting it back for some while. He'll attack while we take a boat to the northern end of Kehannasekke.'

I frowned. 'Which leaves us with a cursed long walk, if I'm remembering the map right, over barren land at that.'

'The central uplands are passable in summer, according to Olret.' Sorgrad was unconcerned. 'Anyway, we want to give Ilkehan a few days to send all his muster off to fight and leave his keep unguarded.'

'But how do we get to kill Ilkehan?' demanded 'Gren.

'There'll be time enough to work that out as we travel.' Sorgrad shot his brother a piercing blue look. 'Your feet are always running faster than your boots.'

And if we made our plans as we went, I thought, no one here could betray them, by accident or design.

'You don't plough a field by turning it over in your mind,' 'Gren retorted. But he dropped the subject as we found Olret in the main hall with Ryshad and Shiv poring over a map on the long table.

'I'll gather men and boats here and here.' Olret stabbed a finger at the parchment. 'We can attack tomorrow.'

'Then we leave today.' Sorgrad looked at Ryshad.

I ducked under Ryshad's arm, sliding a hand around his waist as he nodded to Sorgrad. 'Well soaped is half shaved.'

Olret frowned with what could be suspicion or just bemusement at that particular piece of homely wisdom. 'So soon?'

Ryshad hugged me before leaning forward to trace a finger down the broken mountains that formed Kehannasekke's spine. 'That'll be hard going. The more time we have in hand the better.'

'How long will you be fighting Ilkehan?' demanded Sorgrad. 'If you've driven him off those rocks before we're barely halfway there, we're all but lost.'

'Or if he drives your lot into the quicksands,' added 'Gren, all polite helpfulness.

Olret scowled at him. 'We will not be driven back.'

'All the more reason for us to be ready to strike as soon as possible,' Ryshad said firmly.

Shiv was still studying the map. 'Could you send some other boats fishing or something, at the same time as we set out? They'll draw any curious eyes away from us.'

'Maedror can arrange that while he finds you a boat and crew,' Olret grudgingly conceded.

Sorgrad shook his head. 'We'll row ourselves. If we're caught, we'll take our chances. If your people are taken, that tells Ilkehan you're helping us.'

'We don't want to bring any more trouble down on your people,' said Shiv earnestly.

Olret's face twisted with resentment. 'Ilkehan thinks himself so powerful, so untouchable.'

'We'll show him different,' 'Gren assured him blithely.

'We'll get our gear, while Maedror arranges a boat.' Ryshad's respectful courtesy left Olret with no option but to summon the guard waiting warily by the far door. By the time we'd packed up our few possessions and returned to the great hall, Maedror was waiting.

'The master will meet us at the water's edge,' he said shortly as he handed us each an oilskin-covered bundle. I found mine contained bread and dried meat as he led us out to the stone jetties where an anonymous hide-covered boat bobbed gently at a tether.

Instead of his earlier ill temper, Olret greeted us with a smile. I wondered if it was as false as my own. 'You have been my guests for so short a time but know that I value the friendship you offer.' He spoke loudly enough for the curious, pausing in their incessant fish gutting, to hear. 'As you depart, I offer gifts in earnest of our future hopes.'

Ryshad and Shiv each got a braided wristlet of pale leather, threaded through beads of dark red stone.

'We call it Maewelin's blood.' Olret offered similar wristlets to 'Gren and Sorgrad. 'The tale has it that the Mother cut herself shaping such sharp mountains.' He chuckled and we laughed dutifully at the pleasantry.

'Does it hold any virtue?' I nearly said Artifice but caught myself just in time.

'Not beyond its beauty.' Olret looked puzzled. 'But it loses its lustre unless it sees the sunlight, which we take as token of the Mother's blessing within it.' He had a pendant on a single thong for me but I stopped him putting it over my head with a deprecating smile. 'May I look?' No one puts something that might strangle me around my neck. I studied the red stone glowing in the bright sun, veins of green and yellow teasing the eye as they disappeared into the piece skilfully shaped to resemble the closed bud of a flower. 'It's beautiful.' I put the thong around my neck with a suitably grateful beam.

'We should leave before those boats get too far away to give us cover.' Ryshad pointed to others already cutting through the water, most with oars, one larger with a single square-rigged sail of ruddy leather. They were heading southwards down the strait towards the dark line scored by a broken row of sandbanks and rocky outcrops rising barely higher than the water. With a final bow to Olret we took up the places we'd become used to in the boat that had brought us here.

'Keep close in to shore,' Shiv ordered as Ryshad pushed us away from the jetty. Sorgrad gritted his teeth and hauled in his oar, 'Gren doing the same beside him.

'Don't blame me if we get covered in bird shit.' Ryshad steered a careful course towards the piled stacks of black rock with their bickering roosts.

I waved a farewell at Olret who was watching us with a

peculiar hunger on his face. 'Goodbye,' I muttered. 'Goodbye warm baths, clean beds and food someone else has cooked, even if it is the strangest I've ever tasted.' 'Gren laughed.

'Mind the outflow from the sluices,' Shiv warned as we passed the mill atop the causeway, water foaming from gates beneath it.

As they all concentrated on oars, tiller and the rush of water beneath the thin hull, we all fell silent, the only sound the rhythmic plash of the oars.

I twisted to check that we were out of sight of Olret and promptly took his pendant off.

'Don't,' said Sorgrad sharply, seeing I was about to toss it into the sea.

'It's the only thing we've seen there worth stealing,' 'Gren agreed. 'Trust me, I looked.'

'I don't trust Olret and so I don't trust his gifts.' I hoped no one asked me to elaborate. I'd still rather not complicate matters by explaining about those Shernasekke women.

'Have you any sense that they're enchanted?' Ryshad looked past me. 'Shiv?'

'I'm the wrong mage again.' Shiv looked chagrined. 'But I can't feel anything awry and I always did handling Kellarin artefacts.'

'It could carry some charm to help him keep track of us,' I warned. 'Or hear what we're saying?'

'If there is some trick, getting rid of the things will just let him know we suspect him.' Sorgrad shipped his oar for a moment.

'He could just have been giving us a gift,' 'Gren mused as he took a rest as well.

I looked quizzically at him. 'And you tell me to live my life trusting nothing and no one until Saedrin tells me different at the end of it.'

'I don't have to trust someone to take their valuables.' 'Gren was unconcerned. 'Anyway, we might want to bribe someone to look the other way before we're done with Ilkehan. Better to use Olret's wealth than our own.'

'We wrap them up at the bottom of someone's pack,' Sorgrad said firmly. 'Then any kind of magic will show him piss all but he won't think we're scorning or deceiving him by getting rid of them. I'll take them.'

I turned to Ryshad who was leaning on the tiller with unseeing eyes. 'Ryshad?'

He smiled at me. 'I just remembered where I've seen this stone before. One of Messire D'Olbriot's sisters has some pieces, passed to her by an aunt from one of the House's cadet lines. She got them from some ancestor who married into a family trading out of Blacklith.'

'When we get back, you might like to ask your D'Olbriot just where his kin by marriage were trading in the Dalasor grassland clans,' Sorgrad remarked as he leant into his oar. 'Now, where are we're heading?'

'Just out of sight of Rettasekke and across the strait,' Ryshad told him. 'I'll be cursed before I flog you all the way up to where Olret suggested.'

'Cursed by me, that's for sure.' 'Gren looked at Ryshad. 'You don't trust him?'

It's always reassuring to have people thinking the same way as me.

'I don't trust his reasoning.' Ryshad checked wind and wave before leaning on the tiller. 'His route would take far too long. I want to be ready to hit Ilkehan as soon as we can.'

'If his attack goes badly, Olret might just give us up to save his own skin,' I pointed out. 'He was discussing some kind of a truce when Ilkehan mutilated his son.'

'That lad'll likely lose the other eye, even if he lives,' grimaced Sorgrad. 'I've seen it before with a blinding.'

The memory of the tortured boy prompted another long silence as we toiled up the Rettasekke coast.

'This is our closest approach,' Ryshad announced some while later. 'Shiv, you and Livak take the second set of oars and for all our sakes, match your stroke to hers.'

Rettasekke reached out into the sea, rising up to a head-land faced with sheer cliffs. Distant Kehannasekke lurked just visible, a long sweep of low land among the ever-present mists across the open water. I made my way gingerly up the boat to join Shiv on the forward thwart.

'I'll keep us balanced,' Shiv assured me.

'What do you think we'll find when we land?' asked 'Gren. 'Do you think Ilkehan truly has Eldritch Kin to call up and do his will?'

I was regretting telling him what the children had said. 'Let's just get safely ashore, shall we?'

'As long as the mist hobs don't get us first,' chuckled 'Gren.

'What's one of those, when it's at home?' I demanded.

'They blow in with the fogs and tempt away children and goatlings and foolish hounds,' said 'Gren with relish. 'They carry them off on the back of the north wind.'

'Do you suppose these people share many myths with yours?' Shiv asked 'Gren thoughtfully. 'Childhood nightmares would make useful illusions to clear our path out of there.'

'That's a sound notion,' Ryshad approved.

'What would scare you, 'Gren?' I corrected myself. 'What would scare normal people?'

He laughed. 'There's wraiths. They'll suck the light out of your eyes, given half a chance.'

'Wraiths live in dark holes and you can generally avoid those,' countered Sorgrad. 'Gwelgar always worried me more. They make themselves out of mud and grass and that's everywhere.'

'They rip evildoers limb from limb,' said 'Gren gleefully.

'If the bones of a soke's ancestors feel someone guilty of a mortal crime passing their cave, they summon up a gwelgar,' Sorgrad explained. 'It follows the guilt in their footsteps and nothing stops it, nothing kills it, nothing throws it off the scent.'

'According to our Aunt Mourve,' 'Gren continued sourly, 'after it's killed whoever it's hunting, it goes looking for naughty children to give them a good spanking.'

'I never liked her,' remarked Sorgrad.

I wouldn't exactly call it entertainment but, between them, Sorgrad and 'Gren had enough fables of disconcerting horrors lurking in mountain crevices to take our minds off the backbreaking work of rowing. Even so, by the time we reached Kehannasekke's sprawling maze of salt marsh and treacherous sands, my shoulders were burning and my arms trembled between every time I hauled on the oar.

Ryshad was scanning the shore for somewhere solid enough to set foot. 'Over there.'

As soon as we were all on the dubious safety of a stone-spotted bank of dour grey sand, Sorgrad pulled out a dagger and ripped a rent in the hide hull. 'Cast it adrift,' he ordered. 'We don't want anyone thinking Rettasekke men have landed.'

Ryshad shoved it off into the retreating ripples with one booted foot. He smiled reassurance at me. 'We'll be leaving by magic or not at all.'

'Let's get on.' 'Gren was already heading for the grass-tufted dunes inland, bag slung over his back.

No one wasted breath on idle chatter as we hurried into the shelter of the dunes. The sands gave way to a narrow expanse of close-cropped turf but thankfully any goats were off being coiffed for the summer. I murmured the Forest charm for concealment as we darted across, feeling as vulnerable as any hare started from its form until we reached the broken, hostile land beyond. Stark grey hills rose all around us. Not the raw peaks of Rettasekke, these mountains had been worn to low nubs by countless generations of cold and storm. Screes striped the steeply sloping sides of a cleft that offered our only path.

'Where do we run if we meet trouble?' Sceptical, I looked at treacherous slopes offering scant safe footing.

'We don't,' Ryshad said, drawing his sword.

'We kill it.' 'Gren was scouting eagerly ahead.

Thankfully we didn't meet anyone, just spent an interminable day negotiating ankle-wrenching rock fields, skirting bogs that could swallow a horse and cart and skulking along

the edges of the few patches of land that showed any sign
of tillage or grazing. We ate as we walked until finally the
curious, endless dusk of these northern lands began shrinking
the world around us. Shadows gathered in hollows and dells,
gloom thickening beneath the few spindly trees. Beneath the
translucent lavender sky, darkness shifting and deceiving the
eye, I could see how people might believe in Otherworldly
creatures using such half-light as a path between their realm
and ours. I rather wished 'Gren had kept some of his more
bloodcurdling myths to himself.

'This looks a good place for the night.' Shiv pointed to a
tangle of stunted birch trees, dry earth bare beneath them.

Sorgrad dumped his satchel and rummaged in it for some
food. 'Let's have a plan before the morning,' he suggested.
'Something a bit more definite than "just kill Ilkehan". Surprise will be everything, if we're to get in and out alive, so
we need to know exactly what we're doing and not waste a
breath as we do it.'

Ryshad lay down on the dry ground and stretched his
hands over his head. 'How do we get inside the keep for a
start?'

'How do we find out where he is inside it?' added Sorgrad.
'We don't want to be wandering round, knocking on doors.'

I patted the pouch where my parchment crackled. 'I can
use one of the Forest charms for finding prey to seek out
Ilkehan.'

'You're sure?' Ryshad couldn't help himself.

'Of course she is, and so are we.' 'Gren winked at me.
'Belief's everything with Artifice, isn't it?'

'Remember what Guinalle said about Artifice and Ilkehan?'
Shiv was kneeling by a paltry spring whose flow was soon
sucked back into the thirsty land. 'The more shameful we
can make his death, the more effectively we destroy the power
those enchanters in Suthyfer rely on.'

'You can leave humiliating the corpse to me.' 'Gren looked
disconcertingly eager.

'Is this safe to drink?' At Shiv's nod, I dipped a handful

from the little pool and drank gratefully. 'Lore and Artifice seem centred on these hargeards, these stone circles. Could we destroy Kehannasekke's?'

'It's an obvious thing to do,' Sorgrad agreed.

Ryshad sat up and found himself some food. 'Shiv?'

'If we find the hargeard, I can destroy it.' The mage waved a hand containing a hunk of bread. 'As long as I don't have some Elietimm clawing the wits out of my head.'

'So we need to find the hargeard circle before we move on Ilkehan.' Ryshad pursed his lips. 'As soon as he's dead, we break his stones, so to speak.'

'Gren chuckled at the jest.

'We're sure to be seen, doing all this.' I rubbed wet hands over my face to shed some of the day's grime. 'Let's make that work for us, if we can. You recall the children said Ilkehan's in league with these gebaedim, Eldritch Kin, whatever they are. Is there any way we can go in disguised as vengeful spirits? If we frighten people thoroughly enough, they won't stop to look too closely.'

'More to the point, they won't have the first clue where we came from.' Ryshad nodded.

'If they think we're immortal, maybe they won't bother trying to kill us.' 'Gren liked that idea.

'I'll settle for not missing a sword at my back because I've got this cursed hood up,' I said with feeling.

'The problem is, we can't have Shiv working illusions until Ilkehan's dead.' Ryshad knitted concerned brows.

'If we can find the right plants, I can turn us black haired and blue skinned with no need for magecraft.' The wizard chuckled. 'Living with Pered, I've learned more about dyes and colourings than any sane man could ever need to know.'

Sorgrad laughed. 'That'll be worth doing just to see Halice's face when we get back.'

'What are we looking for?' 'Gren went to root among the plants crouching along the line of the inadequate stream like some oversized truffle hound.

'Flagflowers, if you can find them.' Shiv stood up. He

went foraging and soon returned with his hands full of pale, knobbly roots with dark earth and a few sprigs of spite nettle still clinging to them. 'Mind those leaves, they sting.' He dumped the lot into my startled hands.

'Good thing we're here in the growing season,' I remarked.

Ryshad scratched his head. 'Can I see the map, Shiv, before you start painting us like marionettes?'

Shiv dropped more roots on the grass, and wiped his hands on his breeches before getting out the much-creased parchment. 'We're two, three days' hard march from Ilkehan.' His finger wavered over our general location then touched lightly on a spot just beyond the little castle symbol Pered had used for Kehannasekke's keep. 'That's where we were captured last time.'

'Which would be a good place to find somewhere to hide up,' Ryshad mused. 'In those hillocks just inshore.'

Sorgrad came to look. 'We want a vantage point, so we can keep a good watch for at least a full cycle of the guard.'

'Gren appeared, hands full of dripping roots and Shiv hastily whipped the map out of danger. 'I'm ready to fight anyone, any time of day.'

'We know,' I told him repressively. 'Try for a little patience. Shiv's got to paint us up like Eldritch Kin for a start.'

Sorgrad looked curiously at Shiv. 'Just how are you going to do that?'

'Who's carrying a candle?' Shiv squatted down and began shaving spite nettle roots into fine strips with his belt knife. 'And I need something to hold water.'

Sorgrad sighed as he produced a small silver cup from his belt pouch. 'I generally use this for wine.'

'Don't see a lot of that around here.' 'Gren dug in his pockets and produced a candle end. I found two short stubs in my pack.

Ryshad offered a plain horn cup to Shiv. The wizard took it. 'Thanks. I reckon using magic for this is safer than lighting a fire. Smoke and light will carry and it'll take ten times as long.'

Ryshad nodded reluctantly. 'I suppose Ilkehan would have to suspect someone was using magic to come looking for it, but the faster the better, Shiv. We'll keep watch all the same.'

Apprehension prickled between my shoulder blades as I matched Ryshad walking around the isolated dell, looking up and down the narrow winding valley, straining to hear any hint of booted feet or stifled whispers in the darkening shadows. I sternly curbed my fancy when I found I was dwelling on all the things that could go wrong with this madcap scheme. All right, it was a high stakes game, the highest in fact, but the trick to any hand is playing each throw of runes as they fall. I had plenty of advantages on my side as well; Ryshad's intelligence, Shiv's magic and the brothers' capacity for unflinching mayhem. And it was Sorgrad who'd taught me you win even the most trivial of games by playing as if you were gambling with Poldrion for his ferry fee to the Otherworld.

'Ready.' Shiv called in a low voice. The sight of 'Gren rubbing blue candle grease into this face gave me the first good laugh of this day and a good few since.

'Do you think we'll set a new fashion?' Sorgrad was kneeling with his head bent as Shiv carefully slopped black liquid into his hair.

'How easily will this wash off?' I dipped a suspicious finger into the smoky blue tallow.

'I'm not sure,' Shiv answered frankly. 'Don't put it on too thickly. A little will go a long way and we don't have any to waste.'

'I'll do you, if you'll do me,' invited Ryshad, scooping some into his palm.

'That's the best offer I've had all day.' I fluttered flirtatious eyelashes at him.

Ryshad's hands were gentle on my face as I relished in my turn the feel of bristles roughening his strong jaw and the smoother skin around his hairline. He brushed his lips against the inside of my wrist and we shared a private smile. If this was all the intimacy we could get before we risked our lives, we'd make the most of it.

'So, we watch the keep and work out where Ilkehan will be.' Sorgrad returned to planning the detail of our attack as he lifted his chin to colour his neck. 'What's our actual path in?'

'Through the drains and cellars?' I suggested. 'That's the way we got out last time.'

'We go straight for Ilkehan, hit him as hard as we can, all of us at once,' said Ryshad.

Sorgrad nodded. 'Kill him before he can decide which of us to attack first.'

I couldn't restrain a shiver. 'It's not going to be like last time,' Ryshad promised, holding my gaze.

'We should use some black in the last of the skin paint,' 'Gren said suddenly. 'Fill in the hollows of our eyes, like Sheltya do.' His hair was black as midnight now and his teeth were startling white against a face almost the hue of the dusk sky above.

'That's a sound idea.' I'd forgotten how unearthly that made the Mountain practitioners of Artifice look.

'I wonder what the Sheltya know of the Plains People and the Eldritch Kin,' mused Ryshad.

'We'll ask Aritane when we get back, shall we?' I smiled at him.

'When we get back,' he echoed.

'Who'll be buying the drinks?' demanded 'Gren. It plainly didn't occur to him that there was any doubt we would be getting out of this. I decided to adopt his certainty. Belief was everything in these islands, wasn't it?

Suthyfer, Sentry Island,
7th of For-Summer

'I do not see that you have the authority to tell me I cannot come.' Temar silently cursed whatever god had made Halice taller than him.

'We've made our plan and you agreed it.' Sat on a crude bench outside the cabin, the level strokes of her whetstone didn't vary as the mercenary sharpened her sword. 'Changing horses midstream is a quick and stupid way to drown. Yes, Pered?'

'Sketches of the enchanters.' The artist waved a sheaf of parchment scraps. 'I've done my best from Guinalle's descriptions.'

Halice nodded. 'Given them to Minare and Rosarn. Tell Vaspret I want to see him, if you get a chance.'

Pered swept a mock salute and sauntered off.

'If I come with you, I can lead another assault.' Temar wasn't going to give up that easily.

'Leading assaults isn't your job,' said Halice bluntly. 'You're not leading a cohort any more, you're leading a colony.'

'With every man we can muster, we could finish this tonight,' cried Temar. 'Kill Muredarch and have done.'

'You're forgetting those enchanters,' Halice chided. 'We're hitting the stockade, that's all.' She tilted the blade to catch the firelight and studied the edge. 'I'd like to string Muredarch up by his pizzle for what he did to Naldeth, but all in good time, my lad. Tonight we free as many prisoners as we can and then we run before those enchanters have their hands off their tools long enough to wonder where their boots are.' Halice held the heavy sword's hilt easily in her broad hand

and very carefully shaved a little swathe through the dark hairs on her forearm. 'As soon as Livak tells us Ilkehan's dead, we'll make Elietimm and pirates both sorry they ever set eyes on each other.'

What if Ilkehan couldn't be killed? Temar was trying to find the words to ask this without risking rebuke when Usara came out of the cabin.

'Could you keep the noise down?' the wizard asked with terse politeness. 'Guinalle's overtired and overwrought. You two bickering out here is the last thing she needs.'

'How's Naldeth?' asked Halice.

'Asleep.' The wizard looked weary to the bone. 'If you can get anything more out of Guinalle than "he's as well as can be expected" let me know.'

'Are the pirates still convinced there's no way we can reach them at night?' Halice demanded.

Usara nodded. 'Them and the enchanters as well, apparently.'

'Then she should sleep while we go and prove them wrong.' Halice slid her sword into its sheath. 'Temar, tell Guinalle we'll need her rested if we bring back wounded. She might take heed of that. Darni!'

The burly warrior was a little way down the beach, mercenaries and sailors gathered round him.

'She says she can't rest in case Naldeth suffers some crisis.' Usara's thoughts were still inside the hut with Guinalle. 'He's lost so much blood, she's worried she'll have to strengthen his heart again. I could do that much with wizardry but she won't even let me try.'

Temar's mind was on his own grievances. 'I don't see why Darni is the only choice to lead the other half of this assault.'

Usara wasn't listening, seeing Allin come to join Darni and Halice. Darni laughed abruptly and Halice scrubbed a hand through her short hair, face intrigued. 'What are they up to?'

'Let's find out.' Temar rose and Usara followed as they

hurried to catch Halice and the big warrior disappearing into the shadows behind the cabin.

'Curse it.' Temar stumbled awkwardly on a treacherous tree root. With clouds covering the lesser moon barely at her half and her greater sister waning from her own, the night was a confusion of half-light and shadow.

'I appreciate you want to attack on the darkest night we'll have before Solstice but that hampers your troops just as much as the enemy.' Larissa's cool voice only served to warm Temar's resentment at being excluded.

'I don't have time for admiring clever mages,' Halice warned bluntly. 'Shit!'

Temar felt Usara freeze, as startled as him.

'How did you do that?' Halice asked cautiously after a moment.

'Do what?' demanded Usara with frustration equal to Temar's own.

'Light is made up of varying degrees of heat.' Pride bubbled irrepressibly in Larissa's voice. 'If you see the warmth—'

'I can see in the dark.' Halice's wonder finished the sentence for the mage-girl. 'How long does it last and how many of us can you bespell?'

'Barely half a chime.' Larissa sounded annoyed with herself.

'We can bespell two or three of you,' Allin offered meekly.

'Each of us,' clarified Larissa quickly. 'Call it a handful between us.'

'Better than a poke in the eye with a sharp stick.' Laughter rumbled deep in Darni's chest. 'Kalion had better look to his conjuring when you get back to Hadrumal, ladies, or one of you'll be nominated Hearth Mistress inside the year.'

'It was mostly Allin's idea.' Larissa didn't sound displeased with the praise though. 'Once we decided not to provoke Muredarch by drying up his wells.'

'Larissa saw how to make it work,' insisted Allin.

'We need to refine it before it's a truly effective spell.' The clouds cleared a little and Temar saw Larissa raise a hand. 'Usara? Can you help?'

'How do we make this work for us?' mused Halice. 'How much can I see where there is some light?' She headed back for the beach, the mages close around her, watching alertly.

Temar hurried after them. 'You'd need a second in command whose vision isn't altered.'

'You're not coming.' Darni stretched out an arm like a fence rail to hold him back. 'We can't chance your loss or capture.'

'I can hold my own in a fight,' Temar said stiffly.

'Emperors fall face down in the shit, just the same as peasants.' Darni gave the young nobleman a hard look. 'The rest of us are expendable. You're not.'

'How long would Guinalle hold out if she saw you being dipped for the sharks?' Halice turned the corner of the hut and swore. 'Shit, I can't look anywhere close to a fire. It hurts worse than taking it up the back alley.' She mopped her streaming eyes.

'Stand still.' Larissa passed her hands across the mercenary's face.

'That's better.' Halice grunted with satisfaction 'Mind you, in the right place this could weight the runes for us. Can all three of you do this?'

'It'll be easy enough to show Usara the trick of it,' said Larissa confidently.

'You can't all be going?' Temar stepped around Darni's arm. 'I shall need a mage here, surely. Allin can stay.' Larissa could risk her neck with her ill-concealed ambitions, but Allin was far too precious to him. That abrupt realisation blinded Temar as effectively as the firelight in Halice's bespelled eyes.

'We need all the mages this time,' said Halice with perfunctory apology.

'What if you need to bespeak me?' Temar objected. Was there any way he could insist Allin stayed aboard ship rather than join the actual assault?

'You'll just have to keep a good watch out,' Darni told

him. 'We need the wizards to get us all ashore without lights.'

'There is one thing you can do for us, Messire D'Alsennin.' Halice snapped her fingers at the young man. 'Tell them why we're going. That's a Sieur's job.'

Temar gathered his wits as he saw the array of expectant faces among the campfires on the beach. Catching sight of Allin's hopeful face, radiant with trust, he realised he had to find the words to make these people fight fiercely enough to bring her back safe. He bowed to the waiting men and women, mercenaries, sailors and Kellarin folk, the golden firelight making equals of them all against the velvet blackness of sea and sky. All of them bowed back and Temar cleared his throat.

'I know some of you and you know me, after these last seasons working for Kellarin's benefit. I don't suppose Sieur D'Alsennin means a lot to the rest of you; I'm sorry I've had so little chance to introduce myself as yet. Forgive me; we'll do something about that on your return. You might pick up a few barrels of Kellarin's wine that those thieves have stolen. It's always easier to make new friends over a drink.'

A ripple of appreciative laughter encouraged him. Temar waved a negligent hand.

'You'll be well paid, that goes without saying, but all the gold ever minted can't buy a life and it's the lives of those innocents in that foul stockade you must fight for tonight. You've all heard what was done to Naldeth. You'll not stand to see that done to anyone else, will you?'

A dour chorus of agreement ran around the sands and Temar saw righteous anger on most faces, coloured here and there with ferocious anticipation.

'This isn't the night for making those scum pay for their crimes, mind you. That'll come soon enough, never fear. Tonight you take away the stick they think they can beat us with. Then we wait for friends elsewhere to cut away the prop of their treacherous magic. Once that's gone we'll send them all so fast to the shades there'll be standing room only in Poldrion's ferry. Saedrin himself will have them drawing lots to see who steps up first.'

That didn't get much of a laugh so Temar stopped straining his eloquence.

'Go in, get the prisoners, get back here with your skins whole.' He shrugged. 'It's simple enough. You know what you're doing.'

That won him a rousing cheer and a slap on the shoulder from Halice. 'We'll make a leader of you yet, my lad.'

'Not if you keep calling me that,' he retorted.

'We'll keep it between you and me, then.' She grinned, unapologetic. 'Come on, Allin, Usara.'

Halice didn't look back as she strode down the beach, her handpicked troop gathering around her. She'd stop calling Temar 'lad' when he'd earned the respect to go with the title birth and chance had conferred upon him. Not that he was doing so badly, she allowed, though that romantic streak would have had him long dead in the viciousness of the Lescari wars.

'What's the joke, boss?' Minare was at her elbow, the rest following on behind.

'Nothing.' Halice's smile vanished. 'We're ready for dealing out blood and filth and death and pain?'

'All single minds and no hearts,' Minare confirmed. 'I should have known there'd be a price due for a peaceful life in Kellarin.'

'Make sure anyone within reach of your blade dies there and we can all go back to it.' That's what Halice's mind was set upon. 'Come on, get a move on!' She waved the fighting force towards the waiting boats.

The captain of the *Dulse* was waiting on the main deck when she climbed aboard. 'How close do you want me inshore?'

'We'll tell you when we get there.' Halice looked to check the longboats were being securely lashed to the *Dulse*'s stern. 'Wait for our signal and then come in to get us.'

'It's poor light and worse water,' Master Jevon warned her.

'The wizards have that in hand,' Halice reassured him. 'Usara? This way.'

The mage followed her to the shallow deck of the forecastle where Halice found a dark-haired man with a coil of thin rope in his hands, leather and bone tags marking its length.

'Jil, this is Usara. Right, Master Mage, prove this idea of yours works before I risk all our necks trusting you.' She nodded to Jil who deftly cast the lead weight he held over the prow, fingers noting the thin rope's progress without conscious thought. 'We've got—'

Halice hushed him with a curt hand. 'Usara?'

Usara frowned. 'There's five spans of water beneath the keel. The bottom's sandy here but there are rocks about a plough length that way.' He pointed into the darkness. 'And over there.'

'Jil?'

'That's what the charts say,' admitted the sounding man.

'We'll make a pilot of him yet, won't we?' Halice grinned.

'Good enough to put me out of work.' Jil didn't sound too thrilled.

Halice left the mage to placate the sailor and went down into the waist of the ship, balancing herself as the ship got underway. Her troop was gathered on one side of the deck, Darni's on the other. Halice listened with half an ear as Darni spoke to those under his command. She'd been relieved to see he treated his men well as they'd drilled their motley band into some semblance of a corps. He was appropriately courteous to the few women under his command as well, but cut them no slack that might trip the entire troop. Halice had no quarrel with that.

The *Dulse*'s crew moved round and above them, alert to every peril of night sailing. Master Jevon stood, arms akimbo, on the aftdeck. The helmsman didn't take his eyes off his captain as he felt every movement of sea and ship through the whipstaff.

'Will this be like taking that watchpost?' Halice saw the lad Glane was looking apprehensive.

'Easier, if we all keep our heads,' she told him unemotionally. 'Keep one eye on the enemy, one eye on your mates and one on Vaspret.'

Glane managed a hesitant laugh. 'I'll try.'

'You know where that third eye comes from, lad?' Peyt was sharpening a sword that gleamed brilliantly clean in contrast to his unshaven dishevelment.

Glane shook his head, mystified.

Peyt clutched his groin with a suggestive grin. 'What's got one eye in here?'

'Think with what's between your ears, not between your legs,' Halice interrupted him. 'Chance your arm like you did in Sharlac and I'll leave you behind.'

'Peyt'll just walk back across the open water,' Deglain laughed from his seat in the shadow of the mainsail.

Peyt sneered at him but, before he could reply, Halice bent close to whisper in his ear. 'Don't think you'll get a chance to stay and turn pirate. I've someone ready to put a bolt through your head if I give the nod, you and all your cronies.' She watched him with a dangerous smile as he realised the men he'd relied on to back him in Kellarin were scattered between the two troops. The arrogance faded from his face.

Halice stood in the centre of the deck. 'Tonight, we put a scare into them. Do that well enough and they'll break like reeds when we make our main attack. Check your weapons and be sure you're ready to go as soon as we get there.'

She moved on to the sheltered stretch of deck just below the aftcastle. Rosarn looked up from bundling sheaves of arrows into oiled skins to save them from salt and damp. 'We've less than five quivers a bow,' she warned. 'And fewer spare strings than I'd like.'

'It's a raid, Ros,' Halice reminded her. 'We're not taking the field against the Duke of Parnilesse again.'

Rosarn smiled. 'He's too much sense to fight in the dark.'

'Nobles are supposed to be wise. It's mercenaries are madder than rabid dogs.' Halice watched the crossbowmen checking ratchets, windlasses and quarrels. 'Did you get those pictures from Pered?'

Rosarn patted the breast of her jerkin. 'We'll know them better than their own mothers.'

'If you get a shot, take it but we're not out to kill them at any cost.' Halice raised her voice so all the archers heard her. 'Just keep them scared and ducking their heads as we break the prisoners out.'

'All set?' Darni came up to join them.

'Well enough,' Halice confirmed. 'Yours?'

Darni nodded. 'The experienced lads know we're saving some pottage for another day. They won't let the green ones start a fight to the death.'

'As long as they're blooded before we take them into a real fight.' Halice looked the length of the ship, her gaze halting on Usara still high in the forecastle. 'Fighting was so much simpler without magic to complicate it.'

'Don't blame the mages,' Darni grinned. 'Planir's all for a simple life.'

'Let me know if he manages one,' Halice said drily. 'I'll bottle the secret and hawk it round the fairs. Where's his favourite complication?'

Darni nodded towards the aft cabin. 'Taking a rest, along with little Allin.' The Hadrumal warrior's square face was unreadable in the gloom.

Halice beckoned and he followed her up to the aftdeck. The helmsman and Master Jevon ignored them, intent on guiding the ship safely through the dark waters.

'How is your troop?' Halice asked Darni quietly. 'Who would you send them up against? Who would you run from?'

Darni considered her question before answering. 'They'd hold their own in a skirmish with the Brewer's Boys, as long as we got the drop on them, that is. I wouldn't want to face them in line of battle. I'd be the first one running if we fell foul of Arkady or Wynald.'

'Fair enough.' That Darni had fought in Lescar at the

Archmage's behest was a secondary consideration for Halice,
as long as his judgement agreed with hers.

Darni studied the men down on the main deck. 'We can
still use all the time we can get to drill them but I don't
suppose Sorgrad will dally just to suit our convenience.'
There was respect for the Mountain Man in the warrior's
voice.

'No, I don't suppose he will.' Halice wrinkled her nose
in a private grimace. She'd rather have Sorgrad as her
co-commander on this raid but better a bony fish than an
empty dish. Besides, Darni had won Sorgrad's esteem when
they'd fought together in the Mountains last summer. That
made Darni one of a very select company.

Still, Halice acknowledged, if the big dog's loyalty to his
master's quail got him killed, she wouldn't weep for Darni.
If he got any of hers killed for the mage-girl's sake, she'd
claim a slice of his hide for each and every one of them.
She'd try, anyway. Could she take him? She mentally measured his reach and stride. She hadn't gone up against another
corps commander in a long while. Not since before she'd had
her leg smashed.

Halice rubbed absently at her thigh, feeling as always the
slight thickening of the mended bone. She'd been crippled
as surely as Naldeth until Artifice had reshaped the twisted
and shortened limb. Magic certainly complicated the fighting
life but there was no denying the value of skills like Guinalle's,
and the mages' come to that. If she had to take up her sword
again, better for a cause like this than some mere coffer of
gold.

'Are your banner sergeants clear on their tasks?'

Darni was unscrewing the pommel of his sword.
'Absolutely.' He took a coin out of the hollow in the hilt and
polished it against his jerkin before putting it back. He
grinned at Halice. 'A luck piece from Strell, my wife. What
do you carry?'

Halice smiled briefly. 'A good whetstone.' She looked over
her troop again, satisfying herself that Minare and Vaspret

were best placed to strengthen the less experienced lads like Glane.

The ship ran on through the silent seas, everyone deep in their own thoughts. As the darkness of Suthyfer carved an outline against the stars, every head turned towards the crouching islands and the rushing of the surf. Sailors rushed aloft to furl sails and the ship slowed.

'How close do we go?' Master Jevon asked Halice.

'Watch the wizard.' She pointed to Usara standing shoulder to shoulder in the prow with Jil. The mage was intent on the black sea beneath the bowsprit and the entire ship fell silent, watching him. The helmsman moved the whipstaff with agonising delicacy at every shift of Jil's hand. The ship crept closer and closer to the mouth of the strait where the pirates lurked. Ominous, the islands closed on either side of the *Dulse*, blotting out the few stars breaking through the rents in the cloud above.

'Stir the girls,' Halice said quietly.

Darni slid silently down the ladder to summon Larissa and Allin. They joined him on the deck, faces pale in a passing gleam of the scant moonlight.

'Call up the boats.' At her order, Master Jevon snapped his fingers at the boatswain and the *Dulse*'s crew began hauling up the longboats that had followed her like so many ducklings. The stealthy flap and rustle of canvas overhead was overtaken by the noise of cautious boots on the deck as both troops began climbing down the ladders and netting that the sailors draped over the rails on either side. Only a few whispered oaths broke the hush as somebody was jostled, and then stealthy oars slid into the water.

'See you later, Commander,' said Rosarn. Burdened with arrows and bows, the archers climbed carefully down to a boat crewed by men from the *Dulse*.

Halice went down to the main deck where Allin waited for her, bundled up in a dark cloak. 'Let's go.'

She went down the ladder first, ready to catch the mage-girl if she slipped. The last thing they needed was that kind of commotion. Once they were aboard without mishap, Halice looked across the inky water to find the longboat where Darni hulked massive in the prow, Larissa hooded beside him. She nodded to Minare who silently signalled the men to start rowing. The boats crept forward, silence more precious than speed, sliding into line, each behind the other. Darni led the rest on the other side of the strait.

Halice saw a coppery thread curling through the blackness of the night sea, a sheen like firelight glittering in the very water that should kill it dead, just far enough ahead so the tiller man could see it. Allin sat beside her, round face grave with concentration as the guiding light led them through the rock-strewn shadows of the ever-narrowing strait. Halice rubbed absently at her thigh.

An oar scraped against a hidden rock and a banner sergeant's rebuke was hastily stifled. A scatter of huge stones tumbled down from the cliffs appeared in the water, shadows coming and going beneath the fitful light of the greater moon. Halice scowled upwards. It was a shame these wizards couldn't concoct some means of summoning back the clouds.

The breeze brought the acrid scent of damp, charred wood and Halice dismissed every thought beyond the task ahead of her. She could just make out the stark wrecks of the burnt ships some way down the strait as the thread of magelight coiled in a faint pool of radiance at the very end of the shingle beach. Halice patted Allin's cloaked arm in mute approval before climbing carefully out of the boat. She slid her boots noiselessly through the water, careful of her footing on treacherous stones.

Glancing back, she saw the newer recruits intent on her, anticipation in their shining eyes. Those already blooded under her command were keeping watch for the enemy. Halice studied the sprawling encampment on the far side of the landing. Some of the crooked cabins had spread to two and three rooms and moonlight glinted on windows plundered from the stern cabins of the *Tang* and Den Harkeil's ship. One even boasted a precarious, stubby chimney but most were relying on cook fires scorching the turf or dug into stone-lined pits. Dying back in this stillest watch of the night, they threw up little more than a reddish glow.

There was one fire burning bright, a figure momentarily silhouetted as he threw a log from a handy pile into the flames. Halice watched that single fire as she led her troop ashore. It was a good way off and while it was on higher ground, the indisciplined huts and canvas-covered stores of loot obscured what should have been a clear view of the water. The other side of that coin was Halice couldn't make out just how many raiders were awake and supposedly on watch. A handful? A double handful?

Her foremost men were at the very end of the shingle reach now, creeping closer and closer to the stockade. Minare's men were the first to leave the treacherous stones and move more quickly over the muffling grass. As soon as the timber-walled prison was between her force and the sleeping pirates, Halice divided them with silent hand signals. Minare led his lads up around the stockade to keep watch on the landward side while Halice sent her men the other way, their path curling round close beneath the base of the wall. She fell back behind them, Vaspret at her side, the two of them low to the ground and moving out into the darkness until she could see the whole arc of the beach and the ground rising up to the pirate encampment beyond. She drew her sword.

'Go.'

Her soft command sent Vaspret running low and silent like a coursing hound. The sentry sat idly dozing against the gate of the stockade died before waking without a sound. Vaspret jerked his knife out of the pirate's ribs, keeping one hand still clamped over the corpse's mouth and nose as he wiped the blade clean.

As the rest of the troop waited, Deglain was already moving. With Vaspret keeping watch for him, he brought a formidable pair of blacksmith's pincers to bear on the chain threaded through the gate. He leant all his strength to the task and the link he'd chosen gave way with a sharp crack. Everyone froze but no alarm roused among the oblivious huts.

Vaspret signalled and the rest of the men ran up to vanish inside the gates. Halice watched the distant fire, noting a sharp cry within the stockade followed by sudden hysterical weeping, both sounds silenced moments later. The first of Vaspret's men reappeared, encouraging the more able prisoners, no need to impress upon them the necessity of speed and stealth. They vanished into the black night before the first cries came from a sentry, the startled man silhouetted by the fire at his back. As Vaspret's men dragged and carried more of the prisoners away, commotion boiled up among the pirates' shelters and tents. Vaspret was the last out, an unconscious woman slung over one shoulder.

Halice made a silent bet that she had been the one threatening hysterics. She took a few paces forward, drawing herself to her full height, sword catching the light as she lofted it for all the world like some hero from a ballad penned by a minstrel who'd never so much as lifted a dagger. The pirates were coming on now, some hesitating as to whether they should head for her or the stockade. Minare made that debate irrelevant as the mercenaries lying in wait unseen crashed into the raiders, taking full murderous advantage of their surprise.

'How are we doing?' Halice shouted to Vaspret as he passed her. The time for silence was emphatically past as the clash of steel and cries of pain roused Muredarch's entire contingent.

'Just hold them off till we can get to the boats.' Vaspret halted as he heard battle cries more suited to the Lescari wars.

'If we can.' Halice watched as pirates by the huts and tents began massing for a more coherent attack. They hastily abandoned that ambition as a new attack came howling in to scatter them.

Vaspret chuckled. 'A good man, that Darni.'

'Too good to leave out of this fun.' Halice slapped Vaspret's unburdened shoulder. 'Get those boats loaded.'

Vaspret vanished into the darkness and Halice heard a resounding voice bellowing, the mighty figure of Muredarch appearing for an instant in the light of the watch fire. With him to rally them, the raiders regrouped with more speed and efficiency than she'd have liked.

She looked to see how heavily Minare's men were engaged and tried to judge how Darni's troop was faring from the familiar noises of battle raging on the far side of the encampment. It was time to spite Muredarch before he got his men rallied for a counter attack.

'Withdraw!' Halice bellowed. Minare's men and women kicked and hacked with redoubled ferocity to free themselves. Mercenaries ran past her, taking the most direct line to the unseen boats. Pirates cheered and jeered, some running ahead of the rest, naked swords silver slashes in the darkness as a few of Kellarin's men lagged behind, their lack of experience telling.

'To me!' Halice yelled and a handful of mercenaries instinctively swerved to join their commander, racing back to fall upon the foremost pirates.

The first lost his head entirely to a sideways sweep of Deglain's broadsword, his blood showering the startled Glane. The boy let his sword point drop and was nearly run through by a second raider who'd seen enough death not to mourn his erstwhile comrade. Peyt's thrust pierced the pirate's shoulder and sent the man stumbling backwards. Glane slashed with an edge of panic and the man dropped screaming and pawing at his shattered jaw and a gaping gash in his neck. Peyt finished the man with a thrust through one eye, standing on the corpse's chest to pull his sword free and leaving a bloody footprint clearly visible on the dead pirate's pale shirt.

'Come on!' roared Halice as Glane stumbled towards her, eyes rimmed with white, blood soaking all down one side, shaken beyond reason by the claustrophobic mayhem of battle. She ran to grab him by the arm, dragging him along. 'Are you hurt?'

'They killed Reddig,' the boy gasped. 'Cut him open like a hog.'

'Move before they do the same to you.' Halice shoved him towards the shore, turning back to see more pirates charging across the open ground, Muredarch's shouts driving them on.

A deadly hail rained down. Some died before they hit the ground, shafts clean through heads and bodies. Others collapsed with shrieks of pain, clutching legs or arms torn by razor sharp arrowheads. A second volley came hissing out of the darkness of the far side of the strait as Rosarn and her archers drew down a storm of arrows between the raiders and their unexpected foes. Here and there, crossbow bolts knocked those unlucky enough to present tempting targets clean off their feet.

'Vas!' Halice yelled. 'Are we done?' Rosarn wouldn't have too many arrows left by now.

Vaspret's reply was lost as a new commotion erupted on the far side of the landing. Halice couldn't make out what was happening. 'Allin!' She backed towards the longboats, balancing speed with the need to not fall on her own arse.

'Yes?' Allin appeared at her side, her voice quavering.

'Time to try that new trick of yours,' said Halice, voice calm and reassuring as she held out her hand.

Allin drew a deep breath. She gripped the mercenary commander's fingers with surprising strength and that same obscure sensation crawled over Halice's palm before sinking deep into her bones.

'Thanks.' Halice raised a hand to block the glow of the watch fire and stared into the darkness on the far side of the landing. 'Oh, piss on that!'

'What is it?' Allin's voice was tight with fear.

'Men were sleeping on Den Harkeil's hulk and the *Tang*. They've cut Darni off from his boats.' Halice broke off to knuckle her eyes as fire arrows arched across the strait.

Vaspret came running up. 'That's Ros done, Commander and we're ready to go.'

Halice nodded. 'Back to the boat, lass.'

'What's happening to Darni's troop?' The mage-girl didn't move.

'Get behind me.' Halice held her sword ready as her troop retreated to their boats. Pirates moved closer, wary now. Caution would hold these ones for a few moments longer, Halice judged. All the foolishly bold were dead or bleeding on the scarred and stained turf.

'He's retreating into the woods and we're leaving.' All colour was leached out of the curious half vision the magic bestowed but Halice had watched enough skirmishes to understand what she saw. It was the obvious thing to do and Darni had the sense to see it. What Halice couldn't see was the uneven ground at her feet with the magic enhancing her sight and she nearly fell. 'Undo this spell,' she barked.

The startled wizard slapped Halice's face. Ignoring the sting, the mercenary grabbed Allin and ran with her for the boats, the little mage taking two or three paces to every one of Halice's. They scrambled into the last boat still on the shore, the others already out in the strait. Sobs and heart-felt, exhausted gratitude mingled with the brisk shouts of the mercenaries organising themselves.

'Is everyone accounted for?' yelled Halice as their boat pushed off. A chorus of confirmation from banner sergeants answered her.

'They're coming.' Rosarn's archers stood in their boat to loose a final volley of arrows as pirates came running down to the waterline. Yelps and curses were lost beneath the splash of oars biting deep into the water.

'Get your stroke even!' shouted the banner sergeant furiously. 'Where's that wizard?'

'Here!' Allin scrambled through the boat, hands on all sides urging her forward to the prow.

'Back to the *Dulse*!' Halice bellowed. The longboats surged forward as Allin's magic outlined their path through the rocks and shoals.

Halice looked back, eyes narrowed, but all she could see was confusion around the pirate settlement, fresh wood thrown to rouse slumbering fires, sporadic cries of anger and rebuke ringing out across the waters of the strait. Beyond, she could just make out the crashing of bushes being hacked down.

'Did he get them away?' Vaspret was using a bundle of soiled linen to wipe blood and hair matted with greyish smears from his sword blade.

'I don't hear anyone cheering.' Halice slid her own unsullied weapon back into its sheath. 'I'd say so.'

'When did you last get that dirty?' grinned Minare.

'That's what you scum are paid for, ' Halice retorted with pretended outrage. 'I earn my gold with my brains.'

'Your beauty wouldn't earn you a lead Lescari Mark,' agreed Minare. 'So, is it a price per head or one fee for the lot?' He gestured at the prisoners huddled in the bottom of the boat.

'Did we get them all?' asked Halice.

Minare shrugged. 'All but a handful. A couple were too far gone to bother with and a few just lost their heads and ran away from everyone, friend or foe.'

'Any idea about hurts or losses?' With the elation of the escapade fading, Halice's immediate concern was now her troop.

'Reddig was gutted. Other than that, it's just the usual scars and breaks.' Minare threw the stained rag over the side where it floated for a moment, white on the blackness of the water. 'Reddig was a good man even if he was only a weaver. D'Alsennin better pay us full blood price for him.'

'Halice!' Rosarn stood in the prow as the archer's boat drew alongside. 'Get young Allin to spread her spell around so we can see it. We've not got Larissa.'

'What?' Minare looked up from picking gore out of the binding of his sword hilt. 'She was supposed to stay with you.'

'Where in curses is she?' cried Halice.

'She went ashore with Darni.' Rosarn spread her hands. 'What was I supposed to do? Try to stop her and get fried for my trouble?'

'D'Alsennin's going to be none too pleased about that.' Halice heaved a sigh. 'Usara neither.'

'When was the last time any assault went precisely to plan?' Minare was unconcerned. 'We just have to make it work for us.'

'True enough, as long as Darni got his men and that fool girl of a wizard clear away into the woods.' Halice caught sight of Allin's beseeching, horrified face at the other end of the longboat. She ignored it as she applied herself to the question. As long as she had the answers before Temar, she could keep the upper hand, always an advantage for a mercenary.

Kehannasekke, Islands of the Elietimm, 10th of For-Summer

'I hope Olret's holding his own,' Ryshad muttered.

'He's certainly giving Ilkehan something to worry about, by the looks of it,' I commented.

We lay side by side, peering through the grass topping the dune closest to the sprawling village below Ilkehan's stronghold. The keep itself stood aloof on a rise in the ground, highest point for some distance in any direction, every approach cleared of cover for an advancing army. That didn't matter, I told myself firmly; we weren't an army.

'As long as those are reinforcements because it's going badly for Ilkehan, not additional troops to help him carry his victory on into Rettasekke.' Ryshad kept his spyglass steady.

A metal-barred, solid wooden double gate was opening and a column of black-liveried men marched out with the mindless discipline that Ilkehan terrified into his people. All were armed to the teeth and beyond. The pervasive lack of wood and metals in these islands wasn't inconveniencing Ilkehan to any noticeable degree. 'How many's that gone today?'

'Close on a cohort.' Ryshad's satisfaction reassured me. 'All the fewer for us to trip over.'

I dug myself lower into the sand. The coolness below the top layer was welcome after a long hot day crouched beneath the merciless sun now finally sinking to the horizon. Still, at least we weren't hiking through the desolate heart of the interminable island any more, walking from first light and all through the uncanny dusk, slipping past isolated settlements dotted among the barren hills, taking infuriating detours to avoid the desperate-looking bands that gave the lie to Ilkehan's boast that his lands gave no exiles a refuge. I licked dry lips and wished for some water but we'd emptied our bottles a while back. 'How much longer do we wait?'

'We'll let that lot get clear first, shall we?' Ryshad's eyes shone dark in his blue-tinted face, bristles adding their own shadow to the overall Eldritch effect.

The column marched down to the harbour, cowed villagers ducking their heads before those most thickly studded with signs of rank. I wondered idly what earned these bullies their studs. One for each killing? One for every innocent tortured? 'Can you see any gorgets?'

Ryshad brought his spyglass to bear. 'One at the front, silver. Another at the back, silver.'

'Two less enchanters to worry about.' That was something at least.

'As long as Ilkehan doesn't decide to lead his men into battle for a change.' Ryshad watched through the spyglass as the column waited for boats to ferry them out to larger ships anchored in the deep water of the inlet that bit into the coast just here. 'I wouldn't fancy trying get to him through that lot. How many adepts you think he had to start with? How long does it take to train them?'

'He can't have had that many, surely?' I was looking for reassurance. 'And it's not the number that counts, it's their strength with Artifice.'

'We haven't seen any golden gorgets.' Ryshad took the glass from his eye to smile encouragement at me. 'Guinalle seemed to think he'd sent his best to Suthyfer.'

'Let's hope she's right.' I stifled a groan of frustration. 'I wish we could just get on with it.'

'You sound like 'Gren.' Ryshad returned to looking through his spyglass. 'Why don't you go and keep watch with Shiv?'

'You're trying to get rid of me,' I accused.

'That's right.' A fond smile took the edge off his words but he didn't take his eye off the distant keep. 'You're distracting me. Go and talk to Shiv.'

I scurried backwards down the dune. We'd found this hollow with considerable relief after a tense night of sneaking along this shoreline but I'd be very glad to leave it just as soon as Ryshad and Sorgrad decided we'd learned all we could by watching and agreed it was time to act. All this waiting just gave me time to consider all the things that could go wrong with this plan and wound 'Gren up to an ever more dangerous pitch of frustration.

I crept carefully up the banked sand to where Shiv lay, chin on hands, eyes alert.

Inland, the shifting dunes yielded to more solid land where dark green spiny bushes dotted with yellow flowers clumped together. Dry and gritty with windblown sand, the land rose and fell in shallow swells, mimicking the ocean. A few spotted brown birds foraged for whatever might come wriggling up now that evening was drawing near.

'Any sign of them?' I whispered.

'No.' Shiv was as relaxed as if he lay by his own fireside.

'We'd have heard something, if they'd been taken.' I was starting to tire of hearing my own doubts.

'Screaming, at very least.' A smile quirked at the corner of Shiv's mouth. ''Gren's spoiling for a fight.'

'The trick is making sure he takes on the one you want.' I frowned. 'Is that them?'

Shiv raised himself on his elbows. 'I think so.' Tense, we watched the brothers dart between the spiny green bushes. It was a long run to our hidden hollow from the rise they'd just scrambled over.

'I could cloak them with invisibility,' muttered Shiv, less a suggestion than a comment on the powers we dare not let him use.

I tried to work out if the brothers could see the boat sheds along the shore where the dunes gave way to a stream and hillocks beyond it. If they could, they could be seen in turn.

'Here they come.' Shiv stiffened like a cat undecided whether to pounce or to run. Sorgrad and 'Gren ran across the hostile expanse, scattering the brown birds. I cringed at the thought that someone might hear the squawks of indignation. Sorgrad and 'Gren ran on, barely slowing even in the softer sands of the dunes, throwing themselves past us into hiding.

I spat sand out of my mouth. 'Were you seen?'

'We'll know soon enough.' 'Gren had his hand on his sword hilt, eager face turned towards the unseen boat sheds.

Sorgrad tossed me a few damp and grubby roots. 'There's something to chew on if you're hungry.'

'Thanks,' I said without enthusiasm.

Ryshad turned to see what Sorgrad had brought. 'Burdock?'

He nodded. 'Some sedge as well.'

Between them, Ryshad and Sorgrad had kept our bellies full on the journey through the inhospitable island. With each showing increasing appreciation of the other's foraging skills, I kept my own counsel when faced with food only the truly starving could fully appreciate. I just hoped we got home to some real meals before I wore my teeth down to the gums.

Sorgrad was already lying next to Ryshad. 'Any sign of our friend?'

'Nothing so far,' Ryshad said in a low tone.

'Gren blinked and I shivered involuntarily. He looked curiously at me. 'Maewelin's touch got you?'

'It's your eyes.' I shivered again, icy fingers still stroking my neck. 'Aiten's eyes turned to black pits when Ilkehan's Artifice enslaved him.' That was why I'd had to kill Aiten, Ryshad's long-time friend. Drianon save me from having to make that choice for any of these four.

'Let's not go borrowing trouble.' Sorgrad looked severely at us both. 'Concentrate on the task in hand and worry about other things when they happen.'

'If they happen,' added Ryshad with emphasis. 'Did you find the hargeard?'

Sorgrad nodded. 'It's a fair hike, over beyond that second rise with all the berry bushes.'

'It's enormous,' chuckled 'Gren.

'Folk seeing we're destroying it won't be a problem,' frowned Sorgrad. 'Getting away will be the difficult trick. There's—'

Ryshad tensed. 'The sentries are changing.'

'That's the way in?' Sorgrad brushed sand from his breeches, nodding at a lesser gate cut in the wall.

'What's on the other side?' 'Gren slid his sword a little way out of its sheath, face eager. A wise woman once told him he was born to be hanged, so he always reckoned to come unscathed through any situation not actively involving rope.

'A garden. We'll be going in to the actual keep through a drain.' I swallowed hard on a sudden worry that the cover might be hidden, that I might not be able to find it again, that we might end up trapped like rats in Ilkehan's sewer.

'There's our friend,' Ryshad said slowly. 'That's right, pal, find your nice warm nook.' Keeping ceaseless watch, he'd identified this particular sentry as a lazy bastard who always sheltered from the incessant wind behind the tall crenellations at the corner of the keep. 'Come on!' He shoved the spyglass into his jerkin and slid down the open face of the dune.

'Where's Ilkehan?' 'Gren chewed his lip eagerly as we hurried across the open ground. We had the time it took for six verses of the song Ryshad's mother used to measure the set of her jam before a more dutiful sentry on his rounds would reach this side of the keep.

I drew a deep breath and summoned up the memory of that hated face, dark, pitiless eyes, dead white hair and skin pale and creased with age. '*Tedri na faralir, asmen ek layeran.*' The ancient words might be meaningless in a Forest ballad about Uriol's endless quest for the stag with the silver antlers but here, quick as a blink, Artifice showed me Ilkehan poring over a book taken from packed shelves around him. I'd sneaked around in that keep before and knew for a certainty where he was. 'Still in his study.'

Ryshad picked up the pace. 'We go in, we hit him hard, we leave.'

'Simple,' said 'Gren with happy satisfaction.

Aetheric charms ran through my mind; one to hide us, one just to keep people disinterested, one to make someone worry they'd left an empty pot over a fire. Guinalle had identified a handful of ways for me to distract people but I didn't dare use them so close to Ilkehan. The last thing we needed was Artifice so close alerting him.

We reached the wall and the others flattened themselves on either side of the sally gate as I probed the lock with that fine balance between speed and accuracy that I'd learned over the years. 'Shiv.'

The mage laid a hand on the metal and I pushed the final tumbler over. Since we lacked the Shernasekke women's secrets, we had to risk his magic to supplement my house-breaking skills. There was a faint murmur as the bolts on the far side slid out of their sockets. This was the point of no return. No, I thought furiously, we would be going back. It was Ilkehan who'd be going nowhere once we'd done with him. He owed us and we were here to collect the debt and leave.

Swords drawn, Sorgrad and 'Gren were through in an instant. I followed, Ryshad next, Shiv at his shoulder. A woman screamed, dropping the basket of beans she'd been picking. Sorgrad hissed at her with archaic venom. 'Is it thou hast profaned the unseen world?'

'Will the Mother hide thee from our vengeance or the Maker defend thee?' 'Gren took a pace forward, black haired, blue skinned, eyes piercing.

The woman stumbled backwards, crushing plants heedless underfoot. She screamed as 'Gren menaced her with his sword, tripping, scrambling to her feet and running for a door on the far side of the garden.

'Forget the drains,' ordered Ryshad.

Sorgrad didn't needed telling. He was right behind the hysterical woman fumbling with the latch. She slid through the narrowest of gaps, catching her sleeve and tearing it free in her panic. Sorgrad shoved a boot in the door to stop her slamming it, whatever he was saying sending her fleeing too fast to wonder why an Eldritch man couldn't just walk through any wall he pleased.

'Gren went through the door like a winter storm off the mountains. I followed to find a corridor, the brothers each covering one approach.

Ryshad slammed the door behind Shiv. 'Which way?'

'Up there.' I'd taken the back stairs when I'd crept up and down this keep before but in my new guise of Eldritch Kin, I felt entitled to the main stairs. We ran as if we had vengeful shades at our heels ourselves. Shiv saw the rest of us making ready to drop our bags for a fight and did the same.

'As soon as he's dead, cut off the stairs,' Ryshad told Shiv. We ignored the floor we knew belonged to whatever family Ilkehan had left. As we raced up the next flight, consternation from the kitchen levels floated up after us. A door opened somewhere below and a puzzled voice called out.

This was the floor where Ilkehan had his apartments. Every detail of this place was burned into my memory like the anguish we'd suffered in the stark white dungeons below. Ilkehan knew no such privation, with his polished chests of dark wood lining the corridor, choice pieces of ceramic and bronze displayed on shelves.

'Which door?' 'Gren dropped his pack.

I pointed. 'That one.'

Sorgrad charged through it, veering to one side. 'Gren was a breath behind him, taking the other hand. Ryshad followed, straight as an arrow.

Ilkehan was behind a broad desk, already reaching for a dagger. 'Gren and Sorgrad came at him from either side. Magelight flashed all around, striking reflections from our blades as startling blue as anything the Eldritch Kin might favour. The knives of radiance stabbed the enchanter, piercing him clean through to emerge and careen off the walls, magic dripping like condensation down the pale plaster. The bastard opened his mouth but no sound emerged. Rage twisted his face and his hands clawed towards me and Shiv.

My darts ready, I snapped them off quick as thought. The first bit into Ilkehan's cheek and he recoiled, shoving his chair backwards, dagger now raised. That wasn't about to save him. Ryshad braced a sturdily booted foot against the desk, all his height and strength tipping it up and over to crash down on the enchanter's legs. Ilkehan was trapped, falling as Ryshad sprang over the toppled desk. He brought his sword down into the angle of the enchanter's neck and shoulder, the stroke so hard his blade bit into the boards as Ilkehan hit the floor. As Ryshad wrenched his sword free, I saw the white of shattered bone in the massive wound.

'That's for Aiten.' He had no words foul enough to convey his hatred.

It wasn't a fatal blow, not immediately, the awkward angle had seen to that, but 'Gren and Sorgrad dropped their pennyweight in Raeponin's scales. A sideways slash from 'Gren all but eviscerated the enchanter, entrails spilling out of a bloody gash ripped through his fine woollen tunic and soft shirt. Ilkehan clutched at his stomach, frantic hands already coated with the dark blood pooling around him, oozing beneath the desk that held him down. A man with such a wound should be screaming like a pig at slaughter but even without Shiv's magic to mute him, Ilkehan had no breath for his cries. Scarlet bubbles clustered around his mouth, blood rising in his throat to choke him, more gushing from ribs splintered and broken by Sorgrad's merciless thrust. The man was dead or he would be inside a few moments. I had made certain of that, even without the others' contributions.

'That's silk.' Sorgrad fingered Ilkehan's shirt as he kicked the enchanter's dagger out of reach.

'Nice to see he got something out of the Aldabreshin. Where do you suppose he got this?' 'Gren snatched up the ivory-hilted blade before stepping back with an exclamation of annoyance.

Ilkehan was convulsing, fresh torrents of blood spurting

as the uncontrollable spasms tore apart the wounds inside him. His head whipped from side to side, teeth bared in a snarl like a feral beast's, his hands writhing on the floor, smearing blood ever wider. A faint keening escaped his clenched teeth, blood-flecked foam around his taut lips.

Sorgrad watched the enchanter's final torments with a judicious eye. 'I'll grant you poison's effective but there's always the chance you'll get stabbed while you're waiting for it to take effect.'

'Not if you stay out of stabbing distance.' I coughed and moved away as the stench of voided bowels and bladder joined the acrid reek of blood.

'Shat himself just like that poor little dog,' remarked 'Gren with satisfaction. 'So, what now?'

Shiv was still watching Ilkehan, shaking his head as the enchanter's struggles died away. 'That was quicker than I imagined.'

I saw Ryshad looking down on the body, stony faced. 'Is that recompense for Aiten?' I slipped my arm around his waist.

'No.' He hugged me close. 'Nothing would be. That's the problem with revenge.' Hard satisfaction warmed his expression. 'Which is why I'll settle for justice.'

'Justice, vengeance.' I met his gaze on level terms. 'The important thing is he's dead.'

'How long have we got to dishonour this body?' Sorgrad held out a hand to 'Gren. 'Let's use his own knife.'

'However long it takes that kitchen maid to convince someone she saw Eldritch Kin in the garden?' I hazarded.

Ryshad shook his head. 'You don't have to believe someone to go and see what they're scared of.'

'Then we leave.' I'd have preferred to see Ilkehan suffer longer, just to balance the scales for the torments he'd inflicted on Geris but, vengeance or justice, I was finally ahead of the game. The man whose malice had haunted my nightmares and blighted my hopes with fear was dead at our feet and I was still alive. I intended to keep it that way. 'Come on, let's go.'

'What about all these books?' Shiv was looking at the closely packed ranks of shelves. 'This is a priceless archive. There must be the answers to all Planir's questions and ten times more.'

'Knowledge is power.' I stared round the room. 'Power we don't want to leave for whoever ends up top dog around here.'

Squatting next to Ilkehan's corpse, 'Gren looked up. 'Books burn.'

'I can do that.' Sorgrad snapped his fingers and flame played between them.

'Fire's always a nice distraction for anyone thinking of chasing you.' It wouldn't be the first time the three of us had fled under the cover of a hearty blaze. I opened a coffer beside the desk that proved to be full of parchments. '*Talmia megrala eldrin fres.*' Flames sprang up to dance across the written surfaces, blurring the words. Maybe I would learn a little more Artifice now that Ilkehan was too dead to come picking through my brain.

'Here.' Sorgrad had ripped down a tapestry and tucked it around the coffer. As soon as the wood caught, the tapestry would carry the fire to the carpet.

'Can't we take a few books?' pleaded Shiv.

'Which ones?' I demanded.

'Better hurry.' 'Gren was ripping the binding from a slender tome as we spoke, piling the leaves around the coffer where the parchments now blazed nicely. Sorgrad was breaking open another chest to find three silver gorgets and a golden one along with a considerable spill of coin. He scooped it up, heedless of Ilkehan's blood on the floor.

'We'll share it out later,' 'Gren assured me before belatedly including Ryshad and Shiv in his glance.

Not that my score with the Elietimm could be settled with gold. I added a handful of reed pens to my little fire and 'Gren pocketed the silver cup they'd stood in.

'If Kellarin's to restore the study of Artifice, we need to know so much.' Shiv was looking desperately round the book-lined walls.

'Knowledge can't ever truly be destroyed, Shiv,' Ryshad said impatiently. 'Just lost. Someone, sometime will rediscover it.' He stopped abruptly. 'What we must find are any artefacts Ilkehan's holding.'

'The sleepers in Kellarin!' Saedrin forgive me but I'd clean forgotten. 'Come on Shiv, people are more important than aetheric abstractions.' I left 'Gren happily tending the burning coffer.

'Help me here.' Sorgrad was already trying to lift the toppled desk. Ryshad helped him, both of them levering open the drawers with daggers.

'Let's have anything that'll burn.' 'Gren held out a hand.

A door slamming below us struck us all silent for a moment. The sound of running feet and cries of distress fading into the distance.

'I think there's blood coming through their ceiling,' Sorgrad said thoughtfully.

'Let me bespeak Planir,' begged Shiv. 'If he can raise a nexus, they might save some of the books before they burn.'

Ryshad coughed. The air was thickening. 'We don't want Ilkehan roasted if we're aiming to shock people with Eldritch vengeance on his body. Get him into the corridor and do your worst while we look for any artefacts.' 'Gren and Sorgrad immediately took an arm each and dragged the bloody corpse out of the room.

'Shiv, the plan was your illusions would keep Ilkehan's men scared as we fight our way out.' Ryshad hesitated. 'All right, try reaching Planir as you keep watch but don't get us all killed for a few worm-eaten books.'

'I want my hide whole as much as anyone else,' Shiv assured him. The wizard snatched up a polished silver salver and went into the corridor, green magelight swirling around him.

Ryshad coughed again. 'If there are artefacts here, we need to find them quickly.' The coffer was blazing like a watchman's brazier, scorch marks darkening the plaster above our heads.

Closing my eyes, I pictured the vast irregular cavern of Edisgesset, empty but for those few still bound beneath ancient enchantment. I heard the soft steps of those that kept vigil in the hollow silence. A single shaft of light would be coming down the steps, soft breeze fragrant with the summer's growth outside. I remembered the subtle chill as I passed between that dissolving sunlight and the all-encompassing darkness.

'*Thervir emanet vis alad egadir.*'

It wasn't much of a charm, just a jaunty snatch from a ridiculous tale about a lackwit called Nigadin. He went looking for his knife and, finding it, recalled he'd left his belt somewhere. Finding that reminded him he'd mislaid his boots. Tracking them down, he realised he was without his breeches and so it went on. But I'd used the charm when young Tedin has lost himself and it had led me to the lad. I held those whose bodies rested in that cave in my mind. The old man Gense, sallow face sunk away from his beak of a nose, wisps of hair still surprisingly dark across his bald pate. A boy whose name escaped me, skin pale as milk, tousled hair touched with red that hinted at Forest blood, his head looking too big for the frail body beneath it. Velawe, long a friend of Zigrida's, work-roughed hands with swollen knuckles clasped beneath her sagging breasts, even this enchantment unable to smooth the lines of worry and toil graven between her brows. Porsa, her daughter, beside her, silly, pretty face swathed in a frivolous lace wrap, the curls in her hair still as crisp as the day the tongs had made them.

'*Thervir emanet vis alad egadir.*' Belligerent shouts from the stairs opened my eyes.

'Well?' Ryshad watched me intently.

'Next door.'

The corridor was a scene from an addled drunk's nightmare. Shadows played on the walls like black flames, licking along the floor and up to the ceiling. Shapes came and went on the edge of seeing, distorted heads and bent bodies scampering on unnaturally elongated limbs. One capered in the stairwell, darkness incarnate, eyes of starshine, teeth and nails the pale silver of a mist-shrouded moon. A valiant arrow shot through it, clattering against the wall behind. The figure ducked, huddling in on itself, shadows folding and moulding anew. We heard determined boots thudding on the stairs, shouts urging them upwards.

The darkness reared up with a new mask, a wolf's head snarling and weaving, twice life size and topping a man-shaped body with clawed hands tipped with ice-white talons. The beast snatched up the fallen arrow and threw its head back to howl like a gale from frozen heights. Breath steamed icy from its maw and rolled bodily down the stairs. We heard frantic feet taking flight even before the arrow tumbled down after them.

'Nice to see Shiv paid attention to 'Gren's yarns,' muttered Ryshad.

I was too busy gaping for comment. Startling illusion over-laid Shiv's crude disguise with a vision of Eldritch Kin seen in fever dreams. Too tall and too thin for ease of mind, a shaft of moonlight in one bony hand, his skin was the bottom-less blue of a still pool caught beneath twilight. His hair was shadow darker than those rarest of nights when lesser and greater moons both quit the sky for mysteries of their own. His eyes were black hollows seeing into the very shades, threatening to suck the life from any who caught their gaze.

Sorgrad and 'Gren crouched by his side, visions to terrify Poldrion's own demons. A head appeared in the stairwell and the Elietimm man's jaw dropped as he saw his dread master being butchered by the two eerie apparitions.

'He cut out that lad's stones and eyes. Why don't we swap his round?' 'Gren suggested in a low voice.

Ryshad looked at me and I wondered if I looked as unearthly to him as he did to me.

'You said do your worst.' I spoke before he could. 'We don't look, then we don't have to know. Don't worry. 'Gren's on our side.'

'I'll take your word for that.' Ryshad's tone suggested we'd debate this further when people weren't trying to kill us.

The awesome Eldritch Kin that was Shiv stepped forward, levelling its cold, gold spear. The Elietimm man froze on the stair, white faced and trembling in the darkness.

'Bless the ancestors who chose you to witness our retribution.' 'Gren looked up and hissed with silken spite.

'We curse Ilkehan to the ninth generation. Cursed be all who pervert the sacred lore.' Sorgrad rose, a figure born of nightmares, blood dripping from the ivory-handled knife to be greedily sucked up by scurrying rat-like shadows. 'Thus to all who profane the compact between dead, living and yet unborn.' His words echoed around the stone walls so uncannily Shiv had to be working some magic on them. The reverberations followed the fleeing soldier down the stairs.

Then Shiv winked at me and I could see through the delusion of light and magic to the reality beneath. 'Hurry up.'

We skirted round 'Gren and Sorgrad now chuckling evilly. Ryshad kicked in the door and we found a room dominated by a large table strewn with maps and parchments. A window embrasure held a sturdy chest of unmistakably Tormalin origin.

'In there.' It was locked. I reached for my picks.

'No time.' Ryshad grabbed a handle. 'Dast's teeth!' he rasped as he lifted it on to one shoulder.

Sorgrad appeared in the doorway. 'We need to go now or there'll be too many for us to break through.'

'We're coming,' I assured him.

Scarlet flame danced on his outstretched palm. 'Get clear.'

Sorgrad's handful of fire skidded the length of the table, igniting everything in its path. The wall hangings blazed around us and I swear I felt the hair on my neck crisp as we raced through the doorway. 'Curse it, 'Grad, you nearly fried us!'

'Main stairs or back?' 'Gren was standing by Ilkehan's body, gory to his elbows. I tried not to see what had been done to the body and just about succeeded; apart from realising it wasn't the enchanter's tongue poking from his mouth.

Ryshad glanced down and swallowed hard. Even painted blue, I swear he blenched.

Shiv held the silver salver before him, magical fire from a scrap of burning cloth reflecting oddly on to his painted face. 'I don't have time for this, Planir. Just do what you can.' He shoved the metal inside his jerkin and threw the cloth away.

'Back stairs.' Ryshad jerked his head.

'Sorgrad,' I urged. 'We're leaving.'

'Just a moment.' He was crouched over Ilkehan, his back to me.

I moved to get a clearer look and then thought better of it. 'You've done enough!'

'I promised I'd carve the boy's name in this bastard's forehead.' Sorgrad spoke with slow concentration.

'That won't lead them straight to Olret?' snapped Ryshad.

'Not unless someone hereabouts can read Mandarkin script.' Sorgrad finished with a flourish of his blade sending drops of blood spattering the wall.

'Let's go,' I begged.

'Stay close,' warned Shiv, raising his hands. Drawing them close, he flung another sweep of glittering magic ahead. The shadows took on a mossy hue, shifting into spectres of trees. We moved and they moved with us, dappled darkness shifting and changing, Eldritch shapes on the edge of sight passing all around us.

'Here.' Sorgrad reached for the other handle of the chest and Ryshad let it slide from his shoulder so they could carry it between them.

We reached the back stairwell, narrower and more steeply pitched than the one we'd come up. Shiv and I took the lead as we descended as fast as was still safely cautious, shadows alternately deepening and fading around us. The formless blackness shaped itself into foxes, rats and ravens that ran on ahead. The rushing sound that presages the most violent storms in the wildwood surged around our heads before scouring down the stairs.

'Pered's not the only artist in your household, is he?' At the turn of the stair, I looked back to see Sorgrad and Ryshad balancing the chest between them, each with a blade in their free hand. Rearguard, 'Gren was coming backwards down the stairs, sword and dagger ready. I knew he'd done that often enough not to worry about falling.

As we reached the floor below, a handful of men braver than the rest charged us with viciously flanged maces. Shiv sent them reeling back with a brutal storm of hail crystallising out of the very air. The ice was sharp enough to draw blood from faces and hands before falling to the floor and flowing together to coat the flagstone with lethal slipperiness. The soldiers fell heavily as they struggled to stand, more interested in retreating than pursuit. We ran on down the stairs and along the one corridor we found not peopled with panicked Elietimm. New screams of anguish and horror echoed from the floor where we'd left Ilkehan.

'Over there.' Ryshad nodded to a sturdy double door as we found ourselves in a lofty entrance hall.

Shiv raised a hand and the wood darkened, swelled and ruptured. The metal bands and hasps rusted before our very eyes.

'Come on.' 'Gren brought up his distinctly non-magical boot to kick at it. The rotten wood sagged from splitting hinges now just metal flakes held together by corrosion. I ripped at the wood and we hammered out a hole big enough for Ryshad and Shiv.

'What's out there?' Sorgrad was barely visible as Shiv filled the entrance hall with roiling shadows to baffle our pursuers hesitant on the fringes of the unknown darkness.

I squinted cautiously through the splintered gap. 'Courtyard and the main gate which looks very much locked. Some troops and it's a safe bet more are on their way.'

'How much more have you got in you?' Ryshad looked sharply at the mage.

'Enough,' the wizard assured us. The illusions concealed him as thoroughly as ever but we all heard the weary note in Shiv's voice. 'Sorgrad can try a few of the tricks Larissa taught him, if he likes.'

'No holds barred?' I've never seen Sorgrad at a loss in all the years I'd known him and I was relieved beyond measure to see this was no exception.

'That's battlefield rules, according to Halice.' I glanced at Ryshad.

'It may not be a usual kind of war but they started it.' He shrugged. ''Gren, help me with this.'

The brothers swapped places by the chest and Sorgrad stepped up to the breach in the door. He clapped his hands together and a sheet of flame sprang up, spreading to encircle us all. The damp chunks of broken wood hissed and steamed and the firelight played eerily among the shadows that Shiv was still keeping as black and impenetrable as ever.

'Let's get out of here while they're all still gawping,' I suggested. If Ilkehan's people could barely see us, we could barely see them and that made me nervous.

'Slowly, concentrate.' Shiv's calm voice encouraged Sorgrad and we began walking towards the main gate. Slingshot whizzed into the flames where the stones shattered into razor-sharp, red-hot fragments. I swallowed an un-Eldritch yelp as one stung me on the face.

'What about the gate?' asked Ryshad tightly.

'Just get ready to run,' Sorgrad replied through clenched teeth.

The flames disappeared and the shadows shrivelled. All that protected us were our tawdry disguises and the terrified imaginations of the onlookers. The gate exploded into a ball of fire before anyone could see through our masquerade, shards of burning wood and blistering metal shooting in all directions. People ran for cover, screams from the slowest. The fell rain would have seared us too but for a sandstorm that reared up from the dusty earth to envelop us, sucking the lethal fragments into the maelstrom. We stood in the calm centre of the silently howling winds, a wall of dust and debris concealing us from all the hostile eyes.

I'd kept my bearings, thanks to so many years making my way without benefit of a light to alert a nosy watchman or some indignant householder. 'Forward.' I pointed and we moved, the storm cloaking us.

'Faster,' Sorgrad hissed.

We ran, Ryshad and 'Gren grunting as they lugged the weighty chest between them. Shiv was puffing like a man who'd been on the battlefield all day and even Sorgrad's steps looked leaden as I watched for the changes underfoot that would mean we were through the gate.

'Where do we hide up?' I demanded as soon as we were beyond the wall.

'The hargeard.' Sorgrad looked around, frowning at the constantly shifting veil of wind and dust.

'That way.' I pointed.

'Is there anywhere to hide there?' Ryshad looked at Shiv with concern. 'We can't rely on Gebaedim superstitions to stop them stringing us up if they get their hands on us.'

I shivered. A quick hanging would be the most merciful fate we could hope for.

'Trust me.' Sorgrad's eyes were bright blue against the black that rimmed them.

My fears receded to a manageable level; after all, he'd never let me down before.

CHAPTER SEVEN

From Keran Tonin, Mentor,
To Pirip Marne, Scholar.

Dear Marne,
I hear you're doing some interesting work on the Ancient Races. You might find this useful. I can vouch for it as a genuine copy of an old record; it came from the Isles of the Elietimm a few years ago, when the Archmage's man and those two sworn to D'Olbriot tried to rescue poor Geris. I'd so far rather have had the dear boy home safe instead but at least we're unravelling some notion of what we're dealing with from documents like this.

By the way, have you considered a visit to Kellarin at all? Let me know your thoughts in due course.

With compliments,
      Tonin

Being a true record of the meeting between Itilek of Froilasekke and Jinvejen of Haeldasekke on this sacred night of the empty sky. Let the neutral stones of Heval Islet bear witness to the bones of each clan that both halves of this hide carry the same words.

Itilek tells he has heard of disaster befalling Kehannasekke's bid for the empty lands to the south.

Jinvejen agrees that he has heard the same. The feeling among his clan is that this is Misaen's judgement upon Rekhren for his over-reliance upon Maewelin's priests.

Itilek announces his own priest finds himself powerless.

Jinvejen admits his own councillor is similarly stricken.

Both take time to consider this puzzle.

Jinvejen declares his forefathers have counselled suspicion of Maewelin's priests ever since all in this common exile were driven from our true home by Sheltya malice.

Itilek allows such a sudden and unexpected loss of priestly powers looks like divine retribution but asks what might Misaen's purpose be in doing such a thing?

Jinvejen wonders what does Misaen ask of us all in less troubled times? That we strive to better our lot through hard work and unity of purpose. It was for fear of such uncompromising strength that Sheltya rallied the weaker clans to hound our forefathers from their home. It was only such determination that brought our forefathers across the ice to these isolated rocks. Perhaps Misaen has visited his judgement upon Kehannasekke to rebuke him for seeking a new home to the south rather than returning to reclaim his true inheritance through ingenuity and valour.

Itilek points out how many generations have passed since our forefathers were exiled. Hopes of return to our true home seem ever more distant now the descendants of those that exiled us find themselves assailed by Southrons driven out of their own lands by the men of Tren Ar'Dryen.

Jinvejen reminds Itilek that Southrons are ruled by priests devoted both to Maewelin and to Arimelin and have long counselled retreat rather than making a stand for their sacred places. Cowardice has sewn the seeds of its own destruction.

Itilek asks what Jinvejen proposes.

Jinvejen suggests all ties with Southrons be cut and we tend our own hearths in amity for a full cycle of years. Misaen has shown us plainly that we have no friends but our own blood kindred. Kehannasekke's misadventures prove all other arms will be raised against us. Let us hone our skills and bide our time, raising our sons to strength and singleness of mind. If we prove ourselves worthy, mayhap Misaen will add the edge of true magic to our hard-hitting swords once more.

Itilek agrees to consider this and undertakes to lay the hide with his hargeard that the bones might make their wishes known to him.

The Island City of Hadrumal,
10th of For-Summer

'Thank you so very much, my dear.' Planir lifted his hands from the rim of the silver bowl, face intense. He smiled at Aritane but the courtesy couldn't entirely banish the line between his fine dark brows.

'It is a welcome change to find my talents appreciated.' The Mountain woman's voice was tart, her deep-set blue eyes hard.

'I'd welcome your thoughts on what may happen now,' invited Planir. He rose from his seat across the table from Aritane. 'May I offer you refreshment?'

'Some wine, white if you please.' Aritane smiled at some passing thought before her face returned to its guarded expression.

Planir poured two glasses of a straw-coloured vintage from a dark bottle adorned with a crumbling wax seal. Resuming his seat, he passed one over. 'So Ilkehan is dead. What does that mean for us?' The Archmage was in his shirtsleeves, a silk shirt befitting his rank.

'The manner of his death interests me.' Aritane's exotic accent sat oddly with her everyday gown of Caladhrian cut; serviceable wool dyed a neutral fawn. She raised a hand to brush the corn-coloured sweep of hair falling loose to her shoulders away from her narrow face.

'I take it that savagery has some point beyond simple bloodlust?' Planir gestured towards the empty water. 'And the masquerade?'

'If his people believe Ilkehan's arrogance has summoned retaliation from the Gebaedim—' Aritane pressed her full lips tight together. 'The confidence of his acolytes and thus their power will be all the more thoroughly broken.'

'When can we establish what aetheric strength remains, among the Elietimm or in Suthyfer?' asked Planir slowly. 'I don't want to risk anyone working magic if there's the slightest chance they might suffer Otrick's fate.'

Aritane retreated behind the curtain of her hair. Planir waited patiently.

'I will look for a mind open to true magic tomorrow,' she said finally. 'Then we can judge the consequences of Ilkehan's death.'

'We have many consequences to consider.' Jovial, Planir disregarded Aritane's sour tone. 'Without Ilkehan to menace you or your people, you should consider your opportunities in the world beyond Hadrumal. The universities at Col and at Vanam would welcome your insights into the study of aetheric enchantments.'

'I've met some of these scholars in your libraries. I wouldn't spend a night on a bare mountain with any of them.' Sarcasm tainted Aritane's words. 'So you want rid of me?'

'Not in the least.' Planir's unemotional reply made his sincerity ring all the more true. 'I value your skills highly. Archmage or no, I could never have dared this scrying without your Artifice to defend me.' He waved his wine glass at the silver bowl. 'But I would like to see you find a place where your considerable talents are accorded due respect – and I don't just mean your mastery of aetheric arts.'

Aritane made a non-committal noise before taking a sip of wine. 'Sheltya remain, even if Ilkehan is dead.'

'Is there no way you could make your peace with them?' Planir asked gently.

'When I serve as your scholars' conduit into the secrets of the wise?' Aritane set down her glass with a snap that slopped wine on to the polished table top. 'I hardly think so.'

'The books we've just recovered from Ilkehan's library should hold more than enough secrets to satisfy the mentors of Col, Vanam or anywhere else.' Unperturbed, Planir gestured at a door skilfully concealed in the panelling of the far wall. 'I would see you make peace with the Sheltya so you may be free to live your life as you wish. Until that day comes, I will defend you to the best of my abilities against Sheltya, Elietimm and all who might disparage you hereabouts.'

Aritane blushed a scarlet unbecoming to her pale complexion. 'I will see you tomorrow.'

'As you wish.' Planir rose to bow courteously. 'But remember, my door is always open to you.'

Aritane left without a backward glance, pace audibly increasing as she disappeared down the stairs. Planir stood by the door for a moment, combing long fingers through his hair. He heaved a sigh that could have been frustration, irritation, exhaustion or all three together before kicking the door shut.

Hair in unruly spikes, he ignored his untouched glass of wine and walked to the tall window. He gazed out far beyond the stone-slated roofs of Hadrumal. 'How soon can I go scrying for you, my darling?' he murmured. A mirror stood on the sill beside him, steel-bright within the dark mahogany frame, a silver candlestick beside it, empty.

Something in the courtyard below caught Planir's eye. 'Splendid timing as always, Hearth Master,' he muttered sardonically.

He moved quickly, smoothing his hair to its customary sleekness and catching up his formal robe from its hook on the back of the door. He shrugged it on as he removed Aritane's glass from the table, mopping the spill of wine with his sleeve. His hand hesitated over the scrying bowl but with a smile teasing the corner of his mouth, he let that be.

'Enter.'

Kalion knocked and opened the door, barely waiting for the Archmage's permission before marching in. Planir was sitting in the window seat, glass of wine on the sill beside him, one hand in his breeches pocket while the other held a small book bound in age-worn leather faded to a pale jade. His feet rested on a chair pulled carelessly askew from the table.

'Have you ever read any of Azazir's journals?' Planir

frowned at the crabbed writing still vividly black on the yellowed pages.

Kalion was visibly knocked off his stride. 'Azazir?'

'Yes.' Planir drew the word out absently. 'A menace and a madman but the man had some undeniably interesting ideas.' He shook his head. 'I'd dearly love to know how he summoned that dragon of his but I fear that secret died with Otrick.'

'More's the pity.' Unfeigned regret creased Kalion's fat face. 'Have you found any hints?' Avid, his gaze fastened on the little book.

'Not as yet.' Planir shut the journal with a snap. 'But I think it might make an interesting project. I've been considering the role of Archmage, in the light of what you and Troanna had to say. I'm forced to the rather lowering conclusion that my predecessors and I have spent far too little time actually adding to the sum of wizardry. We become so caught up in the trivia of Hadrumal's daily life that we forget Trydek's first and foremost requirement for this office.' He looked expectantly at Kalion.

The Hearth Master plucked a stray thread from the front of his velvet gown. 'Trydek laid down many precepts when he first brought his school of wizards here. What precisely are you referring to?'

Planir smiled. 'That the Archmage lead the exploration of combining the four elements in quintessential magic.'

Kalion took a chair by the table without waiting for invitation. 'That's an interesting proposal.'

'It's a long-neglected duty of my office.' Planir wasn't smiling any more. 'It's my firm intention to make amends.'

'Is this why you summoned Herion and Rafrid just now? And Sannin.' Kalion's indignation imperfectly masked his suspicion. 'To explore the potential of the nexus as Archmage, you should work with those mages pre-eminent in each element.'

'As Troanna keeps reminding me, we don't have a nexus of mastery, do we?' Planir turned abruptly brisk. 'We've had that out more than often enough. I hope something more interesting brings you here on this sunny afternoon?'

Kalion did his best to recover the determination that had propelled him up the stairs. 'I understand you've had that Aritane woman in here.' He glanced at the scrying bowl with sharp mistrust.

'I see Ely still spends more time at her window than at her books.' The Archmage met Kalion's gaze with level challenge. 'I'd appreciate you moderating your tone. You make it sound as if I were taking my pleasure with her bent over that table. Why should I not consult with the one expert on Artifice we have when the Elietimm threaten us all once more?'

'What has she told you?' demanded Kalion. 'What's going on? We have a right to know, me and Troanna and all the Masters of the Halls.'

'Across the ocean?' Planir shrugged. 'You know how dangerous it would be to scry or bespeak any of the mages out there—'

'Have you any notion what Shiv or Usara might be up to?' Frustration soured Kalion's expression. 'You know they hired a ship full of ruffians culled from dockyards the length of the ocean coast?'

Planir nodded, unperturbed.

'They could be working all manner of magic to the incalculable detriment of wizardry.' Kalion glared at him. 'A great many people disapprove of you letting them take themselves off unsanctioned by the Council to involve themselves in D'Alsennin's affairs.'

'I'd be interested to learn who feels entitled to criticise me in such a high-handed fashion.' Planir looked at Kalion expectantly but the red-faced mage sat obstinately silent. The Archmage shrugged and continued, puzzled. 'I don't understand your objection. You've spent years arguing that Hadrumal's isolation must end, that we must involve ourselves in the concerns of the wider world. You've argued most convincingly that this threat from the Elietimm gives us our opportunity to show what we can do to help and defend the non-mageborn.'

'Under the guidance of the Council,' snapped Kalion. 'Always.'

'That's so often been the sticking point though.' Planir shook his head regretfully. 'Everyone from princes down to pigmen mistrusts mages with their first loyalty to this mysterious Council and all its hidden loyalties and purposes.' The Archmage's expression was guileless. 'Of course, with Artifice to call on, they need not risk that. I rather fear that Artifice may be our undoing without any need for the Elietimm to attack.'

'What do you mean?' Kalion was suspicious.

'I have heard,' Planir raised a hand before tucking it smoothly back in his pocket, 'but bear in mind this is only rumour, that Tadriol has been making overtures to the mentors of Vanam.'

'What kind of overtures?' demanded Kalion instantly.

'I believe he's offering them an Imperial charter to found a new university in a city of their choice,' Planir said thoughtfully. 'Where scholars can cull whatever lore remains among the litany of Tormalin temples, from archive sources like that song book the girl Livak found, and whatever else may be hidden in the records of the great Houses.' Planir sighed. 'Add whatever aetheric knowledge Demoiselle Tor Priminale cares to share and I imagine Tadriol will have his own coterie of enchanters soon enough – and those all bound to him with ties both of gratitude and more material debt.'

Kalion chewed on the unpalatable prospect for a moment before returning to the attack. 'That's all the more reason to rein in Shiv and Usara before they discredit wizardry in the Emperor's eyes.'

Planir smiled. 'You need not concern yourself. I do have some news from Suthyfer—'

'You said you dared not scry,' objected Kalion furiously.

'You didn't let me finish that sentence either.' Planir's voice was cool. 'Thanks to the good offices of the Sheltya maiden Aritane, I can assure you that Shiv and Usara have been working considerable magic that can only resound to Hadrumal's credit.'

Kalion struggled but had to ask the question. 'What have they been doing?'

'All in good time.' Planir waved the hand bearing the ring of his office. 'I'm glad you came to see me because I'm more than a little concerned about Aritane. She doesn't complain but I hear from several sources that Ely continues to be vocal in her contempt for Artifice in general and for Aritane in particular.'

'Who's been saying such things?' asked Kalion with a fair approximation of casual enquiry.

'It's enough that I've been told; I don't care to fan the flames of any feuds Ely may be carrying on.' A hint of contempt coloured the Archmage's tone. 'You might warn your protégée such behaviour does her no credit with wizardry at large and risks my disapproval in particular. I would tell her myself but she'd probably consider me biased against her, after the way she has delighted in spreading unkind gossip about Larissa.' Planir smiled thinly. 'She'd be right at that but we'll save that for another day.'

Kalion cleared his throat, embarrassed. 'I will speak to the girl.'

'I'd appreciate it. If Aritane becomes too unhappy here, there's every possibility she'll retreat to Vanam or whatever new seat of learning Tadriol founds for the study of Artifice. After all, visiting scholars are often the only people being halfway civil to her.' Planir looked thoughtful. 'Sheltya learning would be a considerable addition to whatever aetheric lore Tadriol might amass.'

The Hearth Master's scowl boded ill for the hapless Ely. 'I'll see to it.'

'I'd appreciate it.' Planir picked up his book again but set it down as if a sudden thought had struck him. 'There's something else you can do for me. Well, for Velindre, really.'

'What might that be?' Kalion was puzzled.

'You've encouraged her ambitions to be Cloud Mistress.' Planir smiled ruefully. 'It would be a kindness if you could warn her ahead of time that I shan't be nominating her to the Council.'

'Why not?' Kalion's indignation got the better of him once more.

'Because I'll be nominating Rafrid,' replied Planir simply. 'You cannot deny he's self-evidently the best qualified candidate, both in his elemental proficiencies and with his experience as Master of Hiwan's Hall. He's much more of an age to command respect than Velindre and, even after her recent travels, Rafrid has a far wider circle of friends and acquaintances, here in Hadrumal and beyond. He tells me he's compared notes with alchemists from half the cities between Tormalin and Col.' The Archmage chuckled.

'He cannot hope to continue as Master of the Hall,' Kalion spluttered.

'No indeed.' Planir smiled. 'You and Troanna convinced me of that, rest assured. He's stepping down in favour of Herion.'

'That nonentity?' Kalion's jaw was slack with surprise. 'Whose idea was that?'

'I believe the suggestion came from Shannet.' Planir laughed good-humouredly. 'The old hedge-bird can still surprise us, can't she?'

'She doesn't stir from her own fireside.' Kalion was too taken aback to conceal his chagrin. 'She can barely manage her stairs.'

'That doesn't stop people visiting her,' Planir pointed out. 'She may be old but she still has all her wits and a great many friends besides.'

'I'll tell Troanna,' said Kalion curtly. He rose to leave.

'You can also tell her I've been thinking about her concerns over my own situation.' Planir swung his feet down and leaned forward earnestly. 'She's right, of course. Every Archmage needs a full nexus of Element Masters to back him. I will be nominating a new Stone Master to the Council.'

'Galen?' challenged Kalion.

'No,' The Archmage replied firmly. 'My concerns over his fitness haven't changed and even his closest friends couldn't claim much success from his attempts to ingratiate himself with a wider circle of acquaintances over this last season or so. I'll be nominating Usara.'

'What of my concerns over his fitness? Troanna will most certainly object,' warned Kalion heatedly. He looked sternly at the seated Archmage.

'You know, I really don't think she will,' Planir assured him. 'Not when 'Sar tells the Council about his quite spectacular use of magic in the defence of Kellarin's interests this summer.'

'Just what has he been doing?' asked Kalion through gritted teeth.

Planir hesitated. 'I really should leave that for him to explain, to the Council in full session. We should observe the proprieties.'

'You've seldom bothered about such things before,' retorted Kalion.

'That's a fair criticism.' Planir nodded. 'I do take heed, and of Troanna's rebukes.'

Kalion heaved a heavy sigh. 'So Shiv and Usara are sinking these pirates? These Elietimm enchanters are put to flight?' He sat heavily in the chair he'd just abandoned and crossed his arms over his barrel chest.

'I believe that's the general idea,' Planir assured him. 'Usara's working closely with the Demoiselle Tor Priminale – which is another pennyweight tipping the scales in his favour, of course. With him as Stone Master, that friendship with Guinalle could be invaluable for Hadrumal. As and when Tadriol or whoever looks to unite the study of Artifice, Guinalle will be at the centre of their dealings.'

Kalion nodded grudging agreement. 'When are we to expect more news?'

'Aritane tells me we should be able to scry safely in a few days' time,' replied Planir.

'I look forward to that.' There was an unmistakable edge to Kalion's tone.

'I look forward to the whole business being resolved,' Planir said grimly. 'I want this Elietimm threat removed once and for all.'

'So we can apply ourselves to the proper business of wizardry,' Kalion said with relish. 'Establishing our influence on the mainland.'

Planir laughed. 'Actually, I was more looking forward to having Larissa back again. Did you know she was helping 'Sar and Shiv? I imagine she'll have all manner of insights into the effective use of a double affinity.' He picked up his book again. 'Azazir has some curious theories I'm keen to discuss with her. And, who knows, she may finally agree to marry me.'

'Marry you?' Kalion looked stunned.

'If she'll have me, and all the encumbrances of my office.' Planir smiled fondly. 'I must see if any of the jewellers can supply me with a fitting token of my esteem for her.'

Kalion stood up. 'I'll take my leave of you, Archmage,' he said stiffly. 'I expect to be fully informed as soon as you have any news from Kellarin or Suthyfer.'

'Naturally.' Planir merely sketched a wave of farewell as Kalion stomped out of the room, shoulders stiff with annoyance.

The Archmage leaned back in the window seat, looking for his place in the battered journal. He stopped reading after barely a page, marking his place with a feather and looked at the waiting mirror. Shaking his head, he rose and walked rapidly to the door in the panelling.

'So what did we get?' He slid through the door and wrinkled his nose at the smell of smoke and scorched leather.

'You need someone from the library to catalogue these properly.' A mild-faced mage of middle years studied a scroll that crackled as he unrolled it. 'We nonentities can't be expected to know what we're looking at.' He sounded amused.

'That might be best.' A sturdily built man much of an

age with Planir and Herion knelt by the fireplace stacking badly charred tomes inside the fender. He brushed blackened fragments from a blue cuff. 'You might like to sort these out, Sannin. No one will wonder why you smell of char.' He grinned at the shapely woman who sat on the silk-hung bedstead.

'Thank you, Rafrid, but I don't care to have people think I'm losing my touch.' Sannin tucked a lock of lustrous brown hair behind one ear as she leafed through a small book. 'Will that little masquerade keep Kalion chasing his own tail until we have more definite news?'

'He'll have Troanna chasing him,' chuckled Rafrid. 'And she'll be after anyone else who might conceivably know what we're up to.'

'Quintessential magic's actually something I'm quite interested in pursuing.' Herion glanced up from his scroll.

'Naturally, once we've settled these Elietimm.' Planir leant against the door. 'You don't imagine I was lying to our revered Hearth Master?'

Rafrid set down the seriously burnt book he'd been examining and brushed his hands briskly together. 'The first thing Kalion will be telling Troanna is your plan to elevate me above my peers. For which my sincerest gratitude, Archmage.' He looked rather more resigned than elated.

'You can take it up with Shannet, if you don't want the honour,' Planir offered.

Rafrid pretended to consider this. 'No, I'll take the aggravation of office over her reproaches.'

'She'd never forgive you,' smiled Sannin, still intent on her reading.

'Do you have any ambitions to the honour of Hearth Mistress?' asked Planir idly.

'Me?' Sannin looked up, startled. 'No, none at all.'

'You'd tell people exactly that, if such a curious rumour should start circulating?' Planir's tone was solicitous.

'Just so.' Sannin returned to her book.

'Once word gets round we'll each have half the Council

knocking on our doors.' Herion glanced at Rafrid before looking at Planir. 'We'd better have our answers agreed before the rumours start flying round.'

Planir nodded. 'Go off and learn your verses. These can wait.'

'I'll send someone reliable from Hiwan's library,' Rafrid offered as the two men departed through a second door out on to the staircase.

'Thank you.' Planir went to shut the door but left it ajar, turning to Sannin who was still absorbed in reading. 'Are you willing to risk your reputation by being found alone with the Archmage in his bedchamber?' Bitterness underlay his jest.

'My reputation's safe with anyone whose opinion I value.' Sannin played absently with a button on the nicely rounded bodice of her scarlet dress, not looking up. 'Are you really going to ask her to marry you?'

'I told you I wasn't lying to Kalion.' Planir came to sit beside Sannin on the bed. 'Don't you approve?'

Sannin gazed at him. 'It's not for me to approve or disapprove.' She kissed his cheek with comradely affection before standing up. 'And I gave up pointing out the pitfalls in your chosen path when we were apprentices. Just be careful.'

'I'm touched by your concern.' Planir grinned. 'But what's life without a little risk?'

'Safer. I'm rather more concerned about Larissa,' chided Sannin. 'You've the hide of the village bull and the stones to go with it but she's barely out of her first pupillage. I know she has a double affinity and plenty of intelligence to go with it but she's not as strong as she'd like you to think. She always feels she has to match your measure as well as prove herself to everyone else twice over, just because you favour her. I've seen her overplaying her hand more than once – not that she's the first to do that of course.' Sannin shook her head with rueful amusement. 'I'm glad she's got Usara to rein her in before she comes to grief. Now I'd better get back and see if any of my apprentices have set themselves alight.' She left without a backward glance, pulling the door closed, full skirts swishing on the wooden floor.

Planir sat for a moment before searching beneath his pillows. Tucked in the corner where the yellow silk curtains were tied to the posts, he found a gauzy gossamer wrap embroidered with frivolous blue flowers. He held the delicate cloth to his face and breathed deeply, eyes closed with longing. When he lowered his cupped hands, mischievous determination brightened his fond smile.

Moving to the window he raised the hand bearing the Archmage's great ring. The central diamond caught the strong sunlight and broke it into myriad rainbow shards trapped within the facets. Taking the battered silver circle from his next finger, Planir slid it carefully on beside the insignia of his office. The Archmage's grey eyes narrowed and new light glowed softly in the gems surrounding the diamond. Clear amber light strengthened opposite mysterious emerald radiance and the ruby glowed with increasing warmth opposite the sapphire's cold blue. Planir's face might have been carved from marble as he bent all his concentration on the luminous gems now outshining the very sunlight. The diamond burned ever brighter, drawing colour from the other gems, brilliance fringed with fleeting rainbows. The old silver ring was lost in the blinding light until the magic suddenly flashed into nothingness, leaving Planir gasping, sweat beading his forehead.

He winced as he carefully removed the silver ring, a raw, blistered weal now circling his finger. Shaking, the Archmage studied his handiwork. The once dull and scuffed ring was bright and untarnished, unmarred by any scratch or blemish. It glowed with a rich silver sheen softened with just the faintest hint of gold. Planir left his bedchamber, waving a hand and locks on both doors out on to the corridor snicked softly secure.

Planir slipped the silver ring on his forefinger as he collected a candle from the mantel and took up the mirror and candlestick from the window seat. He winced as snapping his fingertips for a flame pulled painfully at his blisters but the candle burned fiercely all the same. The spreading light shone brilliant in the steel and Planir laid his hands either side of the dark wood frame, concentrating until the spell shrank to little more than a thumbnail disc of vivid brightness.

'Larissa?' whispered Planir. 'Dear heart?'

'Archmage?' Her startled voice rang through the spell.

'Just listen.' He bent close to the mirror. 'Ilkehan is dead. They killed him and cut up his body so D'Alsennin should be able to attack the pirates without fear of Artifice inside a day.'

'I'll bespeak 'Sar,' Larissa began.

'No,' Planir interrupted. 'Not until I know it's safe. Some enchanter may still find a scrap of power somewhere and try to make trouble. Just wait – and I have something for you, to help you when it comes to the fight—'

Frowning, the wizard caught his breath. Then he gasped in sudden shock. He flung the mirror from him, knocking the candle aside, hot wax spattering his hand. The Archmage was oblivious to the searing pain, reeling back senseless in the window seat, a trickle of blood oozing from one nostril. But the silver ring was gone from his finger, leaving only the blistered scar of the burn.

'Usara, wake up!'

The urgent voice roused the mage. 'Guinalle?' He sat bolt upright, then cursed as he slid off the makeshift bed a sailor had lashed together. He hit the ground with a thump that jarred his spine.

'No, it's me, Larissa.'

''Sar?' Hearing voices, Halice came towards the frond-covered canopies she'd ordered built to shade each bed from rain in the night and the earliest light of morning. 'I thought I told you to get some rest.'

'What in the name of all that's holy are you playing at?' Usara stared at the brilliant swirl of blue-white light.

'Ilkehan's dead,' declared the unseen mage-girl, voice high with exultation.

'How do you know?' demanded Halice. The mercenary didn't bother looking towards the magical link, catching up a leather map case from her blankets instead.

'Planir told me.'

Before Usara could wonder at the self-conscious note in Larissa's voice, Temar came running up from the beach, the young Sieur's questions stumbling over Halice's.

'What is it?'

'When did he die?'

'Planir just bespoke me.' Usara thought he heard that bashfulness again.

'What about Livak?' Halice scowled at the blinding radiance, a parchment in her hand. 'Where is she?'

'And Ryshad?' Temar took his sword belt from the stripped

sapling that propped up his shelter, and buckled it on. 'Have they returned to Hadrumal or are they coming here?'

'All Planir told me is Ilkehan's dead,' Larissa said, defensive.

'But Muredarch's enchanters aren't,' Usara remembered hastily. 'We must keep this short.'

'So Planir says we're ready to go? Did he say anything else?' Halice walked to the cook fire by the original pirates' hut.

'Not of significance.' That hint of coyness in Larissa's denial teased Usara again but such curiosity fled at the racket Halice was making with a long metal spoon against the iron cook pot. She bellowed an amicable warning. 'Stir yourselves or I'll stir you with this! I want every man ready to go.'

'We'll bespeak you when we've decided our next move.' Usara addressed the shimmering coil of magic and Larissa's spell spiralled in on itself, vanishing into nothingness.

Allin had come out of the cabin and stared at the empty air. 'When did she learn to do that?' The mage-girl spoke to herself as much as to anyone else.

Usara was sitting on his blankets pulling on his boots but paused to consider this question. 'That was one of Otrick's favourite workings. Was she ever his apprentice?'

'If Ilkehan's dead, why didn't we hear about it from Livak?' Halice picked up a kettle and stuck fingers in her mouth to summon a nearby sailor with an ear-splitting whistle.

'Perhaps Shiv's incapacitated somehow,' said Usara thoughtfully.

'Can't Sorgrad bespeak you?' queried Halice as she handed over the kettle. 'Get that filled.'

Usara shook his head. 'He's not got that skill perfected as yet.'

'If Shiv's hurt, I want to know what's been going on,' said Halice grimly.

'You and me both,' muttered Pered. The artist stood behind Allin, matching the edges of a sheaf of drawings with concentrated precision.

'That's not important – I'm sorry, of course it's important but—' Temar tried to convey apology with a quick look at Pered before turning to Halice. 'If Ilkehan's dead, we must attack, while the pirates' enchanters are still shocked by their master's death.'

'I'm sure Shiv's all right.' Allin gave Pered a reassuring smile and Temar wondered how he could ever have thought her plain.

'The news might have Muredarch off balance as well,' Usara remarked thoughtfully.

Halice nodded slowly. 'As long as we're certain those enchanters are clear off the board and back in the box.'

Allin moved to stir the slumbering cook fire to a cheerful blaze. 'Planir wouldn't have told Larissa to tell us if there was any danger.'

'Larissa's the last person in Hadrumal he'd risk,' agreed Usara with a pang at the truth of his own words.

'Guinalle can tell us how Muredarch's Elietimm stand.' Temar waved a hand at the shuttered wooden hut.

'She got less sleep last night than I did.' Usara realised he had spoken more sharply than he'd intended when he saw Temar's indignation. He managed a milder tone. 'Nursing Naldeth has been tiring. How much are you asking of her?'

'It's simple enough.' Temar's open face betrayed his chagrin. 'If I were but a little more adept, I could do it myself.'

'I'll make her a nice tisane.' Allin rose, brushing sand and ashes from her skirts, and rummaged in a small coffer holding Pered's treasured spice jars. 'You can take it to her, 'Sar.'

'Of course.' Usara hoped he didn't look as self-conscious as he felt when Allin gave him an encouraging smile.

'Let's assume Ilkehan's death has drawn Muredarch's enchanters' teeth.' Temar squared up to Halice. 'We have to decide exactly how to attack. We've spent long enough discussing the options.'

Halice spared a glance for Pered. 'If Livak and Shiv are in trouble, our attack should distract whoever's chasing them, Saedrin willing.'

'As soon as we've seen these pirates to Poldrion's ferry, we can rescue them.' Allin looked hopefully from Halice to Temar.

Halice was frowning, one foot tapping in thought. 'The question we must decide is how best to use Darni and Larissa. He's got the better part of a troop with him and we could certainly use a second attack.'

Temar braced himself. 'I still don't think we can rely on Darni. We've no notion of how many wounded he suffered or how far afield he's fled to evade pursuit.'

'Let me help you, Allin.' Usara went to find the horn cups. He didn't want to get involved in that argument again.

Halice's expression deepened to a scowl. 'It'll take too cursed long to send a boatful of men all the way round to come up the strait from the south.'

'Those two pirate ships we burned all but block the channel anyway,' Usara pointed out. 'A two-handed attack is all very well but we'd gain nothing by splitting our forces and letting Muredarch take on each half as he pleases.'

'Guinalle could call up the *Eryngo* with Artifice, or I could,' Temar amended hastily as he caught Usara's look of rebuke.

'We want every ship holding the blockade.' Halice shook her head. 'We won't net all the rats but I'll be cursed if I'll let them scurry back to Kalaven to plague us in some other season. Send them orders with your Artifice by all means; just to sink any boat that they see.'

'We don't want them fetching up on Kellarin's shores either.' Allin was tying up scraps of muslin filled with miserly spoonfuls of herbs.

'Indeed not.' Temar folded his arms in unconscious imitation of Halice, jaw set. 'So we hit the landing as hard as we can in the first assault. That means you need every man who can hold a sword. I'm coming too.'

'Of course you are.' The mercenary's smile was as fierce as it was unexpected. 'This is your first real fight for your colony. You'll be seen to be leading it, if I have to be standing behind you with a cattle prod.'

Allin's kettle stopped in mid-pour, the wizard looking concerned. 'Couldn't you attack at night again? Wouldn't you all be safer?'

'We won't get away with that trick twice. If Muredarch isn't setting double sentries at sunset, I'm the Elected of Col.' Halice's words were more explanation than rebuke. Temar was glad to see it, though for a fleeting instant he did think it might make a pleasant change if Halice showed him the same forbearance.

'Besides, a raid at night's one thing; a full assault is a whole different hand of runes,' the mercenary continued. 'We need to see what everyone's doing and when those pirates break, we want to know where they run. We'd lose them inside ten strides in those woods in the dark. The whole fight would end up as confused as two cats scrapping in a sack.'

'I can't see us being able to use the archers as effectively as last time.' Usara took a steaming tisane, brow wrinkled in thought.

'No,' agreed Halice, taking a cup from Allin with a nod of thanks. 'They've precious few arrows left, which is another reason we need Darni. 'Sar, when you bespeak Larissa, tell her we want whoever can still walk and wave a stick creating a diversion. If we can split the pirates even just a little, we can drive in a wedge.'

Allin set down her kettle. 'Plenty of the captives we rescued will want to come. They've been saying as much.'

'They're still too weak, however strong their hatred.' Temar's grimace acknowledged that unwelcome truth. 'Naldeth was half dead even before those swine threw him to the sharks.'

'A few days' rest and food won't give them the stamina for a real fight.' Halice turned to the open beach. 'Banner sergeants to me!' she bellowed. 'Let's set about making a proper plan, shall we?' She took another swallow of tisane, grimacing at the heat, before throwing the sodden muslin lump into the fire where it hissed and smouldered. She poured the dregs to dampen the soil and picked up a stick to scrape an outline on the ground.

'Let me do that,' offered Pered but, as he spoke, the earth began to writhe beneath Halice's twig, shaping itself into a representation of the pirates' landing blurred by a misty ochre haze.

'Then let me do that instead.' Pered took one of the cups Allin was still holding and knocked on the door of the hut.

'Enter.' Guinalle's voice was soft and she warned the artist with a finger to her lips. Men snored and shifted on their pallets and the air was rank with the scents of sleep, sweat and injury.

Pered handed her the cup. 'I thought you were supposed to be resting.'

'With Halice shouting fit to be heard in the Otherworld?' She looked quizzically at him. 'What's the news?' She stood in the doorway and looked at Halice, Temar and Usara, dun, black and balding heads bent close together while Allin set about the more prosaic necessity of chopping meat from the island's scurrying rodents to add to the hulled wheat she'd set soaking earlier.

'Planir tells us Ilkehan's dead,' Pered explained.

'Wizards.' Guinalle clicked her tongue with irritation. 'They couldn't wait for me to make sure their path was clear?'

'No one wants to overtax your skills,' said Pered diplomatically. 'Everyone's aware how much your duties ask of you.'

Guinalle smiled into her cup of aromatic tisane. 'Shiv's a lucky man.'

Pered's smile couldn't rise above the apprehension plainly weighing heavily upon him. 'We don't know exactly what's happened in the Ice Islands.'

'So Temar wants me to find out.' Guinalle reached for his blunt and ink-stained hand. 'Let us see together.' She drew him into the frowsty gloom and set her cup down on a cluttered board resting on two trestles. 'With a love such as you share to guide me, I could find Shiv in the Wildlands beyond Solura.' She murmured a soft incantation.

As a sudden vision of Shiv crouching in a thorn bush surprised her, Pered's fingers tightened on her own. 'He's hiding? Are they in danger?' She felt unimaginable pain edge the artist's unspoken thought. 'Something's wrong.'

'It's all right.' Guinalle spoke directly to his common sense to answer the fears of his imagination. 'Whatever they've been doing, it's worn him out but rest will restore him. He seems well content with his work.'

'Where is he?' Pered wondered without speaking and the thought rang in the silence they shared within the bounds of enchantment.

'I cannot tell.' Guinalle shook her head. 'But he feels safe.'

Pered understood her double meaning without need for explanation. Shiv believed himself to be safe and Guinalle sensed no immediate peril threatening him. 'Are they all safe? Livak? Ryshad?'

'As far as I can tell.' Guinalle frowned; it was always so hard to read a mage's thoughts unless they were actively working their own magic. She might be less confused about Usara if she could sense a little more of what he truly felt for her. Then she might not have to rely on someone like Pered to anchor her with his commitments and affections. She hastily set that irrelevance aside before Pered could pick it up and then a flood of images assailed her.

A grief-stricken woman hid hysterical tears behind blood-stained hands and long, tangled hair. Her wild emotions struck Guinalle like a slap in the face. Horror at the death of her protector was twisted by guilty relief that her life would no longer be a nerve-wracking dance around his whims and cruelty. A new brutal truth assailed that scant comfort. Without Ilkehan, who might claim her? If she avoided enslavement or concubinage, how would she eat?

Ruthless, Guinalle broke free of the woman's incoherent thoughts, pulling Pered with her. Noiseless voices and half-glimpsed faces came and went. What manner of Artifice did these Elietimm learn, if they had so little discipline, so little self-control? Theirs was a brutal, caustic art, shocking reactions from people and using such self-betrayal to another's undoing.

As unrestrained Artifice carried emotions hither and thither, Guinalle saw a balding man with solid, wind-scoured features determined to defend his land and people from whatever might follow from Ilkehan's long-hoped-for death. A younger man saw his flank exposed by the loss of his ally. The image in his mind's eye of an undefended keep on an exposed sandbar shifted into a more immediate terror of his own nakedness beneath a descending blade. Vivid imagination saw shining steel cut into white and trembling skin, blood scarlet on the silver blade, flesh and sinew parting. Fear liquefied his belly as he realised no one would care that he had yielded to Ilkehan only to save himself. Guinalle was startled to feel her own bowels gripe in sympathy.

Pered gasped. 'I can't do this, my lady.'

Of course, he was far more susceptible than she. That was why she was so shaken. 'Stay with me.' Guinalle wove an incantation to give him some surcease from the hubbub of emotion. She bolstered her own defences as hopes and fears and guesses and memories swirled through the aether, battering her self-control.

A woman's face creased with age exulted at the death of her enemy. Now she could die content. A younger woman close by was furious with something or someone, struggling against some constraint Guinalle couldn't comprehend and for an instant she saw bars striping that drawn and intent face. Her desperation was her undoing, Guinalle realised with pity, resentment at her situation driving her to impossible pining for what had gone and could never be restored.

The shock of seeing the woman so confined by her regrets distracted Guinalle and she felt the passing brush of a powerful intellect so chilling, it raised gooseflesh on her arms. The impact of this cunning mind swept away all the other whispering emotions and Guinalle hastily shrouded herself with every art that she'd been taught. The questing thought moved on, man or woman Guinalle could not tell, but avaricious, darting from hidden deliberation to masked ambition, eager to take every advantage from this turn of events. Whoever this might be was as well schooled in secrecy as any adept of Ostrin's shrine.

'A face hid from everyone.' With that conclusion Guinalle retreated carefully down the regular paths of rhythmic incantation and led Pered away from the trackless mire of grief, confusion and anticipation. 'Ilkehan's death has caused more chaos among the Elietimm than kicking over an ant heap.'

Pered opened his eyes, and rubbed at stiffness in his neck. 'As you say, my lady.' He winced ruefully. 'I feel as if I've spent half a day bent over a copy desk.'

'That's a fair comparison of the concentration required.' Guinalle gestured to her array of cures, their bottles arranged by height and colour. 'If you've a headache, I can mix you a draught.' It was a shame she had no tincture to still the trembling she felt in her own wits.

'I'll be fine, thank you all the same.' Pered stood rubbing his neck, eyes inward looking. 'That was a remarkable experience, even more so than last time.'

'Guinalle!' Temar's voice startled them both and they turned to see him beckoning her impatiently to the door.

'In a moment.' Guinalle dismissed Temar with a flap of her hand. 'When we have the leisure, you should learn a little Artifice. I believe you could become quite an adept.'

'It's a shame I didn't think of learning such skills before.' Pered didn't bother hiding his bitterness. 'Then I might be of some use here.'

'You can be of use to me and to Naldeth, if you've a mind to it,' Guinalle said with sudden inspiration. 'Ostrin be thanked, his wound is beginning to heal and he has youth and strength to support him while it does.' She spoke in low, confidential tones, gathering up fresh dressings, a pot of salve and a small bottle of dark brown glass from the trestle table. 'What he lacks is the will to live. He believes he has failed his calling, his teachers, Parrail and every other unfortunate lost to the pirates.'

'He's woken?' Pered was visibly taken aback.

'Barely, but I have the arts to hear his thoughts.' Guinalle had to bite her lip at the recollection. She really must get a good night's sleep as soon as possible. Being with Pered was tempting her to weakness as well; his open friendliness disarmed more people than her after all.

Pered shook his head vehemently. 'Their blood's on Muredarch's hands, not Naldeth's.'

'I cannot convince him of that,' sighed Guinalle. She led the way carefully through the pallets to a bed at the back of the hut.

Pered followed. 'What do you want me to do?'

'Talk to him. He can hear you despite his pain and the medicine dulling his senses.' Guinalle laid a hand on Pered's arm. 'Remind him of all there is to live for. Love, beauty, friendship, honesty striving against all that is false.'

'Can't you do that with some Artifice?' asked Pered, curious.

'Not till I have convinced myself.' Guinalle froze and snatched her hand away, unsure if she'd spoken or merely thought that frank admission. Pered's instinctive hug of sympathy startled her still further and she pulled herself abruptly back. 'That would be an abuse of my powers, with him so vulnerable.' He was vulnerable, not her. She couldn't afford to be. Guinalle looked down at Naldeth who lay asleep, wearing only a creased linen shirt, long enough to preserve his modesty. 'Hold this.'

Pered took the dressings and the salve and Guinalle sensed his instinctive sympathy as he watched her carefully remove the bandages from the mage's stump. That was another distraction she could do without, she thought crossly. It must be some consequence of the rude shaking she'd been given by those undisciplined Elietimm.

'That looks a lot neater,' Pered said bracingly.

Guinalle looked closely at the lines of stitches black against

the white skin. 'We had to cut the bone at mid thigh so as
to have enough skin to sew together.' She gently wiped away
dark encrustation. 'That's no bad thing since it meant all the
torn flesh that might have mortified was safely taken off.
There's no hint of rot and the wound is knitting nicely.' She
gave Pered a meaningful look and nodded at the mage, his
face not relaxed in sleep but unnaturally still.

'He's enough leg left to take a prop, if he prefers that to
a crutch.' Pered's voice was warm with encouragement but
he looked anxiously at her.

Guinalle smiled her approval and smoothed fresh salve
over the wound. The mage's whole body tensed beneath her
light touch and she saw Pered cringe in sympathy. Yes, she
decided, he was a good choice to help the wounded and, unlike
her, he wouldn't be battered by Naldeth's constant, unconscious self-reproaches. She took a breath and renewed her
defences once more. She really must get some untroubled
sleep.

'Why's that salve blue?' Pered asked abruptly.

'It's made from woad; it stems bleeding.' Guinalle
re-dressed the wound with deft fingers. 'A most useful plant,
even if preparing it does raise the most appalling stink.' She
tied off the ends of the bandage briskly. 'Sieur D'Alsennin
needs me, Master Mage. Pered is here to watch the wounded
while I'm occupied, so he'll have your dose ready for you
when you need it.' She put her arms around Naldeth with
impersonal efficiency and lifted him more comfortably
against his pillows before gently lifting the dressing on his
arm to assess the healing sore beneath. 'When the pain rouses
him, make him take a spoonful of this. We don't want his
torment setting his elemental powers running loose. Arimelin
grant most of the others will continue to sleep and those that
wake should be content to wait awhile but if anyone is in
great distress, come and get me. I'll be back as soon as I can.'

She won a grin from Pered but Naldeth lay stony faced
as before. Guinalle hid her own misgivings beneath a bland
face and left the hut quickly. She'd achieved something at

least; setting Pered a task to keep his mind off whatever peril Shiv might be facing. If only the artist's vivid appreciation of the life all around him could turn Naldeth from the despondency cutting deeper than the bone saw she'd used on him. As she thought that, some pang she wasn't prepared to identify left her stomach a little hollow.

'What's the matter?' Temar asked sharply as she reached the door of the hut.

Guinalle lifted her chin to meet his challenge. 'I'm concerned for my patients, Naldeth in particular.'

'Oh.' Temar looked sheepish. 'How is he? Has he woken yet?'

'Not to speak with any clarity but Artifice tells me he's wearied by pain and distress,' Guinalle said tightly, ignoring the treacherous thought that the same could be said of herself. What had she been thinking of, betraying her own melancholy like that? There was no comparison. She had a sacred obligation to give her life purpose; to use her skills and learning for the benefit of others.

'Would you like some bread?' Usara appeared with a handful of the long twists of dough the mercenaries were wont to cook over their fires.

'Thank you.' Guinalle wondered when she'd stop missing the fine white loaves she'd been used to. Now that really was a pointless regret, she thought with asperity, worthy of those undisciplined Elietimm women.

'You're entirely welcome.' Usara smiled at her, eyes warm with affection.

Guinalle dropped her gaze and tore a piece off the coarse bread. No matter how fond Usara seemed at present, the mage would return to Hadrumal when this strife was ended, she reminded herself. She would return to her life in Kellarin, meagre as it was. Letting go of lamentations over bread was one thing; risking heartbreak for the chance that Usara might help ease her sorrows was entirely too much to hazard. She'd sought paltry solace in Temar's arms, with all his familiar deficiencies as a suitor and against her better judgement, only to have him make his disdain plain. She wasn't going to lay herself open to such weakness again. But how it would ease all her sorrows to have the support of a love such as Shiv and Pered shared. Oh, this is ridiculous, she scolded herself silently. Get yourself in hand!

'Larissa sent word that Ilkehan is dead,' Temar began as they walked towards the cook fire.

'So Pered said,' Guinalle interrupted. 'From what I can read of the Elietimm, it seems to be so.'

'Seems?' said Halice sharply. 'It could be a lie to deceive us?'

'No.' Guinalle chose her words carefully. 'Ilkehan is truly dead. What I cannot divine is precisely by whose hand or when.'

'Where are Livak and the others?' Halice demanded.

'Safe, for the moment.' Guinalle shrugged. 'Beyond that, those holding power in the islands and who know of Ilkehan's fate are in disarray.'

'We need to know how Muredarch's Elietimm are reacting.' Usara's face was intent on this new question, tenderness for her vanished. Treacherous disappointment piqued Guinalle, but she rebuked herself. This turmoil was folly.

'Guinalle?' Halice was looking curiously at her. 'Are you all right? You seem distracted.'

'I'm tired.' She managed a thin smile. That must be why these idle fancies were distracting her.

'Not too tired?' Usara was concerned.

'Don't worry.' Guinalle waved away Temar's hand as she brushed aside the perplexities that had inexplicably come to plague her. Familiar incantations warded her with the uncomplicated purity of Artifice. Armoured with aetheric magic, she reached out to the pirates' lair and searched for the enchanters.

'They know he's dead.' Guinalle couldn't hide her own elation. 'More, they have lost their grasp on the aether. All their training was focused on Ilkehan, not any understanding of independent enchantment. They're completely at a loss.'

She opened her eyes to see Temar and Usara gazing at her. Halice's face was unreadable as she chewed on a twist of bread. Allin stood beside her, a slowly dripping spoon held above a cauldron over the fire, her round face anxious.

'Can they recover their Artifice?' asked Temar urgently.

'Once they're over the immediate shock, perhaps,' Guinalle allowed. 'But with nothing like the same potential.'

'We need to attack while they're still off balance.' Halice took a pace in the direction of the open beach.

'There's more,' said Guinalle hastily. 'They haven't told Muredarch. If they're of no use to him, they fear he might try to trade their lives for his own and his closest confederates.'

'No danger of that,' spat Temar.

'We definitely have to attack while he doesn't know they're crippled.' Halice accepted a steaming bowl from Allin.

'We set sail as soon as we've filled our bellies.' Temar found a horn spoon in his pocket and took a bowl of the meaty frumenty. 'Thank you, my lady mage.' He ate hungrily, smiling all the while at Allin.

Guinalle accepted a bowl herself, savouring the swollen grain thickening the broth. Allin had even found a little dried apple to add, doubtless for Temar's sake.

Halice jabbed her spoon at him, words muffled by her mouthful of food. 'You need to decide what we're doing about prisoners. If I don't tell my lads while they're still calm enough to heed me, they'll just kill them all as usual and trust Saedrin to sort them out.'

Temar swallowed slowly. 'The pirates' lives are plainly forfeit but we should give those who were captured the chance to surrender. We can mete out justice in due course, can't we?'

Halice shovelled down her food. 'That oath of Muredarch's seemed to bind those who swore it pretty tight.' She looked at Guinalle. 'How will that affect them if they want to turn their coats in a fight?'

Guinalle's spoon hesitated in mid-air. 'I've no idea.' What

a perversion of aetheric power that was. If nothing else, her presence in this age should help put a stop to such foulness. That unbidden thought came as unexpected comfort.

'Your guess?' Temar persisted.

'Guesses are no good and no gold. We could talk till sunset and be no further on than a louse's skip.' Halice dropped her wooden bowl into the emptied cauldron. 'We'll take prisoners but no one's parole, man or woman. Let's be on our way.' Her long stride took her rapidly down the beach where everyone bar the recently freed captives was preparing for battle.

'It's hard to tell the mercenaries and the men of Vithrancel and Edisgesset apart,' mused Guinalle. Men and women checked blades and baldrics, adjusted straps and jerkins, boots and belts, faces set with determination. Some of the sailors were already rowing longboats out to the anchored *Dulse*.

'It's all the drilling.' Usara was at her side. Guinalle blushed with irritation. She hadn't meant to say that aloud either.

'We're all fighting for our future, be it in Kellarin or just on the road with a pocket full of gold.' Temar gave his bowl to Allin who was pouring hot water from the kettle into the cook pot. 'Leave that for someone else. Let's get aboard.'

Allin smiled nervously at him. 'Let's hope we can put an end to all this today.'

'I'll be glad to get back to Kellarin and a proper bed.' Temar took Allin's hand and tucked it through his arm, keeping her close.

'Shall we?' Usara offered Guinalle his arm. 'We're all to go, if this is the final assault.'

Guinalle took a deep breath. 'Will this be an end to it all?'

'If we all give it our very best.' Usara gazed at her intently. 'Then we can look to the future.'

Guinalle had no answer to that so settled for a non-committal smile and resting her hand lightly on the wizard's forearm.

They followed Temar and Allin whose conversation had turned intense.

'I want you safe on the *Dulse*, out of any danger,' he was insisting.

Allin pulled Temar to a halt. 'I can't work the magic Halice needs unless I'm close at hand.'

Temar seized her by the shoulders. 'Then be careful, do be careful.'

She gazed up at him. 'I will and so must you.'

Guinalle watched Temar kiss the mage-girl, her own thoughts in turmoil once more. Was this how he managed to rise above the torments of memory and regret?

'No time for that, Messire,' some anonymous sailor safely out of sight chuckled lewdly.

Allin was scarlet but her eyes were bright and she raised herself on tiptoe to kiss Temar back.

'Nice to see the Sieur doing his bit to boost morale.' Halice grinned as Temar, colour burning on his cheekbones, ran the gauntlet of approving ribaldry and whistles from mercenaries and colonists alike.

He laughed, unconcerned. 'Cohort commanders always reminded us we were fighting for hearth and home, wives and daughters.' Allin giggled as he helped her into the long-boat from the *Dulse*.

'Demoiselle.'

Guinalle followed with Usara, all the doubts and confusion she'd thought she had safely ignored whirling around her mind.

Halice helped her up over the rail with a grim light in her eye. 'Let's get this battle done.'

'Any sign of pursuit?' demanded Ryshad.

'None so far.' Sorgrad was a little way behind us all, searching for any trace we had left in the pathless thickets of berry bushes. Shiv had held up the whirling veil of dust until we were past the first rise beyond the keep. As we'd disappeared like coneys into a heath, he'd sent the dust storm out to dissolve on the seashore. With any luck, the Elietimm would think we'd disappeared with it. Not that we were trusting to luck, naturally. Getting caught and shown up for Planir's assassins painted as Eldritch Kin was not something we were going to risk.

So now we were crouching beneath more berry bushes, on a rise that gave us a view over both keep and the hargeard that was our next target.

'Too busy chasing their tails in there,' 'Gren remarked with satisfaction.

The breeze brought us indistinct shouts from ramparts and courtyard. Tiny figures in black livery and in none ran to and fro across the gaping hole in the wall where the gate had stood.

'Good,' said Shiv fervently. I looked at him with a frisson of concern; he looked exhausted.

'Not necessarily,' frowned Ryshad. 'Not if we want an audience to see us wrecking their hargeard.' He banged his elbow on the salvaged chest and cursed under his breath.

'Are you up to bringing down a whole stone circle?' I asked Shiv. As a general rule, I'm grateful magecraft takes such a toll on its users. It's most reassuring to know any wizard with ambitions to rule the world would die of exhaustion before he managed it but at this particular moment, I felt that Saedrin, Misaen or whatever deity ensured that was being unduly meddlesome.

'Are we still doing that?' 'Gren was redistributing his loot into more secure pockets and tucking the larger items into his pack. 'We could get back in time to fight the pirates, if we didn't.'

'Mercenaries.' Ryshad's sudden grin was white against his blue-painted face 'Never want to finish a job properly.'

'Regular troops,' Sorgrad countered with mock sorrow as he came up to join us. 'No imagination beyond their orders.' He nodded at the chest. 'Get that open, my girl. I'm not carrying it all the way back to Olret.'

'We don't want him cutting himself in for a share.' 'Gren buckled his pack which gave a satisfactory clank. 'You know, we could rob the Tormalin Emperor with a shadow play like that.'

'Try it and you'll have half the sworn men in Toremal after you,' Ryshad growled with half-feigned ferocity.

'You don't think Planir might object, 'Gren?' mused Sorgrad. 'Though he's never short of coin. Maybe that's how he fills his own coffers.'

I had the chest open and lifted the lid to reveal bundles of faded velvet. 'Can we save the banter for a safe fireside?' But I was also feeling the elation that comes after taking an insane risk and getting away with it. 'Ideally one with an inn wrapped round it.'

'Who gets first pick?' 'Gren reached for a close-wrapped lump but I slapped his hand away. 'This isn't loot, 'Gren, it's people's lives and don't you forget it.' I locked gazes with him until I was sure he was heeding me and then stirred the velvet with a careful dagger point to reveal a handful of trinkets. Sorgrad squatted beside me and weighed them in one hand before handing them to his brother.

'I'm already carrying enough weight,' objected 'Gren.

'Then the loot's what you dump,' Sorgrad said in a tone

that brooked no argument. 'You fail to bring someone back to themselves from that cavern and you'll answer to me.'

'And Halice,' I added.

'And half the people of Kellarin.' Ryshad knelt beside me and took my dagger to move the smaller pieces aside, revealing a couple of swords and a handful of daggers.

'One each,' said 'Gren irrepressibly.

'I'd say it's best to spread these around.' Ryshad suited his actions to his words, passing us each a weapon with antique moulding and tarnished decoration. Mine had a particularly fine amethyst for a pommel stone. 'Do your best not to use them though. We don't want unexpected visitors inside anyone's head.' He tried to make light of it but the attempt fell miserably flat.

'As far as Guinalle could make out, it's a sense of danger and strong emotions generally that penetrate the enchantment and stir the hidden mind.' Shiv's face was intent, deep lines drawing down either side of his mouth. 'The people were never meant to be hidden for so long. The enchantment's worn horribly thin.'

From Ryshad's expression, horrible was an apt description of the consequences of the incantations unravelling. He lifted one of the swords with visible reluctance.

'I'll take that.' Shiv stuck the weapon through his belt, velvet wrapping and all.

'Do you know how to use that?' asked 'Gren with a touch of derision.

'No, but that's the whole point,' Shiv retorted. 'I won't be tempted and risk rousing the sleeping mind within it. Who's taking the other one?'

I saw Ryshad steeling himself to what he doubtless saw as his duty and forestalled him. 'I will.'

'Are you sure?' He looked at me, concern darkening his brown eyes.

I wasn't but this wasn't the time to admit it. I avoided his gaze as I adjusted the awkward weapon, trying to make sure it was secure at the same time as not inadvertently stabbing myself in the leg. None of us needed that kind of delay.'

'I'll take it,' 'Gren offered. 'I dealt with Eresken when he came knocking round the back of my mind.'

'You killed him, 'Gren,' I pointed out. 'The whole idea is to bring these people back to life. Anyway, how long do you think you could carry a weapon without using it?'

He nodded sagely. 'You're so good at hiding at the back and letting other people do your fighting.'

I grinned at him. 'Quite right.' He chuckled with appreciation.

'Have you any notion how many people still sleep in Edisgesset?' Shiv frowned, as I shared out the rest of the little parcels, more valuable than ten times their weight in gold or diamonds.

'Thirty or so, wasn't it, at last count?' I felt guilty that I couldn't be more certain. I tucked mine inside the breast of my jerkin, the weight heavy beneath my breastbone, my stomach hollow with the responsibility I now carried.

'Thirty-seven,' said Ryshad with biting emphasis.

Sorgrad scowled. 'Then we're still missing some.'

'That's assuming all these are true Kellarin artefacts,' I pointed out reluctantly.

'So the rest's fair booty?' 'Gren was shaking out the remnants of cloth left in the base of the chest, just to make sure nothing was overlooked.

Shiv and Ryshad were looking back in the direction of Ilkehan's keep.

'They look too busy to send anyone scouting for us,' said Ryshad. 'Let's have that hargeard down to put an end to Muredarch's enchanters.'

Shiv pulled his belt tighter and settled the wrapped sword on his hip. 'Sorgrad, you're going to have to help me with this.'

'Very well.' Sorgrad's voice was unemotional but I could see a gleam of eagerness in his blue eyes. Was this going to be entirely safe? I wondered.

'It's this way.' Sorgrad cuffed his brother lightly round

the head and 'Gren reluctantly abandoned his attempt to pry off the brass fittings of the chest.

More cautious than ermines in the wrong colour coat, we eased our way through thickets of berry bushes thick with leaf, pale pink bell-shaped flowers and squat green berries yet to ripen. I froze with disbelief as I heard a familiar sound from the other side of an upthrust of rock. That first light-hearted jingling was joined by another and then came the clip of small hooves.

I looked at Ryshad who looked at Sorgrad and, at his nod, came to my side. As I drew my dagger and we headed for the far side of the sprawling clump, 'Gren and Sorgrad went in the other direction. Shiv crouched down, catching his breath and keeping watch. I rounded the bushes to find a rocky cleft sheltering the thickest and oldest berry bushes we'd seen and a spring all but dry in the summer's heat.

Being goats, the animals were stripping the berries from the bushes with single-minded determination before moving on to the leaves and any tender twigs they could reach. Being lads, the youths were waving a spray of fruit on the end of a stick to tempt a bold kid out along a weathered knife-edge of outcrop rock. Every time the little goat took another cautious step with small black hooves, the first tow-headed boy edged the berries a little further away. The second boy wanted his turn at the tease, reaching for the branch.

Behind me, Ryshad bent to whisper soundlessly in my ear. 'My father always reckons one lad does the work of one lad, two do the work of half a lad and three gives you no lad at all.'

This pair were so intent on their nonsense, they wouldn't have heard him shout that aloud. They didn't even notice the goats pause in their chewing to stare in their peculiar, slot-eyed way.

Sorgrad and 'Gren appeared at the head of the defile, startling the boys who backed away. The kid sprang lightly down the crumbling rock to bolt the fallen berries with muffled bleats of triumph. One nanny licked a stray leaf from her tufted chin with slow deliberation as she watched me and Ryshad get behind the lads.

It was the work of a moment for me to grab one and Ryshad had the other. The lad froze before easing his head round to see what had snared him. After a sudden gasp, he all but stopped breathing, as entranced as a rabbit by a dancing weasel. I smiled but wondered how effective the disguise might be this close.

If my lad stood stiff as bone, Ryshad's was spineless. He sagged at the knees, hunching over, hands covering his face as Sorgrad and 'Gren advanced with a measured pace. I felt my lad tremble to the very soles of his boots and tightened my grip. He snapped out of his terrified stillness. 'Who are you? What do you want? We're no one, nobody. Take the goats, just don't hurt us.'

Sorgrad reached us and, still silent, laid a finger on the lad's mouth to hush him. The other boy looked up from his half-crouch between Ryshad's merciless hands, blue eyes wide with fear, blond hair tumbled all over his face. If we frightened him any more thoroughly he'd wet himself.

Sorgrad beckoned with one finger before turning to walk back the way he had come. Just as before 'Gren matched his step precisely.

I gave my lad a breath or so before smacking him smartly between the shoulder blades. He stepped forward before he could help himself and I followed close, urging another step with another blow.

The other lad's legs were as useless as if he'd been hamstrung. Ryshad growled deep in his throat, grabbing the lad's tousled hair and pulling back his head to stare deep into his eyes with cold menace. That sent the boy scrambling over the stony ground to cower beside his pal who was now forcing his reluctant feet onward without my intervention.

Ryshad looked a question at me and I shrugged. We followed at the same leaden pace that soon had my nerves twitching. Theatrics were all very well but what if a troop of Elietimm turned up to avenge Ilkehan while we were playing

masquerades? On the other hand, we didn't want this pair
running off to raise the alarm. Shiv appeared at the head of
the defile, standing with 'Gren and Sorgrad. I jerked my head
at the three of them with silent insistence that we get on with
whatever ostentatious destruction they had planned.

Sorgrad led the way over a shoulder of the land, and I
got my first sight of Ilkehan's hargeard. As a symbol of his
might and of the reach of that power, it was daunting enough,
even without ancestral bones and his inescapable Artifice to
sanctify it for his people. We walked round the base of the
great mound, flattened on top like an upturned bowl, so
steeply sided there was no need for a ditch to deter the
profane. A pale scar on the turf showed where countless feet
had made this circuit before us. The boys stumbled; fear tripping both now, terrified whimpers escaping the weaker one.

I slowed to get my bearings. The keep was pretty much
at my back, unseen over the shallow hills that formed a half-
circle here to frame the hargeard. On the shore side, more
hummocks and hillocks hid the dunes and sea. On the far
side, turf reached out to an abrupt wall of unforgiving rock
where the ground had fallen away like a broken piecrust.
The grey stone cut into the land like a knife blade, shallow
enough to step up nearest the hargeard but rising into the
distance until it reached five and six times the height of a
man. Ahead I saw a fan-shaped expanse of grass dotted with
scrubby growth. A road marked with tall grey pillars
marched down this long plain, a flange carved on the inner
face of each one. They were imposing stones but raising
them must have been a mere trifle compared to setting up
the sarsens crowning the mound. I did my best not to gawp
like some country bumpkin on her first visit to Toremal. A
slack jaw wouldn't befit a dread messenger from the Eldritch
Kin.

Steps were cut into the side where the approach road met
the mound. 'Gren, Shiv and Sorgrad stood on successive
treads.

'Kneel,' said 'Gren, lowest and closest to us. The boys fell

to their knees and at 'Gren's gesture, Ryshad and I left them
grovelling to go and flank him.

'All we require is that you bear witness.' Sorgrad's words
were sonorous with the archaic accents I'd heard from the
Sheltya. 'Life cannot thrive without death. Acknowledge this
debt and those who have gone before will guard and guide
you.' I saw the boys pale beneath the tan of their summer
duties, eyes huge.

'But there is a balance to be observed. Ilkehan profaned
it.' Sorgrad's words were as implacable as the tread of the
hangman to the gallows. 'He returned ill for ill thrice and
fivefold. He visited profligate death on the innocent and
defiled the exile of the guilty with blood. He has died at our
hands for these offences.'

The weaker lad huddled ever closer to his companion.
The bolder one gazed at Sorgrad in horrified wonder.

'We will destroy Ilkehan's power root and branch. Malice
and greed desecrate this place and the dead will not suffer
such taint. Bear witness,' Sorgrad repeated. 'Whoever will
rule this land must bring clean hands and raise a new sanctuary or suffer our wrath.'

He turned and walked slowly up the steps, Shiv at his
shoulder. 'Gren and I followed with Ryshad.

'What now?' I asked out of the corner of my mouth.

'Stand in the middle and keep still,' Shiv murmured.

Where Shernasekke had been happy with roughly hewn
stones for their hargeard, Ilkehan's were smooth and regular,
evenly spaced and looked so precisely upright you could test
them with a plumb line. The circle was as perfect as one
drawn with Pered's compasses. Each stone was twice as tall
as Ryshad, maybe more, not squared at the top but cut at an
angle, all the same, edges so sharp you might fear to cut yourself.

The stones were not the tallest monument to Ilkehan's
arrogance. An inner circle was made of wood. Great pines
had been stripped of branches and bark, smoothed and then
more prosaically steeped in pitch to stop them rotting. This

dark, sterile thicket towered above our heads, forbidding, around the innermost sanctuary where four triangular stones waist high and concave on every face marked the corners of a paved square in the centre of the whole edifice.

'What would you say the breadth of this is, compared to Olret's?' Ryshad looked around with a calculating eye. 'There's some constant measure used here, I'd bet on it.'

'Shall we worry about that later?' The five of us stood between the stones; Shiv at the centre, Ryshad behind him and Sorgrad in front. 'Gren and I at either side. I frowned. 'Where are those cursed goatherds?'

'They can't have got far. They'll see this regardless.' Shiv raised his hands and the hargeard responded to the elemental magic with a crashing clangour like a bell tower collapsing. I hastily clapped my hands to my ears. Eldritch dignity be cursed, I didn't want to go home deafened. Unperturbed, Shiv wove his spell and hail hammered down on the stones. Only on the stones. The ice melted and steamed in the evening sun, dark stains trickling down the grey sides before the water paled to frost. Now chill, like the breath of winter, floated off the rocks like smoke. The smooth stones began to split, hairline cracks widening to ragged fissures, flakes and chips of rock falling away.

I saw Shiv concentrating on one particular stone. The great sarsen began to tremble until a blue-green knife of magelight clove it from top to bottom with a sound like the slam of Saedrin's door. Which meant I missed whatever Shiv said to Sorgrad but the results spoke for themselves. Sorgrad rubbed his hands together to summon a ball of magefire and threw it at the wooden pillar on the off-hand side of the steps. The fire wrapped itself around the smooth black surface, bright tendrils spreading like some creeping plant, clinging to every crevice, flames blossoming on the dead wood. Crimson fire writhed, vivid beneath the smoke that billowed up. The ever-present breeze fanned the flames and the erstwhile tree became a column of golden fire and black smoke.

We could feel the all-consuming heat where we stood. I had no desire to end up toasted but bit my tongue on a plea that Sorgrad be careful. Distracting him would be even more dangerous. Then a veil of turquoise mist shimmered all around, cooling us. I mouthed silent gratitude to Shiv.

Sorgrad raised his hand and scarlet fire flowed from the burning timber to the next, flames tumbling down like water, soaking into the pitch. Natural flames took hold as the crimson magefire bowled across the ground, turf unscorched by its passage but the next wooden upright soon blazing.

'Where do you suppose Ilkehan got these trees?' I asked Ryshad.

'Dalasor,' he shrugged. 'A shipyard maybe, raiding someone's mast pond.'

With no more to do than either of us, 'Gren joined the conversation. 'Me and 'Grad were wondering if Ilkehan had been stealing sentinel pines.'

'Interesting idea.' Ryshad had to raise his voice to make himself heard over the roar of flames.

'The trees that mark the drove routes?' What I know about Dalasor can be told in one of Ryshad's mother's jam verses. Grasslands endless enough to lose even the biggest herd of cattle in hold no attraction for me.

'They were planted by the Plains People.' Ryshad shrugged. 'Ilkehan may have known some lore we've lost.'

I looked a little guiltily at Shiv. 'Do you think Planir fetched any of those books away?'

The mage didn't answer, still intent on the destruction of the hargeard. The steady crackle of burning wood raised a menacing threnody all around, the shattering of the great stones a savage counterpoint.

'They'll hear this racket clear over in the keep!' I said with exaggerated loudness.

Shiv grinned. 'They'll see it as well.'

Flames were licking up high into the evening sky, scorching the smoke with red and orange hues. 'I had no idea you could do this kind of magic,' I told him with unfeigned admiration.

'You never know what you can do until you try.' The wizard turned serious. 'That's half the trouble with Hadrumal these days. Libraries and learning are all very well but apprentices end up thinking if some authority doesn't say they can do a given thing, that must mean they can't. We need more mages like Otrick. Unless several sources stated categorically something was impossible and gave clear reasoning why, he reckoned it's always worth a try.'

'That sounds like Otrick.' Agreeing strained my throat. The magefire was spreading ever faster, leaping over the rubble of the disintegrating stones. We'd soon be encircled. 'How are we planning to leave?'

'Over there!' But 'Gren wasn't answering me. He was pointing to a column of black-leathered men running down the approach road. They fanned out, hefting maces in practised hands.

'We wanted witnesses to see Ilkehan's power go up in smoke, didn't we?' Sorgrad weighed a new ball of magefire in one hand, picking out a target.

'Can you see any gorgets?' Ryshad stood beside me, searching the oncoming line.

'I can't tell them apart at this distance, not with the smoke.' I shook Shiv's elbow. 'We can't risk you or Sorgrad to someone with Artifice. We'll never get off these rocks without you.'

'Sorgrad, let the fire go.' Shiv swept his hands around as if cradling an unseen sphere. 'We've got too many elements active and I'm too tired to handle the conflicts.'

The Mountain Man obeyed, which sparked a look of amazement from 'Gren. Azure magelight threaded through the roiling smoke and, ignoring the teasing breezes, wove an impenetrable veil around the blazing wooden pillars.

'Time to disappear,' Sorgrad announced cheerfully.

I looked at Shiv, bracing myself for whatever sorcery had carried us over the ocean and another bout of nausea. Instead, Shiv was on his knees and prying up the slab he'd been standing on. With a scrape to set my teeth on edge it revealed a narrow, stone-lined stair.

I gaped. 'Where does that go?'

'Somewhere not here.' 'Gren was already down the first few steps.

'There's a chamber down there.' Sorgrad cocked his head quizzically at me. 'We found it when we scouted the place.'

'What made you think to look?' I took one step down.

'No one would go to the trouble of building something like this and not make best use of it.' Ryshad urged me on down.

'Build it?' I said stupidly.

'You don't suppose Ilkehan's forefathers just happened to find a perfectly round hillock, do you?' Sorgrad retorted with amusement. 'Get a move on, girl.'

As I followed Shiv I began to see how the mound had been raised from successive layers of that local stone with the useful property of fracturing into handily flat and even pieces. Then I couldn't see anything at all. With another nerve-shredding scrape, Ryshad let the slab fall back into place and we were wrapped in total darkness.

'I know Mountain Men and Forest Folk are known for their night sight but this is a bit excessive.' I reached out a hand until I felt Shiv's shoulder.

I felt rather than heard his low chuckle. A faint glow rose from the stones, as if some moisture reflected a distant light. It vacillated between the palest of greens and a whisper of blue before sliding into a suggestion of red and gold.

'We don't want to give ourselves away,' Ryshad warned from behind me.

'They're bound to know this chamber is here.' Sorgrad nudged me and I moved carefully after Shiv.

The radiance trickled down the stones alongside us. The stairs twisted oddly, curving back and around but the regular pattern of the stacked stones defied my sense of direction. After creeping around in unlit houses on many occasions and never losing my bearings, that unnerved me.

'They can only send down one man at a time.' 'Gren's

voice changed as he spoke, ringing louder in a wider space. 'That means we can kill them all.'

'If they dare come down here.' Shiv stepped carefully off the lowest step, which was an uncomfortable stretch down even for someone with his height. I sat on the bottom tread and swung my feet down to the dark floor below.

Shiv's vaporous magelight slid away to leave the stairs a black void in the wall of a conical chamber. There were other holes, niches an arm span across. Caught unawares, I shuddered as I saw long bones laid haphazard between ribcages still linked to hip bones by spines and leathery cartilage. Skulls tucked to one side or set one atop another regarded us sardonically, sockets dry and empty. Some of the niches were crammed with tumbled bones but no skulls, some all but empty save for several bony faces keeping watch. Something grated between my boot and the flagstoned floor. Looking down, I saw a small bone from a finger or toe.

I swallowed my revulsion. 'Are we giving these people a decent burning?'

'No.' Sorgrad's sharp response echoed round the charnel chamber.

I looked to see what Ryshad thought but he was studying a section of wall. The stones between the niches were large slabs set upright in the layers that made up the mound.

'We're here to destroy the seat of Ilkehan's power.' Shiv looked around before bringing his gaze back to Sorgrad.

'We're not touching these bones.' The Mountain Man was adamant.

'If you say so.' I shivered again. 'So we wait until whoever's up top goes away?'

As I spoke, the sound of the slab at the top being lifted reverberated down the stair. Without magic to fan the flames, someone bold enough or scared enough of his commander must have darted between the burning tree trunks.

'Gren flattened himself to the wall by the entrance, dagger in hand. 'Come and join your ancestors,' he murmured with glee.

'Or we could try this.' Ryshad leaned all his weight on one side of the slab that had so intrigued him. It moved on a hidden pivot to reveal another black void.

'More bones?' I asked with distaste.

Ryshad peered inside as the elemental light explored the darkness. 'No.'

'Looks like a rat trap.' 'Gren barely spared the hole a glance. 'Kill enough of them good and loud and the rest'll think twice about following.'

Sorgrad was already easing past the slanted stone on hands and knees. 'If it's anything like a tyakar, there may be another way out.'

That was good enough for me so I hurried after him, Shiv helping me with a boost to the rump that would have earned anyone else a slap in the face. He wriggled past me to fold himself up next to Sorgrad.

'Get in here, 'Gren,' Ryshad ordered curtly. The Mountain Man obeyed, reluctance just about visible as Shiv's fading illumination chivvied him across the floor. The chamber returned to the silent blackness of before.

'What do we do if they come knocking?' 'Gren grumbled under his breath as he tucked himself opposite me.

'Hush.' Ryshad eased the slab closed with barely more than a whisper of stone on stone. This was a mason's work I could certainly appreciate.

We were sat hunched, shoulder to shoulder, boots uncomfortably tangled. We all tried to calm ourselves, as much to hear what was happening on the other side of the slab as to avoid giving our hiding place away. A faint noise sounded and we all held our breath, straining to hear.

I brought a hand up to my mouth and bit down on the knuckle of my forefinger. Halcarion only knows why but I had a quite insane urge to giggle. I scolded myself silently. That would be ridiculously stupid and quite possibly fatal into the bargain. With us packed like the fish in Olret's barrels, Ryshad felt my shoulders shaking and took my hand, squeezing it in mute reassurance. I closed my other hand over his strong fingers, feeling familiar square-cut nails and the rough skin over his knuckles.

We heard a determined thump as someone jumped that last deceptive step. A second thud and a third joined whoever had drawn the reversed rune and come down first. Emboldened by the fact they weren't yet dead, the newcomers risked some light. A torch flame traced an orange thread around the stone protecting us. I couldn't make out what the muffled voices said but their puzzlement was plain enough as was an encouraging undercurrent of consternation.

'Honoured dead, forgive this intrusion.' A stern voice made us all stiffen. Someone with authority had arrived. A chill gathered like cold sweat in the small of my back as this new voice began what could only be an aetheric chant. What had Sorgrad said about a second way out of this death trap?

'Where am I?' The cry froze the blood in my veins and the enchanter's incantation died on a strangled gasp.

'What do you want?' This second voice was lower and resonant with the rhythms of the Sheltya that Sorgrad had mimicked.

'Where am I?' repeated the first frightened voice and, gathering my wits, I realised it spoke old Tormalin, the tongue of the original settlers. It was a solid gold certainty that these Elietimm in the charnel chamber had no notion what it was saying.

'Is that you?' It was another lost Tormalin voice and I felt Ryshad go rigid beside me. This was a bad enough place for him to find himself in without people from the shades that had so nearly claimed him joining us.

'What do you want with us?' That was the Elietimm bones again, this time several voices resonating through the stone. I screwed my eyes shut but it was no good. I couldn't close my mind's eye on a vision of dry skulls talking, jawbones flapping like some ghastly marionette.

'Where are the people we seek?' That was the enchanter leading our pursuers, his voice was strained with what I sincerely hoped was panic at what he'd started with his incautious Artifice. Gripping Ryshad's hand, I wished fervently for a chance to strangle the bastard with his own gorget.

'Lost, so long lost.' The ancient Elietimm sighed, more voices joining in their lament and sinking the words beneath meaningless ululation.

'I cannot see!' A Tormalin wail rose above the murmur, prompting another despairing cry. 'Are we dead?'

'The darkness, oh, the darkness. I cannot bear it!'

That voice was in the hollow with us. I swear my heart missed a beat and the hairs on my neck bristled like a startled cat. By the greatest good fortune or Misaen's blessing, all five of us jerked so hard in our instinctive desire to flee, we effectively stopped each other from moving at all. Then fear of discovery overrode fear of the disembodied voice and we all froze, still as hiding hares again. Blood pounded in my chest so hard I was surprised not to hear the sound echo back from the stones. The artefacts hidden in my jerkin weighed down on my hollow stomach like lead and a bruise where someone had kicked my leg throbbed.

'The darkness is peace.' The Elietimm bones outside offered rebuke not comfort.

'The darkness is ours.'

'The darkness is knowledge.'

'The darkness is ours to hold and defend.' The menace grew as the voices came thick and fast. The only good thing to be said about that was the noise drowned out the incoherent voice trapped with us.

'Who challenges us?' The dusty rasp had a ring of ritual, something to be said before formal battle or a duel to the death.

'You are demons!'

'We are forsaken.'

'We are lost!'

'Is there no light? Where is the light?'

The Tormalin frenzy nearly, but not entirely, drowned out the sound of boots hammering on the stone steps as the

Elietimm who'd pursued us into the chamber broke and fled. If I hadn't had someone pinning my legs and Ryshad between me and the way out, I'd have followed them and be cursed to the consequences.

The Elietimm voices were shouting now, Tormalin shrieks cutting through the clamour.

'Sorgrad!' I hissed into the darkness. 'You said there was another way out.'

'I said there might be,' he retorted. 'If there is, I can't find it.'

'Use some magelight and look harder,' I told him forcefully.

'I'm not going out through that lot,' 'Gren said with complete certainty.

'I'm not raising any elemental magic until I know how they're going to feel about it,' stated Sorgrad tightly. 'Sheltya ban anyone mageborn from even approaching a tyakar and I'll bet they've good reason.'

'Can shades actually harm the living?' Shiv managed a wizardly tone of detached enquiry for the first half of his question then his voice cracked with concern.

'I've no intention of finding out.' Ryshad's voice was harsh and I caught the scent of fresh sweat. Then I realised my own forehead and breast were damp with cold apprehension.

'Isn't there any Artifice you can use, Livak?' Sorgrad asked with commendable calmness.

'How am I supposed to read it in the dark?' Besides, the parchment in my pocket might as well have been blank, for all I could remember of what was written on it. The chaotic sounds outside rose to a higher pitch and the voice in with us started a low keening like an injured cat.

I hadn't been so terrified since I was a child. This was worse than waking to the impenetrable cold of a winter's night with the candle stub guttered and me scared of the dark but more scared of what might be waiting if I got out of my truckle bed or what might be roused if I called out for someone. At least back then, my mother always had an ear

for me stirring and would appear with a fresh light, putting
the shadows to flight with no-nonsense reassurance mixed
with rebuke. My father, on those rare occasions he stayed
with us on his travels, would use a song, turning the darkness into a comforting blanket wrapping me round. That song
was a Forest song, no jalquezan that I could recall but
anything was worth a try.

> 'Let's run quickly, quickly, quickly, let's run quickly,
>   little lass,
> Let's run quickly, quickly, quickly, let's run quickly,
>   little lass,'

Breath all ragged, I missed more notes than I hit in the
old lullaby but I persevered doggedly.

> 'For the trees still cluster thickly and the shades of night
>   are gathering,
> Let's run quickly, quickly, quickly, let's run quickly,
>   little lass.'

Shiv's tuneless voice told me the song had a place in the
remote Kevil fens. He matched me in slowing the pace of
the jaunty tune to match the words.

> 'Not so fast now, fast now, fast now, not so fast now,
>   little lad,
> Not so fast now, fast now, fast now, not so fast now,
>   little lad,
> See the moons and stars above us and the shades of
>   night are stilling,
> Not so fast now, fast now, fast now, not so fast now,
>   little lad.'

Ryshad's murmured version had a few different words and
turns to the tune but the gist was the same and I fervently
hoped that was all that mattered.

'Walk more slowly, slowly, slowly, walk more slowly, oh
*   my love,*
Walk more slowly, slowly, slowly, walk more slowly, oh
*   my love,*
See the lantern in the window as the shades of night are
*   settling,*
Walk more slowly, slowly, slowly, walking slowly, oh my
*   love.'*

I left the story to the others and concentrated on the soft
harmony my father added as soon as I was old enough to
carry the tune myself, just in case that's where the Artifice
lay. The brothers lent their voices; 'Gren picks up a tune as
easily as he pockets anything else.

'Now we're resting, resting, resting, now we're resting
*   safe at home,*
Now we're resting, resting, resting, now we're resting safe
*   at home,*
Work is done, the day is over and the shades of night
*   are sleeping,*
Now we're resting, resting, resting, now we're resting all
*   at peace.'*

We finished more or less together and sat in the blackness. The voices beyond the slab were silent. That much I'd
hoped for. What I didn't expect to hear was snoring.

'If that's Artifice, it's worked on Shiv,' said 'Gren with
barely repressed hilarity.

I fought a laugh of my own; I could all too easily give way
to inappropriate hysteria.

Ryshad hissed beside me. 'I've got cramp.'

'Let's get out of here,' suggested Sorgrad. 'Anyone after
us must be long gone.'

'It's the longest gone that concern me most.' But I was
eager enough to untangle myself and scramble out of the
confined space once Ryshad had half crawled, half fallen out.

'Dast's teeth!' He stumbled over something that clattered in the darkness.

My heart leapt until I realised it wasn't the hollow ring of bone but the solid clunk of wood. Steel on flint raised sparks that stabbed at my eyes. I rubbed them and then Ryshad had the torch he'd found lit, soft flames warm and reassuring.

'Do you suppose they're keeping watch?' 'Gren moved to the black entrance of the stairway, weapon in hand.

'I would be,' said Ryshad curtly.

'I say we stay put.' Sorgrad was still by the hole we'd hidden in, using his cloak to pillow Shiv's head. The wizard was sleeping as soundly as if he were in the finest inn in Toremal. 'We all need some rest and we're probably safer here than anywhere else in these islands.'

I wished I shared his unconcern. 'Unless the real Eldritch Kin turn up to hold us to account.' That wasn't a joke.

Sorgrad turned to survey the niches with their stacked bones and watchful skulls. 'We should be safe enough, as long as no one uses any kind of magic.'

Ryshad handed me the torch as he bent to dig fingers into his calf and ease his foot up and down. 'That's a curse. We have to get word to Temar and Halice as soon as possible.' His voice strengthened with determination to think about anything but the unnerving experience we'd just shared.

'Tomorrow's soon enough.' 'Gren was pillowing his head on his pack as he lay himself down at the base of the stair. Anyone coming down there would tread on him and that would be the last mistake they made.

'You'll have to wait for Shiv to wake up anyway.' Sorgrad got back into the hollow next to the wizard and settled himself down.

I sat down, concentrating on the torch flame so I wouldn't have to look at the dry bones on all sides. Ordinarily, I'd have my back to a wall if one offered itself but here that meant having bits of ancient skeletons behind me. That notion made my skin crawl. But I soon shuffled round, frowning. There was no way I could sit without some bone-filled void at my back.

'Lean on me.' Ryshad sat back to back with me. We rested on each other, knees drawn up.

'What's a tyakar cave, Sorgrad?' I asked suddenly.

'Where we keep our ancestors' bones in the mountains,' he said sleepily. 'Where Sheltya seek guidance at Solstice.' Grim satisfaction coloured his words. 'What all the low-landers dismiss as superstitious nonsense. Our charlatan priests bamboozling us ignorant fools with their lies and self-serving deceptions.'

Ryshad cleared his throat. 'It's truly necromancy?'

'You'd have to ask Sheltya about that,' yawned Sorgrad. 'If you dare.'

Whoever might go asking, it wouldn't be me. The trivial charms of the Forest or the earnest enchantments to cure and protect that Guinalle excelled in were as much Artifice as I wanted. I'd found the ill-defined powers of the Sheltya unnerving enough without knowing they went around stir-ring up the shades of the dead. That was all too reminiscent of the darker practices of the Elietimm. I'd been right to mistrust magic for so many years, I decided. In all its forms.

Silence hung around us. I was pretty certain Sorgrad and 'Gren were asleep.

'You sleep, if you can,' Ryshad invited. 'I'll look after the torch.'

I settled myself against his broad and reassuring back. 'I couldn't sleep in here if I'd earn a lifetime's gold by it.'

'Me neither,' he admitted.

'I daren't even suggest a game of runes,' I said with a reasonable attempt at a laugh. 'Not seeing the Forest Folk use them for fortune telling.'

'Let's not do anything that might stir up the aether.' I heard a faint grin in his voice.

We sat silent for a while longer.

'So what are we going to do when we get home?' Ryshad asked suddenly. 'The garden will want clearing for a start.'

'Good thing I never got round to planting anything.' I leaned my head back to rub it affectionately against his shoulder. 'Did I tell you I was thinking of going into wine trading?'

'No, I don't think so.' Ryshad reached his hand round, and I laid mine on his upturned palm. He curled his fingers around mine and I did the same. 'You'll need some storage, proper cellarage ideally.'

'I reckon Temar owes me the land to build a warehouse by now.' I feigned concern. 'Have you any notion where I might get the bricks to build that?'

'I think I might know someone who could help out.' I heard the laughter in Ryshad's voice and smiled. 'There are so many wines to choose from,' he continued thoughtfully. 'You should visit the vineyards, see how they store their vintages.'

'And sample them,' I pointed out.

Ryshad squeezed my hand. 'We'll sail for Tormalin as soon as we've settled all this, shall we? Spend Aft-Summer and both halves of autumn putting together a cargo?'

'That's an excellent notion,' I approved. 'Where shall we start?'

Suthyfer, Inner Strait,
10th of For-Summer

Temar stood on the aftdeck and gazed at Allin as she concentrated on filling the sails of the ever-hastening *Dulse*. Her knuckles were white as she gripped the rail.

Halice climbed up from the main deck. 'She may not have Larissa's affinity but she's doing a good job.' She handed Temar his sword. 'You could shave with that if you've a mind to go into battle with a clean chin.'

'I'll wait till we're done and bathe then.' Temar continued to watch Allin whose concentration hadn't wavered in the slightest. He could still feel her lips on his.

Halice was looking at the billowing canvas. ''Sar said something about air and fire being paired in some way.' She turned to check on the *Fire Minnow* cutting a swathe of white foam through the water beside the *Dulse*. Her sails didn't have the constant curve of the *Dulse*'s but she was parting the waves like a sword slicing through silk. Temar followed Halice's gaze to Usara right in the prow of the ship, one hand on the bowsprit as he craned to see the sea beneath.

The door from the aft cabin opened beneath them and Guinalle came out on to the plunging deck. Temar bent over the rail. 'What of the watchpost?'

The demoiselle's eyes fixed on a scar cleared in the all-enveloping forest. 'They're scattered and confused. None will recall their purpose before nightfall.' Guinalle's voice was resolute but her face betrayed distaste.

She could have knocked them senseless at the very least. Temar bit his lip before he voiced such thoughts. No, Guinalle would never forswear her vows with such aggressive Artifice.

'We want to hit them like a storm out of a clear sky,' murmured Halice over the soft sweeps of her whetstone on a dagger.

Temar looked up and saw that the sky, while clear, was perceptibly darkening. 'Is there enough time to win this battle before dusk?'

'If we get a move on,' Halice grinned. 'And I doubt they'll expect an attack this late in the day, so that'll work to our advantage.'

As she spoke, the vessel wheeled and shot into the narrow opening of the inlet, pace barely slackening. Guinalle retreated to the sanctuary of the cabin again.

'Dast's teeth!' A sailor's nervous exclamation made Temar look up. He realised the crew were as tense as cats in a water-mill. Every man moved vigilant among the spars and ropes, making the finest adjustments often before the boatswain's whistled orders.

Pride in Allin's abilities swelled in Temar's chest as the *Dulse* sped through the narrow channel. The little ship raced past looming green hills thick with tangled trees that gripped the very shoreline with belligerent roots. The fighting men ready in the waist of the ship swayed and cursed as the ship heeled and jinked like a bolting horse. More than a few turned pale and Glane dashed for the rail, clutching at his belly, other hand clapped to his mouth. A cry of consternation from the prow prompted anxious looks all round until the boatswain waved reassurance with a broad hand. A swell of nervous laughter ran the length of the boat.

'What is it?' Temar asked Halice.

'Something about the reefs.' She peered over the side rail and surprised Temar with a chuckle. 'Look at this.'

Temar grinned along with Halice when he saw the waters seething furiously as jagged rocks and water-smoothed boulders tumbled over each other to pile against the shore, clearing the channel for the speeding ships. Usara was leaning on the foremost rail of the *Fire Minnow*, head bowed, wizardry turned on the unseen hazards beneath the waters.

'Careful.' The *Dulse* lurched and Halice grabbed Temar's arm.

'Thank you.' Temar took a deep breath as the unrelenting speed and motion made his own stomach protest.

'When we get ashore, you play your part but you watch your back,' Halice warned him sternly. 'You need to stay alive to reap the rewards for Kellarin – and to finish what you seem to have started with young Allin.'

'You keep your hide whole,' Temar retorted. 'I'm not done needing you.'

Halice grinned. 'I'm a mercenary. We're expendable. That's what we're paid for.' Her words won a cheer from the fighting men closest to the aftdeck.

'Just make sure we get paid, Commander!' called Minare.

'First pick of the loot,' shouted Peyt with relish.

'Secure it first and then we'll argue shares.' Challenge rang in Halice's voice.

'We're nearly there.' Allin's strained words drove all other considerations from Temar's mind. The ship lurched as the elemental wind fled. Crewmen scrambled up the ratlines to trim the sails.

'Ready to land!' Halice shouted and her banner sergeants called their troops to order.

'Ready?' The *Fire Minnow* was some way behind but Usara's shout echoed over the waters.

'Yes.' Allin's voice broke on her tension.

'Yes!' Temar drew his sword and waved it. He saw pirates running down to the water, hate-filled weapons catching the sunlight, their shouts soon drowned beneath the abuse the mercenaries on deck were hurling. The foremost brigands stood in the swirling surf, daring the invaders to risk a landing, their taunts raucous.

A deafening roar smashed through the uproar. Flames exploded from the merchant ships broken and dishonoured on the beach. Magefire ripped the masts asunder, wood splitting and metal melting. Burning brands and red-hot splinters scattered the waiting pirates. The troops on the *Dulse* jeered as their ship drove at the shingle, straight as a die. Stones grated beneath the hull, keel biting deep. The sailors caught the last of the wind to force her on, adding their skills to this new magic.

''Sar's pretty good with water,' Halice noted with approval. Temar looked back for Allin. Her feet were firmly planted on the deck, hands tight folded as she turned all her skill to destroying the stolen ships. She didn't flinch, even when someone jumped screaming from the stern of the *Tang*, flames consuming the man even as he fell towards the futile hope of quenching in the sea.

'Ware arrows!' Minare perched on the side rail, sword in one hand, the other holding a rope. The *Fire Minnow* reared up beside the *Dulse*, Usara leaning perilously over the prow as he forced the shingle to bank and hold the hull secure.

Temar put himself between Allin and any hostile arrow but the scattered shower had all but spent its force by the time it clattered among the masts and ropes. Then crossbow quarrels thudded into the wooden side of the *Dulse*, one sending a Kellarin man reeling back clutching his chest and screaming. A second flight of arrows hissed through the air like geese taking fright but this time Allin was ready. A shimmering curtain of magelight swept the shafts toppling and tumbling back to the shore and into the sea.

'Any chance she could use those to pin down a few pirates for us.' Rosarn appeared at Temar's side, her bow strung, reaching for her quiver.

Temar was surprised. 'I thought you'd spent all your arrows.'

'Nearly.' Rosarn narrowed her eyes on a distant target. 'But it's not arrows that makes the archer.' She drew her bow up in one fluid movement and loosed the shaft. A distant scream told Temar it had found its quarry. 'It's the aim,' Rosarn concluded with satisfaction.

Other archers picked to win full value for every precious arrow were on the aftdeck now. A second contingent on the sterncastle of the *Fire Minnow* was picking off enemy cross-bow men.

'Have at them!' Halice roared. Sailors flung ropes and nets over the side of each ship. Some of the mercenaries barely seemed to use them as they poured on to the beach, running to engage those pirates holding their ground despite the flaming embers or spent arrows cascading down on them.

'Go on!' Rosarn shoved Temar towards the main deck. He didn't need her urging, aware of every man's eyes on him. It was he and no other should lead the men of Vithrancel and Edisgesset into this battle. The loyal tenants of D'Alsennin's vast holdings had once trusted him to lead them within the cohorts of the Emperor fighting for Tormalin glory. Now his duty was to lead these men to victory such that as many as possible would live to enjoy it.

By now he was over the side and knee deep in the water. Ahead, Halice led her troop up the sloping shingle. Swirling waves dragging at their boots, the snarling mercenaries fought as one, each man arm's length from the next, ready to defend each other, all while attacking with all the savagery they could muster. The pirates went down like wheat before a scythe, bodies falling to taint the foam with a rush of scarlet.

Temar and his troop followed hard on their heels. 'To me!' he yelled as they gained the solid ground. Halice and her mercenaries met the pirates' main force in the centre of the landing. Immediately in front of Temar, Minare sent his men to either side, long practice spreading claws to crush the enemy. Some of the pirates broke, fleeing to the scatter of huts and tents on the rise beyond. Minare's men fell on the rest like starving dogs on meat.

Blood flung from a sweeping sword spattered Temar's face but he paid it no heed. He saw his moment and ran, blade questing before him. 'Now! For Kellarin!'

Some men echoed his cry. Others settled for wordless screams of hatred as they pursued the fleeing enemy. Temar hacked at a leather-clad back scrambling up the slope. Honed by Halice, his blade slashed a deep gash through jerkin and shirt, skin and flesh. The pirate wheeled round, back arching with the pain and throwing his stroke off so Temar could parry with ease and an upward sweep of his blade. He rolled his wrist round to hack at the man's neck, feeling bone splintering through sliced flesh. Temar pulled the blow short lest his sword bite into the clinging spine as the pirate fell. He ran on, eyes on the enemy, heedless of a body trampled beneath his boots. A man who'd overtaken him felled a pirate in one ferocious sweep of a broadsword. The corpse rolled away and Temar leapt it as he ran, drawing his poniard. His grandsire always said two blades were better than one.

Now they were at the huts and tents, Kellarin's men slashing and cutting with indiscriminate fury at pirates and screaming women.

'Clear every rat hole,' yelled Temar.

A man erupted from a crude shelter walled with the deck grates of a merchant ship. He swung a billhook once destined for peaceful duty in Vithrancel's thickets. Temar swept his sword up to guard his head, thrown on to his back foot as the double-edged and lethally heavy head swung towards him. The man with the bill came on, jabbing forward. Temar feinted to the open side, careful to judge the polearm's reach. The pirate thrust again and Temar darted forward to catch the shaft with his dagger, angling the blade to lock just below the vicious lower spike of the bill's hacking side. In the same movement, he sliced down the shaft with his sword, all but severing the man's foremost hand. The pirate screamed but even as blood gushed from his shattered wrist, he wrenched the gleaming metal head free of Temar's dagger, stumbling backwards. He whirled the bill around his head one-handed, hazel shaft whistling through the air with murderous intent towards Temar's head. Temar jumped back and the bill swept past his face with scant fingers to spare. The heavy head sank toward the ground, the man unable to recover it one-handed. Temar stamped down hard on the flat of the metal. The spike of the bill's crescent face dug deep into the soiled earth pulling the pirate forward, fatally unbalanced. Temar thrust his sword full into the man's belly, ripping it out in a sideways slash.

As he recoiled from the stench of blood and entrails, Temar realised Glane was at his shoulder, an unknown miner from Edisgesset on his other side. 'Bring these down!' he shouted, kicking at the flimsy wall of the billman's shelter. Glane darted forward as a muffled scream came from beneath the tumbled wood. He pulled a young woman out of the wreckage, dark hair tangled over her face, an overlarge bodice laced crooked over a filthy shift. She cowered away from them all, grizzling like a child.

'We're not going to hurt you,' protested Glane, distressed.

'Tie her up,' Temar ordered harshly. 'Trust no one till we have cause.'

Glane hesitated but the miner didn't. He flung the girl face down on the ground, one knee dug into her back as he cut strips of canvas to bind her wrists and ankles, heedless of her sobs.

Temar caught his breath and assessed their situation. Elated, he saw the ramshackle camp falling to Kellarin boots and blades, pirate men and women sprawled in the untidiness of death. Vengeful colonists, eager swords joining them with every passing moment, surrounded the few pirates still fighting.

'Take her yonder, boy.' The miner rolled the tightly trussed girl over with a brutal boot. He jerked his head towards the gravel of the foreshore where Vaspret barked instructions to men standing guard over bound and gagged captives. Glane looked uneasy but hefted the girl on one shoulder, carrying her down the slope like a sack of grain. The miner hastened to join a gang of his fellows who were grappling with some fools who'd thought they could hide in a tent.

Staying alert for any threat, Temar looked along the shore to see Halice's forces fighting the most brutal pirates, men whose only hope was to kill or be killed. They grudged every step of ground, boots digging into bloodstained turf, spitting and cursing at the implacable mercenaries just as determined to force them back. Blades scraped and rasped, scant room to swing freely. Swordplay gave way to punches, fists wrapped around daggers that twisted to gouge at faces and scalps. He looked at the line and lessons from his days in the cohorts rang in his memory.

'They're wheeling, curse it! To me!' Temar bellowed, waving his sword to summon his troop. 'Don't let them reach the shore!' If the circling fight curled round much more, the pirates would have a chance to dash for some weed-covered boats lurking in the rocks beyond the stockade. Sailors from the *Dulse* and the *Fire Minnow* were wrecking everything that could float on the main strand but without the benefit of Temar's higher ground, they hadn't seen those few longboats. Wrathful, he ran, boots thudding on the turf. He'd be cursed if he'd let any of these murderous scum slip away.

Then, as he ran, he saw movement at the stockade. The gates of the rough fortification flung open and Muredarch led a howling mob of his most loyal marauders down on the mercenaries. Those pirates tired by fighting scattered, many paying a heavy price in blood, as the unwearied newcomers hit the mercenary line. The forces met with a crash like the roar of a breaking storm. Muredarch was at the centre of his men, unmistakable with his great height, his immense reach soon leaving dead and wounded littered around him as he swung a two-handed sword in a deathly arc.

Temar wished fruitlessly for a bow, a crossbow and the skills to use either, even as he plunged on with his men. They had to cut the pirates off from the shore. They weren't going to make it. Anguish wracked him. He wasn't going to make it. Another failure would curse him.

Then a shudder ran through the fighting men. The pirates' malice yielded to astonishment that turned visibly to horror. Halice's mercenaries seized the first hint of weakness and smashed into their foes with redoubled violence. Temar and his men forced their way past the end of the battle line, sliding on the shingle but determined to deny the pirates passage.

Temar struggled to see what had rolled the runes of the battle anew. It was Darni and his fugitive troop, crashing out of the trees beyond the encampment. Some carried clubs of green wood instead of swords but the raking stubs of branches scored viciously into exposed arms and faces. There were as few of them as Temar had feared but determination to purge the shame of being put to flight made every man fight with the strength of two.

'Hold fast!' Muredarch's resonant voice pierced the uproar as the pirate line quaked once more. Then it held, pirates bracing themselves in an ominous parody of trained troops.

'Back!' At Muredarch's command, the line began a slow retreat.

'Break 'em!' Halice's roar rose above renewed abuse from the mercenaries.

'To me!' His troop drew up either side of Temar, a solid rank of leather and steel. Temar thrust and cut, intent on blood and revenge but the pirates held their line, trading chances to wound Temar's men for the safety of incoming blows. This was no rout but a disciplined retreat, step by slow step, towards the safety of the stockade.

If Muredarch secured himself in there, Temar thought furiously, they'd have to burn him out. As he thought this, scarlet flames soared beyond the melee, taking him so completely by surprise that a pirate sword darted over his guard to slice deep into his forearm.

'Curse you!' Temar rammed his blade full into the face of the man who'd wounded him, obliterating the bandit's shout of triumph. He ripped his sword free, gouts of blood and mucus on the dulled steel. As the dying man fell backwards, Temar broke free of his own line, men on either side of him instinctively closing the gap. Temar darted this way and that to try and see what was happening by the stockade, straining to hear any clue in the all-encompassing noise.

The stockade was ablaze. Scarlet magefire licked ever higher, black smoke billowing into the clear blue sky. Was this Allin's doing? As Temar wondered, pain erupted inside his head and he staggered with the shock, clapping a hand to his temple expecting to feel some dart or the score of an arrow. He squinted at his palm through tear-filled eyes but there was no blood.

The battle fell into chaos; all-pervasive pain wracking friend and foe alike. Men and women fell to their hands and knees, some clawing at their heads so fiercely they drew their own blood. Others folded around their anguish like wailing babes. Temar's legs wavered beneath him but he forced himself to stay upright. Feet numb, he staggered towards the beached *Dulse*, clumsy waves of his sword sufficient to turn away a shrieking pirate who crossed his path.

'Oh my little son, who will guide you to manhood? I am burning, all is burning, fire all around. I have not the strength of will to turn it aside. Forgive my weakness.' Moin's anguish tore at Temar. Had his own father burned thus with searing grief even as the fever of the Crusted Pox consumed him?

Darige wept for his parents' loss, eyes parching faster than tears could refresh them, sore lids sticky and slow, unable to hide the brilliant death flickering all around. 'How will you live without the bounty I earn you? Who will bring you fuel and food to ward off the killing cold of winter?' Skin reddened, blistered, scored and splitting, Darige envisaged his aged father grey and frozen, starved to death in his bed.

Temar dashed guilty tears from his own eyes. If he hadn't sailed for Kel Ar'Ayen, bold and foolish, he'd have been there to comfort his grandsire on his deathbed. Why had he left the old man to die bereft of any of his blood?

'Why did I never tell you I loved you, Duhel? Now I will die and you'll never know. I'll never know the touch of your lips, your body meeting mine. Ilkehan said we should keep ourselves free from such ties but where is he now I die so utterly alone?' Yalda struggled for breath even as the false air scorched her throat and lungs. Her hair curled in futile retreat from the ascending flames, crumbling to nothingness, all the beauty she'd been so proud of turned hideous.

Screaming with all the living torment of death consumed by fire filled Temar's mind. Fighting the pain, the excruciating memories and regrets, he reached the ship and seized the tarred and knotted netting hanging down the side. Blood from his wound made his sword hand slippery. Howls and weeping assailed him from all sides and the pain in his head felt as if it would crack the very bones of his skull. '*Turryal*,' Temar gasped. '*Tur-ryal en arvenir.*' That gave him enough clarity within the sanctuary of his own mind to haul himself up a few meshes. '*Tur-ryal en arvenir mel edraset.*'

The aetheric ward pushed the pain that surrounded him to the outside of Temar's skin. Even if he still felt flayed alive, it was just sensations of burning assailing him, not the searing bitterness of futile self-recrimination. He gasped, frozen with dread as he felt a death wish pass over him before realising, agony aside, he was of no interest to Muredarch's three adepts. They were intent on spending their final breaths in visiting bloody retribution on the mages who had brought this fiery fate to consume them.

Temar felt the dying Elietimm turn their murderous will on Larissa. Soaring flames filled his vision, eyes open or closed and he saw the girl ringed in silver magelight. Her defences were tarnishing, melting before the Elietimm onslaught and Temar wished with every fibre of his being that he'd studied more Artifice. He racked his memory for any incantation that he might use to aid the embattled wizard. It was no good, he was no use, he just didn't know. That realisation was more painful than the agonies hammering at his half-warded mind. There had to be something he could do. If he couldn't reach Larissa, he had to try to help the other mages. He fell over the rail of the *Dulse* to land with a resounding thud on the deck. Sailors all around were struggling with the overwhelming pain, one man screaming, fallen from the rigging to shatter both legs into splintered bone.

Temar struggled to his feet to see Guinalle on the aftdeck, kneeling beside Allin who lay in a crumpled heap. Temar's heart twisted with the worst torment yet.

'Guinalle,' he rasped, staggering towards her.

'As you hope for Saedrin's grace, help me!' She looked

up, ashen, clinging desperately to Allin's hands. 'It's the Elietimm. I've shielded Allin and 'Sar but I can't reach Larissa.'

Temar nodded and wished he hadn't. 'They're in there.' He pointed towards the inferno that was the stockade and took a deep breath. 'You have to end it. You're the only one who can reach them. It's the only way to save the mages.'

Guinalle looked at him, horror struck.

Temar seized her hands. 'You're the only one who can give them mercy. By Ostrin's very eyes, would you let them die like that?'

If Guinalle had been pale before, now her face was the bloodless ivory of old bone. She crushed Temar's hand against Allin's cold fingers so hard he feared he'd carry the marks for the rest of his days.

'Do what you can for her,' Guinalle whispered hoarsely, screwing her eyes closed, dark bruises in their hollows. 'And 'Sar.'

Temar struggled to wrap his fragile ward around Allin. His inadequate skills were immediately thrown into disarray by an elemental chill, slippery and hard as ice as he tried to reach past it. The still cold of lightless caverns lost beneath the earth penetrated her very bones, refuting the Elietimm Artifice's insidious boast that inexorable fires consumed her. Temar struggled to lend Allin whatever strength he could in denying the insidious appeal to the affinity within her, as the Elietimm sought to let elemental fire loose to destroy the wizard from within. What about Usara? The cold numbed Temar's wits like a fall into freezing water but he tried again, holding Usara in his mind's eye as he sought in vain for the mage. The chill became the bitter burn of midwinter wind and Temar recoiled from it but, before his skills deserted him utterly, he realised the cold protecting Allin was preserving the other wizard too.

'*Eda verlas Moin ar drion eda. Verlas Yalda mal ar drion eda. Darige verlas ar drion eda.*' Guinalle was chanting a litany that Temar had never heard before, tears streaming from her closed eyes. '*Ostrin an abrach nur fel*,' she added in fervent prayer.

The screaming agonies of the dying enchanters faded but slowly. Temar could still feel the scarifying pain through the shreds of his untutored warding as he scrubbed cold tears from his face. Down on the shore, he saw some were recovering faster than others.

Muredarch was one. The big man was charging up the slope towards the edge of the trees where Darni stood swaying over a fallen figure that could only be Larissa. Intent on his prey, the pirate leader didn't realise Halice was pursuing him, mercenaries behind her dragging themselves to their feet with desperate determination.

'Look after Allin.' The effort of leaving her behind nearly broke Temar's resolve but he drove himself to a cable hanging over the side of the ship. He welcomed the burn of the rope on his palms, the throbbing ache of the gash in his forearm; any pain to distract him from his frantic worry for Allin.

He ran past pirates and mercenaries stirring and senseless, the echo of the enchanters' death pangs lessening with every step. Determination to exact full penalty from Muredarch filled him with new energy. The pirate leader had reached Darni now and was hacking at the warrior's guard. The big man was defending himself but with nothing like his customary skill, every block weaker, every movement too slow for safety. Temar nearly cried out to give Darni new heart but seeing Halice was there, he held his tongue. Darni fell and Muredarch roared with triumph but Halice cut his jubilation short. The woman fell on the marauder's unprotected back, her clotted sword sweeping across to lay open bloodied flesh and the white gleam of rib bones.

With a roar like a wounded bull, Muredarch turned on her, great two-handed sword wheeling round. Halice took a double grip on her hand-and-a-half blade and met the stroke with a block that stopped it dead. She stood braced then jabbed at Muredarch's eyes with the pommel of her weapon, sliding out from beneath the killing arc of his sword as he recoiled. He swung at her again, to cut her legs from under her but Halice met the blow with a low parry that turned into a slicing thrust of her own. She moved lithely out of danger and spat at Muredarch.

Temar wanted to shout, to let Halice know he was coming to her aid but dared not lest he distract her. Muredarch raised his mighty blade above his head but the mercenary didn't stay to be poleaxed. She darted forward and sideways and brought her own sword upwards to slice beneath Muredarch's armpit. Temar couldn't restrain a breathless cheer as he saw fresh blood bright in the sunlight.

Halice's move had taken her past Muredarch and the pirate looked murderously at Temar. One arm was clamped to his side but he could wield that colossal sword single-handed. He lunged towards Temar, madness in his eyes. Halice stabbed him in the back, the point of her sword emerging just above his hip. Muredarch fell to his knees and Temar swept a single fluid stroke to cut his mighty head clean from his shoulders. The warm gush of blood from the stump of the pirate's neck soaked Temar's side and thigh. He barely felt it in the hot exultation at the black-hearted villain's death.

'Nicely done, Messire.' Halice wrenched her own blade out of Muredarch's corpse and saluted Temar with it. Beneath the sweat and grime of battle, she was pale. 'I take it that was enchanters trying to split all our skulls?'

Temar grimaced. 'Sharing their death agonies when they were caught in the fire.'

'Did Allin fire the stockade?' asked Halice.

Anguish closed Temar's throat for a moment. 'I don't know. I don't think so. She's hurt.' He moved to head back to the ships. A groan halted him.

'Shit, Darni.' Halice dropped to her knees by the fallen warrior. His face was a ghastly mask of blood, cheek sliced and broken teeth white where a blow had shattered his jaw. Muredarch's second blow had hit lower, cutting a huge gash into the big man's shoulder, muscle and sinew severed. Darni's blood soaked a crumpled figure beneath him.

'Help me,' commanded Halice. 'That's Larissa.'

Temar's hands shook as he stripped off his jerkin and tore off his shirt, damp with sweat and stained with his blood and others'. Darni groaned, chest labouring as they laid him flat on the gory turf. Temar winced as he did his best to staunch the warrior's grievous wounds. 'Will he live?'

'It might be better for him if he didn't.' Halice was grim faced as she felt for the beat of Larissa's heart. 'This one's making her excuses to Saedrin. Shit. Darni could have taken Muredarch. It was trying to defend her body did for him, the fool!' But the woman's tone was more sorrowful than angry.

Temar frowned. 'I can't see any wound.' All the blood on Larissa was Darni's; spent in defence of his master's beloved. He had half expected to find the mage-woman a blackened, contorted corpse.

Halice shook her head in bemusement as she searched the mage's body with careful hands. 'Poldrion only knows what killed her – and he won't tell.'

Darni groaned again, eyes rolling in his head as he tried to blink away the blood blinding him. He hauled his unin-jured arm up to point at the still blazing circle that was now the Elietimm's pyre.

Temar groped for his meaning. 'Larissa fired the stockade?'

Darni's closed his eyes in unmistakable confirmation.

Temar looked at Halice. 'She took the full force of their hatred. I felt it.' He found himself on his feet. 'I have to see Allin and 'Sar.'

He stumbled, running for the ships without waiting for Halice's answer. Mercenaries recovering from the assault of Artifice were slaughtering still-stunned pirates with brutal desperation, not even a thought of offering any chance to surrender. Rosarn on the shore was directing her troop to strip fallen and captive alike of every weapon and anything of value. Temar didn't care. Halice could order division of the spoils as she saw fit. All Temar cared about was Allin.

Every joint and bone in his body protested as he hauled himself up the side of the *Dulse* yet again. The cut in his forearm was a burning gash. 'Demoiselle Guinalle, where is she?' he barked at a sailor slowly coiling a rope more from habit than need.

'Aft cabin,' the man answered in deadened tones.

'Does she live?' Temar demanded as he flung open the door.

Guinalle knelt on the floor, face cupped in her hands, her shoulders shaking. Allin lay motionless in one bunk, face turned to the wall. Usara had been laid on the other side, hands folded neatly on his breast, head tilted back, cheeks hollow and bloodless in the gloom.

'Does she live?' Fury born of terror hardened Temar's tone.

'Barely.' Guinalle scrubbed tears from her face, leaving smears of dirt. 'I can't get them warm,' she sobbed suddenly. 'Neither of them. No matter what I do. I can't get them warm.'

Her eyes rolled up in her head and Temar only just caught her before she crashed to the unforgiving floor.

CHAPTER EIGHT

To Gamar Tilot, Scholar of the University of Col,
From Ely Laisen, Hadrumal.

Dear Gamar,
Some curious things have been turning up in our libraries
lately and our mutual friend thought this might be of interest.
It seems to have been written within the last generation,
possibly even the last handful of years. The original is some
kind of verse but the Mountain lass who translated it is far
too much of a clod to compose anything like it herself.

Tale of the Burning of Haeldasekke

*The men of Dachasekke had long shared the Grey Seal Isle with
the men of Haeldasekke. The isle bore no stones and thus men
of each blood kindred returned to their own circles for justice,
pleas and guidance.*

*So it came to pass on the whitest of nights that his ancestors
sent a vision to the Clan Chief of Dachasekke and he vowed to
raise a circle on the Grey Seal Isle on a rocky knoll where there
was no soil for plough nor yet fodder for grazing. The Clan Chief
of Haeldasekke had no such vision but, though the more influential, would not gainsay Kolbin of Dachasekke's right to honour
the dead within their own bounds.*

*All was well until the time of hay and harvest. Then the men
of Dachasekke invited those of Haeldasekke dwelling on the Grey
Seal Isle to step within their circle to honour those below the
earth. This circle is closer to your homes, they said. Let us hold*

it in common, as we have blood in common. The Clan Chief of Haeldasekke decided he would hold more land in common if Dachasekke was wont to be so generous. He moved boundary cairns to claim the whole of the Lesser Slough once Dachasekke had made harvest.

The Clan Chief of Dachasekke was angered and summoned Scafet of Haeldasekke to meet him on the black sands of treaty that lie in the strait between his fastness and the Grey Seal Isle. He summoned Fedin of Evadasekke to stand as Law Speaker but the men of Haeldasekke would not accept him. Nor yet would they propose a Law Speaker of their own, denying any wrong-doing on their part that would justify a Law Speaker coming within their domain. The Clan Chief of Haeldasekke would not discuss the cairns but told Kolbin of Dachasekke instead of his plans to wed a daughter of Kehannasekke when the time of goat killing came.

Kolbin of Dachasekke saw this would leave him with unfriendly faces to both his flanks. He acquiesced and slew those who had invited men of Haeldasekke within their circle before withdrawing to his fastness. At the time of goat killing Scafet of Haeldasekke's son Osmaeld married Renkana daughter to Rafekan of Kehannasekke beneath an arch of raised turf. He was an able boy with a strong spear arm while she was both promising of body and fair of face. No Law Speaker was called to stand witness to the wedding as Scafet of Haeldasekke and Rafekan of Kehannasekke agreed bride price and dowry were matters best agreed between themselves alone. Both kindreds made merry to the final part of the night.

The days of dark and hunger came and all men withdrew to their firesides. The darkest of nights came and word spread that a scorn pole had been found outside the hall of Kehannasekke's fastness when the sun rose again. It was carved with the likeness of Renkana being used by Scafet as a dog does a bitch. No one knew whose hand raised it. Rafekan burned it and strewed the ashes into the sea, ignoring those who called this unmanly behaviour.

The hall of Haeldasekke's fastness burned the following night.

All within the hall were killed. When the fire cooled, dead were found locked within their bed closets and the main door barred from without. Every bone was charred and broken and none could be buried without dishonour. The Clan Chief of Thrielsekke whose sister was wife to Scafet of Haeldasekke demanded that Rafekan of Kehannasekke summon a Law Speaker to determine the truth of the outrage. The Clan Chief of Kehannasekke refused, saying Scafet had suffered the judgement of his ancestors for dishonouring the wife of his son.

In the early days of the following summer Ilkehan of Kehannasekke threw down his father Rafekan and, being a capable man, was acclaimed as Clan Chief. At the time of hay and harvest, Ilkehan of Kehannasekke and Kolbin of Dachasekke divided the Grey Seal Isle between themselves. The Clan Chiefs of Thrielsekke and Evadasekke both demanded they justify this action before a Law Speaker but none could be found whom all could agree on.

At the time of goat killing, the Clan Chief of Kehannasekke raised a circle for the men of the Grey Seal Isle now of Kehannasekke on a rocky knoll where there was no soil for plough nor yet fodder for grazing.

My first thought on waking was astonishment that I could have closed my eyes long enough to fall asleep. The second was utter determination to get out of this black hole. I was on my feet with my next breath.

'Livak?' Ryshad's voice came from somewhere in the blackness.

'Who are you expecting?' Sorgrad's voice was amused.

'Some long-dead Elietimm?' queried 'Gren with relish.

'That's not funny,' I said severely. Realising Ryshad's jerkin had pillowed my head, I bent down to pick it up. No one could see me so I held it close to breathe in the reassuring scent of him.

The stones began to glow with the nimbus of magelight. 'Good morning.' Shiv unfolded his long limbs from the niche and yawned. 'You wouldn't believe how stiff I am.'

'Trust me, I can.' I stretched my arms above my head in a vain attempt to ease the kinks out of my back. 'Let's sleep in proper beds tonight.'

The strengthening light reached Ryshad sitting at the base of the stair. He smiled at me with unmistakable promise. I winked pertly at him before turning serious. 'Do we have any notion if Elietimm are still netting this burrow?'

'I went up top when I woke.' 'Gren shrugged in the pale light radiating from the far wall. 'I couldn't hear a thing.'

'That's the good news.' Sorgrad perched unconcerned in one of the bone-filled niches. 'The bad news is that's definitely the only way out of here.'

'Definitely.' Ryshad confirmed our predicament. If the brothers brought up in the cave-riddled mountains and

Ryshad with his knowledge of stone working couldn't find another door, there wasn't one to find. 'Shiv, can you tell if there's anyone up above?'

The nondescript light deepened to a pool of mossy green around the mage and a puddle of water coalesced in his cupped hands. He grimaced. 'Can someone drop some ink in here, please?'

Ryshad obliged from his belt pouch.

'Why are you carrying ink?' asked 'Gren with interest.

'You never know when you might want some.' Ryshad was looking at the mage as intently as the rest of us. 'Just a quick look, Shiv. We don't want you falling foul of some adept out to revenge Ilkehan.'

Shiv nodded. 'There's no one waiting for us.' He splashed the water into his face to wash the sleep from his eyes. I was about to point out there'd been ink in it but, with blue paint still coating us all, there wasn't much point.

'Where are we heading?' Sorgrad jumped down to the floor and crossed to the stair, his boots echoing on the stone floor. I joined him, 'Gren ushering Shiv ahead and taking up the rearguard.

'We get well away from here, then we let Halice and Temar know Ilkehan's out of the game. They can set about throwing Muredarch and his wharf rats into the ocean.' Ryshad reached down to my raised hand and pulled me up beside him. I brushed a brief kiss across his cheek as I returned his jerkin.

'I need a shave,' he grimaced.

'I'll forgive you, just this once,' I mocked affectionately.

Sorgrad led the way up the narrow and deliberately disorienting stair. I followed Ryshad, so glad to be leaving this eerie charnel house I had to hold back from shoving him along as he deliberately placed his boots noiselessly on each slab. That reminded me we weren't safe till we were well clear of all the Elietimm with their mysterious powers and intrigues. Until then, we needed to watch our every step. No one ever got hung for being too cautious.

Mind you; no one ever got rich, either. I wondered

privately just what kind of reward the Sieur D'Alsennin might be inclined to give us. With Halice to lead his troops, Temar should win enough booty from the pirates to remedy Kellarin's woeful lack of coin. I'd need a reasonable coffer to get myself launched into the wine trade, after all.

Ahead of me, Ryshad stopped, bringing me rudely back to the here and now. He bent beneath the stone slab, braced to lift it. Sorgrad had a dagger in each hand. He nodded and Ryshad heaved the solid slab up to drop it with a thud.

They were both out of the hole together. Ryshad swung round to his offside, alert for anything unexpected. Sorgrad met him coming the other way.

'All clear.'

'No one here.'

That was enough for me and I scrambled out. It was well into morning up top, the light painfully bright for the first few moments. The sky was pale blue with improbably fluffy clouds rising in serried ranks from the west. The breeze was cool and refreshing on my face after the hushed stillness of the hargeard chamber. Then the acrid sharpness of burnt timber caught me by the throat and I coughed uncontrollably. I tried to stop but only succeeded in half choking myself.

Ryshad caught me by one arm. 'Watch your step.'

Blinking through tears, I saw the top of the mound was strewn with fragments of shattered stone and burnt, splintered timber.

'That's a good job done, I'd say,' remarked Sorgrad with pride.

'Definitely,' Shiv agreed wryly.

'Has anyone got any food?' 'Gren walked cautiously to the edge of the mound, shielding himself behind the broken stump of a sarsen.

I got my coughing under control. 'Not me.'

Ryshad shrugged. 'Sorry.'

'Save the day in a ballad and your hero gets a banquet and a willing princess,' 'Gren grumbled. 'Let's see if we can get back in time to help Halice fight the pirates.'

'The faster we let them know what's happened, the better,' Ryshad allowed.

'Do I work the spell here?' Shiv looked at him.

'Time's pressing,' I pointed out.

Ryshad shrugged. 'Let's see what happens.'

'I'll work the spell with as much finesse as I can.' Shiv dug in his pack for his silver salver and then swore. 'I've no candles.'

Sorgrad picked up a dewed fragment of blackened wood. 'Try this.'

'I'll do my best.' Shiv managed to summon a subdued flicker of scarlet from the brand. 'Usara?'

We all waited expectantly. Nothing happened. Shiv frowned and snuffed out his flame with a workaday gesture. 'He must be asleep.' Squaring his shoulders, he brought renewed fire to the wood. 'Allin? Allin, it's me, Shiv.'

The shining silver stayed obstinately blank. We all looked at Shiv and I wasn't reassured to see his face mirror my own confusion.

'Do you want something else shiny?' 'Gren reached for his pack's buckle.

Shiv frowned. 'That won't make a difference.'

'What would?' Ryshad asked bluntly.

Shiv didn't answer, lifting the salver again and focusing all his attention on it. 'Larissa?' The wood burned with a ferocious crimson. 'Curse it!' Shiv swept the brand through the air to kill the flame, relighting it in the next breath. 'Darni!'

'They can't all be asleep, surely?' I heard concern catch in my voice.

'Is there some aetheric hindrance?' Ryshad asked, perplexed

'There's no power here any more.' Sorgrad spoke up as Shiv shook his head. 'It's like the Shernasekke hargeard; nothing to react to the magic.' He walked round in a slow circle. 'We'd have heard that bell sound if there was.'

Ryshad's thoughts were long leagues away. 'We have to let

Temar and Halice know they can attack the pirates. Shiv, what else can you do? Livak, do you have any Artifice to contact Guinalle?'

'I'm afraid not.' I was sorry to have to disappoint him.

'Let's see what scrying can show us.' Shiv cast aside the blackened wood and knelt on the damp grass. He laid the salver flat and dew sparkled briefly as it rolled across the turf, oozing over the metal to form a thickening emerald skin. Ryshad handed over his pot of ink and Shiv let a single drop fall from the stopper.

We crowded round. It took me a moment to realise the green mists had dissipated because initially all we saw were green leaves of almost exactly the same hue. Shiv drew the vision along the shore until we saw the camp laid out before us, neat campfires with people busy about them.

'That looks orderly enough.' I held both relief and worry firmly in check. There were more campfires than I expected but nowhere near enough people.

Ryshad was seeing the same as me. 'Where's Halice? Temar?'

Shiv wasn't listening. He betrayed a sigh of release as the scrying found Pered standing outside the hut the pirates had left us, deep in conversation with someone I didn't recognise. Whoever he was, someone had given him the worst beating I'd seen outside a mercenary camp.

I held my peace, counting a silent handful of heartbeats so Shiv could be sure his beloved was fine.

'Gren had no such delicacy. 'Where's Halice, curse you!'

'Give me a moment.' Pered's face faded and the water dulled to a stagnant jade before new magic suffused the water with verdant brilliance.

'There she is,' said Shiv with fervent relief.

I squinted at the image confined in the silver platter. 'Where?'

'They've taken the Suthyfer landing,' exclaimed Ryshad.

'They have?' Sorgrad abandoned his thoughtful circuit of the mound to join us.

'We're totally after the fair.' 'Gren was seriously displeased. 'No one to fight and no chance of any share in the loot.'

Shiv was still intent on his spell. 'What do you suppose happened here?' The scrying showed us the burnt-out remnants of the pirates' stockade, a group of mercenaries getting filthy tearing it down.

'Looks like you're not the only ones who got carried away with your fire starting.' I smiled at Sorgrad who was studying the scene with interest.

'How did Halice know they could attack and be safe from the enchanters?' Shiv wondered aloud.

'Good question.' But Ryshad was well enough satisfied. 'Still, the fight's done and we won.'

'It can't have been an easy fight, even without the Elietimm,' I pointed out. 'If 'Sar and the others were using all their wits and wizardry, they're probably still sleeping.'

There was no doubt our friends were masters of the landing. Like those miniature ships that sailors too old to be hired like to sell, we saw the *Dulse* and the *Fire Minnow* riding blithely at safe anchor. Solitary watchmen paced their decks with none of the fearful urgency of men expecting attack. Halice's troops were reclaiming Kellarin's cargoes from the ramshackle remnants of the pirates' encampments, sentries circling with the same desultory stroll.

'Rosarn, Vaspret, Minare.' I ticked off faces I recognised on my fingers before chewing my lip as Shiv's roving spell swept across callously piled bodies. Those had to be pirates. Our dead would be treated with far more respect lest Ostrin turn up in one of his legendary disguises to ask the reason why.

'No mages, nor Guinalle,' observed Ryshad.

'They'll be sitting down to a rich breakfast aboard ship,' said 'Gren scornfully. 'Noble born pay mercenaries to sit and eat their gruel on the cold ground.'

'Shiv, can you see inside the cabins?'

Not without—' The wizard froze and I heard a most unwelcome sound carried by the questing breeze.

'Goat bells.'

'Goat pizzles,' growled 'Gren. 'I'd have bet yesterday scared them off for a season and a half.' He drew his long knife.

'Let's leave them to it,' I pleaded. 'We've seen Suthyfer's secure. Let's not risk our necks in some pointless scrap with the locals.'

'This is supposed to be the work of vengeful Eldritch Kin.' Ryshad waved a hand around the ruined circle. 'Some gutted goatherd will set everyone looking for a man with a blade instead.' He ran a hand through wind-tousled curls. 'Shiv, can you get us back to Suthyfer with Sorgrad's help?'

Shiv shook his head. 'Only one at a time. That would take the better part of two days and I'd need to sleep safe in between times.'

'We're not splitting up,' 'Gren warned. 'Not us and not her.'

'We need to lie up until we can get a nexus worked to lift us out of here together,' said Sorgrad with authority.

'The safest place will be Olret's fiefdom,' Ryshad pointed out.

'I could take us all that far with one spell,' said Shiv confidently.

'About Olret.' I'd pushed him and his secrets to the back of my mind while Ilkehan dominated the foreground. 'Are you suggesting we go back to his keep?' I sat on a convenient stump of rock.

'His laundresses could spare us some soap.' Sorgrad scratched at the soot-smudged and smeary colour still greasy on his forearm. 'I'll never hear the last of it if Halice sees me painted up like a masquerader.'

'Some of those pretty girls might be interested in finding out just how far the blue goes.' 'Gren's lascivious chuckle ruined his air of spurious innocence.

Ryshad looked closely at me. 'What about Olret?'

'Gren was still pursuing his own line of thought. 'He should be a sound bet for a good breakfast.'

'You recall those locked gates on his stairs?' I said casually. That won me everyone's attention.

'Yes,' said Shiv slowly.

This wasn't the time for dancing round the truth. 'Olret keeps a handful of women locked in cages up there, penned like animals in their own filth. They claim to be from Shernasekke, taken captive by Olret when he joined Ilkehan in attacking their house.'

'You didn't think to mention this before?' Shiv was incredulous.

'You didn't believe them?' Ryshad wasn't wasting time with recriminations but the stern glint in his eye warned me to explain myself when we were alone together.

'I didn't know what to believe. They have powerful Artifice but Olret somehow limits their powers to that one room. They wanted me to get word to their kin in Evadasekke.' I racked my memory. 'And Froilasekke and somewhere else.'

'Why's Olret holding them?' Sorgrad demanded as Shiv fumbled for his map.

'To try and get a blood claim on the Shernasekke lands when one of the girls decides his bed is a better place than a prison.' I scowled at 'Gren who looked ready to make some inappropriate quip. 'And it seems they keep their lore very close, these Elietimm adepts. The Shernasekke women reckoned they could work Artifice that Olret couldn't master. Those secrets were something else he wanted.'

Sorgrad shrugged. 'That sounds fair enough, if you're Olret.'

'Or they could have been lying,' Ryshad said reluctantly. 'Olret could have perfectly good reason to keep them locked up. I hate to sound like Mistal but you've only their word to go on.'

'Gren was looking confused. 'Ryshad's brother,' I reminded him. 'The advocate before the law courts.'

Shiv looked up from his map. 'I can't find Evadesekke but I think this may be Froilasekke.' He held up the parchment and pointed.

'That's clear over the other side of the islands,' I said without enthusiasm.

'I'd go further than that for the right kind of gratitude from a rescued maiden.' 'Gren's mood was brightening again.

Ryshad shot him an unreadable glance before returning to me. 'You didn't think we should involve ourselves before. Why tell us now?'

'Those goats are getting nearer,' warned Sorgrad.

'Olret was happy to help us as long as we were going to kill Ilkehan.' I met Ryshad's gaze with a challenge of my own. 'I'm not sure how he'll react to us coming back, if he's got secrets of his own to protect.'

'He doesn't know we know about the women.' Ryshad looked thoughtful.

'I say we steer clear of Olret and let him do as he pleases.' Sorgrad scowled at 'Gren who was predictably bright eyed at the prospect of some new excuse for a fight. 'Rettasekke or Shernasekke, they're nothing to us. We owed Ilkehan a full measure of vengeance and killing him served everyone's purpose. Now that's done, let's go home and reap the rewards.'

'I agree.' I raised my hand to stay Sorgrad's approval. 'But I don't want to find myself coming back here next summer, because Olret's set himself up in Ilkehan's place.'

'So what do you propose to do?' Sorgrad challenged me and Ryshad both. 'Kill Olret as well?'

'I don't know what to do.' I'd had enough of killing, even of those we knew without doubt to be guilty but I didn't bother telling Sorgrad since he wouldn't consider it relevant.

Ryshad sucked his teeth. 'Olret showed us a fair enough face but as our host he would do, of course.'

'And if Olret keeps these women locked up, they're bound to blacken his name.' I spread my hands. 'Now do you see why I didn't muddy the waters stirring all this up?'

'We are going back then?' 'Gren glanced from me to Sorgrad, long knife ready in his hand.

'Not to the keep, not unless we have to.' Ryshad looked

to us each for agreement and then at Shiv. 'Can you take us to some quiet spot inside Olret's boundaries until we can raise Usara and leave this all behind?'

The mage nodded. 'There's a place I saw as we rowed up the coast.'

'What about breakfast?' 'Gren complained.

'What about these women and their claims?' Shiv was looking dour.

'Maybe Guinalle can read the truth of it all in Olret's dreams or some such,' I suggested.

'Shiv, get us out of here, please.' Ryshad cocked his head at goat bells again. 'Whatever Olret may be, his people should be friendly to us and, Dast knows, no one hereabouts will be.'

'Depends what they reckoned to Ilkehan,' countered 'Gren.

His irrepressible voice faded as Shiv wrapped his spell around us. A breeze spiralled ever closer, ever faster, cool against my skin with the soft moisture of wind from the southern sea. The waterfall and grey rocks vanished as the breeze thickened to azure brilliance on the very edge of sight. Then the dizzying spiral seemed to get inside my head and the pleasant cool turned to a chill and wearisome damp making my very bones ache. I closed my eyes and swallowed hard but the sensation of my feet leaving the ground jolted me just that bit too hard. As solid ground lurched beneath my feet once more, I felt my gorge rising and hastily darted to one side.

'Good thing we haven't had breakfast,' said 'Gren cheerily. 'You'd just have wasted it.'

When I'd finished retching, I glowered at him. Ryshad handed me his water bottle and I rinsed my mouth and spat, wiping the back of my hand across my mouth. 'Where are we?'

'Inland and up the coast a way from Olret's settlement.' Shiv had brought us to the edge of some looming barrens, grey rock ripping through the threadbare green on the steep hillsides. We were hidden from the keep by a substantial buttress of rock thrust forward from one of the mountains guarding the interior. It was striped with unusually pale scree and on one face some upheaval had snapped the smooth line of the rock to leave a splintered cliff above a litter of shattered stone.

Sorgrad was peering out towards a long slew of morning mist cloaking the sea. 'How do you suppose that fight for the fort's gone?'

'Gren had other concerns. 'Who do you suppose lives there?' He pointed at a long low house surrounded by a cluster of shabby outbuildings, goatskins nailed up for drying making pale patches on the gable ends. The wind shifted and brought us a whiff of mingled earthy smoke and cooking smells.

'Do you think we could ask for some food?' I looked at Ryshad.

'They can only say no.' He looked at one of the lesser buildings where a puff of steam escaped a window to be swept away by the gusting breezes. 'I'd pay solid coin for the chance of a bath and a shave.'

Sorgrad was already moving towards the isolated homestead. 'We'll get ourselves clean and fed and then we'll try bespeaking 'Sar again.'

'Wait a moment,' Shiv said, irritated. 'Do you want whoever's in there scared out of their wits?'

The air shimmered around us and magic leached much of the colour from our skin and hair. We were still an unnatural hue but, with Halcarion's blessing, a stranger's first thought should be we were just filthy and exhausted rather than dread messengers from the Eldritch Kin.

'Gren picked up the pace as we crossed the wind-scoured turf. People busy about the scatter of buildings paused to stare at us. 'You stay here,' Sorgrad commanded as we reached a low wall of close-fitted stone. He and 'Gren crossed another stretch of grass that yielded to a raggedly cobbled yard in front of the long central house. A couple of men leaned on long narrow spades crusted with dark earth. Both house and the random outbuildings looked built from whatever rock had tumbled down the mountainside, sides bulging with irregular-shaped stones. Few windows pierced the thick walls and those couldn't have admitted much light through their grimy horn panes.

'This doesn't look very promising,' I murmured to Ryshad while trying to look innocuous under the suspicious gaze of the Elietimm men.

'Let's see what Mountain charm can do for us,' he said with a certain sarcasm.

One of the men called into the doorway open on to the blackness inside the dwelling. A thickset woman with a dull orange scarf wound tight around her head appeared fast enough to suggest she'd been keeping a look-out through some peephole. Sorgrad stepped forward with a courteous bow and a sweeping gesture in the general direction of Olret's keep. The woman stepped out of the doorway and waved a hand at one of the outhouses.

'Isn't that where the steam came from?' Shiv looked hopeful.

'Gren turned to wave us forward. I was in a mood to take a gamble as well. 'I don't know about you two but I'm more than ready for a bath.'

The sturdy woman waited with Sorgrad and 'Gren while her sons or whoever they were took themselves off to their daily duties. She stood, feet solid on the irregular cobbles, arms folded across an ample bosom. Her face was creased with age and disillusion, mouth sunken on to almost toothless gums. She was certainly the oldest Elietimm I'd seen thus far and her speech was sufficiently fast and slurred that I understood none of it.

'We can wash in the laundry house,' Sorgrad told us. 'Gren was already unlatching the door. 'She'll send some food out later.'

'Please thank her for us.' I smiled to convey my gratitude but all I got in return was a dour grunt before our grudging hostess stomped off. 'What did you tell her?' I asked in a low tone as Sorgrad ushered me towards the wash house, a low building with an irregular roof ridge and more than one loose slate.

'I said we were travellers who had visited Olret with a view to trading and had been seeing what his lands had to offer in return for our goods.' He was looking thoughtful. 'I said we wanted to make ourselves presentable before returning to his keep.'

'It was Olret's name made the difference,' 'Gren piped up. 'Until then, I thought she'd be setting the dogs on us.'

'I don't suppose they get many visitors hereabouts.' Ryshad unbuttoned his jerkin as we crossed the wash house's threshold. He unlaced his shirt and pulled it over his head, grimacing at both the smell and the ingrained stains of paint and dirt. I wasn't any too taken with him smelling like a hard-ridden horse either but I doubted I smelled of roses or anything close.

'It won't have time to dry, even if you wash it,' I advised reluctantly as I shed my own foetid clothes.

'Shiv?' Ryshad grinned. 'Don't you mages help out in Hadrumal's laundry at all?'

'Are you mocking the arcane mysteries of elemental magic?' The wizard was already stripped to his breeches and unlacing them. 'Actually, apprentices generally work these things out when they've done something stupid or dangerous and need to wash out the evidence.' He laughed at a sudden memory. 'Let's get ourselves clean and then I'll see about the linen.'

'You don't want Pered choking on your stench, do you?' I joked. With the door shut and warm steam hanging around us, I began to relax for the first time since we'd come to these islands. Perhaps it was the familiar scents of damp cloth and harsh lye just like the wash house at home. Knowing Ilkehan was good and dead certainly did a lot to calm my nerves. Now we could get clean and fed and then join the celebrations at Suthyfer. It would be good to swap yarns with Halice now that the danger was safely past. My spirits rose still further.

'Do we get in here?' 'Gren was naked, pale skin stark beneath the paint on his face. He peered into a broad stone basin in the centre of the floor where clouded water steamed.

Sorgrad threw his breeches and underlinen aside and joined him, leaning on the waist-high rim wide enough to rest a bucket on or, in 'Gren's case, a buttock. 'I don't think so. That's a hot spring in there and we don't want to foul it.'

'Do you suppose there might be a wash tub?' I shivered in my shirt as I looked around the laundry. It had bigger windows than the main house with some bladder or membrane dried stiff and yellow and cut to fit the bone frames. The frames were none too tightly fitted and let in wicked draughts as well as a fair amount of light. More cold air whistled along a crude drain running down the centre of the sloping floor to disappear through a hole in one wall.

'You could just about get in here.' Ryshad was stood something halfway between a horse trough and a sink, one of several standing against one wall with long lengths of coarse cloth looped on racks above them. Long and narrow with steep sides, each seemed to have been carved from a single block of pale grey stone veined with faintest white. All but the one at the end were heaped with thick brown blankets soaking in lye and waiting for someone to sluice water through them and beat out the dirt with the bleached bone paddles racked above.

'Find the plug.' I grabbed a pail from a stone ledge and dipped it into the stone basin. The water was hotter than I'd have liked for a bath but I wasn't about to complain.

'Soap root.' Sorgrad was investigating the contents of small baskets and bowls on a shelf. He tossed me a tangled mass of slick fibres.

I wasn't impressed but didn't want to upset our reluctant hostess by using anything better that had taken time and trouble to concoct from her scarce resources. My mother had given me more than one lecture on the costs and aggravation of soap making when my only concern had been simply looking pretty and smelling sweet for whatever swain I'd fancied flirting with.

I sloshed the bucket into the trough and Ryshad did the same. The clouded water smelled faintly reminiscent of a colic draught from an apothecary's shop but that was still preferable to wearing stale sweat and old smoke when we returned triumphant to Suthyfer and everyone's congratulations.

'In you get,' Ryshad smiled at me. Warm with the olive skin of southern Tormalin and dusted with black hair, his broad chest and strong arms looked quite bizarre against the paint staining his hands and forearms.

I dumped my stale shirt on top of my grimy breeches and swung a leg over the hard edge of the trough, careful not to slip on the smooth base. Crouching in the shallow water, I rubbed at my arms with the pulpy root until I won a faint lather that turned a faint blue-grey. 'It's coming off.' I scrubbed hard at my face with the crumbling shreds.

'Close your eyes.'

I barely had time to heed Ryshad's warning before he dumped a bucket of water over me. Once I recovered from the shock, it was wonderful to feel the heat scouring me clean. 'Wait a moment.' I squeezed as much foam from the soap root as I could into my hair.

'Let me.' I closed my eyes, savouring the deft touch of Ryshad's strong fingers. Slick, his hands moved to my shoulders, blunt thumbs digging in gently to loosen muscle knotted by exhausted sleep on a cold stone floor. Just his touch roused my blood and I hoped the others would put my sudden blush down to the heat of the water.

'Eyes closed?' His hands left me and another bucketful came crashing down on my head. I puffed and wiped water from my eyes, appalled at the colour of the water I was kneeling in. Had I really been that filthy?

'Who was that?' Sorgrad was in the middle of soaping his own hair with grated root when a figure went running past the window.

'Gren didn't pause as he scoured his face. 'No idea.'

'Nor me.' I couldn't have said if the person had been male or female, young or grown, not through that clouded excuse for a window.

'Watch out!' 'Gren didn't so much rinse his brother down as slosh a bucket full in his face.

'Did you see?' Ryshad turned to the mage but Shiv was sitting on the rim of the spring's basin, tracing a slow circle in the steaming water with a curious finger. His intense concentration looked ludicrous coupled with his lean nakedness. I tucked away a private observation that Pered was a lucky man.

The mage looked up. 'Sorry?'

'What's so fascinating?' Sorgrad had stripped enough colour from his hair to leave it dun and lifeless but the paint on his arms was proving more stubborn.

Shiv began scrubbing at his own hands. 'The way the fire beneath the rocks reacts with the water. I wonder—' He broke off and looked more closely at the inadequate lather. 'This isn't doing too much good.'

'Can you do better?' 'Gren challenged, lobbing a handful of soap root at the wizard's face.

Shiv caught it deftly and made as if to throw it back, laughing as 'Gren ducked to one side. 'Let's see what a little wizardry can do.' He spun the fresh green of new rushes into the tangle of fibres and tossed me and Ryshad each a clump. Trying to see what we had left 'Gren sufficiently off guard that Shiv managed to hit him full in the face with his. Sorgrad came to his brother's aid and soaked the mage with a pail of water.

'Behave, children,' I chided while trying not to laugh. Whatever Shiv did to the soap roots was remarkably effective and the darkness poured out of my hair when I had another go at washing it. 'How do I look?' I squinted up at Ryshad.

He looked at me, head on one side. 'Muddy brown.'

I stuck my tongue out at him and stood up to let him

sluice the dirty water off me. My arms were still tainted blue but you had to look close to see it. With luck, once I was dressed, people would just think I was feeling the cold.

'Your turn.' I tugged the stopper out of the hole in the bottom of the trough and got out, pleased to see the Eldritch disguise flow down the gully and out beneath the wall. Filling the trough again helped keep me warm but I began to shiver as I washed Ryshad's hair while he scoured his forearms.

'Shiv? Any chance of some fresher linen?' The idea of putting that frowsty shirt on my clean body revolted me.

'Give me a moment.' The wizard's wet hair was black and sleek against his head.

'Can you fetch me my shaving gear?' Ryshad grimaced as he ran a hand over his bristles.

'Gren tested his own chin as I rummaged in Ryshad's bag. 'I don't think I'll bother.'

'You can leave it half a season and no one notices unless your whiskers catch the light,' I teased.

A knock at the door startled us all.

'Hello?' Sorgrad wiped soap from his face.

'Towels?' 'Gren wondered hopefully.

A voice outside said something I didn't catch.

'Food!' 'Gren's face broke into a broad smile. 'Even better.'

I moved to avoid brightening up any passing goatherd's day as 'Gren opened the door entirely heedless of the fact he was bare-arsed and dripping wet. Wiry and muscular, he crouched to pick up a loaded tray.

'What have we got?' Sorgrad picked up a lidded flagon and they set the spoils on the broad rim of the pool. Ryshad finished his cursory shave with a few strokes of his razor and came dripping across the floor.

'You can share that.' A boiled goat's head sitting in broth thick with herbs didn't appeal to me. I prefer my food without an expression. I reached instead for a small plump bird and was agreeably surprised to find it had been stuffed with a sweet dough before baking to succulence.

'Our hostess must be better disposed than she looked.'

Shiv bit into a fat, glistening sausage. The mouthful muffled his curses as sizeable scraps of hot offal spilt down his chest.

Ryshad coughed. 'It looks like everyone wants to get us drunk.' He handed the flagon to me and I took a cautious sip.

'What kind of liquor is that to give travellers?' I coughed. The powerful fumes of the spirit made my eyes water.

'Gren paused, mouth stuffed with flatbread scorched from the skillet. 'There's enough food here to keep us busy for a while.'

'From a woman none too pleased to see us in the first place.' Sorgrad ate a dark blood sausage in a series of rapid bites.

We all looked at each other. Ryshad and I shared a lifetime's habit of suspicion with Sorgrad and 'Gren and even Shiv was looking doubtful.

'What can you see in the yard?' Ryshad scooped a bizarre concoction of cheese pressed with scraps of meat and herbs on to a slab of bread. Chewing, he crossed to a far window and tugged the bone frame just far enough awry for a clear view out.

'There's no one lifting so much as a slop pail out here,' said Sorgrad slowly.

'Where are the people we saw before?' I watched Ryshad rummage in his bag.

'Nowhere.' Sorgrad craned his neck for a better view out of the clouded window.

'That doesn't sound too friendly.' 'Gren stripped the meat from the goat's head with deft fingers and packed it inside a hollow flatbread.

Shiv looked at Ryshad. 'Anything on your side.'

Ryshad rested his spyglass on the sill. 'Men running in ranks like a proper drilled troop are coming this way in a hurry.'

'The old woman sent Olret a message,' said Shiv slowly.

'He's sent us an escort back to the keep?' Sorgrad was sceptical.

'Maybe, maybe not.' Ryshad finished his food in a few swift mouthfuls. 'Let's be ready to meet them, either way.'

We pulled on shirts and jerkins, stepping into breeches and boots, ignoring travel stains and staleness. A shadow caught my eye and as I looked through the yellowed membranes of the nearest window, several furtive figures passed between the blurred outlines of the house and outbuildings. 'The old woman's menfolk are ready to argue the point if we try to leave.'

Sorgrad was stuffing what of the remaining food would travel best into his and 'Gren's bags. 'If it comes to a fight, we take them all on at once.'

'Can't we just leave them gawping at an empty trap?' I asked at Shiv as I laced up my shirt. ''Sar can't still be snoring?'

'What is there to burn?' Shiv dug out his silver salver and looked around. 'I need wood or wax.'

But bone was all there was hereabouts, thanks to the local lack of trees. Wanting trees made me think of the Forest and I threw Shiv one of my everyday rune sticks.

He didn't hesitate, summoning a flame that burned with a strange green tint. He worked his now familiar magic once, then a second time, then a third, the rune stick burning with unnatural rapidity. Growing concern furrowed the mage's brow as I concentrated on securing my bag and Ryshad's to stop myself standing over Shiv. Ryshad was tense at his window while Sorgrad kept watch on the yard outside.

'Well, wizard?' 'Gren demanded, his bag and Sorgrad's slung on his back, knives ready to fight anyone who offered.

'I can't bespeak anyone, not Usara, not Allin, not Larissa.' I heard considerable disquiet in Shiv's voice.

'Can't you rouse Planir or someone in Hadrumal?' Apprehension deepened Ryshad's tone.

'Give me a moment.' Shiv set down his salver and the half-burnt rune stick and heaved a weary sigh. It wasn't paint causing those dark hollows under his eyes, I realised with a sinking feeling. This wasn't the time to find Shiv had spent all his wizardry, not if we couldn't summon help from beyond these islands. What could have happened to the other mages?

'They'll be at the boundary wall any moment now,' Ryshad warned from his vantage point.

'I can see those slackers with their spades hiding round the corner of the house,' Sorgrad said ominously.

'Gren and I stood watching Shiv work his spell once more.

'Planir, it's me, Shiv.' The mage's voice hardened as he bent closer to the amber radiance. 'Open to my spell, curse you! I have to speak to you!'

But the light faded inexorably from the cold metal. 'Don't do this to me!' spat Shiv, heedless of the rune stick burning his fingers. He gripped the salver so hard the silver buckled. With a snap that startled us all, it twisted out of his hands to fall blackened to the floor. Shiv stared at it aghast. 'The magic turned against me.'

A horrible notion struck me. 'Was it the rune stick? The Forest Folk foretelling is Artifice even if they don't call it that—'

Shiv wasn't listening. 'There's something very wrong.'

'There will be if we can't fight a way out of here.' Ryshad snapped his spyglass shut and shoved it in a pocket. We all drew our blades as we heard running feet on the stones of the yard.

'It's only a double handful or so,' said 'Gren scornfully.

'Shiv, can't you just lift us out of here?' I asked.

'Where to?' he asked, exasperated. 'Olret's keep? That's the only other place around here I know well enough to carry us to – and that'll just about finish me.'

'We've fought our way out of tighter corners than this.' 'Gren was unconcerned but then 'Gren was always unconcerned. Moving figures passed by the windows.

'It's whoever Olret's sent that we have to worry about.' Sorgrad assessed the situation calmly. 'If we deal with them, farm boys aren't going to stand up to us.'

Ryshad didn't take his eyes off the door. 'How do we do this?'

Sorgrad used his dagger to loosen the bone frame in the stone aperture beside him. 'We let them in through the door.' The window loosened. 'Then we go out this way.'

Ryshad scowled. 'You three, maybe. Not me and Shiv.'

'I can slow them down,' the mage assured him.

'Once we're out, we attack them from the back.' I resolutely ignored my own misgivings.

'No more time to worry about it.' 'Gren leapt for the door as someone lifted the latch on the other side. He ripped it open and the Elietimm soldier fell into the wash house, taken unawares. He took that surprise to whatever afterlife awaited him as 'Gren struck his head clean off before darting out of the reach of the second man's naked blade.

'Go!' Sorgrad stood between me and the Elietimm forcing their way into the cramped building, bent on ugly slaughter. I used a pail as a step and, tossing the loosened frame aside, I went through the window feet first. 'Gren dived after me to roll on the bruising ground with all the skill of a fairground tumbler. He was on his feet, blades bright in the morning sun before Olret's men realised what was happening.

Most were already inside the wash house. Three were left outside to gawp at our sudden arrival. Two went for 'Gren and the last ran at me. I wasn't about to start swordplay with someone half a head taller so I ducked down and caught up a loose stone the size of my fist. Catching him full in the cheek wasn't as good as a strike to the temple but it sent him staggering back. He fell hard on his arse so I could shove my sword under his jaw to leave him twitching on the dusty ground. I don't kill with 'Gren's insouciance but if someone tries to kill me, I'll answer to Saedrin for his death when my times comes. It was only then I realised I'd taken the insane risk of using the ancient Kel Ar'Ayen blade I carried.

With deft footwork and vicious swordplay, 'Gren added the other two to a tally that'll keep the elder god busy and everyone else waiting in line. Hearing their cries, one came back out of the door and I retreated rapidly, shoving the sword into my belt and reaching into my pouch for darts.

But he wasn't interested in fighting, running so fast even 'Gren couldn't catch him before he jumped the boundary wall and fled.

Curiosity warred with caution and I risked going a little closer. Two Elietimm in the doorway had their backs to me and whoever they were fighting had to be one of my friends so I darted in to hamstring the closest with my longest dagger. He fell, to be killed by Sorgrad and I caught a glimpse of Ryshad struggling with someone further in.

A scream of agony shocked us all to stillness but me and Sorgrad recovered first. As I slashed at the other man's knees from behind, Sorgrad caught the enemy under the breast-bone. The man died, vain pleading silenced by a gush of blood. Sorgrad tried to throw the body back off his blade. I stepped forward to help, holding the corpse down with one boot and saw Ryshad hacking at two men unaccountably tangled in choking coils of sodden cloth.

'Shiv got the laundry on our side,' grinned Sorgrad over the corpse between us.

Shiv was standing on the rim of the pool, a narrow column of scalding steam untroubled by the cold air from the open door and coiling down and around a man whose face was pale, pulpy and undeniably dead. I spoke without thinking. 'You cooked him like a pudding.'

'Pretty much.' The mage sighed. 'And I really am all but spent.'

Ryshad kicked the swathed bodies at his feet to make sure they were good and dead. Blood oozed from rents in the blankets and flowed across the floor to join water and lye seeping down the drain. 'Let's get out of here.'

He and Sorgrad were first out of the door, me following with an arm ready in case Shiv needed support. 'Gren was in the centre of the yard, proud and belligerent as a cockerel ready to leave all comers bleeding in the dust.

'Let me repay your hospitality,' he taunted the unseen inhabitants of the steading. 'My mother throws better bread than your women make to the dogs!'

'We're leaving,' Sorgrad warned him as we passed. 'Gren took a moment to piss copiously on the ground and then ran to catch up.

Ryshad fell back to let the two of them go on ahead. 'Shiv?'

'I'll be all right,' said the wizard tightly. 'I just need some rest and to work out why my magic's not reaching as it should.' He sounded quite as annoyed as weary.

'Rest may solve it. How often does a mage do half what you've done these past few days?' Still, I was starting to share his concern that something, somewhere must be very wrong if we couldn't contact any other mage.

We passed the boundary wall, Ryshad checking all the while to be sure we weren't pursued. 'We'll find somewhere to hide up and work out our next move,' he said decisively. 'And we don't want to be disturbed. Livak, can you work that aetheric charm against being tracked?'

I did my best to sing the jaunty tune as we ran, hoping the Artifice was proof against my ragged breath and the jolting of the uneven, stony ground.

'Y ou're building pyres already?' Temar felt distantly proud that he could keep his voice level.

'No reason to delay.' Halice sounded weary.

'I'd forgotten what it was like.' Temar didn't mind Halice hearing his shame. 'I fought with the cohorts for a year and a half but we were never involved in clearing the carrion, not esquires from the noblest Houses. We were all honour and valour and rushing to leave the battlefield as soon as our commanders gave us leave. It's the comrades you remember, the fooling in the camps, the celebrations and the grateful whores. Not the death.'

'You're a commander this time,' said Halice without censure. 'Now you know why wiser men than us call a battle won the closest evil to a battle lost.'

The two of them watched shrouded bodies being respect-fully laid in a line along the crest of the rising land. The only sound was from the pry bars and axes breaking up what remained of the hulks of the *Tang* and Den Harkeil's ill-fated ship.

'Did Peyt live?' Temar asked after a while.

Halice shook her head. 'Not beyond midnight.'

A sullen line of those pirates who'd escaped summary slaughter carried the salvaged wood up to the burning ground.

'They should burn cleanly enough,' Temar remarked when the burden of silence weighed too heavily for him to bear. He plucked unaware at the edge of the bandage dressing the wound on his arm.

'I reckon so.' Halice watched other captives sewing sailcloth winding sheets around the dead to be honoured with cleansing fire. Minare and his troop stalked among them, cudgels ready to chastise any who failed to show respect to the fallen. 'Though a little magecraft couldn't hurt. Has Allin recovered at all?'

'Not as yet.' Temar couldn't say that in an even tone and didn't even try.

'We'll have to keep the burning hot enough without her then.' Halice pointed at the pyres being built with sombre efficiency by a bloodstained gang of mercenaries. 'Deg knows how to catch the wind to best advantage.'

'What do we put the ashes in?' asked Temar with sudden consternation.

'We'd better talk to Rosarn. She's inventorying the salvage,' Halice replied. 'There must be pickle jars, butter crocks, wide-necked carafes, that kind of thing.'

'You'd send someone's son home in a pickle jar?' Temar was appalled, both at the notion and the realisation he had nothing better to suggest.

'I've sent people home as no more than a few charred bones in a twist of greased sacking before now.' Halice turned her gaze from the measured destruction of the beached ships and Temar saw tears in her eyes. 'I always told myself it was better their family know what had happened than be left with hope and fear from season to season.'

'I'm sorry.' Temar couldn't think what else to say.

Halice smiled without humour, her sorrow retreating. 'I wasn't sorry to think I'd left all that behind. Me and Deg and all the rest of us who opted to stay in Kellarin.'

'Will you still be staying?' Temar wondered aloud.

'Oh yes,' Halice assured him. 'We've shed too much blood to give up on you now.'

'In the cohorts, any man wounded in battle was recompensed according to the severity of his wounds,' said Temar distantly. 'I don't know if the custom still holds but I intend to abide by it.'

They watched the work continue for a while longer in the same pensive stillness. Other captives were dumping their fallen comrades in long boats with scant ceremony. The *Fire Minnow* waited in the middle of the strait to tow the carrion into open water. Her crew made ready to sail, with billows of white canvas and the D'Alsennin pennant jaunty at her masthead.

'They're taking those well clear?' asked Temar, concerned. 'We don't want corpses washing back on the tide!'

'The sharks will make short work of that lot,' said Halice with grim satisfaction. 'Remind me to tell Naldeth what we've done.'

Temar looked again at the pyres being built, running an idle finger over his bandage until he inadvertently touched the tender sore beneath it. He banished the treacherous thought that Guinalle could heal the hurt for him. Her talents were needed elsewhere. He could heal as time and Ostrin allowed. 'We need a shrine,' he said with sudden decision. 'If we keep these ashes in humble containers, so be it but we should at least give them the sanctity of a proper shrine.'

'Agreed.' Halice nodded firm approval. 'Some families will want to leave the ashes where their loved ones fell anyway. We should make sure a roll of the dead goes back on the first ships to Tormalin. Do you think Tadriol would let us use the Imperial Despatch to send word to the families in Lescar and Caladhria?'

'It's not for the Emperor to permit or deny couriers to an acknowledged Sieur,' Temar retorted with some spirit. 'The Imperial Despatch can take word of your losses to the far side of Solura or answer to me for it.'

'Word to Bremilayne will reach Toremal quicker but the quickest way to get news to Caladhria and Lescar will be sending someone to Zyoutessela, so a courier can take passage on to Relshaz. Someone needs to take word to Hadrumal as well.' She reached into her jerkin and dug in an inside pocket to retrieve a thick silver ring. 'This was Larissa's. It should go back with her ashes.'

Temar was puzzled. 'I don't recall her wearing that.'

'Nor me.' Pity and apprehension mixed uneasily in Halice's words. 'I think it belonged to Planir.'

'We'll discuss who goes where when we have all the ships together.' Temar knew he was avoiding the question but he'd face down Emperor Tadriol and the entire Convocation of Princes before he'd tell Planir the woman he'd loved was dead. 'We should bring them all in here, and everyone from the sentry island.'

'Not today,' Halice said firmly. She nodded at the gangs of toiling mercenaries. 'They'll end up roaring drunk tonight and meaner than privy house rats. You should make sure any prisoners you don't want lynched are locked safely in the *Dulse*'s hold as well.'

'Oh.' Temar hesitated. 'Do you think that's wise, letting the men have such liberty? What if some of the pirates who fled sneak back in hopes of more mischief or stealing a boat?'

'Then they'll live to regret it just so long as it takes someone to sling a rope over a tree or gut them like a fish.' New vigour sounded in Halice's voice. 'Still, you're right. One spark makes a lot of work if it catches. Rosarn can take out her scouts tomorrow.'

'As soon as Guinalle can spare the time, she can drill me in the Artifice to search out any stragglers.' Temar straightened his back, shoulders square. 'Ros can start a survey as well as clearing out vermin. Vaspret can help. The sooner we know what we hold here, the better we can plan how to use these islands.'

Halice smiled. 'You'll be telling Tadriol Kellarin claims these islands? In your capacity as Sieur?'

'Yes,' Temar said firmly. 'Do you have some objection?'

'None at all.' Halice looked at the steadily rising pyres. 'It'll be nice to see a battleground showing something more permanent than burn scars for winter storms to wash away.'

For all his newfound determination, Temar's thoughts turned inexorably sorrowful, so he was accordingly grateful for an apologetic cough at his elbow. It was Glane.

'Beg pardon, Messire, Commander but what are we to do with the prisoners that aren't working? Some are saying they were never pirates, only captives. And then there's the wounded—'

'I'll see to the wounded.' Halice clapped Temar on the shoulder. 'Justice and mercy are your prerogative, Messire.'

Temar bit his lip as the tall mercenary strode away.

'Rosarn! Do we have any kind of inventory yet? I want decent food for the wounded,' Halice called out. She kicked at a rickety remnant of some hovel and it collapsed with a clatter. 'And somewhere a cursed sight better than this to sleep!'

Temar turned to Glane. 'Where are these prisoners?'

The boy led him across gravel and dusty turf to a sullen gathering guarded by grim-faced men from Edisgesset. Some were blank faced with fear, staring dejected at the ground, some not even easing the painful bonds constraining them. Others huddled in twos and threes warily alert for any chance to flee, eyes vicious as feral dogs. One woman sat silent, hugging her knees, green dress bloodied around the hem and scorched on one sleeve, the skin beneath red and blistered. Temar felt she was not so much beaten as slyly husbanding her strength. Her hair was still secure in a tidy black braid pinned around her head.

'Build a gallows,' he said in matter-of-fact tones. 'Fit to hang a handful at a time.'

A few faces disintegrated into sickened rage or wretched whimpers, his words confirming their worst fears. Consternation wracked the rest, several trying to stand for all the bonds hampering them. Their protests came thick and fast.

'No, your honour—'

'Your mercy, we beg you—'

'They forced me—'

'Silence!' Temar held up his hands. 'You'll all have your chance to plead for pardon.'

'And to bear witness?' A bedraggled girl struggled to her bruised feet, tied hands awkwardly clutching a blanket some mercenary had thrown her to cover her ragged chemise. 'Hang me if you wish, Messire. I don't care but don't let that bitch escape the death she deserves!' She turned on the woman in the green dress whose eyes were still fixed on the ground. 'Muredarch's whore, the filthy slut, she kept all his secrets.' She broke into wild sobs, kicking at the silent woman. 'She made a whore out me! Let any of them use me—' As she lashed out again, the woman in green tripped her with a deft foot. The hysterical girl fell hard and other prisoners turned on the woman in green and then on each other.

'Break it up!' Temar ordered. Edisgesset men were already wading into the melee, pulling apart the struggling bodies, merciless with some, more gentle with others.

One stood, the trampled girl unconscious in his arms. 'What do I do with her, Sieur?'

'Take her to join the wounded.' Temar gestured towards the edge of the woods where those hurt were being nursed away from the bloodstained battleground. He studied the woman in the green dress who was sitting still and silent once more. Her braid was ripped askew and a bruise purpled one cheek.

'What's your name?' asked Temar.

'Ingella,' one of the other prisoners snarled.

'Were you truly Muredarch's woman?' Temar demanded.

Ingella did not answer, her gaze not wavering from a tuft of grass that seemed to fascinate her.

Temar was aware that every other eye was on him. 'Keep your own counsel,' he said mildly. 'Muredarch wasn't the only one with Artifice to call on. We will have your guilt or innocence out of you one way or another.'

Ingella's face came up with a jerk, horror in her dark eyes.

Temar indicated the others who betrayed new terror with rapid jabs of his finger. 'Those, take them and lock them securely in the bottom hold of the *Dulse*. No one will escape punishment for their crimes here. As for the rest of you, I won't hang any who don't deserve it. You may work or you may be confined in the cargo deck of the ship.'

Some looked at him with faint hope rising above their despair and Temar walked briskly away before anyone could see the sudden tremor in his hands or the quake in his spine as the full weight of his responsibility bore down on him.

'What is it?' Halice appeared at his side. He hadn't even seen her approaching.

'My grandsire was always determined to tell me rank brings duty as well as privilege. Now I know why.' Temar gritted his teeth. 'I must see Guinalle. We'll have to set up a proper assize. If we're to separate those who went willingly to Muredarch from those who were coerced, I need her to work a truthsaying and a powerful one at that.' Temar saw Halice was looking even grimmer than she had before. He wouldn't have thought that was possible. 'What is it?'

'Darni's died,' Halice said shortly.

Temar realised it was possible to feel worse than he did already. 'Perhaps it was for the best,' he said after a long pause. 'His face was smashed beyond hope of repair.'

'And his arm. I was all but ready to give him a clean death myself once he'd seen us kill Muredarch.' Halice sighed. 'Then I wondered if Artifice might save him.' She scowled. 'It was easier when there was no chance of such things.'

Black despair threatened to overwhelm Temar. 'He has a wife, doesn't he? And a child?'

'Two.' Halice bit the word off.

'I wish Ryshad was here.' The words came unbidden from Temar's lips.

'And Livak.' Halice scrubbed a sketchily washed hand through her short, unruly hair. 'Have you been aboard this morning? Usara might be awake by now, or Allin.'

'I think Guinalle would have sent word.' Temar looked at Halice. 'We should see how they are though.' They were walking towards the shingle strand, pace increasing with every step, Temar matching Halice stride for stride.

'You there!' She hailed a sailor pushing off a laden longboat with a single oar over the stern. 'We're for the *Dulse!*'

Temar stayed silent for the short crossing to the ship, nothing to say as he climbed the rope ladder up to the deck.

'Demoiselle Guinalle?' Halice caught a passing sailor with her question.

'Cabin.' He nodded backwards before going on his way.

Temar's feet felt leaden. Halice looked back at him. 'Not knowing won't make any difference.' She opened the door like the best-trained lackey in his grandsire's house. He took a deep breath and went in.

'Temar.' Female voices greeted him, both fraught with emotion and exhaustion.

'Guinalle.' He felt weak with relief. 'Allin. How are you, both of you?'

The demoiselle sat on a low stool, leaning back against the wooden hull of the ship. 'Weary but time will mend that.'

Allin was sitting on her bunk, hair tangled around her pale face. Temar knelt and held her close. The mage-girl drew a long shuddering breath, slipped her arms around him and held tight.

'If you're going to hug me, Halice, do be careful.' Lying on the other bunk, Usara attempted to prop himself on one elbow. 'I feel as if I might snap.'

'You look like a death's head on a mopstick,' Halice told him with friendly concern.

'I rather thought I might.' Usara gave up the uneven struggle and lay back down.

'What happened?' Temar realised that was a foolish question even as he sat on the bunk beside Allin.

'Guinalle saved us.' Allin's reply was muffled as she hid her face against Temar's neck.

'I couldn't let any mage suffer Otrick's fate.' Guinalle did her best to sound matter-of-fact. 'And your own defences proved themselves against the Artifice.'

'Nice to know I hadn't been wasting my time with Aritane,' remarked Usara.

'Larissa's dead, isn't she?' Allin clung to Temar. 'I felt her die, didn't I?'

He eased free of her embrace so he could see her face. 'Yes, my love. I'm so sorry.'

Grief welled up in Allin's eyes. Temar held her close again and felt her warm tears on his skin.

'The adepts found her first,' Guinalle explained with bitter regret. 'That's what alerted me to their plan for you all to share their death. She held out long enough for me to ward you two from the worst of their malice.'

'That's scant consolation for her loss.' Usara rolled his head to look at them all. 'There must be some reason we're so cursed vulnerable to Artifice when we're working wizardry.'

Temar opened his mouth to try and describe what he had seen of Larissa's fate but Guinalle spoke first. 'I believe I have some insight into that now.'

Allin stiffened in Temar's arms, her words putting any other considerations to flight. 'If the pirates are dead, can't we get them home, Livak and Ryshad and Shiv?'

'And Sorgrad and 'Gren.' Halice did her best to contain her impatience. 'When might one of you be strong enough to bespeak them?'

'No time like the present,' said Usara with grim determination. He swung his legs over the side of the bunk and pushed himself upright with visible effort.

'You're hardly in a fit state for magic,' Temar protested but Allin was already moving out of the protective reach of his arm.

She knelt on the floor to pull a small coffer out from beneath the bunk. 'Let me, Usara. Fire's my element.' Allin had already summoned a modest flame from the candle she took from the coffer. She handed Temar a small silver gilt mirror and her expression warned him not to protest. He swallowed his objections as the rising golden light of magic played on Allin's face. Temar wondered again how he could ever have thought her plain. The amber gleam turned the brown of her eyes into a pleated tapestry of light and shade looking into this mystery he could never comprehend.

'Curse it.' She blew out the candle with a chagrined puff. 'I can't reach either of them.'

'Is there something wrong?' demanded Halice. 'With them, I mean.'

'No, I'm just too tired.' Allin looked absurdly cross.

All at once Temar was hard put not to laugh. 'Will you mages ever accept someone else's word without having to prove a thing for yourselves?'

'Not before we get our third set of teeth, according to Otrick.' Usara managed a grin. 'I'll try scrying. That's an easier spell.'

Allin reached into her coffer for a shallow silver bowl and Guinalle fetched the wide-bottomed, narrow-necked ewer from the table. Usara rested the bowl carefully on his knees and studied it as she filled it.

'Let's see what we can see,' Usara murmured, taking a small vial from Allin with a nod of thanks. He let delicate drops of herb-scented green oil fall on to the water before cupping his hands around the bowl, taking a deep breath.

Temar waited tensely for the glow of magelight in the water. His heart sank as a feeble radiance barely reached the low rim of the bowl. Usara scowled and the circling swirl of oil began to whirl faster but just when Temar thought the shimmering light might break into the unearthly brilliance of magecraft, the spiral broke to leave blobs of oil floating aimlessly on the stubborn water.

Usara's lips narrowed to invisibility. 'I'm faring no better than you, Allin.'

'We just need some rest.' Woebegone, the mage-girl looked at Temar and Halice. 'I'm so sorry. It's just we've—'

'Hush, sweetheart.' Temar reached for her hand. 'No one blames you, either of you!' He was about to elaborate on all that the fighting men owed the wizards when Guinalle began a soft incantation. 'What are you doing?'

'Seeing what my skills can do for us.' The demoiselle sat on her stool, eyes closed as she concentrated. '*Tiadar vel aesar lel, Livak eman frer. Sorgren an vel arimel, lek al treradir.*'

Her rhythmic chant was the only sound in the cabin. Usara leant forward, eyes fixed on Guinalle and full of questions. Temar put his arm round Allin's shoulders as she still agonised over her own failure to work the magic he needed. Halice folded her arms and leaned against the door, face impassive.

'I cannot find either of them.' Guinalle threw up her hands in uncharacteristic exasperation. 'So much for the superiority of Artifice over wizardry.'

'You're weary, just the same as Usara and Allin,' Temar pointed out.

'Could you seek out Ryshad instead, or Shiv?' suggested Usara.

Guinalle shook her head. 'Any wizard is horribly hard to find – unless he's working magic of course, and Ryshad's distrust of Artifice is such that it's almost a defence in itself. Anyway, that's not the problem.'

'Then what is?' Temar asked, frustrated.

'Livak's working a charm to conceal them.' Guinalle's brows knitted. 'She doesn't want to be found by anyone's Artifice, not just mine.'

'But Ilkehan's dead,' began Temar.

'So she's hiding from someone else,' said Halice from the door. 'Which likely means some trouble's chasing them.'

'Someone probably took offence at them killing Ilkehan,' Usara said drily.

'What can we do?' cried Allin.

'Rest and restore yourselves and then you can bespeak Shiv or Sorgrad.' Temar tried to keep the vexation he felt out of his words.

'There's only so much you can do before you overtax yourself. That's what the masters say, isn't it, Allin?' Usara let slip a wordless growl of anger. 'This is a pissing inconvenient time for Otrick to be proved right!'

Halice snapped her fingers with exasperation and dug in her breast pocket. 'Would this help either of you?'

'Where did you get that?' Usara was astonished.

'Otrick's ring,' said Allin in the same breath.

'Otrick's and Azazir before him.' Usara held out a hand and Halice handed it over. 'But polished like new. Planir's ensorcelled it.' He looked at the unblemished circle with wonder.

'Which means what?' asked Temar keenly.

'This is a ring of elemental power.' Usara slipped it on the central finger of his off hand and studied it. New colour rose in his drawn face and he laughed. 'Kalion would have four kinds of fit if he knew about this!'

'Why so?' Guinalle sat forward, curiosity getting the better of her weariness.

'Wizards haven't instilled inherent magic into things for a handful of generations, maybe more.' Usara held up his hand. 'People like Kalion have decreed it degrades the mystery of wizardry to allow the non-mageborn any sense of magic.'

'One of us could cast spells wearing that?' Halice was incredulous. 'That sounds like something out of a bad ballad!'

'No, that's truly a minstrel's myth.' Usara took off the ring and tossed it to Allin who fumbled but caught it. 'But a mage can bespeak a non-mageborn person wearing such a thing.'

'That could be useful.' Temar's interest grew.

'Oh!' Allin blushed with surprise as she tried the ring on. Temar looked at her with some concern.

Usara grinned. 'What Kalion and his ilk don't appreciate is the main use of such things isn't to favour the mundane with some taste of mageborn power but to share and renew elemental powers between wizards.'

'Does it give you the strength to scry for Livak and the others?' Halice demanded at once.

'It's worth another try.' Usara held out a hand to take the ring from Allin but paused and looked intently at Guinalle.

'What is it?' She coloured slightly.

'I was just wondering,' the mage said slowly, 'what might happen if you tried it on.'

Rettasekke, Islands of the Elietimm, 11th of For-Summer

'Are you ready?' Sorgrad looked at Ryshad and Shiv.

'It's all right. We've done this before.' I smiled at Ryshad with a reassurance rather more feigned than sincere. Beneath his studied calm, I could see enough concern for both of us.

'Come on!' 'Gren was already barely concealed by the thorn bushes fringing the long pond between us and Olret's demesne. Water lapped at the dam. The recent tide had brought it surging through the open gates and now the sluices held it until it was needed. We had plans for that water.

'Go,' Sorgrad ordered and 'Gren ran, long knives out and ready. Sorgrad and I were a bare stride behind him, boots scuffing dust from the trampled top of the causeway. The tall block of the mill house shielded us from the keep's view but we weren't about to take any chances.

The door wasn't locked; there was no need, after all. 'Gren went through it without pause for breath, cutting down the man gaping at our unexpected arrival. He fell hard, blood dark against the flour spilling all around, mouth gaping like the sack he'd been filling from the chute beside him. I didn't wait to see if 'Gren took a second stroke to kill the man, racing after Sorgrad up the ladders to the upper floors of the wide building.

The miller tending the great millstones heard the commotion below but with nothing to serve as a weapon at hand, he had no choice but death beneath Sorgrad's impersonal blade. When we were done I could spare a pang for two poor bastards dead for simply being in the wrong place but, for now, I was more concerned with saving my own skin.

'Shut off the grain,' ordered Sorgrad.

I was already at the chute carrying kernels down from the hopper on the floor above. The bone slide poised to stop the cascade was immediately apparent and I rammed it home. Sorgrad was busy with the levers that governed the cogs driven by the shafts and axles turned by the waterwheels far below us. As he worked, I heard the rising roar of water gushing through the sluices.

'Gren found the right ropes.' I had to raise my voice above the rumble of the mill now rapidly gathering pace.

'He's no fool.' Sorgrad did something that set the grindstones racing. 'Not when he sees the chance of this kind of fun.'

I watched the grain already between the stones being ground to fine powder falling over the edge of the stone in dwindling trails. 'We're nearly done here.'

Sorgrad was pulling open the trap doors serving the various hoists that carried sacks up and down between the floors of the mill. Pale clouds puffed up from below and he coughed. 'Close those shutters.'

Doing as he bade, I kept a close eye on the grindstones. A squeak like a knife scraping across an earthenware plate told there was barely any grain left for the rough-keyed gritstone to bite on.

'Time to go,' I warned him.

Sorgrad knew as well as I did what would happen when those harsh stones struck sparks from each other for lack of grist. We didn't bother with the ladders, each grabbing a braided leather rope and sliding through the nearest trap to the floor below. I coughed and squinted through air opaque with flour. 'Gren was still slashing sacks with his knife, tossing handfuls into the air. 'Come on!'

He didn't need telling twice either. As white as if he'd been caught in a snowstorm, 'Gren ran for the door without delay. I was hard on his heels with Sorgrad a scant pace behind.

'How sharp were those stones?' Sorgrad yelled as we hared back along the causeway. 'How hard?'

'I didn't stop to look!' Ahead, I could see Ryshad's set face behind the thorn bushes, Shiv rose beside him, apprehension more plainly written on his raw-boned face.

'Get down!' I waved to them.

As I spoke, the mill house behind us exploded. The noise was incredible, a thunderclap that struck like a box to the ears and left my head ringing. A buffet like a sudden wind made me stumble, 'Gren ahead of me was jarred just the same as a surge of air ran past to rattle the bushes where Shiv and Ryshad waited, racing beyond to be lost in the scrubland. Birds rose in startled shrieking clouds from the rippling waters of the pond and the rocky shores beyond the causeway.

Debris rained down all around. Shutters from the ranks of unglazed windows were ripped off whole, sailing far out across the millpond or splashing into the newly liberated waters racing for the sea. Shards of slate hissed through the air, rattling on the rocks of the dam. A sizeable piece struck me full in the back and I hunched my shoulders as I cursed it. Lesser pieces pattered against my head and shoulders. A monumental crash made the causeway shudder beneath our feet and told us a floor or a wall had given way. I didn't turn to look until we reached the comparative safety of the thorn bushes. Ryshad stepped out to catch me as I flung myself off the edge of the causeway. I rested in his arms, panting for breath.

'Gren threw himself to the ground beside us, chest heaving, face alight with exultation. 'There you are, Shiv. Not a sniff of wizardry needed!'

Shiv gazed at the wreck of the mill with a nice confusion of shock and laughter. 'No wonder you don't feel a need to study in Hadrumal, Sorgrad.'

He was looking back with a curious expression. 'You mages could probably tell me why a spark can make powder in the air go up like firedamp.'

I twisted round in Ryshad's arms to see just what we'd achieved. The only time I'd let 'Gren talk me into this before, it had been a little windmill we'd reduced to kindling. I was startled to see how comprehensively such a big, solid building had been wrecked.

'These people don't use enough wood to fuel a really good fire.' 'Gren sounded disappointed.

'We can settle for this.' Ryshad shook his head at the devastation. Each side of the mill had a gaping hole punched through the wall, masonry still tumbling down. The beams and struts of the roof were broken and falling into the midst of the ruin of the shafts and axles and cogs that had driven the millstones, hoisted the sacks and worked all the other mysteries of the miller's craft. A rapidly growing fire filled the hollow heart of the stricken building, voracious flames licking ever higher. As the ever-present breeze helpfully fanned the blaze, its greedy roar rose above sharp sounds of further collapse.

'You say you've done that before?' Ryshad's embrace tightened round me.

'Twice, 'Gren confirmed gleefully.

'Just the once with me,' I reminded him.

'Why?' Ryshad's bemusement made me turn my head to look at him.

'We needed a distraction,' I shrugged.

'Which is what we wanted here.' Sorgrad still wasn't quite sharing 'Gren's uncomplicated jubilation but his eyes were bright with elation. 'I'd say we've got one.'

Beyond the causeway, the abrupt devastation of the mill had thrown Olret's people into utter confusion. Girls ran screaming from the goat sheds, too startled to secure the gates so they were instantly pursued by their yammering herds. Girls and goats alike collided with men and women pouring out of the storehouses by the keep, some rushing for the shore, others pausing to look at the mountains inland, wild gestures eloquent of their fear that some fire from beneath the earth was about to erupt and destroy them. Wiser heads might have got some grip on the situation but went unheard as folk rushing from the long sheds down by the jetties added to the uproar with questions no one could answer.

Men in twos and threes headed unbidden towards the destruction but were diverted almost at once as the goats seized the chance to run loose among the yards and fields. Some leapt the walls surrounding the banked and enclosed fields, eager to gorge themselves on the precious crops. Others jinked around the troughs of gutted fish, heads high and noses questing. Several tried to evade capture by running out on to the landing stages only to misjudge their footing and fall with a splash into the sea or on to a boat and cause yet more chaos.

'Time to go, Shiv.' Ryshad held me closer still.

'This has to be quick so it'll be rough,' the wizard warned.

'Hold on to your breakfast,' 'Gren advised.

I would have stuck out my tongue at him but on balance thought clamping my jaws shut more sensible. The magic was different this time; a rapid blanket of cold mist shot through with blue that enveloped us inside half a breath. Thorn bushes, dam and millpond all vanished into whiteness. The shift was a brutal one, jarring me from head to heels but paradoxically, I felt less inclined to throw up. Fog was still filling my eyes and I rubbed at them.

'Ah!' Shiv let out a harsh gasp. 'I've one more spell in me.'

'Let's make it count,' suggested 'Gren.

'Where are we?' Sorgrad demanded urgently.

As my vision cleared, I saw we stood in the corridor below the floor with the captive women. I headed for the stairs, Ryshad at my side, his sword drawn. 'Gren said something I didn't catch. I turned to see him and Sorgrad racing down the corridor in the other direction.

'Where are they going?' demanded Ryshad.

''Gren's just remembered something,' was all Shiv had to say with sharp annoyance.

'Leave them to it.' I was sorting lock picks and knelt by the metal gate.

'We agreed a plan,' Ryshad fumed.

'It's only ever a plan as long as they choose to go along

with it.' I glanced up to see he'd dearly love to expand on the dangers of such ill-discipline. 'Keep watch and let me open this.'

Shiv stood where he could see down the corridor and Ryshad moved for a better view of the stairs. Turmoil was coming and going in waves below us, urgent shouts beating down wrathful voices answering impossible queries. People ran and doors slammed but, as we'd intended, everyone's attention was on the inexplicable catastrophe over on the causeway. That's where everyone was heading, either to help or more likely just to gawp and exclaim over the misfortune of it all.

'Can you work that concealment charm?' Ryshad asked, voice low and cautious.

'Would you like me to juggle a few knives while I'm at it?' I muttered the arcane words under my breath and did my best to hold the refrain in my mind while probing at the workings of the lock. I closed my eyes the better to concentrate, my fingers remembering the pattern I'd teased out of the hidden shapes before. The lock snicked open. 'That's it.' I stood and pushed the gate open.

'Lock it behind us,' Ryshad ordered.

'What about 'Grad and 'Gren?' I objected.

'Leave it.' Shiv was already taking the stairs two at a time. 'If Olret comes after us, he'll have a key.'

I shrugged as Ryshad hissed through his teeth and we both went after the mage.

'It's me.' I knocked on the bolted door a brisk double tap. Ryshad knelt to pull the lower bolt aside, Shiv reaching for the upper one. 'With friends.' I hastily wiped any wish for concealment from my mind and sincerely hoped someone within had the skills to read my intent for the truth. Otherwise we were in more trouble than I wanted to contemplate with no ally at our backs. I took a deep breath before I had to brave the stench within and lifted the latch.

'Do you bring help?' As before, Shernasekke's lady wasn't wasting time on pleasantries. 'Have you spoken to our kin?'

'We'll help you if you help us,' I matched her directness. 'We've killed Ilkehan and now Olret wants us dead. Give me your word your friends will defend us and we'll get you out of there.'

'I swear by the duty I owe the land of my line and those of my blood within it.' The woman's blue eyes were pale in her drawn and filthy face.

'That sounds good enough.' Ryshad moved warily towards the cage that held her. 'Stand back.' He kicked hard at the crude lock with his booted heel once, twice and with a curse, a third time. It might have been proof against the women's fingers but this onslaught twisted it sufficiently for Ryshad to wrench the door aside. The woman seized her little daughter's hand and pulled her out of their prison, slipping on the ordure underfoot.

Shiv was keeping watch by the door. 'How far do you need to be from here to use your Artifice to contact your kin?'

She looked blankly at him.

'Your lore.' I remembered the Mountain word for the aetheric enchantments of the Sheltya. 'True magic.'

The woman's face cleared, then she grimaced. 'Do you have anything to eat? I'm famished beyond all reason.'

I was about to say we didn't have time to dine when Ryshad pulled a flatbread stuffed with goat meat out of his bag. 'My lady.' He proffered it with the instinctive courtesy drilled into him by years in D'Olbriot's service.

'I'm no one's lady now, good sir.' She managed a wry smile around a mouthful of food before bolting the rest with far from ladylike grace. 'Just Frala Shernasdir.'

'Get us out,' the grandmother demanded urgently. 'If we can touch hands, we can work together!'

Ryshad broke her free and I tripped the locks of a cage that held one of Frala's sisters. She gripped my hand as I let the door swing open. 'You have the lifelong gratitude of Gyslin Shernasdir.' Her fervent words had a formality ill suited to her stained green dress and grimy face.

'You're entirely welcome.' I moved on to the next sister

who was all but rattling her bars in her desperation. Ryshad released the younger girls, both rushing to cling to each other in a shaky embrace.

'Get your wits about you,' their grandmother snapped. 'Forget your aches and your bellies and concentrate on what has to be done.'

Of course, I realised belatedly. Olret wasn't just being a vindictive bastard keeping them in this squalor. He was making certain sufficient physical discomfort hampered their capacity to use Artifice, if not curbed it all together. I dug in my own bag for whatever food 'Gren had cached there and shared it out as best I could between Gyslin, her sister and their daughters.

Ryshad handed the grandmother a battered hunk of sausage and unhooked his water bottle from his belt. 'Shiv—'

The wizard cut him short with an impatient hand. 'Someone's coming up the stairs.' He moved behind the door, keeping watch through the crack at the hinges.

The women froze, food forgotten. Ryshad flattened himself on the open side of the door, sword ready. 'Shiv, can you bolt it?'

An urgent whistle pierced the tense silence. 'No, wait.' I left my last few darts still in my belt pouch. 'It's them.'

Ryshad muttered something under his breath. Shiv didn't close the door and I risked a quick look around it. Sorgrad and 'Gren came running down the corridor from the opposite stairway, each with a cloth-swathed bundle over one shoulder, swords in hand.

'Here!' I beckoned them in and each dropped their burden with a muffled clatter.

'This is hardly the time to go thieving,' I told Sorgrad forcefully.

Sorgrad raised innocent eyebrows, plainly unrepentant. 'Not even for more Kellarin artefacts?' The patterned cloth fell aside to reveal the gleam of old steel and the copper binding of a dagger handle. 'Maybe even the last ones you need?'

'Gren was smirking too. 'Whatever Guinalle doesn't want is ours, remember that.'

'You'll cut me a share or I'll know the reason why.' I couldn't help smiling until I saw the blood on 'Gren's blade. 'Who did you kill to get it?'

'No one,' 'Gren protested, injured. 'That's from the miller. The nurse all but pissed herself and ran like a scolded dog.'

'I guessed he'd hide valuables in that room where his son lies.' Sorgrad answered Ryshad's unspoken question, daring the swordsman to challenge him.

'Gren had already dismissed the matter, turning to sweep a low bow to the women who were looking at the two of them with lively curiosity. 'My ladies, my duty to you.' He winked at me. 'We needn't have worried about finding a bath.'

Ryshad had more important things on his mind. 'Shiv, take us out of here now.'

Before the mage could reply, the grandmother choked on her meat. 'Olret comes,' she gasped.

Her three daughters instantly joined hands, Frala in the middle.

'Quickly.' Gyslin beckoned urgently to her daughter and niece. The grandmother hobbled to the other end of their line and the little girl hid her face in Frala's skirts.

'We'll just have to risk it.' Shiv set his jaw.

'No!'

'Guinalle?' I couldn't help myself; I actually looked round to see if the demoiselle was there in the room.

'What?' Ryshad and Shiv stared at me as if I'd lost my wits.

'Livak, it's me.' I heard the noblewoman's voice again but from the bemused faces all around, I was plainly the only one. 'Don't let Shiv work any magic,' she went on urgently. 'Olret will kill him.'

'No spells, Shiv. Guinalle says no spells.' I struggled to hear her words at the same time as I was trying to explain. 'Usara's scrying for us and Guinalle's working her Artifice through his spell.'

'How are they working that?' Shiv was intrigued.

'Can't that wait?' I glared at him. 'Just remember you can't do any magic without Artifice to ward you or Olret will kill you!'

'Swords'll kill us a cursed sight faster.' Sorgrad was next to the door, 'Gren beside him. 'Half a cohort's on its way.' The tramp of nailed boots echoed ominously up the stone stairwells.

'Shut the door,' Ryshad ordered. 'Bolt it, one of you.' He swept his sword at the women.

I heard the bolts slam home as I tried to concentrate on Guinalle's far-distant voice. 'I have to speak to the adepts you've found. Join their line.'

I really didn't want to do that and not only because the girl's hand closest to me was so filthy, but we were running out of options fast so I grabbed for her.

The room turned dim around me and for one appalling moment I thought I was fainting. Then I realised I was somehow locked in a corner of my own mind with Guinalle's will controlling my body, my voice, my gestures. I could look out through my own eyes but in a peculiar, cramped fashion, only able to look directly ahead and as if through Ryshad's spyglass. I did my best to quell the panic rising within me and then realised that it would do me no good to yield to the impulse to scream, to protest, to fight the enchantment. I had no voice to cry for help, no strength to hit back.

'I am Guinalle Tor Priminale, acolyte of Larasion, sworn to the discipline of Ostrin.' She spoke with my lips and raised my hand to the grandmother. 'Will you aid me in the name of all that you hold sacred?'

'We will.' The voices of all six Elietimm adepts echoed around me as the grandmother took Guinalle's hand to complete the inward-looking circle. The room was instantly overlaid with new images; glimpses of Suthyfer and the newly reclaimed landing, Vithrancel and the busy market place, Edisgesset and the no-nonsense realm of the miners. Each place and person within them was as abiding and as ephemeral as the reality I could no longer feel beneath feet that no longer belonged to me. Something froze around me then Guinalle smashed it like someone breaking winter ice to reveal the fast flowing mysteries of the river beneath. My mother had warned me never to play on a frozen river with graphic tales of children carried away beneath the ice and drowned unable reach the light and air above. The fear I'd felt then was nothing to the terror paralysing me now, even as I felt the women of Shernasekke reaching for the aetheric power long denied them with all the desperate thirst of travellers lost in a waterless waste.

I wanted none of it, struggling not to fall into that torrent of mystery and peril, straining to see the world beyond the enchantment trapping me. Ryshad and Shiv were breaking apart the cages as best they could, 'Gren and Sorgrad piling the twisted bars and frames against the door, wedging broken bits of metal under the bottom, into the hinges, under the latch.

All that was less real than Guinalle now standing before me, dressed in the proud elegance of the Old Empire. Rings shone on every finger, a crescent of gold set with diamonds in her hair, more diamonds around her neck brilliant with fire struck by some unseen light shining on the silk of her flame-coloured gown. The soiled faces of the starved women each faded behind some simulacrum of how they wished to be seen. Frala's hair lightened to the pale gold of sun-bleached straw, piled high on her head with bone pins tipped with blood-red gems. Her full-skirted gown was a maroon rich against her milky skin. Gyslin and the other sister were dressed in the same style, in differing shades of blue, a many stranded rope of curious milky gemstones twisted around Gyslin's neck. The younger women wore less costly shades of green, dresses cut to display nubile charms instead of matronly modesty. The grandmother wore black made all the more severe by a few silver ornaments. With her thin face and sharp nose, she looked more like a crow than ever. Only the little girl was left in her grubby chemise, still clinging to her mother's skirts with one filthy hand and her bedraggled animal in the other.

A booming assault on the door helped pull my wits back to the real world where Ryshad and Shiv were bracing themselves against the wood with 'Gren and Sorgrad still reinforcing their stubborn barricade.

'If we are not all to die at Olret's hand, we must have help,' Guinalle began.

Civility be cursed, I thought furiously. Get on with it!

'*Seldviar namayenar ek tal rath*,' chorused the Elietimm women and their questing dragged me along with them. Now a third layer of reality or illusion overlaid everything and I knew without question I was in very real danger of being swept away by the currents of aether coiling around me.

'*Har dag Vadesorna abrigal*.' Frala summoned up a thickset man as bald as an egg, shoulders bunching in anger as she spoke to him so rapidly I hadn't a hope of understanding her. He turned and stormed off into invisibility, melting like a shape imagined in smoke.

'*Edach ger vistal mor din*.' Gyslin and her daughter were pleading with a nervous-looking woman whose jaw dropped in shock, shadowy shapes hurrying to cluster round her.

'*Olret evid enames Froilasen ral Ashernasen*.' The grandmother wasn't about to stand any nonsense from the well-muscled youth her enchantment had lighted upon. Fortunately he seemed as much inclined for action as her, a spear appearing in his hands in answer to his unspoken wish and his shirt dissolving into a dark cuirass of hardened leather.

Frala turned to Guinalle. 'We have summoned aid. They come as fast as they may.'

Was that going to be fast enough? Even through the Artifice clouding my perception, I heard the splintering crash of an axe hitting the far side of the door. I forced a memory of the room before my mind's eye, picturing Ryshad's face and Sorgrad's, Shiv's lanky frame and 'Gren's short, wiry one. Thought became reality and I saw the wood splintering as blows came hard and fast, Ryshad and Shiv forced back lest they lose an eye or worse.

'Olret comes!' Gyslin's simulacrum turned towards the door even as her true form remained locked in the circle.

Even through the wall, I felt Olret's complete conviction that his intent was strong enough to overwhelm the physical constraints of wood and metal barring his way. He wasn't wrong. The door shattered into kindling almost as completely as the mill had done, splinters gashing Ryshad and the others. Their swords met those of Olret's men who could reach through the narrow doorway. Ryshad and 'Gren took on the foremost guards while Sorgrad and Shiv used twisted lengths of metal on the second rank.

Olret's Artifice slammed into the circle of women but that held. I could see the bastard lurking behind the skirmish in the doorway, face twisted with hate.

'Guinalle! Guinalle!' He sounded as if he were half a league away but that was definitely Usara speaking. 'Give me the ring! Temar, put it on!'

'I can only shield you for a short time.' That was Temar's voice, grim with determination and warning in equal measure.

'That'll be enough.' I was startled to hear Allin sounding so forceful. 'Shiv! Sorgrad! We're going to form a nexus so make ready.'

A sphere of light appeared between the two of them; long-schooled wizard and untrained mageborn. It burned with a ruddy fire, not the crimson of elemental flame but darker, more ominous, weighted with the power of the earth. Shiv reached a hand out towards it and the colour darkened still further yet paradoxically burning all the more fiercely as his own magelight surrounded him with an emerald aura. Shiv nodded to Sorgrad who set his jaw, no more about to duck this challenge than any other he'd ever faced. He spread his hands in an oddly defiant gesture and blue radiance surrounded him, his fine hair blown about as if he stood exposed to a winter storm. Ducking his head like a bull about to charge, Sorgrad thrust his hands, palm out towards the roiling nexus of power. The spell sucked at the caerulean light and the confusion of colour burned away to leave only an eye-scorching whiteness.

'Now!' commanded Usara.

The nexus burst outward into a sheet of flame. It ripped through the room to set Olret's men alight, sending them screaming from the doorway even as the first to be hit burned to fragments of charred flesh and naked bone tumbling to the untouched floor. The spell left Ryshad and 'Gren happily unscorched and free to rush at Olret who was also somehow proof against the magic.

Olret raised a hand and unseen power threw 'Gren backwards into Ryshad. The two of them fell hard among the litter of the ruined door and wrecked cages. The Elietimm advanced, menace plain on his face. In the curious double vision of Artifice, I saw he considered himself a good deal taller and more handsome than a mirror would ever show him. Every detail of the simulacrum was precise, his skin smooth and freshly bathed, a brown cloak richly patterned with orange weave slung back from his shoulders to show a livery of grey leather ornamented with copper studs.

Every instinct screamed at me to move, to run, to draw dagger, darts, even throw the filth from the floor at the man but with Guinalle in control of my body I couldn't move. I would have wept with frustration, if I'd still had the use of my own eyes.

Shiv and Sorgrad moved to stand between Olret and the circle of motionless women. He snarled something, hands moving as if he were swatting flies but a swathe of white light wrapped around them both and nothing happened that I could see.

Olret's remorseless advance slowed. He looked like a man struggling through a bog. Sorgrad raised a hand and lightning cracked out like a whip. Brow twisted with fury, Olret waved it away but a blackened score appeared down his sleeve all the same. Sorgrad lashed him again and again and, for the first time, consternation shadowed Olret's eyes.

Shiv squared his shoulders and now Olret's boots were all but sticking to the floor. He could barely manage to scrape his feet across the boards, struggling like a prisoner shackled to a dragging weight. But that was only the real Olret. His simulacrum came storming onwards, brushing through Shiv and Sorgrad and the light surrounding them as if they weren't even there.

The aetheric embodiments of the women whirled round to form a new circle, faces outward, elbows linked, expressions determined. Olret's arrogant opinion of himself marched through the ring of their physical forms, plainly no barrier and slapped Gyslin's simulacrum hard in the face. She screwed her eyes shut and gritted her teeth and this time he punched her full in the mouth.

'You will not!' Frala's fury earned her Olret's hand twisting in her hair and wrenching her head sideways with a violence that would have snapped a real woman's neck.

'Curse you,' she gasped. 'You and your seed to the ninth generation!'

'I'll kill you!' he roared, wrenching her head to and fro and hammering at her with his other fist. With her arms pinioned, Frala couldn't defend herself. I watched with mounting horror as her image didn't bleed or bruise but began to blur and fade beneath this onslaught.

'You will not!' This was not one new voice but three. The people I'd seen Frala and the others asking for help suddenly appeared. Now Olret was surrounded. The younger man seized his raised arm, twisting it behind his back as the older baldpate unwound the bastard's fingers from Frala's hair. They pulled Olret away, forcing him round to face the hesitant woman who slapped him full in the face.

It wasn't a hard blow but whatever power lay behind it did more damage than a broadsword through the side of his head. Olret's face was ripped askew, left twisted like a child's clay model crossly squashed for not coming out right. The woman slapped him again and the colour began to bleed from his clothes, brown, grey and copper running together into dull and muddy uncertainty. She struck him a third time, no harder than before and now he began to fade. Not all at once, not like an evil dream as you realise you're waking but with great rents appearing in his head and body, soon big enough to see through to the room beyond. His simulacrum tore into sinking fragments that vanished as they hit the floor. His distorted head was the last to disappear, eyes rolling wildly, lolling tongue lashing.

The bald-headed man looked down then turned to Frala. 'We come,' he said simply and all three of them vanished.

'I can't stay,' Guinalle gasped and her image fled into nothingness, leaving me collapsing. I ripped my hands free of the grandmother's merciless grasp and from the girl on my other side. As soon as the circle was broken, everyone fell to the floor, panting like animals. The only one left standing was the little girl, bemused as she looked at the crumpled figures around her.

'Mama?' She knelt to push at Frala's shoulder.

I was on my knees and couldn't have got to my feet if Saedrin himself had asked for it but there was still the noise of fighting in the corridor. I scrubbed at my eyes so fiercely it hurt but I was determined to clear every vestige of aetheric blurring from my vision. I fumbled at my belt, reaching for darts, dagger, anything to use against whatever might come through the door.

I forced my head up, blinking furiously as tears filled my eyes. Olret stood just beyond the doorway; the real Olret. He was held stock-still and from the flickering patterns of many hued light wheeling round him, this was some magical coil worked by the nexus of wizardry. His remaining men were doing their best to reach him but Ryshad and 'Gren stood on either side, barring their way with lethal effectiveness.

That bastard wasn't dead yet no matter what had happened to his aetheric counterpart. I took a deep breath and reached carefully for a dart, reminding myself that poisoning myself by accident would be a monumentally stupid thing to do. I need not have troubled.

Sorgrad threw a handful of lightning at Olret and this time it scored him from head to toe, raising blisters down his blackened face and shattering his forward foot. If wizardry hadn't held him up, he'd have collapsed. Even with the magic pinioning him, he cried out in agony.

'Nothing to save you now, shithead,' crowed Sorgrad.

'Let's just kill him,' said Shiv wearily.

The wheeling light closed in around Olret and he burst into flames. The fire burned odourless and so hot I could feel it on my face and the brightness of the ruby, emerald, amber and sapphire in the flickering blaze was too painful to behold.

Ryshad and 'Gren stumbled in through the door as everyone fighting them fell away, fear more potent than loyalty for Olret's men. Both were bleeding or covered with someone else's blood, I couldn't tell which.

'Burn him, burn every bone in his body. Scatter him on the winds to be lost in the trackless ocean.' It was the grand-mother, crouching on her hands and knees with more of the poised cat than the whipped cur about her. The white fire consuming Olret reflected in her hungry eyes.

Ryshad staggered towards me, falling to his knees, bleeding from a handful of shallow nicks on arms and legs. I clung to him and together we watched Olret die. The old woman got her wish. When the flames closed in on themselves to finally vanish, all that was left was a twisting column of ash. Shiv shattered the windows with a rattle of hailstones and Sorgrad swept all that was left of Olret out to oblivion on a rush of icy air.

'Are we done?' I was shaking so much I could barely get the words out.

'Dast's teeth, we'd better be.' Ryshad wrapped his arms around me, cruelly tight but I didn't mind as his strength damped down the tremors wracking me. I could do without breath for the moment. He pressed his head close to mine and whispered words for me alone. 'It's all right, it's all right. I know, I know.' That was no meaningless reassurance and I clung to the distant promise of calm. Ryshad knew. I heard the truth of it in every beat of his heart hammering beneath his ribs. He'd been imprisoned by Artifice, used by another's will. I'd never be impatient with his distrust of enchantments again, I vowed. I should have stuck to my old beliefs; all magic brings is trouble.

'I need clean linen and water!' Sorgrad's urgent shout roused me from these incoherent thoughts.

'What?'

'Where?'

Sorgrad was kneeling over 'Gren. He was face down on the filthy floor as Sorgrad sliced off his jerkin, already ripped through and soaked in blood. 'One of them got him as he turned,' he explained tersely.

'Shit.' Ryshad tried to wipe away the blood coating 'Gren's back but there was just too much, soaking his breeches, pooling on the floor around Ryshad's knees. Sorgrad was already bloodied to the elbows.

I lifted 'Gren's head out of the muck, cradling his face, biting my lip so hard I drew blood, welcoming the pain as it cleared my mind enough to still my shaking hands.

'Just hold on.' I told him with a smile that hid pain twisting inside me like a hot knife. Drianon, Halcarion, Saedrin, Poldrion, any cursed god who might be listening, please don't let this happen, please don't let him die. We'd won, hadn't we? Why couldn't we just walk away with our victory? Why did it have to be stained with blood?

'Gren squinted up at me with one blue eye glazed with pain. 'It hurts, girl. Curses, it hurts.' He tried to grin but could only manage a puzzled grimace.

'Give me some room.'

Ryshad moved to let Shiv get closer and water poured from the wizard's hands on to 'Gren's naked back. Washed clean, we all saw a deep, ragged gash slicing deep into his side just above his hip. It vanished again as 'Gren's lifeblood came welling out. Ryshad ripped off his jerkin and shirt, Sorgrad doing the same and bundling the linen tight.

'Come on, you skinny little bastard,' Ryshad muttered. 'Put that bloodymindedness to good use for a change. Tell Poldrion where he can stick his ferry pole.' 'Gren meant precious little to Ryshad but Aiten had been his closest friend for ten or more years and I could see the memory of that loss darkening my beloved's brow.

'Let me see him.' The grandmother was at my side.

'You don't touch this wound with those foul hands,' snarled Sorgrad and if he hadn't been fully occupied trying to staunch the flow, I swear he would have hit her.

But she didn't want to touch the wound. Rather she laid a gentle hand on 'Gren's head as it rested in my hands. 'What manner of man are you?' she wondered softly.

'Gren was barely conscious. 'What Misaen made me.'

'And that is—'

I knew the reason for the grandmother's sharp intake of breath. I loved 'Gren like a brother but that didn't blind me to his blithe lack of conscience. Then there was the uncomplicated delight he took in bedding any girl willing and fighting any man fool enough to think 'Gren wouldn't kill him just for the excitement of proving his prowess and filling his purse by way of a bonus.

'He's my friend,' I begged her. 'And he risked his life to save you all.'

The woman looked at me stony faced. 'Which might count for something if he valued what he risked, if he valued what he fought for, if he ever looked beyond the moment he dwells in.'

All at once I was furious with the skinny old crone. What did she know about 'Gren and what he meant to me, no matter what he was? Nor was I about to leave someone else dead on these god-cursed rocks, not after losing Geris and Aiten to this horrible place and its cruel people with their ice-coated hearts.

'Whatever you can do, you just do it.' I wasn't begging

now, I was telling her and I started to rack my brains for some way of forcing her to act. Unfortunately all I could think of was knocking her on her bony arse, which didn't promise to be either effective or overly safe for the rest of us.

She tried to rise but stumbled. Frala caught her arm, helping her to her feet and something passed between them that replaced Frala's look of confusion with one of wary distaste. 'Who are you to make such demands on us?' she snapped curtly. 'Outdwellers all and tainting true magic with your corrupted touch.'

Shiv's distress turned to bitter rage. 'Without our wizardry, my lady, Olret would have ripped your head off!'

'Silence!' The grandmother cut off Frala's reply with a sweep of her hand.

'It's slowing, the bleeding's slowing.' Relief and disbelief mingled in Ryshad's voice.

I looked from the old woman to the horrible wound and saw that the blood was indeed lessening. As I watched, it stopped altogether; gore clotting around the ugly gash already beginning to knit together, swiftly closing to a lumpy purple scar.

'Thank you,' said Sorgrad tightly.

'I don't want your thanks.' The grandmother fixed him with a cold glare. 'I would not have his blood stake any claim to this land, not even though it be that of my worst enemy. Nor yet will I condemn mine own hargeard to have such ill-omened bones entombed within it.'

'The life of your friend settles all debts between us,' Frala declared with finality and a hint of hostility. 'Make no more claims upon us.'

'They're here, Vadesor and his men.' Gyslin had managed to drag herself to the window and was peering out to the court below. I realised I could hear a distant commotion. 'Olret's men are surrendering.'

The younger women looked towards the windows and at each other, their fearful expressions saying more plainly than words that they'd rather take their chances with whatever army had turned up downstairs than the four of us still standing.

'You may leave,' said Frala, uncompromising. 'As soon as you may.'

'Then we will.' Sorgrad threw away the blood-soaked remains of his shirt and nodded at 'Gren, still prostrate and unconscious on the floor. 'Help me get him up.'

Ryshad laid a firm hand between 'Gren's shoulder blades. 'No. We don't want to move him any more than we can avoid.'

I began to shake again, exhausted, too tired to deal with any quarrel between Ryshad and Sorgrad, too scared and too angry to tell these ungrateful bitches what I thought of them, too furious with myself for ever suggesting we come back to these god-cursed islands.

'Shiv,' I forced the words out. 'Just use that pissing nexus to get us home.'

Even as my gorge rose within me under the assault of the magic, I welcomed the nausea.

CHAPTER NINE

To Keran Tonin, Mentor at the University of Vanam,
From Casuel D'Evoir, residing in the House of D'Olbriot,
Toremal, by the grace of the Designate.

Esteemed Mentor Tonin, my compliments.

My researches into those archives that reach back to the
Chaos continue to turn up documents of considerable
interest. I copy to you an open letter circulated at the final
Convocation held in the reign of Nemith the Seafarer, by
Hafrein Den Fellaemion. I am not surprised that Nemith the
Last looked askance at such radical aspirations for the Kel
Ar'Ayen colony but perhaps the time has come for Temar to
realise something of these wishes. I have accordingly sent a
copy for the Sieur D'Alsennin to include in his own archive.

Your humblest of associates
   Casuel, Esquire D'Evoir

Be it known to all men of courage and virtue that
I am lately returned from my voyages into the
deep ocean and bring news to hearten all men of
virtue and valour.

I bring news of an empty land across the seas where broad grass-
lands rich in deer and deep for the plough stretch between generous
rivers offering safe harbour in their wide mouths and giving easy

access to thick forests, flush with game and timber ripe for felling. Beyond rise hospitable hills where we have already found stone for cutting, ores for milling and even gems in the gravels of the streambeds.

Let us turn to this new land, revealed by Dastennin's grace and Saedrin's bounty rather than struggle to shore up the crumbling bounds of our old provinces, in the face of rebellious ingratitude and selfish spite. Let us not squander the strength of our youth on ventures that Talagrin and Raeponin alike have turned their faces from, leaving our cohorts with scant choice but retreat in disarray.

I invite all men, bold and unafraid, to join me in taming this wild and beautiful land. Noble born yet dispossessed of their ancestral lands by the long years of calamity may repair their fortunes. Merchants and craftsmen impoverished by recent constrictions of trade may find both new markets and new resources. The commonalty with but broad backs and strong arms to offer will find their labours rewarded with unencumbered land to till for themselves.

Let none who sail shirk any duty from false expectation of privilege. Respect is to be earned in this new land just as surely as bread and meat will reward those who sow and those who hunt. Those that meet and exceed their obligations will rise, not to be held back by those who will not make shift for themselves or the dead weight of outmoded custom. Every man will be called upon to shoulder responsibility both for himself and his fellows.

I do not promise ease or luxury. I offer you toil and sweat. What such labour will win you is an untrammelled future and the right to make of that all that you can, in the certain knowledge of full title to pass all you might gain on to your heirs and assigns.

Suthyfer, Fellaemion's Landing, 29th of For-Summer

Some mercenaries can carry balance and coordination learned in close-quarter fighting over into dancing. A lot can't but that never seems to stop them. I watched ragged squares and circles form and break and hurriedly change direction, cries ringing above the miscellany of pipes and drums. A reasonable excuse for music rose into the late afternoon sky along with a sudden burst of laughter as three mercenaries got the figure spectacularly wrong.

'Do you reckon they'll have it right by Solstice?' I asked, amused. 'Or are we celebrating mid-summer early for some reason?' I'd been out with a hunting party since first light and hadn't expected to find an impromptu festival on our return.

'Just a little merrymaking to mark the double full moon.' Halice waved an expansive hand towards the spits by the shoreline where Minare's lads were roasting joints from the impressive array of game we'd culled from the islands' forests. Rosarn and Deglain were busy around a collection of pots seething roots and spices and a large cauldron frothed with boiling shellfish. Dotted with whatever early fruits the woods had to offer, huge slabs of travel bread baked on scrubbed boards propped to catch the heat of the fires.

'Have a drink.' Halice offered me a horn cup.

I sniffed suspiciously but was agreeably surprised by the fragrance of Califerian red. 'This isn't something Vaspret's been concocting from berries, sugar and hope.'

'D'Alsennin had the *Maelstrom* load up what was left of his cellar.' Halice gestured towards the ships at anchor in the strait. 'There was plenty of space for the return voyage.'

'They made good time on the journey.' I took an appreciative swallow. 'If Temar's emptied his cellar, he'll be in the market to buy some wine from me, just as soon as Charoleia gets a cargo organised.'

'You'd better think what else you're going to ship over,' said Halice with some amusement.

I didn't understand. 'How so?'

Halice's grin broadened. 'D'Alsennin's latest decree: anyone bringing luxuries over to sell has to pay for the privilege with a few of the boring essentials that barely pay for their carriage.'

'Nails and the like?' I'd heard Ryshad bemoaning their lack often enough. 'Whose bright idea was this?'

'Grandsire D'Alsennin's apparently. Seems this was his rule when the House had properties scattered over half Dalasor.' Halice, ever the warrior, had her own notion of necessities. 'I'd suggest bow staves and a wagon load of arrows myself.'

'I'll write to Charoleia,' I said without enthusiasm.

'She'll be turning all this news to advantage first.' Halice surveyed the landing site. No trace of the stockade remained and Ryshad's involvement meant the properly built wooden huts replacing the debris of the pirates' brief occupation already had a determined air of permanence.

'She's plenty of titbits to tempt the right folk to open their purses.' I looked over to the empty gibbet black against the sky. The last of the hanged had been cut down and thrown to the sharks. 'How do you think the Inglis guilds will react to news of Muredarch's death?'

'Temar will be writing to their council.' Halice looked amused. 'Claiming the bounty on Muredarch's head as well as setting out the concessions on tariffs he expects for doing them such a service.'

'That's certainly what Charoleia would recommend,' I laughed. 'Whose idea was it?'

'Sorgrad may have given him a hint but the lad's getting the bit between his teeth good and proper.' She looked around for Temar. 'We'd best keep an eye out for him tonight. He's a fair few unpleasantnesses to drown and this is the first chance he's allowed himself.'

'The double full moon's as good an excuse as any.' It was a solid gold certainty this was Halice's idea, to give us all a night to eat, drink and forget the tribulations of this past half season. Those that could be were reunited; those bereaved could share their grief. What property could be restored had been and Temar had made handsome restitution for the losses from Muredarch's coffers. Tonight, the moons, greater and lesser could shine down on some uncomplicated fun and then Halcarion would show us all a new path to follow. All of us, every last one of Kellarin's people now that Guinalle had roused the last of Edisgesset's sleepers with the artefacts we had brought back.

I realised Halice was looking askance at me. 'What?'

'Will you be crawling inside a wineskin and tying it closed behind you?' Halice challenged.

'No,' I told her firmly. 'It's not worth the morning after, even drinking D'Alsennin's finest.'

Still, splitting headaches and a sour stomach had been small price to pay for the oblivion I'd won from liquor scrounged from the mercenaries on our return. Ryshad had convinced Halice to leave me be, put me to bed when my words slurred into incoherence, found me cold water, dry bread and a shady place to regret my folly the following day. He had understood the paralysing fear of going to sleep only to find myself back in the confines of Artifice, terrified that waking would find me still locked within my own head, someone else ruling my limbs. Halice nodded with satisfaction and poured me more wine.

'Has he said anything about Ingella?' I asked.

'Temar?' Halice shook her head. 'He did well there, when it came to it.'

'Justice is a Sieur's duty.' I glanced involuntarily at the gibbet. 'Mind you, I don't think it did him any harm, for people to see how reluctant he was to hang a woman.'

'Not as long as he went through with it.' Halice's voice was hard. 'She was condemned beyond question.'

Ingella and the other survivors of Muredarch's scum had faced Temar's assize. He'd judged them with grim-faced authority, impressing us all. Unsavoury duty done, he deserved all the wine he wanted to blot out memories of the condemned struggling, weeping and cursing their way to the gallows.

'It's not for us to look out for Temar,' I pointed out to Halice. 'That's Allin's job these days.'

Halice chuckled into her cup. 'That news in the right quarter should be gold for Charoleia.'

I raised an eyebrow at her. 'How do you think the noble Houses of Toremal will react to a wizard as maitresse to Temar's Sieur?'

'We're the other side of the ocean and there's nothing they can do about it,' said Halice with considerable satisfaction.

'They're wedding at Solstice?' I asked. 'Here or in Vithancel?' That would forestall any prince wanting to make trouble but I couldn't help feeling Allin deserved better than such a rushed affair.

'No, it'll be autumn Equinox,' Halice told me. 'With all honour to Drianon in the old style, all the Sieurs and their ladies and esquires invited to Vithrancel.'

'And to bring their best bid for the new trade,' I continued for her.

'And breaking their journey here, just so they see these islands are well and truly claimed,' concluded Halice. 'Anyone out to argue the point can expect magefire scorching their toes.'

'Not that anyone would be so crass as to say so. This could be an interesting place, given a year or so,' I mused.

'Even more so when Usara brings word back from Hadrumal,' agreed Halice. 'Have you seen Guinalle today?'

I shook my head. 'Not that I recall.'

'You're avoiding her?' Halice's words were halfway between question and accusation.

'She's been making sure Pered looked after the wounded properly while she was away.' I could hear the unconvincing defiance in my protest. 'Or she'll be debating magical congruences with Usara.'

'That's what they've been doing, is it?' Halice grinned. I wondered how long it would be before the demoiselle realised the cheerful satisfaction on Usara's face of a morning made such excuses irrelevant. In the meantime, Halice wasn't letting me excuse myself. 'She deserves a drink before all the good wine's drunk. Find her and give her this. I'm going to get some food.' She handed me the wine, walking off before I could protest.

I swung the fat-bellied bottle by its long neck and considered giving it to someone else. Pered and Shiv were arm in arm by the dancing ground, joking with careful kindness among those who'd survived the pirates and were trying to make merry as best they could. Guinalle would be comforting those with memories too raw and painful to be danced away. Halice was right, curse her. The demoiselle deserved a drink and if she had her mouth full of wine, she couldn't be asking for my thoughts on the Elietimm Artifice she'd dragged me into. It was time Guinalle accepted I had no opinion, beyond determination never to get caught up in it again. Walking up the slope towards the woods, I found I was holding the bottle in a manner more suited to a tavern fight. I changed my grip; I was hardly about to hammer the truth into Guinalle's head with it. I'd have a quiet word with Usara when he got back and ask Ryshad to drop a few hints.

I heard talking inside the canvas-roofed hut where Guinalle was living and halted, just out of sight beyond the doorway.

'Everyone says they know how I must feel.' Naldeth's voice was bitter as gall.

'How can they?' Guinalle was unemotional as usual. No, that wasn't fair, I'd seen her smiling latterly, colour in her cheeks it was a safe bet Usara had put there. 'Though I was severed from the life I'd known as surely as your leg was taken.' I was surprised to hear Guinalle be so blunt. 'If you can learn from my mistakes in trying to cope, you may save yourself some grief.'

'You make is sound so easy.' The mage's reply was barely short of insulting.

'It's the hardest thing I've ever done,' retorted Guinalle. 'But the only alternative is despair and you're no more a coward than I am.'

'I don't have your strength, my lady,' Naldeth choked unexpectedly.

'Then take strength from those willing to offer it,' said Guinalle softly. 'Don't repine for what's lost and agonise over what cannot be changed. Don't shut out those who would help you. If that's the cost of closing the door on pain and regret, it's not worth paying.'

'I can't go back to Hadrumal,' said Naldeth, forlorn. 'I can't face the questions, the pity, everyone whispering in corners—'

'Talk to Usara about that,' Guinalle said briskly. 'Anyway, who says you need go back to Hadrumal?'

'I'm hardly going to be building a new life in Kellarin on one leg and a crutch.' Naldeth's uncertain mood veered back to anger. 'People will see Muredarch's handiwork till the end of my days, my lady. You might as well have left his mark on my chest as well.'

They could both do with a drink. I walked away and approached again, humming a snatch of the round dance being played by the shore.

'Halice doesn't want you missing out.' I stuck my head round the doorframe and waved the bottle cheerfully. 'Any glasses not used for medicine round here?'

'I can find a few.' Guinalle rose from the edge of the bed where Naldeth was propped against a bank of rolled blankets. Minare carried him here every morning despite his protests. Guinalle was determined the mage wasn't going to sit in solitude and brood on his injuries.

'You want to ask Halice for a few hints on using that.' I

nodded at the crutch standing in the corner, untouched since Ryshad had put it there.

'She's probably forgotten how.' Naldeth sounded bitter again.

'She spent the best part of a year never walking without one,' I pointed out. 'And wondering what to do with her life. A crippled mercenary has precious few options compared with a mage. You don't need both feet on the ground to work wizardry.'

'I can't decide if you're a good nurse or not, Livak.' Guinalle turned from the chest that held her tinctures and salves. 'Do your patients get well simply to get away from your encouragement?'

That won a grudging laugh from Naldeth so I'd allow the lady her sarcasm, particularly since I saw calculated humour in her eye.

'Enjoy it.' I proffered the bottle and waved Guinalle away when she tried to refill my horn cup. 'No, thanks all the same. I'm looking for Ryshad.'

I sauntered off, well satisfied with my escape. I'd done what Halice asked. I'd tell her Guinalle was busy with Naldeth, and suggest she help get the wizard back on his feet – well, foot and crutch. If Guinalle thought I was unsubtle, she should see Halice dragging someone out of the mopes. I'd seen mercenaries half dead from their wounds sitting up and taking notice, if only because they'd obey Halice before Poldrion's summons.

The cooking meat smelt tempting. Minare and I had a bet on just what the hare-lipped beasts Vaspret found foraging among the narrow valleys would taste like. Minare wagered something akin to rabbit but I reckoned venison looked nearer the mark.

'Livak!' Sorgrad hailed me and waved a bottle. He and 'Gren were leaning against a stack of the firewood everyone was expected to gather daily. Ryshad had set people thatching the piles with brush to keep any rain off.

'Drink?' asked 'Gren.

I shook my head. 'What have you been up to today?'

'Talking to Pered and Shiv.' 'Gren scratched absently at his side where the wound that should have killed him still itched as it healed. 'Have you seen what they're planning for the inside of the shrine?'

'You mean you've been distracting Pered when he's supposed to be drawing up records for D'Alsennin.' Sorgrad fixed me with a sardonic eye. 'Pered's talking about studying Artifice with Guinalle; reckons he could make an adept.'

'That'll make for a lively household.' I shrugged. 'I'll wish him and Shiv every happiness of wizardry and Artifice under the same roof.'

'Scared?' teased 'Gren.

'Witless,' I confirmed. 'Forest tricks are all very well but the demoiselle can keep her Higher Artifice and welcome. I'll stay safe inside my own skin with both feet firmly on the ground, thanks all the same.' I turned to Sorgrad. 'What about you? Have you got a taste for wizardry? Will we wave you off to Hadrumal?'

He didn't rise to the bait, simply smiling lazily. 'I'll wait and see what word 'Sar brings back from Planir.'

'There should be some fight worth joining in Lescar,' 'Gren remarked. 'Once we find out which side's backed by most coin. I want to see what price we can get for those red stones Olret gave us as well.'

'Half a half-season's peace and quiet and you're already bored,' I scoffed. 'You don't know when you're well off.' I'd decided boredom had more merits than I'd allowed it. Besides, my mother always said if you were bored, you just weren't looking hard enough for something to do. I was beginning to think she might have a point. Mind you, I wasn't thinking in terms of her usual ready suggestions that I polish some brass, blacklead grates or darn linen.

'I could write to Lessay, if anyone's got a notion where to send a letter,' mused Sorgrad.

'Gren's thoughts had already moved on. 'They need someone to make up that set. Look after my wine, 'Grad.'

'That wound's not holding him back then.' I watched him bow deftly to a girl who'd been looking uncertainly for a partner. 'Nor yet the notion he should be dead on the Ice Islands?'

'You know 'Gren,' Sorgrad said easily. 'Where there's no sense, there's no feeling.'

The timorous girl was blossoming under 'Gren's charm. 'I take it she's not yet had the chance to learn how much she owes him, see his scar and kiss it better?'

Sorgrad nodded. 'She looks better than she did, doesn't she?'

I studied the girl but beyond a vague recollection of hysterical weeping, I couldn't put a name to her.

'Guinalle's done a good deal for the worst abused,' Sorgrad continued. 'Taking the edge off memories, blunting dreams. Seems Artifice can help heal the mind as well as the body.'

'I'm still not taking any interest in it,' I told him firmly.

'That'll please Ryshad.' Now it was Sorgrad's turn to dangle a provocation.

'When did you last see me hiding behind a man's wishes?' I stuck my empty cup on the top of his wine bottle. 'You won't talk or trick me into sitting for lessons at Guinalle's feet, just so you've got an excuse for hanging round to talk magic with Shiv and 'Sar.'

'It was worth a try.' Sorgrad grinned, unrepentant.

I was watching 'Gren blithely whirling the dark-haired girl around. 'It really doesn't bother him, does it?'

'How am I supposed to take a drink with everyone giving me things to hold?' Sorgrad frowned at the cups and bottle in his hands. 'What? No, you know 'Gren. There's no future in looking at the past, that's what he says.'

'A sound philosophy as far as it goes,' I allowed. 'But a little forward planning doesn't come amiss.'

'Words to warm Ryshad's heart,' mocked Sorgrad.

I still wasn't biting. 'His father's a mason, 'Grad. Making plans means the building won't come tumbling down around your ears.' Everything had so nearly crashed to ruin around all of us. It was high time I went back to a life where the biggest risks were marked by the roll of the runes and the weight of your purse.

'Where is he?' Sorgrad scanned the lively scene by the water. 'You'd best go and find him, let him know there's food for the eating.'

'Don't drink all the good wine.' I looked but couldn't find Ryshad among the dancing or the hungry throng gathering by the fires.

'Try the shrine,' Sorgrad suggested.

The Island City of Hadrumal,
29th of For-Summer

The full heat of the afternoon beat down on Hadrumal's roofs, striking motes of silver from stone slates and turning masonry beneath to warm gold. Planir stood at his window looking down at the bustling courtyard below. Apprentices hurried about the errands they'd been given by their masters. Mages elevated to the status of pupil walked more slowly back to their lodging, weighed down with carefully cherished dignity and the substantial books many carried. Styles of dress and a general predilection for elemental colours were common to all but cut and quality of cloth inevitably distinguished those born to greater wealth whose families refused to let the accident of magebirth divide them.

In plainer clothes and oblivious to the lofty concerns of wizards, the ordinary folk of Hadrumal came and went; laundresses, maidservants, apprentice boys fetching and carrying so that no mundane distractions need divert those with the privilege of affinity from studying their arcane calling.

Planir watched, face cold. When a knock sounded at his door, he didn't stir. 'Enter.'

Usara came into the room. 'Archmage.' He wore everyday breeches in washed-out maroon and a full-sleeved shirt under a buff jerkin with bone buttons. Both had been cut for a man thicker in the waist and broader in the shoulders. He carried a plain leather bag slung over one shoulder by a braided strap.

''Sar.' Planir still didn't move. 'I heard you were back.'

'Just for a day or so. I had some things to bring you.' Usara moved to the table, empty surface glossy with diligent polishing. The whole room was bright as a pin, neat as new paint. 'This letter for one.'

That turned Planir's head. 'From whom?'

Usara winced at the apprehension and hunger in the Archmage's face. 'Just from Temar.'

Planir managed a wintry smile. 'What can I do for the Sieur D'Alsennin?'

'I suspect he wants your permission to wed Allin.' Usara set the sealed letter on the table. 'He thinks you're the one he should ask.'

Planir returned to gazing out of the window. 'It's always been an Archmage's duty to care for those seeking learning and guidance from Hadrumal.' His voice was harsh with self-accusation.

Usara lifted a small copper urn out of his satchel, setting it on the table with gentle hands. The round-bellied vessel was bright with enamelled leaves and birds, mismatched lid secured with wax and cord.

Planir's head turned involuntarily at the slight sound. 'Larissa?'

'She saved countless lives.' Sorrowful, Usara looked at the urn. He reached into the neck of his shirt and pulled a cord over his head. The silver ring was knotted securely on to it. 'We'd never have been able to use Artifice and wizardry together without this and we couldn't have saved those women from Olret.'

'Which, as Archmage, I should of course be glad for.' Planir turned back to the window. 'Forgive me. As yet I cannot appreciate the wider benefits of losing the woman I loved to a horrible death.'

'Halice gave us the urn. It seems she's always carried one, reckoning she'd be killed sooner or later.' Usara set the ring down on the table. 'Temar wants to name one of the Suthyfer islands for Larissa. We've built a shrine and she'll be remembered with honour if that's where her ashes rest.' He hesitated. 'I thought you might want her here, though. It's for you to say.'

'My last duty as her Archmage?' Pain cracked Planir's sarcasm.

'Your right as her lover,' said Usara quietly.

'Is that all?' asked the Archmage curtly.

'No.' Usara ran a hand over his non-existent hair. 'Forgive me but I asked Kalion and Troanna to join us.'

Planir glared at him. 'Just to make my day complete.'

Usara squared his narrow shoulders. 'I have things to tell you all, in your capacities as Archmage and Element Masters.'

'Have you now?' A spark of interest struggled through the grief darkening Planir's grey eyes. 'That Kalion's dream of closer ties with Imperial Tormalin is to be realised now Temar's realised little Allin's loved him for the better part of a year?'

Usara coloured beneath his sandy beard. 'I also have hopes of marrying into that House.'

'Do you?' Planir managed a faint smile. 'Guinalle has accepted you?'

'I haven't exactly asked her,' Usara admitted. 'Not as yet.'

'Temar's her legal overlord.' Planir moved to the high-backed chair by the fender and waved Usara towards the other. 'You'll be asking his permission for her hand. Do you want me to tell him he can't wed Allin if he turns you down?' The notion surprised the Archmage into a brief laugh.

'I hadn't thought of that.' Usara looked shocked. 'That Temar has rights in the matter, I mean.'

Hasty feet sounded on the stairs beyond the open door.

'Kalion's on his way.' Planir settled himself with calculated care, nodding to Usara to do the same. 'I didn't think it would take him long.'

Usara did his best to assume the Archmage's ease but tension kept his spine stiff as the poker in the empty hearth. As the silence in the room was broken only by the approaching footsteps, he grew pale with determination.

'Hearth Master, do come in.' Planir waved as Kalion reached the doorway, scarlet faced, his chest heaving. 'Troanna, do take a seat.'

The Flood Mistress stalked past Kalion who was still getting his breath. Apart from high colour on her round face, she showed no sign of undue hurry. 'Usara, a welcome surprise.' She took one of the upright chairs beside the table, glancing at the letter, the urn and the ring. Her face turned thoughtful.

Kalion dropped heavily down beside her. 'Usara.' He paused to catch his breath again. 'I should tell you, in all friendliness, that I have grave concerns about your fitness for office. I cannot, in all conscience, let your nomination pass to the Council without setting them out.'

Usara frowned, perplexed. 'I beg your pardon?'

Kalion looked at Planir. 'This is about the Stone Mastery?'

'You'd nominate me?' Usara was startled.

Planir smiled enigmatically. 'Usara asked you here. It seems he has something to say to us all.' He shot Usara a look of challenge.

Usara lifted his chin. 'I was not aware that I would even be considered as Stone Master but with all due respect – and considerable gratitude – I would have refused such an honour.'

'What?' exclaimed Kalion. He would have continued but for the combined effects of exertion and indignation.

Troanna slapped his arm. 'Let him speak.'

'I have come to tell you that I will be staying in Suthyfer, as will Shiv and Allin.' Usara cleared his throat.

'Then we wish you well.' Troanna made as if to stand.

'And we will welcome any mage wanting to join us in studying elemental magic as well as Artifice.' Usara spoke a little faster than usual. 'We wish to found a hall for the exploration of magic in all its forms. We'll start by using our various skills to help build new settlements in Suthyfer and Kellarin. I will be spreading the word among the halls here before I leave.'

Kalion gaped. 'I forbid it!'

'Forgive me, Hearth Master, but you have no right to do so.' Usara looked at Planir. 'Nor, as far as I can tell, do we need your permission as such but we'd value your blessing.'

'It's an Archmage's duty to curb any excesses among wizardry,' said Kalion furiously. 'If setting up some rival hall to Hadrumal isn't excessive, I'd like to know what is!'

'Hush.' Troanna's fingers tightened on Kalion's arm hard enough to cut his words short. 'Do you see your enterprise rivalling Hadrumal, Usara? With just you three and any malcontents you can convince to risk themselves?'

'Not at all, Flood Mistress. What we seek is rather to complement the learning here.' The mage waved a hand at the unseen halls and courts beyond the window. 'There is such a burden of knowledge here that it can stifle new thinking. Any apprentice with a curious idea is more inclined to hunt through the libraries for some clue that someone tried it before, than to actually pursue the notion. If they find nothing to guide them in the accumulated lore of Hadrumal, all too often they abandon the idea altogether.'

'You think yourself wiser than all the mages whose lives spent in study have given you and your heedless friends the very skills to master your inborn magic?' Kalion was incensed.

'We wish to use those skills to add to the sum of wizardry,' retorted Usara. 'Which cannot always be done when the weighty traditions of Hadrumal unfortunately smother initiative.'

'That's a grave accusation,' said Troanna sternly. 'What manner of initiative are we discussing? The insane depredations of some menace like Azazir?'

'Of course not,' Usara responded tightly.

'Can you show us a good idea coming to naught?' asked Planir mildly, fingers steepled beneath his chin as he relaxed in his chair.

Usara took a breath before continuing. 'Consider Casuel, Archmage. When Temar and the Sieur D'Olbriot were assaulted last year, he blocked their attackers' escape by making the vines of a carved stone gate grow to tangle their hands and feet. It was most impressive magic and I would dearly love to know how he worked it but he has no clear idea. Worse, he refuses to try it again without sanction from the records of some dead wizard to assure him that it's safe.'

'You intend letting every wild idea run riot on these islands?' Troanna looked sternly at Usara. 'Will you keep yourselves sufficiently far from D'Alsennin's people so you don't all go up in flames and confusion?'

'We will be taking every precaution against folly, Flood Mistress,' Usara said stiffly. 'We'll use all the safeguards so long proven here. We're not turning our backs on Hadrumal, just taking a step away.'

Planir spoke just fast enough to stop Kalion's intemperate response. 'You make an interesting point about Casuel. He's never really realised his potential, has he?' The Archmage looked from Kalion to Troanna. 'He isn't the first we've seen unhappily overawed by all the misbegotten, misinterpreted legends that hang round this place.'

'Casuel was twisted by his own inadequacies before he ever reached these shores,' snapped Kalion.

'Maybe so,' Planir allowed. 'But who's to say he might not have put those behind him if he didn't feel surrounded by predecessors he doubted he could equal? What about Ely, Kalion? She holds back out of fear of failure.' He fixed the Hearth Master with a stern eye. 'She's an affinity as strong as any I've seen but busies herself rumour mongering and poisoning people's lives with her gossip. To be fair, much as I dislike the girl, I simply don't believe she's cut out for debating the flaws and merits of theories. She might do far better with a freer rein to apply her abilities as suits her best.' His words were cutting. 'Tell me, Troanna, how many apprentices have failed to measure up to your expectations or disappointed you by settling for the limited scope of a hedge mage's life? I've seen far too many scurry off to some mundane town half a day from the high road because that's what they grew up with and they couldn't get used to the lofty halls and concerns of Hadrumal.'

'One is one too many,' said Troanna curtly. 'I'll grant you that.'

'You cannot sanction such a renegade enterprise,' cried Kalion. 'I won't allow it. The Council won't allow it!'

'How will they stop it?' Planir queried mildly. 'None of the precepts Trydek laid down for this place preclude mages establishing some other centre of study. None of those precepts entitle the Council to act against other mages. That's the Archmage's duty.'

'With the Council to guide him,' snapped Kalion.

'To make sure he isn't tempted to a course of magical tyranny.' Planir nodded. 'Forbidding 'Sar and Shiv's attempt to broaden the scope of magical learning sounds uncomfortably like tyranny to me.'

'All mages are subject to Hadrumal's authority.' Kalion glared at Usara.

'Which authority is based on consent, as you are so very fond of reminding me.' Planir sat straighter, looking severe. 'If it is seen to be abused for no good reason, that consent will vanish like snow beneath hot sun. Where will wizardry be then?' He thrust a challenging finger at Kalion. 'You're so keen to see magic accepted in the wider world. Won't seeing wizards helping folk with their everyday business ease the fears and superstitions than bedevil us? Powerful mages from a hidden isle visiting only to closet themselves with lords already holding power of life and death over them don't exactly reassure the commonalty. I can see other advantages. Wizards at the centre of what promises to be a substantial trading network will very well placed to hear of discord or harmony among the powers of the mainland.'

Kalion struggled for a reply so Planir continued remorselessly.

'Not everyone's cut out for the learning of Hadrumal but that doesn't tarnish or devalue it. Study will always have its place, Kalion; I don't think we need feel threatened by 'Sar's new venture. In fact, it'll prove a study in itself to keep the papermakers and bookbinders in work. Has Sannin talked to either of you two about her notion that capacity for magecraft strengthens with its actual use? She'll be fascinated to see what comes of 'Sar's venture.' He glanced at Usara. 'Rafrid and Herion will be interested to share a glass of wine with you before you go. They're interested in exploring merging magic, in a formal nexus and in less structured workings. You and Shiv should share what you've learned, even if your workings have been largely luck and accident.' Planir's tone was one of reproof but that didn't please Kalion whose face showed suspicion still winning over indignation.

Troanna had other concerns. 'This hall or whatever you call it would also be a place for the study of Artifice?'

'You've made it clear you consider such studies here a pointless distraction,' Planir answered tersely. 'Besides, if such a hall were set up under D'Alsennin's auspices in Suthyfer, the Emperor would have no reason to charter any new university. As a rival to Hadrumal, I'd have far more concern over a school of Artifice that we had no links with than over Shiv and Usara's venture where tried and tested friends directed both disciplines.'

'We intend to explore every similarity and difference between aetheric enchantment and our own magic,' said Usara firmly.

Kalion snorted with contempt.

'You don't think that's a worthy aim?' demanded Planir. 'You don't want to know how to save yourself from the living death that Otrick suffered or the fatal shock that rebounded upon Larissa? I'll wager every other mage in Hadrumal would be grateful for such knowledge. A good few will appreciate there being some other focus for Elietimm hatred, if it should ever emerge again. I certainly welcome some bulwark against attack or a sanctuary if Hadrumal itself should ever be struck down. We have all our eggs in one basket, Kalion. Hiding ourselves with mists and magic is all very well but you cannot deny it means we cut ourselves off from the mainland more comprehensively than is good for us. You've always been an advocate for greater involvement in the wider world.' He smiled to undercut the harshness of his words. 'This argument's becoming rather circular. Do any of you have anything to add?'

Usara rose to his feet in the resulting silence. 'If you'll excuse me, Archmage, I wish to speak with Aritane.' He couldn't help glancing at Troanna. 'Guinalle has learned something of an ancient rite of exile still practised among the Elietimm. She wishes to appeal to the Sheltya, to argue that they accept it as basis to sentence Aritane to less than death. Then she can come to Suthyfer as well.'

'Wait a moment.' Planir pointed to the table. 'Kalion, if you'd be so good as to pass me that ring.' He sat forward, hand outstretched.

Kalion picked up the cord and frowned, examining the silver circle. 'Otrick's ring?'

'Azazir's before him.' Troanna leaned over to look.

'You've ensorcelled it yourself.' Kalion narrowed his eyes at Planir who merely smiled and raised his hand to show the scar burned into his finger.

'Now it's imbued with three elements out of the four,' mused Troanna. 'Only fire remaining.'

'Which will double and redouble its power.' Planir cocked his head. 'Kalion?'

'I haven't that depth of affinity.' The Hearth Master handed it to Planir.

'You might surprise yourself.' The Archmage shrugged. 'But I yield to your mastery. The question remains, what shall we do with it?'

None of the other three mages dared meet each other's eyes. Usara slowly resumed his seat as Planir put the ring on his forefinger. 'I know you're anxious to assure us you're not setting up in opposition to Hadrumal, 'Sar, but it occurs to me a degree of competition can be a healthy spur to learning. The scholars of Vanam and Col never make so much progress as when their rivals gain some new insight into a common pursuit.' He pursed his lips. 'I'll be interested to see if a mage fit to complete the square in this particular circle emerges from Hadrumal or Suthyfer first. Until then—' he tossed the ring to Usara who caught it, surprised. 'You take it. You said it proved central to defending your mages against aetheric attack. You'll be the first line of defence against that from now on.'

Kalion scowled. 'If you'll excuse me, Archmage. Usara, I'll bespeak you when I have need of that ring.' He stomped out of the room.

'Don't you approve, Troanna?' queried Planir.

'It's little enough to me or my pupils, either way.' The Flood Mistress looked at Usara. 'Do you still consider the Elietimm a threat?'

Usara hesitated. 'For the present, from all Guinalle can read of the situation, no. Hopefully there's no reason for us to be enemies now. There are four or five clans jostling for position among the Elietimm, well enough matched in men, land and adepts. They're all wise enough to realise any one aiming for pre-eminence will be cut down by the rest uniting against any possibility of a new Ilkehan. They have as many misgivings about us as we have about them, so I don't suppose we'll ever be friends, though D'Alsennin's sending the remaining prisoners from Kellarin's mines back, as earnest of his goodwill.'

'That sounds well enough. You wanted to find Aritane. Don't let me keep you.' Troanna made no move to stir from her chair.

'I'll bid you farewell.' Usara stood and sketched a bow to both. 'I need to see Strell as well, Planir. Temar wants her to know she can call on D'Alsennin for anything she might ever need.'

'I hope that's of some comfort.' Planir plainly doubted it. Usara closed the door softly behind him. 'You have something to say to me, Troanna?' The animation left the Archmage's voice.

Troanna surveyed the room. 'Even allowing for the diligence of your servants, there's no sign you've been throwing crocks. Judging by the usual plentiful array of wines and cordials, you've not been drowning your grief. You're thinner in the face but I've seen you dining with your pupils so you're hardly starving yourself into a decline.'

'Your point?' Planir's face was a chilly mask.

'I've buried two husbands and three children, Planir.' Troanna folded her arms. 'I won't say I know what you're feeling because every loss is different and cuts as deep as any gone before. What I do know is you must grieve or Larissa will remain as dead to you as those ashes in that urn.'

Planir's response was scathing. 'You want me to picture her happily dwelling in the Otherworld, her virtues recognised by Saedrin as sufficient to save her from Poldrion's demons?'

'Don't be a fool.' Troanna was unmoved. 'You've no more use for priests and their superstitions than I have.'

'Then what would you have me do?' snapped Planir.

'Acknowledge your loss and the unfairness of it,' Troanna told him forcefully. 'In whatever way gives you release. Go to the highest point on the island and scream your outrage at the wind, the gods or whatever uncaring destiny visited such untimely death on the poor girl. That's what I've done before now. Look honestly at the path that led her there and spare yourself endless reproaches over what you did or didn't do. We're not Aldabreshin barbarians to believe every twist of fortune is foretold by uncanny portents, that every evil can be averted if only we have the skills to read the signs. She died and you are entitled to grieve, but not to endlessly castigate yourself over a fate that was none of your making.'

'I set her on the path that led her to die,' said Planir harshly.

'Horseshit.' Troanna shook her head. 'You diminish her by thinking so. Larissa was young but she was an intelligent girl and she made her own choices. I never approved of your association but no one can accuse you of influencing her decisions.'

'You're too kind,' said Planir coldly. 'Though that was because I loved her rather than out of any respect for your sensibilities. She is still dead.'

'Until you grieve, she will remain so.' Troanna ran a finger over the swell of the brightly decorated urn, apparently not noticing how Planir tensed. 'There's one notion the Archipelagans hold that I've come to share. No one is dead as long as one person who knew them in life still remembers them as they were. Do Larissa that honour.' She got briskly to her feet with a nod of farewell. 'You know where I am if you want to argue this further, as light relief from twisting Kalion's tail. Talk to Shannet. She's outlived nigh on her whole generation and knows all about loss. This is possibly the only thing we'll ever agree on.'

Planir said nothing as the Flood Mistress tossed that last comment over her shoulder. He sat motionless in his chair for a long while until finally, his expression still unchanged, tears coursed down his cheeks.

Suthyfer, Fellaemion's Landing, 29th of For-Summer

'For a stone mason's son, you make a very good carpenter, but can't you hang up your tool belt for one evening?' I was exaggerating; all Ryshad held was a small hammer.

He held out an arm and I stepped into his embrace. 'It looks good, doesn't it?'

I looked around the shrine. Stones chosen for even colour and smoothness gave a solid foundation to close-fitted wooden walls. The roof above was held firm by rafters finished with the same exquisite care. Around the base of the wall the rich scent of new timber breathed life into niches where the incongruously prosaic vessels holding the ashes of Suthyfer's first dead stood. Charcoal marks and faint scores on the wood promised carving yet to come; I could see Saedrin's keys, Drianon's eagle, Halcarion's crown and Raeponin's scales. In the centre of the floor, the palest stones Ryshad and his fellow craftsmen could find raised a plinth waiting for whatever deity this place would be dedicated to. The wide doors stood open and a shaft of sunlight lit up the empty circle.

I slid my arm around Ryshad's waist to feel the reassuring strength and warmth of him. 'Has Temar said anything about a statue yet?'

Ryshad shook his head. 'Guinalle suggested Larasion.'

I could see the sense in that. 'Sailors heading in both directions will always want to pray for fair weather.'

'Dastennin's the Lord of the Sea and four men out of five in Zyoutessela swear by him before any other.' Ryshad held me close with absent affection. 'Guinalle changed her mind, anyway. Talking about this new hall she and 'Sar want to set up reminded her that Ostrin's shrine held most of the aetheric lore in the Old Empire.'

'Build a bigger plinth,' I suggested. 'Let them share, like the temple in Relshaz.'

Ryshad laughed. 'It'll be a while before Suthyfer can boast anything that splendid. You could fit this whole landing inside that place.'

'It'll be as fine as any Imperial fane when it's finished.' I pulled Ryshad with me to look more closely at the faint designs on the inner face of the wall. 'If Pered's got anything to say about it. Is that Larissa beside Halcarion?'

Ryshad nodded. 'He's trying to include as many of those lost as he can.'

I studied the broad sweep of the mural Pered was planning for the first half of the circle. It followed the lie of the land outside so closely that, when it was finished, it would almost seem as if the shrine had windows not walls. Those coming for solace would see the gods and goddesses reassuringly engaged with the folk of the landing. Trimon sat with his harp, framed by dancing children. Larasion wove garlands for the girls who sat with Halcarion, all dressing their hair in the reflection of a still pool that, thinking about it, didn't actually exist hereabouts. Never mind, Ryshad would doubtless dig one. Drianon wove reeds into baskets by the door of a solid little house, goodwives busy about her. Talagrin stood some way off with a group of men about to go hunting for something to fill the pots that Misaen was hammering at his forge.

'I like it,' I said.

'So do I.' Ryshad kissed my hair.

An array of lidded pots surely too small to be serving as urns caught my eye. 'What's that?'

'Shiv's helping Pered with his pigments.' Ryshad grinned. 'He says Flood Mistress Troanna would be appalled at such mundane use of his affinity but she's not here to see.'

'So it can't hurt her.' I finished the sentence for him. Awkward silence hung between us.

'Pered's talking about studying Artifice,' Ryshad said with careful casualness.

'He can have that song book.' I chose my words with equal care. 'I won't be needing it any more.'

'No?' Ryshad looked down at me.

'Forest riddles and charms hidden in songs, that was fun,' I told him. 'Sheltya, Elietimm, Guinalle and her adepts, that's all too serious for me.' An involuntary shudder surprised me. 'Far too dangerous. They can keep their secrets and welcome.'

'So what are you going to do?' Ryshad's dark eyes searched my face.

'Vithrancel's boring.' I met his gaze unblinking. 'But it's got our house and that's got walls, a roof and a decent privy so it'll do for the moment. As soon as Suthyfer can offer as much and more besides, like taverns for sailors to spend their pay in and market halls for trading and barter, I want to come back here. I've already written to Charoleia to send me a cargo of wine on the first ship she can.' I grinned at him. 'I'm going to try my hand at being a merchant. It's just another way of gambling.'

Ryshad nodded slowly. 'Then I can take the job Temar's been trying to thrust in my hands.'

I felt a sudden qualm. 'He's offering you service with D'Alsennin? An oath?'

'No, and I wouldn't take it if he did,' said Ryshad firmly. 'Temar knows that. He wants me to act as Suthyfer's steward. Someone's got to get things organised around here and he reckons I'm the man for it.'

I couldn't decide if Ryshad was flattered or embarrassed by this accolade. 'You've served D'Olbriot, you know Zyoutessela inside out, you know more about Kellarin than anyone else. He couldn't make a better choice.'

'I hope you're right.' Ryshad hugged me.

'Of course I am.' I frowned. 'But you're not to be sworn to him?' I didn't want any ties pulling Ryshad and me apart, not any more.

'No.' Ryshad kissed my hair again. 'It's time to be my own

man. Besides, the Emperor will be happier to see Suthyfer with a measure of independence from D'Alsennin. It'll make it easier for him to sell to the Convocation of Princes.'

The Sieur D'Olbriot would back Ryshad's integrity and ability against anyone else's arguments for one thing. 'So who will you answer to?' I wondered just what possibilities this notion might present.

'In due course, there'll be merchant's guilds and more shrine fraternities, craftsmen's companies. They'll all want their say. If 'Sar and Guinalle set up their hall, they'll stick their spoon in the pot.' Ryshad looked down at me and grinned. 'I'll be needing to know just what's being said over the ale tankards and round the trading halls if I'm to keep one move ahead of the game.'

'Naturally,' I agreed, my own smile widening. Pride that Ryshad's talents had finally won due recognition warmed me even more than the prospect of the fun ahead.

'For the moment,' continued Ryshad, 'I'll be answering to myself first and foremost. Temar's said as much. He'll make his case when he wants something done, or send the captain of his cohort.' I felt a chuckle deep in Ryshad's chest. 'I should have made a bet with you, against us ever seeing Halice take a Tormalin Sieur's oath.'

'Halice?' I gaped. 'She's to be his captain, oaths given and received and the full ceremony?'

'He asked her today and she said yes. She'll be wearing D'Alsennin's badge just as soon as he can find a silversmith to make it.' Ryshad's approval was evident. 'He reckons she's proven herself five times over. She's more than ready to take his amulet and earn some rights in the land she's been fighting over for a change.'

'Sorgrad and 'Gren won't be impressed,' I said without thinking. 'They want to see what the summer's fighting's turned up in Lescar.'

I felt Ryshad stiffen. 'You're staying this side of the ocean though.'

'I am,' I assured him. 'I'm with Halice on this one. Sorgrad and 'Gren can go off with some hare-brained scheme to get rich quick and welcome. We reckon it's time to play the long game.'

'We'll all make sure the rewards are worth the costs.' Ryshad let his arm fall from my shoulder and reached into the inner pocket of his jerkin. He brought out a bronze medallion. It wasn't the one I'd seen him wear because he'd handed that back to Messire D'Olbriot along with his oath.

'Aiten would have liked it here,' I said softly.

'He would, him and Geris, wouldn't you say?' Ryshad sorted through a handful of nails to find one for the loop where leather thong had hung the medallion around his friend's neck.

I smiled. 'He'd have been desperate to get involved with 'Sar and Guinalle's studies.'

Ryshad shifted the door so he could see the inner face. One day it would be invisible beneath tokens of vows made and boons sought from the gods but for the moment it was unblemished. 'Have we settled that score with the Elietimm?'

'I think so.' There was no incense here yet but I found a few fragrant curls of wood shavings and piled them on the plinth. Ryshad watched me take a sparkmaker out of my pocket. He struck the nail square on the head and Aiten's amulet was fixed to the door. I lit the shavings and hoped the smoke would carry the sound to the Otherworld. Maybe somehow, somewhere, they'd know they were avenged.

Ryshad slowly lowered his hammer, gazing out of the doorway. 'Will you marry me?'

It wasn't a proposal, not with the weight of the question all on the first word nor yet one of those challenges that dares you to say no. He sounded merely curious but I knew my answer had to strike that same balance between lightness and significance. It wasn't a question he was asking idly, not now we could see a life ahead of us that we might share on equal terms.

'This mid-summer? No. My hair would be nowhere near long enough for a wedding plait and it'll probably still be this horrible colour. Equinox? Winter Solstice? Unlikely. I can't see me wanting to get caught up in such a fuss. Next year? The year after? Five years hence? I've no idea. I don't know that I'll ever want to wed.' My heart pounded as I gambled on complete honesty. 'I can be certain I don't want to be without you. I can't imagine my life without you. I won't be going anywhere without you at my side.'

Ryshad nodded slowly but did not speak.

'That's the best answer I can give you.' I waited.

Ryshad turned and tossed the hammer aside so he could fold me in his arms. 'That's more than enough for me. As long as I have you, I have everything I could ever want.'

I kissed him and it was enough, more than enough, for that blissful moment and, as far as I could see, it always would be.

Orbit titles available by post:

❏ The Thief's Gamble	Juliet E. McKenna	£6.99
❏ The Swordman's Oath	Juliet E. McKenna	£6.99
❏ The Gambler's Fortune	Juliet E. McKenna	£6.99
❏ The Warrior's Bond	Juliet E. McKenna	£6.99
❏ The Assassin's Edge	Juliet E. McKenna	£6.99

The prices shown above are correct at time of going to press. However the publishers reserve the right to increase prices on covers from these previously advertised, without further notice.

ORBIT BOOKS
Cash Sales Department, P.O. Box 11, Falmouth, Cornwall, TR10 9EN
Tel: +44 (0) 1326 569777, Fax: +44 (0) 1326 569555
Email: books@barni.avel.co.uk.

POST AND PACKING:
Payments can be made as follows: cheque, postal order (payable to Orbit Books) or by credit cards. Do not send cash or currency.

U.K. Orders under £10	£1.50
U.K. Orders over £10	**FREE OF CHARGE**
E.E.C. & Overseas	25% of order value

Name (Block Letters) _____

Address _____

_____

Post/zip code: _____

❏ Please keep me in touch with future Orbit publications

❏ I enclose my remittance £_____

❏ I wish to pay Visa/Access/Mastercard/Eurocard

Card Expiry Date

